# On Her Majesty's Occult Service

# Other Books by Charles Stross

**Eschaton**
*Singularity Sky*
*Iron Sunrise*
(combined as the omnibus *Timelike Diplomacy*)

**The Merchant Princes**
*The Family Trade*
*The Hidden Family*
*The Clan Corporate*

**Other Novels**
*Accelerando*
*Glasshouse*

**Short Fiction**
*Toast*

# On Her Majesty's Occult Service

## The Atrocity Archives
## The Jennifer Morgue

## Charles Stross

SCIENCE
FICTION

# Contents

GOVERNMENT I.T. SERVICES

# Introduction:
# Charlie's Demons

**"T**HE ATROCITY ARCHIVE" IS A SCIENCE FICTION NOVEL. Its form is that of a horror thriller with lots of laughs, some of them uneasy. Its basic premise is that mathematics can be magic. Its lesser premise is that if the world contains things that (as Pratchett puts it somewhere) even the dark is afraid of, then you can bet that there'll be a secret government agency covering them up for our own good. That last phrase isn't ironic; if people suspected for a moment that the only thing Lovecraft got wrong was to underestimate the power and malignity of cosmic evil, life would become unbearable. If the secret got out and (consequently) other things got in, life would become impossible. Whatever then walked the Earth would not be life, let alone human. The horror of this prospect is, in the story, linked to the horrors of real history. As in any good horror story, there are moments when you cannot believe that anyone would dare put on paper the words you are reading. Not, in this case, because the words are gory, but because the history is all too real. To summarise would spoil, and might make the writing appear to make light of the worst of human accomplishments. It does not. Read it and see.

Charlie has written wisely and well in the Afterword about the uncanny parallels between the Cold War thriller and the horror story. (Think, for a moment, what the following phrase would call to mind if you'd never heard it before: "Secret intelligence.") There is, however, a third side to the story. Imagine a world where speaking or writing words can literally and directly make things happen, where getting one of those words wrong can wreak unbelievable havoc, but where with the right spell you can summon immensely powerful agencies to work your will. Imagine further that this world is administered: there is an extensive division of labour, among the magicians themselves and between the magicians and those who coordinate their activity. It's bureaucratic, and also (therefore) chaotic, and it's full of people at desks muttering curses and writing invocations, all beavering away at a small part of the big picture. The coordinators, because they don't understand what's going on, are easy prey for smooth-talking preachers of bizarre cults that demand arbitrary sacrifices and vanish with large amounts of money. Welcome to the IT department.

It is Charlie's experience in working in and writing about the Information Technology industry that gives him the necessary hands-on insight into the workings of the Laundry. For programming is a job where Lovecraft meets tradecraft, all the time. The analyst or programmer has to examine documents with an eye at once skeptical and alert, snatching and collating tiny fragments of truth along the way. His or her sources of information all have their own agendas, overtly or covertly pursued. He or she has handlers and superiors, many of whom don't know what really goes on at the sharp end. And the IT worker has to know in their bones that if they make a mistake, things can go horribly wrong. Tension and cynicism are constant companions, along with camaraderie and competitiveness. It's a lot like being a spy, or necromancer. You don't get out much, and when you do it's usually at night.

Charlie gets out and about a lot, often in daylight. He has no demons. Like most people who write about eldritch horrors, he has a cheerful disposition. Whatever years he has spent in the cellars haven't dimmed his enthusiasm, his empathy, or his ability to talk and write with a speed, range of reference, and facility that makes you want to buy the bastard a pint just to keep him quiet and slow him down in the morning, before he gets too far ahead. I know: I've tried. It doesn't work.

I first encountered Charles Stross when I worked in IT myself. It was 1996 or thereabouts, when you more or less had to work in IT to have heard about the Internet. (Yes, there was a time not long ago when news about the existence of the Internet spread by word of mouth.) It dawned on me that the guy who was writing sensible-but-radical posts to various newsgroups I hung out in was the same Charles Stross who'd written two or three short stories I'd enjoyed in the British SF magazine Interzone: "Yellow Snow," "Ship of Fools," and "Dechlorinating the Moderator" (all now available in his collection TOAST, Cosmos Books, 2002).

"Dechlorinating the Moderator" is a science fiction story about a convention that has all the trappings of a science fiction convention, but is (because this is the future) a science fact convention, of desktop and basement high-energy fundamental physics geeks and geekettes. Apart from its intrinsic fun, the story conveys the peculiar melancholy of looking back on a con and realising that no matter how much of a good time you had, there was even more that you missed. (All right: as subtle shadings of emotion go this one is a bit low on universality, but it was becoming familiar to me, having just started going to cons.) "Ship of Fools" was about the Y2K problem (which as we all know turned out not to be a problem, but BEGIN_RANT that was entirely thanks to programmers who did their jobs properly in the first place back when only geeks and astronomers believed the twenty-first century would actually arrive END_RANT) and it was also full of the funniest and most authentic-sounding insider yarns about IT I'd ever read. This Stross guy sounded like someone I wanted to meet, maybe at a con. It turned out he lived in Edinburgh. We were practically neighbours. I think I emailed him, and before too long he materialised out of cyberspace and we had a beer and began an intermittent conversation that hasn't stopped.

He had this great idea for a novel: "It's a techno-thriller! The premise is that Turing cracked the NP-Completeness theorem back in the forties! The whole Cold War was really about preventing the Singularity! The ICBMs were there in case godlike AIs ran amok!" (He docsn't really talk like this. But that's how I remember it.) He had it all in his head. Lots of people do, but he (and here's a tip for aspiring authors out there) actually wrote it. That one, Burn Time, the first of his novels I read, remains unpublished—great concept, shaky execution—but the raw talent was there and so was the energy and application and the astonishing range of reference. Since then he has written a lot more novels and short stories. The short stories kept getting better and kept getting published. He had another great idea: "A family saga about living through the Singularity! From the point of view of the cat!" That mutated into the astonishing series that began with "Lobsters," published in Asimov's SF, June 2001. That story was short-listed for three major SF awards: the Hugo, the Nebula, and the Sturgeon. Another, "Router," was short-listed for the British Science Fiction Association (BSFA) Award. The fourth, "Halo," has been short-listed for the Hugo.

Looking back over some of these short stories, what strikes me is the emergence of what might be called the Stross sentence. Every writer who contributes to, or defines, a stage in the development of SF has sentences that only they could write, or at least only they could write first. Heinlein's dilating door opened up a new way to bypass explication by showing what is taken for granted; Zelazny's dune buggies beneath the racing moons of Mars introduced an abrupt gear-change in the degrees of freedom allowed in handling the classic material; Gibson's television sky and Ono-Sendai decks displayed the mapping of virtual onto real spaces that has become the default metaphor of much of our daily lives. The signature Stross sentence (and you'll come to recognise them as you read) represents just such an upward jump in compression and comprehension, and one that we need to make sense not only of the stories, but of the world we inhabit: a world sentenced to Singularity.

The novels kept getting better too, but not getting published, until quite recently and quite suddenly three or four got accepted more or less at once. The only effect this has had on Charlie is that he has written another two or three while these were in press. He just keeps getting faster and better, like computers. But the first of his novels to be published is this one, and it's very good.

We'll be hearing, and reading, a lot more from him.

Read this now.

Ken MacLeod
West Lothian, U.K.
May 2003

# On Her Majesty's Occult Service

# The Atrocity Archives

For my Parents, David and Cecilie Stross

## Acknowledgements

Authors write, but not in a vacuum. Firstly, I owe a debt of gratitude to the usual suspects—members of my local writers workshop all —who suffered through first-draft reading hell and pointed out numerous headaches that needed fixing. Paul Fraser of *Spectrum SF* applied far more editorial muscle than I had any right to expect, in preparation for the original magazine serialization; likewise Marty Halpern of Golden Gryphon Press, who made this longer edition possible. Finally, I stand on the shoulders of giants. Three authors in particular made it possible for me to imagine this book and I salute you, H. P. Lovecraft, Neal Stephenson, and Len Deighton.

♦   ♦   ♦

# 1
## Active Service

Green sky at night; hacker's delight.

I'm lurking in the shrubbery behind an industrial unit, armed with a clipboard, a pager, and a pair of bulbous night-vision goggles that drench the scenery in ghastly emerald tones. The bloody things make me look like a train-spotter with a gas-mask fetish, and wearing them is giving me a headache. It's humid and drizzling slightly, the kind of penetrating dampness that cuts right through waterproofs and gloves. I've been waiting out here in the bushes for three hours so far, waiting for the last workaholic to turn the lights out and go home so that I can climb in through a rear window. Why the hell did I ever say "yes" to Andy? State-sanctioned burglary is a lot less romantic than it sounds—especially on standard time-and-a-half pay.

(You bastard, Andy. "About that application for active service you filed last year. As it happens, we've got a little job on tonight and we're short-staffed; could you lend a hand?")

I stamp my feet and blow on my hands. There's no sign of life in the squat concrete-and-glass block in front of me. It's eleven at night and there are still lights burning in the cubicle hive: Don't these people have a bed to go home to? I push my goggles up and everything goes dark, except the glow from those bloody windows, like fireflies nesting in the empty eye sockets of a skull.

There's a sudden sensation like a swarm of bees throbbing around my bladder. I swear quietly and hike up my waterproof to get at the pager. It's not backlit, so I have to risk a precious flash of torchlight to read it. The text message says, *MGR LVNG 5 MINS*. I don't ask how they know that, I'm just grateful that there's only five more minutes of standing here among the waterlogged trees, trying not to stamp my feet too loudly, wondering what I'm going to say if the local snouts come calling. Five more minutes of hiding round the back of the QA department of Memetix (UK) Ltd.—subsidiary of a multinational based in Menlo Park, California—then I can do the job and go home. Five more minutes spent hiding in the bushes down on an industrial estate where the white heat of technology keeps the lights burning far into the night, in a place where the nameless horrors don't suck your brains out and throw you to the Human Resources department—unless you show a deficit in the third quarter, or forget to make blood sacrifice before the altar of Total Quality Management.

Somewhere in that building the last late-working executive is yawning and reaching for the door remote of his BMW. The cleaners have all gone home; the big servers hum blandly in their air-conditioned womb, nestled close to the service core of the office block. All I have to do is avoid the security guard and I'm home free.

A distant motor coughs into life, revs, and pulls out of the landscaped car park in a squeal of wet tires. As it fades into the night my pager vibrates again: GO GO GO. I edge forward.

No motion-triggered security lights flash on. There are no Rotweiller attack dogs, no guards in coal-scuttle helmets: this ain't that kind of movie, and I'm no Arnold Schwartzenegger. (Andy told me: "If anyone challenges you, smile, stand up straight, and show them your warrant card—then phone me. I'll handle it. Getting the old man out of bed to answer a clean-up call will earn you a black mark, but a black mark's better than a cracked skull. Just try to remember that Croxley Industrial Estate isn't Novaya Zemlya, and getting your head kicked in isn't going to save the world from the forces of evil.")

I squish through the damp grass and find the designated window. Like the briefing said, it's shut but not locked. A good tug and the window hinges out toward me. It's inconveniently high up, a good four feet above the concrete gutter. I pull myself up and over the sill, sending a tiny avalanche of disks scuttering across the floor. The room is ghostly green except for the bright hot spots of powered-down monitors and fans blowing air from hot CPU cases. I stumble forward over a desk covered in piles of kipple, wondering how in hell the owner is going to fail to notice my great muddy boot-print between the obviously confidential documents scattered next to a keyboard and a stone-cold coffee mug. Then I'm on the floor in the QA department, and the clock is ticking.

The pager vibrates again. *SITREP.* I pull my mobile out of my breast pocket and dial a three-digit number, then put it back again. Just letting them know I've arrived and everything's running smoothly. Typical

Laundry—they'll actually include the phone bill in the event log to prove I called in on schedule before they file it somewhere secret. Gone are the days of the impromptu black-bag job . . .

The offices of Memetix (UK) Ltd. are a typical cubicle hell; anonymous beige fabric partitions dividing up little slices of corporate life. The photocopier hulks like an altar beneath a wall covered with devotional scriptures—the company's code of conduct, lists of compulsory employee self-actualization training courses, that sort of thing. I glance around, hunting cubicle D14. There's a mass of Dilbert cartoons pinned to the side of his partition, spoor of a mildly rebellious mind-set; doubtless middle managers prowl round the warren before any visit from the upper echelons, tearing down such images that signal dissent. I feel a minor shiver of sympathy coming on: Poor bastard, what must it be like to be stuck here in the warren of cells at the heart of the new industrial revolution, never knowing where the lightning's going to strike next?

There's a desk with three monitors on it: two large but otherwise ordinary ones, and a weird-ass piece of machinery that looks at least a decade old, dredged out of the depths of the computer revolution. It's probably an old Symbolics Lisp machine or something. It tweaks my antique gland, but I don't have time to rubberneck; the security guard's due to make another round in just sixteen minutes. There are books leaning in crazy piles and drifts on either side: Knuth, Dijkstra, Al-Hazred, other less familiar names. I pull his chair back and sit down, wrinkling my nose. In one of the desk drawers something's died and gone to meet its maker.

Keyboard: check. Root account: I pull out the filched S/Key smartcard the Laundry sourced from one of Memetix's suppliers and type the response code to the system's challenge. (One time passwords are a bitch to crack; once again, give thanks to the Laundry's little helpers.) Then I'm logged in and trusted and it's time to figure out just what the hell I'm logged in to.

Malcolm—whose desk I sit at, and whose keyboard I pollute—is running an ant farm: there are dead computers under the desk, scavenged for parts, and a dubious Frankenstein server—guts open to the elements—humming like a generator beside it. For a moment I hunt around in panic, searching for silver pentacles and glowing runes under the desktop—but it's clean. Logged in, I find myself in a maze of twisty little automounted filesystems, all of them alike. *Fuck shit curse dammit*, I recite under my breath; it was never like this in *Cast a Deadly Spell*. I pull out the phone and dial.

"Capital Laundry Services, how may we help you?"

"Give me a hostname and target directory, I'm in but I'm lost."

"One sec . . . try 'auto slash share slash fs slash scooby slash netapp slash user slash home slash malcolm slash uppercase-R slash catbert slash world-underscore-domination slash manifesto.'"

I type so fast my fingers trip over each other. There's a faint clicking as the server by the desk mounts scooby's gigantic drive array and scratches its read/write heads, looking for what has got to be one of the most stupidly named files anywhere on the company's intranet.

"Hold on . . . yup, got it." I view the sucker and it's there in plaintext: *Some Notes Toward a Proof of Polynomial Completeness in Hamiltonian Networks*. I page through the text rapidly, just skimming; there's no time to give it my full in-depth attention, but it looks genuine. "Bingo." I can feel an unpleasant slimy layer of sweat in the small of my back. "I've got it. Bye for now."

"Bye yourself." I shut the phone and stare at the paper. Just for a moment, I hesitate . . . What I'm here to do isn't fair, is it? The imp of perversity takes over: I bang out a quick command, mailing the incriminating file to a not-so-dead personal account. (Figure I'll read it later.) Then it's time to nuke the server. I unmount the netapp drive and set fire to it with a bitstorm of low-level reformatting. If Malcolm wants his paper back he'll have to enlist GCHQ and a scanning tunneling microscope to find it under all the 0xDEADBEEF spammed across the hard disk platters.

My pager buzzes again. *SITREP*. I hit three more digits on the phone. Then I edge out of the cubicle and scramble back across the messy desk and out into the cool spring night, where I peel off those damned latex gloves and waggle my fingers at the moon.

I'm so elated that I don't even remember the stack of disks I sent flying until I'm getting off the night bus at home. And by then, the imp of perversity is chuckling up his sleeve.

I'm fast asleep in bed when the cellphone rings.

It's in my jacket pocket, where I left it last night, and I thrash around on the floor for a bit while it chirps merrily. "Hello?"

"Bob?"

It's Andy. I try not to groan. "What time is it?"

"It's nine-thirty. Where are you?"

"In bed. What's—"

"Thought you were going to be in at the debrief? When can you come in?"

"I'm not feeling too wonderful. Got home at about two-thirty. Let me think . . . eleven good enough?"

"It'll have to be." He sounds burned. Well, Andy wasn't the one freezing his butt off in the woods last night, was he? "See you there." The implicit *or else* doesn't need enunciating. Her Majesty's Extra-Secret Service has never really been clear on the concept of flexitime and sensible working hours.

I shamble into the bathroom and stare at the thin rind of black mold growing around the window as I piss. I'm alone in the house; everyone else is either out—working—or *out*—gone for good. (That's out, as in working, for Pinky and the Brain; *out*, as in fucked off, for Mhari.) I pick up my senescent toothbrush and perform the usual morning ritual. At least the heating's on. Downstairs in the kitchen I fill a percolator with nuclear-caffeinated grounds and nudge it onto the gas ring. I figure I can make it into the Laundry by eleven and still have time to wake up first. I'll need to be alert for that meeting. Did last night go off properly, or not? Now that I can't do anything about them I remember the disks.

Nameless dread is all very well when you're slumped in front of the TV watching a slasher movie, but it plays havoc with your stomach when you drop half a pint of incredibly strong black coffee on it in the space of fifteen minutes. Brief nightmarish scenarios flit through my head, in order of severity: written reprimands, unemployment, criminal prosecution for participating in a black-bag job for which authorization is unaccountably retroactively withdrawn; worst of all, coming home to find Mhari curled up on the living room sofa again. Scratch that latter vision; the short-lived sadness gives way to a deeper sense of relief, tempered by a little loneliness. The loneliness of the long-distance spook? Damn, I need to get my head in order. I'm no James Bond, with a sexy KGB minx trying to seduce me in every hotel room. That's about the first thing they drum into you at Capital Laundry Services ("Washes cleaner than clean!"): life is not a spy movie, work is not romantic, and there's nothing particularly exciting about the job. Especially when it involves freezing your balls off in a corporate shrubbery at eleven o'clock on a rainy night.

Sometimes I regret not having taken the opportunity to study accountancy. Life could be so much more fun if I'd listened to the right recruiting spiel at the university milk round . . . but I need the money, and maybe one of these days they'll let me do something interesting. Meanwhile I'm here in this job because all the alternatives are worse.

So I go to work.

The London underground is famous for apparently believing that human beings go about this world owning neither kidney nor colon. Not many people know that there's precisely one public toilet in Mornington

Crescent station. It isn't signposted, and if you ask for it the staff will shake their heads; but it's there all the same, because we asked for it.

I catch the Metropolitan line to Euston Square—sharing a squalid rattle-banging cattle car with a herd of bored commuters—then switch to the Northern line. At the next stop I get out, shuffle up the staircase, go into the gents, and step into the right-hand rear stall. I yank *up* on the toilet handle instead of down, and the back wall opens like a big thick door (plumbing and all), ushering me into the vestibule. It's all a bit like a badly funded B-movie remake of some sixties Hollywood spy thriller. A couple of months ago I asked Boris why we bothered with it, but he just chuckled and told me to ask Angleton—meaning, "Bugger off."

The wall closes behind me and a hidden solenoid bolt unlocks the stall door: the toilet monster consumes another victim. I put my hand in the ID scanner, collect my badge from the slot next to it, and step across the red line on the threshold. It's another working day at Capital Laundry Services, discreet cleaning agents to the government.

And guess who's in hot water?

First stop: my office. If you can call it an office—it's a sort of niche between a row of lockers and a herd of senile filing cabinets, into which the Facilities gnomes have jammed a plywood desk and a swivel chair with a damaged gas strut. I drop my coat and jacket on the chair and my computer terminal whistles at me: *YOU HAVE MAIL.* No shit, Sherlock, I *always* have mail. It's an existential thing: if I don't have mail it would mean that something is very wrong with the world, or maybe I've died and gone to bureaucratic hell. (I'm a child of the wired generation, unlike some of the suits hereabouts who have their secretaries print everything out and dictate their replies for an audio-typist to send.) There is also a cold, scummy cup of over-milked coffee on my desk; Marcia's been over-efficient again. A yellow Post-it note curls reproachfully atop one of my keyboards: *MEETING 9:30am CT ROOM B4.* Hell and damnation, why didn't I remember?

I go to meeting room B4.

There's a red light showing so I knock and wave my badge before entering, just in case Security is paying attention. Inside, the air is blue; it looks like Andy's been chain-smoking his foul French fags for the past couple of hours. "Yo," I say. "Everyone here?"

Boris the Mole looks at me stonily. "You're late."

Harriet shakes her head. "Never mind." She taps her papers into a neat stack. "Had a good sleep, did we?"

I pull out a chair and slump into it. "I spent six hours being one with a shrubbery last night. There were three cloudbursts and a rain of small and very confused frogs."

Andy stubs out his cigarette and sits up. "Well, now we're here . . ." he looks at Boris enquiringly. Boris nods. I try to keep a straight face: I hate it when the old guard start playing stiff upper lip.

"Jackpot." Andy grins at me. I nearly have a heart attack on the spot, "You're coming to the pub tonight, Bob. Drinks on me. That was a straight A for results, C-plus for fieldwork, overall grade B for execution."

"Uh, I thought I made a mess going in—"

"No. If it hadn't been a semicovert you'd have had to burn your shoes, but apart from that—well. Zero witnesses, you found the target, there's nothing left, and Dr Denver is about to find himself downsized and in search of a job somewhere less sensitive." He shakes his head. "Not a lot more to say, really."

"But the security guard could have—"

The security guard was fully aware there was going to be a burglary, Bob. He wasn't going to move an inch, much less see anything untoward or sound the alarm, lest spooks come out of the woodwork and find him crunchy and good with ketchup."

"It was a set-up?" I say disbelievingly.

Boris nods at me. "Is a *good* set-up."

"Was it worth it?" I ask. "I mean, I just wiped out some poor bastard's last six months of work—"

Boris sighs mournfully and shoves an official memo at me. It's got a red-and-yellow chevron-striped border and the phrase MOST SECRET DE-STROY BEFORE READING stamped across its cover. I open it and look at the title page: *Some Notes Toward a Proof of Polynomial Completeness in Hamiltonian Networks*. And a subtitle: *Formal Correctness Report.* One of the departmental theorem-proving oracles has been busy overnight. "He duplicated the Turing result?"

"Most regrettably," says Boris.

Harriet nods. "You want to know if last night was worth it. It was. If you hadn't succeeded, we might have had to take more serious measures. That's always an option, you know, but in general we try to handle such affairs at the lowest possible level."

I nod and close the folder, shove it back across the table toward Boris. "What next?"

"Timekeeping," says Harriet. "I'm a bit concerned that you weren't available for debriefing on schedule this morning. You really need to do a bit better," she adds. (Andy, who I think understands how I tick, keeps quiet.)

I glare at her. "I'd just spent six hours standing in a wet bush, and breaking into someone else's premises. *After* putting in a full day's work in preparation." I lean forward, getting steamed: "In case you've forgotten, I was in at eight in the morning yesterday, then Andy asked me to help with this thing at four in the afternoon. Have you ever tried getting a night bus from Croxley to the East End at two in the morning when you're soaked to the bone, it's pouring wet, and the only other people at the bus stop are a mugger and a drunk guy who wants to know if you can put him up for the night? I count that as a twenty hour working day with hardship. Want me to submit an overtime claim?"

"Well, you should have phoned in first," she says waspishly.

I'm not going to win this one, but I don't think I've lost on points. Anyway, it's not really worth picking a fight with my line manager over trivia. I sit back and yawn, trying not to choke on the cigarette fumes.

"Next on the agenda," says Andy. "What to do with Malcolm Denver, Ph.D. Further action is indicated in view of this paper; we can't leave it lying around in public. Cuts too close to the bone. If he goes public and reproduces it we could be facing a Level One reality excursion within weeks. But we can't do the usual brush and clean either, Oversight would have our balls. Ahem." He glances at Harriet, whose lips are thin and unamused. "Could have us all cooling our heels for months in a diversity awareness program for the sensitivity-impaired." He shudders slightly and I notice the red ribbon on his lapel; Andy is too precious by half for this job, although—come to think of it—this isn't exactly the most mainstream posting in the civil service. "Anyone got any suggestions? Constructive ones, Bob."

Harriet shakes her head disapprovingly. Boris just sits there, being Boris. (Boris is one of Angleton's sinister gofers; I think in a previous incarnation he used to ice enemies of the state for the Okhrana, or maybe served coffee for Beria. Now he just imitates the Berlin Wall during internal enquiries.) Andy taps his fingers on the desk. "Why don't we make him a job offer?" I ask. Harriet looks away: she's my line manager—nominally—and she wants to make it clear that this suggestion does not come with her approval. "It's like—" I shrug, trying to figure out a pitch. "He's derived the Turing-Lovecraft theorem from first principles. Not many people can do that. So he's bright, that's a given. I think he's still a pure theory geek, hasn't made any kind of connection with the implications of being able to specify correct geometric relations between power nodes—maybe still thinks it's all a big joke. No references to Dee or the others, apart from a couple of minor arcana on his bookshelf. This means he isn't directly dangerous, and we can offer him the opportunity to learn and develop his skills and interests in a new and challenging field—just as long as he's willing to come on the inside. Which would get him covered by Section Three at that point."

Section Three of the Official Secrets Act (1916) is our principal weapon in the endless war against security leaks. It was passed during a wartime spy scare—a time of deep and extreme paranoia—and it's even more bizarre than most people think. As far as the public knows, the Official Secrets Act only has two sections; that's because Section Three is itself classified *Secret* under the terms of the preceding sections, and merely knowing about Section Three's existence—without having formally signed it—is a criminal offence. Section Three has all kinds of juicy hidden provisions to make life easy for spooks like us; it's a bureaucratic cloaking field. Anything at all can go on behind the shroud of Section Three as if it simply hasn't happened. In American terms, it's a black operation.

"If you section him we have to come up with a job and a budget," Harriet accuses.

"Yes, but I'm sure he'll be useful." Andy waves languidly. "Boris, would you mind asking around your section, see if anyone needs a mathematician or cryptographer or something? I'll write this up and point it at the Board. Harriet, if you can add it to the minutes. Bob, I'd like a word with you after the meeting, about timekeeping."

*Oh shit*, I think.

"Anything else? No? Meeting over, folks."

Once we're alone in the conference room Andy shakes his head. "That wasn't very clever, Bob, winding Harriet up like that."

"I know." I shrug. "It's just that every time I see her I get this urge to drop salt on her back."

"Yes, but she's technically your line manager. And I'm not. Which means you are supposed to phone in if you're going to be late on a day when you've got a kickoff meeting, or else she will raise seven shades of low-key shit. And as she will be in the *right*, appeals to matrix management and conflict resolution won't save you. She'll make your annual performance appraisal look like it's the Cultural Revolution and you just declared yourself the reincarnation of Heinrich Himmler. Am I making myself clear?"

I sit down again. "Yes, for very bureaucratic values of clear."

He nods. "I sympathize, Bob, I really do. But Harriet's under a lot of pressure; she's got a lot of projects on her plate and the last thing she needs is to be kept waiting two hours because you couldn't be bothered to leave a message on her voice mail last night."

Putting it that way, I begin to feel like a shit—even though I can see how I'm being manipulated. "Okay, I'll try harder in future."

His face brightens. "That's what I wanted to hear."

"Uh-huh. Now I've got a sick Beowulf cluster to resurrect before Friday's batch PGP cluster-fuck kicks off. And then a tarot permutator to calibrate, and a security audit for another of those bloody collecting card games in case a bunch of stoned artists in Austin, Texas, have somehow accidentally produced a great node. Is there anything else?"

"Probably not," he murmurs, standing. "But how did you like the opportunity to get out and about a bit?"

"It was wet." I stand up and stretch. "Apart from that, well, it made a change. But I might get serious about that overtime claim if it happens too regularly. I wasn't kidding about the frogs."

"Well, maybe it will and maybe it won't." He pats me on the shoulder. "You did all right last night, Bob. And I understand your problem with Harriet. It just so happens that there's a place on a training course open next week; it'll get you out from under her feet and I think you'll enjoy it."

"A training course." I look at him. "What in? Windows NT system administration?"

He shakes his head. "Computational demonology for dummies."

"But I already did—"

"I don't expect you to *learn* anything in the course, Bob. It's the other participants I want you to keep an eye on."

"The others?"

He smiles mirthlessly. "You *said* you wanted an active service job . . ."

We are not alone, the Truth is Out There, yadda yadda yadda. That kind of pop-culture paranoia is mostly bunk . . . except there's a worm of truth at the heart of every fictional apple, and while there may be no aliens in the freezer room at Roswell AFB, the world is still full of spooks who will come through your window and trash your hard disk if you discover the wrong mathematical theorem. (Or worse, but that's another kind of problem, one the co-workers in Field Ops get to handle.)

For the most part, the universe really does work the way most of the guys with Ph.D.s after their names think it works. Molecules are made out of atoms which are made out of electrons, neutrons, and protons— of which the latter two are made out of quarks—and quarks are made out of leptoquarks, and so on. It's turtles all the way down, so to speak. And you can't find the longest common prime factors of a number with many digits in it without either spending several times the life of the entire universe, or using a quantum computer (which is cheating). And there really are *no* signals from sentient organisms locked up in tape racks at Arecibo, and there really are *no* flying saucers in storage at Area 51 (apart from the USAF superblack research projects, which don't count because they run on aviation fuel).

But that isn't the full story.

I've suffered for what I know, so I'm not going to let you off the hook with a simple one-liner. I think you deserve a detailed explanation. Hell, I think *everybody* deserves to know how tenuous the structure of reality is—but I didn't get to make the rules, and it is a Very Bad Idea to violate Laundry security policy. Because Security is staffed by things that you really don't want to get mad at you—in fact, you don't even want them to notice you exist.

Anyway, I've suffered for my knowledge, and here's what I've learned. I could wibble on about Crowley and Dee and mystics down the ages but, basically, most self-styled magicians know shit. The fact of the matter is that most traditional magic doesn't work. In fact, it would all be irrelevant, were it not for the Turing theorem —named after Alan Turing, who you'll have heard of if you know anything about computers.

*That* kind of magic works. Unfortunately.

You haven't heard of the Turing theorem—at least, not by name — unless you're one of us. Turing never published it; in fact he died very suddenly, not long after revealing its existence to an old wartime friend who he should have known better than to have trusted. This was simultaneously the Laundry's first ever success and greatest ever disaster: to be honest, they overreacted disgracefully and managed to deprive themselves of one of the finest minds at the same time.

Anyway, the theorem has been rediscovered periodically ever since; it has also been suppressed efficiently, if a little bit less violently, because nobody wants it out in the open where Joe Random Cypherpunk can smear it across the Internet.

The theorem is a hack on discrete number theory that simultaneously disproves the Church-Turing hypothesis (wave if you understood that) and worse, permits NP-complete problems to be converted into P-complete ones. This has several consequences, starting with screwing over most cryptography algorithms—translation: *all your bank account are belong to us*—and ending with the ability to computationally generate a Dho-Nha geometry curve in real time.

This latter item is just slightly less dangerous than allowing nerds with laptops to wave a magic wand and turn them into hydrogen bombs at will. Because, you see, everything you know about the way this universe works is correct—except for the little problem that this isn't the only universe we have to worry about. Information can leak between one universe and another. And in a vanishingly small number of the other universes there are things that listen, and talk back—see Al-Hazred, Nietzsche, Lovecraft, Poe, etcetera. The many-angled ones, as they say, live at the bottom of the Mandelbrot set, except when a suitable incantation in the platonic realm of mathematics—computerized or otherwise—draws them forth. (And you thought running that fractal screen-saver was good for your computer?)

Oh, and did I mention that the inhabitants of those other universes don't play by our rule book?

Just solving certain theorems makes waves in the Platonic over-space. Pump lots of power through a grid tuned carefully in accordance with the right parameters—which fall naturally out of the geometry curve I mentioned, which in turn falls easily out of the Turing theorem—and you can actually amplify these waves, until they rip honking great holes in spacetime and let congruent segments of otherwise-separate universes merge. You really don't want to be standing at ground zero when that happens.

Which is why we have the Laundry . . .

I slink back to my office via the coffee maker, from which I remove a mug full of a vile and turgid brew that coats my back teeth in slimy grit. There are three secret memos waiting in the locked pneumatic tube, one of which is about abuse of government-issue toothpaste. There are a hundred and thirty-two email messages waiting for me to read them. And on the other side of the building there's a broken Beowulf cluster that's waiting for me to install a new ethernet hub and bring it back online to rejoin our gang of cryptocrackers. This is my fault, for being the departmental computer guy: when the machines break, I wave my dead chicken and write voodoo words on their keyboards until they work again. This means that the people who broke them in the first place keep calling me back in, and blame me whenever they make things go wrong again. So guess what gets my attention first? Yes, you guessed right: it's the institutional cream and off-green wall behind my monitor. I can't even bring myself to read my mail until I've had a good five minutes staring at nothing in particular. I have a bad feeling about today, even though there's nothing obviously catastrophic to lock onto; this is going to be one of those Friday the Thirteenth type occasions, even though it's actually a rainy Wednesday the Seventeenth.

To start with there's a charming piece of email from Mhari, laundered through one of my dead-letter drops. (You'd better not let the Audit Office catch you sending or receiving private email from work, which is why I don't. As I'm the guy who built the departmental firewall, this isn't difficult.) *You slimy scumbag don't you ever show your nose round my place again.* Oh yes, as if! The last time I was round the flat she's staying in was at the weekend, when she was out, to retrieve my tube of government-issue toothpaste. I somehow resisted the urge to squirt obscene suggestions on the bathroom mirror the way she did when she came round and repo'd my stereo. Maybe this was an oversight on my part.

Next message: a directive on sick leave signed (digitally) by Harriet, pointing out that if more than half an hour's leave is taken a doctor's note must be obtained, preferably in advance. (Why do I feel a headache coming on?)

Thirdly, there's a plea from Fred in Accounting—a loser, basically, who I had the misfortune to smile at last time I was on hell desk duty: "Help, I can't run my files anymore." Fred has just about mastered the high art of the on/off switch but is sufficiently proficient with a spreadsheet to endanger your payroll. Last time I got mail from him it turned out he'd reinstalled an earlier version of some critical bits 'n' pieces over his hard disk, trashing everything, and had the effrontery to be mailing virus-infested jokes around the place. (I bounce the plea for help over to the hell desk, where the staffer on call will get to grapple with it and curse me vilely for trying to be helpful to Fred.)

I spend a second stretch of five minutes staring at the chipped cream paint on the wall behind my monitor. My head is throbbing now, and because of various Health and Safety directives there isn't so much as an aspirin on the premises. After yesterday's inane fiasco there doesn't seem to be anything I can do here today that conjures up any enthusiasm: I have a horrible gut-deep feeling that if I stay things will only get worse. Besides, I put in two days' worth of overtime yesterday, regs say I'm allowed to take time off in lieu, my self-help book says I should still be grieving for my pet hamster, and the Beowulf cluster can go fuck itself.

I log out of the secure terminal and bunk off home early: your taxes at work.

It's eight in the evening and I still have a headache. Meanwhile, Pinky is down in the cellar, preparing another assault on the laws of nature.

The TV console in the living room of Chateau Cthulhu—the geek house I share with Pinky and Brains, both of whom also work for the Laundry—is basically brain candy, installed by Pinky in a desperate attempt to reduce the incidence of creative psychosis in the household. I think this was during one of his rare fits of sanity. The stack contains a cable decoder, satellite dish, Sony Playstation, and a homemade webTV receiver that Brains threw together during a bored half hour. It hulks in the corner opposite the beige corduroy sofa like a black-brushed postmodern sculpture held together with wiring spaghetti; its purpose is to provide a chillout zone where we can collapse after a hard day's work auditing new age websites in case they've accidentally invented something dangerous. Cogitating for a living can result in serious brain-sprain: if

you don't get blitzed on beer and blow or watch trash TV and sing raucously once in a while, you'll end up thinking you're Sonic the Hedge-
hog and that ancient Mrs Simpson over the road is Two-Tails. Could be
messy, especially if Security is positively vetting you at the time.

I am plugged into the boob tube with a can of beer in one hand and
a pizza box in my lap, watching things go fast and explode on the
Discovery Channel, when there's a horrible groaning sound from beneath the carpet. At first I pay no attention because the program currently showing is a particularly messy plane-crash docudrama, but when
the sound continues for a few seconds I realize that not even Pinky's
apocalyptic stereo could generate that kind of volume, and maybe if I
don't do something about it I'm going to vanish through the floorboards.
So I stand up unsteadily and weave my way into the kitchen. The cellar
door is ajar and the light's on and the noise is coming from down below;
I grab the fire extinguisher and advance. There's an ominous smell of
ozone . . .

Chateau Cthulhu is a mid-Victorian terrace, an anonymous London
dormitory unit distinguished mainly by having three cellar rooms and a
Laundry residential clearance, meaning that it's probably not bugged by
the KGB, CIA, or our enemies in MI6. There is a grand total of four
double-bedrooms, each with a lock on the door, plus a shared kitchen,
living room, dining room, and bathroom. The plumbing gurgles ominously late at night; the carpet is a peculiarly lurid species of paisley print
that was the height of fashion in 1880, and then experienced an unde-
served resurrection among cheap-ass landlords during the 1980s.

When we moved in, one of the cellars was full of lumber, one of
them contained two rusting bicycle frames and some mummified cat
turds, and the third had some burned-out candle stubs and a blue chalk
pentacle inscribed on the floor. The omens were good: the house was
right at the corner of an equilateral triangle of streets, aligned due east-
west, and there were no TV aerials blocking the southern roofline.
Brains, pretending to be a God-botherer, managed to negotiate a 10 percent discount in return for exorcising the place after convincing Mr
Hussein that a history of pagan activities could severely impact his rev-
enues on the rental market. (Nonsense, but profitable nonsense.) The
former temple is now Pinky's space, and if Mr Hussein could see it he'd
probably have a heart attack. It isn't the dubious wiring or the three six-
foot-high racks containing Pinky's 1950s vintage Strowger telephone exchange that make it so alarming: more like the way Pinky replaced the
amateurish chalk sketch with a homemade optical bench and properly
calibrated beam-splitter rig and five prisms, upgrading the original student séance antics to full-blown functionality.

(Yes, it's a pentacle. Yes, he's using a fifty kilovolt HT power supply and some mucking great capacitors to drive the laser. Yes, that's a flayed goatskin on the coat rack and a half-eaten pizza whirling round at 33 rpm on the Linn Sondek turntable. This is what you get to live with when you share a house with Pinky and the Brain: I *said* it was a geek house, and we all work in the Laundry, so we're talking about geek houses for very esoteric—indeed, occult—values of geek.)

The smell of ozone—and the ominous crackling sound—is emanating from the HT power supply. The groaning/squealing noise is coming from the speakers (black monoliths from the 2001 school of hi-fi engineering). I tiptoe round the far wall from the PSU and pick up the microphone lying in front of the left speaker, then yank on the cord; there's a stunning blast of noise, then the feedback cuts out. *Where the hell is Brains?* I look at the PSU. There's a blue-white flickering inside it that gives me a nasty sinking feeling. If this was any other house I'd just go for the distribution board and pull the main circuit breaker, but there are some capacitors next to that thing that are the size of a compact washing machine and I don't fancy trying to safe them in a dark cellar. I heft the extinguisher—a rather illegal halon canister, necessary in this household—and advance. The main cut-off switch is a huge knife switch on the rack above the PSU. There's a wooden chair sitting next to it; I pick it up and, gripping the back, use one leg to nudge the handle.

There's a loud *clunk* and a simultaneous *bang* from the PSU. Oops, I guess I let the magic smoke out. Dumping the chair, I yank the pin from the extinguisher and open fire, remembering to stand well clear of those big capacitors. (You can leave 'em with their terminals exposed and they'll pick up a static charge out of thin air; after half an hour, if you stick a screwdriver blade across them you'd better hope the handle is well-insulated because you're sure as hell going to need a new screwdriver, and if the insulation is defective you'll need a couple of new fingers as well.)

The smoke forms a thin coil in midair, swirling in an unnaturally regular donut below the single swinging light bulb. A faint laughter echoes from the speakers.

"What have you done with him?" I yell, forgetting that the mike isn't plugged in. The pentacle on the optical bench is powered down and empty, but the jar beside it is labelled *Dust from ye Tombe of ye Mummy* (*prop. Winchester Road Crematorium*) and you don't need to be a necromancer to figure out what that means.

"Done with whom?"

I nearly jump right out of my skin as I turn round. Pinky is standing in the doorway, holding his jeans up with one hand and looking annoyed.

"I was having a shit," he says. "Who's the fuss about?"

I point at the power supply, wordlessly.

"You didn't—" he stops. Raises his hands and tugs at his thin hair. "My capacitors! You bastard!"

"Next time you try to burn the house down, and/or summon up a nameless monstrosity from the abyss without adequate shielding, why don't you give me some warning so I can find another continent to go live on?"

"Those were fifty quid each in Camden Market!" He's leaning over the PSU anxiously, but not quite anxiously enough to poke at it without insulated gloves.

"Doesn't matter. First thing I heard was the feedback howl. If you don't shut the thing down before answering a call of nature, don't be surprised when Mrs Nature comes calling on you."

"Bugger." He shakes his head. "Can I borrow your laser pointer?"

I head back upstairs to carry on watching my plane-crash program. It's at times like this that I think I really need to find a better class of flatmate—if only the pool of security-cleared cohabitants was larger.

## 2
## Enquiry

It's the afternoon of day two of the training course Andy sent me on, and I have just about hit my boredom threshold. Down on the floor of the cramped lecture theatre our teacher is holding forth about the practicalities of summoning and constraining powers from the vasty deeps; you can only absorb so much of this in one sitting, and my mind is a million kilometers away.

"You need to remember that all great circles must be terminated. Dangling links are potent sources of noise in the circuit, and you need to stick a capacitor on the end to drain it and prevent echoes; sort of like a computer's SCSI bus, or a local area network. In the case of the great circuit of Al-Hazred, the terminator was originally a black goat, sacrificed at midnight with a silver knife touched only by virgins, but these days we just use a fifty microfarad capacitor. You, Bob! Are you falling asleep back there? Take some advice: you don't want to do that. Try this and get the termination wrong and you'll be laughing on the other side of your face—because your face will be on the other side of your head. If you still have a head."

*Bloody academic theoreticians . . .* "Yes," I said. I've been over this before with Brains; electrical great circles are a bad thing, best shunned by anyone with easy access to decent quality lasers and a stabilised platform. Electricity, for ages the primary tool of the experimental vitalists, is now pretty much obsolete—but it's so well-understood that these ivory-tower types prefer to use it as a vehicle for their research, rather than trying more modern geometry engines based on light, which doesn't have any of the nasty side effects of electrical invocations. But that's the British school for you. Over in the States, when they're not dangling stupid "remote viewing" disinformation tricks in front of the press corps the Black Chamber is busy running experiments on the big Nova laser at Los Alamos that everyone thinks is for bomb research. But do we get to play with safe opto-isolated geometry engines and invocation clusters here? Do we, fuck: we're stuck with Dr Volt and his thuggish friend Mr Amp, and pray we don't get a stray ground loop while the summoning core is present and active.

"Anyway, it's time to break for coffee. After we come back in about fifteen minutes, I'm going to move along a bit; it's time to demonstrate the basics of a constraint invocation. Then this afternoon we'll discuss the consequences of an uncontrolled summoning." (Uncontrolled summonings are Bad—at best you'll end up with someone going flatline, their brain squatted by an alien entity, and at worst you'll end up with a physical portal leading somewhere else. So don't do that, m'yeah?)

Teacher claps his hands together, brushing invisible chalk dust from them, and I stand up and stretch—then remember to close my file. The one big difference between this training course and a particularly boring stretch at university is that everything we learn here is classified under Section Three; the penalty for letting someone peek in your notebook can be draconian.

There's a waiting room outside, halfway between the lecture theatres, painted institutional cabbage with frumpy modular seating in a particularly violent shade of burnt orange that instantly makes me think of the 1970s. The vending machine belongs in an antique shop; it appears to run on clockwork. We queue up obediently, and there's a shuffle to produce the obligatory twenty-pence pieces. A yellowing dog-eared poster on the wall reminds us that CARELESS TALK COSTS LIVES—it might be indicative of a sardonic institutional sense of humor but I wouldn't bet on it. (Berwick-upon-Tweed was at war with the Tsar's empire until 1992, and it wouldn't surprise me in the slightest to discover that one of the more obscure Whitehall departments—say, the Ministry of Transport's Department of long-reach electric forklift vehicle Maintenance Inspectorate, Tires Desk—is still locked in a struggle to the death with the Third Reich.)

It is quite in keeping with the character of the Laundry to be aware of the most peculiar anomalies in our diplomatic heritage— the walking ghosts of conflicts past, as it were—and be ready to reactivate them at a moment's notice. That which never lived sleeps on until awakened, and it's not just us citizens of old-fashioned Einsteinian spacetime who make treaties, right?

A fellow trainee shuffles up to me and grins cadaverously. I glance at him and force myself to resist the urge to sidle away: it's Fred from Accounting, the pest who's always breaking his computer and expects me to fix it for him. About fifty-something, with papery dry skin that looks as if a giant spider has sucked all the juice out of him, he's still wearing a suit and tie on the second day of a five-day course—like he's wandered out of the wrong decade. And it looks slept in, if not lived in to the point of being halfway through a second mortgage and a course of damp-proofing. "Dr Vohlman seems to have it in for you, eh?"

I sniff, and decide to stop resisting the urge to sidle away. "Metaphorically or sexually?"

An expression of deep puzzlement flits across Fred's face. "What's

that? Metawatchically? Nah. He's a bad-tempered old bastard, that's all."
He leans closer, conspiratorially: "This is all beyond me, you know?
Dunno why I'm on this junket, our training budget is just way over the
top. Got to use the course credits or we lose them next year. Irene's off
studying Eunuch device drivers, whatever they are, and I got posted
here. Luck of the draw. But it doesn't mean anything to me, if you know
what I mean. You look like one of those intellectual types, though. You
probably know what's going on. You can tell me . . ."

"Eh?" I try to hide behind my coffee cup and manage to burn my fingers. While I'm cursing, Fred somehow ends up standing behind my left
shoulder.

"See, Torsun in HR told me he was sending me here, to learn to be
the departmental system administrator so those people in Support can't
pull the wool over our eyes. But his Vohlman-ness keeps cracking these
weird jokes about devils and knives and things. Is he one of them sa-
tanists we got briefed on four years ago, do you suppose?"

I boggle as discreetly as I can manage. "I'm not sure you should be in
this course. The material gets technical quickly and it can be dangerous
if you're not familiar with the appropriate laboratory safety precautions.
Are you sure you want to stay here?"

"Sure? I'm sure! 'Course I'm sure. But I ain't too happy with the content. For one thing, where's all the stuff about license terms and support?
That comes first. I mean, pacts with the devil is all very well, but I need
to know who to phone for real technical support. And has CESG certified all this stuff for use on government networks?"

I sigh. "Go have a word with Dr Vohlman," I suggest, and—a trifle
rudely—turn away. I know there's always one person who's in the wrong
course, but we're two days in and he still hasn't figured it out—that's got
to be some kind of record, hasn't it?

Everyone drinks up and the smokers magically reappear from wherever they vanished to and we troop back into the lecture theatre.
Teacher—Dr Vohlman—has rolled an archaic test bench in; it looks like
a couple of Tesla coils fucking a Wheatstone bridge next to what I'll
swear is a distributor hub nicked from an old Morris Minor. The wiring
on the pentacle is solid silver, tarnished black with age.

"Right, better put your coffee cups down now, because we're going to
actually put some of the stuff we were discussing before break into practice."

Vohlman is all business, attacking his curriculum with the gusto of a
born schoolteacher. "We're going to try a lesser summoning, a type three
invocation using these coordinates I've sketched on the blackboard. This
should raise a primary manifestation of nameless horror, but it'll be a

fairly *tractable* nameless horror as long as we observe sensible precautions. There will be unpleasant visual distortions and some protosapient wittering, but it's no more intelligent than a *News of the World* reporter—not really smart enough to be dangerous. That's not to say that it's safe, though—you can kill yourself quite easily by treating the equipment with disrespect. Just in case you've forgotten, this current is carrying fifteen amps at six hundred volts, and the baseboard is insulated and oriented correctly along a north-south magnetic axis. The geometry we're using for this run is a modified Minkowski space that we can derive by setting pi to four; there's no fractal dimension involved, but things are complicated slightly because the space to which we're map-ping this diagram has a luminiferous aether. Gather round, please, you need to be inside the security cordon when I power up the circuit. Manesh, if you could switch on the ABSOLUTELY NO ENTRY sign . . ."

We gather round the test bench. I hover near the back. I've seen similar experiments before: in fact, I've done much more exotic ones in the basement back at Chateau Cthulhu. Compared to the insanely complex summonings Brains assembles inside his laser grid this is introductory level stuff, just an official checkpoint on my personnel record. (Did I tell you about the friend of mine who was turned down for a job as a trainee scientific officer because he was unqualified? His Ph.D. was no good—the job description said "three GCSE passes" and he'd long since lost all his high school certificates. That's the way the civil service works.)

Still, it's interesting to watch the other students in this course. Babs, blonde bubble-and-squeak with big-framed spectacles, is treating the bench like an unexploded bomb; I think she's new to this and still too much under the influence of *The Exorcist*, probably expects heads to start spinning round and green slime to start spewing at any moment. (Vohlman should have told the students that's what we keep the Ectoplasm Wallahs around for. Impresses the brass no end. But that's another course.) John, Manesh, Dipak, and Mike are behaving just like bored junior technical staff on another week-away-from-the-desk-is-as-good-as-a-holiday training course. Fred from Accounting looks confused, as if he's mislaid his brain, and Callie's found a pressing reason to go powder her nose. Can't say I blame her; this kind of experiment is fun, the same way that demonstrating a thermite reaction in a chemistry lab is fun—it can blow up in your face. I make damn sure that the electrical fire extinguisher is precisely two paces behind me and one pace to my right.

"Okay, everybody pay attention. Don't, whatever happens, touch the grid. Don't, under any circumstances, say anything once I start. Don't, on pain of your life, step outside the red circle on the floor—we're on top of an earthed cage here, but if we go outside it—"

Topology is everything. The idea of a summoning is simple: you create an attractor node at point A. You put the corresponding antinode at point B. You stand in one of 'em, energize the circuit, and something appears at the other. The big "gotcha" is that a human observer is required—you can't do it by remote control. (Insert some quantum cat mumbo-jumbo about "collapsing the wave function" and "Wigner's Friend versus the Animal Liberation Front" here.) Better hope you picked the right circle to stand in, otherwise you're going to learn far more than you ever wanted to know about applied topology—like how the universe looks when you're turned inside-out.

It's not quite as bad as it sounds. For added security, you can superimpose the attractor node and the safety cell, locking in the summoned agency—which means they shouldn't be able to get to us at the antinode. Which is why Herr Doktor Vohlman mit der duelling scars unt ze bad attitude has plonked the test bench right in the middle of the red pentagram painted on the lecture theatre floor and is enjoining us all to stand tight.

Of course, to get to the fire extinguisher I'd have to step out of the circle . . .

"Is this practice approved by the Health and Safety officer?" Fred asks.

"Quiet, please." Vohlman shuts his eyes, obviously psyching himself up for the activation sequence. "Power." He shoves a knife switch over and a light comes on. "Circuit two." A button is depressed. "Is there anybody there?"

Green vapor seems to swirl at the edges of my vision as I focus on the pentagram of silver wire. Lights glow beneath it, set in a baseboard made of timber harvested from a (used) gallows; setup is everything.

"Three." Vohlman pushes another button, then pulls a twist of paper out of his pocket. Tearing it, he exposes a sterile lancet which he shoves into the ball of his left thumb without hesitation. The hair on the back of my neck is standing on end as he shakes his hand at the attractor and a bead of blood flicks away from it, bounces off the air above one wire, rolls back toward the centre—and hovers a foot above it, vibrating like a liquid ruby beneath the fluorescent lights.

"Is anybody there?" mimics Fred. Abruptly his face crinkles in a grin. "Good joke! I almost believed it for a minute!" He reaches out toward the drop of blood and I can feel vast forces gathering in the air around us—and all of a sudden I can feel a headache coming on, like the tension before an electrical storm.

"No!" squeaks Babs, realising it's too late to stop him even as she speaks.

I see Vohlman's face. It's a mask of pure terror: he doesn't dare move a muscle to stop Fred because touching Fred will only spread the contagion. Fred is already lost and the last thing you do to someone who's in contact with high tension is grab them to pull them away—that is, if you do it, it's the last thing you'll *ever* do.

Fred stands still, and his jacket sleeve twitches as if his muscles are writhing underneath it. His hand is over the attractor, and the drop of blood begins to drift toward his fingertip. He is still smiling, like a man with his foot clamped to the third rail of the underground before the smoke and sparks appear. He opens his mouth. "Yes," he says, in a high, clear voice that is not his own. "We are here."

There are luminous worms writhing behind his eyes.

"What did you do next?" asks Boris.

I lean back and stare up at the slowly roiling smoke-dragons that curl under the fluorescent tubes. It takes me a few seconds to find my voice; my throat is raw, and not from smoke.

"Analyzed the situation very fast, the way they train you to: LEAP methodology. Look, evaluate, assign priorities. Fred had grounded the containment field and the level three agency inside it flood-filled him. Level threes aren't sapient but the universe they come from has a much faster timebase than ours; as soon as he crossed the containment they mapped his nervous system and cracked it like a rotten walnut. Full possession in two to five hundred milliseconds."

"But what did you *do?*" Andy pushes at me.

I swallow. "Well, I was opposite him, and he'd grounded the containment. At that point neither the attractor or the antinode were up and running, so we were all targets. The obvious priority was to shut down the possession, fast. You do that by physically disabling the possessed before the agency can construct a defense in depth. I'd been worried by the electrics and made sure I knew where the fire extinguisher was, so that was what I grabbed first."

Boris: "It was the first thing that come to hand?"

"Yes."

Andy nods. "There's going to be a Board of Enquiry," he says. "But that's basically what we needed to know. It fits with what we're hearing from the other witnesses."

"How badly was he hurt?"

Andy looks away. My hands are shaking so much that my coffee cup rattles against its saucer. "He's dead, Bob. He was dead the moment he crossed the line. You and everybody else there would be dead, too, if you hadn't punched his ticket. You've got one colleague who wasn't there, two who didn't notice what was going on, and five—including the instructor—who swear blind that you saved their lives." He looks back at me: "But we have to put you through the enquiry process all the same because it was a fatal incident. He was married with two kids, and there's a pension and other residuals to sort out."

"I didn't know." I stop, before I say something silly. Fred was a jerk, but no man is an island. I feel sick, thinking about the consequences of what happened in that room. Maybe if I'd explained things to him during the break, patted him on the back and sent him away to find a course that would use up his departmental training credits harmlessly—

Andy cuts into my introspection: "Oh, it's a real mess, all right. Always is, when something goes pear-shaped in the line of duty. I'll go so far as to say I expect the enquiry to be a formality in this case—you'll probably come out of it with a commendation. But in the meantime, I'm afraid you're going back to your office where Harriet will formally notify you that you're suspended on full pay pending an enquiry and possible disciplinary action. You're going to go home and cool your heels until next week, then we'll try to get it over with as fast as possible." He leans back from his desk and sighs. "This sucks, really and truly, but there's no getting around it. So I suggest you treat the suspension as time to chill out and get your head together, get over things—because after the enquiry I expect we'll be resurrecting your application for active duty training and field ops, and looking at it favourably."

"Huh?" I sit up.

"Ninety percent of active duty consists of desk work. You can do that, even if the hat doesn't fit too well. Another 9 percent is sitting around in bushes while the rain drips down your collar, wondering what the hell you're doing there. I figure you can do that, too. It's the other 1 percent—a few seconds of confused danger—that's hard to get right, and I think you've just demonstrated the capability. To the extent that it's my call, you've got it—" he stands up "—if you want it."

I stand up too. "I'll think about it," I say, and I walk out the door before I start mouthing obscenities, because I can't get Fred's expression out of my head. I've never seen someone die before. Funny, isn't it? Most of us go through life and never really see someone die, much less die violently. I should be on a high, knowing that I'm going to qualify for field ops, and if this interview had happened yesterday I would be. But now I just want to throw up in a corner.

Brains is in the kitchen when I get home, attempting to cook an omelette without breaking the eggshell.

It's raining, and my jacket is drenched from the short run between the tube station and the front door; give thanks once more to the invisible boon of contact lenses, without which I would be staring at the world through streak-befuddled spectacles. "Hi," says Brains. "Can you hold this for me?"

He hands me an egg. I stare.

The normally not-so-clean kitchen worktop is gleaming and sterile, as if in preparation for a particularly fussy surgeon. At one side of it sits a syringe and needle preloaded with a grey, opaque liquid—essence of concrete. At the other side of it sits a food processor, its safety shutoff hacked and something that looks worryingly like half an electric motor bolted to the drive shaft that normally turns its blades. I stand there dripping and staring: even for Brains's projects, this is distinctly abnormal.

I hand the egg back. "I'm not in the mood."

"C'mon. Just hold it?"

"I mean it. I've just been suspended, pending an enquiry." I unzip my jacket and let it tumble to the floor. "Game over, priority interrupt, segmentation fault."

Brains cocks his head toward one side and stares at me with big bright eyes, like a slightly demented owl. "Seriously?"

"Yeah." I hunt around for the coffee jar and begin ladling scoopfuls into the cafeteria. "Water in the kettle?"

"Suspended? On pay? Why?"

In goes the coffee. "Yes, on pay. I saved six people's lives, plus my own. But I lost the seventh, so there's going to be an enquiry. They say it's a formality, but—" *Click*, the kettle is now on, heating up to a steam explosion.

"Something to do with that training course?"

"Yeah. Fred from Accounting. He grounded a summoning grid—"

"Gene police! You! Out of the pool, now!"

"It's not funny."

He looks at me again and loses his levity. "No, Bob, it's not funny. I'm sorry." He offers me the egg. "Here, hold this, I implore you."

I take it and nearly drop it; it's hot, and feels slightly greasy. There's also a faint stench of brimstone. "What the hell—"

"Just for a moment, I promise you." He pulls out a roughly made copper coil, the wire wrapped around a plastic pie cutter and hooked up to some gadget or other, and gingerly threads it over the egg, around my wrist and back again. "There. The egg should now be degaussed." He puts the coil down and takes the egg from my nerveless hand. "Observe! The first prototype of the ultimate integral ovine omelette." He cracks it on the side of the worktop and a yellow, leathery curdled sponge flops out. The smell of brimstone is now pronounced, tickling at my nostrils like the aftereffect of a fireworks show. "It's still at the development stage—I had to use a syringe on it, but next on the checklist is gel-diffusion electrophoresis using flocculated hemoglobin agglutinates pending in-ovo polymerisation of the rotor elements—so how did your pet luser autodarwinate?"

I pull up a trash can and sit down. Maybe Brains isn't as monumentally self-obsessed as he looks? At least he slipped the question in painlessly enough.

"You know how there's always someone who ends up in the wrong course? It was that dumb accounts clerk I'm always bitching about. He got in the Intro to Occult Computing course by mistake. I shouldn't have been there, anyway, but Harriet managed to convince Andy I needed it; getting her own back for last month, I think." Harriet has been having problems with her email system and asked my advice; I don't know quite what went wrong, but she ended up blowing five days of the departmental training budget attending a course on sendmail configuration. Took her three weeks to stop twitching every time somebody mentioned rules. "Well and all, I guess what he did qualifies as a massive self-LART, but . . ."

I realize I'm not talking anymore and shudder convulsively.

"His eyes were full of worms."

Brains turns, silently, and rummages in the cupboard above the sink. He pulls down a big bottle labelled *Drain Fluid*, rinses out a couple of chipped cups that are languishing on the draining board, then fills them from the bottle. "Drink this," he says.

I drink. It isn't bleach: my eyes don't quite bulge out, my throat doesn't quite catch fire, and most of the liquid doesn't evaporate from the surface of my tongue. "What the hell is this stuff?"

"Sump degreaser." He winks at me. "Stops Pinky dipping his wick in it, right?" I wink back, a bit nonplussed; I do not think that phrase means what Brains thinks that it means, but if I told him I doubt he'd give me any more of this stuff, so I'm not going to enlighten him. Right now I've got a strong urge to get blindingly drunk—which he seems to have sensed. If I'm blind drunk I won't have to think. And not thinking for a while will be a good thing.

"Thank you," I say, as gravely as I can—it's Brains's secret, after all, and he's confided it in me. I'm obscurely touched, and if I didn't keep seeing Fred grinning at me whenever I closed my eyes it might actually get to me.

Brains peers at me closely. "I think I know your problem," he says.

"What's that?"

"You need—" he's already topping up my cup "—to get pissed. Now."

"But what about your—" I wave feebly at the worktop.

He shrugs. "It's an early success; I'll get it working properly later."

"But you're busy," I protest, because this whole thing is very un-Brains-like; at his worst he's a borderline autist. To have him paying attention to someone else's emotional upsets is, well, eerie.

"I was only trying to prove that you can make an omelette without breaking eggs. That's just a dumb metaphor or a silly practical experiment; you're real, and a classic example of what it means, too. You're broken, in the course of scrambling a body-snatcher's zero point outbreak, and I figure we need to see if all the king's men can fix you, or at least make you feel better. Then you can help me with my egg-sacting project."

I do not throw the glass at him. But I make him refill it.

An indeterminate but nonzero number of semifull vodka glasses later, Pinky appears, looking tall and gangly and slightly flustered. He demands to know where the nearest bookshop is.

"Why?"

"For my nephew." (Pinky has a brother and sister-in-law who live on the other side of London and who have recently spawned.)

"What are you getting him?"

"I'm buying an A to Z and a bible."

"Why?"

"The A to Z is a christening present and the bible is so I know the way to the church." Brains groans; I scrabble drunkenly behind the sofa for a sponge bullet for the Nerf gun, but they all seem to have fallen through the wormhole that leads to the planet of lost paper clips, pencils, and irreplaceable but detachable components of weird toys. "Say, what's going on here?"

"I'm taking a break from my cunning plan to help Bob get drunk, because that's what he needs," says Brains. "He needs distracting and I was doing my best until you came in and changed the subject." He stands up and throws one of the suckers at Pinky, who dodges.

"That's not what I meant; there's a weird smell in the kitchen and something that's, er, squamous and rugose—" a household catch-phrase, and we all have to make the obligatory Cthulhu-waggling-tentacles-on-chin gesture with our hands "—and yellow tried to eat my shoe. What's up?"

"Yeah." I struggle to sit up again; one of the straps under the sofa cushions has failed and it's trying to swallow me. "Just what was that thing in the kitchen?"

Brains stands up: "Behold—" he hiccups "—I am in the process of disproving a law of nature; to wit, that it is impossible to make an omelette without breaking eggs! I have a punning clan—"

Pinky throws the (somewhat squashed, but definitely formerly spherical) omelette at his head and he ducks; it hits the video stack and bounces off.

"I have a cunning plan," Brains continues, "which if you'll let me finish—"

I nod. Pinky stops looking for things to throw.

"That's better. The question is how to churn up an egg without breaking the shell, then cook it from the inside out, correct? The latter problem was solved by the microwave oven, but we still have to whisk it up properly. This usually means breaking it open, but what I figured out was that if I inject it with magnetized iron filings in a lecithin emulsion, then stick it in a rotating magnetic field, I can churn it up quite effectively. The next step is to do it without breaking the shell at all—immerse the egg in a suspension of some really tiny ferromagnetic particles then use electrophoresis to draw them into it, then figure out some way of making them clump together into long, magnetized chains inside it. With me so far?"

"Mad, *mad* I say!" Pinky is bouncing up and down. "What are we going to do tonight, Brains?"

"What we do every night, Pinky: try to take over the world!" (Of haute cuisine.)

"But I've got to buy a couple of books before the shops close," says Pinky, and the spell is broken. "Hope you feel better, Bob. See you guys later." And he's gone.

"Well that was useless," sighs Brains. "The lad's got no staying power. One of these days he'll settle down and turn all normal."

I look at my flatmate gloomily and wonder why I put up with this shit. It's a glimpse of my life, resplendent in two-dimensional glory, from an angle that I don't normally catch—and I don't like it. I'm just about to say so when the phone chirrups.

Brains picks it up and all expression drains from his face. "It's for you," he says, and hands me the phone.

"Bob?"

My free hand starts to shake because I really don't need to hear this, even though part of me wants to. "Yes?"

"It's me, Bob. How are you? I heard the news—"

"I feel like shit," I hear myself saying, even though a small corner of my mind is screaming at me. I close my eyes to shut out the real world. "It was horrible. How did you hear?"

"Word gets around." She's being disingenuous, of course. Mhari has more tentacles than a squid, and they're all plugged into the Laundry grapevine. "Look, are you okay? Is there anything you need?"

I open my eyes. Brains is staring at me blankly, pessimistically. "I'm getting as drunk as possible," I say. "Then I plan to sleep for a week."

"Oh," she says in a small voice, sounding about as cute and appealing as she ever did. "You're in a bad state. May I come round?"

"Yes." In an abstract sort of way I notice Brains choking on his drain fluid. "The more the merrier," I say, hollow-voiced. "Party on."

"Party on," she echoes, and hangs up.

Brains glares at me. "Have you taken leave of your senses?" he demands.

"Very probably." I toss back what's left in my cup and reach for the bottle.

"That woman's a psychopath."

"So I keep telling myself. But after the tearful reconciliation, hot passionate bunny fucks on the bedroom floor, screaming pentacle-throwing tantrum, and final walkout number four, at least she'll give me something concrete and personal to feel *really* depressed about, instead of this gotta-save-'em-all shit I'm kicking my own arse over."

"Just keep her out of the cellar this time." He stands up unsteadily. "Now if you'll excuse me, I've got some omelettes to nuke . . ."

A week later:

"This is an M11/9 machine pistol, manufactured by SW Daniels in the States. In case you hadn't figured it out, it's a gun. Chambered to take 9mm and converted to accept a sten magazine, it has a very high cyclic rate of 1600 rounds per minute, muzzle velocity 350 meters per second, magazine capacity thirty rounds. This cylinder is a two-stage wipeless suppressor, *not* what you might have seen in the movies as a 'silencer'; it doesn't silence the gun, but it cuts the noise by about thirty decibels for the first hundred or so rounds you put through it.

"You need to know three things about this machine. One: if someone points one at you, do whatever they tell you, it is not a fashion accessory. Two: if you see one lying around, don't pick it up, unless you know how to carry it safely. You might blow your feet off by accident. Three: if you need one, dial the Laundry switchboard and ask for 1-800-SAS—our lads will be happy to oblige, and they train with these things every day of the week."

Harry isn't joking. I nod, and jot down some notes, and he sticks the submachine gun back in the rack.

"Now this—tell me about *this*."

I look at the thing and rattle off automatically: "Class three Hand of Glory, five charge disposable, mirrored base for coherent emission instead of generalised invisibility . . . doesn't seem to be armed, maximum range line-of-sight, activation by designated power word—" I glance sidelong at him. "Are you cleared to use these things?"

He puts the Hand of Glory down and picks up the M11/9 carefully. He flicks a switch on its side, looks round to make sure he's clear, points it downrange, and squeezes the trigger. There's a shatteringly loud crackle of gunfire followed by a tinkle of brass on concrete around our feet. "Your call!" he shouts.

I pick up the hand. It feels cold and waxy, but the activation code is scribed on the sawn-off radius in silver. I step up beside him, point it downrange, focus, and concentrate on the trigger string, knowing that it sometimes takes a few seconds—

WHUMP.

"Very good," Harry says drily. "You realize it cost an execution in Shanxi province to make that thing?"

I put it down, feeling queasy. "I only used one finger. Anyway, I thought our suppliers used orangoutangs. What happened?"

He shrugs. "Blame the animal rights protesters."

I'm not back on duty—I'm suspended on full pay. But according to Boris the Mole there's a loophole in our official procedures which means that I'm still eligible for training courses that I was signed up for before being suspended, and it turns out that Andy signed me up for a full package of six weeks of prefield training: some of it down at the village that used to be called Dunwich, and some at our own invisible college in Manchester.

The full package is a course in law and ethics (including International Relations 101: "Do whatever the nice man with the diplomatic passport tells you to do unless you want to start World War Three by accident."), the correct use of petty cash receipts, basic tailing and surveillance, timesheets, how to tell when you're being T&S'd, travel authorization requests, locks and security systems, reconciliation and write-offs, police relations ("Your warrant card will get you out of most sticky situations, if they give you time to show it."), computer security (roll around the floor, laughing), software purchase orders, basic thaumaturgic security (ditto), and use of weapons (starting with the ironclad rule: "Don't, unless you have to and you've been trained."). And so I find myself down on the range with Harry the Horse, a middle-aged guy with an eye patch and thinning white hair who thinks nothing of blowing things away with a submachine gun but seems somewhat startled at my expertise with a HOG–3.

"Right." Harry ejects the magazine from his gun and pulls the cocking handle to get rid of the chambered round. "I think we'll keep you off the firearms list then, and pencil you in for training to COWEU–2—certification of weaponry expertise, unconventional, level two. Permission to carry unconventional devices and use them in self-defense when authorised on assignment to hazardous duty. I take it that bullseye wasn't an accident?"

I pick up the hand and remember to disarm it this time. "Nope. You realize you don't need an anthropoid for this? Ever wondered why there are so many one-legged pigeons in central London?"

Harry shakes his head. "You young 'uns. Back when I was getting going we used to think the future would be all lasers and food pills and rockets to Mars."

"It's not that different," I remonstrate. "Look, it's a science. You try using a limb from someone who died of motor neurone disease or MS and you'll find out in a hurry! What we're doing is setting up a microgrid that funnels in an information gate from another contiguous continuum. Information gates are, like, easy; with a bit more energy we can crank it open and bring mass through, but that's more hazardous so we don't do it very often. The demonic presences—okay, the extraterrestrial sapient fast-thinkers on the other side—try to grab control over the proprioceptive nerves they can sense the layout of on the other side of the grid. The nerves are dead, like the rest of the hand, but they still act as a useful channel. So the result is an information pulse, raw information down around the Planck level, that shows up to us as a phase-conjugated beam of coherent light—"

I point the hand at the downrange target. Two smoking feet.

"What will you do if you ever have to point that thing at another human being?" Harry asks quietly.

I put it back on the rack hastily. "I really hope I'm never put in that position," I say.

"That's not good enough. Say they were holding your wife or kids hostage—"

"The enquiry hasn't been held yet," I reply. "So I don't know if I've still got a job. But I hope I never get put in that kind of position again."

I try to keep my hands from shaking as I padlock the case and reactivate the ward field. Harry looks at me thoughtfully and nods.

"Committee of enquiry will come to order."

I shuffle the papers in front of me, for no very good reason other than to conceal my nervousness.

It's a small conference room, walled in thick oak panels and carpeted in royal blue. I've just been called in: they're grilling people in order of who was there and who was responsible, and after Vohlman I'm number two. (He was running the course and conducted the summoning; I merely terminated it.) I don't recognise the suits sitting behind the table, but they look senior, in that indefinable way that somehow says, "I've got my KCMG; how long until you get yours?" The third is a senior mage from the Auditors, which would be enough to make my blood run cold if I were guilty of anything worse than stealing paper clips.

They ask me to stand on the centre of the crest of arms in the carpet: sewn with gold thread, some kind of Latin motto, very nice. I feel the hairs on my arms prickle with static and I know it's live.

"Please state your name and job title." There's a recorder on the desk and its light is glowing red.

"Bob Howard. Darkside hacker, er, Technical Computing Officer grade 2."

"Where were you on Thursday the nineteenth of last month?"

"Er, I was attending a training course: Introduction to Applied Occult Computing 104, conducted by Dr Vohlman."

The balding man in the middle makes a doodle on his pad then fixes me with a cold stare. "Your opinion of the course?"

"My—er?" I freeze for a moment; this isn't in the script. "I was bored silly—um, the course was fine, but it was a bit basic. I was only there because Harriet was pissed off at me for coming in late after putting in a twenty-hour shift. Dr Vohlman did a good job, but really it was insanely basic and I didn't learn anything new and wasn't paying much attention—" *Why am I saying this?*

The man in the middle looks at me again. It's like being under a microscope; I feel the back of my neck burst out in a cold, prickly sweat. "When you weren't paying attention, what were you doing?" he demands.

"Daydreaming, mostly." What's going on? I can't seem to stop myself answering everything they ask, however embarrassing. "I can't sleep in lecture theatres and you can't read a book when there are only eight students. I kept an ear open in case he said something interesting but mostly—"

"Did you bear Frederick Ironsides any ill will?"

My mouth is moving before I can get control: "Yes. Fred was a fuckwit. He kept asking me stupid questions, was too dumb to learn from his own mistakes, made work for other people to mop up after him, and held a number of opinions too tiresome to list. He shouldn't have been in the course and I told him to tell Dr Vohlman, but he didn't listen. Fred was a waste of airspace and one of the most powerful bogon emitters in the Laundry."

"Bogons?"

"Hypothetical particles of cluelessness. Idiots emit bogons, causing machinery to malfunction in their presence. System administrators absorb bogons, letting the machinery work again. Hacker folklore—"

"Did you kill Frederick Ironsides?"

"Not deliberately—yes—you've got my tongue—no—dammit, he did it himself! Damn fool shorted out the containment wards during a practical so I hit him with the extinguisher, but only after he was possessed. Self-defense. What kind of spell is this?"

"No opinions, Robert, facts only and just the facts, please. Did you hit Frederick Ironsides with the fire extinguisher because you hated him?"

"No, because I was scared shitless that the thing in his head was going to kill us all. I don't hate him—he's just a bore but that isn't a capital offence. Usually."

The woman on his right makes a note on her pad. My inquisitor nods: I can feel chains of invisible silver holding my tongue still, chains binding me to the star chamber carpet I stand upon. "Good. Just one more question, then. Of the students on your training course, who least belonged there?"

"Me." Before I can bite my tongue, the compulsion forces me to finish the sentence: "I could have been teaching it."

The sea crashes on the shore endlessly, a grey continuum of churning water that meets the sky halfway to infinity. Shingle crunches as I walk along what passes for a beach here, past the decaying graveyard that topples gently down the slope to the waters below. (Every year the water claims another foot off the headland; Dunwich is slowly sinking beneath the waves, until finally the church bells will toll with the tide.)

Seagulls scream and whirl and snap in the air above me like dervishes.

I came here on foot to get away from the dormitory and the training units and the debriefing offices built from what used to be two rows of ramshackle cottages and a big farmhouse. There are no roads in or out of Dunwich; the Ministry of Defense took over the entire village back in 1940 and redirected the local lanes, erasing it from the map and the collective consciousness of Norfolk as if it never existed. Ramblers are repulsed by the thick hedges that surround us on two sides and the cliff that protects its third flank. When the Laundry inherited Dunwich from MI5, they added subtler wards; anyone approaching cross-country will begin to develop a deep sense of unease a mile or so outside the perimeter. As it is, the only way in or out is by boat—and our watery friends will take care of any unwelcome visitors smaller than a nuclear submarine.

I need space to think. I've got a lot to think about.

The Board of Enquiry found that I was not responsible for the accident. What's more, they approved my transfer to active status, granted my course completion certificate, and blew through the department like a hot desert wind driving stinging sand-grains of truth before it. With their silvertongue bindings and executive authority the old broom swept clean and left everything behind tidy—if a little shaky, with all the nasty unwashed linen exposed to the cold-eyed view of authority. I would not have liked to answer to their jackal-headed servitors if I were guilty. But, as Andy pointed out, if being a smart-arse was an offence, the Laundry would not exist in the first place.

Mhari moved back into my room after the night of the party and I haven't dared tell her to move back out again. So far she hasn't thrown anything at me or threatened to slash her wrists, in any particular order. (Two months ago, the last time she polled my suicide interrupt queue, I was so pissed off I just said, "Down, not across," using a fingernail to demonstrate. That's when she broke the teapot over my head. I should have taken that as a warning sign.)

What I've got to think about now is a lot larger. The business with Fred was a real eye-opener. Do I still want to put my name on the active service list? Join the Dry Cleaners, visit strange countries, meet exotic people, and cast death spells at them? I'm not sure anymore. I *thought* I was sure, but now I know it amounts to shivering in a rainstorm most of the time and having to watch people with worms waggling behind their eyes the rest of it. Is this what I want to do with my life?

Maybe. And then again, maybe not.

There's a large boulder on the shingle ahead of me; beyond it, a decaying upside-down boat marks the no-go border within our security perimeter. This is as far away as I can get without tripping alarms, drawing down security attention, and generally looking stupid in public. I place a hand on the boulder; it's heavily weathered and covered in lichen and barnacles. I sit on it and look back down the beach, back toward Dunwich and the training complex. For a moment, the world looks hideously solid and reliable, almost as if the comforting myths of the nineteenth century were true, and everything runs on clockwork in an orderly, unitary cosmos.

Somewhere down in the village, Dr Malcolm Denver is undergoing induction briefings, orientation lectures, shoe-size measurements, pension adjustments, and being issued with his departmental toothpaste tube and identification dog tags. He's probably still a bit pissed off, the way I was four years ago when I was pulled in after someone—they never told me who—caught me systematically dumpster-diving through files that were off-limits but inadequately guarded from network infiltration. It was really just a summer vacation job between finishing my CS degree and starting postgrad work: making ends meet doing contract work for the Department of Transport. I smelt a rat in the woodpile and began to dig, never quite suspecting the full magnitude of the rodent whose tail I had grabbed hold of. I was pissed off at first, but over the following four years, spent immersed in the Laundry Basket—our strange collective ghetto of secret knowledge—I acquired the basics of this calling. Thaumaturgy is quite as fascinating as number theory, thank you very much, the hermetic disciplines descended from Trismegistus as engrossing as the sciences he dabbled in. But do I want to dedicate myself to working in a secret field for life?

I can't very well go back to civvy street; they'll let me if I ask nicely, but only as long as I agree to have nothing to do with a wide range of occupations—including everything I can possibly earn a living at. This will cause problems, family problems as well as money problems—mum will probably ignore me and dad will yell about slacking and layabout hippies. Having a son in the civil service suits them down to the ground: they both get to ignore the inconvenient evidence of their mistaken marriage and carry on with their lives, secure in the knowledge that at least they did the parental thing successfully. Meanwhile, I haven't served long enough to earn a pension yet. I suppose I could stagnate in tech support indefinitely, or mutate into management; a generous portion of the Laundry's payroll is devoted to buying the silence of incompetent lambs, manufacturing work for people who need something to fill the time between their first, accidental exposure and final retirement. (There's nothing kindhearted about this; bumping off talkative voices is an expensive, dangerous business with hideous political consequences if you get caught, and it makes for an unpleasant working environment. Paying dead wood to sit at a desk and not rock the boat is comparatively cheap and painless.) But I'd like to think life isn't quite so . . . meaningless.

Seagulls wheel and squawk overhead. There's a faint thud behind me; one of them has dropped something on the beach. I turn round to watch, just in case the bastards are trying to toilet-bomb me. At first glance that's what it looks like: something small, like a starfish, and faintly green. But on closer inspection . . .

I stand up and lean over the thing. Yes, it's starfish-shaped: radial symmetry, five-fold order. Seems to be a fossil, some kind of greenish soapstone. Then I look closer. I know that only two hundred miles away most of the nuclear reactors in Europe are sitting on the Normandy coast, where the prevailing winds would blow a fallout plume out toward us. (And you wonder why the British government insists on keeping its nuclear weapons?) Nevertheless, this is weirder than any radiation mutant has a right to be. Each tentacle tip is slightly truncated; the whole thing looks like a cross-section through a sea cucumber. It must be a representative of an older order, a living fossil left over from some weird family of organisms mostly rendered extinct by the Cambrian biodiversity catastrophe—when the structures that lie buried two kilometers below a nameless British Antarctic Survey base were built.

I stare at the fossil, because it seems like an omen. A thing transported from its natural environment, washed up and left to die on an alien beach beneath the gaze of creatures incomprehensible to it: that's a good metaphor for humanity in this age, the humanity that the Laundry is sworn to defend. Never mind the panoply of state and secrecy, the cold-war trappings of village and security cordon—what it's about, when you get down to it, is this: our appalling vulnerability, collectively, before the onslaught of beings we can barely comprehend. A lesser one, not even one of the great Old Ones, would be enough to devastate a city; we play under the shadow of forces so sinister that a momentary relaxation of vigilance would see all that is human blotted out.

I can go back to London, and they will let me go back to my desk and my stuffy cubicle and my job fixing broken office machines. No recriminations, just a job for life and a pension in thirty-years time in return for a promise of silence to the grave. Or I can go back to the office in the village and sign the piece of paper that says they can do whatever they like with me. Unthanked, possibly fatal service, anywhere in the world: called on to do things which may well be repugnant, and which I will never be able to talk about. Maybe no pension at all, just an unmarked grave in some isolated defile on a central Asian plateau, or a sock-shod foot washed up, unaccompanied, on a Pacific beach one morning while the crabs dine heavy. Nobody ever volunteered for field ops because of the pay and conditions. On the other hand . . .

I look at the starfish-thing and see eyes, human eyes, with worms moving inside them, and I realize that there is no choice. Really, there never was a choice.

# 3
# Defector

Three months later to the nearest minute I am loosely attached to the US desk, working on my first field assignment. This would normally be an extremely stressful point in my career, except that this is very much a low-stress training mission, as Santa Cruz is one of the nicest parts of California, and right now having my fingernails pulled out by the Spanish Inquisition would be more pleasant than putting up with Mhari. So I'm making the most of it, sitting in a tacky bar down on a seaside pier, nursing a cold glass of Santa Cruz Brewing Company wheat beer, and watching the pelicans practice their touch-'n'-gos on the railing outside.

It's early summer and the temperature's in the mid-twenties; the beach is covered in babes, boardwalk refugees, and surf nazis. This being Santa Cruz I'm wearing cut-off jeans, a psychedelic T-shirt, and a back-to-front baseball cap—but I can't kid myself about passing for a native. I've got the classic geek complexion—one a goth would kill for—and in Santa Cruz even the geeks get out in the sun once in a while. Not to mention wearing more than one earring.

My contact is a guy called Mo. Actually, I'm not sure that isn't a pseudonym. Nobody seems to know very much about the mysterious Mo, except he's an expatriate British academic, and he's having trouble coming home. All of which makes me wonder why the Laundry is involved at all, as opposed to the Consulate in San Francisco.

A bit of background is in order; after all, aren't the UK and the USA allies? Well, yes and no. No two countries have identical interests, and the result is a blurred area where self-interest causes erstwhile allies to act toward one another in a less than friendly manner. Mossad spies on the CIA; in the 1970s, Romania and Bulgaria spied on the Soviet Union. This doesn't mean their leaders aren't slurping each other's cigars, but . . .

In 1945 the UK and the USA signed a joint intelligence-sharing treaty that opened their most secret institutions to mutual inspection and exchange: at the time they were fighting a desperate war against a common enemy. Not many people outside the secret services understand just how close to the abyss we stood, even as late as April 1945: there's nothing like facing a diabolical enemy set on your complete destruction to cement an alliance at the highest level . . . and for the first few postwar years, the UK-USA treaty kept us singing from the same hymn book.

But UK-USA relations deteriorated over the following decade. Partly this was a side effect of the Helsinki Protocol; when even Molotov agreed that occult weapons of the type envisaged by Hitler's Thule Society minions were too deadly to use, a lot of the pressure came off the alliance. When it became apparent that the British intelligence system was riddled with Russian spies, the CIA turned the cold shoulder; thus, a background of shifting superpower politics was established, in which the moth-eaten British lion was unwillingly taught his place in the scheme of things by the new ringmaster, Uncle Sam. I suppose you could blame the Suez crisis and the Turing debacle, or Nixon's paranoia, but in 1958, when the UK offered to extend the 1945 treaty to cover occult intelligence, the US government refused.

My colleagues in GCHQ listen in on domestic US phone calls, compile logs, and pass them across the desk to their NSA liaisons—who are forbidden by charter from spying on domestic US territory. In return, the NSA Echelon listening posts give GCHQ a plausibly deniable way of monitoring every phone conversation in western Europe—after all, they're not actually listening; they're just reading transcripts prepared by someone else, aren't they? But in the twilight world of occult intelligence, we aren't allowed to cooperate overtly. I don't have a liaison here, any more than I'd have one in Kabul or Belgrade: I'm technically an illegal, albeit on a tourist visa. Any nasty reality excursions are strictly my problem.

On the other hand, the days of midnight insertions—bailing out of the back door of a bomber by midnight and trying not to hang your parachute up on the Iron Curtain—are gone for good. Gone, too, are the days of show trials for captured spies: if I get caught, the worst I can expect is to be questioned and put on the first flight home. My way into the country was more prosaic than a wartime parachute drop, too: I flew in on an American Airlines MD-11, filled out the visa waiver declaration ("occupation: civil servant; purpose of visit: work assignment," and no, I was not a member of the German Nazi Party between 1933 and 1945), and entered via the arrival hall at San Francisco Airport.

Which is how I find myself watching the pelicans on the pier at Santa Cruz, sipping my beer sparingly, waiting for Mo to manifest himself, and trying to figure out just why a British academic should be having so much trouble coming home as to need our help—not to mention why the Laundry might be taking him seriously.

I'm not the only customer in the bar, but I'm the only one with a beer and a copy (unopened) of *Philosophical Transactions on Uncertainty Theory* lying in front of me. That's my cover; I'm meant to be a visiting postgrad student come to talk to the prof about a possible teaching post. So when Mo walks in he should have no difficulty identifying me. There are six professors of philosophy at UCSC: one tenured, two assistant, and three visiting. I wonder which of them he is?

I glance around idly, just in case he's already here. There are two grunge metal skateboard types in the far corner, drinking Bud-Miller-Coors and comparing body piercings; the town's swarming with 'em, nothing to take note of. A gentleman in a plaid shirt, chinos, and short haircut sits on a bar stool on his own, back ramrod-straight, reading the *San Jose Mercury News*. (That dings my suspicion-o-meter because he looks very Company in a casual-Friday kind of way—but if they were tailing me why in hell would they make it so obvious? He might equally well be an affluent local businessman.) A trio of nrrrd grrrlzz with shaven scalps and unicorn forelocks compare disposable tattoos and disappear into the toilet one by one, going in glum and coming out giggly: must be a Bolivian marching powder dispenser or a mendicant sin-eater or something in there. I shake my head and sip my beer, then look up just as a rather amazing babe with classic red hair leans over me.

"Mind if I take this chair?"

"Um—" I'm trying desperately to think of an excuse, because my contact is looking for a single man with a copy of *PTUT* on the table in front of him. But she doesn't give me time:

"You can call me Mo. You would be Bob?"

"Yeah. Have a seat." I blink rapidly at her, stuck for words. She sits down while I study her.

Mo is striking. She's a good six feet tall, for starters. Strong features, high cheekbones, freckles, hair that looks like you could wrap it in insulation and run the national grid through it. She's got these big dangly silver earrings with glass eyeballs, and she's wearing combat pants, a plain white top, and a jacket that is so artfully casual that it probably costs more than I earn in a month. Oh, and there's a copy of *Philosophical Transactions on Uncertainty Theory* in her left hand, which she puts down on top of mine. I can't estimate her age; early thirties? That would make her a real high-flyer. She catches me staring at her and stares back, challenging.

"Can I buy you a drink?" I ask.

She freezes for a moment then nods, emphatically. "Pineapple juice." I wave at the bartender, feeling more than a little flustered. Under her scrutiny I get the feeling that there's something of the Martian about her: a vast, unsympathetic intelligence from another world. I also get the feeling that she doesn't suffer fools gladly.

"I'm sorry," I say, "nobody told me who to expect." The local businessman looks across from his newspaper expressionlessly: he sees me watching and turns back to the sports pages.

"Not your problem." She relaxes a little. The bartender appears and takes an order for a pineapple juice and another beer—I can't seem to get used to these undersized pints—and vanishes again.

"I'm interested in a teaching post," I find myself saying, and hope her contact told her what the cover story is. "I'm looking for somewhere to continue after my thesis. UCSC has a good reputation, so . . ."

"Uh-huh. Nice climate too." She nods at the pelicans outside the window. "Better than Miskatonic."

"Really? You were there?"

I must have asked too eagerly because she looks at me bleakly and says, "Yes." I nearly bite my tongue. (Foreign female professor of philosophy in the snobbish halls of a New England college. Worse: non-WASP, judging from the Irish accent.) "Some other time. What was the topic of your thesis again?"

Is it my imagination or does she sound half-amused? This isn't part of the script: we're meant to go for a walk and talk about things where we can't be overheard, not ad-lib it in a café. Plus, she thinks I'm from the Foreign Office. What the hell does she expect me to say, early Latin literature? "It's about—" I mentally cross my fingers "—a proof of polynomial-time completeness in the traversal of Hamiltonian networks. And its implications."

She sits up a bit straighter. "Oh, *right*. That's interesting."

I shrug. "It's what I do for a living. Among other things. Where do your research interests lie?"

The businessman stands up, folds his newspaper, and leaves.

"Reasoning under conditions of uncertainty." She squints at me slightly. "Not prior probabilities stuff, Bayesian reasoning based on statistics—but reasoning where there are no evidential bases."

I play dumb: suddenly my heart is hammering between my ribs. "And is this useful?"

She looks amused. "It pays the bills."

"Really?"

The amusement vanishes. "Eighty percent of the philosophical logic research in this country is paid for by the Pentagon, Bob. If you want to work here you'll need to get your head around that fact."

"Eighty percent—" I must look dumbfounded, because something goes *click* and she switches out of her half-sardonic *Brief Encounter* mode and into full professorial flow: "A philosophy professor earns about thirty thousand bucks and costs maybe another five thousand a year in office space and chalk. A marine earns around fifteen thousand bucks and costs maybe another hundred thousand a year in barrack space, ammunition, transport, fuel, weapons, VA expenses, and so on. Supporting all the philosophy departments of the USA costs about as much as funding a single battalion of marines." She looks wryly amused: "They're looking for a breakthrough. Knowing how to deconstruct any opponent's ideological infrastructure and derive self-propagating conceptual viruses based on its blind spots, for example. That sort of thing would give them a real strategic edge: their psych-ops people would be able to make enemies surrender without firing a shot, and do so reliably. Cybernetics and game theory won them the Cold War, so paying for philosophers is militarily more sensible than paying for an extra company of marines, don't you think?"

"That's—" I shake my head "—logical, but weird." *No weirder than what they pay me to do.*

She snorts. "It's not exceptional. Did you know that for the past twenty years they've been spending a couple of million a year on research into antimatter weapons?"

"Antimatter?" I shake my head again: I'm going to get a stiff neck at this rate. "If someone figured out how to make it in bulk they'd be in a position to—"

"Exactly," she says, and looks at me with a curiously satisfied expression. Why do I have a feeling she's seen right through me?

(Antimatter isn't the most exotic thing DARPA has been spending research money on by a long way, but it's exotic enough for the average college professor; especially a philosopher who, reading between the lines, has any number of reasons for being cheesed off with the military-academic complex.)

"I'd like to talk about this some more," I venture, "but maybe this isn't the right place?" I take a mouthful of beer. "How about a walk? When do you have to get back to your office?"

"I have a lecture to deliver at nine tomorrow, if that's what you're asking." She pauses, delicately, tongue slightly extended: "You're thinking about coming to work here, why don't I show you some of the sights?"

"That would be great." We finish our drinks and leave the bar—and the bugs, real or imagined—behind.

I can be a good listener when I try. Mo—a diminutive of Dominique, I gather, which is why I couldn't find her on the university's staff roster—is a good talker, or at least she is when she has a lot to unload. Which is why we walk until I have blisters.

Seal Point is a grassy headland that abruptly turns into a cliff, falling straight down to the Pacific breakers. Some lunatics in wetsuits are trying to surf down there; I wouldn't want to underwrite their life insurance policies. About fifty feet away there's a rocky outcrop carpeted in sea lions. Their barking carries faintly over the crash of the surf. "My mistake was in signing the nondisclosure agreements the university gave me without getting my own lawyer to check them out." She stares out to sea. "I thought they were routine academic application agreements, saying basically the faculty would get a cut from any commercial spin-offs from inventions I made while employed by them. I didn't read the small print closely enough."

"How bad was it?" I ask, shifting from one foot to another.

"I didn't find out until I wanted to go visit my aunt in Aberdeen." So much for my ear for accents. "She was sick; they wouldn't give me a visa. Would you believe it, an exit visa from the USA? I was turned back at the security gate."

"They're usually more worried about people trying to immigrate," I say. "Isn't that the case?"

"I'm not a US citizen; I've got British citizenship and a green card residence permit. I just happen to work here because, well, there aren't a lot of research posts in my speciality elsewhere. If I'd stayed with my ex-husband I'd be eligible for Israeli citizenship, too. But they won't let me leave. I didn't realize it would be like this." She falls silent for a moment; seabirds squawk overhead. "When the Immigration Service made trouble the Pentagon sorted them out, can you believe it? Told them to get off my case."

I nod silently: this isn't good news. It means that someone, somewhere, thinks Mo is a strategic asset—*special treatment, kid gloves, do* not *let this one out of your sight.* We do similar things, sometimes: I'm not allowed to go on vacation outside the EU without written permission from my head of department. But that's because I do secret work for the government. Mo is just a professor, isn't she? I wish she'd be a bit more specific, and say which bit of the Pentagon is giving her grief, rather than just using it as a generic category for big government.

"When did the trouble start?" I ask.

She laughs. "Which trouble?"

*Me and my big mouth.* "Uh, the current batch. I'm sorry; nobody briefed me."

She looks at me oddly. "Just what kind of Foreign Office employee are you?"

I shrug. "If you don't ask me any questions, I won't have to tell you any lies. I'm sorry, but I can't discuss my work. Let's just say that when you started complaining someone with a bit more clout than the consulate was listening. They sent me to see if there's anything we can do for you. All right?"

"Bizarre." She looks askance at me. "Let's walk." She turns, and I follow her back toward the road. There's a footpath leading out of town, shaded by trees; we take it. "The trouble started in Miskatonic," she says. "David and I—we're divorced, now—well, it didn't work out. I didn't play the politics right; Miskatonic is really bad for internal backbiting. When it was obvious they weren't going to open the tenure track up any time soon, I got a feeler from someone at UCSC. Nice research grant, an interesting field close to my own, and a promise of the fast track if I got results."

Tenured professorship is the academic holy grail: a job for life, supposedly to let first-class researchers poke into any corner they feel like, regardless of how popular it is with the administration. Which is, of course, why they're trying to abolish it. "How did it go?"

"I flew over for the interview. I got the job. Only there was a lot of paper to sign. David is a lawyer, but by then—" she falls silent. I can fill in some of the gaps, I think.

We're walking uphill now, and the path narrows. Dappled patterns of light and shade ripple across the dusty track. It's midafternoon and the day is hot and bright. A couple of surf dudes wander past and look at us curiously. "How did you get into your current field of research?" I ask.

"Oh, it was a natural progression. In Edinburgh I was working on inferential reasoning. When I got the job in Arkham I started out doing more of the same, but the belief systems field has been undersubscribed for years, and it seemed like a good place to stake my claim, especially given the interesting closed archives in their stacks: Arkham has a really unique library, you know? I began publishing papers, and that's about when the shit began happening inside the department. Maybe it was departmental politics, but now I'm beginning to wonder."

"They've got long tentacles, not to mention other nameless organs. It would help if I could see the documents you signed."

"They're at the office. I can go in and pick them up later." We're on a steep slope now, going uphill and I'm breathing hard. Mo has long legs and evidently walks a lot. Exercise or habit?

"Your research," I say. "You're certain it's not about any specific military applications?"

I know immediately that I've made a mistake. Mo stops and glares at me. "I'm a philosopher, with a sideline in folk history," she hisses angrily. "What do you take me for?"

"I'm sorry." I take a step back. "I've got to make sure. That's all."

"I shan't be offended then." I get a creepy feeling that she means exactly what she says. "No. It's just, I'm certain—no, positive, in the exact meaning of the word—that it's not that. A calculus of belief, a theory for deriving confidence limits in statements of unsubstantiated faith, can't have any military applications, can it?"

"Did you say *faith?*" I ask, hot and cold chills running up and down my spine. "Specifically, you can analyze the validity of a belief, without—" I stop.

"Let's not get too technical without a whiteboard, hmm?"

"Faith can mean several things, depending on who uses the word," I say. "A theologian and a scientist mean different things by it, for example. And 'unsubstantiated' has a dismayingly technical ring to it. But let's take a hypothetical example. Suppose I assert that I believe in flying pigs. I haven't seen any, but I have reason to believe that flying peccaries, a related species, exist. You're saying you could place confidence limits on my belief? Quantify the probability of those porcine aviators existing?"

"It works." She shrugs. "The numbers are out there. It's a platonic universe; all we can see are the shadows on the wall of the cave, but there are real numbers out there, they have an existence in and of themselves. I just began looking into probabilistic metrics that can be applied to assertions of a theological nature. There are some interesting documents in the Wilmarth folklore collection at Miskatonic . . ."

"Aha." We round a corner and there's an odd little clearing ahead, ringed with trees, with a hillside rising from the far end. "So we're back to the old idea of a real universe, and an observable one, and all we know about is what we can observe. So the department of strategic folklore in the Pentagon was concerned about you showing other people where to find their high-altitude hams?"

She stops and looks at me, frankly sizing me up. She comes to some sort of decision because after a moment she answers: "I think they were more worried about the creatures that cast the shadows on the walls. In particular, the ones that ate the USS *Thresher* and a certain Russian *Whisky*-class hunter-killer about thirty years ago . . ."

When I return to my motel room that evening the man in the plaid shirt from the bar is waiting for me. He's got a federal ID card, a warrant, and an attitude problem.

"Sit down, shut up, and listen," he begins. "I'm going to say this once, and once only. Then you're going to get the hell out of town because if you're still on this continent in twenty-four hours I'm going to have you arrested."

I drop my jacket on the back of my chair. "Who are you and what are you doing here?"

"I said shaddup." He produces a laminated card and I make a show of looking at it. It says, basically, that someone who may or may not be in front of me works for the Office of Naval Intelligence—assuming I'd know an ONI pass if I tripped over one by accident. I think for a moment that he's unusually trusting for a law enforcement officer—they usually make with the guns before they go in—then I realize why and stifle a shudder. His eyes are dead, and there's a funny-looking scar on his forehead, which means the mind animating the body is probably in a bunker miles away. "As far as I'm concerned, today you are a tourist. If you're still here tomorrow I will have to investigate the possibility that you are a foreign national engaged in activities detrimental to the security of this nation. But unless you tell me you're working for the Laundry right here and now, I don't have to act on that information until eighteen hundred hours tomorrow. Am I making myself clear?"

"What's the Laundry?" I ask, doing my best to look puzzled.

He snorts. "Wise guy, huh? Get this through your head—we have wards and sensoids and watchers. We know who you people are, we've got you covered. We know where you live; we know where your dog goes to school. Get it?"

I shrug. "I think you're making a mistake."

"Well." He tries the number four Marine Sergeant glare again, but it bounces off me. "You're *wrong*. We don't make mistakes. You've just spent the past two hours speaking to a national security asset and we don't like that, Mr Howard, we don't like it at all. Normally we'd just pull her security clearance and sling her ass on the next flight out, but the piece you've been talking to may be carrying around some items in her head that are not going to be allowed out of this country. Understand? The matter is under review. And if you happen to have overheard anything you shouldn't have, we're not going to let you out either. Luckily for you we happen to know she didn't tell you anything important. Now make yourself a history of not being here, and you'll be all right."

I sit down and start taking my trainers off. "Is that all you've got to say?" I ask.

Plaid Shirt snorts again: "Is that all?" He walks over to the door. "Yeah buddy, that's all," he says, and opens it. Then there's a wet slapping sound and he falls over backward, leaking blood onto the carpet from both ears.

I roll sideways, out of the line of sight of the door, and grab for the small monkey's paw I wear on a leather thong round my neck. Electricity jolts the palm of my hand as the ward activates. ("Try not to get yourself killed on friendly territory," said Andy: some joke *that* turned out to be!) Plaid Shirt is blocking the suite door from closing and this is one of those

California motels where all the doors open off balconies. I steady my nerves, then get myself turned round behind the bathroom sidewall and make a grab for his nearest arm.

They never tell you how heavy a corpse is in training school. I lean forward thoughtlessly to take a two-handed grip under his shoulder and that's when a mule punches my exposed shoulder. I fall over backward, dragging Plaid Shirt behind me, and the door swings shut.

The pool of blood is growing, but I have to be sure; the bullet hole is somewhere above his hairline. I force myself to look closer—

There are faint letters inscribed on his forehead in an ancient alphabet. They glow briefly then fade as I watch.

I do not feel good about sharing a motel room with a ballistically decommissioned intelligence agency spy. Unfortunately there appears to be a lunatic with a rifle waiting for me outside. I have an edgy feeling that the other shoe is about to drop within the next ninety seconds, and if I don't get out of here I'm going to be answering some pointed questions. Of course, I'm not really meant to last that long—or am I? Did they know about the standard-issue ward? Maybe if I'm lucky the ward will keep on working; they don't like taking direct hits, but they lose efficacy bit by bit, not all at once.

There's a loud blat of engine noise from outside the balcony; a motorbike with a blown muffler revs up then shrieks out of the car park on a trail of rubber. I grab my trainers, yank them on (wincing every time I flex my left arm), grab my jacket, wrap a hand around the dry-dusty object in the right front pocket, and yank the door open—

Just in time to see the bike vanishing down the road, and not a single cop in sight.

I duck into the bathroom and run the taps, then thrust my hands under them to rinse the blood away. They're shaking, I notice distantly. After a moment I start thinking very fast; then I dry my hands and go into the bedroom and pick up my mobile phone. The number I want is already programmed in.

"Hello? Winchester Waste Management?"

"Hi, this is Bob H-Howard speaking," I say. "I've had a bit of an accident and I could do with some cleaning services."

"What did you say your address was?" asks the receptionist. I rattle off the hotel address. Then: "What sort of cleaning do you require?"

"The bedcovers will need changing." I think for a moment. "And I cut myself shaving. I'm going to have to go to work now."

"Okay, our crew will be around shortly." She hangs up on me.

The coded message I sent translates as follows: "Warning, my cover is shot. I've got to get out urgently, things are going bad, and under no circumstances should anyone approach me." *I cut myself shaving:* "Things turned bloody." This sort of code, unlike a cypher, is virtually impossible to crack—as long as you never use it twice. With luck it'll take whoever's tapping the line a few minutes to realize that I've pushed the panic button.

I drop the bathroom towels over Plaid Shirt's leaking head, then grab my jacket and flight bag and cautiously nudge the front door open. Nothing nasty happens. I step out onto the balcony, lock the door behind me, and head down to the car park. All thought of getting Mo's travel arrangements in hand is gone: my immediate job is to drive north, drop the rental off at the airport, and bump myself onto the next available flight.

When I zap the car it doesn't explode: the doors unlock and the lights come on. Clutching my lucky monkey's paw I get in, start the engine, and drive away into the night, shaking like a leaf.

"Hello? Who is this?"

"Mo? This is Bob."

"Bob—"

"Yeah. Look, about this afternoon."

"It's so good to hear—"

"It was great seeing you too, but that's not what I'm calling about. Something's come up at home and I've got to leave. We'll be reviewing your case notes and seeing what pressure we can—"

"You've got to help me."

"What? Of course we'll—"

"No, I mean right *now!* They're going to kill me. I'm locked up in here and they didn't search me so they didn't find my phone but—"

CLICK.

"What the fuck?"

I stare at the phone, then hastily switch it off and yank out the battery in case someone's trying to trace my cell.

"What the *fuck?*"

My head whirls. Oh yeah, a redheaded maiden in distress just asked me to rescue her: a chunk of me is cynically thinking that I must be *really* hard up. There's a pithed spy in my hotel suite and my welcome mat is going to be withdrawn with extreme prejudice when his owners find out about it, just in time to get a cryptic phone call from my target who seems to be in fear for her life. What the—*whatever*—is going on, here?

In the Laundry we supposedly pride ourselves on our procedures. We've got procedures for breaking and entering offices, procedures for reporting a shortage of paper clips, procedures for summoning demons from the vasty deeps, and procedures for writing procedures. We may actually be on track to be the world's first ISO-9000 total-quality-certified intelligence agency. According to our written procedure for dealing with procedural cluster-fucks on foreign assignment, what I should do at this point is fill out Form 1008.7, then drive like a bat out of hell over Highway 17 until it hits the Interstate, then take the turnoff for San Francisco Airport, and use my company credit card to buy the first available seat home. Not forgetting to file Form 1018.9 ("expenses unexpectedly incurred in responding to a situation 1008.7 in the line of duty") in time for the end of month accounting cycle.

Except if I do that—and if Mo's abductors are as friendly as my second visitor of the evening—I've just vaped the mission, screwed the pooch, written off the friendly I was supposed to be extracting, and blown my chances of a second date. (And we'll never find out whether the last thought to pass through the mind of the captain of the *Thresher* was, "It's squamous and rugose," or simply, "It's squamous!")

Looking around, I see the parking lot is still empty. So I pull out, and roll through a U-turn across the railway tracks, and back into town. It's time to apply a little thought to the situation.

Mo lives in a rented flat not that far from the university campus. Now that I know her true name it takes me ten minutes with a map and a phone book to find it and drive over. There are no police cars outside and no sign of trouble; just a flat that's showing no lights. I know she's not home but I need something—anything—of hers so I park the car and briskly walk up the path to her front door, and knock as if I expect a welcome, hoping like hell that her abductors haven't left me a nasty surprise.

The screen door is shut but the inner door gapes open. Ten seconds with the blade of a multitool and the screen door's gaping too. The place is a mess—someone tipped over a low table covered in papers, there's a laptop inverted on the floor, and as my eyes become accustomed to the gloom I see a bookcase face down on the carpet in front of a corridor. I step over it, one hand in my pocket, looking for the bedroom.

The bedroom's a mess: maybe someone searched it in a hurry, or maybe she's the nesting kind. There's a pile of clothing by the bed that looks worn, so I bundle a T-shirt into my bag and head back to the car. Skin flakes, that's what I need; I try not to think too hard about what might be happening to her right now.

As I'm going down the path I see someone coming the other way. Middle-aged, male, thickset. "Howdy," he says, slightly suspiciously.

"Hi," I say, "just dropping by. Mo asked me to water her plants."

"Oh." Instant boredom, conjured by her name. "Well, try not to leave your car there, it's blocking the disabled space."

"I'll be gone before anyone notices," I promise, and do my best to do just that.

Parked safely round the corner I pull out the T-shirt. In the dashboard light it looks faded; hopefully that'll do. I reach into my travel bag and pull out my hacked Palm computer, call up a specialized application that will erase itself if I don't enter a valid password within sixty seconds, pop open the expansion slot on its back, and swipe the concealed sensor across the fabric. *Oh great:* the arrow on the screen is pointing right back at me—I must have contaminated that swatch with my own biomagnetic whatever. Swearing, I restart the program and the machine promptly crashes. It takes another three tries before I get an arrow that's pointing somewhere else, and points in the same direction no matter which way I hold the gadget.

The wonders of modern technology.

An hour later I'm lying on my belly in the undergrowth at the edge of a stand of trees. I'm clutching a monkey's paw, a palmtop computer, and a cellphone; my mission, unless I choose to reject it, is to prevent a human sacrifice in the house in front of me—with no backup.

The hiss and crash of Pacific surf drowns out any noise from the road behind me. There's an onshore breeze, and along with the dampness of the ground—it rained earlier—it is making me shiver. The bruise on my left shoulder smarts angrily: I probably won't be able to move it in the morning. (My damn fault for getting in the way of a bullet. The kinetic impact binding worked its intended miracle but I'm not covered anymore.)

There's a truck parked in front of the carport, the house lights are on, and the curtains are drawn. Ten minutes ago a couple of guys came out the front door, took the dirt bike from the garage, drove straight across the lawn and onto the main road without pausing for traffic. I didn't get a good look at them, but an applet on my palmtop is screaming warnings at me: huge, honking great summoning fields are loose in the area, and judging by the subtype it's a gateway invocation that they're planning. They're actually going to try and open a mass-transfer gate to another universe—seriously bad juju. I've no idea who the hell these people are, or why they snatched Mo, but this is not looking good.

A flicker of light from the road; there's the snarl of a two-stroke engine, then the bike is turning back into the carport with its two passengers on board. One of them has a backpack . . . they've picked something up? Something they don't want to store too close to home? I hunker down lower, trying to make myself invisible. Take another reading, like the others I've made around this side of the garden. I think I've got a feel for it; a complex spiral of protection more than two hundred feet across, centred on the house. Major League paranoia, to protect something big that they're planning. This is where they've brought Mo—I wonder why? I sneak closer to a large window at the side, trying to keep the bushes between myself and the road, and hope like hell that there aren't any dogs here.

They've got the curtains drawn but the window itself is open—although there's some kind of bug screen in the way. I can hear voices. I don't recognize the language and they're muffled by the curtain, but there are more than two speakers. One of them laughs, briefly: it's not a pleasant sound. I settle back against the wall and take stock, trying not to breathe too loudly. Item: I'm sure Mo is in here, unless she's in the habit of lending her T-shirts out to strange swarthy men who perform major summoning rituals whenever she's kidnapped by somebody else. Item: they're not with ONI, or the Laundry. In fact, they're presumed hostile until proven otherwise. Item: there are at least four of them—two on the bike, two or more who stayed in here with Mo. I am not a one-man SWAT team and I am not trained in dealing with hostage-rescue situations, and like Harry said, setting out to be a hero without knowing what you're doing is a good way to end up dead. Hmm. What I need right now *is* a SWAT team, but I don't happen to have one up my sleeve. And aren't SWAT teams supposed to figure out where the hostage is and what's going on before they go storming through the building?

There is, of course, one constructive thing I can do, though it's going to get me yelled at when I go home. I switch my mobile phone back on, then fumble my way through its menus until I find the call log and tell it to dial the last caller. That would be Mo, and if ONI hasn't put a wiretap on her I'm a brass monkey's stepfather. It rings three times before there's an answer and I listen carefully, but there's nothing audible from inside the house.

"Who is this?" It's a man's voice, rather harsh-sounding.

I hold the mouthpiece very close to my lips: "You're looking for Mo," I say.

"Who is this?" he repeats.

"A friend. Listen. Where you find this phone you will find a house. There are several perps in the vicinity, at least four in the building. They've kidnapped Mo, they're building a Dho-Nha circle, at least level four, and you will want to take defensive precautions—"

"Stay right there," says the man on the other end of the phone, so I carefully put it down under the window and scramble round to the back of the house on hands and knees. The front door bangs open. A different voice calls out, "Is that you, Achmet?"

No answer. I hold my breath, heart pounding in my chest. Footsteps on gravel. "The American bitch, she is secure." I back away from the house toward the nearest clump of bushes—the men loom out of the shadows—but the footsteps halt. "I stay out here. Cigarette."

*Bastard's on a fag break!* I glance up at the sky, which is dark as a marketing hack's heart and full of coldly distant stars. *How am I going to get past him?* I grip the monkey's paw in my pocket, carefully withdraw it, and point it at the ground. A red-eyed coal glowers from the doorway, just visible round the side of the house. A distant buzzing bike engine grows louder, heading up the hills far above. Apart from that, the night is silent. *Too* silent, I realize after a minute; that's a road over there—where's the traffic? I begin to edge backward, trying to get farther into the bushes, and that's when everything blanks.

4
The Truth Is in Here

"You don't remember what happened next?"

"Yes, that's what I've been telling you for the past hour." There's no point getting angry with them; they're just doing their job. I resist the temptation to rub my head, the dressing covering the sore patch behind my right ear. "All I remember after that is waking up in hospital the next day."

"Harrumph." I blink; did I really hear someone say *harrumph?* Yes—it's the guy who looks like something the gravedigger's cat dragged in, Derek something or other. He blinks right back at me with watery eyes. "According to page four of the medical notes, paragraph six—"

I watch while they all obediently shuffle their notes. Nobody thought to give me a copy, of course, even though they're mine. "Contusion and hairline fracture on the right occipital hemisphere, some bruising and abrasion consistent with a weighted object." I turn my head, wincing slightly because of the pain in my neck, and point to the dressing. It's been nearly a week; one thing they don't tell you in the detective potboilers is how bad being whacked on the head with a cosh hurts. No, not a cosh: an Object, Weighted, Black Chamber Field Operatives for the Use of, Complies with US-MILSTD-534-5801.

"I suppose we can consider this to be substantiated, then," says the talking corpse. "Please continue where you left off."

I sigh. "I woke up in a hospital room with a needle in my arm and a goon from one of their TLAs baby-sitting me. After about an hour someone who claimed to be running Plaid Shirt turned up and started asking pointed questions. Seems they were already running a stakeout. After the third time that I explained what happened at the motel he agreed that I hadn't waxed their asset and demanded to know why I'd been round at the house. I told him that Mo phoned me and asked for help and it sounded urgent, and after I repeated myself another couple of dozen times he left. The next morning they shipped me to the airport and stuck me on the plane."

The battle-axe from Accounting who's sitting next to Derek glares at me. "*Business* class," she hisses. "I suppose that was your idea of a good ride home?"

*Huh?* "That was nothing to do with me," I protest. "Did they bill—"

"Yes." Andy twirls his pen idly as a fly batters itself against the energy-saving lightbulb overhead.

"Uh-oh." Unsanctioned expenditure isn't quite a hanging offense in the Laundry, but it's definitely up there with insubordination and mutiny. During the Thatcher years they were even supposed to have had paper clip audits, before someone pointed out that the consequences of poor employee morale in this organization might be a trifle worse than in, say, the Ministry of Agriculture, Fisheries, and Food. "Not guilty," I say automatically, before I can stop myself. "I didn't ask them for that, it happened after the assignment went pear-shaped, and I wasn't conscious at the time."

"Nobody's accused you of authorizing budgetary variances beyond your level of authorization," Andy says soothingly. He casts a quelling glance at Derek from Accounting, and then asks: "What I'd like to know is why you went after her, though. SOP was to leave the area as soon as you were blown. Why did you stick around?"

"Uh—" My lips are dry because I've been expecting this one. "I was going to leave. I was in the rental car and heading for the road out of town back to the airport, just as soon as I got out of the kill zone. I'd have done it too, except that Mo rang."

I lick my lips again. "I was sent to see if I could facilitate an extraction. I figured that meant someone thought Mo was worth extracting. My apologies if that isn't actually the case, but what I heard on the phone sounded like Mo had been abducted, and in the wake of the shooting I figured this was an even worse outcome than a blown mission and withdrawal. So I improvised, went round to her house and used my locator on her.

"I've been thinking about it a lot since then. What I should have done, I mean. I could have found where she was being held then driven back to the motel to find whoever was running that spy. Or something. Or headed for the airport and phoned from the departure lounge. All I can say is I was too involved. Some bastard had just tried to kill me; I mean, ONI was bugging Mo. When I phoned, they had put a diversion on her line, which is how come I was able to tell them where to look. But they probably already *knew*, I mean, when Mo called me on her pocket mobile that would have tipped them off."

I empty the glass of water down my throat and put it back on the table in front of me.

"Look, I figure ONI or some other TLA outfit—say, the Black Chamber pretending to be ONI investigators—was watching Mo and picked up on me as soon as we made contact. It was a stitch-up. Whoever tried to shoot me and snatch her took them by surprise. That wasn't in the script. I know I should have come home then, but at that point I think everyone was off balance. Who the fuck *were* those loons, anyway? A major summoning in public—"

"You have no need to know," Derek says snippily. "Drop it!"

"Okay." I lean back in my chair, tipping it on two legs; my head aches abominably. "I get the picture."

My third interrogator pipes up in a reedy voice: "This isn't the whole story, is it, Robert?"

I stare at her, annoyed. "Probably not, no."

Bridget is a blonde yuppwardly-mobile executive, her sights fixed on the dizzying heights of the cabinet office in seeming ignorance of the bulletproof glass ceiling that hovers over all of us who work in the Laundry. Her main job description seems to be making life shitty for everybody farther down the ladder, principally by way of her number one henchperson, Harriet. She holds forth, strictly for the record: "I'm un-happy about the way this assignment was set up. This was supposed to be a straightforward meet-and-pitch session, barely one rung up from hav-ing our local consul pay a social call. With all due respect, Robert is not a particularly experienced representative and should not have been sent into such a situation without mentoring—"

"It's friendly soil!" Andy interrupts.

"As friendly as it gets without a bilateral arrangement, which is to say, *not* an *active* joint-intelligence-sharing, committee-sanctioned, liaison environment. Foreigners, in other words. Robert was pushed out in the cold without oversight or adequate support from higher management, and when things went off the rails he quite naturally did his best, which wasn't quite good enough." She smiles dazzlingly at Andy. "I'd like to minute that he needs additional training before being subjected to solo exercises, and I'd also like to say that I think we need to review the cir-cumstances leading up to this assignment closely in case they are symp-tomatic of a weakness in our planning and accountability loop."

*Oh great.* Andy looks almost as disgusted as I feel. Bridget has just damned us—everyone else, in fact—with faint praise. I did "as well as could be expected" and need extra supervision before I can be let out of the kindergarten to go pee-pee. Derek and Andy and everyone else in-volved get to have Bridget poke her long, inquisitive nose into their pro-cedural compliance and see if they're exercising due diligence. As for Bridget, if she turns up anything that even whiffs of negligence she gets to look good to the top brass by cleaning shop, and anyone who disagrees is being "grossly unprofessional." Office politics, the Laundry remix.

"My head aches," I mutter. "And my body is telling me that it's two in the morning. Do you have any more questions? If you don't mind, I'm going to go home and lie down for a day or two."

"Take all week," Andy says dismissively. "We'll have everything sorted out when you get back." I stand up fast; in my current state I don't think to ask what "I'd like to see a written report of your trip," Bridget adds before I can close the door behind me. "Documented in accordance with Operations Manual Four, chapter eleven, section C. No need to hurry, but I want it on my desk by the end of next week."

Evidence, Written, Bureaucrats for the Malicious Use of. I head for home, anticipating a long hot bath and then eighteen hours in the sack.

Home is much as I left it seven days ago. There's a pile of bills slowly turning brown at the corner propping up one of the kitchen table legs. The bin is overflowing, the kitchen sink likewise, and Pinky hasn't cleaned out his bread-maker since the last time he used it. I look in the fridge and find a limp tea bag and a carton of milk that's good for another day or so before it starts demanding the vote, so I make myself a mug of tea and sit at the kitchen table playing Tetris on my palmtop. Colored blocks fall like snowflakes in my mind, and I drift for a while. But reality keeps intruding: I've got a week's washing in my suitcase, another week of washing in my room, and while Pinky and the Brain are at work I can get to the washer/dryer. (Assuming nobody's left a dead hamster in it again.)

Deliberately ignoring the bills, I get up and drag my suitcase upstairs. My room is much the way I left it, and I suddenly realize that I hate living this way: hate the second-hand furniture designed by aliens from Planet Landlord, hate sharing my personal space with a couple of hyper-intelligent slobs with behavioral problems and explosive hobbies, hate feeling my future possibilities hemmed in by my personal vow of poverty—the signature on my Laundry warrant card. I drag the suitcase into my room through a fog of fatigue and mild despair, then open it and begin to sort everything into piles on the floor.

Something snuffles behind me.

I spin round so fast I nearly levitate, hand fumbling for a mummified monkey's paw that isn't there—then recognition cuts in and I breathe again. "You startled me! What are you doing in there?"

Just the top of her head is visible. She blinks at me sleepily. "What does it look like?"

I consider my next words carefully. "Sleeping in my bed?"

She pulls down the duvet far enough to yawn, mouth pink and grey in the dim light that filters through the new curtains. "Yeah. Heard you were due back today so I, mmm, pulled a sickie. Wanted to see you."

I sit down on the side of the bed. Mhari's hair is mousy-brown with blonde highlights she puts in it every few weeks; it's cut in short flyaway locks that tangle around my fingers when I run my hand over her scalp. "Really?"

"Yeah, really." A bare arm reaches out of the bedding, wraps around my waist, and pulls me down. "Been missing you. Come here."

I'm meaning to sort my dirty clothing into piles for the washing machine, but instead all my clothing ends up in a heap in the middle of the floor, and I end up in a heap under Mhari, who is naked under the duvet and seemingly intent on giving me a very warm welcome home, if not a rinse and tumble-dry. "What *is* this?" I try to ask, but she grabs my head and holds my mouth against one generously proportioned nipple. I get the message and shut up. Mhari is in the mood, and this is about the one situation in which our relationship functions smoothly. Besides, it's more than a week since the last time I've seen her, and being ambushed this way is the best thing that's happened to me in quite a while.

About an hour later, fucked-out and completely exhausted—to say nothing of sweaty—we're lying in a tangle on the bed (the duvet seems to have decided to join the washing pile) and she's making buzzing noises in the back of her throat like a cat. "What brought this on?" I ask.

"I needed you," she says, with the kind of innocent egotism that a cat could only envy. Grabs at my back: "Mmm. Hmm. Had a bad week."

"A bad week?" I'm practicing being a good listener; it's usually opening my mouth that gets me into trouble with her.

"First there was a complete mess at the office: Eric was off sick and dropped the ball on a case he was handling and I had to pick up the pieces. Ended up working late three nights running. Then there was a party at Judy's. Judy got me drunk, introduced me to a friend of hers. He turned out to be a real shit, but only after—"

I roll away. "I wish you wouldn't do this," I hear myself saying.

"Do what?" She looks at me, hurt.

I sigh. "Never mind." Never *fucking* mind, I try not to say. I suddenly feel really dirty. "I'm going to have a shower," I say, and sit up.

"Bob!"

"Never mind." I get up, grab a dirty towel from the pile on the floor, and head for the bathroom to wash her off me.

Mhari has a problem: her problem is me. I should just tell her to fuck off and die, sever all links, refuse to talk to her—but she's good company when we're on speaking terms, she can push all my buttons correctly when we're in bed, and she can get right under my skin and leave me feeling about five and a half inches high. My problem is that she wants to trade me in on New Boyfriend, model 2.0, one with a fast car and a Rolex Oyster and prospects. (Warped senses of humor and dead-end Laundry postings are strictly optional.) She's permanently on the re-

bound, either toward me or away from me—I can't always tell which—
and in between she uses me the way a cat uses a scratching post. Partying
at Judy's place, for example: Judy is a mindless management functionary
bimbo friend of hers who is somehow always impeccably turned out and
manages to make me feel like a dirty little schoolboy, although she's far
too polite to ever say anything. So when Mhari traps off with some dou-
ble-glazing salesman she meets via Judy and he turfs her out of his bed
the next morning, I'm supposed to be around as a friendly consolation
fuck the next day.

*My* problem is that she doesn't seem to appreciate that I hate being
on the receiving end of this. If I try to make a big deal of it she'll accuse
me of being jealous and I'll end up feeling obscurely guilty. If I don't
make a big deal of it she'll continue to act like I'm some kind of door-
mat. And who knows? Maybe I'm just being paranoid and she *isn't* looking around for Mr New Boyfriend. (Yeah, and wild boars have been
spotted in the holding pattern over Heathrow with an engine under each
wing.)

I haven't had to chase any strangers out of my bed yet, but with Mhari
around I keep wondering when it'll happen. The worst of it is, I don't
want to just cut things dead; I'd rather she stopped playing games than
she stopped seeing me. Perhaps it's self-deception, but I think we could
make things work. Maybe.

I'm in the shower cubicle washing my hair when I hear the door
open. "I do not appreciate hearing about your one-night stands," I say,
eyes closed to avoid the sting of shampoo. "I don't understand why the
fuck you hang around me when you're obviously so eager to find someone else. But will you please leave me alone for a bit?"

"Oops, sorry," says Pinky, and closes the door.

He's waiting on the landing when I finish in the bathroom; we stu-
diously avoid each other's eyes. "Uh, it's okay to go into your room," he
volunteers. "She's gone out."

"Oh good."

He hurries after me as I head downstairs. "She asked me to have a
word with you," he calls breathlessly.

"That's fine," I say distantly. "Just as long as she isn't asking you to
share my bed."

"She says you need to check out the alt.polyamory FAQ," he says, and
cringes.

I switch the kettle on and sit down. "Do you really think *I* have a
problem?" I ask. "Or does *Mhari* have a problem?"

He glances around, trapped. "You have incompatible lifestyle
choices?" he ventures.

The kettle hisses like an angry snake. "Very good. Incompatible lifestyle choices is such a fucking *civilized* way of putting it."

"Bob, do you think she might be doing this to get your attention?"

"There are good ways and bad ways to get my attention. Whacking on my ego with a crowbar will get my attention, sure, but it's not going to leave me well disposed to the messenger." I pour more hot water into my mug of tea, then stand up and rummage in the cupboard. *Ah, it's right where I left it.* I upend a generous dollop of Wray and Nephew's overproof Jamaican rum into the mug and sniff: brown sugar crossed with white lightning. "The male ego is a curious thing. It's about the size of a small continent but it's extremely brittle. Drink?"

Pinky sits down opposite me, looking as if he's sharing the kitchen table with an unexploded bomb. "Why not look on the bright side?" he says, holding out a coke glass for the rum.

"There's a bright side?"

"She keeps coming back to you," he says. "Maybe she's doing it to hurt herself?"

"To—" I bite off the snide reply I was working on. When Mhari gets depressed she gets *depressed:* I've seen the scars. "I'll have to think about that one," I say.

"Well, then." Pinky looks pleased with himself. "Doesn't that look better? She's doing it because she's depressed and hates herself, not because there's anything wrong with you. It's not a reflection on *your* virile manhood, you big hunk of beefcake. Go get yourself a one nighter of your own and she'll have to make her mind up what she wants."

"Is that in the FAQ?" I ask.

"I dunno; I don't pay much attention to breeder reproductive rituals," he says, fingering his moustache.

"Thank you, Pinky," I say heavily. He does a little wave and bow, then tips the contents of his glass down his throat. I spend the next minute or two helping save him from choking, and then we have another wee dram. The rest of the afternoon becomes a blur, but when I wake up in bed the next morning I have a stunning hangover, a vague memory of drunkenly talking things over with Mhari for hours on end until it blew up into a flaming row, and I'm on my own.

Situation normal: all fucked up.

Two days later, I am booked into an Orientation and Objectivity seminar at the Dustbin. Only God and Bridget—and possibly Boris, though he won't say anything—know *why* I'm booked into an O&O course three days after getting off the plane, but something dire will probably happen if I don't turn up.

The Dustbin isn't part of the Laundry, it's regular civil service, so I try to dig up a shirt that isn't too crumpled, and a tie. I own two ties—a Wile E. Coyote tie, and a Mandelbrot set tie that's particularly effective at inducing migraines—and a sports jacket that's going a bit threadbare at the cuffs. Don't want to look too out of place, do I? Someone might ask questions, and after the *auto-da-fé* I've just been through I do not want anyone mentioning my name in Bridget's vicinity for the next year. I'm halfway to the tube station before I remember that I forgot to shave, and I'm on the train before I notice that I'm wearing odd socks, one brown and one black. But what the hell, I made the effort; if I actually owned a suit I'd be wearing it.

The Dustbin is our name for a large, ornate postmodernist pile on the south bank of the Thames, with green glass curtain walls and a big, airy atrium and potted Swiss cheese plants everywhere there isn't a security camera. The Dustbin is occupied by a bureaucratic organization famous for its three-hour lunches and impressive history of KGB alumni. This organization is persistently and mistakenly referred to as MI5 by the popular media. As anyone in the business knows, MI5 was renamed DI5 about thirty years ago; like those Soviet-era maps that misplaced cities by about fifty miles in order to throw American bombers off course, DI5 is helpfully misnamed in order to direct freedom of information requests to the wrong address. (As it happens there *is* an organization called MI5; it's in charge of ensuring that municipal waste collection contracts are outsourced to private bidders in a fair and legal manner. So when your Freedom of Information Act writ comes back saying they know nothing about you, they're telling the truth.)

The Dustbin cost approximately two hundred million pounds to construct, has a wonderful view of the Thames and the Houses of Parliament, and is full of rubbish that smells. Whereas we loyal servants of the crown and defenders of the human race against nameless gibbering horrors from beyond spacetime have to labor on in a Victorian rookery of cabbage-colored plasterboard walls and wheezing steam pipes somewhere in Hackney. That's because the Laundry used to be part of an organization called SOE—indeed, the Laundry is the sole division of SOE to have survived the bureaucratic postwar bloodletting of 1945—and the mutual loathing between SIS (aka DI6) and SOE is of legendary proportions.

I turn up at the Dustbin and enter via the tradesman's entrance, a windowless door in a fake-marble tunnel near the waterfront. A secretary who looks like she's made of fine bone china waves me through the biometric scanner, somehow manages to refrain from inhaling in my presence (you'd think I hailed from the Pestilence Division at Porton Down), and finally ushers me into a small cubicle furnished with a hard wooden bench (presumably to make me feel at home). The inner door opens and a big, short-haired guy in a white shirt and black tie clears his throat and says, "Robert Howard, this way please." I follow him and he drops one of those silly badge-chains over my head then pushes me through a metal detector and gives me a cursory going over with a wand, airport security style. I grit my teeth. They know exactly who I am and who I work for: they're just doing this to make a point.

He relieves me of my Leatherman multitool, my palmtop computer, my Maglite torch and pocket screwdriver set, the nifty folding keyboard, the MP3 walkman, the mobile phone, and a digital multimeter and patch cable set I'd forgotten about. "What's all this, then?" he asks.

"Do you guys ever go anywhere without your warrant card and handcuffs? Same difference."

"I'll give you a receipt for these," he says disapprovingly, and shoves them in a locker. "Stand on this side of the red line for now." I stand. Something about him makes my built-in police detector peg out; Special Branch acting as uniformed commissionaires? *Yeah, right.* "Present this on your way out to collect your stuff. You may now cross the red line. Follow me, do not, repeat *not*, open any closed doors or enter any areas where a red light is showing, and don't speak to anyone without my say-so."

I follow my minder through a maze of twisty little cubicle farms, all alike, then up three floors by elevator, then down a corridor where the Swiss cheese plants are turning yellow at the edges from lack of daylight, and finally to the door of what looks like a classroom. "You can talk now; everyone else in this class is cleared to at least your level," he says. "I'll come collect you at fifteen hundred hours. Meanwhile, go anywhere you want on this level—there's a canteen where you'll have lunch, toilet's round that corner there—but don't leave this floor under any circumstances."

"What if there's a fire?" I ask.

He looks at me witheringly: "We'd arrest it. I'll see you at three o'clock," he says. "And not before."

I enter the classroom, wondering if teacher is in yet.

"Ah, Bob, nice to see you. Have a seat. Hope you found us okay?"

I get a sinking feeling: it's Nick the Beard. "I'm fine, Nick," I say. "How's Cheltenham?" Nick is some sort of technical officer from CESG, based out at Cheltenham along with the other wiretap folks. He drops round the Laundry every so often to make sure all our software is licensed and we're only running validated COTS software purchased via approved suppliers. Which is why, whenever we get word that he's about to visit, I have to run around rebooting servers like crazy and loading the padded-cell environments we keep around purely to placate CESG so they don't blacklist our IT processes and get our budget lopped off at the knees. Despite that, Nick is basically okay, which is why I get the sinking feeling; I don't enjoy treating nice guys like they're agents of Satan or Microsoft salesmen.

"They moved me out of the hole on the map two months ago," he says. "I'm based here full-time now. Miriam's got a job in the city, so we're thinking of moving. Have you met Sophie? I think she's running this course today."

"Don't think so. Who else is coming? What do you know about, um, Sophie? Nobody even showed me a course synopsis; I'm not sure why I'm here."

"Oh, well then." He rummages in his brief case and pulls out a sheet of paper, hands it to me: *Orientation and Objectivity 120.4: Overseas Liaison.*

I start reading: *This seminar is intended to provide inductees with the correct frame of mind for conducting negotiations with representatives of allied agencies. Common pitfalls are discussed with a view to inculcating a culture of best practice. A proactive approach to integrating operational agreements with extraterritorial parties is deprecated, and correct protocol for requesting diplomatic assistance is introduced. Status: completion of this seminar and associated coursework is mandatory for foreign postings in Category 2 (nonallied) positions.*

"Ah, really," I say faintly. "How interesting." (Thank you, Bridget.)

"All I wanted was to visit the factory that supplies our PCs out in Taiwan," Nick mutters darkly. "All part of our ISO certification cycle, assuring that they're following best industry practices in motherboard assembly and testing . . ."

The door opens. "Ah, Nick! Nice to see you! How's Miriam?"

It's a new arrival. He's the very image of a schoolteacher: a thin, weedy-looking guy with big horn-rimmed spectacles and thinning hair. Except, when he positively leaps into the room, he gives the impression of being made of springs. Nick obviously knows him: "She's fine, fine — and how are you yourself? Uh, Bob, have you met Alan?"

"Alan?" I stick out a hand tentatively. "With what department? If I'm allowed to ask?"

"Umm—" he pumps my hand up and down then looks at me oddly as I nurse my bruised fingertips—he's got a grip like a vise. "Probably not, but that's okay," he announces. "Let's not get carried away, eh!" Over his shoulder to Nick: "Hillary's fine, but she's having a devil of a time with the guns. We're going to need a new cupboard soon, and the rental in Maastricht is horrible."

*Guns?* "Alan and I belong to the same shooting club," Nick explains diffidently. "With all the fuss a few years ago we had to either move our guns out of the country to somewhere where it's legal to own them, or turn them in. Most of us turned ours in and use the club facilities, but Alan's a holdout."

"Handguns?"

"No, long arms. That's recreational shooting, by the way. I'm just an amateur but Alan takes it a bit more seriously—trained for the Olympics a way back."

"What's the club?" I ask.

"Damned impudent infringement of our civil rights," Alan huffs. "Not trusting their own citizens to own automatic weapons: a bad sign. But we do what we can. Artists' Rifles, by the way. Drop in if you're ever in the neighborhood, ha ha. So we're just waiting for Sophie now."

"Could be worse." Nick ambles over to the table beside the door and prods at what looks like a thermos jug. "Ah, coffee!" I kick myself mentally for not noticing it first.

"You going anywhere?" asks Alan.

"Just back." I shrug. "Didn't even know this course existed."

"Business or pleasure?"

"Milk or sugar, Alan?"

"Business. I wish it *had* been pleasure. They didn't brief me and nothing was the way I expected it—"

"Ha ha. Milk, no sugar. Typical Laundry turf war, by the sound of it. So your boss's boss's first cousin sent you for remedial classes, stay late after school, dunce cap in the corner, the usual rigmarole?"

"That's about it. Hey, pour me one too?"

"Seen it a dozen times before," offers Nick. "Nobody ever thinks to *tell* anyone when they're expected—" I yawn. "You tired?"

"Still jetlagged, thanks." I blow on my coffee.

The door opens and a woman in a brown tweed suit—Sophie, I presume—walks in. "Hello, everybody," she says. "Alan, Nick—you must be Bob." A brief grin. "Glad you're all here. Today we're going to go over some basic material by way of reminding you of the proper protocol for dealing with foreign agencies while posted abroad on neutral or friendly but not allied territory." She plonks a bulging briefcase down on the desk at the front of the classroom.

"If I can just confirm—all three of you are due to fly out to California in the next few days, is that right?"

*Uh-oh.* "I'm just back," I say.

"Oh dear. You've done the 120.4 course before, then? This is just a refresher?"

I take a deep breath. "I can honestly say that the fact that this seminar exists is news to both myself and my immediate supervisors. I think that's why I'm here now."

"Oh well!" She smiles brightly. "We'll soon see about that. Just as long as your trip was productive and nothing went wrong! This course is about procedures that should only be necessary in event of an emergency, after all." She digs into the case and hands us each a hefty wedge of course notes. "Shall we begin?"

It's been six weeks since I was certified fit for active duty, and three weeks since I came back from Santa Cruz in business class with a bandage around my head. Bridget has had her little joke, I've suffered through about two weeks of seminars intended to bolt, padlock, and weld shut the stable door in the wake of the equine departure, and I'm slowly going out of my skull with boredom.

For my sins I've been posted to a pokey little office in the Dansey Wing of Service House—little more than a broom closet off a passageway under the eaves, roof wreathed in hissing steam pipes painted black for no obvious reason. There's a valuable antique that Services claims is a computer network server, and when I'm not nursing it from one nervous breakdown to the next I am expected to file endless amounts of paperwork, prepare a daily abstract based on several classified logs and digests that cross my desk. The abstract is forwarded to some senior executives, then shredded by a guy in a blue suit. In between, I'm expected to make the tea. I feel like a twenty-six-year-old office boy. Over-qualified, naturally. To add insult to injury, I have a new job title: Junior Private Secretary.

I would, I think, be right out of my skull and halfway down the road by now, chased by men in white coats wielding oversized butterfly nets, were it not for the fact that the word "secretary" means something very different from its normal usage in the steamy little world of the Laundry. Y'see, before the 1880s, a secretary was a gentleman's assistant: someone who kept the secrets. And there are secrets to be kept, here in the Arcana Analysis Section. In fact, there's a whole bloody wall of filing cabinets full of 'em right behind my cramped secretarial chair. (Some wag has plastered a Post-it note on one of the drawers: THE TRUTH IS IN HERE, SOMEWHERE.) I'm learning things all the time, and apart from the bloody filing work, not to mention the coffee pot from hell and the network server from heck, it's mostly okay. Except for Angleton. Did I mention Angleton?

I'm standing in for Angleton's junior private secretary, who is on sab-batical down at the funny farm or taking a year out doing an MBA or something. And therein lies my problem.

"Mister Howard!" That's Angleton, calling me into the inner sanc-tum.

I stick my head round his door. "Yes, boss?"

"Enter." I enter. His office is large, but feels cramped; every wall — it's windowless—is shelved floor-to-ceiling in ledgers. They're not books, but microfiche binders: each of them contains as much data as an ency-clopaedia. His desk looks merely odd at first sight, an olive-drab mono-lith bound with metal strips, supporting the TV-sized hood of a fiche reader. It's only when you get close enough to it to see the organlike ped-als and the cardhopper on top that, if you're into computational archae-ology, you realize that Angleton's desk is an incredibly rare, antique Memex—an information appliance out of 1940s CIA folklore.

Angleton looks up at me as I enter, his face a blue-lit washout of text projected from the Memex screen. He's nearly bald, his chin is two sizes two small for his skull, and his domed scalp gleams like bone. "Ah, Howard," he says. "Did you find the material I requested?"

"Some of it, boss," I say. "Just a moment." I duck out into my office and pick up the hulking dusty tomes that I've carried up from the stacks, two basements and a fifty-metre elevator ride below ground level. "Here you are. *Wilberforce Tangent* and *Opal Orange.*"

He takes the tomes without comment, opens the first of them, and starts sliding card-index sized chunks of microfilm into the Memex input hopper. "That will be all, Howard," he says superciliously, dismiss-ing me.

I grit my teeth and leave Angleton to his microfilm. I once made the mistake of asking why he uses such an antique. He stared at me as if I'd just waved a dead fish under his nose, then said, "You can't read Van Eck radiation off a microfilm projector." (Van Eck radiation is the radio noise emitted by a video display; with sophisticated receivers you can pick it up and eavesdrop on a computer from a distance.) Back then I hadn't learned to keep my mouth shut around him: "Yeah, but what about Tempest shielding?" I asked. That's when he sent me off to the stacks for the first time, and I got lost for two hours on sublevel three before I was rescued by a passing vicar.

I go into my outer office, pull out the file server's administration con-sole, log on, and join the departmental Xtank tournament. Fifteen min-utes later Angleton's bell dings; I put my game avatar on autopilot and look in on him.

Angleton positively glowers at me over his spectacles. "Check these files back into storage, sign off, then come back here," he says. "We need to talk."

I take the tomes and back out of his office. Gulp: he's *noticed* me! Whatever next?

The elevator down to the stacks is about to depart when I stick my foot in the door, holding it. Someone with a whole document trolley has got her back to me. "Thanks," I say, turning to punch in my floor as the door closes and we begin our creaky descent into the chalk foundations of London.

"No bother." I look round and see Dominique with the doctorate from Miskatonic: Mo, whom I last saw stranded in America, phoning me for help on a dark night. She looks surprised to see me. "Hey! What are you doing here?"

"It's a long story, but to cut it short I was shipped home after you phoned me. Seems those goons who were watching you picked me up. What about you? I thought you were having trouble getting an exit visa?"

"Are you kidding?" She laughs, but doesn't sound very amused. "I was kidnapped, and when they rescued me I was *deported!* And when I got back here—" Her eyes narrow.

The lift doors open on subbasement two. "You were conscripted," I say, sticking my heel in the path of one door. "Right?"

"If you had anything to do with it—"

I shake my head. "I'm in more or less the same boat, believe it or not; it's how about two-thirds of us end up here. Look, my *Obergruppenführer* will send his SS hellhounds after me if I'm not back in his office in ten minutes, but if you've got a free lunchtime or evening I could fill you in?"

Her eyes narrow some more. "I'll bet you'd like that." *Ouch!* "Have some good excuses ready, Bob," she says, rolling her file cart toward me. I notice absently that it's full of *Proceedings of the Scottish Society of Esoteric Antiquaries* from the nineteenth century as I dodge out of the lift.

"No excuses," I promise, "only the truth."

"Hah." Her smile is unexpected and enigmatic; then the lift doors slide shut, taking her down farther into the bowels of the Stacks.

The Stacks are in what used to be a tube station, built during World War Two as an emergency bunker and never hooked up to the underground railway network. There are six levels rather than the usual three, each level built into the upper or lower half of a cylindrical tube eight meters in diameter and nearly a third of a kilometre long. That makes for about two kilometers of tunnels and about fifty kilometers of shelf space. To make matters worse, lots of the material is stored in the form of microfiche—three by five film cards each holding the equivalent of a hundred pages of text—and some of the more recent stuff is stored on gold CDs (of which the Stacks hold, at a rough guess, some tens of thousands). That all adds up to a *lot* of information.

We don't use the Dewey Decimal Catalogue to locate volumes in here; our requirements are sufficiently specialized that we have to use the system devised by Professor Angell of Brown University and subsequently known as the Codex Mathemagica. I've spent the past few weeks getting my head around the more arcane aspects of a cataloguing system that uses surreal number theory and can cope with the N-dimensional library spaces of Borges. You might think this a deadly boring occupation, but the ever-present danger of getting lost in the stacks keeps you on your toes. Besides which, there are rumors of ape-men living down here; I don't know how the rumors got started, but this place is more than somewhat creepy when you're on your own late at night. There's something weird about the people who work in the stacks, and you get the feeling it could be infectious—in fact, I'm really hoping to be assigned some other duty as soon as possible.

I locate the stack where the *Wilberforce Tangent* and *Opal Orange* files came from and wind the aisles of shelving apart to make way; they are both dead agent files from many years ago, musty with the stench of bureaucratic history. I slide them in, then pause: next to *Opal Orange* there's another file, one with a freshly printed binding titled *Ogre Reality*. The name tickles my silly gland, and in a gross violation of procedure I flip it out of the shelves and check the contents page. It's all paper, at this stage, and as soon as I see the MOST SECRET stamp I move to flip it shut—then pause, my eyeballs registering the words "Santa Cruz" midway down the first page. I begin speed-reading.

Five minutes later, the small of my back soaked in a cold sweat, I replace the file on the shelf, wind them back together, and head for the lift as fast as my feet will carry me. I don't want Angleton to think I'm late— *especially* after reading that file. It seems I'm lucky enough to be alive as it is . . .

"Pay attention to this, Mr Howard. You are in a privileged position; you have access to information that other people would literally kill for. Because you stumbled into the Laundry through a second-floor window, so to speak, your technical clearance is several levels above that which would be assigned to you if you were a generic entrant. In one respect, that is useful; all organizations need junior personnel who have high clearances for certain types of data. On another level, it's a major obstacle." Angleton points his bony middle finger at me. "Because you have no *respect*."

He's obviously seen *The Godfather* one time too many. I find myself waiting for a goon to step out of the shadows and stick a gun in my ear. Maybe he just doesn't like my T-shirt, a picture of a riot cop brandishing a truncheon beneath the caption "Do not question authority." I swallow, wondering what's coming up next.

Angleton sighs deeply, then stares at the dark greenish oil painting that hangs on his office wall behind the visitor's hot seat. "You can fool Andrew Newstrom but you can't fool me," he says quietly.

"You know Andy?"

"I trained him when he was your age. He has a commitment that is in short supply these days. I know just how devoted to this organization *you* are. Draftees back in my day used to understand what they'd got themselves into, but you young ones . . ."

"Ask not what you can do for your country, but what your country has ever done for you?" I raise an eyebrow at him.

He snorts. "I see you understand your deficiencies."

I shake my head. "Not me—that's not my problem. I decided I want to make a career here. I know I don't have to—I know what the Laundry's for—but if I just sat around under the cameras waiting for my pension I'd get *bored*."

Those eyes are back on me, trying to drill right through to the back of my head. "We know that, Howard. If you were simply serving your time you'd be back downstairs, counting hairs on a caterpillar or something until retirement. I've seen your record and I am aware that you are intelligent, ingenious, resourceful, technically adept, and no less brave than average. But that doesn't alter what I've said one bit: you are routinely, grossly insubordinate. You think you have a *right* to know things that people would—and do—kill for. You take shortcuts. You aren't an organization man and you never will be. If it was up to me you'd be on the outside, and never allowed anywhere near us."

"But I'm not," I say. "Nobody even noticed me until I'd worked out the geometry curve iteration method for invoking Nyarlathotep and nearly wiped out Birmingham by accident. Then they came and offered me a post as Senior Scientific Officer and made it clear that 'no' wasn't on the list of acceptable answers. Turns out that nuking Birmingham overrides the positive vetting requirement, so they issued a reliability waiver and you're stuck with me. Shouldn't you be pleased that I've decided to make the best of things and try to be useful?"

Angleton leans forward across the polished top of his Memex desk. With a visible effort he slews the microfiche reader hood around so that

I can see the screen, then taps one bony finger on a mechanical keypress. "Watch and learn."

The desk whirs and clunks; cams and gears buried deep in it shuffle hypertext links and bring up a new microfilm card. A man's face shows up on the screen. Moustache, sunglasses, cropped hair, forty-something and jowly with it: "Tariq Nassir al-Tikriti. Remember that last bit. He works for a man who grew up in his home town around the same time, who goes by the name of Saddam Hussein al-Tikriti. Mr Nassir's job entails arranging for funds to be transferred from the Mukhabarat— Saddam's private Gestapo—to friendly parties for purposes of inconveniencing enemies of the Ba'ath party of Iraq. Friendlies such as Mohammed Kadass, who used to live in Afghanistan before he fell foul of the Taliban."

"Nice to know they're not all religious fundamentalists," I say, as the Memex flicks to a shot of a bearded guy wearing a turbanlike something on his head. (He's scowling at the camera as if he suspects it of holding Western sympathies.)

"They deported him for excessive zeal," Angleton says heavily. "Turns out he was marshalling resources for Yusuf Qaradawi's school. Do I need to draw you a diagram?"

"Guess not. What does Qaradawi teach?"

"Originally management studies and economics, but lately he's added suicide bombing, the necessity for armed struggle preceded by *Da'wa* and military preparation in order to repel the greater *Kufr*, and gauge metrics for raster-driven generative sepiroth on vector processors. Summoning the lesser shoggothim in other words."

"Nng," is all I can say to that. "What's this got to do with the price of coffee?"

Another photograph clicks up on the screen: this time a gorgeous redhead wearing an academic gown over a posh frock. It takes me a moment to recognise Mo. She looks about ten years younger, and the guy in a tux whose arm she's draped over looks—well, lawyerly seems to fit what she told me about her ex. "Dr Dominique O'Brien. I believe you've met?"

I glance up and Angleton is staring at me.

"Do I have your *complete* attention now, Mr Howard?" he rasps.

"Yeah," I concede. "Do you mean the kidnappers in Santa Cruz—"

"Shut up and listen and you may learn something." He waits for me to shut up, then continues. "I'm telling you this because you're in it already, you've met the prime candidate. *Now*, when you were sent over there we didn't know what you were dealing with, what Dr O'Brien was sitting on. The Yanks did, which was why they weren't letting her go, but they seem to have changed their minds in view of the security threat. She's not a US citizen and they've got her research findings; interesting, but nothing fundamentally revolutionary. Furthermore, with enough information about her out in the public domain to attract nuisances like the Izzadin al-Qassem hangers-on who tried to snatch her in Santa Cruz, they don't much want her around anymore. Which is why she's over here, in the Laundry and under wraps. They didn't simply deport her, they asked us to take care of her."

"If it's not fundamentally revolutionary research, why are we interested in her?" I ask.

Angleton looks at me oddly. "I'll be the judge of that." It all clicks into place, suddenly. Suppose you worked out how to build a Teller-Ullam configuration fusion device—a hydrogen bomb. That wouldn't qualify as revolutionary these days, either, but that doesn't mean it's unimportant, does it? I must give some sign of understanding what Angleton's getting at because he nods to himself and continues: "The Laundry is in the nonproliferation business and Dr O'Brien has independently rediscovered something rather more fundamental than a technique for landscaping Wolverhampton without first obtaining planning permission. In the States, the Black Chamber took an interest in her—don't ask about where they fit in the American occult intelligence complex, you really don't want to know—but verified that it wasn't anything new. We may not have a bilateral cooperation treaty with them, but once they worked out that all she'd come up with was a variation on the Logic of Thoth there was really no reason to keep her except to prevent her falling into the hands of undesirable persons like our friend Tariq Nassir. It's their damned munitions export regulations again; the contents of her head are classified up there with nerve gas and other things that go bump in the dark. Anyway, once the mess was cleared up—" he glares at me as he hisses the word *mess* "—they really had no reason not to let her come home. After all, we're the ones who gave them the Logic in the first place, back in the late fifties."

"Right . . . so that's all there is to it? I *heard* those guys, they were going to open a major gateway and drag her through it—"

Angleton abruptly switches off the Memex and stands up, leaning over the desk at me. "Official word is that nothing at all like that happened," he snaps. "There were no witnesses, no evidence, and nothing happened. Because if anything *did* happen there, that would tend to indicate that the Yanks either fucked up by releasing her, or threw us a live hand grenade, and we know they never fuck up, because our glorious prime minister has his lips firmly wrapped around the presidential cigar in the hope of a renewal of the bilateral trade agreement they're talking about in Washington next month. Do you understand me?"

"Yeah, but." I stop, "Ah . . . yes. Official report by Bridget, no?"

For the first time ever Angleton turns an expression on me that might, in a bright light, if you squinted at him, be interpreted as a faint smile. "I couldn't possibly comment."

I spin my wheels for a moment. "Nothing happened," I say roboti-cally. "There were no witnesses. If anything happened it would mean we'd been passed a booby prize. It would mean some bunch of terrorists came arbitrarily close to getting their hands on a paranormal H-bomb designer, and someone at ONI figured they could count coup by passing the designer to us for safe keeping, meaning they expect us to fuck up to their political advantage. And that couldn't possibly happen, right?"

"She's in the Library, on secondment to Pure Research for the dura-tion," Angleton says quite casually. "You might want to invite the young lady out for dinner. I'd be quite interested in hearing about her research at second hand, from someone who obviously understands so much about predicate calculus. Hmm, five-thirty already. You might want to go now."

Taking my cue I stand up and head for the door. My hand is out-stretched when Angleton adds, tonelessly: "How many made it back from the raid on Wadi al-Qebir, Mr Howard?"

I freeze. *Shit.* "Two," I hear myself saying, unable to control my trai-tor larynx: it's another of those auditor compulsion fields. *Bastard's got his office wired like an interrogation suite!*

"Very good, Mister Howard. They were the ones who didn't try to sec-ond-guess their commanding officer. Can I suggest that in future you take a leaf from their book and refrain from poking your nose into things you have been told do not concern you? Or at least learn not to be so predictable about it."

"Ah—"

"Go away before I mock you," he says, sounding distantly amused.

I flee, simultaneously embarrassed and relieved.

I find Mo by the simple expedient of remembering that my palmtop is still attuned to her aura; I bounce around the basement levels in the lift, doing a binary search until I zero in on her in one of the reading rooms of the library. She's poring over a fragile illuminated manuscript, in-scribed with colors that glow brilliantly beneath the hooded spotlight she uses. She seems to be engrossed, so I knock loudly on the door frame and wait.

"Yes? Oh, it's you."

"It's ten to six," I say diffidently. "Another ten minutes and an orangoutang in a blue suit will come round and lock you in for the night. I know some people enjoy that sort of thing, but you didn't strike me as the type. So I was thinking, could you do with a glass of wine and that explanation we were talking about?"

She looks at me deadpan. "Sounds better than facing the urban gorillas. I've got to get home for nine but I guess I can spare an hour. Do you have anywhere in mind?"

We end up at an earning-facilitated nerd nirvana called Wagamama, just off New Oxford Street: you can't miss it, just look for the queue of fashion victims halfway around the block. Some of them have been waiting so long that the cobwebs have fossilised. My impressions are of a huge stainless steel kitchen and Australian expat waiters on rollerblades beaming infrared orders and wide-eyed smiles at each other from hand-held computers as they skate around the refectory tables, where earnest young things in tiny rectangular spectacles discuss Derrida's influence on alcopop marketing via the next big dot-sad IPO, or whatever it is the "in" herd is obsessing about these days over their gyoza and organic buckwheat ramen. Mo is crammed opposite me at one end of a barrack-room table of bleached pine that looks as if they polish it every night with a microtome blade; our neighbours are giggling over some TV studio deal, and she's looking at me with an analytical expression borrowed from the laboratory razor's owner.

"The food's very good," I offer defensively.

"It's not that—" she gazes past my shoulder "—it's the culture. It's very Californian. I wasn't expecting the rot to have reached London yet."

"We are Bay Aryans from Berkeley: prepare to be reengineered in an attractive range of color schemes for your safety and comfort!"

"Something like that." A waitron whizzes past and smart-bombs us both with cans of Kirin that feel as if they've been soaked in liquid nitrogen. Mo picks hers up and winces at me as it bites her fingertips. "Why do they call it the Laundry?"

"Uh . . ." I think for a moment. "Back in the Second World War, they were based in a requisitioned Chinese laundry in Soho, I think. They got Dansey House when the Dustbin's new skyscraper was commissioned." I pick up my beer carefully, using a mitten improvised from my sleeve, and tip the can into a glass. "Claude Dansey, he was stuck in charge of SOE. Former SIS dude, didn't get on well with the top nobs—it was all politics; SOE was the cowboy arm of British secret ops during the war. Churchill charged SOE with setting Europe ablaze behind German lines, and that's exactly what they tried to do. Until December 1945, when SIS got their revenge, of course."

"So the bureaucratic infighting goes that far back?"

"Guess so." I take a sip of beer. "But the Laundry survived more or less intact after the rest of SOE was gutted, like the way GCHQ survived even though the Bletchley Park operation was wound up. Only more secretively." Hmm. This is *not* stuff we should be talking about in public; I pull out my palmtop and tap away at it until a rather useful utility shows up.

"What's that?" she asks interestedly, as the background clatter and racket diminishes to a haze of white noise.

"Laundry-issue palmtop. Looks like an ordinary Palm Pilot, doesn't it? But the secret's in the software and the rather unusual daughterboard soldered inside the case."

"No, I mean the noise—it isn't just my ears, is it?"

"No, it's magic."

"Magic! But—" she glares at me. "You're not kidding, are you? What the hell is going on around here?"

I look at her blankly: "Nobody told you?"

"*Magic!*" She looks disgusted.

"Well okay, then, it's applied mathematics. I thought you said you're not a Platonist? You should be. These boxes—" I tap the palmtop "—are the most powerful mathematical tools we've developed. Things were done on an ad-hoc basis until about 1953, when Turing came up with his final theorem; since then, we've been putting magic on a systematic basis, on the QT. Most of it boils down to the application of Kaluza-Klein theory in a Linde universe constrained by an information conservation rule, or so they tell me when I ask. When we carry out a computation it has side effects that leak through some kind of channel underlying the structure of the Cosmos. Out there in the multiverse there are listeners; sometimes we can coerce them into opening gates. Small gates we can transfer minds through, or big gates we can move objects through. Even really huge gates, big enough to take something huge and unpleasant— some of the listeners are *big*. Giants. Sometimes we can invoke local reversals or enhancements of entropy; that's what I'm doing right now with the sound damper field, fuzzing the air around us, which is already pretty random. That's basically the business the Laundry is in."

"Ah." She chews her lower lip for a moment, appraising me. "So that's why you were so interested in me. Say, do you have any references for this work of Turing's? I'd like to read up on it."

"It's classified, but—"

"Wtyjdfshjwrtha rssradth aeywerg?"

I turn and look at the waitress who's beaming at me inscrutably. "'Scuse me." I tap the "pause" button on screen. "What was that again?"

"I said, are you ready to order yet?"

I shrug at Mo, she nods, and we order. The waitron skids off and I tap the "pause" button again. "I didn't originally volunteer for the Laundry," I feel compelled to add. "They drafted me much the same way they drafted you. On the one hand, it sucks. On the other hand, the alternatives are a whole lot worse."

She looks angry now. "What do you mean, worse?"

"Well—" I lean back "—for starters, your work on probability engineering. You probably thought it was mostly irrelevant, except to theoretical types like Pentagon strategic planners. But if we mix it up with a localised entropy inversion we can make life *very* hot for whoever or whatever is on the receiving end. I'm not clear on the details, but apparently it's at the root of one particularly weird directed invocation: if we can set up a gauge field for probability metrics we can tune in on specific EIs fairly—"

"EIs?"

"External Intelligences. What the mediaeval magic types called demons, gods, spirits, what have you. Sentient aliens, basically, from those cosmological domains where the anthropic principle predominates and some sort of sapient creatures have evolved. Some of them are strongly superhuman, others are dumb as a stump from our perspective. What counts is that they can be coerced, sometimes, into doing what people want. Some of them can also open wormholes—yes, they've got access to negative matter—and send themselves, or other entities, through. As I understand it, general indeterminacy theory lets us target them very accurately: it's the difference between dialing a phone number at random and using a phone book. I think."

A crescent-shaped plate of *gyoza* appears on the table between us, and for a couple of minutes we're busy eating; then bowls of soup arrive and I'm busy juggling chop sticks, spoon, and noodles that are making a bid for freedom.

"So." She drains her bowl, lays the chopsticks across it, and sits up to watch me. "Let's summarize. I've stumbled across a research field that's about as critical to your—the Laundry—as if I'd been working on nuclear weapons research without realising it. In this country, everyone who works on this stuff works for the Laundry, or not at all. So the Laundry has sucked me in and you're here to give me an update so I know what I'm swimming in."

"Other people's dirty underwear, mostly," I say apologetically.

"Yeah, right. And this concern for keeping me updated was all your own idea too, huh? Just what the hell was going on in Santa Cruz? Who were those guys who snatched me, and what were *you* doing?"

"I won't say I wasn't asked to have a discreet chat with you." I put my spoon down, then turn it over. Then over again. "Look, the Laundry is first and foremost a self-perpetuating bureaucracy, like any other government agency, right? SOP, when shit hits the fan in the field, is to protect head office by pulling back feelers." I turn the spoon over. "When I got home I was carpeted for going after you—given a going over in front of my boss."

"You were what?" Her eyes widen. "I don't remember you—"

I pull a face. "Standard protocol if something goes down is to get the hell out of town, Mo. But you were obviously in over your head when you rang, so I went round your place and followed you to that safe house they were holding you in. Phoned your mobile, expecting a diversion tap, and the next thing I knew I was sitting up in hospital with a hangover and no alcohol to show for it, being grilled by the Feds. Very clever of me, but at least they pulled us both out alive. Anyway, when I got home it turned out that officially none of that shit happened. You were not abducted by, ahem, Middle Eastern gentlemen who might or might not have been working for a guy called Tariq Nassir, with connections to Yusuf Qaradawi. You were not being kept under surveillance by the Black Chamber. Because if either of those things were true, it would be Bad, and if it was Bad, it would put a black mark on my boss's record book. And she wants her KCMG and DBE so bad you can smell it when she walks in the door."

Mo is silent for a while. "I had no idea," she says presently. There's a slightly wild look in her eyes: "They were talking about killing me! I heard them!"

"Officially it didn't happen, but unofficially—Bridget isn't the only poker player in the Laundry." I shrug. "One of the other players wants to hear your side of the story, off the record." I glance round. "This is not the place for it. Even with a fuzzbox."

"I—huh." She checks her watch. "An hour to go. Look, Bob. If you've got time to come back to my place for a coffee before I turf you out, we should talk some more." She looks at me warningly: "I'm going to have to kick you out at nine-thirty, though. Got a date."

"Well okay." I don't think I show any sign of guilty disappointment—or relief that I won't have an opportunity to outscore Mhari at her own game this once. Besides which, I think Mo is too nice to play that kind of dirty trick on. I raise a hand and a waiter zips over, swipes my credit card through her handheld, and wishes me a nice day.

We head over to Mo's place and I get a bit of a surprise; she's renting a flat in a centralish part of Putney, all wine bars and bistros. We catch the tube over and end up walking downstairs from an overhead platform:

you know you're entering suburbia when the underground trains poke their noses up into the open air. She walks very fast, forcing me to hurry to keep up. "Not far," she remarks, "just round a couple of corners from the tube stop."

She marches up a leaf-messed street in near darkness, hemmed in to either side by parked cars, everything washed out by orange sodium lights. I can feel the first chilly fingers of autumn in the air. "It's up here," she says, gesturing at a front door set back from the road, with a row of buzzers next to it. "Just a sec. I'm on the third floor, by the way; I've got the attic." She fumbles with a key in the lock and the door swings open on a darkened vestibule as the skin on the back of my neck begins to prickle, while the sound goes flat and the light deadens.

"Wait—" I begin to say, and something uncoils from the shadows and lashes out at Mo with a noise like an explosion in a cat factory.

She barely makes a noise as it grabs her with about a dozen tentacles—no suckers here—and yanks her into the darkened vestibule. I scream, "Shit!" and jump back, then yank at my belt where I happen to have clipped my multitool: the three-inch blade flips out and locks as I fumble around the inside of the door for a light switch, left-handed, holding the knife in front of me.

Now I hear a muffled squeaking noise—Mo is on the floor up against an inner doorway, screaming her head off. What looks like a nest of pythons has wriggled under the woodwork and is trying to drag her in by the neck. But whatever field is damping my hearing is also stifling her cries, and the thing has got her arms and torso. Behind her, the door is bulging; the light from the bulb overhead is attenuated to a dull, candle-like flicker.

I step back, yank out my mobile phone, and hit a quick-dial button, then throw it into the roadway outside. Then I take a deep breath and force myself to go back inside.

"*Get it off me!*" she mouths, thrashing around. I lean over her and try sawing at one of the tentacles. It's dry and leathery and squirms underneath the blade, so I jab the point of the knife into it and force my weight down.

The thing on the other side of the door goes apeshit: a banging and crashing resounds through the floor as if something huge is trying to break down the wall. The tentacles around Mo tighten until her mouth opens and I'm terrified she's going to turn blue. Something black begins to ooze out around my knife so I concentrate on ramming the thing down against the floor and slicing from side to side. It feels as if I'm trying to skewer a rubber band big enough to power a wind-up freight locomotive.

Mo thrashes around until her back is against the door; her eyes roll and I give a desperate yank on the tentacle with my free hand. The pain is indescribable: it feels like I've just grabbed hold of a mass of razor blades. Something black and oily is squirting out around the knife blade and I try to keep my hand out of it. How long is it going to take Capital Laundry Services to answer the sodding phone and get a Plumber out here? Too fucking long—a quarter of an hour at least. Maybe I can do something else—

A steel vise closes around my left ankle and yanks my shin against the doorframe so hard I scream and drop the knife. Another one wraps around my waist like an animated hawser and constricts violently. Mo valiantly lends a hand and succeeds in elbowing me under the chin: I see stars for a second or two and fumble around with a left hand that feels like a lump of raw meat for that dropped multitool. There's got to be a better way. If I've remembered my Gadget Man cigarette lighter . . . I reach into my pocket and, instead, find my palmtop. Illumination dawns.

The light of its display is a mycoid green glow in the darkness. A thousand miles away something is roaring at me. Icons shimmer, hovering above the screen. I thumb one of them, an ear with a red line through it, smearing blood across the glass as I cut in the antisound field and pray that it works.

## 5
## Ogre Reality

I wake up to discover my back feels as if the All Blacks have been performing a victory dance on it, my ankle's been turned on a lathe, and my left hand worked over with a steak tenderiser. I open my eyes; I'm lying on the floor, legs stretched out, and Mo is leaning over me. "Are you all right?" she asks, in a ragged voice.

"Death shouldn't hurt like this," I croak. I blink painfully and wonder what the hell happened to her shirt—it looks as if it's been used as a nest by a family of hungry ferrets. "It had you for longer—"

"Once you began hacking at it," she begins, then pauses to clear her throat. "It let go. Think you can stand up? You turned that gadget on and the thing just *vanished*. Whipped back under the door and sort of faded out. Turned translucent and—went away."

I look round. I'm lying in a sticky black puddle of something that isn't blood, thankfully—or, at least, not human blood. The light is normal for a dingy vestibule with an energy-saver bulb, and the tentacles have gone from the walls. "My phone," I say, pushing my back up against the wall. "I threw it out—"

Mo heaves herself upright and staggers to the front door, bends down and picks something up delicately. "You mean this?"

She drops it beside me, in about three separate pieces.

"Fuck. That was meant to call the Plumbers."

"Come upstairs, you'd better explain." She pauses. "If you think it's safe?"

I try to laugh but a vicious stabbing pain in my ribs stops me. "I don't think that thing will be coming back any time soon: I fuzzed its eigenvector but good."

She unlocks the inner door and we stumble up three flights of stairs, then she opens another door and I somehow end up slumped across another overstuffed sofa from the Planet of the Landlords, gasping with pain. She double-locks and deadbolts the door then flops into an armchair opposite me. "What the hell was that?" she asks, rubbing her throat.

"That was what we call in the trade an Unscheduled Reality Excursion, usually abbreviated to 'Oh fuck.'"

"Yes, but—"

"What I said earlier? We live in an Everett-Wheeler cosmology, all possible parallel universes coexisting. That thing was an agent someone summoned from elsewhere to, um—"

"Fuck with our metabolic viability," she suggests.

"Yeah, that." I pause and take stock of my ribs, ankle, and general frame of mind. My hands are shaking slightly and I feel clammy and cold with the aftershock, but not entirely out of control. Good. "You mentioned something about coffee." I lever myself upright. "If you tell me where it is . . ."

"Kitchen's over there." I realize there's a breakfast bar and a cramped cooking niche behind me. I shamble over, fumble for the light switches, check there's water in the kettle, and begin scooping instant out of the first available jar. Mo continues: "My neck hurts. Do you have lots of, uh, reality excursions in this line of work?"

"That's the first I've ever had follow me home," I say truthfully. Fred the Accountant doesn't count.

"Well I am glad to hear that." Mo stands up and goes somewhere else—bathroom, at a guess; I need the caffeine so badly that I don't really notice. While the kettle boils I root out a couple of mugs and some milk, and when I turn round she's back in the armchair wearing a clean T-shirt. I fill the mugs. "Milk, no sugar. Bathroom's behind you on the left," she adds, noncommittally.

One splash of water on my face later I'm back on the sofa with a mug of coffee, beginning to feel a bit more human—Neanderthal, maybe.

"What was that thing doing here?" she asks me.

"I don't know, and I'm not sure I want to know."

"Really?" She glares at me. "Trouble has a bad habit of following you around. First time I meet you, an hour later some Middle Eastern thugs stick me in the trunk of their car, drive me halfway round Santa Cruz, lock me in a cupboard, and gear up to sacrifice me. Second time I meet you, an hour later some random bad dream with too many tentacles ambushes me in my front hall." She pauses for a thoughtful moment. "Now granted, you seem to turn up in time to stop them, but, on the balance of prior probabilities, there appears to be a statistical correlation between you appearing in my life and horrible things happening. What's *your* excuse?"

I shrug painfully. "What can I say? There seems to be a positive correlation in my life between people telling me to talk to you and horrible things happening to me. I mean, it's not as if I make a habit of letting random nightmares with too many tentacles come along on a date, is it? Parenthetically speaking," I add hastily.

"Huh. Well then. Got any ideas as to why this is happening, mister spy guy?"

"I am *not* a spy," I say, nettled, "and the answer—" is right in front of my pointy nose if I'd bloody well focus on it, I suddenly realize.

"Yes?" she prompts, noticing my pause.

"Those guys who officially didn't abduct you." I take a sip of coffee and wince; I'm not used to the instant stuff she uses. "And who weren't officially talking about sacrificing you. I want you to tell me everything you didn't officially tell anyone who debriefed you. Like the whole truth."

"What makes you think I didn't tell—" she stops.

"Because you were afraid nobody would believe you. Because you were afraid they'd think you were a nut. Because there were no witnesses and nobody wanted to believe anything had happened to you in the first place because they'd have had to fill in too many forms in triplicate and that would be bad. Because you didn't owe the bastards anything for fucking up your life, if you'll excuse my French." I wave a hand in the general direction of the doorway. "*I* believe you. I know something really stinks around here. If I can figure out what it is, stopping it features high on my list of priorities. Is that enough for you?"

Mo grimaces, a strikingly ugly expression. "What's to say?"

"Lots. Your call: if you won't tell me what happened, I can't try and sort things out for you."

She sips her coffee as it cools. "After we met, I went home thinking everything was going to be okay. You, or the Foreign Office, or whoever, would sort things out so I could come home. It was all just a mix-up, right? I'd get my visa sorted out and be allowed to go back home without any more problems."

Another mouthful of coffee. "I walked back to my condo. That's one of the things I liked about UCSC: the town's small enough you can walk anywhere. You don't have to drive as long as you don't mind getting to SF being a royal pain. I was turning over a problem I'm working on, a way to integrate my probability formalism with Dempster-Shaffer logic. Anyhow, I stopped off at a convenience store to buy some stuff I was running out of and who should I run into but David? At least, I *thought* it was David." She frowns. "I thought he was out east, and I really didn't want to see him anyway—I mean, I'm over him. He's history."

"What makes you think it wasn't your ex-husband?" I ask.

"Nothing, at the time. He just turned round from the counter and smiled at me and said, 'Can I give you a lift home?' and I sort of . . ." she trails off.

"It offered you a lift home," I echo.

"What do you mean, *it*?"

I close my eyes. "You got yourself into some really smelly shit there.

Say some son of a bitch wants to abduct somebody. They have to get a victim profile, samples from the victim—it's not simple, not just messing around with hair or fingernail clippings for the DNA—but suppose they get it. Then they invoke, um, generate a vector field oriented on the victim's—"

"Yeah, yeah, I'll take that bit on trust."

"Okay then. I'll give you some references tomorrow. Basically it's what used to be called an incubus: a demon lover. Something the victim won't resist because they don't *want* to resist. It's not actually a demon; it's just a hallucination, like a website generated by customer relationship management software from hell."

"A lure?"

"Yes, that's it exactly. A lure." I placed my unfinished mug down between my feet.

She shudders, looks worried. "Maybe I wasn't over him as thoroughly as I wanted to be."

"I know the feeling," I say, thinking of Mhari.

She shakes herself. "Anyway. Next thing I know I'm sitting in the back of a Lincoln and some guy I don't know who's wearing a Nehru suit and a beard is sticking a pistol in my side. And he says something like, 'American bitch, you have been selected for a great honor.' And I say, 'I'm not American,' and he just sneers."

Her hand is shaking so badly that coffee slops on the floor.

"He just—"

"It doesn't matter, what happens next?" I ask, trying to get her over the emotional hump. Over there they hold grudges for a long time. Some of the Pathans are probably still plotting their revenge for Lord Elphinstone's expedition.

"We drive around for a bit and head out of town, northbound on Highway 1, then the car pulls up to this house and the driver opens the door and they push me in through a side door into the house. The driver's wearing that long, baggy shirt and trousers you see on TV, and a scarf around his head, and he's got a beard, too. They push me through the kitchen and into a closet with a light then shut the door, and I hear them chain the door handles together. Someone else comes in and they talk for a bit, then I hear a door slam. That's when I pulled out my mobile phone and called you."

"You overheard them talking. What about?"

"I—wasn't concentrating much. Tell the truth—" she puts the cup down on the floor; its saucer is swimming in coffee "—I was afraid they were going to rape me. *Really* afraid; I mean, this was kidnapping, what would you expect? When they didn't, when they were talking, it was almost worse. Does that make any kind of sense? The waiting. But he—the one I didn't see—he had a deep voice, some accent—sounded German to me. Thick, gravelly, lots of sibilants. Had to keep repeating himself to the others, the Middle Eastern men. 'The Opener of the Ways requires the wisdom,' he kept saying. 'It needs information.' I think one of the Middle Eastern guys was objecting because after a bit there was a noise like—" she pauses, and swallows. "Like downstairs. And I didn't hear him again."

I shake my head. "This isn't making any sense so far—" Hastily: "No, I'm not saying you're wrong, I just can't figure out how it fits together. That's *my* problem, not yours."

I drain my coffee and wince as it hits my stomach and sits there, burning like a lump of molten lead. "Sounds like they were talking about a blood sacrifice. That's the Sacrifice of Knowledge rite. Middle Eastern guys. An incubus. German accent. You're sure it was German?"

"Yes," she says gloomily. "At least, I think it was German; Middle European for sure."

"That really *is* odd." Which distracts me and catapults my train of thought right into terra incognita because there are *no* usual suspects in the occult field in Germany; the Abwehr's Rosenberg Gruppe and any survivors of the Thule Gesellschaft were "shot trying to escape" by late June 1945. The camp guards were mostly executed or pulled long prison sentences, the higher-ups responsible for the Ahnenerbe-SS were executed, the whole country turned into a DMZ as far as the occult is concerned. After the Third Reich's answer to the Manhattan Project came so close to completion, that was about the one thing that Truman and Stalin and Churchill all saw eye-to-eye on—and the current government shows no desire to go back down that route of blood and madness.

"He went on a bit," Mo adds unexpectedly.

"Really? What about?"

"He wanted to go home, to take help home, something like that. I think."

I sit up, wince as my ribs remind me not to move too fast. "Help. Did he say what kind?"

Mo frowns again. Her thick, dark eyebrows almost join in the middle, looming like thunderclouds. "He went on about the Opener of the Ways a bit more. Oddly, as if he was talking about me. Said that help for the struggle against the Dar-al-Harb would wait until the ceremony of, uh, 'Unbinding the roots of Ig-drazl'? Then he would 'Open the bridge and bring the ice giants through.' He was very emphatic about the bridge, the bridge to living space. That was his term for it: *living space*. Does that make any sense?"

"It makes an *oh-shit* kind of sense." I watch as she picks up her mug and rolls it round between her hands. "Was that all?"

"All? Yes. I waited until I heard them go out, then I phoned you. I obviously got things wrong, though, because the next thing I knew they yanked open the door and the one with the gun grabbed the phone and stamped on it. He was *angry*, but the other—with the accent—" she judders to a stop.

"Can you describe him?"

She swallows. "That's the crazy thing. From the voice I kind of expected Arnie Schwarzenegger in *The Terminator*, except he *wasn't*. There were just these four Middle Eastern guys, and one of them had—I can't, uh, can't remember his face. Just those eyes. They seemed to glow, sort of greenish. Like marbles. Like there was something luminous and wormy behind his face. He—the one with the eyes and this weird German accent—he was *angry* and yelled at me and I was so afraid, but they just smashed my phone then shut the door on me again. Chained the door shut and overturned a table or something against it. And I—hell." She finishes her coffee. "That was about the worst hour of my life." Pause. "It could have been worse." Pause. "They could have." Pause. "You might not have answered." Pause. "They might not have found me."

"All in a day's work," I say with forced lightheartedness, which has nothing to do with the way I feel. "When the cops brought you out, did you see anything?"

"I wasn't paying much attention," she says shakily. "There were gunshots, though. Then what looked like a whole SWAT team kicked the cupboard door in and pointed their toys at me. You ever had two guys point assault rifles at your head, so close you can see the grooves on the inside of the barrels? You just lie there very still and try very hard not to look threatening." Pause. "Anyway, one of the agents in charge figured out I was the hostage in about three seconds flat and they led me out through the front. There was blood everywhere and two bodies, but not the guy with the weird eyes. I'd recognize him. Thing is, there were strange symbols all over the wall; it was whitewashed and it looked like they'd been painting on it in thick black paint, or blood, or something. A low table under it, with a trashed laptop and some other stuff. Candlesticks, an arc-welding power supply. It was weird, I guess you'd know how weird it looked. Then they drove me away."

My bad feeling is getting worse. In fact, it's not setting off alarm bells in my head anymore: it's sounding the Three Minute Warning. "Mind if I use your phone?" I ask, carefully nonchalant. "I think we still need the Plumbers."

\* \* \*

Due to the miracles of matrix management Bridget is my head of department and writes my personal efficiency assessments, and Harriet is her left hand of darkness and handles administrative issues like training; but since I moved to active service, Andy is now my line manager with overall responsibility for my effectiveness and work assignment, and Angleton is just the guy I'm acting as temporary private secretary for. I decide to start at the bottom of the seniority queue, consign Harriet to the pits of operational ineffectiveness—I mean, this is a woman who would give you a written reprimand for wasting departmental funds if you used silver bullets on a werewolf—and conclude that my best chance of survival is to throw myself on Andy's mercy.

Which means I nobble him absolutely as soon as I can, first thing in the morning.

"Mind if I have a word?" I ask, sticking my head around his door without asking—the red light is off.

Andy is slumped behind his desk, nursing his starter-motor coffee mug. He raises an eyebrow at me. "You look—" He stabs a finger at his keyboard, raises another eyebrow at his email. "Oh. So it was *you* who called the Plumbers out last night."

I sit down in the chair opposite his desk without asking permission. "Angleton told me to pump Mo after work—" I see his expression "—for information, dammit!"

Andy hides behind his coffee. "Do go on," he says warmly, "this is the best entertainment I'm going to get all morning."

"Then you must be hard up. We ate out, then went back to her place for some more sensitive discussions about the, uh, non-events last month. Something was waiting for us in the lobby."

"Something." He looks skeptical. "And you called out the Plumbers for that?"

I yawn: it's been a long night. "It tried to rip her fucking head off and I've got a cracked rib to show for it. If you'd read that goddamn report you'd see what forensics found in the carpet; they're never going to get the ichor stains out—"

"I'll read it." He puts his coffee mug down. "First, give me the basics. How did you deal with it?"

I produce the wreckage of my Laundry-issue palmtop. "I'll be needing a new PDA, this one's fucked. Mind you, it's not as fucked as the malevolent mollusc from Mars that jumped us; I bumped the fuzz diffuser up to full power and piped the entire entropy pool into it over wide-spectrum infrared. It decided it didn't like that and discorporated instead of sticking around to finish the job, otherwise you'd be spending this morning watching them hoover me off the walls and ceiling."

I take as deep a breath as the strapping around my ribs will permit. "Anyway, afterward I got the whole story out of Mo. The bits she was afraid of telling anyone for fear they wouldn't believe her. And that's why I called the Plumbers. See, the Yank field group who rescued her didn't tell us what the hell was going on. The leader was some Arab guy with a German accent, talking about help for the struggle with the Dar-al-Harb once the roots of Yggdrasil are unbound. Only they didn't get him—or she didn't see his body. Boss, do we have anything on German terror groups using Beckenstein-Skinner actor theory to possess their victims? Hell, anything about any German terror groups more recent than the Ahnenerbe using occult techniques?"

Andy looks at me with a stony expression. "Wait here. Do *not* move." He pushes the DNI button (turning on the red warning light outside the door—WARNING: CLASSIFIED ACTIVITIES: DO NOT IN-TRUDE) then stands up and hurries out.

I sit there and let my eyes roam around Andy's cubbyhole. The contents are prosaic: one institutional desk (scratched), one swivel chair (used), two armless visitor chairs (ditto), one bookcase, and a classified document safe (basically a steel cabinet with lockable metal doors on it). His PC is five years old and running a password-locked screensaver, and his desk is clear—no papers lying around. In fact, if it wasn't for the classified document safe and the lack of papers it could be a low-level manager's office in any cash-pinched business in corporate Britain.

I'm leaning back in my chair and inspecting the flecks of institutional paint smeared on the frosted glass in the high window when the door opens again. Andy enters, closely followed by Derek and—shock, horrors—Angleton. I'm surrounded! "Here he is," says Andy.

Angleton claims Andy's chair behind the desk—the privilege of the senior inquisitor—and Andy sits down next to me, while Derek stands at parade rest in front of the door, as if to stop me escaping. He's got some kind of box like a small briefcase, which he parks on the floor next to his feet.

"Speak," says Angleton.

"I did as you told me. Mo and I were talking. I kept it to nonclassified while we were in public; I convinced her I needed to hear the full story, not just the official version, so we went back to her place. We were jumped in the hallway. Afterward, she told me enough that I thought there was a clear and present danger to her life. Did Andy tell you—"

Angleton snaps his fingers at Derek. Derek, who is not my idea of an obedient flunky, nevertheless obediently passes him the briefcase, which he opens on the desk. It turns out to contain a small mechanical type-writer with a couple of sheets of paper already wound around the roller.

He laboriously taps out a sentence, then turns the typewriter toward me: it says *SECRET OGRE CARNATE GECKO*, and I get an abrupt sinking feeling in my stomach.

"Before you leave this office you will write down everything you remember about last night," he says tersely. "You will not leave this office until you have finished and signed off on the report. One of us will stay with you until the job is done, and countersign that this is a true transcript and that there were no uncleared witnesses. Once you leave this office you will not see this document again. You will not, repeat *not*, discuss last night's events with anyone other than the participants and the people in this room without first obtaining written permission from one of us. Do you understand?"

"Uh, yeah. You're classifying everything under *OGRE CARNATE GECKO* and I'm not to discuss it with anyone who isn't cleared. Can I ask why the typewriter? I could email—"

Angleton looks at me witheringly: "Van Eck Radiation." He snaps his fingers. *But we're in the Laundry*, I protest silently, *the whole building is Tempest-shielded.* "Start typing, Bob."

I start typing. "Where's the delete key on this—oh."

"You're typing on carbon paper. In triplicate. Once you finish, we burn the carbons. And the typewriter ribbon."

"You could have offered a quill pen: that'd be more secure, wouldn't it?" I peck away at the keyboard in a purposeful manner. After a minute or two Angleton silently rises and ghosts out of the room. I peck on, occasionally swearing as I catch a fingernail under a key or jam a bunch of letters together. Finally I'm done: one page of single-spaced, densely printed text, detailing the events of last night. I sign each copy and present them to Andy, who countersigns, then carefully inserts them into a striped-cover folder and passes it to Derek, who writes out receipts for them and hands a copy to each of us. He leaves without a word.

Andy walks round the desk, stretches, then looks at me. "What am I going to do with you?"

"Huh? What's wrong?"

Andy looks morose. "If I'd known you'd show such a well-developed talent for raking up the mud . . ."

"Comes of my hacking hobby before I came to the attention of . . . look. I called the Plumbers because I had reason to be afraid that Mo— Professor O'Brien—was in serious danger. Would you rather I hadn't?"

"No." He sighs. For a moment he looks old. "You did the right thing. It's just that the Plumbing budget is chargeable to departmental accounts. That leaves us open to some rather nasty maneuvering if the

usual suspects decide it's an opportunity to extend their little empires.
I'm wondering how the hell we're going to spin it past Harriet."

"Why don't you just tell—oh."

"Yes." He nods at me. "You're beginning to catch on. Now run along
and get back to work. I'm sure your in-tray is overflowing."

I'm working my way through that overcrowded in-tray late in the afternoon when Harriet stalks in without knocking. (Actually, I'm up to my
eyeballs in a clipping from the *Santa Cruz County Sentinel*. It makes for
fascinating reading: TWO DEAD IN MURDER, SUICIDE. Two
unidentified males, one believed to be a Saudi Arabian national, found
dead in a house out toward Davenport. Police investigating weird occult
symbols smeared on the walls in blood. Drugs suspected.) "Ah, Bob," she
coos with malevolent solicitude. "Just the person I was looking for!"

Oh shit. "What can I do for you?" I ask.

She leans over my desk. "I understand you called out the Plumbers
last night," she says. "I happen to know that you're currently assigned to
Angleton as JPS, which is a nonoperational role and therefore doesn't
give you release authority for wet-and-dry issues. You are no doubt aware
that cleanup funds are allocated on a per-department basis, and require
prior authorization from your head of department, in writing. You didn't
obtain authorization from Bridget, and funnily enough, you didn't approach me for a release either." She smiles with chilly insouciance.
"Would you like to explain yourself?"

"I can't," I say.

"I—*see*." Harriet looms over me, visibly working on her anger. "You
realize that last night you cost our working budget more than seven *thousand* pounds? That's going to have to be justified, Mr Howard, and *you*
are going to justify it to the Audit Commission when they come round
next month. Let's see—" she flips through what looks for all the world
like a commercial invoice "—cleaning up Professor O'Brien's front door,
sweeping her apartment for listeners and actors, *rehousing* Professor
O'Brien in a secure apartment, armed escort, medical expenses. What
on earth have you been up to?"

"I can't tell you," I say.

"You're going to tell me. That's an order, by the way," she says in conversational tones. "You're going to tell me in writing *exactly* what happened there last night, and explain why I shouldn't take the expenses out
of your pay packet—"

"Harriet."

We both look round. Angleton's door is ajar; I wonder how long he's
been standing there.

"You don't have clearance," he says. "Let it drop. *That's* an order."

The door shuts. Harriet stands there for a moment, her jaw working soundlessly as if she's forgotten how to speak. I commit the spectacle to memory for future enjoyment. "Don't think this is the last you'll hear of this," she snaps at me as she leaves, slamming the door.

*TWO DEAD IN MURDER, SUICIDE*. Hmm. Ahnenerbe. Thule Gesellschaft. Incubi. German accents. Opener of the Ways. Double-hmm. I pull my terminal closer; it's only got access to low-classification and public sources, but it's time to do some serious data mining. I wonder . . . just what have Yusuf Qaradawi's friends and the Mukhabarat got to do with the last and most secret nightmares of the Third Reich?

The next day I go into the office and find Nick waiting for me at my desk like an overexcited trainee schoolmaster. This is an unscheduled intrusion in my plans, which mostly revolve around applying some security patches to the departmental file server and digging out the maintenance schematics to Angleton's antique Memex.

"Come along now! I've got something to show you," he says, in a tone that makes it clear I don't have any choice. He leads me up a staircase carpeted in a thick bottle-green pile that I haven't seen before, then along a corridor with dark, oak-panelled walls like a provincial gentlemen's club from the 1930s, except that gentlemen's clubs don't come with closed circuit TV cameras and combination locks on the doors.

"What *is* this place?" I ask.

"Used to be the director's manor," he explains. "When we had a director." When we had a director: I don't ask. He stops at a thick oak door and punches some digits into the lock, then opens it. "After you," he says.

There's a conference table and a modern—by Laundry standards—laptop set up at one end of it. A whole shitload of electronics racked up on shelves behind, along with some thick leather-bound books and a bunch of stuff like silver pencils, jars of mouldy dust, and what looks for all the world like a polygraph. As I go in I notice that the doorframe is unusually thick and there are no outside windows. "Is this shielded?" I ask.

Nick nods jerkily. "Well spotted, that man! Now sit down," he suggests.

I sit. The top shelf of the equipment rack is dominated by a glass bell jar with a human skull in it; I grin back at it. "'Alas, poor Yorick.'"

"Carry on like you have been and maybe your head will fetch up in there one day," Nick says, grinning. "Ah." The door opens. "Andy."

"Why am I here?" I ask. "All this cloak and dagger shit is—"

Andy drops a fat lever-arch file on the table in front of me. "Read and enjoy," he says dryly. "One day you, too, can have the fun of maintaining this manual."

I open the cover to be confronted by a sheet which basically says I can be arrested for so much as thinking about disclosing the contents of the next page. I flip to page two and read a paragraph that essentially says 'Abandon hope all ye who enter here,' so I turn *that* one over and get to the title page: *FIELD OPERATIONS MANUAL FOR COUNTER-OCCULT OPERATIONS.* Below it, in small print: *Approved by Departmental Quality Assurance Team* and then *Complies with BS5750 standard for total quality management.* I shudder. "Since when have we been into mummification?" I ask.

"Embalming—" Andy frowns for a moment. "Oh, you mean total quality—" he stops and clears his throat. "One of these days your sense of humor is going to get you into trouble, Bob."

"Thanks for the advance warning." I look at the manual gloomily. "Let me guess. I'm to do as we discussed earlier—by the book. *This* book, right? Why wasn't I issued it before Santa Cruz?"

Andy pulls out the chair beside me and flops down in it. "Because that wasn't officially an operation," he says in tones of sweet reason. "That was an informal information-gathering exercise involving a non-classified source. Operations require sign-off at director level. Informal information-gathering exercises don't."

I put the folder down on the table. "Does Bridget have anything to do with this?"

"Tangentially."

Nick sniffs, loudly, from his post by the door. "Arse-covering, boy. *That* was meant to be a risk-free chat. *This* is about what you do when you're ordered to stick your head in the lion's mouth. Or up its arse to inspect the hemorrhoids."

I look round at him. "You're planning on sending me on an op?" I ask. "Happy joy. Not."

Andy glances at Nick. "He's beginning to get it," he comments.

"Are you planning on involving Professor O'Brien in this?" I ask. "I mean, it seems to me that she's the one under threat. Isn't she?"

"Well." Andy glances at Nick, then back at me. "You're on active service, so you need to know this stuff inside out and upside down. But you're right, the specific reason for this session is what happened the other night. I can't confirm or deny the identities of anyone else involved, though."

"Then I've got a problem," I tell him. "I don't know if I should bring it up right now, but if I sit on it and I'm wrong . . . well, way I see it is, Mo is the one who's under threat and in need of protection. Right? I mean, *I* can cope with being drooled over by things with more tentacles than brains, but it's not exactly part of her job description, is it? You're supposed to be responsible for her safety. If you've got me going over rules of engagement, and she's involved, then when the shooting starts—"

Andy is nodding. It's a bad sign when your boss starts nodding at you before you finish each sentence.

"As a matter of fact I agree with your concerns completely," he says. "And yes, I agree we've got a problem. But it's not quite what you think it is." He leans forward and makes a steeple out of his fingers, elbows together on the table. The steeple leans sideways at an architecturally unsound angle. "We can probably keep her safe indefinitely, as long as she's locked down under a protection program and resident in one of our secure accommodation units. That's not in question; if nobody can see or track her, they can't attack her—although I'm not sure about the inability to track given that they must have obtained samples in order to spring that incubus on her last month. What concerns me is that such a posture is essentially defensive. We don't know for sure just what we're defending *against*, Bob, and that's bad."

Andy takes a deep breath, but Nick jumps in before he can continue: "We've dealt with Iraqi spies before, boy. This doesn't smell like them."

"Uh." I pause, unsure what to say. "What do you mean?"

"He means that the Mukhabarat simply don't have the technology to summon an incubus. Nor do they generally manage incarnations that leave Precambrian slime all over the carpet; about all they're up to is interrogation and compulsion of Watchers and a little bit of judicious torture. No real control of phase-space geometry, no Enochian deep grammar parse-tree generators—at least none that we've seen the source code to. So we can't make any assumptions about the attacks on Mo. Someone tried to grab her for whatever purpose. By now, they must know we're onto them. The next logical step is for them to pull back and switch track to whatever they were working on in the first place—which is extremely dangerous for us because if they were trying to snatch her, they were probably working on weapons of mass destruction. We badly need to get them out in the open and our only bait is Professor O'Brien. But if she knows she's bait, she'll keep looking round for sharks—which will tip them off. So we're assigning you to shadow her, Bob. You keep an eye on her. We'll keep an eye on you. When they bite, we'll reel them in. You don't need to know how, or when, but you'll do well to read this manual so you know how we set up this kind of situation. Clear?"

I crane my neck round at Nick, whose expression is uncharacteristically flat: he stares right through me with eyes like gunsights. "I don't like it. I *really* don't like it."

"You don't have to," Andy says flatly. "We're *telling* you what to do. Your job is—I shouldn't be telling you this, it should be Angleton, this afternoon, but what the hell—you're going to be assigned to shadow Mo. We'll do the rest. All I want to hear from you now is that you're going to do as you're told."

I tense. "Is that an order?"

"It is now," says Nick.

When I get home after receiving my mission orders and preemptive chewing-out from Angleton I find my key doesn't turn in the lock. It's dark and it's raining so I lean on the doorbell continuously until the door swings open. Pinky stands behind it, one hand on the latch. "What took you so long?" I ask him.

He steps back. "These are yours, I believe," he says, handing me a bunch of shiny new keys. He clanks as he walks; he's wearing black combat boots, matching trousers, what looks like a leather vest, and enough chains to stock a medium-sized prison. "I'm off clubbing tonight."

"Why the new keys?" I close the door and shake my hair, shrug off my coat, and try to find room to hang it in the hall.

"They changed the locks today," he says conversationally, "departmental orders, apparently." There's a new mat inside the front door, and when I look closely I see silvery lettering in a very small font stitched into its edges. "They came and swept the house for listeners and actors then renewed the wards on all the windows, the doors, the air vents—even the chimney. Any idea why?"

"Yeah," I grunt. I head for the kitchen, squeezing past someone's battered suitcases that are parked in the hall.

"We've got a new flatmate, too," he adds. "Oh, Mhari's fucked off again, but this time she says she's moving into House Orange for good."

"Ah-hum." *Twist the knife in the wound, why don't you?* I inspect the kettle, then poke around inside my cupboard to see if there's any food more substantial than a pot noodle.

"You'll probably like the new flatmate, though," Pinky continues. "She's helping Brains with his omelettes in the front cellar—he's using high-intensity ultrasound, this time."

I find a pot noodle and a desiccated supermarket pizza base. There's cheese and tomato paste in the fridge, and a pork sausage I can chop up to go on top of it, so I turn the grill on. "Any newspapers?" I ask.

"Newspapers? Why?"

"I have to book a flight. I'm taking a week's leave next Monday, and it's already Wednesday."

"Going anywhere interesting?"

"Amsterdam."

"Cool!" There's a pair of fur-lined handcuffs on the bread board; Pinky picks them up and eyes them critically, then starts polishing them on a square of kitchen roll. "Party on?"

"I have some research to do at the Oostindischehuis. And in the basement of the Rijksmuseum."

"Research." He rolls his eyes and tucks the handcuffs into a belt clip. "What a *boring* use for a holiday in Amsterdam!"

I chop bits of pork sausage up and sprinkle them over my garbage pizza, oblivious. The cellar door swings open. "Did somebody mention Amsterdam—hey, what are *you* doing here?"

I drop my knife. "Mo? What are *you*—"

"Bob? Hey, have you guys met?"

" 'Scuse me, would you mind moving? I need to get through—"

With four people in the kitchen it's distinctly cozy, not to say crowded. I move my pizza up under the grill and switch the kettle on again. "Who put you up here?" I ask Mo.

"The Plumbers—they said this was a secure apartment," she says, rubbing the side of her nose. She peers at me suspiciously. "What's going on?"

"It *is* a secure apartment," I say slowly. "It's on the Laundry list."

"Bob's girlfriend just moved out for the fourth time," Pinky explains helpfully. "They must have thought the spare room needed filling."

"Oh, this is too much." Mo pulls out a chair and sits down with her back against the wall, arms crossed defensively.

"Guys?" I ask. "Could you take it outside?"

"Certainly," Brains sniffs, and disappears back into the cellar.

Pinky smiles. "I knew you'd hit it off!" he says, then ducks out of the room hastily.

A minute later the front door slams. Mo fixes me with a magistrate's stare. "You live here? With those two?"

"Yeah." I inspect the grill. "They're mostly harmless, when they're not trying to take over the world each night."

"Trying to—" she stops. "That one. Uh, Pinky? He's out clubbing?"

"Yes, but he never brings any rough trade home," I explain. "He and Brains have been together for, oh, as long as I've known them."

"*Oh*." I see the light bulb go on above her head: some people are a bit slow on the uptake about Pinky and Brains.

"Brains doesn't get out a lot. Pinky is a party animal, a bit of rubber, a bit of leather. Every few weeks, whenever the moon is in the right phase, hairs burst from the palms of his hands and he turns into a wild bear with a compulsion to terrorize Soho. Brains doesn't seem to notice.

They're like an old married couple. Once a year Pinky drags Brains out to Pride so he can maintain his security clearance."

"I *see*." She relaxes a little but looks puzzled. "I thought the secret services sacked you for being homosexual?"

"They used to, said it made you a security risk. Which was silly, because it was the practice of firing homosexuals that made them vulnerable to blackmail in the first place. So these days they just insist on openness—the theory is you can only be blackmailed if you're hiding something. Which is why the Brain gets the day off for Gay Pride to maintain his security clearance."

"Ah—I give up." She smiles. The smile fades fast. "I've still got to move my stuff in. They're packing up the flat and I didn't have much anyway, most of my furniture is in a shipping container somewhere on the Atlantic . . . Why Amsterdam, Bob?"

I prod at the pizza, which is beginning to melt on top as the grill strains to heat it up. "I've been doing a bit of digging." I wince: my rib stabs at me. "Things you said last night. Oh, has anyone said anything to you?"

"No." She looks puzzled.

"Well, don't be surprised if in the next couple of days Andy or Derek drops by and gets you to sign a piece of paper saying that you'll cut your own throat before talking to anyone without clearance. That's what they did to me; they're taking it seriously."

"Well *that's* a relief," she says with heavy irony. "Did you learn anything?"

The pizza is bubbling away on top; I turn the grill down so that it can heat right through. "Coffee?"

"Tea, if you've got it."

"Okay. Um, I did some reading. Did you know that what you overheard is completely impossible? As in, it can't happen because it's not allowed?"

"It's not—hang on." She glares at me. "If you're pulling my leg—"

"Would I do a thing like that?" I must look the image of hurt innocence because she chuckles wickedly.

"I wouldn't put anything past you, Bob. Okay, what do you mean by 'it's not allowed'? As your professor I am ordering you to tell me everything."

"Uh, isn't it my job to say, 'Tell me, professor'?"

She waves it off: "Nah, that would be a cliché. So tell me. What the fornicating hell is happening? Why does someone or something try to render me metabolically incompetent whenever I meet you?"

"Well, it goes back to around 1919," I say, dropping tea bags into a chipped pot. "That was when the Thule Gessellschaft was founded in Munich by Baron von Sebottendorff. The Thule Society were basically mystical whack-jobs, but they had a lot of clout; in particular they were heavily into Masonic symbolism and a load of post-Theosophical guff about how the only true humans were the Aryan race, and the rest—the *Mindwertigen*, 'inferior beings'— were sapping their strength and purity and precious bodily fluids. All of this wouldn't have mattered much except a bunch of these goons were mixed up in Bavarian street politics, the Freikorps and so on. They sort of cross-fertilized with a small outfit called the NSDAP, whose leader was a former NCO and agent provocateur sent by the Landswehr to keep an eye on far-right movements. He picked up a lot of ideas from the Thule Society and when he got where he wanted he told the head of his personal bodyguard—a guy called Heinrich Himmler, another occult obsessive—to put Walter Darre, one of Alfred Rosenberg's protégés, in charge of the Ahnenerbe Society. Ahnenerbe was originally independent, but rapidly turned into a branch of the SS after 1934; a sort of occult R&D department cum training college. Meanwhile the Gestapo orchestrated a pretty severe crackdown on all nonparty occultists in the Third Reich; Adolf wanted a monopoly on esoteric power, and he got it."

I switch off the grill. "All this would have amounted to exactly zip except that some nameless spark in the Ahnenerbe research arm unearthed David Hilbert's unpublished Last Question. And from there to the Wannsee Conference was just a short step."

"Hilbert, Wannsee—you've lost me. What did the calculus of variations have to do with Wannsee, wherever that is?"

"Wrong question, right Hilbert; it's not one of the Twenty-Three Questions on unsolved problems in mathematics, it's something he did later. Thing is, Hilbert was experimenting with some very odd ideas toward the end, before he died in 1943. He'd more or less pioneered functional analysis, he came up with Hilbert Space—obviously—and he was working toward a 'proof theory' in the mid-thirties, a theory for formally proving the correctness of theorems. Yeah, I know, Gödel holed that one under the waterline in 1931. Anyhow, you know Hilbert's published work dropped off sharply in the 1930s and he didn't publish *anything* in the 1940s? And yes, he'd read Turing's doctoral thesis. Do I need to draw you a diagram? No? Good.

"Now, Wannsee . . . that was the conference in late 1941 that set the Final Solution in motion. Before then, it was mostly an alfresco atrocity—*Einsatzgruppen*, mobile murder units, running around behind the front line machine-gunning people. It was the Ahnenerbe-SS, with the Numerical Analysis Department founded on the back of that unpublished work by Hilbert—he pointedly refused to cooperate any further once he realized what was going on, by the way—which provided the seed for the Wannsee Invocation. The Wannsee Conference was attended by delegates from about twenty different Nazi organizations and ministries. It set up the organization of the Final Solution. The Ahnenerbe ran it behind the scenes, using Karl Adolf Eichmann—at the time, head of Section IV B4 of the Reich Main Security Office—as organizational head, a kind of Nazi equivalent of General Leslie Groves. In the USA, General Groves was a Corps of Engineers officer; he organised the massive logistical and infrastructure mobilisation needed to build the Manhattan Project. In Vienna, Eichmann, an SS *Obersturmbannführer*, was in charge of providing raw material for the largest necromantic invocation in human history.

"The goal of what the Ahnenerbe called Project Jotunheim, and what everyone else called the Wannsee Invocation, was what we'd today designate the opening of a class four gate—a large, bidirectional bridge to another universe where the commutative operation, opening gates back to our own, is substantially easier. A bridge big enough to take tanks, bombers, U-boats. Can you spell 'counterstrike'? We're not sure quite what their constraint requirements were, or what the Wansee Invocation was intended to accomplish, but they'd have been pretty drastic; Wannsee cost the Nazi state a greater proportion of its wealth than the Manhattan Project cost the US, and would have had similar or bigger military implications if they'd succeeded. Of course, their spell was grotesquely unoptimised; you could probably do it with a budget of a million pounds for equipment and only use a couple of sacrifices if you had a proper understanding of the theory. They tried to do a brute-force attack on the problem, and failed—especially when the Allies got wind of it and bombed the crap out of the big soul-capacitors at Peenumünde. But that's not the point. They failed, and those deaths, all ten million or so of the people they murdered in the extermination camps that fed the death spell, didn't suffice to pull their heads out of the noose."

Mo shivers. "That's *horrible.*" She stands up and walks over to inspect the tea. "Hmm, needs more milk." She leans against the counter next to me. "I can't believe Hilbert would have cooperated with the Nazis willingly on that kind of project."

"He didn't. And when the Allies found out, they, um, demilitarised Germany with extreme prejudice. In the occult field, anyway. None of the Ahnenerbe-SS researchers from the Numerical Analysis Division survived; if the SOE death squads didn't get them, it was the OSS or the NKVD. That's what the Helsinki Protocol was about: *nobody* wanted to see systematic mass murder of civilians adopted as a technique in strategic warfare, especially given some of the more unpleasant and extreme effects the weapon Ahnenerbe-SS were working on could give rise to. Like collapsing the false vacuum or letting vastly superhuman alien intelligences gain access to our universe. This stuff made atom bombs and ballistic missiles look harmless."

"Oh." She pauses. "Which is why what happened to me is impossible, right? I think I begin to see. Curiouser and curiouser . . ."

"I'm going to Amsterdam next Monday, soon as I've booked a flight," I say slowly. "Want to come along?"

I feel like a real shit. Andy told me I would, and Angleton ground the message home; but it doesn't help any as I tell her half the reasons why I'm going to Amsterdam—the half she's cleared for.

"The Reijksmuseum has an interesting basement," I say lightly. "It's off-limits to civ—to people who don't have need-to-know on the Helsinki Protocols. Thing is, Holland is part of the EUINTEL agreement, a treaty group that provides for joint suppression operations directed against paranormal threats. I'm not allowed to visit the USA on business without a specific invitation, but Amsterdam is home territory. As long as it's official and I've established a liaison relationship I can call for backup and expect to get it. And if I want to examine the basement library, well, it's the best collated set of Ahnenerbe-SS memorabilia and records this side of Yad Vashem."

"So if you get a hankering to go look at some old masters and disappear through a side door for a couple of hours—"

"Exactly."

"Bullshit, Bob." She frowns at me, eyebrows furrowing. "You've just been lecturing me about the history of this bunch of Nazi necromancers. You obviously think there's some connection with the Middle Eastern guys in Santa Cruz, the one with the weird eyes and the German accent. Your flatmates have just been telling me how safe this house is, and how all the wards have just been updated. If you're afraid of something, why not just sit tight at home?"

I shrug. "Well, leaving aside that the bastards seem to want you for something—I'm not sure. Look, there's some other stuff I'm not allowed to talk about, but right now Amsterdam looks like the right place to be, if I want to find these idiots before they try and kidnap you again."

I pull the grill tray out and slide my garbage pizza onto a plate. "Slice of pizza?"

"Yes, thank you."

I cut the thing in two pieces and slide one onto another plate, pass it to her. "Look, there's a connection between those goons who kidnapped you in Santa Cruz and something my boss has been keeping an eye on for a couple of years. It turns out that they're connected to the Mukhabarat, the Iraqi secret police; there's a proliferation spin on the whole thing, rogue state trying to get its hands on weapons forbidden by treaty. Right?" She nods, mouth too full to reply. "From that perspective, kidnapping you makes perfect sense. What I don't understand is the sacrifice bit. Or the attempt to kill you. It just doesn't make sense if it's simply a Mukhabarat technology transfer deal. Those guys are vicious but they're not idiots."

I take a deep breath. "No, the trouble you've got is something related to the Ahnenerbe-SS's legacy. Which is deep, dark shit. I wouldn't put it beyond Saddam Hussein to be dealing in such things—the Ba'ath party of Iraq explicitly modelled their security apparatus on the Third Reich, and they've got a real down on Jews—but it puzzles me. I mean, the possessed guy you saw who wasn't in the flat when the Black Chamber SWAT team stormed it—was he something to do with the Mukhabarat or one of their proxies summoning up some psychotic Nazi death magic or something? If so, the question is who they are, and the answer may be buried in the Rijksmuseum basement. Oh, and there's one other thing."

"Oh? What would that be?"

I can't look her in the eye; I just can't. "My boss says he'd value your insight. On an informal basis."

Which is only half the truth. What I *really* want to say to her is: *It's you they're after. As long as you're here in a Laundry safe house they can't get to you. But if we trail you in front of them, in the middle of a city that happens to be the Mukhabarat's headquarters for Western Europe, we might be able to draw them out. Get them to try again, under the guns of a friendly team. Be our tethered goat, Mo?* But I'm chicken. I don't have the guts to ask her to bait my hook. I hold my tongue and I feel about six inches tall, and in my imagination I can see Andy and Derek nodding silent approval, and it still doesn't help. "Given enough pairs of eyes, all problems are transparent," I say, falling back to platitudes. "Besides, it's a great city. We could maybe study etchings together, or something."

"You need to work on your pickup lines," Mo observes, yanking a particularly limp segment of pizza base loose and holding it up. "But for the sake of argument, consider me charmed. How much will this trip cost?"

"Ah, now that's the good bit." I drain my mug and push it away from me. "There aren't many perks that come from working for the Laundry, but one of them is that it happens to be possible to get a cheap travel pass. Special arrangement with BA, apparently. All we have to pay is the airport tax and our hotel bill. Know any decent B&Bs out there?"

6

## The Atrocity Archives

Three days flick by like microfiche cards through the input hopper of Angleton's Memex. Mo has settled into the vacant room on the second floor of our safe house like a long-term resident; as a not very senior academic, her Ph.D. years not long behind her, she probably spent years in flat-shares like this. I focus on my day-to-day work, fixing broken network servers, running a security audit of some service department's kit (two illicit copies of Minesweeper and one MP3 music jukebox to eliminate), and spending the afternoons up in the secure office in the executive suite, learning the bible of field operations by heart. I try not to think about what I'm getting Mo into. In fact, I try not to see her at all, spending long hours into the evening poring over arcane regulations and petty incantations for coordinating joint task-force operations. I feel more than a little bit guilty, even though I'm only obeying orders, and consequently I feel a little bit depressed.

At least Mhari doesn't try to get in touch.

The Sunday before we're due to leave I have to stay home because I need to pack my bags. I'm dithering over a stack of T-shirts and an electric toothbrush when someone knocks on my bedroom door. "Bob?"

I open it. "Mo."

She steps inside, hesitant, eyes scanning. My room often has that effect on people. It's not the usual single male scattering of clothes on every available surface—aggravated by my packing—so much as the groaning, double-stacked bookcase and the stuff on the walls. Not many guys have anatomically correct life-sized plastic skeletons hanging from a wall bracket. Or a desk made out of Lego bricks, with the bits of three half-vivisected computers humming and chattering to each other on top of it.

"Are you packing?" she asks, smiling brightly at me; she's dressed up for a night out with some lucky bastard, and here's me wondering when I last changed my T-shirt and looking forward to a close encounter with a slice of toast and a tin of baked beans. But the embarrassment only lasts for a moment, until her wandering gaze settles in the direction of the bookcase. Then: "Is that a copy of Knuth?" She homes in on the top shelf. "Hang on—volume *four*? But he only finished the first three volumes in that series! Volume four's been overdue for the past twenty years!"

"Yup." I nod, smugly. Whoever she's dating won't have anything like *that* on his shelves. "We—or the Black Chamber—have a little agreement with him; he doesn't publish volume four of *The Art of Computer Programming*, and they don't render him metabolically challenged. At least, he doesn't publish it to the public; it's the one with the Turing Theorem in it. Phase Conjugate Grammars for Extra-dimensional Summoning. This is a very limited edition—numbered and classified."

"That's—" she frowns. "May I borrow it? To read?"

"You're on the inside now; just don't leave it on the bus."

She pulls the book down, shoves a bundle of crumpled jeans to one side of my bed to make room, and perches on the end of it. Mo in dress-up mode turns out to be a grownup designer version of hippie crossed with Goth: black velvet skirt, silver bangles, ethnic top. Not quite self-consciously pre-Raphaelite, but nearly. Right now she's destroying the effect completely by being 100 percent focused on the tome. "Wow." Her eyes are alight. "I just wanted to see if you were, like, getting ready? Only now I don't want to go; I'm going to be up all night!"

"Just remember we need to be out the door by seven o'clock," I remind her. "Allow two hours for getting to Luton and check in . . ."

"I'll sleep on the plane." She closes the book and puts it down, but keeps one hand on the cover, protectively close. "I haven't seen you around much, Bob. Been busy?"

"More than you can imagine," I say. Setting up scanners that will slurp through the Laundry's UPI and Reuters news feeds and page me if anything interesting comes up while I'm away. Reading the manual for field operations. Avoiding my guilty conscience . . . "How about you?"

She pulls a face. "There's so *much* stuff buried in the stacks, it's unbelievable. I've been spending all my time reading, getting indigestion along the way. It's just such a waste—all that stuff, locked up behind the Official Secrets Act!"

"Yeah, well." It's my turn to pull a face now. "In principle, I kind of agree with you. In practice . . . how to put it? This stuff has repercussions. The many-angled ones live at the bottom of the Mandelbrot set; play around with it for too long and horrible things can happen to you." I shrug. "And you know what students are like."

"Yes, well." She stands up, straightening her skirt with one hand and holding the book with the other. "I suppose you've got more experience of that than I have. But, well." She pauses, and gives a little half-smile: "I was wondering if, if you'd eaten yet?"

Ah. Suddenly I figure it out: I'm *so* thick. "Give me half an hour?" I ask. *Where the hell did I leave that shirt?* "Anywhere in particular take your fancy?"

"There's a little bistro on the high street that I was meaning to check out. If you're ready in half an hour?"

"Downstairs," I say firmly. "Half an hour!" She slips out of my room and I waste half a minute drooling at the back of the door before I snap out of it and go in search of something to wear that doesn't look too shop-soiled. The sudden realisation that Mo might actually enjoy my company is a better antidepressant than anything I could get on a prescription.

I'm brought to my senses by the shrill of my alarm clock: it's eight in the morning, the sky's still dark outside, my head aches, and I'm feeling inexplicably happy for someone who this afternoon will be baiting the trap for an unknown enemy.

I pull on my clothes, grab my bags, head downstairs still yawning vigorously. Mo is in the kitchen, red-eyed and nursing a mug of coffee; there's a huge, travel-stained backpack in the hall. "Been up all night with the book?" I ask. She was thinking about it all through what was otherwise a really enjoyable quiet night out.

"Here. Help yourself." She points to the cafeteria. She yawns. "This is *all* your fault." I glance at her in time to catch a brief grin. "Ready to go?"

"After this." I pour a mug, add milk, shudder, yawn again, and begin to work on it. "Somehow I'm not hungry this morning."

"I think that place goes on the visit-again list," she agrees. "I must try the couscous next time . . ." She mounts another attack on her mug and I decide that she's just as attractive wearing jeans and sweat shirt and no warpaint first thing in the morning as in the evening. I'll pass on the red eyes, though. "Got your passport?"

"Yeah. And the tickets. Shall we go?"

"Lead on."

Some hours later we've emerged from Arrivals at Schiphol, caught the train to the Centraal Station, grappled with the trams, and checked into a cutesy family-run hotel with a theme of hot and cold running philosophers — Hegel on the breakfast room place mats, Mo in the Plato room on the top floor, and myself relegated to the Kant basement. By early afternoon we're walking in the Vondelpark, between the dark green grass and the overcast grey sky; a cool wind is blowing in off the channel and for the first time I'm able to get the traffic fumes out of my lungs. And we're out of sight of Nick and Alan who, until the hotel, tailed us all the way from the safe house to the airport and then onto our flight — I suppose they're part of the surveillance team. It's bad practice to acknowledge their presence and they made no attempt to talk to me; as far as I can tell, Mo doesn't suspect anything.

"So where is this museum then?" asks Mo.

"Right there." I point. At one end of the park, a neoclassical lump of stonework rears itself pompously toward the sky. "Let's check in and get our restricted area passes validated, huh? Give it an hour or so and we can try and find somewhere to eat."

"Only a couple of hours?"

"Everywhere closes early in Amsterdam, except the bars and coffee shops," I explain. "But don't go in a coffee shop and order a coffee or they'll laugh at you. What we call a café is an *Eethuis*, and what they call a café we call a pub. Got it?"

"Clear as mud." She shakes her head. "Good thing for me everyone seems to speak English."

"It's a common affliction." I pause. "Just don't let it make you feel too secure. This isn't a safe house."

We walk past a verdigris-covered statue while she considers this. "You have another agenda for coming here," she says finally.

My guts feel cold. "Yes," I admit. I've been dreading this moment.

"Well." Unexpectedly she reaches out and takes my hand. "I assume you're prepared for the shit to hit the fan, right?"

"All feco-ventilatory intersections are covered. They assure me."

"*They*." She shrugs, uncomfortably. "This was their idea?"

I glance round, keeping a vague eye on the other wanderers in the park; a couple of elderly pensioner types, a kid on a skateboard, that's about it. Of course that doesn't mean we aren't being tailed—a raven that's had its central nervous system hijacked by a demonic imperative, a micro-UAV cruising silent a hundred meters overhead with cameras focused—but at least you can do something about human tradecraft, as opposed to the esoteric or electronic kinds.

"They're not keen on letting whoever's tracking you get a chance to say 'third time lucky,' " I try to explain. "This is a setup. We're on friendly territory and if anyone tries to grab you, I'm not the only one on your case."

"That's nice to know." I look at her sharply but she's got her innocent face on, the absent-minded professor musing over a theorem rather than focusing on the world, the flesh, and the devils of Interpol's most-wanted list.

"You never did tell me about the *Thresher*," I comment as we cross the road to the museum.

"Oh, what? The submarine? I didn't think you were interested."

"Huh." I lead her along the side of the building instead of climbing the steps, and I keep an eye open for the side entrance I'm looking for. "Of course I'm interested."

"I was kidding, you know." She flashes me a grin. "Wanted to see if it would make you pull your finger out. You spooks are just so *focused*."

There's a blank door set between two monolithic granite slabs that form one flank of the museum; I rap on it thrice and it opens inward automatically. (There's a camera in the ceiling of this entrance tunnel: unwanted visitors will not be made welcome.) "What *is* this?" Mo asks, "Hey, that's the first secret door I've seen!"

"Nah, it's just the service entrance," I say. The door closes behind us and I lead her forward, round a bend, and up to the security desk. "Howard and O'Brien from the Laundry," I say, placing my hand on the counter.

The booth is empty, but there are two badges waiting on the counter and the door ahead of us opens anyway. "Welcome to the Archive," says a speaker behind the counter. "Please take your ID badges and wear them at all times except when visiting the public galleries."

I take them and pass one to Mo. She inspects it dubiously. "Is this solid silver? What's the language? This isn't Dutch."

"It probably came from Indonesia. Don't ask, just wear it." I pin mine on my belt, under the hem of my T-shirt—it doesn't need to be visible to human guards, after all. "Coming?"

"Yeah."

The cellars under the Rijksmuseum remind me of an upmarket version of the Stacks at Dansey House—huge tunnels, whitewashed and air-conditioned, chock-full of shelves. There's a difference: almost all the contents at Dansey House are files. Here there are boxes, plastic or wooden, full of evidence, left over from the trials that followed a time of infinite horrors.

The Ahnenerbe-SS collection is in a subbasement guarded by locked steel doors; one of the curators—a civilian in jeans and sweater—takes us down there. "Don't you be staying too long," she advises us. "This place, it gives me creeps; you not sleeping well tonight, yah?"

"We'll be all right," I reassure her. The Ahnenerbe collection has about the strongest set of guards and wards imaginable—nobody involved in looking after it wants to worry about lunatics and neo-Nazis getting their hands on some of the powerfully charged relics stored here.

"You say." She looks at me blackly, then one eyebrow twitches. "Sweet dreams."

"Just what are we looking for?" asks Mo.

"Well, to start with—" I clap my hands. We're facing a corridor with numbered storage rooms off to either side. It's well lit and empty, like a laboratory where everyone has just nipped out for afternoon tea. "The symbols painted on the walls of the apartment in Santa Cruz," I say. "Think you'd recognise them if you saw them again?"

"Recognise? I, uh . . . maybe," she says slowly. "I wouldn't like to say for sure. I was half out of my head and I didn't get a real good look at them."

"That's more than I got, and the Black Chamber didn't send us any postcards," I say. "Which is why we've come here. Think of it as a photofit session for necromancy." I read the plaque on the nearest door, then push it open. The lights come on automatically, and I freeze. It's a good thing the lights are bright, because the contents of the room, seen in shadow, would be heart-stopping. As it is, they're merely heart-breaking.

There's a white cast-iron table, a thing of curves and scrollwork, just inside the doorway. Three chairs sit around it, delicate-looking white assemblies of struts and curved sections. I blink, for there's something odd about them, something that reminds me of the art of Giger, the film set of *Alien*. And then I realize what I'm looking at: the backs of the chairs are vertebrae, wired together. The chairs are made of scrimshaw, carved from the thigh bones of the dead; the decorative scrollwork of the table is a rack of human ribs. The tabletop itself is made of polished, interlocking shoulder blades. And as for the cigarette lighter—

"I think I'm going to be sick," whispers Mo. She looks distinctly pale.

"Toilet's down the corridor," I bite out, gritting my teeth while she hurries away, retching. I take in the rest of the room. *They're right*, I think in some quiet, rational recess of my mind, *some things you just can't tell the public about*. The Holocaust, even seen at arm's length through newsreel footage, was bad enough to brand the collective unconscious of the West with a scar of indelible evil, madness on an inconceivable scale. Hideous enough that some people seek to deny it ever happened. But *this*, this isn't something you can even begin to describe: this is the dark nightmare of a diseased mind.

There were medical laboratories attached to the death camp at Birkenau. Some of their tools are stored here. There were other, darker, laboratories behind the medical unit, and their tools are stored here too, those that have not been destroyed in accordance with the requirements of disarmament treaties.

Next to the charnel house garden furniture sits a large rack of electronics, connected to a throne of timber with metal straps at ankle and wrist—an electric chair; the Ahnenerbe experimented with the destruction of human souls, seeking a way to sear through the Cartesian bottleneck and exterminate not only the bodies of their victims, but the informational echoes of their consciousness. Only the difficulty of extinguishing souls on a mass production basis kept it from featuring prominently in their schemes.

Beyond the soul-eater there's a classical mediaeval iron maiden, except that the torturers of the Thirty Years War didn't get to play with aluminium alloy and hydraulic rams. There are other machines, all designed to maim and kill with a maximum of agony: one of them, a bizarre cross between a printing press and a rack made of glass, seems to have materialized from a nightmare of Kafka's—

They were trying to generate pain, I realize. They weren't simply killing their victims but deliberately *hurting* them in the process, hurting them as badly as the human body could stand, squeezing the pain out of them like an evil seepage of blood, hurting them again and again until all the pain had been extracted—

I'm sitting down but I don't remember how I got here. I feel dizzy; Mo is standing over me. "Bob?" I close my eyes and try to control my breathing. "Bob?"

"I need a minute," I hear myself saying.

The room reeks of old, dead terror—and a brooding malevolence, as if the instruments of torture are merely biding their time. *Just you wait,* they're saying. I shudder, open my eyes, and try to stand up.

"This was what the . . . the Ahnenerbe used?" asks Mo. She sounds hoarse.

I nod, not trusting my voice. It's a moment before I can speak. "The secret complex. Behind the medical block at Birkenau, where they experimented with pain. Algemancy. They took Zuse's Z-2 computer, you know? It was supposed to have been bombed by the Allies, in Berlin. That was what Zuse himself was told, he was away at the time. But they took it . . ." I swallow. "It's in the next room."

"A computer? I didn't know they had them."

"Only just; Konrad Zuse built his first programmable computer in 1940. He independently invented the things: after the war he founded Zuse Computer Company, which was taken over by Siemens in the early sixties. He wasn't a bad man; when he didn't cooperate they stole his machine, demolished the house where he had built it, and claimed the destruction was an Allied bomb. The cabbalistic iterations, you see—they rebuilt it at Sobibor camp, using circuits soldered with gold extracted from the teeth of their victims." I stand up and head for the door. "I'll show you, but that's not really why we're . . . hell. I'll show you."

The next room in the Atrocity Archive contains the remains of the Z-2. Old nineteen-inch equipment racks tower ceiling-high; there are mounds of vacuum tubes visible through gaps in the front panels, dials and gauges to monitor power consumption, and plug-boards to load programs into the beast. All very quaint, until you see the printer that lurks in the shadowy recess at the back of the room. "Here they ran the phase-state calculations that dictated the killing schedule, opening and closing circuits in time to the ebb and flow of murder. They even generated the railway timetables with this computer, synchronizing deliveries of victims to the maw of the machine." I walk toward the printer, look round to see Mo waiting behind me. "This printer." It's a plotter, motors dragging an Ouija-board pen across a sheet of—it would have been parchment, but not from a cow or a sheep. I swallow bile. "They used it to inscribe the geometry curves that were to open the way of Dho-Na. All very, very advanced: this was the first real use of computers in magic, you know."

Mo backs away from the machines. Her face is a white mask under the overhead strip lighting. "Why are you showing me this?"

"The patterns are in the next room." I follow her out into the corridor and take her by the elbow, gently steering toward the third chamber—where the real Archive begins. It's a plain-looking room, full of the sort of file drawers you find in architects' offices—very shallow, very wide, designed to hold huge, flat blueprints. I pull the top drawer of the nearest cabinet out and show her. "Look. Seen anything like this before?" It's very fine parchment inscribed with what looks like a collision between a mandala, a pentagram, and a circuit diagram, drawn in bluish ink. At the front and left, a neat box-out in engineering script details the content of the blueprint. If I didn't know what it was meant to be, or what the parchment was made of, I'd think it was quite pretty. I take care not to touch the thing.

"It's—yes." She traces one of the curves with a fingertip, carefully holding it an inch above the inscription. "No, it wasn't this one. But it's similar."

"There are several thousand more like this in here," I say, studying her expression. "I'd like to see if we can identify the one you saw on the wall?" She nods, uneasily. "We don't have to do it right now," I admit. "If you would rather we took a breather there's a café upstairs where we can have a cup of coffee and relax a bit first—"

"No." She pauses for a moment. "Let's get it over and done with." She glances over her shoulder and shudders slightly. "I don't want to stay down here any longer than I have to."

About two hours later, while Mo is halfway through the contents of drawer number fifty-two, my pager goes off. I scrabble at the waistband of my jeans in a momentary panic then pull the thing out. One of the newsgreppers I left running on the network servers back home has paged me: in its constant trawl through the wire feeds it's come across something interesting. *KILLING IN ROTTERDAM*, it says, followed by a reference number.

Got to go upstairs," I say, "think you'll be okay here for twenty minutes?"

Mo looks at me with eyes like bruises. "I'll take you up on that coffee break if you don't mind."

"Not at all. Not having much luck?"

"Nothing so far." She yawns, catches herself, and shakes her head. "My attention span is going. Oh God, coffee. I never realized it was possible to be horrified and bored out of your skin at the same time."

I refrain from calling her on the unintentional pun; instead I make a note of where she's got up to—at this rate we could be here for another week, unless we get lucky—and slide the drawer shut. "Okay. Time out."

The coffee shop is upstairs, attached to the museum shop; it's all whitewash and neat little tables and there's a stand with patisseries on it next to the counter. All very *gezelig*. A row of cheap PCs along one wall offer Internet access for the compulsives who can't kick their habit for a day of high culture. I home in on one and begin the tedious process of logging into one of the Laundry's servers by way of three firewalls, two passwords, an encrypted tunnel, and an S/Key challenge. At the end of the day I'm onto a machine that isn't exactly trusted—the Laundry will not allow classified servers to be connected on the net, by any arrangement of wires or wishful thinking—but that happens to run my news trawler. Which, after all, is fishing in the shallow waters of Reuters and UPI, rather than the oceanic chasm of state secrets.

So what made my pager go off? While Mo is drinking a mug full of mocha and contemplating the museum's catalogue of forthcoming attractions, I find myself reading an interesting article from the AP wire service. DOUBLE KILLING IN ROTTERDAM (AP): Two bodies discovered near a burned-out shipping container in the port appear to be victims of a brutal gangland-style slaying. Blood daubed on the container, victims—ah, a correlation with a restricted information source, something sucked out of the Police National Computer and not available in the usual wire service bulletin. One victim is a known neo-Nazi, the other an Iraqi national, both shot with the same gun. *Is that all?* I wonder, and go clickety-click, sending out a brief email asking where was the shipping container sent from and where was it bound for because you never know . . .

I shake my head. The article dinged my search filter's "phone home" bell by accumulating little keyword matches until it passed a threshold, not because it's obviously important. But something nags at the back of my mind: there's seawater nearby, graffiti in blood on the wall, an Iraqi connection. Why Rotterdam? Well, it's one of the main container-port gateways into Europe, that's for starters. For seconds, it's less than fifty kilometers away.

There's no other real news. I log out and leave the terminal; time to drink a coffee and get back to work.

Three hours later: "Found it," she says.

I look up from the report I'm reading. "Are you sure?"

"Certain." I stand up and walk over. She's leaning over an open drawer and her arms are tense as wires. I think she'd be shaking if she wasn't holding herself still and stiff. I look over her shoulder. The drawing is a geometry curve all right. Actually, I've seen ones like this before. The aborted summoning Dr Vohlman demonstrated in front of the class that day—was it only a few weeks ago?—looked quite similar. But that one was designed to open a constrained information channel to one of the infernal realms. I can't quite see where this one is directed, at least not without taking it home and studying it with the aid of a protractor and a calculator, but a quick glance tells me it's more than a simple speakerphone to hell.

*Here* we see a differential that declares a function of tau, the rate of change of time with distance along one of the Planck dimensions. *There* we see an admonition that this circuit is not to be completed without a cage around it. (A good thing the notation we use, and that of the Ahnenerbe, is derived from the same source, or I wouldn't be able to figure it out.) *This* formula looks surprisingly modern, it's some sort of curve through the complex number plane—each point along it is a different Julia set. And *that* is where the human sacrifice is wired into the diagram by its eyeballs while still alive, for maximum bandwidth—

I blank for a second, flashing on the evil elegance of the design. "Are you *sure* this is it?" I mumble.

"Of course I'm sure!" Mo snaps at me. "Do you think I'd—" she stops. Takes a deep breath. Mutters something quietly to herself, then: "What *is* it?"

"I'm not 100 percent certain," I say, carefully placing the notepad I was reading from down on my chair and moving to one side so I can inspect the diagram from a different angle, "but it looks like a resonator map. A circuit designed to tune in on another universe. This one is similar to our own, in fact it's astonishingly close by; the energy barrier you have to tunnel through to reach it is high enough that nothing less than a human sacrifice will do."

"Human sacrifice?"

"It doesn't take much energy to talk to a demon," I explain. "They're pretty much waiting to hear from us, at least the ones people mostly want to talk to. But they come from a long way away—from universes with a very weak affinity to our own. Information leakage doesn't imply an energy change in our own world; it's concealed in the random noise. But if we try to talk to a universe close to home there's a huge potential energy barrier to overcome—this sort of prevents causality violations. The whole thing is mediated by intelligence—observers are required to collapse the wave function—which is where the sacrifice comes in: we're eliminating an observer. Done correctly, this lets us talk to a universe that isn't so much next door as lying adjacent to our own, separated by a gap less than the Planck length."

"Oh." She points at the map. "So this thing . . . it's a very precise transformation through the Mandelbrot set. Which you guys have used as a map onto a Linde continuum, right? Why don't they just set up an n-dimensional homogeneous matrix transformation? It's so much more intuitively obvious."

"Uh—" She manages to surprise me at the damnedest times. "I don't know. Have to read up on it, I guess."

"Well." She pauses for an instant and looks very slightly disappointed, as if her star pupil has just failed a verbal test. "This is very like what I saw. Got any suggestions for what to do next, wise guy?"

"Yes. There's a photocopier upstairs. Let's call the curator and run off a copy or two. Then we can get someone back home to compare it to the photographs of the shipping container at that murder site in Rotterdam. If they're similar we have a connection."

Our hotel has a bijou bar and a breakfast room, but no restaurant; so it seems natural that after running off our copies we should go home, head for our respective rooms, freshen up, and head out on the town to find somewhere to eat. (And maybe share a drink or two. Those hours in the basement of horrors are going to give me bad dreams tonight, and I'd be surprised if Mo is any better.) I spend half an hour soaking in the bathtub with a copy of *Surreal Calculus and the Navigation of Everett-Wheeler Continua*—hoping to brush up on my dinner-table patter— then dry myself, pull on a clean pair of chinos and an open-necked shirt, and head upstairs.

Mo is waiting at the bar with a cup of coffee and a copy of the *Herald Tribune*. She's wearing the same evening-out-on-the-town outfit as last time. She folds the newspaper and nods at me. "Want to try that Indonesian place we passed?" I ask her.

"Why not." She finishes the coffee quickly. "Is it raining outside?"

"Wasn't last time I looked."

She stands up gracefully and pulls her coat on. "Let's go."

The nights are drawing in, and the evening air is cool and damp. I'm still self-conscious about navigating around the roads—not only do they run on the wrong side, but they've got separate bike lanes everywhere, and, to make matters worse, separate tram lanes that sometimes don't go in the same direction as the rest of the traffic. It makes crossing the road an exercise in head-twitching, and I nearly get mown down by a girl on a bicycle riding without lights in the dusk—but we make it to the tram stop more or less intact, and Mo doesn't laugh at me out loud. "Do you always jerk around like that?"

"Only when I'm trying to avoid the feral man-eating mopeds. Is this tram—ah." Two stops later we get off and head for that Indonesian place we passed earlier. They have a vacant table, and we have a meal.

I turn on my new palmtop's antisound and Mo talks to me over her satay: "Was that what you were hoping to find at the museum?"

I dribble peanut sauce over a skewer before replying. "It was what I was hoping *not* to find, really." She has her back to the plate-glass window and I have a decent view of the main road behind her shoulder. Which is important, and I keep glancing that way because I am on edge—our friendly nieghborhood abductors seem to go to work at dusk, and when all's said and done this is a stakeout and Mo is the goat. I look back at her. She's very decorative, for a goat: most goats don't wear ethnic tops, large silver earrings, and friendly expressions. "On the other hand, at least we know we're dealing with something profoundly unpleasant. Which means that *Carnate Gecko* gets something solid to chew on and we've got a lead to follow up."

"Assuming it doesn't follow *us* up instead." Her expression clouds over in an instant: "Tell me the truth, Bob?"

My mouth turns dry: this is a moment I've been dreading even more than the discovery in the basement. "What?"

"Why are they after me?"

Oh, *that* truth. I manage to breathe again. "Your . . . research. And the stuff you were really working on in the States."

"You know about that." She looks tense and I suddenly wonder, *How many secrets are we keeping from each other?*

"Angleton told me about it. Black Chamber notified us when they deported you. Don't look so startled. About the restricted theoretical work on probability manipulation—lucky vectors, fate quantisation? It's all classified, but it's not—no, what I mean to say is, they don't like us running around on their turf, but information sharing goes on at different levels."

I point my skewer at her and dissemble creatively. "That stuff is fairly serious juju in our field. The Pentagon plays with it. We've got it. A couple of other countries have occult operations groups who make use of destiny entanglement fields. But the likes of Yusuf Qaradawi can't get his hands on it without a hell of a lot of reverse engineering, any more than the provisional IRA ever got their hands on cruise missile technology. The difference is, to build a cruise missile takes a ton of aerospace engineers, an advanced electronics industry, and factories. Whereas to build a scalar field that can locally boost probability coefficients attached to a Wigner's Friend observer—say, to allow a suicide bomber to walk right through a ring of bodyguards as if they aren't there—takes a couple of theoreticians and one or two field ops. Occult weapons are so much more *portable* that you can think in terms of stealing the infrastructure— if you've got people who can understand it. As most nongovernmental activist groups rely on cannon fodder so dumb they have 'mom' and 'dad' tattooed on their knuckles so the cops know who they belong to, that isn't usually much of a threat."

"But." She raises her last satay and swallows the skewered morsel. "This time there is." I see motion outside the window: see a familiar face, little more than a pale blur in the darkness, glance inside as it walks past.

"Evidently," I mumble, feeling guilty.

"So your bosses decided to trail me in public and see what they picked up while trying to identify the group by way of the museum basement," she adds briskly. "How many people are watching us, Bob?"

"At least one right now," I say, heart bouncing around my rib cage. "That I know of, I mean. This is supposed to be a full top-and-tail job, guards outside the hotel and round the clock watch on your movements. Same as most politicians at risk of assassination get. Not that we're expecting any suicide bombers," I add hastily.

She smiles at me warmly: "I'm *so* pleased to know that. It really makes me feel secure."

I wince. "Can you suggest any alternatives?" I ask.

"Not from your boss's—what's his name? Angleton? His point of view. No, I don't suppose there is." A waiter appears silently and removes our plates. She looks at me with an expression that I can't read. "Why are *you* here, Bob?"

"Uh . . ." I pause to get my thoughts in order. "Because it's my mess. I got roped in because I didn't follow procedures and hang you out to dry in California, and then I was there when things turned nasty, and this

whole mess is classified up to stupid levels because there's a turf war going on between project management and operational executive—"

"That's not what I meant." She's silent for a moment. Then: "Why
did you break the rules in Santa Cruz? Not that I object, but . . ."

"Because—" I inspect my wineglass, "I like you. I don't think leaving
people I like in the shit is a good way to behave. And, frankly, I don't
have a very professional attitude to my work. Not the way the spooks
think I should."

She leans forward. "Do you have a more professional attitude to your
work now?"

I swallow. "No, not really."

Something—a foot—rubs up and down my ankle and I nearly jump
out of my skin. "Good." She smiles in a way that turns my stomach to
jelly, and the waiter arrives with a precariously balanced pile of dishes
before I can say anything and risk embarrassing myself. We just stare at
each other until he's gone, and she adds: "I hate it when people let their
professionalism get in the way of real life."

We eat, and we talk about people and things, not necessarily in compli-
mentary terms. Mo explains what it's like to be married to a New York
lawyer and I commiserate, and she asks me what it's like to live with a
manic-depressive psycho bitch from hell, and evidently she's been talking to Pinky and Brains about things because I find myself describing my
relationship with Mhari with sufficient detachment that it might as well
be over—ancient history. And she nods and asks if running into Mhari
in Accounts and Payroll isn't embarrassing and this leads to a long discourse on how working for the Laundry is about as embarrassing as
things can get: from the paper clip audits to the crazy internal billing system, and about how I hoped that getting into field ops would get me out
from under Bridget's thumb, but no such luck. And Mo explains about
tenure track backbiting politics in small American university departments, and about why you can kiss your career goodbye if you publish
too much—as well as too little—and about the different ways in which a
dual-income no-kiddies couple can self-destruct so messily that I'm left
thinking maybe Mhari isn't that unusual after all.

We end up walking back to the hotel arm in arm, and under a broken streetlamp she stops, wraps her arms around me, and kisses me for
what feels like half an hour. Then she rests her chin on my shoulder, beside my ear. "This is so good," she whispers. "If only we weren't being followed."

I tense. "We're—"

"I don't like being watched," she says, and we let go of each other simultaneously.

"Me neither." I glance round and see a lone guy on the street behind us looking in the window of a closed shop, and all the romance flees the evening like gas from a punctured balloon. "Shit."

"Let's just . . . go back. Hole up and wait for morning."

"I guess."

We start moving again and she takes my hand. "Great evening out. Try it again some time?"

I smile back at her, feeling both regret and optimism. "Yeah."

"*Without* the audience."

We reach the hotel, share a last drink, and head for our separate rooms.

I dream of wires. Dark landscape, cold mud. Something screams in the distance; lumpy shapes strung up on barbed wire stretched before the fortress. The screams get louder and there's a rumbling and crashing and somewhere in the process I become aware that I'm not dreaming— someone is screaming, while I lie in bed halfway between sleeping and waking.

I'm on my feet almost before I realize I'm awake. I grab a T-shirt and jeans, somehow slide my feet into both legs simultaneously and I'm out the door within ten seconds. The corridor is silent and dim, the only lighting coming from the overhead emergency strips; it's narrow, too, and by night the pastel-painted walls form a claustrophobic collage of grey-on-black shadows. Silence—then another scream, muffled, coming from upstairs. It's definitely human and it doesn't sound like anything you'd expect to hear from a hotel room at night. I pause for a moment, feeling silly as I consider that particular possibility—then duck back into my room and grab the multitool and the palmtop I've left atop the dresser. *Now* I head for the staircase.

Another scream and I take the steps two at a time. A door opens behind me, a tousled head poking out and mumbling, "I'm trying to sleep . . ."

The hair on my arms stands on end. The stair rail is glowing a faint, eerie blue; sparks sting my bare feet as I climb, and the handle of the fire door at the top of the stairs gives me a nasty shock. Air sighs past me, a thin breeze blowing along the corridor where blue flickering outlines the door frames in darkness. Another scream and this time a thudding noise, then a muffled crash; I hear a door slam somewhere below me, then the shattering whine of a fire alarm going off.

Mo is in the Plato suite. That's where the screams are coming from, where the wind blows—I hit the door with my shoulder as hard as I can, and bounce.

"What is going on?"

I glance round. A middle-aged woman, thin-faced and worried. "Fire alarm!" I yell. "I heard screaming in here. Can you get help?"

She steps forward, waving a big bunch of keys: she must be the concierge. "Allow me." She turns the door handle and the key, and the door slams open inward as a gust of wind grabs us both and tries to yank us into the room. I grab her arm and brace my feet against the door-frame. Now there's a scream right in my ear, but she grabs my wrist with another hand and I wrestle her back into the corridor. A howling gale is blowing through the doorway, as if someone's punched a hole in the universe. I risk a glance round it and see—

A hotel bedroom in chaos and disarray—wardrobe tumbled on the floor, bedclothes strewn everywhere—all the hallmarks of a fight, or a burglary, or something. But where in my room there's another door and then a cramped bathroom, here there's a *hole*. A hole with lights on the other side of it that cast sharp shadows across the damaged furniture. Stars, harsh and bright against the darkness of a flat, alien landscape shrouded in twilight.

I pull my head back and gasp into the woman's ear: "Get everybody out of here! Tell them it's a fire! I'll get help!" She's half doubled-over from the wind but she nods and stumbles toward the staircase. I turn to follow, shocked, half-dazed. *Where the hell have the watchers gone? We're supposed to be under surveillance, dammit!* I look back toward the bedroom for a final glance through that opening that shouldn't be there. The wind batters at my back, a gale howling past my ears. The opening is the size of a large pair of doors, ragged bits of lath and wallpaper showing where the small gate ripped through the wall. Beyond it, rolling ground, deep cold; a valley with a still lake beneath the icy, unwinking stars that form no constellations I can recognize. Something dim frosts the sky; at first I think it's a cloud, but then I recognise the swirl—the arms of a giant spiral galaxy raised above a dim landscape not of this world.

I'm freezing, the wind is trying to rip me through the doorway and carry me into the alien landscape—and there's no sign of Mo, nor of her abductor. She's in there somewhere, that's for sure. Whoever, whatever opened it was waiting for her to go to bed when we came back to the hotel. They left fragments of their geometry inscribed in bloody runes on the walls and floor. They'll have planned this, taken her for their own purposes—

A hand grabs my arm. I jerk round: it's Alan, looking just as much like a schoolteacher as ever, wearing an expression that says the head-master is angry. His other hand is wrapped around the grips of a very large pistol. He bends close and yells, "Let's get the fuck out of here!"

No argument. He pulls me toward the fire door and we make our way down the stairs, shocked and frostbitten. The wind quietens behind us as we rush down to the ground floor, all the way to the bar where Angleton is waiting to be briefed.

7
## Bad Moon Rising

The emergency gathers pace over the next three hours.

When I glance out the front door I see a fire-control truck—a big lorry with a control room mounted on its load bed—squatting in the middle of the street outside the hotel, blue lights strobing against the darkness; a couple of pumps are drawn up on either side, and a gaggle of police vans are parked round the corner. Cops are busy buzzing around, evacuating everyone on the block from hotel and dwelling alike. The cover story is that there's a gas leak. The pump engines are real enough, but the control vehicle has nothing to do with the fire brigade: Angleton had it shipped into Holland before Mo and I arrived, just in case. It belongs to OCCULUS—Occult Control Coordination Unit Liaison, Unconventional Situations—the NATO occult equivalent of a NEST, or Nuclear Emergency Search Team. But while NEST operatives are really only trained to look for terrorist nukes, OCCULUS has to be ready for Armageddon in a variety of guises. I only just found out about OC-CULUS and I really don't know whether or not I want to punch Angleton or just be grateful for his foresight.

There's rack after rack of specialized communication equipment in the back of the truck, and a scarier bunch of paramilitaries than I've ever seen outside of a movie. They're poking around the hotel right now—sending in robots with cameras, installing sensors on the way up the staircase—laying the groundwork for whatever comes next.

Alan leads me into the bar, where Angleton is waiting. Angleton has dark hollows under his eyes; his tie is loose and his collar unbuttoned. He's scribbling notes on a yellow pad in between snapping instructions on a mobile phone that's just about glued to his ear. "Sit down," he gestures as he listens to someone at the other end.

"We ought to pull back to the amber zone," Alan says, "there's structural damage."

"Later." Angleton waves him off and goes back to talking on the phone. "No, there's no need to go to Rung Four yet, but I want the backup wagon on twenty-four by seven alert, and we'll need Plumbers crawling over everything. And Baggers, but especially Plumbers. Tell Bridget to fuck off." He glances at me. "Grab a drink from the bar and get ready to tell me everything." Back to the phone: "I'll expect hourly updates." He puts the phone down and turns to me. "Now. Tell me exactly what happened."

"I don't *know* what happened," I say. "I went to bed. Next thing, I hear screams and wake up—" I clench my fists to stop my hands shaking.

"Fast forward. What did you find in her room?" Angleton leans forward intently.

"How did you know . . . hell. I got up there, heard whistling like wind. So I tried to break the door down. Then the concierge showed up, unlocked the door and nearly got sucked in; I grabbed her and sent her back down. There's a gate in there, class four at least—it's about two-plus meters in diameter, runs straight through the wall, and it's stable. Furniture was thrown around as if there was a fight, but there's a big wind blowing. On the other side of the gate there's no atmosphere to speak of."

"No atmosphere." Angleton nods and makes a note as two firemen—I think they're firemen—enter the bar and begin setting up something that looks like a rack of industrial scaffolding in the middle of the room. "The source of the wind?"

"I think so. It was bloody cold, which suggests expansion into vacuum." I shiver and glance up; above our heads the whistle of wind through rubble continues unabated. "She wasn't there," I add. "I think they took her."

Angleton's lips quirk. "That is not an unreasonable deduction." His expression hardens. "Describe the other side of the gate."

"Twilight, a shallow valley. I couldn't see the ground very clearly; it sloped down to a distant lake, or something that looked like one. The stars were very clear, not twinkling at all, and I could see they weren't familiar. There was a huge galaxy covering, uh, about a third of the sky."

Alan sticks a glass between my fingers: I take an experimental swallow. Orange juice spiked with something stronger. I continue: "No air on the other side. Alien starscape. But there *are* stars, and at least one planet; that means it's pretty damn close to us, it's not one of those universes where the ratio of the strong nuclear force to the electromagnetic force prevents fusion." I shiver. "Whoever they are, they've got her and they've got an open mass-transfer gate. What do we do now?"

Alan silently leaves the room. Angleton looks at me oddly. "That's a very good question. Do you have any ideas to contribute?" he asks.

I swallow. "I have one idea. It's the Ahnenerbe, isn't it? That's the connection. The Middle Eastern guy, the one with the luminous eyes that she described—it's a possession. Something left over from the war,

an Ahnenerbe revenant of some kind, possessing the leader of a
Mukhabarat strike cell in California. And now they've snatched Mo."

He closes his eyes. "Your email this afternoon. You are *sure* she positively identified the scan you sent me from California? You'd bet your
life on it?"

"Pretty sure." I nod. "Was it—"

"We found the same pattern in Rotterdam." He sighs and opens his
eyes again. "The very same; my complements on your search criteria.
Was there something similar in her room?"

"I honestly can't say; it was dark, I was trying not to be dragged in by
the wind, and the gate had instantiated in the middle of it. I don't think
so, but if you can get a photograph from up there I can confirm—"

"In progress."

Alan comes back in; he's wearing a bright orange overall and carrying a bulky box, some kind of sensor gear. "You'll have to move now," he
tells Angleton. "The top floor's in danger of collapsing. Hole up in the
van and stay out of the way; we need to sweep the block for werewolves."

"Were—"

I must look surprised because Alan barks a brief laugh at me.
"Leftovers from the authors of this incursion, old boy, not hairy-palmed
wolf-men with a silver allergy. Come on, shift yourself."

"Shit—" I find myself on my feet, Angleton holding my elbow in a
viselike grip.

"Come now, Mr Howard. This is no time to lose your self-control."
He steers me out into the street (barefoot, the tarmac under my toes
makes me wince) and then up the steps into the OCCULUS command
vehicle. A guard waves us in, insect-eyed in respirator. "A spare overall
for Mr Howard here," Angleton calls, and a minute later I'm loaded
down with enough survival gear to equip a small polar expedition, from
the y-fronts out.

"You're going to send people in to try and close the gate," I predict in
the general direction of the back of Angleton's head as he dials a phone
number. "I want to go with them."

"Don't be silly, boy. What do you think you can achieve?"

"I can try to rescue her," I say.

There's a burst of static from farther up the compartment and one of
the men in black (black turtleneck, black fatigues, black face-paint, and
MP-10 slung over his chair) turns and calls out: "Message for the captain!" Alan mutters a curse and squeezes past me. I begin pulling on a
sock. There are one-way windows along one side of the cabin and outside in the road I see some kind of large truck squeezing past us.

"I'm serious," I tell Angleton. "I know what's going on here, or most of it. Or I can guess. Werewolves, he said. Holdovers from the Reich, huh? And the Mukhabarat connection. That gate doesn't go into the dark anthropic zone; it stops short, somewhere where humans can exist. Really *evil* humans, whoever survived from the Ahnenerbe-SS after the war was lost." I begin to wriggle into the bottom half of my survival suit shell. "I've been studying Sheet 45075 from Birkenau, you know. If it's the same one they used over there, I can shut it down safely—without a massive discharge when it arcs to ground."

He's on the phone again. "Very good, any survivors? Two, you say, and three sacrifices? That's excellent. Have you identified—"

I tap him on the shoulder. "Mo told me what she was researching on the Black Chamber contract," I say. "You really don't want them to get their hands on it."

Angleton's head whips round— "One minute, boy." Back to the phone: "Get them to sing. I don't care how you do it; by dawn I want to know who they thought they were summoning." He puts the phone down and glares at me. "Tell me."

"Probability manipulation," I say.

"Close, but not close enough," Angleton says coldly. He stands up, leaving the armless chair swinging—in the confined space of the truck this is not a good idea. "You got some of it right and the rest wrong. And what makes you think I can afford to risk you? This is an OCCULUS job now: straight in, find out what's there, plant demolition charges, straight out."

"Demolition charges." I look past his shoulder. The door opens and a familiar face is coming in. Odd, I'd never imagined what Derek the Accountant would look like in battle dress. (Worried, mostly.)

"The commander's due in half an hour," Derek says by way of introduction. "What's the goat doing here?"

"Enough." Angleton waves me to follow as he heads for the door. I slide my feet into moon boots, follow him without bothering to fasten the straps. I hurry down the steps into a flashing hell of red and blue lights, Dutch police escorting sleepy hotel guests and residents to safety, firemen gearing up with breathing apparatus in the road. Angleton pulls me aside. "Interrupt if you see Captain Barnes—"

"Who?"

"Alan Barnes," he says impatiently. "Listen." He fixes me with a beady stare: "This is not a game. There's a very good chance that Dr O'Brien is already dead—in case you hadn't noticed, there's no air on the other side of that gate, and unless her abductors wanted her alive they won't have bothered with niceties like a respirator for her. That lack of air is one of the reasons we must close it as fast as possible, the other being to stop the people who opened it from making use of it as a stable egress portal."

"You say *people*," I mutter. "Who? The Ahnenerbe-SS?"

"I hope so," he replies grimly. "Anything else would be infinitely worse. At the end of the war, Himmler ordered a number of so-called werewolf units to continue the struggle. We've never been able to track down the Ahnenerbe's final redoubt, but the suspicion that it lies on the other side of a gate goes back a long way—you've read *OGRE REALITY*, you can imagine why the Mukhabarat might want to get in touch with them."

"So the other side of that gate is—" my mind races "—a hold-out from the Third Reich, a colony intended to keep the dark flame burning and exact revenge on the enemies of Nazism in due course . . . One that's had fifty years to fester and grow on an alien world . . . But they lost the coordinates for the return journey, didn't they? Something went wrong and they were trapped there until—" I stop and stare at Angleton. "You *hope* that's what's on the other side of the gate?"

He nods. "The alternatives are all much worse."

On further thought I have to admit he's right: a colony of leftover Nazi necromancers and their SS bodyguards are trivially dangerous compared to things like the one that took over Fred the Accountant. And *they* are small beer by the standards of the sea of universes, where malignant intelligences wait only for an invitation to surge through a knothole in the platonic realm and infect our minds.

"How are you going to deal with them?" I ask. Angleton leads me around the truck; I can get a good view of the big low-loader that squeezed past us, and there's some sort of tracked vehicle sitting on its load bed. There's a crane, too. I peer closer, but the cordon of cops around it bars my view. "How the hell are you going to get that through a third-floor window?" I ask.

Angleton shrugs. "I'm sure the hotel owners will file a claim on their building insurance." He looks at me. "Alan's men are professionals, Robert. They're not used to being slowed down by civilians like you—or me. What can you do that they can't?"

I lick my lips. "Can they open a temporary gate back home if the door there slams shut behind them? Can they safely disarm a live geometry node?"

"They're the Artists' Rifles," Angleton says witheringly. "They're the bloody SAS, boy, 21st Battalion Territorial Army; what did you think they were, a gun club? Who else do you think we'd trust with a hydrogen bomb wired up to a dead man's handle?"

I stare at the low-loader and realize that the cops around it are all carrying HK–4s and facing outward. "I can provide you with a different kind of insurance policy. Give me the charts and I'll see they make it back alive—with Mo, if I have any say in the matter. Plus, aren't you just a little *curious* about what the Ahnenerbe might have been doing with a Z–2 and its descendants for the past fifty years?"

"Do you want me to strangle him now, or wait till he's finished annoying you?" asks Alan, who has sneaked up behind me so quietly I never even noticed. Needless to say I almost jump out of my skin.

"Leave him be." Angleton almost looks amused. "He's still young enough to think he's immortal—and he's cleared for active. All waivers signed, next of kin on file, carries an organ donor card, that sort of thing. Can you use him?"

I have to turn my head to keep both of them in view: Angleton, the old, dried-up ghost of intelligence spooks past, and Alan—Captain Barnes, that is—schoolmasterly and intense. "That depends," Alan tells Angleton. Then he focuses on me. "Bob, you can come along on this trip on one condition. The condition is that if you get any of my men killed by arsing around, I will personally shoot you. Do you understand and agree?"

Somehow I manage to nod, although my mouth's gone very dry all of a sudden. "Yup, got it. No arsing around."

"Well, that's all right then!" He claps his hands together briskly, then softens very slightly. "As long as you do what you're told, you'll pass. I'm going to give you to Blevins and Pike; they'll look after you. I know what your specialities are: weird alien runes, ancient Nazi computers, esoteric rocket science, that sort of thing. Boffin city. If we run into anything like that I'll let you know. What's your weapons clearance, if any?"

"I'm certified to level two, unconventional." I frown. "What else do you need?"

"Ever used scuba gear?"

"Er, yes." I neglect to add that it was on a holiday package deal, an afternoon of training followed by supervised swimming near a coral reef, with instructors and guides on hand.

"Okay, then I'll leave Pike to check you out on the vacuum gear. You'll be issued with a weapon; you are not, repeat *not*, to use it under any circumstances while any soldiers are left alive unless you are explicitly ordered to. Got that?"

"Find Pike. Learn how to use vacuum gear. Do not use weapon without orders."

"That'll do." Alan glances at Angleton. "He'll make a good Norwegian Blue, don't you think?"

Angleton raises an eyebrow. "Bet you he'll be 'pining for the fjords' within hours."

"Hah! Hah!" Alan doesn't bray: his laughter is oddly fractured, as if it's escaping from a broken muffler. Loss of control, that's what it is. He's thin, wiry, intense, and looks like the kind of schoolmaster who's spent years slitting throats in strange countries, and took to teaching as a way of passing on his knowledge. A weird breed, not uncommon in the British public schools, who recycle their own graduate cannon fodder to train the next generation in an ethos of military service. And whose mannerisms are aped lower down the academic ladder. Artists' Rifles indeed!

I try telling myself that Mo will be all right, that they wouldn't have bothered abducting her if they didn't want her alive, but it's no good: whenever I get some idle time my brain keeps looping on the fact that someone I feel strongly about has been snatched and may already be dead. Luckily I don't have much time to obsess because Alan immediately drags me back inside the OCCULUS control truck and throws me to Sergeant Martin Pike, who takes one look at me, mutters something about the blessings of Loki, and starts grilling me about nitrogen narcosis, the bends, partial pressure of oxygen, and all sorts of other annoying things I haven't studied since school. Pike is a sergeant. He's also a Ph.D. in mechanical engineering and designs things that go fast and explode, when he isn't being a weekend soldier in a special unit hung off the SAS. He's met people like me before and knows how to deal with them.

A second—and then a third—fire-control truck has drawn up outside the evacuated hotel and we're in the back of vehicle number two, which seems to be a mobile armory. I'm stripping off the survival gear and struggling into something like a bastard cross between a body stocking and a piece of bondage rubberwear from hell—low pressure survival gear, Pike tells me—a lycra and silk contraption that seems to consist mostly of straps and is designed to do the same job as a space suit in terms of holding me together and helping me breathe.

"Vacuum isn't as hostile as you probably imagine if you've read too much bad science fiction," he says while I'm grunting and wheezing over the upper half of the suit. "But you'd have real fun breathing without a decent gas seal around your regulator, and without this suit and pressurized goggles you'll end up half-blind and covered in blood blisters within ten or twenty minutes. The real problems are heat dissipation—there's no air around you to keep you cool by convection and insulated from the ground, which is going to be *fucking* cold—and maintaining your breathing. Cooling we can deal with—this cloth is porous, you start sweating and the sweat will evaporate and keep you cool, and there's a drinking bottle in your helmet. Don't let it run dry, because running one of these suits is a bit like running a noddy suit in the Iraqi desert—you will sweat like hell, you will drink a pint of water and electrolytes every hour, and if you forget to do that you will keel over from heat stroke. Turn round, now." I turn round and he starts tightening straps all the way up my back as if I'm wearing a corset. "These are to keep your rib cage under a bit of elastic tension, help you breathe out."

"What if I need to take a piss?" I ask.

He chuckles. "Go ahead. There's enough adsorbent padding that you probably won't freeze your wedding tackle off."

Trussed up in the pressure suit, I feel like a fifties comic-book hero who's blundered through a fetish movie's wardrobe. Pike passes me a bunch of elbow and knee protectors, a tough overall, and a pair of massively padded moon boots. Somehow I struggle into them. Then he comes up with a lightweight backpack frame with air tanks and—"A rebreather? Isn't that dangerous?" I ask.

"Yup. We aren't NASA and we can't waste five hours depressurising you down to run on pure oxygen. 'Sides, you're not wearing a hard-shell suit. You're going to breathe a seventy/thirty nitrogen-oxygen mix; we scrub the carbon dioxide out with these lithium hydroxide canisters and recycle the nitrogen, adding oxygen to order."

"Uh-huh. How do I change tanks?"

"On your own? You don't—there's a trick to it and we don't have time to teach you. You cut over from tank one to tank two with the regulator valve here, then you ask me to change tanks for you. If someone wants you to change their tank, which they won't unless things go pear-shaped in a big way, you do it like this—" He demonstrates on an unmounted backpack and I try to keep track of it. Then he shows me the helmet and the chest-mounted monitors that keep track of my gas supply, temperature, and so on. Finally he seems satisfied. "Well, if you remember all that you're not going to die by accident—at least not immediately. Still happy?"

"Um." I think about it. "It'll have to do. What about radio?"

"Don't worry about it—it's automatic." He flicks a switch or two on my chest panel, evidently making sure of that. "You're on the general channel—everyone will be able to hear you unless they explicitly shut you out. Now . . ." He picks up a gadget that looks like a pair of underwater digital video cameras strapped with gaffer tape to either side of a black box gizmo of some kind. "Have you ever seen one of these before?"

I peer closely, then unclip the lid on the box and look inside. "I didn't know they'd successfully weaponized that."

He looks surprised. "Can you tell me what it is and how it works?"

"Can I—yeah, I've seen this arrangement before but only in the lab. This chip *here* is a small custom-built ASIC processor that emulates a neural network that was first identified in the *cingulate gyrus* of a medusa. Turns out you can find the same pathways in a basilisk, but . . . well. There's a load of image processing stuff on the front end, behind those video cameras. Now, I would guess that the two cameras are the optical component of this gadget: we're performing some sort of wave superposition on the target, so . . ."

"Fine, fine." He passes me a somewhat shop-soiled video camera manual. "Give this a read. And this." He hands me a bundle of typed pages with bright red *SECRET* headers, then passes me the lash-up. I look it over dubiously: there's an arrow on top of the neural network box with the caption THIS SIDE TOWARD ENEMY, and a flat-panel camcorder viewfinder on the back so you can pretend it's just a computer game you're playing with while you kill people.

What this gadget does violates the second law of thermodynamics: nobody's quite sure why it's so specific, but the medusa effect seems to be some kind of observationally mediated quantum tunnelling process. It turns out that something like 0.01 percent of all the atomic nuclei of carbon in the target zone acquire eight extra protons and a balancing number of neutrons, turning 'em into highly electronegative silicon ions. A roughly balancing proportion of carbon nuclei just seem to vanish, wrecking whatever bonds they were part of.

"How much damage can this thing do to a person?" I ask.

"How much damage will a stubby shotgun do?" Pike responds. "Enough. Silicon-hydrogen bonds aren't stable. Don't point it at anyone and don't switch it on and most of all don't hit the OBSERVE button unless I tell you to. Which I won't, unless you are very, very unlucky. Or unless you decide to blow your feet off by accident, which is your own lookout."

"Understood." I switch off the viewfinder and power down both cameras then gingerly put the gadget down. "You aren't expecting trouble by any chance?"

Pike stares at me. "No, it's my job to see that you don't get into trouble," he says. I take a second to recognise the expression: he's wondering if I'm going to be a liability.

"Tell me what to do and I'll do it," I say. "You're the expert on this."

"Am I?" He looks skeptical. "You're the occult specialist, you tell me what we're up against." He bends down, picks up a rebreather regulator, begins stripping off the insulation panels in an absentminded sort of way. "I mean it. What are you expecting to find on the other side of this gate?"

Something clicks in my mind: "You've gone through gates before, right?"

He glances at me. "Maybe. Maybe not." I realize that he isn't looking at the rebreather as he strips it: he's got it down to a set of motions he can run through in total darkness. Then it hits me: I'm going to be hopelessly dependent on these guys for just about everything more challenging than breathing. Liability, me? Maybe I don't know what I'm getting myself into after all. But it's a bit late to back out now.

"Well." I lick my suddenly dry lips. "This one, we *hope* the only things waiting for us are a bunch of superannuated Nazis who've kidnapped one of our scientists. Trouble is, this bunch sent someone through to California, and London, and maybe to Rotterdam, who isn't too superannuated to be banging heads. So I'll take a rain check on the predictions, if you don't mind—expect the worst and hope you're disappointed."

"Indeed." His tone is dry as he adds, "I love these bastard colostomy-fucking reconnaissance jobs, I really do."

They force me to catch a couple or three hours sleep by sticking a needle full of phenobarbitone into my left arm and making me count backward from ten. I never make it past five; then there's a pain in my other arm and Pike is shaking my shoulder. "Wake up," he says. "Briefing in five minutes, action in half an hour."

"Euurgh," I say, or something equally coherent. He passes me a mug full of something that might be mislabelled as coffee and I sit up and try to drink it while he disposes of the used antidote syrette. I have a vague memory of dreams: eyes with luminous worms swimming in them, eyes like a friendly death staring at me across an electrodynamic summoning trap. I shudder as a little rat-faced guy sits down opposite me and opens up a zippered and incongruously expensive-looking golf bag.

Pike takes it upon himself to introduce us. "Bob, this is Lance-Corporal Blevins. Roland, this is Bob Howard, a Laundry necromancer."

Rat-face looks at me and grins, baring unfeasibly large and yellow incisors. "Pleased ter meet yer," he says, pulling an iron out of his golf bag—one with telescopic sights and thick foam insulation over most of the visible surfaces. Vacuum-adapted, I realize: these guys *have* been exploring gates before. "Allus nice ter 'ave a bit of animal with us."

"Animal?"

"Magic," Pike explains. "Listen, you stay close to me or Roland unless I tell you otherwise. He's the squadron backup: what this means is, he'll either be in the rear or deployed to cover a quick in-and-out. He'll park you somewhere safe and keep an eyeball on you if I'm too busy to nursemaid."

"Diamond geezer, mate," Blevins says, winking horribly, then he pulls out a bunch of jeweller's screwdrivers and goes to work on his gun, fiddling with the sights.

What I think is, *You guys really know how to make someone feel wanted*, but I end up saying nothing because, once I get my ego out of the way, Pike is right. I am not a soldier, I know nothing about what to do and what not to do, and I'm not even in good physical condition. Fundamentally, I guess I am a liability to these guys, except for my specialist expertise. It's not a very pleasant thought, but they're not going out of their way to rub it in, so the least I can do is be polite. And hope Mo is all right.

"Wot you fink I should load up on?" Roland asks. "I got silver bullets in seven point sixty-two, but they tend to tumble in low pressure regimes like wot's on the other side of this gate—"

"Briefing first," Pike says. "Let's go."

The hotel bar is barely recognizable. Scaffolding and jacks in every corner support a protective raft just under the ceiling; there's a nest of wiring and monitors on the bar top, and some sort of stair-climbing robot camera waiting just inside the doorway. Alan—Captain Barnes—is waiting next to a woman who's sort of slumped all over the robot's control panel, muttering to it and twiddling a circuit tester in a meaningful way. A dozen other men in pressure suits and camouflage overalls are leaning against the walls or sitting down: half of them have backpacks and full face-covering helmets to hand, but there's a surprising shortage of guns and I'm the only one in the room without a notepad—until I pull out my palmtop, which I've been carrying in a pocket more or less continuously since I was ejected from my bedroom.

There's not much idle chatter: the mood in the room is pretty sombre, and Alan gets down to business at once, like a headmaster conducting a staff meeting. "The situation we're facing is an open gate, class four, with unknown—but undesirable—parties on the other side. They've snatched one of our scientists. A secondary mission goal is to get her back alive. But the primary goal is to identify the parties responsible and, if they are who we think they are, neutralize them and then withdraw, ensuring the gate closes behind us. Let me stress that we are not 100 percent certain who we're up against, so identification and threat characterization are our first tasks. This isn't as clear-cut a job as we'd like, so I want you all to focus on it and give it a bit of thought. First, the situation. Derek?"

Derek from the Laundry, Derek the dried-up old accountancy clerk, stands up and delivers a terse, comprehensive sitrep as if he's done it a thousand times before. Who'd have thought it? "Ahnenerbe werewolf colony left over from Himmler's last stand." Mumble. "Mukhabarat." Cough. "Republican guard." Mutter. "Kidnapped scientist." Mumble. I don't need to take notes; near as I can tell I've heard it all before. Glancing round I try to catch Angleton's eye—just in time to see him slipping out the back. Then Derek finishes. "Back to you, Captain."

"Our mission is to take a look on the other side of the hill," says Alan. "Bringing back kidnapped scientists and neutralising undesirables are tactical tasks, but our number one strategic priority is to do a full threat evaluation and ensure word gets back home. So, step one is to send through a crawler and make sure there isn't a welcome party waiting for us on the other side. If it's clear, we insert. Step two—" he pauses "—we secure the other side, emplace the demolition package in case things go to pieces on us, then improvise depending on what we find." He grins, briefly. "I love surprises. Don't you?"

Well, yes, otherwise I'd never have volunteered for active duty in the first place. Which is why, half an hour later, I find myself standing on a purple-painted hotel staircase beneath a portrait of Martin Heidegger, breathing through an oxygen mask and waiting to follow a dumpy little tracked robot, half a platoon of territorial SAS, and an armed hydrogen bomb through a rip in the spacetime continuum.

Blurred shadows dance across the video screen, grey and black textures like ripped velvet laid over volcanic ash. On the floor in front of my feet the coil of cable unspools, snaking into darkness. Hutter, the equipment tech with the control panel, is hunched over it like a video game addict, twitching her joystick with gloved hands. I lean over behind Alan, who has the ringside view; I have to lean because the backpack is a solid mass, thirty kilograms pushing me forward if I even think about relaxing.

"One metre forward; now pan left."

The screen jerks. There's a thin wail as air vents through the doorframe and the cable reels out, then the scenery on screen begins to rotate. We see more blurred grey rubble, then a view that swoops away, down to a distant sea. As the camera pans round further the back of the robot comes into view, trailing a white umbilical back into the incongruous side of a wall. There isn't enough light to examine the wall, or enough scan lines: it's a night-vision camera, but we're operating in starlight. The camera continues to rotate until it's pointing back to its original bearing. There is no sign of life.

"Looks clear," someone whispers in my ear, voice tinny and half-masked by static.

"If you want to go first, feel free to volunteer," Alan says dryly. "Mary. See any hot spots?"

"Nothing," the tech reports.

"Okay. Bearing zero six zero, forward ten or until you see anything, then halt and report."

She follows through and the little robot lurches forward into the grey and black landscape on the other side of the gate. "Ambient air pressure, ten pascals. Ambient temperature—thermocouple gives an error, FLIR is flat lined, but that backup sensor is claiming somewhere between forty-five and sixty Kelvin. Gravimetric—it's Earth-like. Uh, I'm worried about the power, boss. Battery load is normal, but we're losing power like crazy—I think it's in danger of freezing solid. We never designed a robot to do this kind of environment—it's colder than summer on Pluto."

Someone whistles tunelessly until Pike tells them to shut up.

"How does this affect our environment model?" Alan asks aloud. "The suits are only certified down to a hundred and twenty Kelvin."

Someone else clears their throat. "Donaldson here. I think we should be okay, sir. We're only going to be in contact with the ground via the feet, and we've got plenty of insulation—and heating—there. No air means no convective loss, and we're not going to radiate any faster just because ambient is cooler. Our regulators use a counter-current loop to warm incoming air from whatever we breathe out, so they're not in danger of icing up. The real risk is that we're going to be more visible on infrared, and if we get into a firefight and have to take cover we are going to get frostbitten so fast it isn't funny. That lake is probably liquid nitrogen—don't walk on any shiny blue ice, it'll be frozen oxygen and the heat from your feet will flash-boil it. Oh, and it's diamagnetic: your compasses won't work."

"Thank you for that reminder, Jimmy," says Alan. "Any more compelling insights into why the laws of physics are not our friends?"

The camera pans round: same landscape, but now we see the gate framed by a low mound of dirt heaped up on one side, and a broken-down wall on the other. The lake is clearer, and some sort of rectilinear structure is just visible over the crest of the ridge.

"I don't understand the temperature," Donaldson says pensively. "There's something about it I can't quite put my finger on."

"Well, you're going to get a chance to put your finger on it quite soon. Mary, still no hot spots? Good. Alpha team—ready, insert."

On the other side of the doorway three guys wearing dark, insulated suits and backpacks quickly duck through the open gate and are gone from our universe. The robot's camera, pointing backward, catches them for posterity: ghosts leaping over it and passing out of view to either side.

"Chaitin: clear, over."

"Smith: nothing in view. Over."

"Hammer: clear, over."

The camera pans round and takes in three shapes hunched low behind the bluff, one of them pointing a stubby pipe back past the robot.

"Don, if you'd be so good as to take a look round the rear of the gate. Mike, Bravo team insert."

Three anonymous bulky figures push past behind me, through the pressure doors erected in front of the hotel room: a gust of wind howls past my helmet as they enter the gate. The camera pans—

"Chaitin: nothing behind the gate. Landscape is clear, rising to hills in the middle distance. I see some kind of geometric inscription on the ground and one, no, two bodies. Male, naked, gutted with a sharp implement. They look to be frozen—handcuffed behind their backs."

My heart flops over and I begin to breathe again, ashamed but relieved that neither of them is Mo. "Howard here: that'll be the human sacrifices they used to open the gate," I say. "Is there a kind of metal tripod nearby with an upturned dish on top?"

"Chaitin: nope, somebody's cleaned up around here."

"Bloody typical," somebody mutters out of turn.

"Charlie, insert," says Andy. He taps me on the arm: "C'mon, Bob. Time to party."

Ahead of us, Pike picks up the controls on something that looks like an electric street cleaner—the kind of wheeled cart you walk behind— and drives it forward toward the doors. It nudges through and the gale almost sucks me forward; I follow in his wake, trying not to think about the cart's payload. You can make a critical mass out of about six kilos of plutonium, but you need various other bits and pieces to make a bomb; while they've been fitted inside an eight-inch artillery shell before now, nobody has yet built a nuke that you can carry easily—especially when you're wearing a thirty-kilo life-support backpack.

Mist spurts out around me as I walk through the gate, and suddenly the ground under my feet isn't carpet anymore: it's crumbly, crunchy, like a hard frosted snowfall over gravel. I hear a faint buzz as heat exchangers switch on in my helmet, using the warmth of my breath to heat the air I'm breathing in. My skin prickles, abruptly feeling tight, my suit seems to contract all around me, and I emit an enormous and embarrassing fart. External air pressure: zero. Temperature: low enough to freeze oxygen. Jesus, it *is* springtime on Pluto.

Pike drives his gadget forward about five meters, halfway to the parked robot, then stops and begins unreeling a spool of cable from on top of it. He almost backs into me before I get out of his way. "Bob, take this." He hands me some kind of joystick-like gadget with a trigger built into it, plugged into the wire.

"What is it?" I ask, thumbing my intercom to his channel.

"Dead man's handle. We use two of them to detonate while we're out of range of the permissive action link signal—this side of the gate. Go on, pull the trigger, I've got the other one. It's perfectly safe to let go of one trigger at a time, it only goes bang if both triggers are released for ten seconds at the same time."

"Gee, thanks. How long did you say this wire is?"

I lumber in a circle, taking care not to let the wire get twisted around my feet as I take in the view. The gate is inscribed in a low wall; our footsteps have obscured the transient map in front of it, but behind the wall that supports the aperture the pattern is more or less intact (along with the two victims who were sacrificed to open it). The ground is crunchy, like loose soil after a heavy frost. Behind us and to the left and right it slopes up toward a low ridge; in front, the ground slopes down and broadens out into a valley. The stars overhead are unwinking, dimensionless points of light in a harsh vacuum. They look reddish, demonic eyes staring down at me; a universe of red dwarves, long after the sun has burned down.

Alpha and Bravo teams have fanned out ahead and behind the wall, advancing in a curious duck-walking crouch from cover to cover. I spot a lump sticking out of the ground about five meters away, and plod over to inspect it. It's a tree stump, shattered half a metre above the ground and hard as ice. I reach out to touch it and a thin mist bursts from the wood—I yank my fingers back before the stream of gas can chill them into frostbite. Wood crumbles and falls away from the stump, shattered by the warmth. I shudder inside my layers of compression fabric and insulation, and fart again.

There are boot imprints in the ground behind the gate, and they don't look like ours.

"Howard, get back to the gate. Don't tangle up the wire you're holding."

"Understood." I stomp back toward the gate, collecting loops of wire from the handle (which I have carefully avoided arming).

"Give." An anonymous, bulky figure holds out a hand: above the visor I see the name BLEVINS. I pass Roland the trigger and he attaches it to his chest with a Velcro pad, then heads for the low rise behind the gate.

"Howard, Barnes here. I'm on the rise behind you, twenty meters upslope. Come tell me what you think of this." A *click* as he hops frequency, to check on everybody else in turn.

I come up beside him on the rise and find him hefting a heavily insulated camera in front of his faceplate. Someone—Sergeant Howe, I think—is crouching farther up the slope with some kind of shotgun or grenade launcher in his arms. "Come on and look at this," Alan says; he sounds mildly amused as he waves me forward. "Keep your head low and no sudden movements. That's far enough, Bob."

I can just peep over the ridge, which falls away abruptly in front of me. More dead tree stumps; the ground beneath me, the crunching—now I can see that it's grass, freeze-dried and mummified beneath a layer of carbon dioxide frost. Hills or low mounds of some kind rise in the near distance, and then—

"Disneyland?" I hear myself saying.

Alan laughs quietly. "Not Disneyland. Think Mad King Ludwig's last commission, as executed by Buckminster Fuller." Cheesecake crenellations, battlements with machicolations, moat and drawbridge and turrets. Spiky pointed roofs on the towers—like the police stations in West Belfast, designed to deflect incoming mortar fire. Arrow slots filled with mirror glass half a metre thick. Radomes and antenna masts in the courtyard where you'd expect armored knights to mount up.

"I didn't know the RUC were Cthulhu-worshippers."

"They're not, laddie," says Howe, and I flush. "Check out the slope up to that moat. Probably got rammed earth behind those walls, but they're not really expecting direct artillery fire. Intruders on foot, rockets, I don't know what—but not tanks or direct fire."

"They won," Alan says distantly. "This isn't a fortification. Bob, I should apologize: it *is* a police station." Light glistens on the Gestapo battlements as I try to understand what he means.

"What happened to them?" I ask.

"Look," says Howe, pointing off to the left. I follow his direction and get my first inkling of just how far beyond our experience this world is. From up here the moon is visible, gibbous and close to the horizon; but the familiar man-in-the-moon pattern of marias and seas has been erased, replaced by a shadow-scribed visage carved across the entire lunar surface in runes ten kilometers deep. It's astonishing to behold, a miracle testimonial to one man's vanity on a scale that makes Mount Rushmore or the pyramids look like a child's sandcastle. And from the small tuft of moustache to the keynote cowlick of hair, the face is instantly recognizable.

From a quarter of a million miles away, Hitler's image stares at me across a land given over to ice and shadow. And I know the Ahnenerbe can't be far away.

8
## Storming Mount Impossible

The Artists' Rifles storm the Ahnenerbe's secret fortress with speed and élan, moderated only by tactical caution and a degree of perplexity that deepens as they determine that the castle is, in fact, unoccupied.

First in is the little reconnaissance robot, portaged into position and released by a couple of tense soldiers half a kilometre away from the rest of the expedition. As it rolls onto the flat killing apron around the redoubt, Bravo team moves like ghosts through the petrified forest on the other side of the castle. Everybody is tense: nobody talks on radio while they're line of sight on the castle, and nobody wants to be visible, either—on infrared against this chill landscape, a human being will stand out like a magnesium flare.

The robot rolls out onto the killing apron in front of the castle, little puffs of snow fountaining up behind its treads. At this point if anyone is guarding it we'd expect to see fireworks, but nothing happens: nobody shoots, nothing lights up. I hunch over behind Hutter's shoulder, watching the video feed via the secure fiber-optic cable. The castle is dark, except for a central building that glows red hot, two hundred and fifty degrees hotter than the ambient temperature. It silhouettes the battlements, towers, and radomes nicely.

Alan circles a hand above his head twice, and a long way away a sleeping dragon erupts. A dot of light sizzles across the frozen landscape on a jet of flame and slams into the outer door of the gatehouse: lumps of stone and metal tumble silently through the empty vacuum above it. Things begin to happen very quickly as Alpha team lays down fire on the gatehouse and Bravo team skids out across the ice behind the castle and makes for the forbiddingly high walls. A chain of fireworks erupts from the ground and bursts over the battlements in front of them, then—

Nothing. Nothing but silence and the jerky movements of Alan's men. They reach the foot of the wall and swarm up it as if they aren't wearing heavy backpacks, while a second Dragon launcher pops a rocket off at the front of the castle and someone—Sergeant Howe, I think—beats the courtyard with machine-gun fire that makes small mushroom clouds of white vapor burst from the ground. And there's *still* no answering fire.

"Alpha secure," someone grunts in my headphones. Then: "Bravo secure. Cease fire, cease fire, we've got an empty venue."

"Empty? Confirm." It's Alan's voice. He doesn't sound perturbed, but—

"Alpha here, the place is *empty*," insists whoever's using that call sign. "As in abandoned."

"Bravo confirms, Mike here. There's a dead truck in the courtyard but no sign of life up here. Dunno about the central target, but if they've retreated in there they aren't coming out. They wouldn't have heard us, anyway." He sounds nervous, breathy.

"Mike, keep under cover, don't assume anything. Hammer, close in fast and secure the gatehouse. Chaitin, lay on the central blockhouse but hold fire on my word. Charlie team move in."

Alan stands up and runs forward, crouching close to the ground; across the landscape I can see the others moving toward the castle's shattered gates—popping up and lunging forward for a few seconds then diving flat to the ground, ready to fire.

Still nothing happens. *What's going on?* I wonder. Only one way to find out: I stand up and jog forward heavily, feeling the backpack ramming my feet down onto the frozen ground. The empty killing apron is about a hundred meters wide and I feel really naked as I step out onto it, out of the cover of the petrified forest. But there's no sign of life in the castle. Nothing at all untoward happens as I trot forward and, panting, heave myself into the shadow of the gatehouse.

It looms overhead, a grey mound of concrete or stone in the darkness; a narrow window, dark as the crypt, overlooks the entranceway. The gates are solid slabs of wood bound in metal, but they lean drunkenly away from the huge hole that the Dragon blew between them. I pause, and someone whacks me in the back: "Howard, get *down!*"

I get down and feel icy cold through the thick padding on my knees and elbows. There's some radio chatter: terse announcements as each team makes its way through a series of checkpoints. "Chaitin, keep the blockhouse covered. Hutter, any signs of life?"

"Hutter: nothing, boss. Blockhouse is warm, but nothing's moving outside it. Uh, correction. I have a temperature fix on the courtyard; it's a couple of degrees warmer than outside. Probably heat from the blockhouse." The blockhouse is glowing brightly on infrared, a surer sign of life than anything else we've seen.

I edge through the tunnel under the walls—rammed earth overhead, frozen like cement—and peer round the corner at the blockhouse. The name doesn't do it justice; it's the central building in the complex and it's built like a small castle. Windows, high up, big dome erupting from the roof, small doors shut tight against the chill. Some kind of small vehicle, like a weird cross between a tank and a motorbike, is parked against the wall, dusty with a sprinkling that isn't snow.

"Cool, I always wanted a Kettenkrad," someone remarks on the common channel.

"Morris, shut the fuck up; the cylinder heads are probably vacuum welded anyway. Chaitin, check out the doors. Scary Spice, cover with the M40."

Someone who doesn't look at all like one of the Spice Girls moves up beside me and levels something that looks like a drainpipe fucking a submachine gun at the blockhouse. Someone else, anonymous in winter camouflaged pressure gear, jogs forward and then dashes at the door. Bazooka man whacks me on the shoulder to get my attention: "Get back!" he hisses.

"Okay, I'm back," I say. Funnily enough I don't feel afraid at all, which surprises me. "Say, are you sure this isn't Castle Wolfenstein?"

"Fuckin' dinna say that else ye can live with the fuckin' consequences," someone rumbles in my ears. Soldier #1 raises something that looks like a plumber's caulking gun and squirts white paste around the frame of the blockhouse door. Still no sign of a welcoming committee. I glance up at the hostile red stars above the battlements and wonder why I can't see very many of them. A thought strikes me just as the guy with the plumber's mate sticks a timer into the goop and bounds back our way then crouches: "Cover!" The ground bounces and smoke and gas puffs out from the edges of the door—the gunk is a high-brisance explosive and it cuts through the reinforced steel door like a blowtorch through butter. I see the door getting bigger and beginning to squash vertically— then it slams past us and the escaping gush of air bowls me right over and nearly rolls me along the frigid ground.

"*Jesus*," someone says, and I turn round to see where the door landed behind me. Something is *wrong* my nerves are screaming—where the hell are the Ahnenerbe? *There should be people here*, that's what's wrong.

Scary Spice has his grenade launcher leveled on the chamber behind the door, but the air flow has stopped and when Chaitin tosses in a flare it lights up a bare, empty room the size of a garage, with sealed doors to either side. "Spooky," I remark. "Looks empty. Anyone home?"

The SAS aren't waiting around to find out; the whole of Bravo team piles into the empty vestibule in a hurry and Chaitin moves forward. More chatter: "Airlocks, this is a fucking death trap get us in *get us in* . . ."

"Castle fucking Wolfenstein, eh?" Alan remarks in my ear, and according to my chest panel he's on a private channel. I join him.

"Why isn't anybody here?" I ask.

"Who the fuck knows? Let's just get inside, fast. You got any ideas?"

"Yeah. If you depressurize this building and Mo's inside you'll have lost us our best clue yet."

"If I *don't* depressurize that building and some fucking Nazi revenant ices my people I'll have lost more than just our best clue." Someone taps me on the shoulder and I jump, then turn far enough to recognise Alan. "Remember that," he says.

"We're here for information first—" I say, but he's cut over to another channel already so I don't know if he hears me. In any case, he taps me on the shoulder again and waves me toward the vestibule. Where Bravo team has sprung a door with a big locking wheel, hopped through, and the wheel is now spinning behind them. Airlock door, at a guess.

"Bravo, Mike here, we have atmosphere—half a kilopascal at only twenty below freezing. Pressure's coming up: lock safety is tripped. Everything here looks to be in working order, but dusty as hell. We're ready to go through on your word."

I follow Alan and Alpha squad into the vestibule. Scary Spice is busy laying strips of some kind of explosive gunk all around the airlock door, while one of the other soldiers lines up on it with a heavily insulated light machine gun. I flick to the main channel and listen to the crackly chatter; something seems to be wrong with my radio because I'm picking up a lot of noise. Noise—

"Howard here, anybody else picking up a lot of radio hash?"

"Hutter here, who was that? Repeat please, I'm reading you strength three and dropping."

"Hutter, Bob, cut the chatter and use your squelch. We've got a job to do here." Alan sounds distinctly preoccupied; I decide interrupting is a bad idea and focus instead on my suit radio in case there's a problem with it. A minute of fiddling tells me that there isn't. It's a really cute UHF set, able to hop around about a zillion sidebands at high speed—analogue, not digital, but the pinnacle of that particular technology. If it's picking up hash then the hash is spread far and wide.

I walk back to the vestibule entrance and look up at the sky. The stars are really prominent; the smoky red whirlpool of the galaxy stares down at me like a malignant red eye, startlingly visible against the night. I hunt around for the moon but it's out of direct sight, casting knife-edged black shadows across the pale blue snowscape. I blink, wishing I could rub my eyes. *Blue?* I must be seeing things. Or maybe the optical filters on my helmet are buggering my color sensitivity—I've had it happen with computer screens before now.

I turn back to face the interior and someone is waving me forward; the airlock door gapes open. "Howard, Hutter, Scary, your cycle." I move forward carefully. The concrete floor is chipped and scarred, stained with old grease marks. I look round: something large is inching toward the gates—Pike, and the cart with the H-bomb. "I'll follow you through with the charge," Alan adds. I step through into the airlock room, boggling at the array of pipework on view—it's like something out of a war movie, the interior of a beached U-boat, all plumbing and dials and big spinner wheels. Hutter pushes the door closed behind us and cranks a handle. The airlock is narrow, and dark except for our helmet lamps; I shudder, and try not to think about what would happen if the door jams. On my other side Scary Spice yanks a valve-lever in the opposite door, and there's a thin hissing as fog spills into the room from vents along the floor. A needle in my suit's chest instrument panel quivers and begins to move—air pressure. After a few more seconds I feel my suit going limp and clammy around me, and hear a distinct *clank* as the hissing stops.

"Going through," says Scary Spice, and he spins the locking wheel on the inner door and pushes it open.

I'm not sure what I am expecting to see; Castle Wolfenstein is a definite maybe, and I was subjected to the usual run of second-rate war movies during my misspent childhood, but the last thing on my list would have been a kennel full of freeze-dried Rottweilers. Someone has powered up an overhead light bulb which is swinging crazily at the end of its cord, casting wild shadows across the emaciated-looking corpses of a dozen huge dogs. Next to the airlock is a table, and behind it a wall of lockers; ahead of us, a wooden door leading onto a corridor. The light doesn't reach far into those shadows. Hutter prods me in the back and as I step forward something crunches under my boot heel, leaving a nasty brownish stain on the floor. "Yuck." I look round.

"You can switch your transmitter off," says Hutter, "we've got air." She fiddles with her suit panel: "Looks breathable, too, but don't take my word for it."

"Quiet." Scary Spice looks round. "Mike?"

"Mike here." My radio isn't crackling as much now we're indoors. "No signs of life so far—lots of dusty offices, dead dogs. We've swept the ground floor and it looks as if there's nobody home." He sounds as puzzled as I feel. Where the hell *are* the bad guys?

"Roger that, Hutter and yon boffin are with me in the guardhouse. We're waiting on reinforcements."

I hear a squeal of metal and look round; Hutter is closing the airlock door again, and it sounds like it hasn't been oiled for fifty years.

"Uh, we have bodies." I jump; it's a different voice, worryingly shaky. Chaitin? "I'm in the third door along on corridor B, left wing, and it isn't pretty."

"Barnes here. Chaitin, sitrep." Alan sounds purposeful.

"They're—looks like a mess room, boss. It's hard to tell, temperature's subzero so everything's frozen but there's a lot of blood. Bodies. They're wearing—yeah, SS uniforms, I'm vague on the unit insignia but it's definitely them. Looks like they shot themselves. Each other. O Jesus, excuse me sir, need a moment."

"Take ten, Greg. What's so bad? Talk to me."

"Must be, uh, at least twenty of them, sir. Freeze-dried, like the doggies: they're kind of mummified. Can't have happened recently. There's a pile against one wall and a bunch around this table, and—one of them is still holding a pistol. Dead as they come. There's some papers on the table."

"Papers. What can you tell me?"

"Not much sir, I don't speak German and that's what they look to be in."

Someone swears creatively. After a moment I realize that it's Chaitin.

"*Status*, Chaitin!"

"Just trod in—" more swearing. "Sorry, sir." Sound of heavy breathing. "It's safe but, but anyone who comes here better have a strong stomach. Looks like some kind of black magic—"

Hutter taps me on the shoulder and motions me forward: "Howard coming through. Don't touch anything."

The building is a twilight nightmare of narrow corridors, dust and debris, too narrow to turn round in easily with the bulky suit backpacks. Scary Spice leads me through a series of rooms and a mess hall, low benches parked to either side of a wooden table in front of a counter on which sit pans that have tarnished with age. Then we're into a big central hall with a staircase leading up and down, and another corridor, this one with gaping doors—and Chaitin waiting outside the third door with someone else inside.

The scene is pretty much what Chaitin described: table, filing cabinets, pile of withered mummies in grey and black uniforms, black-brown stains across half of them. But the wall behind the door—

"Howard here: I've seen these before," I transmit. "Ahnenerbe-issue algemancy inductance rig. There should be—ah." A rack of stoppered glass bottles gleams from below the thing like a glass printing press with chromed steel teeth. There's a wizened eyeless horror trapped in it, his jaws agape in a perpetual silent scream, straining at manacles drawn tight by dehydrating muscle tissue. I carefully pay no attention to it: throwing up inside a pressure suit would be unwise. Bulldog clips and batteries and a nineteen-inch-wide rack—where's the trough? Answer: below the blood gutters.

"One last summoning, by the look of it, before they all died. Or shot themselves." I trace a finger along the boundary channel of the arcane machine, careful not to touch it: they probably filled the channel with liquid mercury—a conductor—but it's long since evaporated. If it was a possession, that tends to spread by touch, or along electrical conductors. (Visuals, too, although that usually takes serious computer graphics work to arrange.) I turn away from the poor bastard impaled on the torture machine and look at the table. The papers there are brittle with age: I turn one page over, feeling the binder crackling, and see a Ptath transform's eye-warping geometries. "They were summoning something," I say. "I'm not sure what, but it was definitely a possessive invocation." For some reason I have an unaccountable sense of wrongness about the scene. What have I missed?

The mummy with the pistol in its hand seems to be grinning at me.

I flick my radio off and rely on plain old-fashioned speech to keep my words local: "Chaitin," I say slowly, "that corpse. The one with the gun. Did he shoot everyone else here—or could it have been someone else? Was he defending himself?"

The big guy looks puzzled. "I don't see—" he pauses, then sidles round the table until he's as close to the corpse as he can get. "Uh-huh," he says. "Maybe there was someone else here, but he sure looks as if he shot himself. That's funny—"

My radio drowns him out. "Barnes to all: we've found Professor O'Brien. Howard, get your arse downstairs to basement level two, we're going to need your expertise to get her out. Everyone else, eyes up: we have at least one bad guy unaccounted for."

My skin crawls for a moment: What the hell can be wrong with Mo if they need me to help rescue her? Then I notice Chaitin watching me. "Take care," he says gruffly. "You know how to use that thing?"

"This?" I clumsily pat the basilisk gun hanging from my chest pack. "Sure. Listen, don't touch that machine. I mean, like really *don't touch* it. I think it's dead but you know what they say about unexploded bombs, okay?"

"Go on." He waves me past him at the door and I go out to find Scary Spice crouched in the corridor, eyes swivelling like a chameleon on cocaine.

"Let's go." We head for the stairs, and I can't shed the nagging feeling that I've missed something critically important: that we're being sucked into a giant cobweb of darkness and chilly lies, doing exactly what the monster at its centre wants us to do—all because I've misinterpreted one of the signs around me.

The basement level is colder than the surface rooms and passages. I find Sergeant Pike there, helmet undogged, breath steaming and sparkling in the light of a paraffin lamp someone has coaxed into oily, lambent life. "What kept you?" he asks.

I shrug. "Where is she and how is she?"

He points at the nearer of two corridor entrances; this one is lit by a chain of bioluminescent disposables, so that a ghastly chain of green candlelight marks the route. My stomach feels suddenly hollow. "She's conscious but nobody's touching her till you've given the okay," he says.

*Oh great.* I follow the chain of ghost lights to the open door—

The door may be wide open but there's no mistaking it for anything other than a cell. Someone's stuck another lantern on the floor, just so I can see what else is inside. The room is almost completely occupied by some kind of summoning rig—not a torture machine like the one upstairs, but something not that far away from it. There's a wooden framework like a four-poster bed, with elaborate pulleys at each corner. Mo is spread-eagled on her back, naked, tied to the uprights, but the effect is just about anything other than kinky-sexy—especially when I see what's suspended above her by way of more pulleys and the same steel cables that loop through her manacles. Each of the uprights is capped by a Tesla coil, there's some kind of bug-fuck generator rig in the corner, and half the guts of an old radar station's HF output stage arranged around the perimeter of a crazy pentacle surrounding the procrustean contraption. It's like a bizarre cross between an electric chair and a rack.

Her eyes are closed. I think she's unconscious. I can't help myself: I fumble with the locking ring on my helmet then raise my visor and take a breath. It's cold in here—it's been about eight hours since she was abducted, so if she's been there that long she's probably halfway to hypothermia already.

I shuffle closer, careful not to cross the solder-dribbled circuit inscribed on the stone floor. "Mo?"

She twitches. "Bob? Bob! Get me out of here!" She's hoarse and there's an edge of panic in her voice.

I take a shuddering, icy breath. "That's exactly what I'm going to do. Only question is *how.*" I glance around. "Anyone there?" I call.

Be with you in a sec," replies Hutter from outside the door. "Waiting for the boss."

I go fumbling in my padded pocket for the PDA, because before I go anywhere near that bed I want to take some readings. "Talk to me, Mo. What happened? Who put you here?"

*"Oh, God, he's out there—"*

She just about goes into spasm, straining at the cables in panic. "Stop that!" I shout, on edge and jittery myself. "Mo, stop *moving*, that thing could cut loose any moment!"

She stops moving so suddenly that the bed-rack-summoning-bench shakes. "What did you say?" she asks out of one corner of her mouth.

I squat, trying to see the base of the frame she's lying on. "That thing. I'm going to untie you just as soon as I've checked that it isn't wired. Dead man's handle. Looks like a Vohlman-Knuth configuration—powered down right now, but stick some current through those inductors and it could turn very nasty indeed." I've tapped up an interesting diagnostic program on the palmtop and the Hall-effect sensor embedded in the machine is giving back some even more interesting readings. Interesting, in the sense of the Chinese proverb—"May you live in interesting times"—or more likely die in them. "You use it for necromantic summonings. Demons, they used to call them: now they're primary manifestations, probably 'cause that doesn't frighten the management. Who put you on it?"

"This skinny guy, with a suntan and a German accent—"

"From Santa Cruz?"

"No, I'd never seen him before."

"Shit. Did he have any friends? Or do anything to set up that rack over there?"

I inspect the top of the framework. The chandelier-thing hangs from the roof of the execution machine like a bizarre, three-dimensional guillotine blade: cut any of the ropes holding Mo to the bed and it will fall. I'm not sure what it's made of—glass and bits of human bone seem to figure in the design, but so do color-coded wires and gears—but the effect will be about as final as flicking the switch on a frog in a liquidizer. Trouble is, I'm not sure the damned thing won't fall anyway, if someone switches on the device.

"No," Mo says, but she sounds doubtful.

I'm checking around the foot of the necromantic bed now, and it's a good thing the instrument's got a log display: lots of *very* bad shit has gone down here, ghosts howling in the wires, information destroyed and funnelled out of our spacetime through weirdly tangled geometries of silver wire and the hair of hanged women. Bastards. I really ought to keep Mo talking.

"I was asleep," she says. "I remember a dream—howling air, very cold, being carried somewhere, unable to move. Like being paralyzed, scary as hell and I couldn't breathe. Then I woke up down here. *He* was leaning over me. My head aches like the mother of all hangovers. What happened?"

"Did he say anything?" I ask. "Make any adjustments?"

"He said I'd served my purpose and this would be my final contribution. His eyes, they were *really* weird. Luminous. What do you mean, make adjust—" she tries to raise her head and the bed creaks. There's an ominous buzzing sound from the control panel at the far side of the room and a red light comes on.

"Oh shit," I say, as the door opens and two soldiers in vacuum gear come in and the lights flicker. I see the chandelier-like thing above Mo sway on its ropes, hear the bedframe creak. As she gathers breath to scream I clumsily jump onto the bed and brace myself on hands and knees above her. "Someone cut the fucking cables, pull her out, and *cut the fucking wires!*" I yell. I'm kneeling on one of them when the descending mass of obsidian and bone and wire lands on my backpack with a crunch—and I discover the hard way that the thing is electrified, and Mo is wired to earth.

My head is spinning, I feel nauseous, and my right knee feels like it's on fire. *What am I doing—*

"Bob, we're going to pull it off you now. Can you hear me?"

Yeah, I can hear you. I want to throw up. I grunt something. The crushing weight on my back begins to lift. I blink stupidly at the wooden slats in front of me, then someone grabs my arm and tries to pull me sideways. Their touch hurts; someone, maybe me, screams, and someone else yells "Medic!"

Seconds or minutes later I realize that I'm lying on my back and someone is pounding on my chest. I blink and try to grunt something. "Can you hear me?" they say.

"Yeah—*oof.*"

The pounding stops for a moment and I force myself to breathe deeply. I know I should be lying on something, but what? I open my eyes properly. "Oh, that wasn't good. My knee—"

Alan leans over my field of view; people are bustling about behind him. "What was that all about?" he asks.

"Is Mo—"

"I'm all right, Bob." Her voice comes from right behind me. I start, and it feels like someone's clubbed me behind the ear again—my head is about to split open. "That—thing—" her voice is shaky.

"It's an altar," I say tiredly. "Should have recognised the design sooner. Alan, the bad guy is loose here. Somewhere. Mo was bait for a trap."

"Explain," Alan says, almost absent-mindedly. I roll my head round and see that Mo is sitting with her back to the wall, legs stretched out in front of her; someone's given her one of the red survival suits, no good in vacuum but enough to keep her warm, and she's got a silver foil blanket stretched around her shoulders. Behind her, the altar is a splintered wreck.

"It's not so hard to open a gate and bring an information entity through, especially if you've got a body ready and waiting for it at the other end, right? Physical gates are harder, and the bigger you want 'em, the more energy or life you have to expend to stabilize it. Anyway, this is an altar; there are a couple like it in the basement of that museum we came to visit. You put the sacrifice on the altar, wire it to an invocation grid, and kill the victim—that's what the chandelier was for—channelling what comes back out. Only this one—the guards and wards around the altar are buggered. They'd offer no protection at all once the summoning was manifest, and the thing would take over anyone it could come into contact with. Transfer by electrical conduction, that's how a lot of these things spread."

"So you tried to shield her with your body," says Alan. "How touching!"

"Huh." I cough and wince at the answering pain in my head. "Not really; I figured the scaffold wouldn't be able to cut through my air tanks. And if it killed her we'd all be dead, anyway."

"What was it set up to summon?" Mo asks. Her voice still hoarse.

"I don't know." I frown. "Nothing friendly, that's for sure. But then, this isn't the Ahnenerbe, is it? Even though they built this place, they've been dead for a long time. Suicide, by the look of it. This bastard's some kind of possessor entity—jumps from body to body. It's been shadowing you from the States, but when it got you all it did was use you as raw material in a summoning sacrifice. Doesn't make sense, does it? If it wanted you so bad, why not just walk up to you, shake hands, and move into your head?"

"It doesn't matter right now." Alan stands. "We're leaving soon. According to Roland the gate's shrinking; we've got about four hours to pull out, and your mystery kidnapper hasn't tried to make a break for it. What we're going to do is put a guard on the gate, get the hell out of here, and leave the demo charge ticking. He won't be able to sneak back around us, and the gadget will toast what's left of this place."

"Uh-huh. How's my tankage?"

"Dented, and your suit front panel is blown—it took the brunt of the charge, otherwise you'd be a crispy critter right now. Look, I'm going to get things organised in person, seeing all our radios are flaking out." Alan looks round. "Hutter, get these people sorted out and ready to pull back; I want them both mobile within the hour, we've got a lot of shit to move out of here." He glances down at me and winks. "You've done well."

Over the course of the next fifteen minutes I recover enough to sit up against the wall, and Mo just about manages to stop shivering. She leans against me. "Thank you," she says quietly. "That went *way* beyond—"

Hutter and Chaitin bang in through the door, heaving a couple of bulky kit-bags full of assorted gear: vacuum support underwear, heated outer suit, a new regulator and air tank for my framework, a new backpack and helmet for Mo. "Look at the lovebirds," Chaitin says, apparently amused by us. "On your feet, pretties, got to get you ready to move and ain't nobody going to carry you."

While Hutter is getting Mo into her pressure gear I stumble around the wreckage of the procrustean bed and hunt for my palmtop—dropped when I had to leap for her life. I find it lying on the concrete floor, evidently kicked into a corner of the room, but it's undamaged, which is a big relief. I pick it up and check the thaum level absently, and freeze: something is really *not* right around here. Following the display I trail around the walls until I find an inexplicably high reading in front of that rack of high tension switchgear. *Something* is happening here: local entropy is sky-high as if information is being destroyed by irreversible computation in the vicinity. But the rack is switched off. I pocket the small computer and give the rack an experimental yank; I'm nearly knocked off my feet when it slides toward me.

"Hey!" Chaitin is right behind me, shoving me out of the way and pointing his gun into the dark cavity behind the rack.

"Don't," I say tersely. "Look." I switch on my suit headlamp, and promptly wish I hadn't.

"Oh Jesus." Chaitin lowers his gun but doesn't look away. The room behind the instrument rack is another cell: it must have been undisturbed for a long time, but it's so cold that most of the body parts are still recognizable. There's a butcher's shop miasma hanging over it, not decay, exactly, but the smell of death. Enough spare parts for Dr Frankenstein to make a dozen monsters lie heaped in the room, piled in brown-iced drifts in the corners. "Shut the fucking door," he says distantly, and steps out of my way.

"Anyone got a hacksaw?" I ask.

"You can't be serious—" Chaitin pushes up his visor and stares at me. "Why?"

"I want to take samples from the top few bodies," I say slowly. "I think they may be something to do with the Mukhabarat's Santa Cruz operation."

"You're nuts," he says.

"Maybe, but don't you want to know who these people were?"

"No fucking way, mate," he says. Then he breathes deeply. "Look, I was in Bosnia, y'know, the mass graves?" He glances down and scuffs the floor. "Spent a couple of weeks guarding the forensics guys one summer. The worst thing about those pits, you scrubbed like crazy but in the end you had to throw your boots away. Once that smell gets into the leather it won't leave." He looks away. "You're fucking out of your skull if you think I'm going to help you take trophies."

"So just get me an axe," I snap irritably. (Then I wince again and wish I hadn't.) He looks at me oddly for a moment, as if trying to make his mind up whether or not to get physical, then turns and stomps off.

When Chaitin returns he's carrying a fireman's axe and an empty kit-bag. He leaves me alone for ten minutes while I discover just how difficult it is to chop through the wrist bones of a corpse that's been frozen for days or months. I find that I'm angry, very angry indeed—so angry, in fact, that the job doesn't upset me. I want to find the bastard who did this and give him a taste of his own medicine, and if chopping off dead hands is the price then it's a price I'm happy to pay—with interest.

But why do I still feel as if I'm missing something obvious? Like, maybe, what the demon—dybbuk, possessor, whatever-you-call-it—lured us here for?

## 9
## Black Sun

When I come out of the cellar clutching my grisly handbag, Hutter and Mo are gone. Chaitin is stooging around, shuffling from foot to foot as he waits for me. "Let's go," he says, so I heft the bag at him.

"Got it." We head back up the corridor past the glow-tubes and I glance over my shoulder just once, breath steaming in the frigid air. Then I lower my visor and lock it in place, check my regulator, and listen to the hiss of cool air through my helmet. "Where is everybody?"

"Boss man's up top arming the gadget; your squeeze is on her way back to the gateway."

"Great," I say, and I mean it. This place is getting to me; I almost want to dance a little jig at the thought of blowing it to atoms. "Did anybody find any documentation?"

"Documentation? Tons of it. These guys were Germans, dude. You ever worked with the fucking Wehrmacht, you'd be able to tell a story about documentation, too."

"Huh." We hit the bottom of the stairs. Scary Spice is waiting for us.

"Go on up," he says to Chaitin. He stops me: "You, wait." He twists a dial on my chest pack: "Hear me?"

"Yeah," I say, "loud and clear. Has anyone seen any sign of the bastard who kidnapped Mo?"

"The target, you mean?" Scary hefts his heavily insulated gun and for a moment I'm glad I can't see through his face mask. "Naah, but you're going up the stairs right now and I'm following you, and if you see anyone behind me yell like hell."

"That," I say fervently, "is fine by me." Already the shadows are lengthening as the glow-tubes slowly burn out.

There's crosstalk and terse chatter all over the radio channel Scary has tuned me to; I get the impression of three teams retreating to prearranged positions, keeping their eyes peeled for company. Some evil bastard demon has been here in the past couple of hours, wearing a stolen body: Can't we move faster? Evidently not. "Timer set to seven thousand seconds by my mark," Alan cuts in on the common channel. "This is your hundred and ten minute warning, folks. I've pulled the spoiler chain and the initiator is now live; anyone still here in two hours better have some factor one-billion sunblock. Sound off by name."

Everyone seems to be accounted for, except the three outside. "Okay, pull out in LIFO order. Scary, Chaitin, make sure Howard's in tow and cycle when ready."

"Right boss." Chaitin. "C'mon, you, let's go."

"Okay." I wait while Chaitin cycles through the airlock into the garage, then open the door and squeeze into the cramped closetlike space. "I'm on tank one, everything working."

"It better be. Okay, cycle yourself through."

I wait for a tense two minutes while the air hisses out of a tiny tube and I feel the pressure suit tightening around me. Oddly, I begin to feel warmer once I'm in partial vacuum; the chilly air in the redoubt was sapping my body heat. Presently the outer door swings open. "Move, move!"

I walk out into the garage, open doors gaping at the ink-black sky, then out into the courtyard in front of the building. Chaitin's waiting there. Someone's parked that electric trolley next to the wall, but the little half-track thing with a motorcycle's front wheel is missing. "Someone taking souvenirs?" I ask.

A burst of static that I just about decode as "What?" tells me that the interference is worse than before; I glance up and see red stars, a dull red swirl of galaxy overhead . . . a distinct pink tinge to the moon, in fact.

I point at where the Kettenkrad was parked. "There, it's gone," I say. "Who took it?"

Chaitin shrugs. I look round. "Go there." He points at the main gatehouse. I start walking. The moonlight is dim, rosy: either I'm feeling lightheaded or . . . or what?

It's about a kilometre to the wall where our unseen enemy opened the gate to Amsterdam, and with no sign of him in the vicinity I have time to do a little bit of thinking. Looking straight up I see only darkness; the visible stars mostly stretched in a wide belt above the horizon, the moon an evil-faced icon staring down at us. The power to suck all the life and heat out of a planet like this—it's horrifying. While a sacrificial murder will get you a hot-line to a demon capable of possessing you, or a window to some universe so alien you can't comprehend its physical laws, it takes a lot of power to open a physical gate to another version of the Earth. Shadow Earths interfere with each other, and it's very difficult to generate congruence. But whatever happened here . . .

I try to picture what might have happened. I can only come up with two scenarios:

Scenario one. An Ahnenerbe detachment in Germany, some time in April of 1945. They know they're losing, but defeat is not an acceptable option to them. They quickly gather all the supplies they can: foodstuffs, machine tools, seeds, fuel. Using a handful of captured enemy POWs, a gate is opened to somewhere cold and airless where they can wait out the hue and cry before making a break for home.

Nope, that doesn't work. How'd they build this fortress? Or mess with the moon?

Scenario two. A divergent history; a different branch of our own universe, so close to our own timeline that the energy it takes to open a full bridge between the two realities approximates the mass-energy of the universe itself. The point of departure, the fork in the river of time, is an invocation the Ahnenerbe attempted late in the war—but not too late. It's an act of necromancy so bloody that the priests of Xipe Totec would have cringed in horror, so gruesome that Himmler would have protested. They opened a gateway. We thought it was just a tactical move, a way to move men and materials about without being vulnerable to Allied attack—shunt them into another world, travel across it bypassing their enemies, then open a gateway back to our own continuum. But what if they were doing something more ambitious? What if they were trying to open a channel to one of the nameless places where the infovores dwell: beings of near-infinite cold, living in the darkened ghosts of expanded universes that have succumbed to the ancient forces of proton decay and black hole evaporation? Invoking Godlike powers to hold their enemies at bay, the forces of the Red Army and the Western Allies are held in check . . .

What happened next?

Pacing through the petrified forest I can see it as clearly as a television documentary. A wind of desolation and pain screams out of the heart of Europe, hurling bombers from the skies like dandelion seeds. A darkness rises in the west, a maelstrom that sucks Zukhov's divisions in like splinters of a shattered mast sent flying in a hurricane. The SS necromancers are exultant: their demons harrow the Earth in stolen bodies, scouring it clean of enemy forces, eating the souls of the *untermenschen* and spitting up their bones. Snow falls early as *fimbulwinter* sets in, for the ice giants of legend have returned to do the bidding of the thousand-year Reich, and the Führer's every dream shall be made real. A pale sun that warms nothing gazes down across a wilderness of ice and fire, ravaged by the triumph of the will.

They only realize how badly they'd miscalculated some months later as the daylight hours shorten, and shorten further—until the equinox passes, the temperature continues to fall as the sunlight dims, and the giants cease to do their bidding.

*Götterdämmerung* has come for the victorious Third Reich . . .

Up the low rise with the wall on the other side, I turn round and look back at the redoubt, at the last island of warmth in a cold world that's been sucked dry. I contemplate it for a minute or so. "Had a thought," I say aloud, and get a burst of static in return.

I look round. Chaitin is standing farther up the hillside; he waves at me. More static. "You there?" I ask, fiddling with my radio controls "Can you hear me?"

He walks toward me, brandishing something. I focus on a coil of cable with a plug on the end, but as he approaches the static begins to clear up. He pokes it at my chest pack but I bat his hand away. "Speak," he says roughly.

I take a deep breath: "I need to make some measurements. There is something very, very wrong with this whole picture, you know? Why is it so cold? Why are our suit radios all malfunctioning? What killed everyone in that bunker? Seems to me that Alan needs to know. Hell! I need to know—it's important."

Through his suit helmet Chaitin's expression is unreadable. "Explain."

I shiver with a sudden realisation. "Look, they summoned something that hunkered down and sucked all the fucking energy out of this universe, and if Alan sets off an H-bomb—what do you think is going to happen?"

"Talk more." Chaitin offers me the cable again.

I point to my damaged chest pack, then point my finger straight up. "Look, the stars are all reddish, and they're too far apart. That's number one. Red shift means they're all flying away from each other like crazy! That, or the energy in the light they're emitting is being sapped by something. I figure that effect is also what's screwing with our radios: in this universe the Planck constant is changing. Number two, the sun—the sun's gone out. It went out a few decades ago, that's why the temperature's down to forty absolute and dropping; the only thing keeping the Earth above cosmic background temperature is the fact that it's a honking great reservoir of hot rocks, with enough thorium and uranium mixed in that decay heat will keep it simmering for billions of years. But that's losing energy faster than it should, too, because something here is distorting the laws of physics. Third: for all we know all the other suns have gone out, too—the light we see from the stars is fossil radiation, it's been travelling for years, centuries."

I take a deep breath and shift my feet. Chaitin isn't saying anything; he's just looking around, looking for signs in the sky or the earth. "Something is eating energy, and information," I say. "Our primary objective—in coming here—is to find out what's going on and report back. I'm saying we haven't found out yet, and what the captain doesn't know can hurt us all."

Chaitin turns back to face me.

"It makes sense, doesn't it?" I say. "Like, it all hangs together?"

He holds up a torch to illuminate his face through his visor. He's grinning at me with a face I haven't seen before: "*Sehr gut,*" he says, then he drops the torch, releases the catches, and lifts his helmet off. Luminous worms of light writhe soundlessly behind his eyelids, twisting in the empty space of his skull, just like the thing that took Fred from Accounting. The out-gassing air from his suit wreathes him in vapor as he leans toward me, grabbing, trying to make a close flesh-to-flesh contact seeing as his comms-cable gambit has failed. Just one moment of electrical conduction—

The thing that occupies Chaitin's skin and bone is not very intelligent: it's forgotten that I'm wearing a suit too, and that these suits are designed to take a fair bit of abuse. Still, it's pretty freaky. I drop my sack and hop backward, nearly going arse-over-ears as gravity seems to suck at my backpack. The possessed body scrabbles toward me and I can see, very clearly, a trickle of blood bubbling from his nose as I fumble for the basilisk gun at my waist, grab onto it with both hands, and punch both red buttons with my thumbs. For a panicky moment I think that it's dead, batteries drained by the chilling cold out here—then all hell breaks loose.

Roughly one in a thousand carbon nuclei in the body that used to belong to Chaitin spontaneously acquire an extra eight protons and seven or eight neutrons. The mass deficit is bad enough—there's about as much energy coming out of nowhere as a small nuke would put out—but I'll leave that to the cosmologists. What's bad is that each of those nuclei is missing a whopping eight electrons, so it forms a wildly unstable carbosilicate intermediary that promptly grabs a shitload of charge out of the nearest electron donor molecules. Then it destabilizes for real, but in the process it's set off a cascade of tiny little acid/base reactions throughout the surrounding hot chemical soup that used to be a human body. Chaitin's body turns red, the kind of dull red of an electric heating element—then it *steams*, bits of his kit melting as his skin turns black and splits open. He begins to topple toward me and I yell and jump away. When he hits the ground he shatters, like a statue made of hot glass.

The next thing I know I'm on my knees on the frozen ground, breathing deeply and trying desperately to tell my stomach to be still. I can't afford to throw up because if I vomit in my face mask I will die, and then I won't be able to tell Alan what kind of mistake he'll be making if he sets off the demolition charge.

This whole world has been turned into a mousetrap: a body-snatching demon, patient and prepared, waiting for us little furry folk with beady black eyes to stick our curious noses inside.

I pick myself up, watching the steamy vapor pour from the ground around the molten depressions my kneepads melted in the permafrost as I take more deep, laborious breaths. Static ebbs and flows in my ears like bacon frying, the distorted sidebands of a transmission counting down the minutes to the artificial sunrise. I try not to look at what's left of Chaitin.

They summoned an infovore: something that eats energy and minds. A thing—I don't know what sort—from a dead cosmos, one where the stars had long since guttered into darkness and evaporated on a cold wind of decaying protons, the black holes dwindling into superstring-sized knots on a gust of Hawking radiation. A vast, ancient, slow thinker that wanted access to the hot core of a youthful universe, one mere billions of years from the Big Bang, poised for a hundred trillion years of profligate star-burning before the long slide into the abyss.

On my feet now, I check my air supply: good for two and a quarter hours. That will see me through—the bomb's going to blow in just over an hour. I look round, trying to work out which way to go. Thoughts are clamoring in my head, divergent priorities—

The thing was hungry. First it did what it was invited to do, sucked the minds and life from the Ahnenerbe's enemies, occupied their bodies, and learned how to pass for human. Then it pulled more of itself through the gate than they'd expected. It's big—far too big to fit through a man-sized gate—but it had access to all the energy it wanted, and all the minds to sacrifice, more than enough power to force it wide open and squirm through into this new, rich cosmos.

The monster they summoned gave the Ahnenerbe more than they asked for. As well as damping the fusion phoenix at the heart of every star, it started to drain energy directly out of spacetime, messing with the Planck constant, feeding on the false vacuum of space itself. Light stretched, grew redder; the gravitational constant became a variable, dropping like a barometer before a storm. Fusion processes in the sun guttered and died, neutrons and protons remaining stubbornly monogamous. The solar neutrino flux disappeared first, though it would take centuries for the sun itself to show signs of cooling, for the radiation-impeded gravitational collapse to a white dwarf core to resume. Meanwhile, the universe began to expand again, prematurely ageing by aeons in a matter of years.

Back to the here-and-now. Here I am with a corpse. And a gun. And the corpse manifestly killed using the gun in my hands. *Shit.* I twiddle the squelch on my radio but get nothing but loud hissing and incoherent bursts of static. What am I going to tell Alan— "Look, I know I appear to have shot one of your men, but you've got to abort the mission"?

I glance up at the sky. It's night, but maybe the sun would be visible if I knew where to look. Visible—and shrunken, farther away than it is back home, for as the creature sucks energy out of spacetime, space itself is getting bigger, and emptier. Losing energy. *Find Alan. Stop the bomb. Get everybody out fast.* It took a lot of energy for the thing to fully open the gate to its original home and bring itself through to this shattered Earth; energy that is no longer available in this drained husk of a universe, energy that it needs if it's to move on to pastures new. About all it's capable of on its own right now was to listen for an invitation—from the terror cell in Santa Cruz—and answer their call. What will it do if we dump more energy into it? Open a gate back to its original home? Expand the gate to *our* Earth? There's a worst-possible-case scenario here that I don't even want to think about—I'm going to have nightmares about it for years, *if* I have any years ahead of me to have nightmares in.

Having dragged its huge, cold presence through to squat in the ruins of the victorious Reich, it settled down to wait: patient, for it has waited for an infinity of infinities already, waiting for a hot, fast thinker to open the gate to the next universe. Focused in one place, it will be able to move far faster this time—no need for a sacrifice of millions to get its attention. Once invited—by the clever stupidity of a terrorist cell, perhaps—it can take possession of a body and, using what it has learned of the nature of humanity from the Ahnenerbe-SS, manipulate those around it. The possessed, its agent on the other side of that first gate, must arrange to open a connection, then find an energy source to crack it wide open, big enough to admit the rest of the eater. Opening a gate wide enough for a human body, with an agent at both ends, would take about as much energy as it had left—the lives of all the remaining Ahnenerbe-SS survivors in this world, hoarded against such an eventual need. But to open a gate so that it can admit an ice giant—a being big enough to carve monuments on the moon and suck dry a universe—will take much more energy: energy gained from either a major act of necromancy or a singularly powerful local source.

I look around. I'm at the foot of a hill; on the other side of it there's a wall, and a couple of pathetic corpses, and half a platoon of SAS specialists. Behind me there's a petrified forest and a castle of shadows, populated with nightmares. (Oh, and a hydrogen bomb that's going to go off in about seventy minutes.) Where is everybody? Strung out between the castle and the gate, that's where.

*Got to tell Alan not to set off the bomb.* I pick up my sack of hands and stagger downhill toward the skeletal trees, feet and ankles tensed with that walking on glass sensation you get when you're afraid there's nothing but black ice underfoot, one hand clutching the basilisk gun at arm's reach. Branches claw at me in the twilight, making me flinch inside my helmet; they snap and tinkle against my visor, rigid bundles of mummified twigs with all the heat sucked out of them. *If there's more than one of the body snatchers here . . .*

I skid and go down on one thigh, hard. Something crunches underfoot, like twigs snapping. I lever myself upright, rub my leg and wince, breath loud in my ears. Looking down I see a hump of frozen brown, a small rabbit or a rat or something else that's been dead for years. *Dead.* I stoop and pick up my bag of severed hands, tagged for identification at a later date. *Wouldn't this be a good time to think about precautions?* In case there are other demons stalking this frozen plain in stolen bodies?

Well, yes. I cast a glance in the direction of the redoubt, racking my brains for a half-forgotten lecture on occult stealth technologies.

Fifteen minutes later—ten precious minutes of which expire in a feverish rush of poking clumsily at a severed ulna and radius with my multitool and a roll of duct tape—I'm standing in the middle of the dead ground in front of the redoubt. Things have clearly gone very pear-shaped indeed. I clutch the talisman like a drowning man and try to figure out what to do now.

(The talisman glows dimly, an eerie blue light chewing away at the fingertips. To get it lit, I used the basilisk gun on a tree stump and thrust it against the glowing coals. The deep incisions in the palm are the red of firelight reflected in freshly spilt blood. I grip the grisly artifact by its exposed wrist bones and hope like hell that it performs as advertised. See, if you stick a phase-conjugate mirror on the base of a Hand of Glory you can make it spit light; but that's a modern perversion of its original function . . .)

Overhead, the stars are going out one by one. The moon is a blood-soaked red disk; shadows are creeping across the landscape, settling across the hills I can glimpse through my night-vision goggles. And something like a fire is burning on the roofline above the last redoubt of the Ahnenerbe-SS: What's going on?

I try the radio again. "Howard to anyone, anyone still out there, please respond." The hissing, frying interference crashes in on my ears, obscuring any answer. I stumble forward on the icy ground just as something that might once have been human dashes around the side of the building, heading in the direction of the gate. It doesn't see me, but someone inside sees it: sparks blossom on the cold ground behind it, and I see brief muzzle flashes coming from a window-slit on the second floor.

It was one of ours originally, but no human being can sprint around a building with their helmet off and backpack missing in a *fimbulwinter* cold enough to freeze liquid oxygen.

The possessed soldier raises something blocky to its shoulder and sprays cartridge cases all over the night. Maybe one or two of the bullets come close to the upstairs window, but if so they don't stop whoever's upstairs from catching it with their next burst: for a moment it capers across the ice, then it flops down and lies still. "Shit," I mutter, and find myself stumbling into a clumsy trot toward the gaping garage door with its welcoming airlock.

Nobody shoots at me; the talisman is doing its job, fogging the senses of anyone who can see me. I skid to a halt just outside, a nasty suspicion blossoming in my mind, and very carefully inspect the threshold. Yup, there it is: a black box taped to the wall, thin wire stretched taut across the threshold at knee level. Some wag has stenciled THIS SIDE TOWARD LIFE INSURANCE CLAIMANT on its case. I very carefully step over the tripwire then try the radio again. "Howard to anyone. What's going on? Who's shooting?"

A crackling whine flattens the answer, but at least this time there *is* one: "Howard! What's your condition? Report." I try to remember who it is, those clipped tones: Sergeant Howe.

"I'm in the garage with a Hand of Glory," I say. I swallow. "It got Chaitin while I wasn't watching him, but I got away—shot it while it was trying to assimilate me. A demon, that is. They take possession if they can touch you—it takes skin-to-skin or electrical contact. There was more than one out here but I'm not sure any are still up. I improvised a stealth talisman to get me back in here; you've got to put me through to Alan, *immediately.*"

"Wait right there." He sounds tense. "You in the garage?"

I try to nod, then answer: "Yeah, I'm in the garage—I spotted the spring surprise in time. Look, this is urgent; we've got to disable the demo gadget before we get out of here. If it blows—"

The outer airlock door edges open. "Get your ass in the airlock *now*, Howard. Close and lock the door. When it cycles, put anything you're carrying down and raise your arms. When the door opens, don't move until I say so. Don't even *breathe* until I say so. Got it?"

"Got it," I say, and open the airlock door. I freeze—then carefully put the Hand of Glory down outside the lock, power down the basilisk gun and isolate the charge circuit, drop the sack of severed hands, and make sure my palmtop is asleep before I look inside the chamber again. I swallow. There's a green spheroid taped to the inner door, a fine wire stretching from one end to the rubberized gasket that seals the lock. Below it, there's another gadget: a thaumometer, a sensor that monitors spatiotemporal disturbances indicative of occult activity. That, too, has a wire vanishing inside the gasket. I swallow again. "I'm stepping inside the lock now," I say. My legs don't want to move. "I'm closing the outer door."

I tell myself I know Alan, and he's not going to do anything stupid. I tell myself that Sergeant Howe is a professional. Locking myself in a room the size of a shower cubicle with a live hand grenade on the end of a string still gives me the cold shudders.

Air hisses through vents and I raise my arms, stiffly forcing the suit to comply. At the last moment I think to turn and make sure that I'm leaning against the side of the lock, not facing the inner door. Then the door clicks—audible, there must be air pressure inside—and swings open. Someone is kneeling outside, pointing a gun at me from behind a body that's sprawled on the floor right in front of the lock.

"Bob." It's Alan. "If that's you, I want you to tell me who else was in the classroom with us."

*Phew.* "It was taught by Sophie, and we were in it with Nick from CESG."

"That's good. And you're still wearing your helmet. That's good, too. Now I want you to turn around slowly, keeping your hands up—that's right. Now, I want you to slowly raise your visor. Hold it—keep your hands still." The guy with the gun keeps it leveled on my face. Mo was right: I never realized you could see the grooves—lands—of a rifle barrel at three meters; it looks huge, large enough to drive a freight train down.

Something jabs at my left leg and I nearly stumble, then: "He's clean," announces someone who was right next to me all the time—I never noticed—and I lower my arms. The guy who's been keeping me covered points his gun at the floor, and suddenly I'm breathing normally again.

"Where's Alan?" I ask. "What's been happening here?"

"I was hoping you could tell me," Alan says in my left ear. I look round and he grins tensely. The grin doesn't reach his eyes, which are the color of liquid oxygen and just as warm. "Tell me *exactly* what happened to you when you went outside. Tell it like your life depends on it."

"Uh, okay." I shuffle away from the lock door and someone—Scary Spice?—swings it shut again.

I spill the beans, including the way Chaitin jumped me. I figure they already know that something's taking over brains and bodies wherever possible. My eyes keep being drawn back to the floor. It's Donaldson, the guy who was speculating about meteorology earlier. He doesn't look real, somehow, as if he ought to get up and walk away in a minute or two, peel off the rubber gore applied by the special effects people and have a laugh with us over a pint. "I figure the whole thing is a trap," I finish. "We were lured here deliberately. Only one of the possessors came through to our world, and it could only control one body at a time, but there may be more here. They're working for, or are part of, something that's not human, but that's had years to study us—to study the survivors from the Ahnenerbe-SS. It took over some useful idiots who tried to summon it from our side in order to use it for a terrorist incident; then it stalked us, kidnapped Mo as bait. It did that because it wants us to provide a power source that'll allow it to expand the gate and push its main body through into our universe. It's a lot bigger than the possessors we've seen so far— it's, like, it's achieved a limited beachhead but it needs to grab an entire harbour from the defenders—us—before it can land the main body of its forces."

"Right." Alan looks pensive. "And how do you think it's going to do this?"

"The demolition gadget. What yield have you set it to?" I ask.

Howe raises an eyebrow. "Tell him," says Alan.

"It's a selective yield gadget," says Howe. "We can set it to anything from fifteen kilotons to a quarter of a megaton—it's a mechanical process, screw jacks adjust the gap between the fusion sparkplug and the initiator charge so that we get more or less fusion output. Right now it's at the upper end of the yield curve, dialled all the way up to city-buster size. What's this got to do with anything?"

"Well." I lick my lips; it's really cold in here now and my breath is steaming. "To open a gate big enough to bring through a large creature like whatever ate this universe takes a whole lot of entropy. The Ahnenerbe did it in this universe by ritually murdering roughly ten million people: information destruction increases entropy. But you can do it in other ways—an H-bomb is a really great entropy *and* energy generator, it minimizes the information content of *lots* of stuff." They look blank: I glare at them. "Look, it's the intersection between thermodynamics and information theory, right? Information content is inversely proportional to entropy, entropy is a measure of how well randomized a system is—that's one of the core assumptions of magic, right? That you can transfer energy between universes via the platonic realm of ordered information—mathematics. I think what this monster has been doing all along was raising enough hell via its minor agents to provoke a response—one in which we'd lash out, giving it all the juice it needs to expand the gate. As it is, the minor gate it yanked Mo through is shrinking; I figure that was all it could manage. It's drained so much energy from this universe already that it had to wait for precisely the right moment before it dared open that one; this place is falling apart, and there may not be enough power for the monster to open even one more minor gate. Have you noticed how the stars are going out and we're getting radio interference? I think what we're seeing is fossil starlight—what's left of this universe may only be a bit larger than the solar system, and it's shrinking at close to light-speed. Give it another few hours and it'll collapse like a soap bubble, taking the ice giant with it. Unless we feed it, or them, or whatever the hell it is, enough energy to shore open the gate to our own world and expand it until they can squeeze through."

"Ah." Alan looks as if he's just swallowed something unpleasant. "So. It's your considered opinion that our best course of action would be to disable the bomb and retire, hmm?"

"That's about the size of it," I agree. "Where did you plant the gadget anyway?"

"Downstairs; but that's a bit of a sore point," Alan comments airily. "The bomb's armed and we've switched over from manual detonation control via the dead man's handle to the internal timer. But there's a catch. You see, Her Majesty's Government doesn't *really* like the idea of leaving armed hydrogen bombs lying around the place without proper supervision. PAL control is fine, and so is a detonation wire and dead man's handle, but these things are designed in case they might get overrun, and we wouldn't want to hand an H-bomb on a plate to some random troublemaker, what?"

Alan begins to pace. Alan pacing, that's a bad sign. "Once we've inserted the initiator, dialled a yield, armed the detonators, punched in the permissive action codes, set the timer, *then* removed the control wires, nothing's going to stop it. Can't even open it up: someone messes with the tamper piece, it calls 'tilt' and the game's over. Y'see, we might be a Soviet Guards Motor Rifle formation that's just captured the bridge it's strapped to. Or a bunch of uglies from the backwoods behind the Khyber Pass. So, as you can understand, even conceding that letting it blow here and now might be a very bad idea, it's going to go. Unless you fancy trying your hand at dissecting a booby-trapped, ticking H-bomb, and I don't recall seeing UXB training on your resumé."

He glances at his watch. "Only another fifty-seven minutes to go, lad. We can probably make it to the gate if we leave in less than half an hour, as long as there aren't too many of the blighters left outside—so I'd hurry up if I was you."

"Could we take it with us?" I ask.

He barks a short laugh. "What, you think they'd thank us for dragging a live quarter-megaton bomb back into one of the most densely populated cities in Europe?"

"They can't stop it then?"

"Take an act of God to stop it now," Howe says with gloomy satisfaction. "Take an act of God to get us all out of here alive, too. Bet you're wishing you hadn't come back!"

I lick my lips, but my tongue seems to have turned to dry leather. Leathery, like one of Brains's weirdly scrambled-in-its-own-shell eggs. Which reminds me: suddenly what I have to do comes crystal clear. "I think I know how to get your people out regardless of whether there are any revenants outside," I say. "Same way I got in here without anyone spotting me. As for the bomb—what if just a bit of the implosion charge goes off prematurely? Say, at one end of it?"

Alan looks at me oddly. "How are you going to do that?"

"Never mind. What happens *if?* If, if. Way I remember it, all nuclear weapons these days use a core of plutonium and a set of shaped charges that interlock around it. When they go off, they have to be really precisely timed or the core doesn't implode properly, and if it doesn't implode it doesn't reach critical mass, and if it doesn't go supercritical it doesn't go bang. Right?" I'm almost bouncing up and down. "There's some stuff I need just outside the airlock—a bag of severed hands, a basilisk gun. I've got the rest of the kit here. How many of us are there upstairs, roundabout, who need to walk out? The sack has enough samples cut from execution victims to make Hands of Glory for everyone— walk right past the lurkers in the forest. *If* someone goes and gets them right now. As for the bomb . . ."

I'm still thinking about the bomb as Sergeant Howe wordlessly ducks into the airlock and I hear the hiss of depressurisation. Ticking, ticking. The bomb's booby-trapped. I need to figure out a way of reaching through the case, reaching past the wires and the polystyrene foam spacers around the plutonium rod, past the surrounding parcels of lithium deuteride wrapped in depleted uranium, through the steel casing of the A-bomb trigger—

Alan is standing in front of me, leaning in my face. "Bob."

"Yeah." *The basilisk gun is the solution. I think . . .*

"Hand of Glory. Tell me what the hell I need to know."

"A Hand of Glory is fabricated from the hand and wrist of someone who has been wrongly executed. A fairly simple circuit is inscribed around the radius and ulna and the fingertips are ignited. What it does is a limited invocation that results in the bearer becoming invisible. In effect. There are variations, like the inversion laser—stick a phase-conjugate mirror on the base and it makes a serious mess of whatever the hand's pointed at—but the original use of the hand is as a disintermediating tool for observer/subject interactions. Or so Eugene Wigner insisted. How many people have you got?"

The airlock door is cycling: Alan crouches, gun leveled on the door. He waves me off to one side impatiently.

It's Howe. No luminous worms behind his face plate; he hefts a lumpy, misshapen sack and my basilisk gun as he steps through the door.

"Seven, plus yourself. You were saying?" Alan asks.

"Give me." I take the sack. *It's like peeling potatoes,* I tell myself, *just like peeling potatoes.* "Anyone got a roll of duct tape? And a pen? Great, now clear the fuck away and give me room to breathe." Just like peeling potatoes, strange vegetables that grow in a soil of horror, watered with blood. A lot of the original bits of folklore surrounding the Hand of Glory are just that. You don't need a candle made of human fat, horse dung, and suchlike, with a wick made of the hair of a hanged man. You don't need fingers from the fetus of a hanged pregnant woman, amputated stealthily at midnight. All you need is a bunch of hands, some wire or solder, a pen, a digital-analogue converter, a couple of programs I carry on my palmtop, and a strong stomach. Well, I can fake the stomach: just tell myself I'm peeling spuds, sticking bits of wire in Mr Potato Head, triggering ghost echoes in a decaying neural network, feeding something arcane. Howe pushes in and insists on copying what I do; it's annoying at first, but monkey-see monkey-do gets results and between us we make short work of the sack. A couple of the hands are washouts but in twenty minutes flat I've got a shrunken bag and a row of ghastly trophies arranged on the guardroom table.

"Here," I say. Scary Spice—who has been shuffling nervously and keeping one eye on the airlock door—jumps.

"What's up?"

Howe watches with silent interest.

I hold up a hand. "Look." Thank Cthulhu for pocket soldering irons: the fingertips ignite neatly, that crypt-glow dancing around them.

Scary Spice looks confused. "Where are you? What's up?" His eyeballs are sliding around like greased marbles; he instinctively raises his gun.

"Safe that!" snaps Howe. He winks in my general direction.

"Hold out your left hand, Scary," I say.

"Okay." He shuts his eyes; I shove the stump of the hand into his glove. "What the fuck *is* this?"

I blink and try to focus on him, but he's slipping away. It's weird; I try to track him but my eyes refuse to lock on. "What you're holding is called a Hand of Glory. While you're holding it, nobody can see you—it works on the possessors outside, too, or I wouldn't be here."

"Uh, yeah. How long's it good for?"

"How the fuck should I know?" I reply. I glance at Howe.

"Put it down *now*," he says. A hand appears on the table and I find I can focus on Scary again. Howe glances at me. "This is a bloody miracle," he says morosely. "Pity we didn't have it a couple of years ago in Azerbaijan." He keys his mike: "Howe to all, we've got a ticket home. Alpha, Bravo, Charlie, everyone downstairs *now*. Captain, you're going to want to see this too."

It's like being at school again, sitting one fucking exam after another, sure that if you don't finish the question in the set time it's going to screw your life. *This* exam, the fail grade is anything short of 100 percent and you get the certificate, with no appeal possible, milliseconds after you put your pen down.

I'm crouching in the basement with Alan and a thing that looks like a steel dustbin on a handcart, if steel dustbins came painted green and neatly labelled THIS WAY UP and DO NOT DROP. I will confess that I'm sweating like a pig, even in the frigid air of the redoubt, because we are now down to about fifteen minutes and if this fails we won't have time to reach the gate.

"Take five," says Alan. "You're doing really well, Bob. I mean that. You're doing *really* well."

"I bet you say that to all the boys," I mutter, turning the badly photocopied page of arming instructions—the pamphlet that comes with the bomb has a blue cardboard cover, like a school exercise book that's been classified top secret by mistake.

"No, really." Alan leans back against the wall. "They got away, Bob. Everyone but us. Maybe you don't think that's a big deal, but they do; they'll remember it for the rest of their lives, and even if we don't follow them they'll be drinking a toast to your memory for a long time to come."

"That's reassuring." I flip another page. I didn't know H-bombs came with user manuals and cutaway diagrams, exploded views of the initiator core. "Look, this is where the pit goes, right?" I point at the page and then at a spot about five centimeters above the base of the dustbin.

"No." Alan moves my hand right up to the top of the bomb casing. "You've got it upside down."

"Well, that's a relief," I say lightly.

"At least, I *think* it's upside down," he says in a worried tone of voice.

"Uh-huh." I move my finger over the diagram. "Now *this* is where the detonation controller goes, right?"

"Yes, that's right," he says, much more reassuringly. I give the green dustbin a hard glance.

Atom bombs aren't that complicated. Back in the late 1970s an American high school physics teacher got together with his class. They designed and built an A-bomb. The US Navy thanked them, trucked it away, added the necessary plutonium, and detonated it down on the test range. The hard bit about building an A-bomb is the plutonium, which takes a specialized nuclear reactor and a chemical reprocessing plant to manufacture and which tends to be kept behind high barbed-wire fences patrolled by guys with guns.

However, atom bombs do have one interesting trait: they go "bang" when you squeeze a sphere of plutonium using precisely detonated explosive lenses. *Conventional* explosives. And if those lenses don't detonate in exactly the right sequence, if you scramble them, you may get a fizzle, but you don't get a firework. It's like an egg, with a yolk (the A-bomb detonator) and a white (the fusion spark plug and other bang-amplifying widgets) inside it.

So here I am, sitting next to a rogue H-bomb with fourteen minutes to run on its clock; and when Alan passes me a magic marker I draw a big fat X on its casing, because I intend to do to this bomb exactly what Brains did to his eggs—scramble it without breaking the shell.

"How many lenses in this model?"

"Twenty. Dodecahedral layout, triangular sections. Each of 'em is a slab of RDX with a concave centre and a berylide-alloy facing pointing inward."

"Gotcha." More chalk marks. RDX is mondo nasty high explosive; its detonation speed is measured in kilometers per second. When they blow, those explosive lenses will punch the beryllium-alloy sheet inward onto a suspended sphere of plutonium about the size of a large grapefruit or a small melon. If you blow them all within a microsecond or so, the shock wave closes around the metallic core like a giant fist, and squeezes. If they go off asymmetrically, instead of squeezing the plutonium until it goes bang, they squirt it harmlessly out the side. Well, harmlessly unless you're standing nearby. A slug of white-hot supercritical plutonium barreling out of a ruptured bomb casing at several hundred meters per second is not exactly fun for all the family. "That puts the top half of the hemisphere about—here."

"Very good. What now?"

"Fetch a chair and some books or boxes or something." I pick up the basilisk gun and begin fiddling with it. "I need to align this on the hemisphere and tape it in position."

When the beryllium-alloy sphere assembles it squishes the plutonium pit inward. Plutonium is about twice as dense as lead, and fairly soft; it's a metal, warm to the touch from alpha particle decay, and it exhibits some of the weirdest heavy-metal chemistry known to science. It exists in half a dozen crystalline forms between zero and one hundred Celsius; what it gets up to inside an imploding nuclear core is anybody's guess.

"Chair."

"Duct tape."

"What next?"

"Get me a cordless drill, a half-inch bit, and a pair of scissors."

At the core of the grapefruit there's a hollow space, and inside the hollow there's a pea-sized lump of weirdly shaped metal alloy, the design of which is a closely guarded secret. When the molten-hot compressed plutonium hits it, it vomits neutrons. And the neutrons in turn start a cascade reaction inside the plutonium; every time a plutonium nucleus is hit by a neutron it wobbles like jelly, splits in two, and emits a bunch more neutrons and a blast of gamma radiation. This happens in a unit of time called a "shake"—about a tenth of a thousandth of a millionth of a second—and every plutonium nucleus in the core will have been blasted into fragments within fifty shakes of the core shockwave hitting the initiator and triggering that initial neutron burst. (*If* it collapses symmetrically.) And maybe a few milliseconds later the devil will be free to dance in our universe.

Twelve minutes to go. I position the chair in front of the bomb. The back of the chair is made of plywood—a real win—so I drill holes in it at the right separation, then get Alan to hold the basilisk box while I chop strips of duct tape off the reel and bind it to the chair immediately in front of the X where I think the explosive lenses lie.

"Bingo." One chair. One basilisk gun—a box with a camcorder to either side—taped to the back of the chair. One ticking hydrogen bomb. The back of my neck itches, as if already feeling the flash of X-rays ripped from the bleeding plasma of the bomb's casing when the pit disassembles in a few scant shakes of Teller's alarm clock. "I'm powering up the gun now." The gun's sensors face the bomb through the holes I've drilled in the chair's back. I switch it on and watch the charge indicator. Damn, the cold doesn't seem to have done the batteries any good. It's still live, but close to the red RECHARGE zone.

"Okay," I say, leaning back. "One more thing to do: we have to trip the observe button."

"Yes, that seems obvious," says Alan. "Um, mind me asking why?"

"Not at all." I close my eyes, feeling as if I've just run a marathon. "The basilisk spontaneously causes about 1 percent of the carbon nuclei in the target in front of it to tunnel into silicon. With one hell of an energy release at the same time, of course."

"But plutonium isn't carbon—"

"No, but the explosive lenses are made of RDX, which is a polyni-trated aromatic hydrocarbon compound. You turn 1 percent of the RDX charge into silicon and it will go bang very enthusiastically indeed. If we offset it to one side like *this*—" I nudge the chair a couple of centimeters "—one side of the A-bomb's explosive lenses predetonate, totally out of sequence, causing a fizzle. Imagine a giant's fist, squeezing the pluto-nium core; now imagine he's left his thumb off the top. Molten pluto-nium squirts out instead of compressing around the initiator and going bang. You get a messy neutron pulse but no supercriticality excursion. Maybe explosive disassembly of the case, and a mess of radiation, but no mushroom cloud."

Alan glances at his watch. "Nine minutes. You'd better be going."

"Nine—what do you mean?"

He looks at me tiredly. "Laddie, unless there's a timer on this basilisk gadget, *someone* has to stay here and pull the trigger. You're a civilian, but I signed up for the Queen's shilling."

"Bullshit!" I glare at him. "You've got a wife and kids. If anyone's dis-posable around here it's me."

"Firstly, I seem to remember you saying you'd do whatever I said be-fore you came along on this road trip. Secondly, you understand what's going on: you're too bloody important to leave behind. And thirdly, it's my job," he says heavily. "I'm a soldier. I'm paid to catch bullets, or neu-trons. You're not. So unless you've got some kind of magic remote con-troller for—"

I blink rapidly. "Let me look at it again," I say.

The basilisk gun is a bunch of customized IC circuits bolted to a pair of digital camcorders. I lean closer. The good news is they have fast in-terfaces. The bad news—

Shit. No infrared. The TV remote control program on my palmtop won't work. I straighten up. "No," I say.

"Get the hell out of here then," says Alan. "You've got six minutes. I'm going to wait sixty seconds after you leave the room, then hit the but-ton." He sounds very calm. "Go on, now. Unless you think losing two lives is better than losing one."

*Shit.* I punch the door frame twice, oblivious to the pain in my wrist.

"Go!" he yells.

Upstairs, I pause in the guardroom, about to ignite one of the two Hands of Glory that are waiting for me on the table. I wonder if I'm far enough away from the bomb. (That American scientist—Harry Dagnian, wasn't it?—who did something similar by accident in the Manhattan Project: dropped a neutron reflector on top of a weapon core during an experiment. He died a couple days later, but a guard just ten feet away wasn't affected.) There's a muffled thud that I feel through the soles of my boots; a split second later I hear a noise like a door slamming.

I hear my pulse racing erratically. I hear it, therefore I am still alive. I heard the explosion, therefore the bomb fizzled. There will be no nuclear fireball to energize the conquest dreams of the ancient evil that lurks in this pocket universe. All I have to do is pick up the Hand and walk back to the slowly evaporating gate before it closes . . .

A minute passes. Then I put down the Hand of Glory and wait for another minute. It's no good. My feet carry me back inside and I fasten down my faceplate, switching to my canned air supply as I head down the corridor that leads to the staircase.

At the top of the stairs I key my microphone. "Alan? Are you there?"

A momentary pause, then: "Right you are." He chuckles hoarsely. "Always knew I'd die in my own bed, laddie." Another pause. "Make sure you're buttoned up before you come downstairs. This isn't a sight most people ever get to see."

# 10
# Inquest

Three days later I am back in London. Most of the intervening time seems to be spent in interview rooms, doing debriefs and going over every last aspect of events. When I'm not talking myself hoarse I am fed institutional food and sleep in a spartan institutional bed. Officer's Mess or something. The flight back to London is an anticlimax, and I go straight from the airport to Alan's hospital bed.

It's in a closed bay off a ward devoted to tropical diseases in one of the big London teaching hospitals. There's a staff nurse on the desk out in front, and a police officer on the door. "Hi," I say. "I'm here to see Alan Barnes."

The nurse barely looks up. "No visitors for Mr Barnes." He goes back to studying someone else's medication chart.

I lean on the front of the nursing station. "Look," I say. "Personal friend *and* coworker. It's visiting hours. Please."

This time the nurse looks at me. "You really don't want to see him," he says. The cop straightens up and takes notice of me for the first time.

I pull my warrant card. "How is he?" I ask.

The nurse exhales sharply. "He's stable for now but we may have to move him to the ICU at short notice; it isn't pretty." He glances at the cop. "We can arrange to call you if there's any change."

I glance at the officer of the law, who is inspecting my warrant card as if it's the clue to a particularly nasty murder: "Are you going to let me in or not?"

The cop looks at me sharply. "You can go in, Mr Howard." She opens the door and steps inside first, not bothering to give me back the card.

"No more than five minutes!" calls the nurse.

It's a small room with no window; fluorescent lights and a trolley bed surrounded by machines that have far too many dials and knobs for comfort. A trolley beside the bed is draining bags of transparent fluid into the arm of the bed's occupant by way of a vicious-looking cannula. The bed's occupant is reclining on a mound of pillows; his eyelids flicker open as I come in. He smiles. "Bob."

"I came as soon as they let me go," I say. I reach into my inner pocket for the card, barely noticing the policewoman behind me tense; when she sees the envelope she relaxes again. "How are you feeling?"

"Like shit." He grins cadaverously. "Like the world's worst-ever case of Montezuma's revenge. Have you been all right, lad?"

"Can't complain much. They haven't given me a chance to talk to Mo, and I spent the first day back being prodded by the witch doctors— I think they liked the color of my bile or something." I'm babbling. *Get a grip.* "Guess there was enough concrete between you and me. Have they let you talk to, uh, Hillary? Is the food okay?"

"Food—" he turns his head to look at the cannula in his arm. His skin is brown and ulcerated and seems to be hanging loose, patchy white flakes falling from the underlying reddish tissue. "Seem to be eating through a hose these days, Bob." He closes his eyes. "Not seen Hillary. Shit, I'm tired. Feverish, too, some of the time." His eyes open again. "You'll tell her?"

"Tell her what, Alan?"

"Just tell her."

The policewoman clears her throat behind me. "Yeah, I'll tell her," I say. Alan doesn't give any sign of showing that he's heard me; he just nodded right off, like an eighty-year-old on Valium. I open the envelope and put the card in it on his bedside table, where he'll see it when he wakes up. If. He always knew he'd die in his own bed. *Tell Hillary?*

I turn and walk through the door, blind to the world. The cop follows me out, shutting it carefully. "Do you know who did that to him, Mr Howard?" she asks quietly.

I stop. Clench my fists behind my back. "Sort of," I say quietly. "They won't be doing it to anyone else, if that's what you're asking. If you'll give me back my card now, I have to go in to the office and make sure someone's told his wife where he is. I take it you'll let her in?"

She glances at the nurse. "Up to him." She nods at me, then some misplaced piece of Metropolitan Police customer relations training kicks in on autopilot: "Have a nice day, now."

I check into the Laundry via the back door. It's three in the afternoon and a light rain is falling: mild breeze from the southeast, cloud cover at 90 percent, a beautiful match for my mood. I head for my cubicle and find it unchanged from when I was last here, more than a week ago: there's a coffee cup containing some amazingly dead dregs, a pile of un-read unclassified memos, and a bunch of yellowing Post-it notes saying *SEE ME* plastered all over my terminal and keyboard.

I drop into the chair in front of the terminal and poke listlessly at the decaying hayrick of email that's cluttering up my user account. Oddly, there doesn't seem to be a lot from more than one day into the trip. That's kind of strange: I should be deluged with stupid nonsense from

HR, requests for software upgrades from the losers in Accounting, and peremptory reports for the GDP of Outer Mongolia in 1928 from Angleton—well, not the latter.

I kick back for a moment and stare at the ceiling. There are a couple of coffee-colored stains up there, relics of who-knows-what mishap, deep in the Precambrian era of Laundry history. Rorschach-like, they call up the texture of Alan's skin: brown, loose, looking burned from the inside out. I glance away. For a moment even the fossil Post-it notes are preferable to thinking about what I have to do next.

Then the door opens. "Robert!" I look round. It's Harriet, and I know something's wrong because Bridget is lurking behind her, face a contemplative middle-management mask, and she's clutching a bunch of blue-covered files. "Where've you been hiding? We've been looking for you for days."

"I don't know if you're cleared," I respond wearily. I think I can see what's coming.

"Would you please come with us?" says Bridget, voicing the order as a request. "We have some things to talk about."

Harriet backs out of the cramped doorway and I haul myself upright and let them march me down the corridor and up the stairs to a vacant conference room, all dusty pine veneer and dead flies trapped between perpetually closed venetian blinds. "Have a seat." There are four chairs at the table, and as I glance round I notice that we seem to have picked up an escort: Eric the Ancient Security Officer, a dried-up prune of a former RAF sergeant whose job is to lock doors, confiscate papers left lying on unoccupied desks, and generally make a pestilential nuisance of himself—a sinecure for the irreformably officious.

"What's this about?" I place both hands palms-down on the table.

"It's about several things, as a matter of fact," begins Harriet. "Your controller and I have been worried for some months now about your timekeeping." She plonks a thin blue file down on the table. "We note that you're seldom in the department before 10 A.M., and your observance of core hours falls short of the standard expected of an employee."

Bridget picks up the tag-team prosecution: "Now, we understand that you're used to working occasional off-shift hours, being called out on those odd occasions when there's a problem with one of the servers. But you haven't been filling out variance form R-70 each time you've put in these hours, and without an audit trail I'm afraid we can't automatically accept requests for time off in lieu. According to our records you've been taking off an average of two unscheduled days per month—which could get us, your supervisors, into serious trouble if Audit Bureau were to get interested."

Harriet clears her throat. "Simply put, we can't cover for you any-more. *In* fact—"

Bridget is shaking her head. "This latest escapade is unacceptable, too. You've absented yourself from work for five consecutive working days without following either the approved sick/leave-of-absence proce-dure or applying to your department head for a holiday variance or even compassionate leave. This sort of thing is not only antisocial—think of the additional work you've made for everybody else who's been covering your absence!—but it's a gross violation of procedures." She pronounces the last phrase with the sort of distaste usually reserved by the tabloid press for ministers caught soliciting on Hampstead Heath. "We simply cannot overlook this."

Harriet nods. "And then there's what Eric found in your mailbox."

By this time my neck is aching as I try to keep my eyes on all three of them at the same time. *What the hell's going on?* Harriet and Bridget ad-ministering a procedural mugging is all very well, and I'm damned if I'll let them plant a written warning on my personnel file without an appeal. But Eric's the departmental security officer. What's he in here for?

"Very bad indeed, young fellow," he quavers. And now Bridget barely tries to conceal a triumphant, somewhat feral grin as she plants a raw printout of an email message on the tabletop. "Subject: Some Notes Toward a Proof of Polynomial Completeness in Hamiltonian Networks." My mind goes blank for a moment, then I remember the black-bag job, Croxley Industrial Estate, the hum of servers at midnight and security guards hiding under their desks. And my stomach goes icy cold.

"What's this about?" asks Bridget.

"I think you've got some explaining to do," opines Eric, peering at me with watery blue eyes like an elderly vulture contemplating a wildebeest that's just made the terminal mistake of drinking from a poisoned water-ing hole.

My stomach feels like ice, but the sense of gathering outrage at the back of my head is like a red-hot band. As I see them watching me with varied degrees of expectancy I feel a flash of raw anger: I press my hands down on the tabletop because I really feel like punching somebody in the face, and that wouldn't be the right way to handle this situation.

"You have no need to know," I say as firmly as possible.

Harriet's smile slips first. "I'm your team leader," she says sternly. "You aren't in a position to tell me what I need to know."

"Fuck that." I stand up. "Minute this, if you're going to start writing it down: I want it noted that I deny all accusations, that my actions are justified. I am not going to be party to a procedural lynch mob held on spurious grounds. You don't have need to know and I don't have permission to tell you. If you want to take this further I insist that you take it up with Angleton."

"Angleton—" Now Bridget's smile has slipped, too. Eric is blinking rapidly, confused. I pick on him.

"Let's put this on Angleton's desk," I say soothingly. "He'll know what to do with it."

"If you say so—" Eric looks uncertain. He's been around so long that he doesn't have to imagine the reasons behind Angleton's mystique: he *knows*. He almost looks afraid.

"Come on."

I grab the papers off the table, yank the door open and march out. Behind me, Bridget protests: "You can't!"

"I bloody can," I snarl over my shoulder, speeding up to a trot as I head for his basement lair. "You bloody see if I can!" I've got a fistful of accusations and a startled Harriet flapping after me: that's all I need. Fucking departmental politics, see where it gets you.

Angleton's outer vestibule: the door gapes open. I barge right in, startling the spotty young geek who's threading microfilm between the Memex's rollers. "Boss!" I call.

The inner door swings open. "Howard. We were just discussing you. Enter."

I slide to a halt on the green carpet, in front of the great olive-colored metal desk. I hold up the papers. "Bridget and Harriet," I say. "Oh, and Eric."

Andy leans against the wall next to Angleton's desk and whistles quietly. "You sure know how to make friends and influence people."

"Silence, please." Angleton leans forward. "Miz Brody. May I ask what you're trying to pin on our young friend here?"

Bridget parks herself on the other side of the desk from Angleton, and leans over him. "Violation of departmental procedures. Security breaches. Misuse of Internet access. Poor timekeeping. Absence without official leave. Breach of protocol and abusive behavior toward a superior amounting to gross misconduct."

"I . . . see." Angleton's voice is cold enough to freeze liquid hydrogen.

Out of the corner of my eye I find Andy trying to catch my eye. He seems to be twitching his cheek in Morse code—telling me to keep my mouth shut.

"He's a loose cannon," Bridget insists, in a Thatcheresque tone of total conviction. "He's a menace. Can't even fill out a time sheet accurately."

"Miz Brody." Angleton leans back, looking up at Bridget across the expanse of his desk. *That's odd, why is he relaxing?* I wonder.

He holds something up. "You appear to have overlooked something." The thing in his hand is small and walnut colored: a tuft of hair sticks out of one end of it, bristly and dry. Bridget inhales sharply. "Howard works for me now. He's on your budget allocation, I agree, but he works for *me*, and you will henceforth confine your relationship with him to issuing monthly payslips and ensuring that his office is not accidentally reallocated, unless you wish to wind up emulating the fate of your illustrious predecessor." He jiggles the thing in his hand.

Bridget's eyes are fixed on the thing. She swallows. "You wouldn't."

"My dear, I assure you that I am an equal-opportunity executioner. Eric!" The elderly security officer shuffles forward. "Please remove Miz Brody from my office before she makes me say something I might regret."

"You *bastard*," she snarls, as Eric places a hand on her shoulder and urges her away from the room. "Just because you think you can go outside channels and talk to the director, don't let that fool you—"

The door shuts behind her. Angleton puts the wizened thing down on his blotter. "Do you think I'm bluffing, Robert?" he asks me, his tone deceptively mild.

I swallow. "Uh-huh. No way. Never."

"Good." He smiles at the shrunken head before him. "Something the pen-pushers never seem to get straight: don't threaten, don't bluff. Isn't that right, Wallace?"

The shrunken head seems to nod, or maybe it's just my imagination. I take a deep breath. "Actually, I was meaning to see you. It's about Alan."

Angleton nods. "He took five hundred rems, boy. They tell me that ten years ago that would probably have been fatal."

"Has anyone told Hillary yet?"

Andy coughs. "I'm going round there in a couple of hours." My expression must be skeptical because he adds, "Who do you think was best man at their wedding?"

"Oh. Okay." I feel an enormous letdown, as if some tension I'd barely been aware of has been released. "Well, then. That's the main thing."

"Not really."

I glance back at Angleton. "There's more?"

"Bad timekeeping." He looks contemplative. "So you visited Alan first off, then came in to work. I'd say you've done a full day's work today already, Howard. Better go home before you're too late."

"Home?" Then I realize. "How long has she been back?"

"Two days." His cheek twitches. "Better hope she isn't angry with you."

*   *   *

As I stick the key in the front door lock, I look up at the roofline—both infinitely familiar and strangely alien. *I've only been away one week*, I tell myself. *What can have changed?*

The front hall is full of petite tank tracks. They're about twenty centimeters wide, covered in dried-up mud, and they run past the hulking Victorian coat rack and the living room door to stop just short of the kitchen. I stumble between them as I close the outer and inner doors, try to find somewhere to stow my bag that isn't covered in leftovers from the retreat from Moscow, and remove my coat.

There's most of an engine block on the kitchen table. Whoever put it there for dissection had the good sense to spread a couple of copies of *The Independent* under it; a headline peeps out from under one oily corner: AMSTERDAM HOTEL GAS BLAST KILLS FOUR. Yeah, right. Depression crashes down on me like a black tide: I suddenly feel very ancient, old beyond my years' span in centuries. The kitchen sink is full of unwashed dishes; I turn on the hot tap and swirl it around in search of a mug that's more or less cleanable, then go rummage in my cupboard for some tea bags.

A new crop of bills has sprouted in the fertile soil of the cork notice board. I'll have to read them sooner or later—later will do. There's a small pile of letters with my name on them in the usual place—half of them look to be junk mail, judging by the glossy envelopes. And there's no water in the kettle. I fill it, then sit down next to the engine block and wait for enlightenment to spring on me. I am, I realize, tired; also depressed, lonely, and afraid. Until a couple of months ago I never saw anyone die; for the past couple of nights I haven't been able to dream about anything else. It's exhausting, physically and emotionally. One of the doctors said something about stress disorders but I wasn't listening properly at the time. I wonder if the engine block belongs to Pinky or Brains: I've got a mind to give them a chewing out over it when they come home. It's antisocial as hell—what if someone wanted to eat lunch in here?

The kettle boils, then clicks off. I sit in silence for a moment, feeling a chill in the air, then stand up to pour a mug of tea.

"Make one for me, too?"

I nearly scald myself but control the kettle in time. "I didn't hear you come in."

"That's okay." She moves a chair behind me. "I didn't hear you come in, either. Been back long?"

"Back in the country?" I'm rummaging in the sink for another mug as my mouth freewheels without human intervention, seemingly autonomous, as if it isn't a part of me. "Only since this morning. I had to visit Alan in hospital first, then I went in to work for a couple of hours. Been in meetings. They've kept me in meetings ever since . . ."

"Did they tell you not to talk about it—to anybody?" she asks. I detect a note of strain in her voice.

"Not . . . exactly." I rinse the mug, drop a tea bag in it, pour on hot water, put it down, and turn round to face her. Mo looks the way I feel: hair askew, clothes slept-in, eyes haunted. "I can talk to you about it, if you like. You're cleared for this by default." I drag another chair out from the table. She drops into it without asking. "Did they tell you what was going on?"

"I—" she shakes her head. "Tethered goat." She sounds faintly disgusted, but her face is a mask. "Is it over?"

I sit down next to her. "Yes. Definitely and forever. It's not going to happen again." I can see her relaxing. "Is that what you wanted to hear?"

She looks at me sharply. "As long as it's the truth."

"It is." I look at the engine block gloomily. "Whose is this?"

She sighs. "I think it belongs to Brains. He brought it home yesterday; I don't know where he got it from."

"I'm going to have words with him."

"Won't be necessary; he said he's going to take it away when he moves out."

"What?"

I must look puzzled, because she frowns: "I forgot. Pinky and Brains are moving out. By the end of the week. I only found out yesterday, when I got back."

"Oh great." I glance at the collection of papers, pinned like butterflies to the corkboard: there's nothing like a change of flatmates to induce feelings of fear and loathing over the phone bill. "That's kind of short notice."

"I think it's been brewing for some time," she says quietly. "He said something about your attitude . . ." she trails off. "Hard to live with, so they're going to leave you to your cozy domesticity, unquote." Her eyes sparkle for a moment, angry and hard. "Know any sensitivity training camps with watchtowers and armed guards? I think he could do with an enforced vacation."

"Him and my line manager, both. At least, my old manager." The mugs of tea have been brewing long enough; I fish the bags out and add milk. "Here. You didn't tell me what else you've been doing."

"Doing?" She stares at me. "I've been passed around in a pressurized plastic sack by a bunch of soldiers, poked and prodded by doctors, grilled by security officers, and packed off home like a naughty little girl. I haven't exactly done much *doing*, if you follow. In fact—" she shakes her head in disgust. "Forget it."

"I can't." I can't meet her eyes, either. I'm staring at a cooling mug of tea, and all I can see are worms of pale light, writhing slowly. "I think this was important, Mo. To people other than us, people who'll sleep better at night now."

"Why. Me." She's gritting her teeth; platitudes won't work.

"Because you were there," I say tiredly. "Because someone in your town was trying to carry out a petty act of terrorism, and summoned up an ancient evil they couldn't control. Because you were close and were thinking the unthinkable on a regular, professional basis. A mind is a dangerous thing to taste, and sometimes—only sometimes—things come out of the woodwork that like the flavour of our thoughts. This particular thing was relying on our stupidity, or on our failure to recognise what it was, and used you as bait to sucker us in. We thought *we* were using *you* as bait, but all the time it was playing us like a fish on a line. In the end, at least five people died because of that mistake, and another is in hospital right now and maybe isn't going to make it."

"Thanks." Her tone of voice is like granite. "Whose mistake was it?"

"Committee decision." I put my mug down and look at her. "If we hadn't come after you, those other guys would still be alive. So I guess, from a purely utilitarian point of view everyone in the Laundry fucked up, all the way down the line, from start to finish. I shouldn't have come after you in Santa Cruz: end of story."

"Is that what you really think?" she asks, wonderingly.

I shake my head. "Sometimes we make mistakes for all the right reasons. If Angleton had run this according to the book, by our wonderful ISO-9000-compliant recipe for intelligence operations in the occult sphere, you'd be dead—and the ice giant would still have come through. We'd *all* have been dead, soon enough."

"Angleton broke the rules? I didn't think he was the type. Dried-up old bureaucrat."

"A vintage that sometimes isn't what it seems."

She stands up. "Why were *you* there?" she asks.

I shrug. "Did you expect me to leave you?"

She looks at me for a moment that feels like eternity. "I didn't know you long enough to guess the answer to that, before. Funny what a crisis teaches you about other people." She holds out a hand. "Brains probably isn't going to get back until seven and I need to go back to my flat in half an hour; give me a hand moving this thing off the table?" She gestures at the engine block.

"Guess so. Um, what are you planning on doing, if I may be so bold?"

"Doing?" She pauses with one hand on the Kettenkrad engine block: "I'm moving the rest of my stuff into Brains's room once he's gone. You didn't think you could get rid of me that easily, did you?" She grins, suddenly. "Want to help me pack?"

# The Concrete Jungle

✧ ✧ ✧

THE DEATH RATTLE OF A MORTALLY WOUNDED TELEPHONE is a horrible thing to hear at four o'clock on a Tuesday morning. It's even worse when you're sleeping the sleep that follows a pitcher of iced margueritas in the basement of the Dog's Bollocks, with a chaser of nachos and a tequila slammer or three for dessert. I come to, sitting upright, bare-ass naked in the middle of the wooden floor, clutching the receiver with one hand and my head with the other—purely to prevent it from exploding, you understand—and moaning quietly. "Who is it?" I croak into the microphone.

"Bob, get your ass down to the office right away. This line isn't secure." I recognize that voice: I have nightmares about it. That's because I work for its owner.

"Whoa, I was asleep, boss. Can't it—" I gulp and look at the alarm clock "—wait until morning?"

"No. I'm calling a code blue."

"Jesus." The band of demons stomping around my skull strike up an encore with drums. "Okay, boss. Ready to leave in ten minutes. Can I bill a taxi fare?"

"No, it can't wait. I'll have a car pick you up." He cuts the call, and *that* is when I start to get frightened because even Angleton, who occupies a lair deep in the bowels of the Laundry's Arcana Analysis Section— but does something far scarier than that anodyne title might suggest—is liable to think twice before authorizing a car to pull in an employee at zero-dark o'clock.

I manage to pull on a sweater and jeans, tie my shoelaces, and get my ass downstairs just before the blue and red strobes light up the window above the front door. On the way out I grab my emergency bag—an overnighter full of stuff that Andy suggested I should keep ready, "just in case"—and slam and lock the door and turn around in time to find the cop waiting for me. "Are you Bob Howard?"

"Yeah, that's me." I show him my card.

"If you'll come with me, sir."

Lucky me: I get to wake up on my way in to work four hours early, in the front passenger seat of a police car with strobes flashing and the driver doing his best to scare me into catatonia. Lucky London: the streets are nearly empty at this time of night, so we zip around the feral taxis and somnolent cleaning trucks without pause. A journey that would normally take an hour and a half takes fifteen minutes. (Of course, it comes at a price: Accounting exists in a state of perpetual warfare with the rest of the civil service over internal billing, and the Metropolitan Police charge for their services as a taxi firm at a level that would make you think they provided limousines with wet bars. But Angleton has declared a code blue, so . . .)

The dingy-looking warehouse in a side street, adjoining a closed former primary school, doesn't look too promising—but the door opens before I can raise a hand to knock on it. The grinning sallow face of Fred from Accounting looms out of the darkness in front of me and I recoil before I realize that it's all right—Fred's been dead for more than a year, which is why he's on the night shift. This isn't going to degenerate into plaintive requests for me to fix his spreadsheet. "Fred, I'm here to see Angleton," I say very clearly, then I whisper a special password to stop him from eating me. Fred retreats back to his security cubbyhole or coffin or whatever it is you call it, and I cross the threshold of the Laundry. It's dark—to save light bulbs, and damn the health and safety regs—but some kind soul has left a mouldering cardboard box of hand torches on the front desk. I pull the door shut behind me, pick up a torch, and head for Angleton's office.

As I get to the top of the stairs I see that the lights are on in the corridor we call Mahogany Row. If the boss is running a crisis team then that's where I'll find him. So I divert into executive territory until I see a door with a red light glowing above it. There's a note taped to the door handle: *BOB HOWARD ACCESS PERMITTED.* So I "access permitted" and walk right in.

As soon as the door opens Angleton looks up from the map spread across the boardroom table. The room smells of stale coffee, cheap cigarettes, and fear. "You're late," he says sharply.

"Late," I echo, dumping my emergency bag under the fire extinguisher and leaning on the door."'Lo, Andy, Boris. Boss, I don't think the cop was taking his time. Any faster and he'd be billing you for brown stain removal from the upholstery." I yawn. "What's the picture?"

"Milton Keynes," says Andy.

"Are sending you there to investigate," explains Boris.

"With extreme prejudice," Angleton one-ups them.

"*Milton Keynes?*"

It must be something in my expression; Andy turns away hastily and pours me a cup of Laundry coffee while Boris pretends it's none of his business. Angleton just looks as if he's bitten something unpleasant, which is par for the course.

"We have a problem," Angleton explains, gesturing at the map. "There are too many concrete cows."

"Concrete cows." I pull out a chair and flop down into it heavily, then rub my eyes. "This isn't a dream is it, by any chance? No? Shit."

Boris glowers at me: "Not a joke." He rolls his eyes toward Angleton. "Boss?"

"It's no joke, Bob," says Angleton. His normally skeletal features are even more drawn than usual, and there are dark hollows under his eyes. He looks as if he's been up all night. Angleton glances at Andy: "Has he been keeping his weapons certification up-to-date?"

"I practice three times a week," I butt in, before Andy can get started on the intimate details of my personal file. "Why?"

"Go down to the armory right now, with Andy. Andy, self-defense kit for one, sign it out for him. Bob, don't shoot unless it's you or them." Angleton shoves a stack of papers and a pen across the table at me. "Sign the top and pass it back—you now have GAME ANDES REDSHIFT clearance. The files below are part of GAR—you're to keep them on your person at all times until you get back here, then check them in via Morag's office; you'll answer to the auditors if they go missing or get copied."

"Huh?"

I obviously still look confused because Angleton cracks an expression so frightening that it must be a smile and adds, "Shut your mouth, you're drooling on your collar. Now, go with Andy, check out your hot kit, let Andy set you up with a chopper, and *read* those papers. When you get to Milton Keynes, do what comes naturally. If you don't find anything, come back and tell me and we'll take things from there."

"But what am I looking for?" I gulp down half my coffee in one go; it tastes of ashes, stale cigarette ends, and tinned instant left over from the Retreat from Moscow. "Dammit, what do you expect me to find?"

"I don't expect anything," says Angleton. "Just go."

"Come on," says Andy, opening the door, "you can leave the papers here for now."

I follow him into the corridor, along to the darkened stairwell at the end, and down four flights of stairs into the basement. "Just what the fuck *is* this?" I demand, as Andy produces a key and unlocks the steel-barred gate in front of the security tunnel.

"It's GAME ANDES REDSHIFT, kid," he says over his shoulder. I follow him into the security zone and the gate clanks shut behind me. Another key, another steel door—this time the outer vestibule of the armory. "Listen, don't go too hard on Angleton, he knows what he's doing. If you go in with preconceptions about what you'll find and it turns out to be GAME ANDES REDSHIFT, you'll probably get yourself killed. But I reckon there's only about a 10 percent chance it's the real thing—more likely it's a drunken student prank."

He uses another key, and a secret word that my ears refuse to hear, to open the inner armory door. I follow Andy inside. One wall is racked with guns, another is walled with ammunition lockers, and the opposite wall is racked with more esoteric items. It's this that he turns to.

"A prank," I echo, and yawn, against my better judgement. "Jesus, it's half past four in the morning and you got me out of bed because of a student prank?"

"Listen." Andy stops and glares at me, irritated. "Remember how you came aboard? That was *me* getting out of bed at four in the morning because of a student prank."

"Oh," is all I can say to him. *Sorry* springs to mind, but is probably inadequate; as they later pointed out to me, applied computational demonology and built-up areas don't mix very well. *I* thought I was just generating weird new fractals; *they* knew I was dangerously close to landscaping Wolverhampton with alien nightmares. "What kind of students?" I ask.

"Architecture or alchemy. Nuclear physics for an outside straight." Another word of command and Andy opens the sliding glass case in front of some gruesome relics that positively throb with power. "Come on. Which of these would you like?"

"I think I'll take this one, thanks." I reach in and carefully pick up a silver locket on a chain; there's a yellow-and-black thaumaturgy hazard trefoil on a label dangling from it, and NO PULL ribbons attached to the clasp.

"Good choice." Andy watches me in silence as I add a Hand of Glory to my collection, and then a second, protective amulet. "That all?" he asks.

"That's all," I say, and he nods and shuts the cupboard, then renews the seal on it.

"Sure?" he asks.

I look at him. Andy is a slightly built, forty something guy; thin, whispy hair, tweed sports jacket with leather patches at the elbows, and a perpetually worried expression. Looking at him you'd think he was an Open University lecturer, not a managerial-level spook from the Laundry's active service division. But that goes for all of them, doesn't it? Angleton looks more like a Texan oil-company executive with tuberculosis than the legendary and terrifying head of the Counter-Possession Unit. And me, I look like a refugee from CodeCon or a dot-com startup's engineering department. Which just goes to show that appearances and a euro will get you a cup of coffee. "What does this code blue look like to you?" I ask.

He sighs tiredly, then yawns. "Damn, it's infectious," he mutters. "Listen, if I tell you what it looks like to me, Angleton will have my head for a doorknob. Let's just say, *read* those files on the way over, okay? Keep your eyes open, count the concrete cows, then come back safe."

"Count the cows. Come back safe. Check." I sign the clipboard, pick up my arsenal, and he opens the armory door. "How am I getting there?"

Andy cracks a lopsided grin. "By police helicopter. This is a code blue, remember?"

I go up to the committee room, collect the papers, and then it's down to the front door, where the same police patrol car is waiting for me. More brown-pants motoring—this time the traffic is a little thicker, dawn is only an hour and a half away—and we end up in the northeast suburbs, following the roads to Lippitts Hill where the Police ASU keep their choppers. There's no messing around with check in and departure lounges; we drive round to a gate at one side of the complex, show our warrant cards, and my chauffeur takes me right out onto the heliport and parks next to the ready room, then hands me over to the flight crew before I realize what's happening.

"You're Bob Howard?" asks the copilot. "Up here, hop in." He helps me into the back seat of the Twin Squirrel, sorts me out with the seat belt, then hands me a bulky headset and plugs it in. "We'll be there in half an hour," he says. "You just relax, try to get some sleep." He grins sardonically then shuts the door on me and climbs in up front.

Funny. I've never been in a helicopter before. It's not quite as loud as I'd expected, especially with the headset on, but as I've been led to expect something like being rolled down a hill in an oil drum while maniacs whack on the sides with baseball bats, that isn't saying much. *Get*

*some sleep* indeed; instead I bury my nose in the so-secret reports on
GAME ANDES REDSHIFT and try not to upchuck as the predawn
London landscape corkscrews around outside the huge glass windscreen
and then starts to unroll beneath us.

REPORT 1: Sunday September 4th, 1892
CLASSIFIED MOST SECRET, Imperial War Ministry,
September 11th, 1914
RECLASSIFIED TOP SECRET GAME ANDES, Ministry of
War, July 2nd, 1940
RECLASSIFIED TOP SECRET REDSHIFT, Ministry of
Defense, August 13th, 1988

My dearest Nellie,
    In the week since I last wrote to you, I have to confess that I
have become a different man. Experiences such as the ordeal I
have just undergone must surely come but once in a lifetime; for
if more often, how might man survive them? I have gazed upon
the gorgon and lived to tell the tale, for which I am profoundly
grateful (and I hasten to explain myself before you worry for my
safety), although only the guiding hand of some angel of grace
can account for my being in a position to put ink to paper with
these words.
    I was at dinner alone with the Mehtar last Tuesday evening—
Mr Robertson being laid up, and Lieutenant Bruce off to Gilgut
to procure supplies for his secret expedition to Lhasa—when we
were interrupted most rudely at our repast. "Holiness!" The runner, quite breathless with fear, threw himself upon his knees in
front of us. "Your brother . . . ! Please hasten, I implore you!"
    His excellency Nizam ul Mulk looked at me with that wicked
expression of his: he bears little affection for his brutish hulk of a
brother, and with good reason. Where the Mehtar is a man of re-
fined, albeit questionable sensibilities, his brother is an uneducated coarse hill-man, one step removed from banditry. Chittral
can very well do without his kind. "What has happened to my
beloved brother?" asked ul Mulk.
    At this point the runner lapsed into a gabble that I could
barely understand. With patience the Mehtar drew him out—
then frowned. Turning to me, he said, "We have a—I know not
the word for it in English, excuse please. It is a monster of the

caves and passes who preys upon my people. My brother has gone to hunt it, but it appears to have got the better of him."

"A mountain lion?" I said, misunderstanding.

"No." He looked at me oddly. "May I enquire of you, Captain, whether Her Majesty's government tolerates monsters within her empire?"

"Of course not!"

"Then you will not object to joining me in the hunt?"

I could feel a trap closing on me, but could not for the life of me see what it might be. "Certainly," I said. "By Jove, old chap, we'll have this monster's head mounted on your trophy room wall before the week is out!"

"I think not," Nizam said coolly. "We burn such things here, to drive out the evil spirit that gave rise to them. Bring you your *mirror*, tomorrow?"

"My—" Then I realized what he was talking about, and what deadly jeopardy I had placed my life in, for the honor of Her Majesty's government in Chittral: he was talking about a Medusa. And although it quite unmans me to confess it, I was afraid.

The next day, in my cramped, windowless hut, I rose with the dawn and dressed for the hunt. I armed myself, then told Sergeant Singh to ready a squad of troopers for the hunt.

"What is the quarry, sahib?" he asked.

"The beast that no man sees," I said, and the normally imperturbable trooper flinched.

"The men won't like that, sir," he said.

"They'll like it even less if I hear any words from them," I said. You have to be firm with colonial troops: they have only as much backbone as their commanding officer.

"I'll tell them that, sahib," he said and, saluting, went to ready our forces.

The Mehtar's men gathered outside; an unruly bunch of hillmen, armed as one might expect with a mix of flintlocks and bows. They were spirited, like children, excitable and bickering; hardly a match for the order of my troopers and I. We showed them how it was done! Together with the Mehtar at our head, kestrel on his wrist, we rode out into the cold bright dawn and the steep-sided mountain valley.

We rode for the entire morning and most of the afternoon, climbing up the sides of a steep pass and then between two towering peaks clad in gleaming white snow. The mood of the party was uncommonly quiet, a sense of apprehensive fortitude settling over the normally ebullient Chittrali warriors. We came at last to a mean-spirited hamlet of tumbledown shacks, where a handful of scrawny goats grazed the scrubby bushes; the hetman of the village came to meet us, and with quavering voice directed us to our destination.

"It lies thuswise," remarked my translator, adding: "The old fool, he say it is a ghost-bedevilled valley, by God! He say his son go in there two, three days ago, not come out. Then the Mehtar—blessed be he—his brother follow with his soldiers. And that two days ago."

"Hah. Well," I said, "tell him the great white empress sent me here with these fine troops he sees, and the Mehtar himself and his nobles, and we aren't feeding any monster!"

The translator jabbered at the hetman for a while, and he looked stricken. Then Nizam beckoned me over. "Easy, old fellow," he said.

"As you say, your excellency."

He rode forward, beckoning me alongside. I felt the need to explain myself further: "I do not believe one gorgon will do for us. In fact, I do believe we will do for it!"

"It is not that which concerns me," said the ruler of the small mountain kingdom. "But go easy on the hetman. The monster was his wife."

We rode the rest of the way in reflective silence, to the valley where the monster had built her retreat, the only noises the sighing of wind, the thudding of hooves, and the jingling of our kits. "There is a cave halfway up the wall of the valley, here," said the messenger who had summoned us. "She lives there, coming out at times to drink and forage for food. The villagers left her meals at first, but in her madness she slew one of them, and then they stopped."

Such tragic neglect is unknown in England, where the poor victims of this most hideous ailment are confined in mazed bedlams upon their diagnosis, blindfolded lest they kill those who nurse them. But what more can one expect of the half-civilized children of the valley kingdoms, here on the top of the world?

The execution—for want of a better word—proceeded about as well as such an event can, which is to say that it was harrowing and not by any means enjoyable in the way that hunting game can be. At the entrance to the small canyon where the woman had made her lair, we paused. I detailed Sergeant Singh to ready a squad of rifles; their guns loaded, they took up positions in the rocks, ready to beat back the monster should she try to rush us.

Having thus prepared our position, I dismounted and, joining the Mehtar, steeled myself to enter the valley of death.

I am sure you have read lurid tales of the appalling scenes in which gorgons are found; charnel houses strewn with calcined bodies, bones protruding in attitudes of agony from the walls as the madmen and madwomen who slew them gibber and howl among their victims. These tales are, I am thankful to say, constructed out of whole cloth by the fevered imaginations of the degenerate scribblers who write for the penny dreadfuls. What we found was both less—and much worse—than that.

We found a rubble-strewn valley; in one side of it a cave, barely more than a cleft in the rock face, with a tumbledown awning stretched across its entrance. An old woman sat under the awning, eyes closed, humming to herself in an odd singsong. The remains of a fire lay in front of her, logs burned down to white-caked ashes; she seemed to be crying, tears trickling down her sunken, wrinkled cheeks.

The Mehtar gestured me to silence, then, in what I only later recognized as a supremely brave gesture, strode up to the fire. "Good evening to you, my aunt, and it would please me that you keep your eyes closed, lest my guards be forced to slay you of an instant," he said.

The woman kept up her low, keening croon—like a wail of grief from one who has cried until her throat is raw and will make no more noise. But her eyes remained obediently shut. The Mehtar crouched down in front of her.

"Do you know who I am?" he asked gently.

The crooning stopped. "You are the royal one," she said, her voice a cracked whisper. "They told me you would come."

"Indeed I have," he said, a compassionate tone in his voice. With one hand he waved me closer. "It is very sad, what you have become."

"It *hurts*." She wailed quietly, startling the soldiers so that one of them half-rose to his feet. I signaled him back down urgently as I approached behind her. "I wanted to see my son one more time . . ."

"It is all right, aunt," he said quietly. "You'll see him soon enough." He held out a hand to me; I held out the leather bag and he removed the mirror. "Be at peace, aunt. An end to pain is in sight." He held the mirror at arms length in front of his face, above the fire before her: "Open your eyes when you are ready for it."

She sobbed once, then opened her eyes.

I didn't know what to expect, dear Nellie, but it was not this: somebody's aged mother, crawling away from her home to die with a stabbing pain in her head, surrounded by misery and loneliness. As it is, her monarch spared her the final pain, for as soon as she looked into the mirror she *changed*. The story that the gorgon kills those who see her by virtue of her ugliness is untrue; she was merely an old woman—the evil was something in her gaze, something to do with the act of perception.

As soon as her eyes opened—they were bright blue, for a moment—she changed. Her skin puffed up and her hair went to dust, as if in a terrible heat. My skin prickled; it was as if I had placed my face in the open door of a furnace. Can you imagine what it would be like if a body were to be heated in an instant to the temperature of a blast furnace? For that is what it was like. I will not describe this horror in any detail, for it is not fit material for discussion. When the wave of heat cleared, her body toppled forward atop the fire—and rolled apart, yet more calcined logs amidst the embers.

The Mehtar stood, and mopped his brow. "Summon your men, Francis," he said, "they must build a cairn here."

"A cairn?" I echoed blankly.

"For my brother." He gestured impatiently at the fire into which the unfortunate woman had tumbled. "Who else do you think this could have been?"

A cairn was built, and we camped overnight in the village. I must confess that both the Mehtar and I have been awfully sick since then, with an abnormal rapidity that came on since the confrontation. Our men carried us back home, and that is where you find me now, lying abed as I write this account of one of the most horrible incidents I have ever witnessed on the frontier.

I remain your obedient and loving servant,<br>Capt. Francis Younghusband

As I finish reading the typescript of Captain Younghusband's report, my headset buzzes nastily and crackles. "Coming up on Milton Keynes in a couple minutes, Mr Howard. Any idea where you want to be put down? If you don't have anywhere specific in mind we'll ask for a slot at the police pad."

*Somewhere specific . . . ?* I shove the unaccountably top-secret papers down into one side of my bag and rummage around for one of the gadgets I took from the armory. "The concrete cows," I say. "I need to take a look at them as soon as possible. They're in Bancroft Park, according to this map. Just off Monk's Way, follow the A422 in until it turns into the H3 near the city centre. Any chance we can fly over them?"

"Hold on a moment."

The helicopter banks alarmingly and the landscape tilts around us. We're shooting over a dark landscape, trees and neat, orderly fields, and the occasional clump of suburban paradise whisking past beneath us — then we're over a dual carriageway, almost empty at this time of night, and we bank again and turn to follow it. From an altitude of about a thousand feet it looks like an incredibly detailed toy, right down to the finger-sized trucks crawling along it.

"Right, that's it," says the copilot. "Anything else we can do for you?"

"Yeah," I say. "You've got infrared gear, haven't you? I'm looking for an extra cow. A hot one. I mean, hot like it's been cooked, not hot as in body temperature."

"Gotcha, we're looking for a barbecue." He leans sideways and fiddles with the controls below a fun-looking monitor. "Here. Ever used one of these before?"

"What is it, FLIR?"

"Got it in one. That joystick's the pan, this knob is zoom, you use this one to control the gain, it's on a stabilized platform; give us a yell if you see anything. Clear?"

"I think so." The joystick works as promised and I zoom in on a trail of ghostly hot spots, pan behind them to pick up the brilliant glare of a predawn jogger, lit up like a light bulb — the dots are fading footprints on the cold ground. "Yeah." We're making about forty miles per hour along the road, sneaking in like a thief in the night, and I zoom out to take in as much of the side view as possible. After a minute or so I see the park ahead, off the side of a roundabout. "Eyes up, front: Can you hover over that roundabout?"

"Sure. Hold on." The engine note changes and my stomach lurches, but the FLIR pod stays locked on target. I can see the cows now, grey shapes against the cold ground — a herd of concrete animals created in 1978 by a visiting artist. There should be eight of them, life-sized Friesians peacefully grazing in a field attached to the park. But something's wrong, and it's not hard to see what.

"Barbecue at six o'clock low," says the copilot. "You want to go down and bring us back a take-away, or what?"

"Stay up," I say edgily, slewing the camera pod around. "I want to make sure it's safe first . . ."

REPORT 2: Wednesday March 4th, 1914
CLASSIFIED MOST SECRET, Imperial War Ministry, September 11th, 1914
RECLASSIFIED TOP SECRET GAME ANDES, Ministry of War, July 2nd, 1940
RECLASSIFIED TOP SECRET REDSHIFT, Ministry of Defense, August 13th, 1988

Dear Albert,
Today we performed Young's double-slit experiment upon Subject C, our medusa. The results are unequivocal; the Medusa effect is both a particle *and* a wave. If de Broglie is right . . .
But I am getting ahead of myself.
Ernest has been pushing for results with characteristic vim and vigor and Mathiesson, our analytical chemist, has been driven to his wits' end by the New Zealander's questions. He nearly came to blows with Dr Jamieson who insisted that the welfare of his patient—as he calls Subject C—comes before any question of getting to the bottom of this infuriating and perplexing anomaly.
Subject C is an unmarried woman, aged 27, of medium height with brown hair and blue eyes. Until four months ago, she was healthy and engaged as household maid to an eminent KC whose name you would probably recognize. Four months ago she underwent a series of seizures; her employers being generous, she was taken to the Royal Free Infirmary where she described having a series of blinding headaches going back eighteen months or so. Dr Willard examined her using one of the latest Roentgen machines, and determined that she appeared to have the makings of a tumor upon her brain. Naturally this placed her under Notification, subject to the Monster Control Act (1864); she was taken to the isolation ward at St Bartholomew's in London where, three weeks, six migraines, and two seizures later, she experienced her first Grand Morte fit. Upon receiving confirmation that she was suffering from acute gorgonism, Dr Rutherford asked me to proceed as agreed upon; and so I arranged for the Home Office to be contacted by way of the Dean.
While Mr McKenna was at first unenthusiastic about the

prospect of a gorgon running about the streets of Manchester, our reassurances ultimately proved acceptable and he directed that Subject C be released into our custody on her own cognizance. She was in a state of entirely understandable distress when she arrived, but once the situation was explained she agreed to cooperate fully in return for a settlement which will be made upon her next of kin. As she is young and healthy, she may survive for several months, if not a year, in her current condition: this offers an unparalleled research opportunity. We are currently keeping her in the old Leprosarium, the windows of which have been bricked up. A security labyrinth has been installed, the garden wall raised by five feet so that she can take in the air without endangering passers-by, and we have arranged a set of signals whereby she can don occlusive blindfolds before receiving visitors. Experiments upon patients with acute gorgonism always carry an element of danger, but in this case I believe our precautions will suffice until her final deterioration begins.

Lest you ask why we don't employ a common basilisk or cockatrice instead, I hasten to explain that we do; the pathology is identical in whichever species, but a human source is far more amenable to control than any wild animal. Using Subject C we can perform repeatable experiments at will, and obtain verbal confirmation that she has performed our requests. I hardly need to remind you that the historical use of gorgonism, for example by Danton's Committee for Public Safety during the French revolution, was hardly conducted as a scientific study of the phenomenon. This time, we will make progress!

Once Subject C was comfortable, Dr Rutherford arranged a series of seminars. The New Zealander is of the opinion that the effect is probably mediated by some electromagnetic phenomenon, of a type unknown to other areas of science. He is consequently soliciting new designs for experiments intended to demonstrate the scope and nature of the gorgon effect. We know from the history of Mademoiselle Marianne's grisly collaboration with Robespierre that the victim must be visible to the gorgon, but need not be directly perceived; reflection works, as does trivial refraction, and the effect is transmitted through glass thin enough to see through, but the gorgon cannot work in darkness or thick smoke. Nobody has demonstrated a physical mechanism for gorgonism that doesn't involve an unfortunate creature afflicted with the characteristic tumors. Blinding a gorgon appears to control the effect, as does a sufficient visual distortion. So why does Ernest insist on treating a clearly biological phenomenon as one of the greatest mysteries in physics today?

"My dear fellow," he explained to me the first time I asked, "how did Madame Curie infer the existence of radioactivity in radium-bearing ores? How did Wilhelm Roentgen recognize X-rays for what they were? Neither of those forms of radiation arose within our current understanding of magnetism, electricity, or light. They had to be something else. Now, our children of Medusa apparently need to behold a victim in order to injure them—but how is the effect transmitted? We know, unlike the ancient Greeks, that our eyes work by focusing ambient light on a membrane at their rear. They used to think that the gorgons shone forth beams of balefire, as if to set in stone whatever they alighted on. But we know that cannot be true. What we face is nothing less than a wholly new phenomenon. Granted, the gorgon effect only changes whatever the medusoid can see directly, but we know the light reflected from those bodies isn't responsible. And Lavoisier's calorimetric experiments—before he met his unfortunate end before the looking glass of l'Executrice—proved that actual atomic transmutation is going on! So what on earth mediates the effect? How can the act of observation, performed by an unfortunate afflicted with gorgonism, transform the nuclear structure?"

(By nuclear structure he is of course referring to the core of the atom, as deduced by our experiments last year.)

Then he explained how he was going to seat a gorgon on one side of a very large device he calls a cloud chamber, with big magnetic coils positioned above and below it, to see if there is some other physical phenomenon at work.

I can now reveal the effects of our team's experimentation. Subject C is cooperating in a most professional manner, but despite Ernest's greatest efforts the cloud chamber bore no fruit— she can sit with her face pressed up against the glass window on one side, and blow a chicken's egg to flinders of red-hot pumice on the target stand, but no ionization trail appears in the saturated vapor of the chamber. Or rather, I should say no direct trail appears. We had more success when we attempted to replicate other basic experiments. It seems that the gorgon effect is a continuously variable function of the illumination of the target, with a sharply defined lower cut-off and an upper limit! By interposing smoked glass filters we have calibrated the efficiency with which Subject C transmutes the carbon nuclei of a target into silicon, quite accurately. Some of the new electrostatic counters I've been working on have proven fruitful: secondary radiation, including gamma rays and possibly an elusive neutral particle, are given off by the target, and indeed our cloud chamber has produced an excellent picture of radiation given off by the target.

Having confirmed the calorimetric and optical properties of the effect, we next performed the double-slit experiment upon a row of targets (in this case, using wooden combs). A wall with two thin slits is interposed between the targets and our subject, whose gaze was split in two using a binocular arrangement of prisms. A lamp positioned between the two slits, on the far side of the wall from our subject, illuminates the targets: as the level of illumination increases, a pattern of alternating gorgonism was produced! This exactly follows the constructive reinforcement and destruction of waves Professor Young demonstrated with his examination of light corpuscles, as we are now supposed to call them. We conclude that gorgonism is a wave effect of some sort—and the act of observation is intimately involved, although on first acquaintance this is such a strange conclusion that some of us were inclined to reject it out of hand.

We will of course be publishing our full findings in due course; I take pleasure in attaching a draft of our paper for your interest. In any case, you must be wondering by now just what the central finding is. This is not in our paper yet, because Dr Rutherford is inclined to seek a possible explanation before publishing; but I regret to say that our most precise calorimetric analyzes suggest that your theory of mass/energy conservation is being violated—not on the order of ounces of weight, but by enough to detect. Carbon atoms are being transformed into silicon ions with an astoundingly high electropositivity, which can be accounted for if we assume that the effect is creating nuclear mass from somewhere. Perhaps you, or your new colleagues at the Prussian Academy, can shed some light on the issue? We are most perplexed, because if we accept this result we are forced to accept the creation of new mass *ab initio*, or treat it as an experimental invalidation of your general theory of relativity.

> Your good friend,
> Hans Geiger

A portrait of the agent as a (confused) young man:

Picture me, standing in the predawn chill in a badly mown field, yellowing parched grass up to the ankles. There's a wooden fence behind me, a road on the other side of it with the usual traffic cams and streetlights, and a helicopter in police markings parked like a gigantic cyborg beetle in the middle of the roundabout, bulging with muscular-looking sensors and nitesun floodlights and making a racket like an explosion in a noise factory. Before me there's a field full of concrete cows, grazing safely and placidly in the shadow of some low trees which are barely visible in the overspill from the streetlights. Long shadows stretch out from the fence, darkness exploding toward the ominous lump at the far end of the paddock. It's autumn, and dawn isn't due for another thirty minutes. I lift my modified camcorder and zoom in on it, thumbing the record button.

The lump looks a little like a cow that's lying down. I glance over my shoulder at the chopper, which is beginning to spool up for takeoff; I'm pretty sure I'm safe here but I can't quite suppress a cold shudder. On the other side of the field—

"Datum point: Bob Howard, Bancroft Park, Milton Keynes, time is zero seven fourteen on the morning of Tuesday the eighteenth. I have counted the cows and there are nine of them. One is prone, far end of paddock, GPS coordinates to follow. Preliminary surveillance indicated no human presence within a quarter kilometre and residual thermal yield is below two hundred Celsius, so I infer that it is safe to approach the target."

One unwilling foot goes down in front of another. I keep an eye on my dosimeter, just in case: there's not going to be much secondary radiation hereabouts, but you can never tell. The first of the cows looms up at me out of the darkness. She's painted black and white, and this close up there's no mistaking her for a sculpture. I pat her on the nose. "Stay cool, Daisy." I should be safely tucked up in bed with Mo—but she's away on a two-week training seminar at Dunwich and Angleton got a bee in his bonnet and called a code blue emergency. The cuffs of my jeans are damp with dew, and it's cold. I reach the next cow, pause, and lean on its rump for a zoom shot of the target.

"Ground zero, range twenty meters. Subject is bovine, down, clearly terminal. Length is roughly three meters, breed . . . unidentifiable. The grass around it is charred but there's no sign of secondary combustion." I dry-swallow. "Thermal bloom from abdomen." There's a huge rip in its belly where the boiling intestinal fluids exploded, and the contents are probably still glowing red-hot inside.

I approach the object. It's clearly the remains of a cow; equally clearly it has met a most unpleasant end. The dosimeter says it's safe—most of the radiation effects from this sort of thing are prompt, there are minimal secondary products, luckily—but the ground underneath is scorched and the hide has blackened and charred to a gritty, ashlike consistency. There's a smell like roast beef hanging in the air, with an unpleasant undertang of something else. I fumble in my shoulder bag and pull out a thermal probe, then, steeling myself, shove the sharp end in through the rip in the abdomen. I nearly burn my hand on the side as I do so—it's like standing too close to an open oven.

"Core temperature two six six, two six seven . . . stable. Taking core samples for isotope ratio checks." I pull out a sample tube and a sharp probe and dig around in the thing's guts, trying to tease a chunk of ashy, charred meat loose. I feel queasy: I like a well-cooked steak as much as the next guy, but there's something deeply wrong about this whole scene. I try not to notice the exploded eyeballs or the ruptured tongue bursting through the blackened lips. This job is quite gross enough as it is without adding my own dry heaves to the mess.

Samples safely bottled for analysis, I back away and walk in a wide circle around the body, recording it from all angles. An open gate at the far end of the field and a trail of impressions in the ground completes the picture. "Hypothesis: open gate. Someone let Daisy in, walked her to this position near the herd, then backed off. Daisy was then illuminated and exposed to a class three or better basilisk, whether animate or simulated. We need a plausible disinformation pitch, forensics workover of the paddock gate and fence—check for exit signs and footprints—and some way of identifying Daisy to see which herd she came from. If any livestock is reported missing over the next few days that would be a useful indicator. Meanwhile, core temperature is down to under five hundred Celsius. That suggests the incident happened at least a few hours ago—it takes a while for something the size of a cow to cool down that far. Since the basilisk has obviously left the area and there's not a lot more I can do, I'm now going to call in the cleaners. End."

I switch off the camcorder, slide it into my pocket, and take a deep breath. The next bit promises to be even less pleasant than sticking a thermocouple in the cow's arse to see how long ago it was irradiated. I pull out my mobile phone and dial 999. "Operator? Police dispatch, please. Police dispatch? This is Mike Tango Five, repeat, Mike Tango Five. Is Inspector Sullivan available? I have an urgent call for him . . ."

REPORT 3: Friday October 9th, 1942
CLASSIFIED TOP SECRET GAME ANDES, Ministry of
War, October 9th, 1942
RECLASSIFIED TOP SECRET REDSHIFT, Ministry of
Defense, August 13th, 1988

ACTION THIS DAY:
Three reports have reached SOE Department Two, office
337/42, shedding new light on the recent activities of Dr Ing
Professor Gustaf Von Schachter in conjunction with RSHA Amt.
3 and the inmates of the Holy Nativity Hospital for the Incurably
Insane.

Our first report ref. 531/892-(i) concerns the cessation of action by a detached unit of RSHA Amt. 3 Group 4 charged with
termination of imbeciles and mental defectives in Frankfurt as
part of the Reich's ongoing eugenics program. An agent in place
(code: GREEN PIGEON) overheard two soldiers discussing the
cessation of euthanasia operations in the clinic in negative terms.
Herr Von Schachter had, as of 24/8/42, acquired a Führer Special
Order signed either by Hitler or Borman. This was understood by
the soldiers to charge him with the authority to requisition any
military resources not concerned with direct security of the Reich
or suppression of resistance, and to override orders with the effective authority of an *obergruppenführer*. This mandate runs in conjunction with his existing authority from Dr Wolfram Sievers,
who is believed to be operating the Institute for Military
Scientific Research at the University of Strasbourg and the processing centre at Natzweiler concentration camp.

Our second report ref. 539/504-(i) concerns prescriptions dis-
pensed by a pharmacy in Frankfurt for an unnamed doctor from
the Holy Nativity Hospital. The pharmaceutical assistant at this
dispensary is a sympathizer operated by BLUE PARTRIDGE and
is considered trustworthy. The prescriptions requisitioned were
unusual in that they consisted of bolus preparations for intrathe-
cal (base of cranium) injection, containing colchicine, an extract
of catharanthides, and morphine. Our informant opined that this
is a highly irregular preparation which might be utilized in the
treatment of certain brain tumors, but which is likely to cause
excruciating pain and neurological side effects (ref. GAME AN-
DES) associated with induction of gorgonism in latent individuals suffering an astrocytoma in the cingulate gyrus.

Our final report ref. 539/504-(ii) comes from the same informant and confirms ominous preparatory activities in the Holy Nativity Hospital grounds. The hospital is now under guard by soldiers of Einsatzgruppen 4. Windows have been whitewashed, *mirrors* are being removed (our emphasis) or replaced with one-way observation glass, and lights in the solitary cells rewired for external control from behind two doors. Most of the patients have disappeared, believed removed by Group 4 soldiers, and rumors are circulating of a new area of disturbed earth in the countryside nearby. Those patients who remain are under close guard.

**Conclusion**: The preparation referenced in 539/504-(i) has been referred to Special Projects Group ANDES, who have verified against records of the suppressed Geiger Committee that Von Schachter is experimenting with drugs similar to the catastrophic Cambridge IV preparation. Given his associate Sievers's influence in the Ahnenerbe-SS, and the previous use of the Holy Nativity Hospital for the Incurably Insane as a secondary centre for the paliative care of patients suffering seizures and other neuraesthenic symptoms, it is believed likely that Von Schachter intends to induce and control gorgonism for military purposes in explicit violation of the provisions for the total suppression of stoner weapons laid out in Secret Codicil IV to the Hague Convention (1919).

**Policy Recommendation**: This matter should be escallated to JIC as critical with input from SOE on the feasibility of a targeted raid on the installation. If allowed to proceed, Von Schachter's program shows significant potential for development into one of the rumoured *Vertlesgunswaffen* programs for deployment against civilian populations in free areas. A number of contingency plans for the deployment of gorgonism on a mass observation basis have existed in a MOW file since the early 1920s and we must now consider the prospects for such weapons to be deployed against us. We consider essential an immediate strike against the most advanced development centres, coupled with a strong reminder through diplomatic back channels that failure to comply with all clauses (secret and overt) of the Hague Convention *will* result in an allied retalliatory deployment of poison gas against German civilian targets. We cannot run the risk of class IV basilisks being deployed in conjunction with strategic air power . . .

By the time I roll into the office, four hours late and yawning with sleep deprivation, Harriet is hopping around the common room as if her feet are on fire, angrier than I've ever seen her before. Unfortunately, according to the matrix management system we operate she's my boss for 30 percent of the time during which I'm a technical support engineer. (For the other 70 percent I report to Angleton and I can't really tell you *what* I am except that it involves being yanked out of bed at zero four hundred hours to answer code blue alerts.)

Harriet is a back-office suit: mousy and skinny, forty-something, and dried up from spending all those years devising forms in triplicate with which to terrorize field agents. People like Harriet aren't supposed to get excited about anything. The effect is disconcerting, like opening a tomb and finding a break-dancing mummy.

"Robert! Where on earth have you been? What kind of time do you call this? McLuhan's been waiting on you—you were supposed to be here for the licence policy management committee meeting two hours ago!"

I yawn and sling my jacket over the coat rack next to the "C" department coffee station. "Been called out," I mumble. "Code blue alert. Just got back from Milton Keynes."

"Code blue?" she asks, alert for a slip. "Who signed off on it?"

"Angleton." I hunt around for my mug in the cupboard over the sink, the one with the poster on the front that says CURIOUS EYES COST LIVES. The coffee machine is mostly empty, full of black tarry stuff alarmingly similar to the toxic waste they make roads out of. I hold it under the tap and rinse. "His budget, don't worry about it. Only he pulled me out of bed at four in the morning and sent me off to—" I put the jug down to refill the coffee filter "—never mind. It's cleared."

Harriet looks as if she's bitten into a biscuit and found half a beetle inside. I'm pretty sure that it's not anything special; she and her boss Bridget simply have no higher goal in life than trying to cut everyone else down so they can look them in the eye. Although, to be fair, they've been acting more cagy than usual lately, hiding out in meetings with strange suits from other departments. It's probably just part of their ongoing game of Bureaucracy, whose goal is the highest stakes of all—a fully vested Civil Service pension and early retirement. "What was it about?" she demands.

"Do you have GAME ANDES REDSHIFT clearance?" I ask. "If not, I can't tell you."

"But you were in Milton Keynes," she jabs. "You told me that."

"Did I?" I roll my eyes. "Well, maybe, and maybe not. I couldn't possibly comment."

"What's so interesting about Milton Keynes?" she continues.

"Not much." I shrug. "It's made of concrete and it's very, very boring."

She relaxes almost imperceptibly. "Make sure you get all the paperwork filed and billed to the right account," she tells me.

"I will have before I leave this afternoon at two," I reply, rubbing in the fact that I'm on flexitime; Angleton's a much more alarming, but also understanding, manager to work for. Due to the curse of matrix management I can't weasel out completely from under Bridget's bony thumb, but I must confess I get a kick out of having my other boss pull rank on her. "What was this meeting about?" I ask slyly, hoping she'll rise to it.

"You should know, you're the administrator who set up the mailing list," she throws right back at me. *Oops.* "Mr McLuhan's here to help us. He's from Q Division, to help us prepare for our Business Software Alliance audit."

"Our—" I stop dead and turn to face her, the coffee machine gurgling at my back. "Our audit with *who?*"

"The Business Software Alliance," she says smugly. "CESG outsourced our COTS application infrastructure five months ago contingent on us following official best practices for ensuring quality and value in enterprise resource management. As you were *too busy* to look after things, Bridget asked Q Division to help out. Mr McLuhan is helping us sort out our licencing arrangements in line with guidelines from Procurement. He says he's able to run a full BSA-certified audit on our systems and help us get our books in order."

"Oh," I say, very calmly, and turn around, mouthing the follow-on *shit* silently in the direction of the now-burbling percollator. "Have you ever been through a BSA audit before, Harriet?" I ask curiously as I scrub my mug clean, inside and out.

"No, but they're here to help us audit our—"

"They're funded by the big desktop software companies," I say, as calmly as I can. "They do that because they view the BSA as a *profit centre.* That's because the BSA or their subcontractors—and that's what Q Division will be acting as, they get paid for running an audit if they find anything out of order—come in, do an audit, look for *anything* that isn't currently licensed—say, those old machines in D3 that are still running Windows 3.1 and Office 4, or the Linux servers behind Eric's desk that keep the departmental file servers running, not to mention the FreeBSD box running the Daemonic Countermeasures Suite in Security—and demand an upgrade to the latest version under threat of lawsuit. Inviting them in is like throwing open the doors and inviting the Drugs Squad round for a spliff."

"They said they could track down all our installed software and offer us a discount for volume licensing!"

"And how precisely do you think they'll do that?" I turn round and stare at her. "They're going to want to install snooping software on our LAN, and then read through its take." I take a deep breath. "You're going to have to get him to sign the Official Secrets Act so that I can formally notify him that if he thinks he's going to do that I'm going to have him sectioned. Part Three. Why do you *think* we're still running old copies of Windows on the network? Because we can't afford to replace them?"

"He's already signed Section Three. And anyway, you said you didn't have time," she snaps waspishly. "I asked you five weeks ago, on Friday! But you were too busy playing secret agents with your friends downstairs to notice anything as important as an upcoming audit. This wouldn't have been necessary if you had time!"

"Crap. Listen, we're running those old junkers because they're so old and rubbish that they can't catch half the proxy Internet worms and macro viruses that are doing the rounds these days. BSA will insist we replace them with stonking new workstations running Windows XP and Office XP and dialing into the Internet every six seconds to snitch on whatever we're doing with them. Do you *really* think Mahogany Row is going to clear that sort of security risk?"

That's a bluff—Mahogany Row retired from this universe back when software still meant silk unmentionables—but she isn't likely to know that, merely that I get invited up there these days. (Nearer my brain-eating God to thee . . .)

"As for the time thing, get me a hardware budget and a tech assistant who's vetted for level five Laundry IT operations and I'll get it seen to. It'll only cost you sixty thousand pounds or so in the first year, plus a salary thereafter." Finally, *finally*, I get to pull the jug out of the coffee machine and pour myself a mug of wake-up. "That's better."

She glances at her watch. "Are you going to come along to the meeting and help explain this to everybody then?" she asks in a tone that could cut glass.

"No." I add cow juice from the fridge that wheezes asthmatically below the worktop. "It's a public/private partnership fuck-up, film at eleven. Bridget stuck her foot in it out of her own free will: if she wants me to pull it out for her she can damn well ask. Besides, I've got a code blue report meeting with Angleton and Boris and Andy and that trumps administrative make-work any day of the week."

"Bastard," she hisses.

"Pleased to be of service." I pull a face as she marches out the room and slams the door. "Angleton. Code blue. Jesus." All of a sudden I remember the modified camcorder in my jacket pocket. "Shit, I'm running late . . ."

REPORT 4: Tuesday June 6th, 1989
CLASSIFIED TOP SECRET GAME ANDES REDSHIFT,
Ministry of Defense, June 6th, 1989

ABSTRACT: Recent research in neuroanatomy has characterised the nature of the stellate ganglial networks responsible for gorgonism in patients with advanced astrocytoma affecting the cingulate gyrus. Tests combining the "map of medusa" layout with appropriate video preprocessing inputs have demonstrated the feasibility of mechanical induction of the medusa effect.

Progress in the emulation of dynamically reconfigurable hidden-layer neural networks using FPGA (fully programmable gate array) technology, combined with real-time digital video signal processing from binocular high-resolution video cameras, is likely within the next five years to allow us to download a "medusa mode" into suitably prepared surveillance CCTV cameras, allowing real-time digital video monitoring networks to achieve a true line-of-sight look-to-kill capability. Extensive safety protocols are discussed which must be implemented before this technology can be deployed nationally, in order to minimize the risk of misactivation.

Projected deployment of CCTV monitoring in public places is estimated to result in over one million cameras *in situ* in British mainland cities by 1999. Coverage will be complete by 2004–06. Anticipated developments in internetworking and improvements in online computing bandwidth suggest for the first time the capacity of achieving a total coverage defense-in-depth against any conceivable insurgency. The implications of this project are discussed, along with its possible efficacy in mitigating the consequences of CASE NIGHTMARE GREEN in September 2007. . . .

Speaking of Mahogany Row, Angleton's picked the boardroom with the teak desk and the original bakelite desk fittings, and frosted windows onto the corridor, as the venue for my debriefing. He's sitting behind the desk tapping his bony fingers, with Andy looking anxious and Boris imperturbable when I walk in and flip the red MEETING light on.

"Home movies." I flip the tape on the desktop. "What I saw on my holiday." I put my coffee mug down on one of the disquietingly soft leather mats before I yawn, just in case I spill it. "Sorry, been up for hours. What do you want to know?"

"How long had it been dead?" asks Andy.

I think for a moment. "I'm not sure—have to call Pathology if you want a hard answer, I'm afraid, but clearly for some time when I found it after zero seven hundred. It had cooled to barely oven temperature."

Angleton is watching me like I'm a bug under a microscope. It's not a fun sensation. "Did you read the files?" he asks.

"Yes." Before I came up here I locked them in my office safe in case a busy little Tom, Dick, or Harriet decided to do some snooping. "I'm really going to sleep well tonight."

"The basilisk, is found." Boris.

"Um, no," I admit. "It's still in the wild. But Mike Williams said he'd let me know if they run across it. He's cleared for OSA-III, he's our liaison in—"

"How many traffic cameras overlooked the roundabout?" Angleton asks almost casually.

"Oh—" I sit down hard. "Oh shit. *Shit.*" I feel shaky, very shaky, guts doing the tango and icy chills running down the small of my back as I realize what he's trying to tell me without saying it out loud, on the record.

"That's why I sent you," he murmurs, waving Andy out of the room on some prearranged errand. A moment later Boris follows him. "You're not supposed to get yourself killed, Bob. It looks bad on your record."

"Oh shit," I repeat, needle stuck, sample echoing, as I realize how close to dying I may have been. And the crew of that chopper, and everyone else who's been there since, and—

"Half an hour ago someone vandalized the number seventeen traffic camera overlooking Monk's Road roundabout three: put a .223 bullet through the CCD enclosure. Drink your coffee, there's a good boy, do try not to spill it everywhere."

"One of ours." It comes out as a statement.

"Of course." Angleton taps the file sitting on the desk in front of him—I recognize it by the dog-ear on the second page, I put it in my office safe only ten minutes ago—and looks at me with those scary grey eyes of his. "So. The public at large being safe for the moment, tell me what you can deduce."

"Uh." I lick my lips, which have gone as dry as old boot leather. "Some time last night somebody let a cow into the park and used it for target practice. I don't know much about the network topology of the MK road traffic-control cams, but my possible suspects are, in order: someone with a very peculiar brain tumor, someone with a stolen stoner weapon—like the one I qualified for under OGRE REALITY—or someone with access to whatever GAME ANDES REDSHIFT gave birth to.

And, going from the questions you're asking, if it's GAME ANDES REDSHIFT it's unauthorized."

He nods, very slightly.

"We're in deep shit then," I say brightly and throw back the last mouthful of coffee, spoiling the effect slightly by nearly coughing my guts up immediately afterward.

"Without a depth-gauge," he adds drily, and waits for my coughing fit to subside. "I've sent Andrew and Mr B down to the stacks to pull out another file for you to read. Eyes only in front of witnesses, no note-taking, escort required. While they're signing it out I'd like you to write down in your own words everything that happened to you this morning so far. It'll go in a sealed file along with your video evidence as a deposition in case the worst happens."

"Oh shit." I'm getting tired of saying this. "It's internal?"

He nods.

"CPU business?"

He nods again, then pushes the antique portable manual typewriter toward me. "Start typing."

"Okay." I pick up three sheets of paper and some carbons and begin aligning their edges. "Consider me typing already."

**REPORT 5: Monday December 10th, 2001**
**CLASSIFIED TOP SECRET GAME ANDES REDSHIFT,**
Ministry of Defense, December 10th, 2001
**CLASSIFIED TOP SECRET MAGINOT BLUE STARS,**
Ministry of Defense, December 10th, 2001

**Abstract**: This document describes progress to date in establishing a defensive network capable of repelling wide-scale incursions by reconfiguring the national closed-circuit television surveillance network as a software-controlled look-to-kill multi-headed basilisk. To prevent accidental premature deployment or deliberate exploitation, the SCORPION STARE software is not actually loaded into the camera firmware. Instead, reprogrammable FPGA chips are integrated into all cameras and can be loaded with SCORPION STARE by authorised MAGINOT BLUE STARS users whenever necessary.

. . .

**Preamble**: It has been said that the US Strategic Defense Initiative Organization's proposed active ABM defense network will require the most complex software ever developed, characterised by a complexity metric of >100 MLOC and heavily criticized by various organizations (see footnotes [1][2][4]) as unworkable and likely to contain in excess of a thousand severity-1 bugs at initial deployment. Nevertheless, the architectural requirements of MAGINOT BLUE STARS dwarf those of the SDIO infrastructure. To provide coverage of 95 percent of the UK population we require a total of 8 million digitally networked CCTV cameras (terminals). Terminals in built-up areas may be connected via the public switched telephone network using SDSL/VHDSL, but outlying systems may use mesh network routing over 802.11a to ensure that rural areas do not provide a pool of infectious carriers for demonic possession. TCP/IP Quality of Service issues are discussed below, along with a concrete requirement for IPv6 routing and infrastructure that must be installed and supported by all Internet Service Providers no later than 2004.

There are more than ninety different CCTV architectures currently on sale in the UK, many of which are imported and cannot be fitted with FPGAs suitable for running the SCORPION STARE basilisk neural network prior to installation. Data Disclosure Orders served under the terms of the Regulation of Investigatory Powers Act (2001) serve to gain access to camera firmware, but in many regions upgrades to Level 1 MAGINOT BLUE STARS compliance is behind schedule due to noncompliance by local police forces with what are seen as unreasonable Home Office requests. Unless we can achieve a 340 percent compliance improvement by 2004, we will fail to achieve the target saturation prior to September 2007, when CASE NIGHTMARE GREEN is due.

. . .

Installation has currently been completed only in limited areas; notably Inner London ("Ring of Steel" for counter-terrorism surveillance) and Milton Keynes (advanced next-generation MAN with total traffic management solution in place). Deployment is proceeding in order of population density and potential for catastrophic demonic takeover and exponential burn through built-up areas . . .

. . .

**Recommendation**: One avenue for ensuring that all civilian CCTV equipment is SCORPION STARE compatible by 2006 is to exploit an initiative of the US National Security Agency for our own ends. In a bill ostensibly sponsored by Hollywood and music industry associations (MPAA and RIAA: see also CDBTPA), the NSA is ostensibly attempting to legislate support for Digital Rights Management in all electronic equipment sold to the public. The implementation details are not currently accessible to us, but we believe this is a stalking-horse for requiring chip manufacturers to incorporate on-die FPGAs in the one million gate range, reconfigurable in software, initially laid out as DRM circuitry but reprogrammable in support of their nascent War on Un-Americanism.

If such integrated FPGAs are mandated, commercial pressures will force Far Eastern vendors to comply with regulation and we will be able to mandate incorporation of SCORPION STARE Level Two into all digital consumer electronic cameras and commercial CCTV equipment under cover of complying with our copyright protection obligations in accordance with the WIPO treaty. A suitable pretext for the rapid phased obsolescence of all Level Zero and Level One cameras can then be engineered by, for example, discrediting witness evidence from older installations in an ongoing criminal investigation.

If we pursue this plan, by late 2006 any two adjacent public CCTV terminals—or private camcorders equipped with a digital video link—will be reprogrammable by any authenticated MAGINOT BLUE STARS superuser to permit the operator to turn them into a SCORPION STARE basilisk weapon. We remain convinced that this is the best defensive posture to adopt in order to minimize casualties when the Great Old Ones return from beyond the stars to eat our brains.

"So, what this boils down to is a Strategic Defense Initiative against an invasion by alien mind-suckers from beyond spacetime, who are expected to arrive in bulk at a set date. Am I on message so far?" I asked.

"Very approximately, yes," said Andy.

"Okay. To deal with the perceived alien mind-sucker threat, some nameless genius has worked out that the CCTV cameras dotting our green and pleasant land can be networked together, their inputs fed into a software emulation of a basilisk's brain, and turned into some kind of omnipresent look-to-kill death net. Even though we don't really know how the medusa effect works, other than that it relies on some kind of weird observationally mediated quantum-tunneling effect, collapse of the wave function, yadda yadda, that makes about 1 percent of the carbon nuclei in the target body automagically turn into silicon with no apparent net energy input. That right?"

"Have a cigar, Sherlock."

"Sorry, I only smoke when you plug me into the national grid. Shit. Okay, so it hasn't occurred to anyone that the mass-energy of those silicon nuclei has to come *from* somewhere, somewhere else, somewhere in the Dungeon Dimensions . . . damn. But that's not the point, is it?"

"Indeed not. When are you going to get to it?"

"As soon as my hands stop shaking. Let's see. Rather than do this openly and risk frightening the sheeple by stationing a death ray on every street corner, our lords and masters decided they'd do it bottom-up, by legislating that all public cameras be networked, and having back doors installed in them to allow the hunter-killer basilisk brain emulators to be uploaded when the time comes. Which, let's face it, makes excellent fiscal strength in this age of outsourcing, public-private partnerships, service charters, and the like. I mean, you can't get business insurance if you don't install antitheft cameras, someone's got to watch them so you might as well outsource the service to a security company with a network operations centre, and the brain-dead music industry copyright nazis are campaigning for a law to make it mandatory to install secret government spookware in every walkman—or camera—to prevent home taping from killing Michael Jackson. Absolutely brilliant."

"It *is* elegant, isn't it? Much more subtle than honking great ballistic missile submarines. We've come a long way since the Cold War."

"Yeah. Except you're *also* telling me that some script kiddie has rooted you and dialed in a strike on Milton Keynes. Probably in the mistaken belief that they think they're playing MISSILE COMMAND."

"No comment."

"Jesus Fucking Christ riding into town on top of a pickup truck full of DLT backup tapes—what kind of idiot do you take me for? Listen, the ball has gone *up*. Someone uploaded the SCORPION STARE code to a bunch of traffic cams off Monk's Road roundabout and turned Daisy into six hundred pounds of boiled beef on the bone *a la* basilisk, and all you can say is *no comment?*"

"Listen, Bob, I think you're taking this all too personally. I can't comment on the Monk's Road incident because you're officially the tag-team investigative lead and I'm here to provide backup and support, not to second-guess you. I'm trying to be helpful, okay?"

"Sorry, sorry. I'm just a bit upset."

"Yes, well, if it's any consolation that goes for me, too, and for Angleton believe it or not, but 'upset' and fifty pence will buy you a cup of coffee and what we really need is to finger the means, motive, and murderer of Daisy the Cow in time to close the stable door. Oh, and we can rule out external penetration—the network loop to Monk's Road is on a private backbone intranet that's firewalled up to the eyeballs. Does that make it easier for you?"

"No shit! Listen, I happen to agree with you in principle, but I am *still* upset, Andy, and I want to tell you—no shit. Look, this is so not-sensible that I know I'm way the hell too late but I think the whole MAG-INOT BLUE STARS idea is fucking insane, I mean, like, bull-goose barking-at-the-moon hairs-on-the-palm-of-your-hands crazy. Like atomic landmines buried under every street corner! Didn't they know that the only unhackable computer is one that's running a secure operating system, welded inside a steel safe, buried under a ton of concrete at the bottom of a coal mine guarded by the SAS and a couple of armored divisions, and *switched off*? What did they think they were *doing*?"

"Defending us against CASE NIGHTMARE GREEN, Bob. Which I'll have you know is why the Russians are so dead keen to get Energiya flying again so they can launch their Polyus orbital battle stations, and why the Americans are getting so upset about the Rune of Al-Sabbah that they're trying to build censorware into every analogue-to-digital converter on the planet."

"Do I have CASE NIGHTMARE GREEN clearance? Or do I just have to take it on trust?"

"Take it on trust for now, I'll try and get you cleared later in the week. Sorry about that, but this truly . . . look, in this instance the ends justify the means. Take it from me. Okay?"

"Shit. I need another—no, I've already had too much coffee. So, what am I supposed to do?"

"Well, the good news is we've narrowed it down a bit. You will be pleased to know that we just ordered the West Yorkshire Met's computer crime squad to go in with hobnailed boots and take down the entire MK traffic camera network and opcentre. Official reason is a suspicion of time bombs installed by a disgruntled former employee—who is innocent, incidentally—but it lets us turn it into a Computer Misuse case and send in a reasonably clueful team. They're about to officially call for backup from CESG, who are going to second them a purported spook from GCHQ, and that spook is going to be you. I want you to crawl all over that camera network and figure out how SCORPION STARE might have got onto it. Which is going to be easier than you think because SCORPION STARE isn't exactly open source and there are only two authorised development teams working on it on the planet that we know of, or at least in this country, one of them is—surprise—based in Milton Keynes, and as of right this minute you have clearance to stamp all over their turf and play the Gestapo officer with our top boffin labs. Which is a power I trust you will not abuse without good reason."

"Oh great, I always fancied myself in a long, black leather trench coat. What will Mo think?"

"She'll think you look the part when you're angry. Are you up for it?"

"How the fuck could I say no, when you put it that way?"

"I'm glad you understand. Now, have you got any other questions for me before we wrap this up and send the tape to the auditors?"

"Uh, yeah. One question. Why me?"

"Why—well! Hmm. I suppose because you're already on the inside, Bob. And you've got a pretty unique skill mix. Something you overlook is that we don't have many field qualified agents, and most of those we have are old school two-fisted shoot-from-the-hip-with-a-rune-of-destruction field necromancers; they don't understand these modern Babbage engine Internet contraptions like you do. And you've already got experience with basilisk weapons, or did you think we issued those things like toothpaste tubes? So rather than find someone who doesn't know as much, you just happened to be the man on the spot who knew enough and was thought . . . appropriate."

"Gee, thanks. I'll sleep a lot better tonight knowing that you couldn't find anyone better suited to the job. Really scraping the barrel, aren't we?"

"If only you knew . . . if only you knew."

The next morning they put me on the train to Cheltenham—second class of course—to visit a large office site, which appears as a blank spot on all maps of the area, just in case the Russians haven't noticed the farm growing satellite dishes out back. I spend a very uncomfortable half hour being checked through security by a couple of Rottweilers in blue suits who work on the assumption that anyone who is not known to be a Communist infiltrator from North Korea is a dangerously unclassified security risk. They search me and make me pee in a cup and leave my palmtop at the site security office, but for some reason they don't ask me to surrender the small leather bag containing a mummified pigeon's foot that I wear on a silver chain round my neck when I explain that it's on account of my religion. The idiots.

It is windy and rainy outside so I have no objection to being ushered into an air-conditioned meeting room on the third floor of an outlying wing, offered institutional beige coffee the same color as the office carpet, and to spending the next four hours in a meeting with Kevin, Robin, Jane, and Phil, who explain to me in turn what a senior operations officer from GCHQ detached for field duty is expected to do in the way of maintaining security, calling on backup, reporting problems, and filling out the two hundred and seventeen different forms that senior operations officers are apparently employed to spend their time filling out. The Laundry may have a bureaucracy surfeit and a craze for ISO-9000 certification, but GCHQ is even worse, with some bizarre spatchcock version of BS5720 quality assurance applied to all their procedures in an attempt to ensure that the Home Office minister can account for all available paper clips in near real-time if challenged in the House by Her Majesty's loyal opposition. On the other hand, they've got a bigger budget than us and all they have to worry about is having to read other people's email, instead of having their souls sucked out by tentacular horrors from beyond the universe.

"Oh, and you really ought to wear a tie when you're representing us in public," Phil says apologetically at the end of his spiel.

"And get a haircut," Jane adds with a smile.

Bastards.

The Human Resources imps billet me in a bed and breakfast run by a genteel pair of elderly High Tory sociopaths, a Mr and Mrs MacBride. He's bald, loafs around in slippers, and reads the *Telegraph* while muttering darkly about the need for capital punishment as a solution to the problem of bogus asylum seekers; she wears heavy horn-rimmed glasses and the hairdo that time forgot. The corridors are wallpapered with an exquisitely disgusting floral print and the whole place smells of mothballs, the only symptom of the twenty-first century being a cheap and nasty webcam on the hall staircase. I try not to shudder as I slouch upstairs to my room and barricade the door before settling down for the evening phone call to Mo and a game of Civ on my palmtop (which I rescued from Security on my way out.) "It could be worse," Mo consoles me, "at least *your* landlord doesn't have gill slits and greenish skin."

The next morning I elbow my way onto an early train to London, struggle through the rush hour crush, and somehow manage to weasel my way into a seat on a train to Milton Keynes; it's full of brightly clad German backpackers and irritated businessmen on their way to Luton airport, but I get off before there and catch a taxi to the cop shop. "There is nothing better in life than drawing on the sole of your slipper with a biro instead of going to the pub on a Saturday night," the lead singer of Half Man Half Biscuit sings mournfully on my iPod, and I am inclined to agree, subject to the caveat that Saturday nights at the pub are functionally equivalent to damp Thursday mornings at the police station. "Is Inspector Sullivan available?" I ask at the front desk.

"Just a moment." The moustachioed constable examines my warrant card closely, gives me a beady-eyed stare as if he expects me to break down and confess instantly to a string of unsolved burglaries, then turns and ambles into the noisy back office round the corner. I have just enough time to read the more surreal crime prevention posters for the second time ("Are your neighbours fox-hunting reptiles from the planet of the green wellies? Denounce them here, free of charge!") when the door bangs open and a determined-looking woman in a grey suit barges in. She looks how Annie Lennox would look if she'd joined the constabulary, been glassed once or twice, and had a really dodgy curry the night before.

"Okay, who's the joker?" she demands. "You." A bony finger points at me. "You're from—" she sees the warrant card "—oh shit." Over her shoulder: "Jeffries, *Jeffries*, you rat bastard, you set me up! Oh, why do I bother." Back in my direction: "You're the spook who got me out of bed the day before yesterday after a graveyard shift. Is this *your* mess?"

I take a deep breath. "Mine and yours both. I'm just back down from—" I clear my throat "—and I've got orders to find an inspector J. Sullivan and drag him into an interview room." Mentally crossing my fingers: "What's the J stand for?"

"Josephine. And it's *detective* inspector, while you're about it." She lifts the barrier. "You'd better come in then." Josephine looks tired and annoyed. "Where's your other card?"

"My other—oh." I shrug. "We don't flash them around; might be a bit of a disaster if one went missing." Anyone who picked it up would be in breach of Section Three, at the very least. Not to mention in peril of their immortal soul.

"It's okay, I've signed the Section, in blood." She raises an eyebrow at me.

"Paragraph two?" I ask, just to be sure she's not bluffing.

She shakes her head. "No, paragraph three."

"Pass, friend." And then I let her see the warrant card as it really is, the way it reaches into your head and twists things around so you want to throw up at the mere thought of questioning its validity. "Satisfied?"

She just nods: a cool customer for sure. The trouble with Section Three of the Official Secrets Act is that it's an offense to know it exists without having signed it—in blood. So us signatories who are in theory cleared to talk about such supersecret national security issues as the Laundry's tea trolley rota are in practice unable to broach the topic directly. We're supposed to rely on introductions, but that breaks down rapidly in the field. It's a bit like lesbian sheep; as ewes display their sexual arousal by standing around waiting to be mounted, it's hard to know if somebody else is, well, you know. *Cleared*. "Come on," she adds, in a marginally less hostile tone, "we can pick up a cup of coffee on the way."

Five minutes later we're sitting down with a notepad, a telephone, and an antique tape recorder that Smiley probably used to debrief Karla, back when men were real men and lesbian sheep were afraid. "This had better be important," Josephine complains, clicking a frighteningly high-tech sweetener dispenser repeatedly over her black Nescafé. "I've got a persistent burglar, two rapes, a string of car thefts, and a phantom pisser, who keeps breaking into department stores, to deal with, then a bunch of cloggies from West Yorkshire who're running some kind of computer audit—your fault, I believe. I need to get bogged down in X-*Files* rubbish right now like I need a hole in my head."

"Oh, it's important all right. And I hope to get it off your desk as soon as possible. I'd just like to get a few things straight first."

"Hmm. So what do you need to know? We've only had two flying saucer sightings and six alien abductions this year so far." She raises one eyebrow, arms crossed and shoulders set a trifle defensively. Who'd have thought it? Being interviewed by higher authorities makes the alpha female detective defensive. "It's not like I've got all day: I'm due in a case committee briefing at noon and I've got to pick up my son from school at four."

On second thought, maybe she really *is* busy. "To start with, did you get any witness reports or CCTV records from the scene? And have you identified the cow, and worked out how it got there?"

"No eyewitnesses, not until three o'clock, when Vernon Thwaite was out walking his girlfriend's toy poodle which had diarrhoea." She pulls a face, which makes the scar on her forehead wrinkle into visibility. "If you want we can go over the team reports together. I take it that's what pulled you in?"

"You could say that." I dip a cheap IKEA spoon in my coffee and check cautiously after a few seconds to see if the metal's begun to corrode. "Helicopters make me airsick. Especially after a night out when I was expecting a morning lie-in." She almost smiles before she remembers she's officially grumpy with me. "Okay, so no earlier reports. What else?"

"No tape," she says, flattening her hands on the tabletop to either side of her cup and examining her nail cuticles. "Nothing. One second it's zero zero twenty-six, the next it's zero seven fourteen. Numbers to engrave in your heart. Dennis, our departmental geek, was most upset with MKSG—they're the public-private partners in the regional surveillance outsourcing sector."

"Zero zero twenty-six to zero seven fourteen," I echo as I jot them down on my palmtop. "MKSG. Right, that's helpful."

"It is?" She tilts her head sideways and stares at me like I'm a fly that's landed in her coffee.

"Yup." I nod, then tell myself that it'd be really stupid to wind her up without good reason. "Sorry. What I can tell you is, I'm as interested in anything that happened to the cameras as the cow. If you hear anything about them—especially about them being tampered with—I'd love to know. But in the meantime—Daisy. Do you know where she came from?"

"Yes." She doesn't crack a smile but her shoulders unwind slightly. "Actually, she's number two six three from Emmett-Moore Ltd, a dairy factory out near Dunstable. Or rather, she was two six three until three days ago. She was getting along a bit, so they sold her to a local slaughterhouse along with a job lot of seven other cows. I followed-up on the other seven and they'll be showing up in your McHappy McMeal some time next month. But not Daisy. Seems a passing farmer in a Range Rover with a wagon behind it dropped by and asked if he could buy her and cart her away for his local family butcher to deal with."

"Aha!"

"And if you believe that, I've got a bridge to sell you." She takes a sip of her coffee, winces, and strafes it with sweeteners again. Responding on autopilot I try a mouthful of my own and burn my tongue. "Turns out that there's no such farmer Giles of Ham Farm, Bag End, The Shire, on record. Mind you, they had a camera on their stockyard and we nailed the Range Rover. It turned up abandoned the next day on the outskirts of Leighton Buzzard and it's flagged as stolen on HOLMES2. Right now it's sitting in the pound down the road; they smoked it for prints but it came up clean and we don't have enough money to send a SOCO and a forensics team to do a full workup on every stolen car we run across. *However*, if you twist my arm and promise me a budget *and* to go to the mat with my boss I'll see what I can lay on."

"That may not be necessary: we have ways and means. But can you get someone to drive me down there? I'll take some readings and get out of your face—except for the business with Daisy. How are you covering that?"

"Oh, we'll find something. Right now it's filed under 'F' for Fucking Fortean Freakery, but I was thinking of announcing it's just an old animal that had been dumped illegally by a farmer who didn't want to pay to have it slaughtered."

"That sounds about right." I nod slowly. "Now, I'd like to play a random word-association game with you. Okay? Ten seconds. When I say the words tell me what you think of. Right?"

She looks puzzled. "Is this—"

"Listen. Case-Nightmare-Green-Scorpion-Stare-Maginot-Blue-Stars. By the authority vested in me by the emissaries of Y'ghonzzh N'hai I have the power to bind and to release, and your tongue be tied of these matters of which we have spoken until you hear these words again: Case-Nightmare-Green-Scorpion-Stare-Maginot-Blue-Stars. Got that?"

She looks at me cross-eyed and mouths something, then looks increasingly angry until finally she gets it together to burst out with: "Hey, what *is* this shit?"

"Purely a precaution," I say, and she glares at me, gobbling for a moment while I finish my coffee until she figures out that she simply can't say a word about the subject. "Right," I say. "Now. You've got my permission to announce that the cow was dumped. You have my permission to talk freely to me, but to nobody else. Anyone asks any questions, refer them to me if they won't take no for an answer. This goes for your boss, too. Feel free to tell them that you can't tell them, nothing more."

"Wanker," she hisses, and if looks could kill I'd be a small pile of smoldering ashes on the interview room floor.

"Hey, *I'm* under a geas, too. If I don't spread it around my head will explode."

I don't know whether she believes me or not but she stops fighting it and nods tiredly. "Tell me what you want then get the hell out of my patch."

"I want a lift to the car pound. A chance to sit behind the wheel of that Range Rover. A book of poetry, a jug of wine, a date tree, and—sorry, wrong question. Can you manage it?"

She stands up. "I'll take you there myself," she says tersely. We go.

I get to endure twenty-five minutes of venomous silence in the back seat of an unmarked patrol car driven by one Constable Routledge, with DI Sullivan in the front passenger seat treating me with the warmth due a serial killer, before we arrive at the pound. I'm beyond introspective self-loathing by now—you lose it fast in this line of work. Angleton will have my head for a key-ring fob if I don't take care to silence any possible leaks, and a tongue-twisting geas is more merciful than most of the other tools at my disposal—but I still feel like a shit. So it comes as a great relief to get out of the car and stretch my legs on the muddy gravel parking lot in the pouring rain.

"So where's the car?" I ask, innocently.

Josephine ignores me. "Bill, you want to head over to Bletchley Way and pick up Dougal's evidence bag for the Hayes case. Then come back to pick us up," she tells the driver. To the civilian security guard: "You, we're looking for BY 476 ERB. Came in yesterday, Range Rover. Where is it?"

The bored security goon leads us through the mud and a maze of cars with POLICE AWARE stickers glued to their windshields then gestures at a half-empty row. "That's it?" Josephine asks, and he passes her a set of keys. "Okay, you can piss off now." He takes one look at her face and beats a hasty retreat. I half-wish I could join him—whether she's a detective inspector or not, and therefore meant to be behaving with the gravitas of a senior officer in public, DI Sullivan looks to be in a mood to bite the heads off chickens. Or Laundry field agents, given half an excuse.

"Right, that's it," she says, holding out the keys and shaking them at me impatiently. "You're done, I take it, so I'll be pushing off. Case meeting to run, mystery shopping centre pisser to track down, and so on."

"Not so fast." I glance round. The pound is surrounded by a high wire fence and there's a decrepit Portakabin office out front by the gate: a camera sits on a motorized mount on a pole sticking up from the roof. "Who's on the other end of that thing?"

"The gate guard, probably," she says, following my finger. The camera is staring at the entrance, unmoving.

"Okay, why don't you open up the car." She blips the remote to unlock the door and I keep my eyes on the camera as she takes the handle and tugs. *Could I be wrong?* I wonder as the rain trickles down my neck. I shake myself when I notice her staring, then I pull out my palmtop, clamber up into the driver's seat, and balance the pocket computer on the steering wheel as I tap out a series of commands. What I see makes me shake my head. Whoever stole the car may have wiped for fingerprints but they didn't know much about paranormal concealment—they didn't use the shroud from a suicide, or get a paranoid schizophrenic to drive. The scanner is sensitive to heavy emotional echoes, and the hands I'm looking for are the most recent ones to have chilled from fright and fear of exposure. I log everything and put it away, and I'm about to open the glove locker when something makes me glance at the main road beyond the chainlink fence and—

"*Watch out! Get down!*" I jump out and go for the ground. Josephine is looking around so I reach out and yank her ankles out from under her. She yells, goes down hard on her backside, and tries to kick me, then there's a loud *whump* from behind me and a wave of heat like an open oven door. "Shit, fuck, shit—" I take a moment to realize the person cursing is me as I fumble at my throat for the bag and rip it open, desperately trying to grab the tiny claw and the disposable cigarette lighter at the same time. I flick the lighter wheel and right then something like a sledgehammer whacks into the inside of my right thigh.

"*Bastard . . . !*"

"Stop it—" I gasp, just as the raw smell of petrol vapor reaches me and I hear a crackling roar. I get the pigeon claw lit in a stink of burning keratin and an eerie glow, nearly shitting myself with terror, lying in a cold damp puddle, and roll over: "*Don't move!*"

"Bastard! What—hey, what's burning?"

"Don't move," I gasp again, holding the subminiature Hand of Glory up. The traffic camera in the road outside the fence is casting about as if it's dropped its contact lens, but the one on the pole above the office is locked right onto the burning tires of the Range Rover. "If you let go of my hand they'll see you and kill you *oh shit—*"

"Kill—*what?*" She stares at me, white-faced.

"You! Get under cover!" I yell across the pound, but the guy in the blue suit—the attendant—doesn't hear me. One second he's running across the car park as fast as his portly behind can manage; the next moment he's tumbling forward, blackening, puffs of flame erupting from his eyes and mouth and ears, then the stumps as his arms come pinwheeling off, and the carbonized trunk slides across the ground like a grisly toboggan.

"Oh shit, oh shit!" Her expression changes from one second to the next, from disbelief to dawning horror. "We've got to help—"

"Listen, *no!* Stay down!"

She freezes in place for a full heartbeat, then another. When she opens her mouth again she's unnaturally cool. "What's going on?"

"The cameras," I pant. "Listen, this is a Hand of Glory, an invisibility shield. Right now it's all that's keeping us alive—those cameras are running SCORPION STARE. If they see us we're dead."

"Are you—the car? What happened to it?"

"Tires. They're made of carbon, rubber. SCORPION STARE works on anything with a shitload of long-chain carbon molecules in it—like tires, or cows. Makes them burn."

"Oh my sainted aunt and holy father . . ."

"Hold my hand. Make skin to skin contact—not that hard. We've got maybe three, four minutes before this HOG burns down. Bastards, *bastards*. Got to get to the control shack—"

The next minute is a nightmare of stumbling—shooting pains in my knees from where I went down hard and in my thigh where Josephine tried to kick the shit out of me—soaking cold damp jeans, and roasting hot skin on my neck from the pyre that I was sitting inside only seconds ago. She holds onto my left hand like it's a lifesaver—yes, it is, for as long as the HOG keeps burning—and we lurch and shamble toward the modular site office near the entrance as fast as we can go. "Inside," she gasps, "it can't see inside."

"Yeah?" She half-drags me to the entrance and we find the door's open, not locked. "Can we get away round the other side?"

"Don't think so." She points through the building. "There's a school."

"Oh shit." We're on the other side of the pound from the traffic camera in the road, but there's another camera under the eaves of the school on the other side of the road from the steel gates out front, and it's a good thing the kids are all in lessons because what's going on here is every teacher's nightmare. And we've got to nail it down as fast as possible, because if they ring the bell for lunch— "We've got to kill the power to the roofcam first," I say. "Then we've got to figure a way out."

"What's going on? What *did* that?" Her lips work like a fish out of water.

I shake my head. "Case-Nightmare-Green-Scorpion-Stare-Maginot-Blue-Stars tongue be loosed. Okay, talk. I reckon we've got about two, three minutes to nail this before—"

"This was all a setup?"

"I don't know yet. Look, how do I get onto the roof?"

"Isn't that a skylight?" she asks, pointing.

"Yeah." Being who I am I always carry a Leatherman multitool so I whip it out and look around for a chair I can pile on top of the desk and stand on, one that doesn't have wheels and a gas strut. "See any chairs I can—"

I'll say this much, detective training obviously enables you to figure out how to get onto a roof fast. Josephine simply walks over to the ladder nestling in a corner between one wall and a battered filing cabinet and pulls it out. "This what you're looking for?"

"Uh, yeah. Thanks." She passes it to me and I fumble with it for a moment, figuring out how to set it up. Then another moment, juggling the multitool and the half-consumed pigeon's foot and looking at the ladder dubiously.

"Give me those," she says.

"But—"

"Listen, *I'm* the one who deals with idiot vandals and climbs around on pitched roofs looking for broken skylights, okay? And—" she glances at the door "—if I mess up you can phone your boss and let him know what's happening."

"Oh," I mumble, then hand her the gadgets and hold the ladder steady while she swarms up it like a circus acrobat. A moment later there's a noise like a herd of baby elephants thudding on the rooftop as she scrambles across to the camera mount. The camera may be on a moving platform but there's a limit to how far it can depress and clearly she's right below the azimuth platform—just as long as she isn't visible to both the traffic camera out back and the schoolyard monitor out front. More shaking, then there's a loud clack and the Portakabin lights go out.

A second or two later she reappears, feet first, through the opening. "Right, that should do it," she says. "I shorted the power cable to the platform. "Hey, the lights—"

"I think you shorted a bit more than that." I hold the ladder as she climbs down. "Now, we've got an immobilized one up top, that's good. Let's see if we can find the controller."

A quick search of the hut reveals a bunch of fun stuff I hadn't been expecting, like an ADSL line to the regional police IT hub, a PC running some kind of terminal emulator, and another dedicated machine with the cameras showing overlapping windows on-screen. I could kiss them; they may have outsourced the monitoring to private security firms but they've kept the hardware all on the same backbone network. The blinkenlights are beeping and twittering like crazy as everything's now running on backup battery power, but that's okay. I pull out a breakout box and scramble around under a desk until I've got my palmtop plugged into the network hub to sniff packets. Barely a second later it dings at me. "Oh, lovely." So much for *firewalled up to the eyeballs*. I unplug and surface again, then scroll through the several hundred screenfuls of unencrypted bureaucratic computerese my network sniffer has grabbed. "*That* looks promising. Uh, I wouldn't go outside just yet but I think we're going to be all right."

"Explain." She's about ten centimeters shorter than I am, but I'm suddenly aware that I'm sharing the Portakabin with an irate, wet, detective inspector who's probably a black belt at something or other lethal and who is just about to really lose her cool: "You've got about ten seconds from *now* to tell me everything. Or I'm calling for backup and warrant card or no you are going in a cell until I get some answers. Capisce?"

"I surrender." I don't, really, but I point at my palmtop. "It's a fair cop, guv. Look, someone's been too clever by half here. The camera up top is basically a glorified webcam. I mean, it's running a web server and it's plugged into the constabulary's intranet via broadband. Every ten seconds or so a program back at HQ polls it and grabs the latest picture, okay? That's in addition to whatever the guy downstairs tells it to look at. Anyway, someone *else* just sent it an HTTP request with a honking great big file upload attached, and I don't think your IT department is in the habit of using South Korean primary schools as proxy servers, are they?

And a compromised firewall, no less. Lovely! Your cameras may have been OwnZOr3d by a fucking script kiddie, but they're not as fucking smart as they *think* they are otherwise they'd have fucking stripped off the fucking referrer headers, wouldn't they?" I stop talking and make sure I've saved the logfile somewhere secure, then for good measure I email it to myself at work.

"Right. So I know their IP address and it's time to locate them." It's the work of about thirty seconds to track it to a dial-up account on one of the big national ISPs—one of the free anonymous ones. "Hmm. If you want to help, you could get me an S22 disclosure notice for the phone number behind this dial-up account. Then we can persuade the phone company to tell us the street address and go pay them a visit and ask why they killed our friend with the key ring—" My hands are shaking from the adrenalin high and I am beginning to feel angry, not just an ordinary day-to-day pissed-off feeling but the kind of true and brutal rage that demands revenge.

"Killed? Oh." She opens the door an inch and looks outside: she looks a little grey around the gills, but she doesn't lose it. Tough woman.

"It's SCORPION STARE. Look, S22 data disclosure order first, it's a fucking murder investigation now, isn't it? Then we go visiting. But we're going to have to make out like it's accidental, or the press will come trampling all over us and we won't be able to get anything done." I write down the hostname while she gets on the mobile to head office. The first sirens start to wail even before she picks up my note and calls for medical backup. I sit there staring at the door, contemplating the mess, my mind whirling. "Tell the ambulance crew it's a freak lightning strike," I say as the thought takes me. "You're already in this up to your ears, we don't need to get anyone else involved—"

Then my phone rings.

As it happens we don't visit any murderous hackers, but presently the car pound is fronted with white plastic scene-of-crime sheeting and a photographer and a couple of forensics guys show up and Josephine, who has found something more urgent to obsess over than ripping me a new asshole, is busy directing their preliminary work-over. I'm poring over screenfuls of tcpdump output in the control room when the same unmarked car that dropped us off here pulls up with Constable Routledge at the wheel and a very unexpected passenger in the back. I gape as he gets out of the car and walks toward the hut. "Who's this?" demands Josephine, coming over and sticking her head in through the window.

I open the door. "Hi, boss. Boss, meet Detective Inspector Sullivan. Josephine, this is my boss—you want to come in and sit down?"

Andy nods at her distractedly: "I'm Andy. Bob, brief me." He glances at her again as she shoves through the door and closes it behind her. "Are you—"

"She knows too much already." I shrug. "Well?" I ask her. "This is your chance to get out."

"Fuck that." She glares at me, then Andy: "Two mornings ago it was a freak accident and a cow, today it's a murder investigation—I trust you're not planning on escalating it any further, terrorist massacres and biological weapons are a little outside my remit—and I want some answers. *If* you please."

"Okay, you'll get them," Andy says mildly. "Start talking," he tells me.

"Code blue called at three thirty the day before yesterday. I flew out to take a look, found a dead cow that had been zapped by SCORPION STARE—unless there's a basilisk loose in Milton Keynes—went down to our friends in Cheltenham for briefing yesterday, stayed overnight, came up here this morning. The cow was bought from a slaughterhouse and transported to the scene in a trailer towed by a stolen car, which was later dumped and transferred to this pound. Inspector Sullivan is our force liaison—external circle two, no need to know. She brought me here and I took a patch test, and right then someone zapped the car—we were lucky to survive. One down out front. We've, uh, trapped a camera up top that I *think* will prove to have firmware loaded with SCORPION STARE, and I sniffed packets coming in from a compromised host. Police intranet, firewalled to hell and back, hacked via some vile little dweeb using a primary school web server in South Korea. We were just about to run down the intruder in meatspace and go ask some pointed questions when you arrived." I yawn, and Andy looks at me oddly. Extreme stress sometimes does that to me, makes me tired, and I've been running on my nerves for most of the past few days.

"All right." Andy scratches his chin thoughtfully. "There's been a new development."

"New development?" I echo.

"Yes. We received a blackmail note." And it's no fucking *wonder* that he's looking slightly glassy-eyed—he must be in shock.

"*Blackmail?* What are they—"

"It came via email from an anonymous remixer on the public Internet. Whoever wrote it knows about MAGINOT BLUE STARS and wants us to know that they disapprove, especially of SCORPION STARE. No sign that they've got CASE NIGHTMARE GREEN, though. They're giving us three days to cancel the entire project or they'll blow it wide open in quote the most public way imaginable unquote."

"Shit."

"Smelly brown stuff, yes. Angleton is displeased." Andy shakes his head. "We tracked the message back to a dial-up host in the UK—"

I hold up a piece of paper. "This one?"

He squints at it. "I think so. We did the S22 soft-shoe shuffle but it's no good, they used the SIMM card from a prepaid mobile phone bought for cash in a supermarket in Birmingham three months ago. The best we could do was trace the caller's location to the centre of Milton Keynes." He glances at Josephine. "Did you impress her—"

"Listen." She speaks quietly and with great force: "Firstly, this appears to be an investigation into murder—and now blackmail, of a government department, right?—and in case you hadn't noticed, organising criminal investigations just happens to be my speciality. Secondly, I do not appreciate being forcibly gagged. I *have* signed a certain piece of paper, and the only stuff I leak is what you get when you drill holes in me. Finally, I am getting really pissed off with the runaround you're giving me about a particularly serious incident on my turf, and if you don't start answering my questions soon I'm going to have to arrest you for wasting police time. Now, which is it going to be?"

"Oh, for crying out loud." Andy rolls his eyes, then says very rapidly: "By the abjuration of Dee and the name of Claude Dansey I hereby exercise subsection D paragraph sixteen clause twelve and bind you to service from now and forevermore. Right, that's it. You're drafted, and may whatever deity you believe in have mercy on your soul."

"Hey. Wait." She takes a step back. "What's going on?" There's a faint stink of burning sulphur in the air.

"You've just talked yourself into the Laundry," I say, shaking my head. "Just try to remember I tried to keep you out of this."

"The Laundry? What are you talking about? I thought you were from Cheltenham?" The smell of brimstone is getting stronger. "Hey, is something on fire?"

"Wrong guess," says Andy. "Bob can explain later. For now, just remember that we work for the same people, ultimately, only we deal with a higher order of threat than everyday stuff like rogue states, terrorist nukes, and so on. Cheltenham is the cover story. Bob, the blackmailer threatened to upload SCORPION STARE to the ring of steel."

"Oh shit." I sit down hard on the edge of a desk. "That is so very not good that I don't want to think about it right now." The ring of steel is the network of surveillance cameras that were installed around the financial heart of the city of London in the late 1990s to deter terrorist bombings. "Look, did Angleton have any other—"

"Yes. He wants us to go visit Site Able right now, that's the lead development team at the research centre behind SCORPION STARE. Um, inspector? You're in. As I said, you're drafted. Your boss, that would be Deputy Chief Constable Dunwoody, is about to get a memo about you from the Home Office — we'll worry about whether you can go back to your old job afterward. As of now, this investigation is your only priority. Site Able runs out of an office unit at Kiln Farm industrial estate, covered as a UK subsidiary of an American software company: in reality they're part of the residual unprivatized rump of DERA, uh, QinetiQ. The bunch that handles Q-projects."

"While you're busy wanking over your cow-burning nonsense I've got a ring of car thieves to—" Josephine shakes her head distractedly, sniffs suspiciously, then stops trying to fight the geas. "*That smell* . . . Why do these people at Kiln Farm need a visit?"

"Because they're the lead team on the group who developed SCORPION STARE," Andy explains, "and Angleton doesn't think it's a coincidence that our blackmailer burned a cow in Milton Keynes. He thinks they're a bunch of locals. Bob, if you've got a trace that'll be enough to narrow it down to the building—"

"Yes?" Josephine nods to herself. "But you need to find the individual responsible, and any time bombs they've left, and there's a small matter of evidence." A thought strikes her. "What happens when you catch them?"

Andy looks at me and my blood runs cold. "I think we'll have to see about that when we find them," I extemporize, trying to avoid telling her about the Audit Commission for the time being; she might blow her stack completely if I have to explain how they investigate malfeasance, and then I'd have to tell her that the burning smell is a foreshadowing of what happens if she is ever found guilty of disloyalty. (It normally fades a few minutes after the rite of binding, but right now it's still strong.) "What are we waiting for?" I ask. "Let's go!"

In the beginning there was the Defense Evaluation and Research Agency, DERA. And DERA was where HMG's boffins hung out, and they developed cool toys like tanks with plastic armour, clunky palmtops powered by 1980s chips and rugged enough to be run over by a truck, and fetal heart monitors to help the next generation of squaddies grow up strong. And lo, in the thrusting entrepreneurial climate of the early nineties a new government came to power with a remit to bring about the triumph of true socialism by privatising the post office and air traffic control systems, and DERA didn't stand much of a chance. Renamed QinetiQ by the same nameless marketing genius who turned the Royal Mail into Consignia and Virgin Trains into fodder for fuckedcompany-

dot-com, the research agency was hung out to dry, primped and beauti-
fied, and generally prepared for sale to the highest bidder who didn't
speak with a pronounced Iraqi accent.

However . . .

In addition to the ordinary toys, DERA used to do development work
for the Laundry. Q Division's pedigree stretches back all the way to
SOE's wartime dirty tricks department—poison pens, boot-heel escape
kits, explosive-stuffed sabotage rats, the whole nine yards of James Bond
japery. Since the 1950s, Q Division has kept the Laundry in more esoteric equipment: summoning grids, basilisk guns, Turing oracles, self-
tuning pentacles, self-filling beer glasses, and the like. Steadily growing
weirder and more specialized by the year, Q Division is far too sensitive
to sell off—unlike most of QinetiQ's research, what they do is classified
so deep you'd need a bathyscaphe to reach it. And so, while QinetiQ was
being dolled up for the city catwalk, Q Division was segregated and spun
off, a little stronghold in the sea of commerce that is forever civil service
territory.

Detective Inspector Sullivan marches out of the site office like a
blank-faced automaton and crisply orders her pet driver to take us to Site
Able then to bugger off on some obscure make-work errand. She sits
stiffly in the front passenger seat while Andy and I slide into the back and
we proceed in silence—nobody seems to want to make small talk.

Fifteen minutes of bumbling around red routes and through trackless
wastes of identical red brick houses embellished with satellite dishes and
raw pine fences brings us into an older part of town, where the buildings
actually look different and the cycle paths are painted strips at the side of
the road rather than separately planned routes. I glance around curiously, trying to spot landmarks. "Aren't we near Bletchley Park?" I ask.

"It's a couple of miles that way," says our driver without taking his
hands off the wheel to point. "You thinking of visiting?"

"Not just yet." Bletchley Park was the wartime headquarters of the
Ultra operation, the department that later became GCHQ—the people
who built the Colossus computers, originally used for breaking Nazi
codes and subsequently diverted by the Laundry for more occult purposes. Hallowed ground to us spooks; I've met more than one NSA liaison who wanted to visit in order to smuggle a boot heel full of gravel
home. "Not until we've visited the UK offices of Dillinger Associates, at
any rate."

Dillinger Associates is the cover name for a satellite office of Q
Division. The premises turns out to be a neoclassical brick-and-glass ed-
ifice with twee fake columns and wilted-looking ivy that's been trained
to climb the facade by dint of ruthless application of plant hormones. We

pile out of the car in the courtyard between the dry fountain and the glass doors, and I surreptitiously check my PDA's locator module for any sign of a match. Nothing. I blink and put it away in time to catch up with Andy and Josephine as they head for the bleached blonde receptionist who sits behind a high wooden counter and types constantly, as unapproachably artificial-looking as a shop window dummy.

"HelloDillingerAssociatesHowCanIHelpEwe?" She flutters her eyelashes at Andy in a bored, professional way, hands never moving away from the keyboard of the PC in front of her. There's something odd about her, but I can't quite put my finger on it.

Andy flips open his warrant card. "We're here to see Doctor Voss."

The receptionist's long, red-nailed fingers stop moving and hover over the keyboard. "Really?" she asks, tonelessly, reaching under the desk.

"Hold it—" I begin to say, as Josephine takes a brisk step forward and drops a handkerchief over the webcam on top of the woman's monitor. There's a quiet *pop* and the sudden absence of noise from her PC tips me off. I sidestep the desk and make a grab for her just as Andy produces a pistol with a ridiculously fat barrel and shoots out the camera located over the door at the rear of the reception area. There's a horrible ripping sound like a joint of meat tearing apart as the receptionist twists aside and I realize that she isn't sitting on a chair at all—she's joined seamlessly at the hips to a plinth that emerges from some kind of fat swivel base of age-blackened wood, bolted to the floor with heavy brass pins in the middle of a silvery metallic pentacle with wires trailing from one corner back up to the PC on the desk. She opens her mouth and I can see that her tongue is bright blue and bifurcated as she hisses.

I hit the floor shoulder first, jarringly hard, and grab for the nearest cable. Those red nails are reaching down for me as her eyes narrow to slits and she works her jaw muscles as if she's trying to get together a wad of phlegm to spit. I grab the fattest cable and give it a pull and she screams, high-pitched and frighteningly inhuman.

*What the fuck?* I think, looking up as the red-painted claws stretch and expand, shedding layers of varnish as their edges grow long and sharp. Then I yank the cable again, and it comes away from the pentacle. The wooden box drools a thick, blue-tinted liquid across the carpet tiles, and the screaming stops.

"Lamia," Andy says tersely. He strides over to the fire door that opens onto the corridor beyond, raises the curiously fat gun, and fires straight up. A purple rain drizzles back down.

"What's going on?" says Josephine, bewildered, staring at the twitching, slowly dying receptionist.

I point my PDA at the lamia and ding it for a reading. Cool, but nonzero. "Got a partial fix," I call to Andy. "Where's everyone else? Isn't this place supposed to be manned?"

"No idea." He looks worried. "If this is what they've got up front the shit's already hit the fan—Angleton wasn't predicting overt resistance."

The other door bangs open of a sudden and a tubby middle-aged guy in a cheap grey suit and about three day's worth of designer stubble barges out shouting, "Who are you and what do you think you're doing here? This is private property, not a paintball shooting gallery! It's a disgrace—I'll call the police!"

Josephine snaps out of her trance and steps forward. "As a matter of fact, I *am* the police," she says. "What's your name? Do you have a complaint, and if so, what is it?"

"I'm, I'm—" He focuses on the no-longer-twitching demon receptionist, lolling on top of her box like a murderous shop mannequin. He looks aghast. "Vandals! If you've damaged her—"

"Not as badly as she planned to damage us," says Andy. "I think you'd better tell us who you are." Andy presents his card, ordering it to reveal its true shape: "by the authority vested in me—"

He moves fast with the geas and ten seconds later we've got mister fat guy—actually Dr Martin Voss—seated on one of the uncomfortable chrome-and-leather designer sofas at one side of reception while Andy asks questions and records them on a dictaphone. Voss talks in a monotone, obviously under duress, drooling slightly from one side of his mouth, and the stench of brimstone mingles with a mouth-watering undertone of roast pork. There's purple dye from Andy's paintball gun spattered over anything that might conceal a camera, and he had me seal all the doorways with a roll of something like duct tape or police incident tape, except that the symbols embossed on it glow black and make your eyes water if you try to focus on them.

"Tell me your name and position at this installation."

"Voss. John Voss. Res-research team manager."

"How many members are there on your team? Who are they?"

"Twelve. Gary. Ted. Elinor. John. Jonathan. Abdul. Mark—"

"Stop right there. Who's here today? And is anyone away from the office right now?" I plug away at my palmtop, going cross-eyed as I fiddle with the detector controls. But there's no sign of any metaspectral resonance; grepping for a match to the person who stole the Range Rover draws a blank in this building. Which is frustrating because we've got his (I'm pretty sure it's a *he*) boss right here, and there ought to be a sympathetic entanglement at work.

"Everyone's here but Mark." He laughs a bit, mildly hysterical. "They're all here but Mark. Mark!"

I glance over at Detective Inspector Sullivan, who is detective inspecting the lamia. I think she's finally beginning to grasp at a visceral level that we aren't just some bureaucratic Whitehall paper circus trying to make her life harder. She looks frankly nauseated. The silence here is eerie, and worrying. *Why haven't the other team members come to find out what's going on?* I wonder, looking at the taped-over doors. *Maybe they've gone out the back and are waiting for us outside. Or maybe they simply can't come out in daylight.* The smell of burning meat is getting stronger: Voss seems to be shaking, as if he's trying not to answer Andy's questions.

I walk over to the lamia. "It's not human," I explain quietly. "It never was human. It's one of the things they specialise in. This building is defended by guards and wards, and this is just part of the security system's front end."

"But she, she spoke . . ."

"Yes, but she's not a human being." I point to the thick ribbon cable that connected the computer to the pentacle. "See, that's a control interface. The computer's there to stabilize and contain a Dho-Nha circuit that binds the Dee-space entity here. The entity itself—it's a lamia—is locked into the box which contains, uh, other components. And it's compelled to obey certain orders. Nothing good for unscheduled visitors." I put my hands on the lamia's head and work my fingers into the thick blonde hair, then tug. There's a noise of ripping Velcro then the wig comes off to reveal the scaly scalp beneath. "See? It's not human. It's a lamia, a type of demon bound to act as a front-line challenge/response system for a high security installation with covert—"

I manage to get out of the line of fire as Josephine brings up her lunch all over the incredibly expensive bleached pine workstation. I can't say I blame her. I feel a little shocky myself—it's been a really bad morning. Then I realize that Andy is trying to get my attention. "Bob, when you're through with grossing out the inspector I've got a little job for you." He pitches his voice loudly.

"Yeah?" I ask, straightening up.

"I want you to open that door, walk along the corridor to the second room on the right—not pausing to examine any of the corpses along the way—and open it. Inside, you'll find the main breaker board. I want you to switch the power off."

"Didn't I just see you splashing paint all over the CCTV cameras in the ceiling? And, uh, what's this about corpses? Why don't we send Doctor Voss—oh." Voss's eyes are shut and the stink of roast meat is getting stronger: he's gone extremely red in the face, almost puffy, and he's shaking slightly as if some external force is making all his muscles twitch simultaneously. It's my turn to struggle to hang onto breakfast. "I didn't know anyone could make themselves *do* that," I hear myself say distantly.

"Neither did I," says Andy, and that's the most frightening thing I've heard today so far. "There must be a conflicted geas somewhere in his skull. I don't think I could stop it even if—"

"Shit." I stand up. My hand goes to my neck automatically but the pouch is empty. "No HOG." I swallow. "Power. What happens if I don't?"

"Voss's pal Mark McLuhan installed a dead man's handle. You'd know all about that. We've got until Voss goes into brain stem death and then every fucking camera in Milton Keynes goes live with SCORPION STARE."

"Oh, you mean we die." I head for the door Voss came through. "I'm looking for the service core, right?"

"Wait!" It's Josephine, looking pale. "Can't you go outside and cut the power there? Or phone for help?"

"Nope." I rip the first strip of sealing tape away from the door frame. "We're behind Tempest shielding here, and the power is routed through concrete ducts underground. This is a Q Division office, after all. If we could call in an air strike and drop a couple of BLU-114/Bs on the local power substations that might work—" I tug at the second tape "—but these systems were designed to be survivable." Third tape.

"Here," calls Andy, and he chucks something cylindrical at me. I catch it one-handed, yank the last length of tape with the other hand, and do a double-take. Then I shake the cylinder, listen for the rattle of the stirrer, and pop the lid off.

"Take cover!" I call. Then I open the door, spritz the ceiling above me with green spray paint, and go to work.

I'm sitting in the lobby, guarding the lamia's corpse with a nearly empty can of paint and trying not to fall asleep, when the OCCULUS team bangs on the door. I yawn and sidestep Voss's blistered corpse—he looks like he's gone a few rounds with Old Sparky—then try to remember the countersign. *Ah, that's it.* I pull away a strip of tape and tug the door open and find myself staring up the snout of an H&K carbine. "Is that a gun in your hand or are you just here to have a wank?" I ask.

The gun points somewhere else in a hurry. "Hey, Sarge, it's the spod from Amsterdam!"

"Yeah, and someone's told you to secure the area, haven't they? Where's Sergeant Howe?" I ask, yawning. Daylight makes me feel better—that, and knowing that there's backup. (I get sleepy when people stop shooting at me. Then I have nightmares. Not a good combination.)

"Over here." They're dressed in something not unlike Fire Service HAZMAT gear, and the wagons are painted cheerful cherry-red with luminous yellow stripes; if they weren't armed to the teeth with automatic weapons you'd swear they were only here because somebody had phoned in a toxic chemical release warning. But the pump nozzles above the cabs aren't there to spray water, and that lumpy thing on the back isn't a spotlight—it's a grenade launcher.

The inspector comes up behind me, staggering slightly in the daylight. "What's going on?" she asks.

"Here, meet Scary Spice and Sergeant Howe. Sarge, Scary, meet Detective Inspector Sullivan. Uh, the first thing you need to do is to go round the site and shoot out every closed circuit TV camera you can see—or that can see you. Got that? And webcams. And doorcams. See a camera, smash it, that's the rule."

"Cameras. Ri-ight." Sergeant Howe looks mildly skeptical, but nods. "It's definitely cameras?"

"Who *are* these guys?" asks Josephine.

"Artists' Rifles. They work with us," I say. Scary nods, deeply serious. "Listen, you go outside, do anything necessary to keep the local emergency services off our backs. If you need backup ask Sergeant Howe here. Sarge, she's basically sound and she's working for us on this. Okay?"

She doesn't wait for confirmation, just shoves past me and heads out into the daylight, blinking and shaking her head. I carry on briefing the OCCULUS guys. "Don't worry about anything that uses film, it's the closed circuit TV variety that's hostile. And, oh, try to make sure that you are *never* in view of more than one of 'em at a time."

"And don't walk on the cracks in the pavement or the bears will get us, check." Howe turns to Scary Spice: "Okay, you heard the man. Let's do it." He glances at me. "Anything inside?"

"We're taking care of it," I say. "If we need help we'll ask."

"Check." Scary is muttering into his throat mike and fake firemen with entirely authentic fire axes are walking around the bushes along the side of the building as if searching for signs of combustion. "Okay, we'll be out here."

"Is Angleton in the loop? Or the captain?"

"Your boss is on his way out here by chopper. Ours is on medical leave. You need to escallate, I'll get you the lieutenant."

"Okay." I duck back into the reception area then nerve myself to go back into the development pool at the rear of the building, below the offices and above the labs.

Site Able is a small departmental satellite office, small for security reasons: ten systems engineers, a couple of manager dogsbodies, and a security officer. Most of them are right here right now, and they're not going anywhere. I walk around the service core in the dim glow of the emergency light, bypassing splashes of green paint that look black in the red glow. The octagonal developer pool at the back is also dimly illuminated—there are no windows, and the doors are triple-sealed with rubber gaskets impregnated with fine copper mesh—and some of the partitions have been blown over. The whole place is ankle deep in white mist left over from the halon dump system that went off when the first bodies exploded—good thing the air conditioning continued to run or the place would be a gas trap. The webcams are all where I left them, in a trash can at the foot of the spiral staircase up to level one, cables severed with my multitool just to make sure nobody tries to plug them back in again.

The victims—well, I have to step over one of them to get up the staircase. It's pretty gross but I've seen dead bodies before, including burn cases, and at least this was fast. But I don't think I'm going to forget the smell in a hurry. In fact, I think I'm going to have nightmares about it tonight, and maybe get drunk and cry on Mo's shoulder several times over the next few weeks until I've got it out of my system. But for now, I shove it aside and step over them. Got to keep moving, that's the main thing—unless I want there to be more of them. And on my conscience.

At the top of the staircase there's a narrow corridor and partitioned offices, also lit by the emergency lights. I follow the sound of keyclicks to Voss's office, the door of which is ajar. Potted cheese plants wilting in the artificial light, puke-brown antistatic carpet, ministry-issue desks—nobody can accuse Q Division's brass of living high on the hog. Andy's sitting in front of Voss's laptop, tapping away with a strange expression on his face. "OCCULUS is in place," I report. "Found anything interesting?"

Andy points at the screen. "We're in the wrong fucking town," he says mildly.

I circle the desk and lean over his shoulder. "Oh shit."

"You can say that again if you like." It's an email Cc'd to Voss, sent over our intranet to a Mike McLuhan. Subject: meeting. Sender: Harriet.

"Oh shit. Twice over. Something stinks. Hey, I was supposed to be in a meeting with her today," I say.

"A meeting?" Andy looks up, worried.

"Yeah. Bridget got a hair up her ass about running a BSA-authorised software audit on the office, the usual sort of make-work. Don't know that it's got anything to do with this, though."

"A *software* audit? Didn't she know Licencing and Compliance handles that on a blanket department-wide basis? We were updated on it about a year ago."

"We were—" I sit down heavily on the cheap plastic visitor's chair "—what are the chances this McLuhan guy put the idea into Harriet's mind in the first place? What are the chances it *isn't* connected?"

"McLuhan. The medium is the message. SCORPION STARE. Why do I have a bad feeling about this?" Andy sends me a worried look.

" 'Nother possibility, boss-man. What if it's an internal power play? The software audit's a cover, Purloined Letter style, hiding something fishy in plain sight where nobody will look at it twice until it's too late."

"Nonsense, Bridget's not clever enough to blow a project wide open just to discredit—" His eyes go wide.

"Are you sure of that? I mean, *really* and *truly* sure? Bet-your-life sure?"

"But the body count!" He's shaking his head in disbelief.

"So it was all a prank and it was meant to begin and end with Daisy, but it got a bit out of control, didn't it? These things happen. You told me the town police camera network's capable of end-to-end tracking and zone hand-off, didn't you? My guess is someone in this office—Voss, maybe—followed me to the car pound and realized we'd found the vehicle McLuhan used to boost Daisy. Stupid wankers, if they'd used one of their own motors we'd not be any the wiser, but they tried to use a stolen one as a cutout. So they panicked and dumped SCORPION STARE into the pound, and it didn't work, so they panicked some more and McLuhan panicked even more—bet you he's the go-between, or even the guy behind it. What is he, senior esoteric officer? Deputy site manager? He's in London so he planted the crazy blackmail threat then brought down the hammer on his own coworkers. Bet you he's a smart sociopath, the kind that does well in midlevel management, all fur coat and no knickers—and willing to shed blood without a second thought if it's to defend his position."

"Damn," Andy says mildly as he stands up. "Okay, so. Internal politics, stupid bloody prank organised to show up Angleton, they use idiots to run it so your cop finds the trail, then the lunatic in chief cuts loose and starts killing people. Is that your story?"

"Yup." I nod like my neck's a spring. "And right now they're back at the Laundry doing who the fuck knows what—"

"We've got to get McLuhan nailed down fast, before he decides the best way to cover his tracks is to take out head office. And us." He smiles reassuringly. "It'll be okay, Angleton's on his way in. You haven't seen him in action before, have you?"

Picture a light industrial/office estate in the middle of anytown with four cherry-red fire pumps drawn up, men in HAZMAT gear combing the brush, a couple of police cars with flashing light bars drawn up across the road leading into the cul-de-sac to deter casual rubberneckers. Troops disguised as firemen are systematically shooting out every one of the security cameras on the estate with their silenced carbines. Others, wearing police or fire service uniforms, are taking up stations in front of every building—occupied or otherwise—to keep the people inside out of trouble.

*Just another day at the office, folks, nothing to see here, walk on by.*

Well, maybe not. Here comes a honking great helicopter—the Twin Squirrel from the Met's ASU that I was in the other night, only it looks a lot bigger and scarier when seen from a couple hundred feet in full daylight as it settles in on the car park, leaves and debris blowing out from under the thundering rotors.

The chopper is still rocking on its skids when one of the back doors opens and Angleton jumps down, stumbling slightly—he's no spring chicken—then collects himself and strides toward us, clutching a briefcase. "Speak," he tells me, voice barely raised to cover the rush of slowing rotors.

"Problem, boss." I point to the building: "Andy's still inside confirming the worst but it looks like it started as a fucking stupid interdepartmental prank; it went bad, and now one of the perps has wigged out and gone postal."

"A prank." He turns those icy blue peepers on me and just for a fraction of a second I'm not being stared at by a sixty-something skinny bald guy in a badly fitting suit but by a walking skeleton with the radioactive fires of hell burning balefully in its eye sockets. "You'd better take me to see Andrew. Fill me in on the way."

I'm stumbling over my tongue and hurrying to keep up with Angleton when we make it to the front desk, where Andy's busy giving the OCCULUS folks cleanup directions and tips for what to do with the broken lamia and the summoning altars in the basement. "Who's—oh, it's you. About time." He grins. "Who's holding the fort?"

"I left Boris in charge," Angleton says mildly, not taking exception at Andy's brusque manner. "How bad is it?"

"Bad." Andy's cheek twitches, which is a bad sign: all his confidence seems to have fled now that Angleton's arrived. "We need to—damn."

"Take your time," Angleton soothes him. "I'm not going to eat you." Which is when I realize just how scared *I* am, and if I'm half out of my tree what does that say about Andy? I'll give Angleton this much, he knows when not to push his subordinates too hard. Andy takes a deep breath, lets it out slowly, then tries again.

"We've got two loose ends: Mark McLuhan, and a John Doe. McLuhan worked here as senior occult officer, basically an oversight role. He also did a bunch of other stuff for Q Division that took him down to Dansey House in a liaison capacity. I can't *believe* how badly we've slipped up on our vetting process—"

"Take your time," Angleton interrupts, this time with a slight edge to his voice.

"Sorry, sorry. Bob's been putting it together." A nod in my direction. "McLuhan is working with a John Doe inside the Laundry to make us look bad via a selective disclosure leak—basically one that was intended to be written off as bad-ass forteana, nothing for anyone but the black helicopter crowd to pay any attention to, except that it would set you up to look bad. I've found some not very good email from Bridget inviting McLuhan down to headquarters, some pretext to do with a software audit. Really fucking stupid stuff that Bob can do the legwork on later. But what I *really* think is happening is, Bridget arranged this to make you look bad in support of a power play in front of the director's office."

Angleton turns to me: "Phone head office. Ask for Boris. Tell him to arrest McLuhan. Tell him, SHRINKWRAP. And MARMOSET." I raise an eyebrow. "Now, lad!"

Ah, the warm fuzzies of decisive action. I head for the lamia's desk and pick up the phone and dial 666; behind me Andy is telling Angleton something in a low voice.

"Switchboard?" I ask the sheet of white noise. "I want Boris. *Now.*" The Enochian metagrammar parsers do their thing and the damned souls or enchained demons or whatever on switchboard hiss louder then connect the circuit. I hear another ring tone. Then a familiar voice.

"Hello, Capital Laundry Services, system support department. Who are you wanting to talk to?"

*Oh shit.* "Hello, Harriet," I say, struggling to sound calm and collected. Getting Bridget's imp at this juncture is not a good sign, especially when she and Boris are renowned for their mutual loathing. "This is a red phone call. Is Boris about?"

"Oh-ho, Robert! I was wondering where you were. Are you trying to pull a sickie again?"

"No, I'm not," I say, taking a deep breath. "I need to talk to Boris urgently, Harriet, is he around?"

"Oh, I couldn't possibly say. That would be disclosing information prejudicial to the good running of the department over a public network connection, and I couldn't possibly encourage you to do that when you can bloody well show your face in the office for the meeting we scheduled the day before yesterday, remember that?"

I feel as if my guts have turned to ice. "Which meeting?" I ask.

"The software audit, remember? You never read the agenda for meetings. If you did, you might have taken an interest in the *any other business* . . . Where *are* you calling from, Bob? Anyone would think you didn't work here . . ."

"I want to talk to Boris. Right now." The graunching noise in the background is my jaw clenching. "It's urgent, Harriet. To do with the code blue the other day. Now you can get him right now or you can regret it later, which is your choice?"

"Oh, I don't think that'll be necessary," she says in what I can only describe as a gloating tone of voice. "After missing the meeting, you and your precious Counter-Possession Unit will be divisional history, and you'll have only yourselves to blame! Goodbye." And the bitch hangs up on me.

I look round and see both Andy and Angleton staring at me. "She hung up," I say stupidly. "Fucking Harriet has a diversion on Boris's line. It's a setup. Something about making an end run around the CPU."

"Then we shall have to attend this meeting in person," Angleton says, briskly marching toward the front doors, which bend aside to get out of his way. "Follow me!"

We proceed directly to the helicopter, which has kept its engines idling while we've been inside. It's only taken, what? Three or four minutes since Angleton arrived? I see another figure heading toward us across the car park—a figure in a grey trouser suit, slightly stained, a wild look in her eyes. "Hey, you!" she shouts. "I want some answers!"

Angleton turns to me. "Yours?" I nod. He beckons to her imperiously. "Come with us," he calls, raising his voice over the whine of gathering turbines. Past her shoulder I see one of the fake firemen lowering a kitbag that had been, purely coincidentally, pointed at DI Sullivan's back. "This bit I always dislike," he adds in a low monotone, his face set in a grim expression of disapproval. "The fewer lives we warp, the better."

I half-consider asking him to explain what he means, but he's already climbing into the rear compartment of the chopper and Andy is following him. I give Josephine a hand up as the blades overhead begin to turn and the engines rise in a full-throated bellowing duet. I get my headset on in time to hear Angleton's orders: "Back to London, and don't spare the horses."

The Laundry is infamous for its grotesque excesses in the name of accounting; budgetary infractions are punished like war crimes, and mere paper clips can bring down the wrath of dead alien gods on your head. But when Angleton says *don't spare the horses* he sends us screaming across the countryside at a hundred and forty miles per hour, burning aviation fuel by the ton and getting ATC to clear lower priority traffic out of our way—and all because he doesn't want to be late for a meeting. There's a police car waiting for us at the pad, and we cut through the chaotic London traffic incredibly fast, almost making it into third gear at times.

"McLuhan's got SCORPION STARE," I tell Angleton round the curve of Andy's shoulder. "And headquarters's security cams are all wired. If he primes them before we get back there, we could find a lockout—or worse. It all depends on what Harriet and her boss have been planning."

"We will just have to see." Angleton nods very slightly, his facial expression rigid. "Do you still have your lucky charm?"

"Had to use it." I'd shrug, if there was more room. "What do you think Bridget's up to?"

"I couldn't possibly comment." I'd take Angleton's dismissal as a putdown, but he points his chin at the man in the driver's seat. "When we get there, Bob, I want you to go in through the warehouse door and wake the caretaker. You have your mobile telephone?"

"Uh, yeah," I say, hoping like hell that the battery hasn't run down.

"Good. Andrew. You and I will enter through the front door. Bob, set your telephone to vibrate. When you receive a message from me, you will know it is time to have the janitor switch off the main electrical power. *And* the backup power."

"Oops." I lick my suddenly dry lips, thinking of all the electrical containment pentacles in the basement and all the computers plugged into the filtered and secured circuit on the other floors. "All hell's going to break loose if I do that."

"That's what I'm counting on." The bastard *smiles*, and despite all the horrible sights I've seen today so far, I hope most of all that I never see it again before the day I die.

"Hey, what about me?" Angleton glances at the front seat with a momentary flash of irritation. Josephine stares right back, clearly angry and struggling to control it. "I'm your liaison officer for North Buckinghamshire," she says, "and I'd really *like* to know who I'm liaising with, especially as you seem to have left a few *bodies* on my manor that I'm going to have to bury, and this jerk—" she means me, I am distraught! Oh, the ignominy! "—promised me you'd have the answers."

Angleton composes himself. "There are no answers, madam, only further questions," he says, and just for a second he sounds like a pious wanker of a vicar going through the motions of comforting the bereaved. "And if you want the answers you'll have to go through the jerk's filing cabinet." *Bastard.* Then there's a flashing sardonic grin, dry as the desert sands in June: "Do you want to help prevent any, ah, recurrence of what you saw an hour ago? If so, you may accompany the jerk and attempt to keep him from dying." He reaches out a hand and drops a ragged slip of paper over her shoulder. "You'll need this."

*Provisional warrant card, my oh my.* Josephine mutters something unkind about his ancestry, barnyard animals, and lengths of rubber hose. I pretend not to hear because we're about three minutes out, stuck behind a slow-moving but gregarious herd of red double-decker buses, and I'm trying to remember the way to the janitor's office in the Laundry main unit basement and whether there's anything I'm likely to trip over in the dark.

"Excuse me for asking, but how many corpses do you usually run into in the course of your job?" I ask.

"Too many, since you showed up." We turn the street corner into a brick-walled alley crowded by wheelie bins and smelling of vagrant piss. "But since you ask, I'm a detective inspector. You get to see lots of vile stuff on the beat."

Something in her expression tells me I'm on dangerous ground here, but I persist: "Well, this is the Laundry. It's our job to deal with seven shades of vile shit so that people like you don't have to." I take a deep breath. "And before we go in I figured I should warn you that you're going to think Fred and Rosemary West work for us, and Harold Shipman's the medical officer." At this point she goes slightly pale—the Demon DIYers and Doctor Death are the acme of British serial killerdom after all—but she doesn't flinch.

"And you're the *good* guys?"

"Sometimes I have my doubts," I sigh.

"Well, join the club." I have a feeling she's going to make it, if she lives through the next hour.

"Enough bullshit. *This* is the street level entrance to the facilities block under Headquarters Building One. You saw what those fuckers did with the cameras at the car pound and Site Able. If my guess is straight, they're going to do it all over again *here*—or worse. From here there's a secure line to several of the Met's offices, including various borough-level control systems, such as the Camden Town control centre. SCORPION STARE isn't ready for nationwide deployment—"

"What the *hell* would justify that?" she demands, eyes wide.

"You do not have clearance for that information." Amazing how easily the phrase trips off the tongue. "Besides, it'd give you nightmares. But you're the one who mentioned hell, and as I was saying     " I stop, with an overflowing dumpster between us and the anonymous doorway "—our pet lunatic, who killed all those folks at Dillinger Associates and who is now in a committee meeting upstairs, could conceivably upload bits of SCORPION STARE to the various camera control centres. Which is why we are going to stop him, by bringing down the intranet backbone cable in and out of the Laundry's headquarters. Which would be easy if this was a bog-standard government office, but a little harder in reality because the Laundry has guards, and some of those guards are very special, and some of those very special guards will try to stop us by eating us alive."

"Eating. Us." Josephine is looking a little glassy. "Did I tell you that I don't do headhunters? That's Recruitment's job."

"Look," I say gently, "have you ever seen *Night of the Living Dead*? It's really not all that different—except that I've got permission to be here, and you've got a temporary warrant card too, so we should be all right." A thought strikes me. "You're a cop. Have you been through firearms training?"

*Click-clack.* "Yes," she says drily. "Next question?"

"Great! If you'd just take that away from my nose—that's better—it won't work on the guards. Sorry, but they're already, uh, metabolically challenged. However, it *will* work very nicely on the CCTV cameras. Which—"

"Okay, I get the picture. We go in. We stay out of the frame unless we want to die." She makes the pistol vanish inside her jacket and looks at me askance—for the first time since the car pound with something other than irritation or dislike. Probably wondering why I didn't flinch. (Obvious, really: compared with what's waiting for us inside a little intracranial air conditioning is a relatively painless way to go, and besides, if she was seriously pissed at me she could have gotten me alone in a nice soundproofed cell back in her manor with a pair of size twelve boots and their occupants.) "We're going to go in there and you're going to talk our way past the zombies while I shoot out all the cameras, right?"

"Right. And then I'm going to try to figure out how to take down the primary switchgear, the backup substation, the diesel generator, *and* the batteries for the telephone switch and the protected computer ring main *all* at the same time so nobody twigs until it's too late. While fending off anyone who tries to stop us. Clear?"

"As mud." She stares at me. "I always wanted to be on TV, but not quite this way."

"Yeah, well." I glance up the side of the building, which is windowless as far as the third floor (and then the windows front onto empty rooms three feet deep, just to give the appearance of occupation). "I'd rather call in an air strike on the power station but there's a hospital two blocks that way and an old folks' home on the other side . . . you ready?"

She nods. "Okay." And I take a step round the wheelie bin and knock on the door.

The door is a featureless blue slab of paint. As soon as I touch it, it swings open—no creaking here, did you think this was a Hammer horror flick?—to reveal a small, dusty room with a dry powder fire extinguisher bolted to one wall and another door opposite. "Wait," I say, and take the spray paint can out of my pocket. "Okay, come on in. Keep your warrant note handy."

She jumps when the door closes automatically with a faint hiss, and I remember to swallow—it only looks like a cheap fire door from the outside. "Okay, here's the fun part." I give the inner door a quick scan with a utility on my palmtop and it comes up blank, so I put my hand on the grab-bar and pull. This is the moment of truth; if the shit has truly hit the fan already the entire building will be locked down tighter than a nuclear bunker, and the thaumaturgic equivalent of a three-phase six-hundred-volt bearer will be running through all the barred portals. But I get to keep on breathing, and the door swings open on a dark corridor leading past shut storeroom doors to a dingy wooden staircase. And that's all it is—there's nothing in here to confuse an accidental burglar who makes it in past the wards in hope of finding some office supplies to filch. All the really classified stuff is either ten storeys underground or on the other side of the cellar walls. Twitching in the darkness.

"I don't see any zombies," Josephine says edgily, crowding up behind me in the gloom.

"That's because they're—" I freeze and bring up the dry powder extinguisher. "Have you got a pocket mirror?" I ask, trying to sound casual.

"Hold on." I hear a dry click, and then she passes me something like a toothbrush fucking a contact lens. "Will this do?"

"Oh wow, I didn't know you were a dentist." It's on a goddamn telescoping wand almost half a metre long. I lean forward and gingerly stretch the angled mirror so I can view the stairwell.

"It's for checking the undersides of cars for bombs—or cut brake pipes. You never know what the little fuckers in the school playground will do while you're talking to the headmistress."

*Gulp.* "Well, I guess this is a suitable alternative use."

I don't see any cameras up there so I retract the mirror and I'm about to set foot on the stairs when she says, "You missed one."

"Huh . . . ?"

She points. It's about waist level, the size of a doorknob, embedded in the dark wooden wainscoting, and it's pointing *up* the stairs. "Shit, you're right." And there's something odd about it. I slide the mirror closer for an oblique look and dry-swallow. "There are two lenses. Oh, tricky."

I pull out my multitool and begin digging them out of the wall. It's coax cable, just like the doctor ordered. There's no obvious evidence of live SCORPION STARE, but my hands are still clammy and my heart is in my mouth as I realize how close I came to walking in front of it. How small can they make CCTV cameras, anyway? I keep seeing smaller and smaller ones . . .

"Better move fast," she comments.

"Why?"

"Because you've just told them you're coming."

"Oh. Okay." We climb the staircase in bursts, stopping before the next landing to check for more basilisk bugs. Josephine spots one, and so do I—I tag them with the mostly empty can of paint, then she blasts their lenses from behind and underneath, trying not to breathe the fumes in before we move past them. There's an unnaturally creaky floorboard, too, just for yucks. But we make it to the ground floor landing alive, and I just have time to realize how badly we've fucked up when the lights come up and the night watchmen come out from either side.

"Ah, Bob! Decided to visit the office for once, have we?"

It's Harriet, looking slightly demented in a black pin-striped suit and clutching a glass of what looks like fizzy white wine.

"Where the fuck is everyone else?" I demand, looking round. At this time of day the place should be heaving with office bodies. But all I see here is Harriet—and three or four silently leaning night watchmen in their grey ministry suits and hangdog expressions, luminous worms of light glowing in their eyes.

"I do believe we called the monthly fire drill a few hours ahead of schedule." Harriet smirks. "Then we locked the doors. It's quite simple, you know."

Fred from Accounting lurches sideways and peers at me over her shoulder. He's been dead for months: normally I'd say this was something of an improvement, but right now he's drooling slightly as if it's past his teatime.

"Who's *that?*" asks Josephine.

"Who? Oh, one of them's a shambling undead bureaucrat and the other one used to work in accounts before he had a little accident with a summoning." I bare my teeth at Harriet. "The game's up."

"I don't think so." She's just standing there, looking supercillious and slightly triumphant behind her bodyguard of zombies. "Actually the boot is on the other foot. You're late and you're out of a job, Robert. The Counter-Possession Unit is being liquidated—that old fossil Angleton isn't needed anymore, once we get the benefits of panopticon surveillance combined with look-to-kill technology and rolled out on a departmental basis. In fact, you're just in time to clear your desk." She grins, horribly. "Stupid little boy, I'm sure they can find a use for you below stairs."

"You've been talking to our friend Mr McLuhan, haven't you?" I ask desperately, trying to keep her talking—I *really* don't want the night watchmen to carry me away. "Is he upstairs?"

"If so, you probably need to know that I intend to arrest him. Twelve counts of murder and attempted murder, in case you were wondering." I almost look round, but manage to resist the urge: Josephine's voice is brittle but controlled. "Police."

"Wrong jurisdiction, dear," Harriet says consolingly. "And I do believe our idiot tearaway here has got you on the wrong message. That will never do." She snaps her fingers. "Take the woman, detain the man."

"Stop—" I begin. The zombies step forward, lurching jerkily, and then all hell breaks loose about twenty centimeters from my right ear. Zombies make excellent night watchmen and it takes a lot to knock one down, but they're not bulletproof, and Josephine unloads her magazine two rounds at a time. I'm dazzled by the flash and my head feels as if someone is whacking me on the ear with a shovel—bits of meat and unspeakable ripped stuff go flying, but precious little blood, and they keep coming.

"When you've *quite* finished," Harriet hisses, and snaps her fingers at Josephine: the zombies pause for a moment then close in, as their mistress backs toward the staircase up to the first floor.

"Quick, down the back corridor there!" I gasp, pointing to my left.

"The—what?"

"Quick!"

I dash along the corridor, tugging Josephine's arm until I feel her running with me. I pull my warrant card and yell, "*Open sesame!*" ahead and doors slam open to either side—including the broom closets and ductwork access points. "In here!" I dive in to one side and Josephine piles in after me and I yank at the door—"*Close, damn you, fuck, close sesame!"* and it slams shut with the hardscrabble of bony fingertips on the outside.

"Got a light?" I ask.

"Naah, I don't smoke. But I've got a torch somewhere—"

The scrabbling's getting louder. "I don't want to hurry you or anything, but—" And lo, there is light.

We're standing at the bottom of a shallow shaft with cable runs vanishing above us into the gloom. Josephine looks frantic. "They didn't drop! I shot them and they *didn't drop!*"

"Don't sweat it, they're run by remote control." Maybe now is not the time to explain about six-node summoning points, the Vohlman exercise, and the minutiae of raising and binding the dead: they're knocking on the door and they want in. But look, here's something even *more* interesting. "Hey, I see CAT-5 cabling. Pass me your torch?"

"This isn't the time to go all geeky on me, nerd-boy. Or are you looking for roaches?"

"Just fucking do it, I'll explain later, okay?" Harriet is really getting to me; it's been a long day and I told myself ages ago that if I ever heard another fucking lecture about timekeeping from her I'd go postal.

"Bingo." It *is* CAT-5, and there's an even more interesting cable running off to one side that looks like a DS-3. I whip out my multitool and begin working on the junction box. The scrabbling's become insistent by the time I've uncovered the wires, but what the fuck. Who was it who said, *When they think you're technical is the time to go crude?* I grab a handful of network cables and yank, hard. Then I grab another handful. Then, having disconnected the main trunk line—*mission accomplished*—I take another moment to think.

"Bob, have you got a plan?"

"I'm thinking."

"Then think faster, they're about to come through the door—"

Which is when I remember my mobile phone and decide to make a last-ditch attempt. I speed-dial Bridget's office extension—and Angleton picks up after two rings. Bastard.

"Ah, Bob!" He sounds positively avuncular. "Where are you? Did you manage to shut down the Internet?"

I don't have time to correct him. Besides, Josephine is reloading her cannon and I think she's going to try a *really* horrible pun if I don't produce a solution PDQ. "Boss, run McLuhan's SCORPION STARE tool and upload the firmware to all the motion-tracking cameras on the ground floor east wing loop *right now.*"

"What? I'm not sure I heard you correctly."

I take a deep breath. "She's subverted the night watchmen.

Everybody else is out of the building. Do it *now* or I'm switching to a diet of fresh brains."

"If you say so," he agrees, with the manner of an indulgent uncle talking to a tearaway schoolboy, then hangs up.

There's a splintering crash and a hand rams through the door right between us and embeds itself in the wall opposite. "Oh shit," I have time to say as the hand withdraws. Then a bolt of lightning goes off about two feet outside the door, roughly simultaneous with a sizzling crash and a wave of heat. We cower in the back of the cupboard, terrified of fire until after what seems like an eternity the sprinklers come on.

"Is it safe yet?" she asks—at least I think that's what she says, my ears are still ringing.

"One way to find out." I take the broken casing from the network junction box and chuck it through the hole in the door. When it doesn't explode I gingerly push the door open. The ringing is louder; it's my phone. I pull it wearily out of my pocket and hunch over it to keep it dry, leaning against the wall of the corridor to stay as far away from the blackened zombie corpses as I can. "Who's there?"

"Your manager." He sounds merely amused this time. "What a sorry shower you are! Come on up to Mahogany Row and dry off, both of you—the director has a personal bathroom, I think you've earned it."

"Uh. Harriet? Bridget? McLuhan?"

"Taken care of," he says complacently, and I shiver convulsively as the water reaches gelid tentacles down my spine and tickles my balls like a drowned lover.

"Okay. We'll be right up." I glance back at the smashed-in utility cupboard and Josephine smiles at me like a frightened feral rat, all sharp teeth and savagery and shining .38 automatic. "We're safe now," I say, as reassuringly as possible. "I think we won . . ."

The journey to Angleton's lair is both up and along—he normally works out of a gloomy basement on the other side of the hollowed-out block of prime London real estate that is occupied by the Laundry, but this time he's ensconced in the director's suite on the abandoned top floor of the north wing.

The north wing is still dry. Over there, people are still at work, oblivious to the charred zombies lying on the scorched, soaked, thaumaturgically saturated wing next door. We catch a few odd stares—myself, soaked and battered in my outdoors gear, DI Sullivan in the wreckage of an expensive grey suit, oversized handgun clenched in a death grip at her side—but wisely or otherwise, nobody asks me to fix the Internet or demands to know why we're tracking muddy water through Human Resources.

By the time we reach the thick green carpet and dusty quietude of the director's suite Josephine's eyes are wide but she's stopped shaking. "You've got lots of questions," I manage to say. "Try to save them for later. I'll tell you everything I know and you're cleared for, once I've had time to phone my fiancée."

"I've got a husband and a nine year old son, did you think of that before you dragged me into this insane nightmare? Sorry. I know you didn't *mean* to. It's just that shooting up zombies and being zapped by basilisks makes me a little upset. Nerves."

"I know. Just try not to wave them in front of Angleton, okay?"

"Who *is* Angleton, anyway? Who does he think he is?"

I pause before the office door. "If I knew that, I'm not sure I'd be allowed to tell you." I knock three times.

"Enter." Andy opens the door for us. Angleton is sitting in the director's chair, playing with something in the middle of the huge expanse of oak desk that looks as if it dates to the 1930s. (There's a map on the wall behind him, and a quarter of it is pink.) "Ah, Mister Howard, Detective Inspector. So good of you to come."

I peer closer. *Clack. Clack. Clack.* "A Newton's cradle; how 1970s."

"You could say that." He smiles thinly. The balls bouncing back and forth between the arms of the executive desktop aren't chromed, rather they appear to be textured: pale brown on one side, dark or blonde and furry on the other. And bumpy, disturbingly bumpy . . .

I take a deep breath. "Harriet was waiting for us. Said we were too late and the Counter-Possession Unit was being disbanded."

*Clack. Clack.*

"Yes, she would say that, wouldn't she."

*Clack. Clack. Clack. Clack.* Finally I can't stand it anymore. "Well?" I demand.

"A fellow I used to know, his name was Ulyanov, once said something rather profound, do you know." Angleton looks like the cat that's swallowed the canary—and the feet are sticking out of the side of his mouth; he *wants* me to know this, whatever it is. "Let your enemies sell you enough rope to hang them with."

"Uh, wasn't that Lenin?" I ask.

A flicker of mild irritation crosses his face. "This was before then," he says quietly. *Clack. Clack. Clack.* He flicks the balls to set them banging again and I suddenly realize what they are and feel quite sick. No indeed, Bridget and Harriet—and Bridget's predecessor, and the mysterious Mr McLuhan—won't be troubling me again. (Except in my nightmares about this office, visions of my own shrunken head winding up in one of the director's executive toys, skull clattering away eternally in a scream that nobody can hear anymore . . .) "Bridget's been plotting a boardroom coup for a long time, Robert. Probably since before you joined the Laundry—or were conscripted." He spares Josephine a long, appraising look. "She suborned Harriet, bribed McLuhan, installed her own corrupt geas on Voss. Partners in crime, intending to expose me as an incompetent and a possible security leak before the Board of Auditors, I suppose—that's usually how they plan it. I guessed this was going on, but I needed firm evidence. You supplied it. Unfortunately, Bridget was never too stable; when she realized that I knew, she ordered Voss to remove the witnesses then summoned McLuhan and proceeded with her palace coup d'état. Equally unfortunately for her, she failed to correctly establish who my line manager was before she attempted to go over my head to have me removed." He taps the sign on the front of the desk: PRIVATE SECRETARY. Keeper of the secrets. Whose secrets?

"Matrix management," I finally say, the lightbulb coming on above my head at last. "The Laundry runs on matrix management. She saw you on the org chart as head of the Counter-Possession Unit, not as private secretary to . . ." *So that's how come he's got the free run of the director's office!*

Josephine is aghast. "You call this a government department?"

"Worse things happen in parliament every day of the year, my dear." Now that the proximate threat is over, Angleton looks remarkably imperturbable; right now I doubt he'd turn her into a frog even if she started yelling at him. "Besides, you are aware of the maxim that power corrupts and absolute power corrupts absolutely? Here we deal every day of the week with power sufficient to destroy your mind. Even worse, we *cannot* submit to public oversight—it's far too dangerous, like giving atomic firecrackers to three-year-olds. Ask Robert to tell you what he did to attract our attention later, if you like." I'm still dripping and cold, but I can feel my ears flush.

He focuses on her some more. "We can reinforce the geas and release you," he adds quietly. "But I think you can do a much more important job here. The choice is yours."

I snort under my breath. She glances at me, eyes narrowed and cynical. "If this is what passes for a field investigation in your department, you *need* me."

"Yes, well, you don't need to make your mind up immediately. Detached duty, and all that. As for you, Bob," he says, with heavy emphasis on my name, "you have acquitted yourself satisfactorily again. Now go and have a bath before you rot the carpet."

"Bathroom's two doors down the hall on the left," Andy adds helpfully from his station against the wall, next to the door: there's no doubt right now as to who's in charge here.

"But what happens now?" I ask, bewildered and a bit shocky and already fighting off the yawns that come on when people stop trying to kill me. "I mean, what's really *happened?*"

Angleton grins like a skull: "Bridget forfeited her department, so the directors have asked me to put Andrew in acting charge of it for the time being. Boris slipped up and failed to notice McLuhan; he is, ah, temporarily indisposed. And as for you, a job well done wins its natural reward—another job." His grin widens. "As I believe the youth of today say, don't have a cow . . ."

# Afterword:
# Inside the Fear Factory

$\diamond$  $\diamond$  $\diamond$

*F*ICTION SERVES A VARIETY OF PURPOSES. AT ITS HEART lies the simple art of storytelling—of transferring ideas and sequences of events and pictures and people from the storyteller's head to that of the audience solely by means of words. But storytelling is a tool, and the uses to which a tool can be put often differs from—and is more interesting than—the uses for which the tool was designed.

Fiction is spun from plausible lies, contrived to represent an abreality sufficiently convincing that we do not question what we hear—and there are different forms within fiction. Consuming fiction is fun, an activity we engage in for recreation. So why, then, do we have an appetite for forms of fiction that make us profoundly uneasy, or that frighten us?

The chances are that if you've got to this afterword, you've done so the long way round—by reading "The Atrocity Archive" and "The Concrete Jungle." This book is a work of fiction, a recreational product. Nobody forced you to read it by holding a gun to your head, so presumably you enjoyed the experience. Now, at risk of demystifying it, I'd like to pick over the corpse, dissect its three major organs, and try to explain just how it all fits together.

## Cold Warriors

I'd like to begin by painting an anonymized portrait of one of the greatest horror writers of the twentieth century—a man whose writing was a major influence on me when I wrote these stories.

D. was born in London in 1929, of working class parents. A bright young man, he was educated at St Marylebone Grammar and William

Ellis, Kentish Town, then worked as a railway clerk before undergoing National Service in the RAF as a photographer attached to the Special Investigation Branch.

After his discharge in 1949, he studied art, achieving a scholarship to the Royal College of Art. Working as a waiter in the evenings, he developed an interest in cooking. During the 1950s he travelled, working as an illustrator in New York City and as an art director for a London advertising agency, before settling down in Dordogne and starting to write. His first novel was an immediate success, going on to be filmed (in a version starring Michael Caine); subsequently he produced roughly a book a year for the rest of the twentieth century. D. is somewhat reclusive, and was notorious at one point for only communicating via Telex machine. He may also hold the record for being the first writer ever to produce a novel entirely using a word processor (around 1972).

D.'s work is coolly observed, with a meticulous eye for background detail and subtle nuance. His narrators are usually anonymous, their cynical inspection of organization and situation infused with a distaste or disdain for their circumstances that some of the other characters find extremely annoying, if not ideologically suspect. The world they find themselves trapped in is a maze of secret histories and occult organizations, entities that overlap with the world we live in, hiding beneath the surface like a freezing cold pond beneath a layer of thin ice. And hovering in the background over it all is a vast grey pall, a nightmare horror of impending *Götterdämmerung*; for the great game of D.'s protagonists, breezily (or depressively) cynical though they might be, is always played for the ultimate stakes.

D. is, of course Len Deighton, perhaps more commonly regarded as one of the greatest masters of the spy thriller (who, with such works as *The Ipcress File, Funeral in Berlin,* and *Billion Dollar Brain,* is considered by some critics to be the equal or even the superior of John Le Carré). And the background to his novels, the world that infused them with tension and provided the stakes for the desperate gambles he described, was the Cold War.

The Cold War came to an abrupt end in 1991 with the Soviet coup that led to the breakup of the Union of Soviet Socialist Republics. Today, just a decade or so after it ended with a whimper instead of a bang, it is increasingly hard to remember just what it was like to live with a face-off of such enormous proportions between two powers that represented the Manichean opposites of industrial civilization. But those of us who grew up during the Cold War have been as permanently scarred by it as any child who watched the events of 9/11 live on CNN; because the Cold

War applied a thin varnish of horror atop any fictional exploration of diplomacy, spying, or warfare.

Going back to the origins of the Cold War is a difficult task; its roots grew from a variety of sources in the fertile, blood-drenched soil of the early twentieth century. What is not in question is the fact that, by 1968, the United States of America and the Union of Soviet Socialist Republics had assembled—and pointed at each other on a hair-trigger— arsenals unprecedented in the history of warfare. During the First World War, all combatants combined expended on the order of eleven million tons of explosives. This was equivalent to the payload of a single B-52 bomber or Titan-2 ICBM of the middle period Cold War, before smart weapons and precision guidance systems began to replace the headsman's axe of deterrence with a surgeon's scalpel.

Many of the children of the Cold War era grew up doubting that they'd ever reach adulthood. Annihilation beckoned, in an apocalyptic guise that was nevertheless anatomized far more precisely than the visions of any mediaeval mystic. We knew the serial numbers, megatonnage, accuracy, flight characteristics, and blast effects of our nemesis, lurking sleeplessly beneath the waves or brooding in launcher-erectors scattered across the tundra under a never-setting sun.

One of Len Deighton's skills was that he infused the personal dilemmas and conflicts of his protagonists—little men and women trapped in seedy, poorly paid bureaucratic posts—with the shadow of the apocalypse. Cold War spy fiction was in some respects the ultimate expression of horror fiction, for the nightmare was *real*. There's no need to hint darkly about forbidden knowledge and elder gods, sleeping in drowned cities, who might inflict unspeakable horrors, when you live in an age where the wrong coded message can leave you blinded with your skin half-burned away in the wreckage of a dead city barely an hour later. The nightmare was very real indeed, and arguably it has never ended; but we have become blasé about it, tap dancing on the edge of the abyss because the great motor of ideological rivalry that powered the Cold War has broken down and we're all business partners in globalization today and forevermore.

Spy fiction, like horror fiction, relies on the mundanity of the protagonist to draw the reader into proximity with the unnatural and occult horrors of alienation. We are invited to identify with the likes of Harry Palmer (as Deighton named him in the film of *The Ipcress File*—significantly, he has no name in the original novel), a low-level civil servant whose occasional duties, in between filing paperwork, involve visiting nuclear test sites, shepherding weapons scientists, and hunting agents of the alien power. Slowly sucked into a ghastly plot by the slow revelation of occult, secret knowledge, Palmer is bewildered and confused and forced to confront his worst fears in a world that the novelist slowly discloses to be under a nightmarish threat from beyond the consensus reality imposed by our society.

We've also become blasé about the apocalyptic nightmares of an earlier age.

Howard Phillips Lovecraft was one of the great pioneers of the spy thriller. Born in 1890, in Providence, Rhode Island, he was the child of well-off parents. However, when Lovecraft was three years old, his father was institutionalized, and Lovecraft suffered a variety of psychosomatic ailments that prevented him attending school. Despite these problems he was self-educated, taking an interest in science as well as literature. After a nervous breakdown in 1908, Lovecraft lived at home with his increasingly deranged mother. Writing rapidly, he became a self-published amateur journalist, and in the late-nineteen-teens began to send out his stories for publication.

Lovecraft brought a cool, analytical eye to the pursuit of espionage. In his writings we frequently encounter the archetype of the scholar as spy, digging feverishly through libraries and colossal archives in search of the lost key to the cryptic puzzle. In *At the Mountains of Madness* Lovecraft prefigures the late-twentieth-century techno-thriller brilliantly, with his tale of highly trained agents of an imperial power infiltrating a forbidden icy continent—not a million miles from the brooding ice plateaux of Siberia—in search of secret knowledge, at peril of death at the hands of the vigilant defenders of the new order should they come to their attention. Echoes of Lovecraft's obsessions abound in the more developed thrillers of the Cold War, from Alistair MacLean's *Ice Station Zebra* to the fervidly luscious garden of biological horrors in Ian Fleming's *You Only Live Twice* (the book, not the film).

Are we confused yet? Just in case, I'll summarize. Len Deighton was not an author of spy thrillers but of horror, because all Cold War-era spy thrillers rely on the existential horror of nuclear annihilation to supply a frisson of terror that raises the stakes of the games their otherwise mundane characters play. And in contrast, H. P. Lovecraft was not an author of horror stories—or not entirely—for many of his preoccupations, from the obsessive collection of secret information to the infiltration and mapping of territories controlled by the alien, are at heart the obsessions of the thriller writer.

(Before I stretch this analogy to breaking point, I am compelled to admit that there *is* a difference between the function and purpose of horror and spy fiction. Horror fiction allows us to confront and sublimate our fears of an uncontrollable universe, but the threat verges on the overwhelming and may indeed carry the protagonists away. Spy fiction in contrast allows us to believe for a while that the little people can, by obtaining secret knowledge, acquire some leverage over the overwhelming threats that permeate their universe. So, although the basic dynamics of both horror and spy fiction rely on the same sense of huge, impersonal forces outside the control of the protagonists, who might initially be ignorant of them, the outcome is often different.)

## The Game of Spy and Dagon

The fictional spy is very unlike the spy in real life.

Every so often, Western intelligence agencies advertise in public for recruits. The profile of the professional agent is that of a government employee: quiet, diligent, punctillious about filling out forms and obeying procedures. Far from having a mysterious past, prospective employees of secret agencies have to provide a complete and exhaustive list of everywhere they've ever lived, and their background will be picked over in detail before the appointment is approved. Far from being men of action, the majority of intelligence community staff are office workers, a narrow majority of them female, and they almost certainly never handle weapons in the line of duty.

The picture changes when you contemplate non-Western organizations such as the Iraqi Mukhabarat, agencies of states that contemplate internal subversion with the cold eye of totalitarian zeal. It changes in time of open warfare, and it changes again when you examine Western agencies concerned with counter-terrorism and organised crime duties, such as the FBI. But the key insight to bear in mind is that in reality, the James Bond of the movie series (and, to a lesser extent, Ian Fleming's original literary wish-fulfillment vehicle) is an almost perfect photographic negative of the real intelligence agent. He is everything that a real spy cannot afford to be—flashy, violent, high-rolling, glamorous, the centre of attention.

So why are spies such fascinating targets of fiction?

Answer: because they know (or want to know) what's really going on.

We live in an age of uncertainty, complexity, and paranoia. Uncertainty because, for the past few centuries, there has simply been far too much knowledge out there for any one human being to get their brains around; we are all ignorant, if you dig far enough. Complexity multiplies because our areas of ignorance and our blind spots intersect in unpredictable ways—the most benign projects have unforeseen side effects. And paranoia is the emergent spawn of those side effects; the world is not as it seems, and indeed we may never be able to comprehend the world-as-it-is, without the comforting filter lenses of our pre-conceptions and our mass media.

It is therefore both an attractive proposition (and a frightening one) to believe that someone, somewhere, knows the score. It's attractive when we think they're on our side, defenders of our values and our lives, fighting in the great and secret wars to ensure that our cozy creature comforts survive undisturbed. And it's terrifying when we fear that maybe, just maybe, someone out there who *doesn't like us*, or even *doesn't* think *like us*, has got their hands on the control yoke of an airliner and is aiming dead for the twin towers of our *Weltanschauung*.

That's not just a tasteless metaphor, by the way. One comment that surfaced a lot in the second half of September 2001 was, "I thought at first it was like something out of a Tom Clancy novel." Tom Clancy is one of the leading exponents of the mega-scale techno-thriller, the big-ger-is-better offshoot of the spy novel and its obsession with gadgets and tools of the trade. For an instant, the fabric of the real world seemed to have been ripped aside and replaced with a terrible fiction—and indeed, the 9/11 hijackers thought that they were *sending a message* to the hated West. It was a message that shocked and horrified (and maimed and murdered); and part of the reason it was so painful was that it struck at our assumption that we knew the score, that we knew what was going on and that our defenders were awake and on the ball.

Sometimes the paranoia can strike too close to home: writing in the near future is a perilous proposition. I began writing "The Atrocity Archive" in 1999. For Bob's trip to California and his run-in with some frighteningly out-of-their-depth terrorists, I went digging and came back with an appropriately obscure but fanatical and unpleasant gang who might, conceivably, be planning an atrocity on American soil. But by the time the novel first came into print in the pages of the Scottish magazine *Spectrum SF*, it was late 2001—and editor Paul Fraser quite sensibly sug-gested I replace Osama bin Laden and al-Qaida with something slightly more obscure on the grounds that, with USAF bombers already pound-ing the hills of Afghanistan, bin Laden didn't appear to have much of a future. (In retrospect, I got off lightly. Who can forget the wave of late-eighties cold war thrillers set in the USSR in the mid-nineties?)

As for the war in Iraq, I make no apologies. The novel was written in 1999–2000, and should be taken as set in 2001, *before* the events of 9/11.

On the other side of the narrative fence from our friend the spy stands our enemy, the destructive Other. The Other comes in a variety of guises, but always means us ill in one form or another. It might be that the Other wants to conquer and subjugate us, enforce our obedience to a religion, ideology, or monarch. Or the Other might simply want to eat our brains, or crack our bones and suck our marrow. Whatever the goal, it is defined in terms profoundly incompatible with our comfort and safety. Sometimes ideology and alienation overlap in alegory; the 1950s classic *Invasion of the Body Snatchers* was superficially about invading aliens, but also served as a close metaphor for Cold War paranoia about Communist infiltrators. Meanwhile, *The Stepford Wives* tore away the mask of an outwardly utopian vision of a conformist community with everyone in their place to reveal a toe-curlingly unpleasant process of alienation worming its way beneath the skin.

There is this about horror: it allows us to confront our fears, dragging the bogeyman out of the closet to loom over us in his most intimidating guise. (The outcome of the confrontation depends on whether the horror is a classical tragedy—in which the protagonist suffers their downfall because of a flawed character and hubris—or a comedy—in which they are redeemed; but the protagonist is still tainted with the brush of horror.)

And there is this about spy fiction: it allows us to confront our ignorance, by groping warily around the elephant of politics until it blows its trumpet, or perhaps stamps one gigantic foot on the protagonist's head. (Again, the outcome depends on the tragicomic roots of the narrative—but it still all hinges on ignorance and revelation.)

And now for something completely different.

## HAX0R DUD35

The fictional hacker is not a real computer geek but a four-thousand-year-old archetype.

There have been trickster-gods running around administering wedgies to authority figures ever since the first adolescent apprentice took the piss out of his elder shaman. From Anansi the spider god through to the Norse trickster-god Loki, the trickster has been the expression of whimsy, curiosity, and occasional malice. Our first detailed knowledge of polytheistic religions comes from the first agricultural civilizations to leave written records behind. Early agricultural societies were conservative to a degree that seems bizarrely alien to us today: they balanced on a Malthusian knife-edge between productive plenitude and the starvation of famine. Change was deeply suspicious because it meant, as often as not, crop failure and starvation. The trickster-god is the one who makes a constant out of change; stealing fire, stealing language, stealing just about anything that isn't nailed down and quite a lot that is, he brought our ancestors most of their innovations.

Let's fast-forward to the present day, where a bewildering rate of change is actually a norm that can be counted upon to continue for decades or centuries. While we don't have trickster-gods and death-gods and crop-gods anymore, we *do* have narratives that serve the purpose of accustoming us to the idea of almost magical social dislocation.

The hot core of recent technological innovation—"recent" meaning since 1970—has been the computer industry. Driven by the inevitable progression of Moore's law, we've seen enormous breakthroughs, the likes of which haven't been seen since the rapid development of aviation between 1910 and 1950. Computers are a pervasive technology, and wherever they go they leave a sluglike trail of connectedness, information-dense and meaning-rich with the distillate of our minds. Unlike earlier technologies computers are general-purpose tools that can be reconfigured to do different tasks at the press of a button: one moment it's a dessert topping, the next it's a floor wax (or a spreadsheet, or an immersive game).

Hackers, in fiction, are the trickster-gods of the realm of computing. They go where they're not supposed to, steal anything that isn't nailed down (or rather, written down in ink on parchment with a quill plucked from a white goose), and boast about it. There is a refreshing immediacy to their activities because they move at the speed of light, cropping up anywhere they wish.

In reality, nothing could be further from the truth. Real hackers—computer programmers in the sense that the word was coined at MIT in the 1960s—are meticulous, intelligent, mathematically and linguistically inclined obsessives. Far from diving in and out of your bank account details, they're more likely to spend months working on a mathematical model of an abstraction that only another hacker would understand, or realize was an elaborate intellectual joke. All engineering disciplines generate a shared culture and jargon. The computing field has generated a remarkably rich jargon, and a shared culture to go with it. In some cases the sense of tradition is astonishingly strong; there are clubs and mutual support groups, for instance, for those people who choose to lovingly nurse along the twenty-year-old minicomputers they rescued from scrapheaps, rather than abandon them and move what software they can to a new generation of hardware.

At the other end of the spectrum are the script kiddies and warez dudes, the orcish adolescent otaku who trash other people's work machines and try to take over chat networks in a fit of asocial misspelled pique. These are the real and mildly destructive hackers who generate most of the newspaper headlines and outrage—tweaking the codebase of moronic email viruses, hanging out online and moaning endlessly, swallowing the image reflected back at them by the magic mirror of the tabloid press.

But if we return for a moment to the fictional hacker, not only do we discover the archetype of the trickster-god lurking just round the corner, but we also discern the outline of our spy/horror protagonist hunched over their keyboard, trying to dig down into the network of dreams and fears to understand what's really going on.

*Every* science-fictional depiction of a hacker at work seems to be about pulling away the rug to reveal a squirming mass of icky truths hiding beneath the carpet of reality. From John M. Ford's *Web of Angels* onward, we've had hackers exploiting networks to find the truth about what's really going on. Sometimes the hacker archetype overlaps with the guy-with-a-gun (as in Ken MacLeod's *The Star Fraction* or William Gibson's *Johnny Mnemonic*), or the gamer-with-a-virtual-gun (in film, Mamoru Oshii's *Avalon*), or even both (Hiro Protagonist, in Neal Stephenson's *Snow Crash*). Mao remarked, "power grows from the barrel of a gun"—both in real life and in fiction—and if guns are about power, then hacking is about secret knowledge, and knowledge is also power. In fact, when you get down to it, what the fictional hacker has come to symbolize is not that far away from the fictional spy—or the nameless narrator of one of H. P. Lovecraft's strange tales of exploration and alienation.

## Hacking the Subconscious, Spying on Horror, Revealing Reality

There's an iron tripod buried in the basement of the Laundry, carved with words in an alien language that humans can only interpret with the aid of a semisentient computer program that emulates Chomsky's deep grammar. Unfortunately the program is prone to fits of sulking, and because it obeys a nondeterministic algorithm it frequently enters a fatal loop when it runs. There is no canonical translation of the inscription. Government linguists tried to decipher the runes the hard way; all those who tried wound up dead or incarcerated in the Funny Farm. After a systems analyst suggested that the carving might really be the function binding for our reality, and that pronouncing it with understanding would cause a fatal exception, Mahogany Row decided to discourage future research along these lines.

The metafictional conceit that magic is a science has been used in fantasy—or science fiction—several times. James Gunn's *The Magicians* is explicitly based upon it. Rick Cook managed to squeeze several books from the idea of a socially clueless programmer stranded in fantasyland

and forced to compete with the magi by applying his unfair expertise in compiler design. There is something *about* mathematics that makes it seem to beg for this sort of misappropriation: an image problem deeply rooted both in the way that the queen of sciences is taught, and in the way we think about it—in the philosophy of mathematics.

Plato spoke of a realm of mathematical truth, and took the view that unearthing a theorem was a matter of discovery: it revealed its truth to us like a shadow cast upon the wall of a cave by a light source and a reality invisible to our eyes. Later Descartes used similar reasoning and a weasely analogical excuse to split the world into things of the spirit and of the flesh. If the body was clearly an organic machine, *someone* had to be in a driving seat controlling it through a switchboard located (he believed) in the pineal gland.

The history of nineteenth- and twentieth-century medical research was a disaster for the idea of an immortal soul. Mind-body dualism sounds good, until you realize that it implies that the body's sensory nerves must in some way transfer information to the soul, and the soul must somehow affect the dumb matter with which it is associated. When the best microscopes could barely resolve nerve fibers, this was not a problem: but the devil lies in the detail, and with electron micrographs taking us down to the macromolecular level of cytology, and with biochemistry finally beginning to explain how everything works, the brain was revealed for what it is—a mass of fleshy endocrine cells squirting their neurotransmitter messages at one another in promiscuous abandon. There is precious little room left for a soul that can remain hidden but nevertheless influence the flesh.

But. Let us take Plato's realm of mathematical abstraction seriously; and with it, let us adopt the Wheeler model of quantum cosmology—that there exists an infinity of possible worlds, and all of them are *real*. Can we, by way of the Platonic realm, transfer signals between our own sheaf of human-friendly realities and others, infinitely distant and infinitely close, where other minds might listen? What if, in other words, the multiverse is leaky? What sort of people might first discover such information leakage, and to what use would they put it, and what risks would they encounter in the process?

This is the twentieth (and early twenty-first) century, an age of spooks and wonder, of conspiracies and Cold War, an age in which the horror of the pulp magazines lurched forth onto the world stage in trillion-dollar weapons projects capable of smashing cities and incinerating millions. This is not the era of the two-fisted hero-scientist putting the finishing touches on his spherical exploration machine before setting off on a flight to Galaxy Z. Nor is it the age of the mad scientist in his castle basement, laboriously stitching together the graveyard trawl while Igor flies a kite from the battlements to bring the animating power down to the thing on the slab. It *is* the decade of the computer scientist, the fast-thinking designer of abstract machines that float on a Platonic realm of thought and blink in or out of existence with a mouseclick.

We can get some ideas about the lives and occupations of these people by extrapolating from the published material about the intelligence services. James Bamford's *Body of Secrets,* a deep and fascinating history of the US National Security Agency, offers some hints from outside—as do other histories of the cryptic profession, such as David Kahn's *The Codebreakers* and Alan Hodges's masterful biography of Alan Turing—for if any agency gets its hands on tools for probing the Platonic realm, it will be a kissing cousin of the kings of cryptography.

We can draw some other conclusions from the unspoken and unwritten history of the secret services. Why, for example, was the British Special Operations Executive disbanded so suddenly in 1945? One version is that the rivalry between SOE and the established Secret Intelligence Service was bitter, and after the 1945 election SIS lobbied the new government to disband SOE. But we know that when other similar organizations have disbanded they have left ghosts behind. US Secretary of State Henry Stimson disbanded the Black Chamber in 1929, with the immortal phrase, "gentlemen do not read each other's mail," but that didn't stop the Black Chamber's secrets ending up in Room 3416 of the Munitions Building, there to become the core of the Army's new Signal Intelligence Service.

British governments are less forthcoming—many of Whitehall's deepest secrets are stored in boxes labelled for release no less than a hundred years after the events they describe—but we can guess at similar revenants of SOE surviving the winter of the war, just as we know that many of the secrets of Bletchley Park's codebreaking operation ended up in Cheltenham, at the new (and unimportant-sounding) Government Communications Headquarters. SOE was deeply engaged with resistance operations against the Nazi occupation of Europe during the Second World War; if by some chance the Ahnenerbe-SS *were* sheltering ghastly secrets, it is unlikely that the subsequent custodians of such knowledge would have joined their comrades mustering out of service at the end of the conflict.

We can extrapolate somewhat from the post-1945 growth of the intelligence agencies. Back in 1930, when William Friedman became the first chief of the US Army Signal Intelligence Service, the new successor to the Black Chamber had just three employees. By the year 2000, Crypto City—the NSA headquarters in Maryland—had a population of

32,000 regular workers and an annual budget on the order of seven billion dollars. The much smaller Government Communications HQ (GCHQ)—Britain's equivalent of the NSA—still has a budget measured in the high hundreds of millions. Information is power, and these agencies wield it without much restraint on the purse strings and without substantial external oversight. We can assume that even a relatively small 1945-vintage occult intelligence operation would have grown over the years into a sprawling organization with either a huge central office or, possibly, multiple secure sites dotted around the country.

Finally, this brings us back to the Laundry. The Laundry squats at the heart of a dark web, the collision between paranoia and secrecy on one hand, and the urge to knowledge on the other. Guardians of the dark secrets that threaten to drown us in nightmare, their lips are sealed as tightly as their archives. To get even the vaguest outline of their activities takes a privileged trickster-fool hacker like Bob, nosy enough to worm his way in where he isn't supposed to be and smart enough to explain his way out of trouble. Some day Bob will grow up, fully understand the ghastly responsibilities that go with his job, shut the hell up, and stop digging. But until then, let us by all means use him as our unquiet guide to the corridors of the Fear Factory.

## Afternote:
## Two Frequently Asked Questions

While I was writing "The Atrocity Archive," my friend Andrew Wilson (science fiction reviewer for *The Scotsman*) kept telling me: "For God's sake, don't read *Declare* by Tim Powers until you finish the novel."

Powers is a remarkable writer, and in *Declare* he explored an arcane world remarkably close to that of "The Atrocity Archive." The points of similarity are striking: rogue departments within SOE that survive the end of the war, operations in the British secret intelligence community that focus on the occult and run independently of anything else for a period of decades—even a protagonist who, with a special SAS team, tries to take on a supernatural horror.

Luckily for me, I listened to Andrew. He was right: if I'd read *Declare* it would have derailed me completely. And that would have been a shame, because in tone and attitude the two novels are very different. *Declare* is perhaps best read as an hommage to John Le Carré, whereas the outlook of "The Atrocity Archive" is perhaps closer to Len Deighton, by way of Neal Stephenson. *Declare* is about disengagement and the abandonment of former responsibility; "The Atrocity Archive" is more interested in coming of age in a world of ghosts and shadows. *Declare* is about the secret services that waged The Great Game; "The Atrocity Archive" is about the agencies that fought the Wizard War. The two novels are sufficiently far apart that they stand on their own merit. I'll just leave the topic by saying, if you liked this book, you'll probably enjoy *Declare*.

About six months *after* the scare over *Declare* another friend said, "Hey, have you ever heard of Delta Green?"

I used to be big on role-playing games, but it's been close to two decades since I was last involved in the scene to any extent. So the whole Chaosium phenomenon had passed me by. It turns out that Lovecraft's horrors have found a fertile field (or swamp) in the shape of the game *Call of Cthulhu*. In *Call of Cthulhu*, gamers role-play their way through one or another 1920s-era scenario that usually involves solving bizarre mysteries before something hideous sucks their brains out through their ears with a crazy straw. "Delta Green" is an almost legendary supplement to *Call of Cthulhu* that attempts to bring the mythos role-playing game up-to-date. There's a rogue intelligence agency battling to prevent infestations of extradimensional horrors . . . sound familiar?

All I can say in my defense is, no: I hadn't heard of "Delta Green" when I wrote "The Atrocity Archive." "Delta Green" has such a markedly American feel that "The Atrocity Archive" is right off the map. (Which is odd, because in tone if not in substance they feel a lot closer than, say, *Declare*.) So I'll leave it at that except to say that "Delta Green" has come dangerously close to making me pick up the dice again.

Charles Stross
Edinburgh, U.K.
April 2003

# The Jennifer Morgue

For Andrew, Lorna, and James

## Acknowledgements

No book gets written in a vacuum, and this one is no exception. I'd like to thank my editors, Marty Halpern at Golden Gryphon and Ginjer Buchanan at Ace, and my agent Caitlin Blasdell, all of whom helped make this book possible. I'd also like to thank my hundreds of test readers—in no particular order: Simon Bradshaw, Dan Ritter, Nicholas Whyte, Elizabeth Bear, Brooks Moses, Mike Scott, Jack Foy, Luna Black, Harry Payne, Andreas Black, Marcus Rowland, Ken MacLeod, Peter Hollo, Andrew Wilson, Stefan Pearson, Gavin Inglis, Jack Deighton, John Scalzi, Anthony Quirke, Jane McKie, Hannu Rajaniemi, Andrew Ferguson, Martin Page, Robert Sneddon, and Steve Stirling. I'd also like to thank Hugh Hancock, who valiantly helped me MST3K my way through the Bond canon.

✦ ✦ ✦

# Prologue:
# Jennifer

August 25, 1975
165° W, 30° N

*T*HE GUYS FROM THE "A" AND "B" CREWS HAVE BEEN
sitting on their collective ass for five weeks, out in the middle
of nowhere. They're not alone; there's the ship's crew, from the captain
on down to the lowliest assistant cook, and the CIA spooks. But the
other guys have at least got something to do. The ship's crew has a vessel to run: an unholy huge behemoth, 66,000 tons of deep-ocean exploratory mining ship, 400 million bucks and seven years in the building.
The CIA dudes are keeping a wary eye on the Russian trawler that's
stooging around on the horizon. And as for the Texan wildcat drilling
guys, for the past couple of days they've been working ceaselessly on the
stabilized platform, bolting one sixty-foot steel pipe after another onto
the top of the drill string and lowering it into the depths of the Pacific
Ocean. But the "A" and "B" teams have been sitting on their hands for
weeks with nothing to do but oil and service the enormous mechanism
floating in the moon pool at the heart of the ship, then twiddle their
thumbs nervously for eighty hours as the drill lowers it into the crushing
darkness.

And now that Clementine is nearly on target, there's a storm coming.

"Fucking weather," complains Milgram.

"Language." Duke is a tight-ass. "How bad can it get?"

Milgram brandishes his paper, the latest chart to come out of the
weather office on C deck where Stan and Gilmer hunch over their

green-glowing radar displays and the telex from San Diego. "Force nine predicted within forty-eight hours, probability sixty percent and rising. We can't take that, Duke. We go over force six, the impellers can't keep us on station. We'll lose the string."

The kid, Steve, crowds close. "Anyone told Spook City yet?" The guys from Langley hang out in a trailer on E deck with a locked vault-type door. Everyone calls it Spook City.

"Nah." Duke doesn't sound too concerned. "Firstly, it hasn't happened yet. Secondly, we're only forty fathoms up from zero." He snaps his fingers at the curious heads that have turned in his direction from their camera stations: "Look to it, guys! We've got a job to do!"

Clementine—the vast, submersible grab at the end of the drill string—weighs around 3,000 tons and is more than 200 feet long. It's a huge steel derrick, painted gray to resist the corrosive effects of miles of seawater. At a distance it resembles a skeletal lobster, because of the five steel legs protruding from either flank. Or maybe it's more like a giant mantrap, lowered into the icy stillness of Davy Jones's locker to grab whatever it can from the sea floor.

Duke runs the engineering office from his throne in the center of the room. One wall is covered in instruments; the other is a long stretch of windows overlooking the moon pool at the heart of the ship. A door at one side of the window wall provides access to a steel-mesh catwalk fifty feet above the pool.

Here in the office the noise of the hydraulic stabilizers isn't quite deafening; there's a loud mechanical whine and a vibration they feel through the soles of their boots, but the skull-rattling throbbing is damped to a survivable level. The drilling tower above their heads lowers the endless string of pipes into the center of the pool at a steady six feet per minute, day in and day out. Steve tries not to look out the window at the pipes because the effect is hypnotic: they've been sliding smoothly into the depths for many hours now, lowering the grab toward the bottom of the ocean.

The ship is much bigger than the grab that dangles beneath it on the end of three miles of steel pipe, but it's at the grab's mercy. Three miles of pipe makes for a prodigious pendulum, and as the grab sinks slowly through the deep-ocean currents, the ship has to maneuver frantically to stay on top of it in the six-foot swells. Exotic domes on top of the vessel's bridge suck down transmissions from the Navy's *Transit* positioning satellites, feeding them to the automatic Station Keeping System that controls the ship's bow and stern thrusters, and the cylindrical surge compensators that the derrick rests on. Like a swan, it looks peaceful on the surface but under the waterline there's a hive of frantic activity.

Everything—the entire 400-megabuck investment, ten years of Company black operations—depends on what happens in the next few hours. When they reach the bottom.

Steve turns back to his TV screen. It's another miracle of technology. The barge has cameras and floodlights, vacuum tubes designed to function in the abyssal depths. But his camera is flaking out, static hash marching up the screen in periodic waves: the pressure, tons per square inch, is damaging the waterproof cables that carry power and signal. "This is shit," he complains. "We're never going to spot it—if . . ."

He trails off. Good-time Norm at the next desk is standing up, pointing at something on his screen. There's a whoop from the other side of the room. He squints at his screen and between the lines of static he sees a rectilinear outline. "Holy—"

The public address system crackles overhead: "Clementine crew. K-129 on screens two and five, range approximately fifty feet, bearing two-two-five. Standby, fine thruster control."

It's official—they've found what they're looking for.

The atmosphere in Spook City is tense but triumphant. "We're there," announces Cooper. He smirks at the hatchet-faced Brit in the crumpled suit, who is smoking an unfiltered Camel in clear violation of shipboard fire regulations. "We did it!"

"We'll see," mutters the Brit. He stubs the cigarette out and shakes his head. "Getting there is only half the struggle."

Nettled, Murph glares at him. "What's your problem?" he demands.

"You're messing with something below 1,000 meters, in strict contravention of Article Four," says the Brit. "I'm here as a neutral observer in accordance with Section Two—"

"Fuck you and your neutral status, you're just sore because you guys don't have the balls to stand on your waiver rights—"

Cooper gets between them before things can escalate again. "Cool it. Murph, how about checking with the bridge again to see if there's been any sign of the commies taking an interest? They'll twig when they see we've stopped lowering the string. James—" He pauses. Grimaces slightly. The Brit's alias is transparent and, to a Company man, borderline insulting: Cooper wonders, not for the first time, *Why the fuck does he call himself that?* "—let's go take a hike down to the moon pool and see what they've found."

"Suits me." The Brit stands up, unfolding like a stick-insect inside his badly fitting gray suit. His cheek twitches but his expression stays frozen. "After you."

They leave the office and Cooper locks the door behind him. The

Hughes GMDI ship may be enormous—it's bigger than a Marine Corps assault carrier, larger than an Iowa-class battleship—but its companionways and corridors are a cramped, gray maze, punctuated by color-coded pipes and ducts conveniently located at shin-scraping and head-banging height. It doesn't roll in the swells but it rocks, weirdly, held solidly on station by the SKS thrusters (a new technology that accounts for a goodly chunk of the cost of the ship). Down six flights of steps there's another passage and a bulkhead: then Cooper sees the dogged-back hatch leading out into the moon pool at the level of the fifty-foot catwalk. As usual it takes his breath away. The moon pool is just under 200 feet long and 75 feet wide, a stillness of black water surrounded by the gantries and cranes required for servicing the barge. The giant docking legs are fully extended below the waterline at either end of the pool. The drill string pierces the heart of the chamber like a black steel spear tying it to the ocean floor. The automatic roughneck and the string handling systems have fallen silent, the deafening clatter and roar of the drill system shut down now that the grab has reached its target. Soon, if all goes well, the derrick above them will begin hauling up the string, laboriously unbolting the hundreds of pipe segments and stacking them on the deck of the ship, until finally Clementine—also known as the HMB-1 "mining barge"—rumbles to the surface of the pool in a flurry of cold water, clutching its treasure beneath it. But for now the moon pool is a peaceful haven, its surface marred only by shallow, oily ripples.

The engineering office is a hive of activity in contrast to the view outside the windows, and nobody notices Cooper and the British spook as they slip inside and look over the operations controller's shoulder at his screens. "Left ten, up six," someone calls. "Looks like a hatch," says someone else. Strange gray outlines swim on the screen. "Get me a bit more light on that . . ."

Everyone falls silent for a while. "That's not good," says one of the engineers, a wiry guy from New Mexico who Cooper vaguely remembers is called Norm. The big TV screen in the middle is showing a flat surface emerging from a gray morass of abyssal mud. A rectangular opening with rounded edges gapes in it—a hatch?—and there's something white protruding from a cylinder lying across it. The cylinder looks like a sleeve. Suddenly Cooper realizes what he's looking at: an open hatch in the sail of a submarine, the skeletonized remains of a sailor lying half-in and half-out of it.

"Poor bastards probably tried to swim for it when they realized the torpedo room was flooded," says a voice from the back of the room. Cooper looks around. It's Davis, somehow still managing to look like a Navy officer even though he's wearing a civilian suit. "That's probably what saved the pressure hull—the escape hatch was already open and the boat was fully flooded before it passed through its crush depth."

Cooper shivers, staring at the screen. "*Consider Phlebas*," he thinks, wracking his brain for the rest of the poem.

"Okay, so what about the impact damage?" That's Duke, typically businesslike: "I need to know if we can make this work."

More activity. Camera viewpoints swivel crazily, taking in the length of the Golf-II-class submarine. The water at this depth is mostly clear and the barge floodlights illuminate the wreck mercilessly, from the blown hatch in the sail to the great gash in the side of the torpedo room. The submarine lies on its side as if resting, and there's little obvious damage to Cooper's untrained eye. A bigger hatch gapes open in front of the sail. "What's that?" he asks, pointing.

The kid, Steve, follows his finger. "Looks like the number two missile tube is open," he says. The Golf-II class is a boomer, a ballistic missile submarine—an early one, diesel-electric. It had carried only three nuclear missiles, and had to surface before firing. "Hope they didn't roll while they were sinking: if they lost the bird it could have landed anywhere."

"Anywhere—" Cooper blinks.

"Okay, let's get her lined up!" hollers Duke, evidently completing his assessment of the situation. "We've got bad weather coming, so let's haul!"

For the next half-hour the control room is a madhouse, engineers and dive-control officers hunched over their consoles and mumbling into microphones. Nobody's ever done this before—maneuvered a 3,000-ton grab into position above a sunken submarine three miles below the surface, with a storm coming. The sailors on the Soviet spy trawler on the horizon probably have their controllers back in Moscow convinced that they've been drinking the antifreeze again, with their tale of exotic, capitalist hyper-technology stealing their sunken boomer.

The tension in the control room is rising. Cooper watches over Steve's shoulder as the kid twiddles his joystick, demonstrating an occult ability to swing cameras to bear on the huge mechanical grabs, allowing their operators to extend them and position them close to the hull. Finally it's time. "Stand by to blow pressure cylinders," Duke announces. "Blow them *now*."

Ten pressure cylinders bolted to the grab vent silvery streams of bubbles: pistons slide home, propelled by a three-mile column of seawater, drawing the huge clamps tight around the hull of the submarine. They bite into the mud, stirring up a gray cloud that obscures everything for a while. Gauges slowly rotate, showing the position of the jaws. "Okay on even two through six, odd one through seven. Got a partial on nine and eight, nothing on ten."

The atmosphere is electric. Seven clamps have locked tight around the hull of the submarine: two are loose and one appears to have failed. Duke looks at Cooper. "Your call."

"Can you lift it?" asks Cooper.

"I think so." Duke's face is somber. "We'll see once we've got it off the mud."

"Let's check upstairs," Cooper suggests, and Duke nods. The captain can say "yes" or "no" and make it stick—it's his ship they'll be endangering if they make a wrong call.

Five minutes later they've got their answer. "Do it," says the skipper, in a tone that brooks no argument. "It's what we're here for." He's on the bridge because the impending bad weather and the proximity of other ships—a second Russian trawler has just shown up—demands his presence, but there's no mistaking his urgency.

"Okay, you heard the man."

Five minutes later a faint vibration shakes the surface of the moon pool. Clementine has blown its ballast, scattering a thousand tons of lead shot across the sea floor around the submarine. The cameras show nothing but a gray haze for a while. Then the drill string visible through the control room window begins to move, slowly inching upward. "Thrusters to full," Duke snaps. The string begins to retract faster and faster, dripping water as it rises from the icy depths. "Give me a strain gauge report."

The strain gauges on the giant grabs are reading green across the board: each arm is supporting nearly 500 tons of submarine, not to mention the water it contains. There's a loud mechanical whine from outside, and a sinking feeling, and the vibration Cooper can feel through the soles of his Oxford brogues has increased alarmingly—the *Explorer's* drill crew is running the machines at full power now that the grab has increased in weight. The ship, gaining thousands of tons in a matter of seconds, squats deeper in the Pacific swell. "Satisfied now?" asks Cooper, turning to grin at the Brit, who for his part looks as if he's waiting for something, staring at one screen intently.

"Well?"

"We've got a little time to go," says the hatchet-faced foreigner.

"A little . . . ?"

"Until we learn whether or not you've gotten away with it."

"What are you smoking, man? Of course we've gotten away with it!" Murph has materialized from the upper decks like a Boston-Irish ghost, taking out his low-level resentment on the Brit (who is sufficiently public-school English to make a suitable whipping boy for Bloody Sunday, not to mention being a government employee to boot). "Look! Submarine! Submersible grab! Coming up at six feet per minute! After the break, film at eleven!" His tone is scathing. "What do you think the commies are going to do to stop us, start World War Three? They don't even god-damn know what we're doing down here—they don't even know where their sub went down to within 200 miles!"

"It's not the commies I'm worried about," says the Brit. He glances at Cooper. "How about you?"

Cooper shakes his head reluctantly. "I still think we're going to make it. The sub's intact, undamaged, and we've got it—"

"Oh shit," says Steve.

He points the central camera in the grab's navigation cluster down at the sea floor, a vast gray-brown expanse stirred into slow whorls of foggy motion by the dropping of the ballast and the departure of the submarine. It should be slowly settling back into bland desert-dunes of mud by now. But something's moving down there, writhing against the current with unnatural speed.

Cooper stares at the screen. "What's that?"

"May I remind you of Article Four of the treaty?" says the Brit. "No establishment of permanent or temporary structures below a depth of one kilometer beneath mean sea level, on pain of termination. No re-moval of structures from the abyssal plain, on pain of ditto. We're tres-passing: legally they can do as they please."

"But we're only picking up the trash—"

"They may not see it that way."

Fine fronds, a darker shade against the gray, are rising from the muddy haze not far from the last resting place of the K-129. The fronds ripple and waver like giant kelp, but are thicker and more purposeful. They bring to mind the blind, questing trunk of an elephant exploring the interior of a puzzle box. There's something disturbing about the way they squirt from vents in the sea floor, rising in pulses, as if they're more liquid than solid.

"Damn," Cooper says softly. He punches his open left hand. "Damn!"

"Language," chides Duke. "Barry, how fast can we crank this rig? Steve, see if you can get a fix on those things. I want to peg their ascent rate."

Barry shakes his head emphatically. "The drill platform can't take any more, boss. We're up to force four outside already, and we're carry-ing too much weight. We can maybe go up to ten feet per minute, but if we try to go much above that we risk shearing the string and losing Clementine."

Cooper shudders. The grab will still surface if the drill string breaks, but it could broach just about anywhere. And *anywhere* includes right under the ship's keel, which is not built to survive being rammed by 3,000 tons of metal hurtling out of the depths at twenty knots.

"We can't risk it," Duke decides. "Keep hauling at current ascent rate."

They watch in silence for the next hour as the grab rises toward the surface, its precious, stolen cargo still intact in its arms.

The questing fronds surge up from the depths, growing toward the lens of the under-slung camera as the engineers and spooks watch anxiously. The grab is already 400 feet above the sea floor, but instead of a flat muddy desert below, the abyssal plain has sprouted an angry forest of grasping tentacles. They're extending fast, reaching toward the stolen submarine above them.

"Hold steady," says Duke. "Damn, I said hold steady!"

The ship shudders, and the vibration in the deck has risen to a tooth-rattling grumble and a shriek of over-stressed metal. The air in the control room stinks of hot oil. Up on the drilling deck the wildcats are shearing bolt-heads and throwing sixty-foot pipe segments on the stack rather than taking time to position them—a sure sign of desperation, for the pipe segments are machined from a special alloy at a cost of $60,000 apiece. They're hauling in the drill string almost twice as fast as they paid it out, and the moon pool is foaming and bubbling, a steady cascade of water dropping from the chilly metal tubes to rain back down onto its surface. But it's anyone's guess whether they'll get the grab up to the surface before the questing tentacles catch it.

"Article Four," the Brit says tensely.

"Bastard." Cooper glares at the screen. "It's ours."

"They appear to disagree. Want to argue with them?"

"A couple of depth charges . . ." Cooper stares at the drill string longingly.

"They'd fuck you, boy," the other man says harshly. "Don't think it hasn't been thought of. There are enough methane hydrates down in that mud to burp the granddaddy of all gas bubbles under our keel and drag us down like a gnat in a toad's mouth."

"I know that." Cooper shakes his head. *So much work!* It's outrageous, an insult to the senses, like watching a moon shot explode on the launch pad. "But. Those bastards." He punches his palm again. "It should be ours!"

"We've had dealings with them before that didn't go so badly. Witch's Hole, the treaty zone at Dunwich. You could have asked us." The British agent crosses his arms tensely. "You could have asked your Office of Naval Intelligence, too. But no, you had to go and get creative."

"The fuck. You'd just have told us not to bother. This way—"

"This way you learn your own lesson."

"The fuck."

The grab was 3,000 feet below sea level and still rising when the tentacles finally caught up with it.

The rest, as they say, is history.

## Chapter 1:
## Random Ramona

If you work for the Laundry long enough, eventually you get used to the petty insults, the paper clip audits, the disgusting canteen coffee, and the endless, unavoidable bureaucracy. Your aesthetic senses become dulled, and you go blind to the decaying pea-green paint and the vomit-beige fabric partitions between office cubicles. But the big indignities never fail to surprise, and they're the ones that can get you killed.

I've been working for the Laundry for about five years now, and periodically I become blasé in my cynicism, sure that I've seen it all—which is usually the signal for them to throw something at me that's degrading, humiliating, or dangerous—if not all three at once.

"You want me to drive a *what?*" I squeak at the woman behind the car rental desk.

"Sir, your ticket has been issued by your employer, it says here und here—" She's a brunette: tall, thin, helpful, and very German in that schoolmarmish way that makes you instinctively check to see if your fly's undone. "The, ah, Smart Fortwo coupé. With the, the kompressor. It is a perfectly good car. Unless you would like for the upgrade to pay?"

*Upgrade.* To a Mercedes S190, for, oh, about two hundred euros a day. An absolute no-brainer—if it wasn't at my own expense.

"How do I get to Darmstadt from here?" I ask, trying to salvage the situation. "Preferably alive?" (Bloody Facilities. Bloody budget airlines that never fly where you want to go. Bloody weather. Bloody liaison meetings in Germany. Bloody "cheapest hire" policy.)

She menaces me with her perfect dentistry again. "If it was me I'd take the ICE train. But your ticket—" she points at it helpfully "—is non-refundable. Now please to face the camera for the biometrics?"

Fifteen minutes later I'm hunched over the steering wheel of a two-seater that looks like something you'd find in your corn flakes packet. The Smart is insanely cute and compact, does about seventy miles to a gallon, and is the ideal second car for nipping about town; but I'm not nipping about town. I'm going flat out at maybe a hundred and fifty kilometers per hour on the autobahn while some joker is shooting at me from behind with a cannon that fires Porsches and Mercedes. Meanwhile, I'm stuck driving something that handles like a turbo-charged baby buggy. I've got my fog lights on in a vain attempt to deter the other road users from turning me into a hood ornament, but the jet wash every time another executive panzer overtakes me keeps threatening to roll me right over onto my roof. And that's before you factor in the deranged Serbian truck drivers, driven mad with joy by exposure to a motorway that hasn't been cluster-bombed and then resurfaced by the lowest bidder.

In between moments of blood-curdling terror I spend my time swearing under my breath. This is all Angleton's fault. He's the one who sent me to this stupid joint-liaison committee meeting, so he bears the brunt of it. His hypothetical and distinctly mythological ancestry is followed in descending order by the stupid weather, Mo's stupid training schedule, and then anything else that I can think of to curse. It keeps the tiny corner of my mind that isn't focused on my immediate survival occupied—and that's a very tiny corner, because when you're sentenced to drive a Smart car on a road where everything else has a speed best described by its mach number, you tend to pay attention.

There's an unexpected lull in the traffic about two-thirds of the way to Darmstadt, and I make the mistake of breathing a sigh of relief. The respite is short-lived. One moment I'm driving along a seemingly empty road, bouncing from side to side on the Smart's town-car suspension as the hair-dryer-sized engine howls its guts out beneath my buttocks, and the next instant the dashboard in front of me lights up like a flashbulb.

I twitch spasmodically, jerking my head up so hard I nearly dent the thin plastic roof. Behind me the eyes of Hell are open, two blinding beacons like the landing lights on an off-course 747. Whoever they are, they're standing on their brakes so hard they must be smoking. There's a roar, and then a squat, red Audi sports coupé pulls out and squeezes past my flank close enough to touch, its blonde female driver gesticulating angrily at me. At least I think she's blonde and female. It's hard to tell because everything is gray, my heart is trying to exit through my rib cage, and I'm frantically wrestling with the steering wheel to keep the roller skate from toppling over. A fraction of a second later she's gone, pulling back into the slow lane ahead of me to light off her afterburners. I swear I see red sparks shooting out of her two huge exhaust tubes as she vanishes into the distance, taking about ten years of my life with her.

"You stupid fucking bitch!" I yell, thumping the steering wheel until the Smart wobbles alarmingly and, heart in mouth, I tentatively lift off the accelerator and let my speed drift back down to a mere 140 or so. "Stupid fucking Audi-driving Barbie girl, brains of a chocolate mousse—"

I spot a road sign saying DARMSTADT 20KM just as something—a low-flying *Luftwaffe* Starfighter, maybe—makes a strafing run on my left. Ten infinitely long minutes later I arrive at the slip road for Darmstadt sandwiched between two eighteen-wheelers, my buttocks soaking in a puddle of cold sweat and all my hair standing on end. Next time, I resolve, I'm going to take the train and damn the expense.

Darmstadt is one of those German towns that, having been land scaped by Allied heavy bombers, rezoned by the Red Army, and rebuilt by the Marshall Plan, demonstrates perfectly that (a) sometimes it's better to lose a war than to win one, and (b) some of the worst crimes against humanity are committed by architecture students. These days what's left of the '50s austerity concrete has a rusticated air and a patina of moss, and the worst excesses of '60s Neo-Brutalism have been replaced by glass and brightly painted steel that clashes horribly with what's left of the old Rhenish gingerbread. It could be Anytown EU, more modern and less decrepit than its US equivalent, but somehow it looks bashful and self-effacing. The one luxury Facilities did pay for is an in-car navigation system (the better to stop me wasting Laundry time by getting lost en route), so once I get off the Death Race track I drive on autopilot, sweaty and limp with animalistic relief at having survived. And then I find myself in a hotel parking bay between a Toyota and a bright red Audi TT.

"The fuck." I thump the steering wheel again, more angry than terrified now that I'm not in imminent danger of death. I peer at it—yup, it's the same model car, and the same color. I can't be certain it's the same one (my nemesis was going so fast I couldn't read her number plate because of the Doppler shift) but I wouldn't bet against it: it's a small world. I shake my head and squeeze out of the Smart, pick up my bags, and slouch towards reception.

Once you've seen one international hotel, you've seen them all. The romance of travel tends to fade fast after the first time you find yourself stranded at an airport with a suitcase full of dirty underwear two hours after the last train left. Ditto the luxury of the business hotel experience on your fourth overseas meeting of the month. I check in as fast and as painlessly as possible (aided by another of those frighteningly helpful German babes, albeit this time with slightly worse English) then beam myself up to the sixth floor of the Ramada Treff Page Hotel. Then I hunt through the endless and slightly claustrophobic maze of air-conditioned corridors until I find my room.

I dump my duffle bag, grab my toilet kit and a change of clothes, and duck into the bathroom to wash away the stink of terror. In the mirror, my reflection winks at me and points at a new white hair until I menace him with a tube of toothpaste. I'm only twenty-eight: I'm too young to die and too old to drive fast.

I blame Angleton. This is all his fault. He set me on this path exactly two days after the board approved my promotion to SSO, which is about the lowest grade to carry any significant managerial responsibilities. "Bob," he said, fixing me with a terrifyingly avuncular smile, "I think it's about time you got out of the office a bit more. Saw the world, got to grips with the more mundane aspects of the business, that sort of thing. So you can start by standing in for Andy Newstrom on a couple of low-priority, joint-liaison meetings. What do you say?"

"Great," I said enthusiastically. "Where do I start?"

Well okay, I should really blame myself, but Angleton's a more convenient target—he's very hard to say "no" to, and more importantly, he's eight hundred miles away. It's easier to blame him than to kick the back of my own head.

Back in the bedroom I pull my tablet PC out of my luggage and plug it in, jack it into the broadband socket, poke my way through the tedious pay-to-register website, and bring up the VPN connection back to the office. Then I download an active ward and leave it running as a screen saver. It looks like a weird geometric pattern endlessly morphing and cycling through a color palette until it ends up in a retina-eating stereoisogram, and it's perfectly safe to sneak a brief glance at it, but if an intruder looks at it for too long it'll Pwnz0r their brain. I drape a pair of sweaty boxer shorts across it before I go out, just in case room service calls. When it comes to detecting burglars, hairs glued to door frames are passé.

Down at the concierge desk I check for messages. "Letter for Herr Howard? Please to sign here." I spot the inevitable Starbucks stand in a corner so I amble over to it, inspecting the envelope as I go. It's made of expensive cream paper, very thick and heavy, and when I stare at it closely I see fine gold threads woven into it. They've used an italic font and a laser printer to address it, which cheapens the effect. I slit it open with my Swiss Army cybertool as I wait for one of the overworked Turkish baristas to get round to serving me. The card inside is equally heavy, but hand-written:

> Bob,
>     Meet me in the Laguna Bar at 6 p.m. or as soon as you arrive, if later.
>     Ramona

"Um," I mutter. *What the fuck?*

I'm here to take part in the monthly joint-liaison meeting with our EU partner agencies. It's held under the auspices of the EU Joint Intergovernmental Framework on Cosmological Incursions, which is governed by the Common Defense provisions of the Second Treaty of

Nice. (You haven't heard of this particular EU treaty because it's secret by mutual agreement, none of the signatories wanting to start a mass panic.) Despite the classified nature of the event it's really pretty boring: we're here to swap departmental gossip about our mutual areas of interest and what's been going on lately, update each other on new procedural measures and paperwork hoops we need to jump through to requisition useful information from our respective front-desk operations, and generally make nice. With only a decade to go until the omega conjunction—the period of greatest risk during NIGHTMARE GREEN, when the stars are right—everyone in Europe is busy oiling the gears and wheels of our occult defense machinery. Nobody wants their neighbors to succumb to a flux of green, gibbering brain-eaters, after all: it tends to lower real estate values. After the meeting I'm supposed to take the minutes home and brief Angleton, Boris, Rutherford, and anyone else in my reporting chain, then circulate the minutes to other departments. *Sic transit gloria spook.*

Anyway, I'm expecting an agenda and directions to a meeting room, not a bar invite from a mysterious Ramona. I rack my brains: *Who do I know who's called Ramona? Wasn't there a song . . . ? Joey Ramone . . .* no. I fold the envelope and stuff it in my back pocket. *Sounds like a porn spammer's alias.* I break out of the slowly shuffling coffee queue just in time to annoy the furiously mustachioed counter dude. *Where the hell is the Laguna Bar?*

I spot a number of dark, glass-partitioned areas clustered around the atrium in front of the check-in desk. They're the usual hotel squeeze joints, overpriced restaurants, and 24-hour shops selling whatever you forgot to pack yesterday morning at four o'dark. I hunt around until I spot the word LAGUNA picked out in teensy gold Fraktur Gothic to one side of a darkened doorway, in an evident attempt to confuse the unwary.

I peek round the partition. It's a bar, expensively tricked out in that retro-seventies style with too much polished Italian marble and sub-Bauhaus chrome furniture. At this time of evening it's nearly empty (although maybe the fact that they charge six euros for a beer has something to do with it). I check my phone: it's 6:15. *Damn.* I head for the bar, glancing around hopefully in case the mysterious Ramona's wearing a cardboard sign saying: I'M RAMONA—TRY ME. So much for subtle spy-work.

"Ein Weissbier, bitte," I ask, exhausting about sixty percent of my total German vocabulary.

"Sure thing, man." The bartender turns to grab a bottle.

"I'm Ramona," a female voice with a vaguely East Coast accent murmurs quietly in my left ear. "Don't turn around." And something hard pokes me in the ribs.

"Is that the aerial of your mobile phone, or are you displeased to see me?" It probably *is* a phone, but I do as she says: in this kind of situation it doesn't do to take chances.

"Shut up, wise guy." A slim hand reaches discreetly under my left arm and paws at my chest. The bartender is taking an awfully long time to find that bottle. "Hey, what is this Scheiss?"

"You found the shoulder holster? Careful, that's my Bluetooth GPS receiver in there. And that pocket's where I keep the noise-canceling headphones for my iPod—hey, watch out, they're expensive!—and the spare batteries for my PDA, and—"

Ramona lets go of my fishing jacket and a moment later the stubby object disappears from the small of my back. The bartender swings round, beaming and clutching a weird-looking glass in one hand and a bottle with a culturally stereotyped label in the other. "Dude, will this do? It's a really good Weizenbock . . ."

"Bob!" trills Ramona, stepping sideways until I can finally see her. "Make mine a dry gin and tonic, ice, but hold the fruit," she tells the barman, smiling like sunrise over the Swiss Alps. I glance at her sidelong and try not to gape.

We're in supermodel territory here—or maybe she's Uma Thurman's stunt double. She's almost five centimeters taller than me, blonde, and she's got cheekbones Mo would kill for. The rest of her isn't bad, either. She has the kind of figure that most models dream about—if indeed that isn't what she does for a living when she isn't sticking guns in civil servants' backs—and whatever the label on her strapless silk gown says, it probably costs more than I earn in a year, before you add in the jewelry dripping from her in incandescent waves. Real physical perfection isn't something a guy like me gets to see up close and personal very often, and it's something to marvel at—then run away from, before it hypnotizes you like a snake staring into the eyes of something small, furry, and edible.

She's beautiful but deadly, and right now she has one slim hand in her black patent-leather evening bag: judging from the slight tension at the corners of her eyes I'll bet hard money she's holding a small, pearl-handled automatic pistol just out of sight.

One of my wards bites me on the back of my wrist and I realize what's come over me: it's a glamour. I feel a sudden pang of something like homesickness for Mo, who at least comes from my own planet, even if she insists on practicing the violin at all hours.

"Fancy meeting you here like this, darling!" Ramona adds, almost as an afterthought.

"How unexpected," I agree, taking a step sideways and reaching for the glass and bottle. The bartender, dazzled by her smile, is already reaching for a shot glass. I manage an experimental grin. Ramona reminds me of a certain ex-girlfriend (okay, she reminds me of Mhari: I admit it, try not to wince, and move on) done up to the nines and in full-on predator mode. As I get used to the impact of her glamour I begin to get an edgy feeling I've seen her before. "Is that your red Audi in the car park?"

She turns the full force of her smile on me. "What if it is?"

*Glub glub . . . chink.* Ice cubes sloshing into gin. "That'll be sixteen euros, man."

"Put it on my room tab," I say automatically. I slide the card over. "If it is, you nearly rubbed me out on the A45."

"I nearly—" She looks puzzled for a moment. Then even more puzzled. "Was it you in that ridiculous little tin can?"

"If my office would pay for an Audi TT I'd drive one, too." I feel a stab of malicious glee at her visible disquiet. "Who do you think I am? And who are you, and what do you want?"

The bartender drifts away to the other end of the bar, still smiling blissfully under her influence. I blink back little warning flickers of migraine-like distortion as I look at her. *That's got to be at least a level three glamour she's wearing,* I tell myself, and shiver. My ward isn't powerful enough to break through it so I can see her as she really is, but at least I can tell I'm being spoofed.

"I'm Ramona Random. You can call me Ramona." She takes a chug of the G&T, then stares down her nose at me with those disquietingly clear eyes, like an aristocratic Eloi considering a shambling, half-blind Morlock who's somehow made it to the surface. I take a preliminary sip of my beer, waiting for her to continue. "Do you want to fuck me?"

I spray beer through my nostrils. "You have got to be kidding!"

It's more tactful than *I'd rather bed a king snake* and sounds less pathetic than *my girlfriend would kill me,* but the instant I come out with it I know it's a gut reaction, and true: *What's under that glamour?* Nothing I'd want to meet in bed, I'll bet.

"Good," says Ramona, closing the door very firmly on that line of speculation, much to my relief. She nods, a falling lock of flax-colored hair momentarily concealing her face: "Every guy I've ever slept with died less than twenty-four hours later." It must be my expression, because a moment later she adds, defensively: "It's just a coincidence! I didn't kill them. Well, most of them."

I realize I'm trying to hide behind my beer glass, and force myself to straighten up. "I'm very glad to hear it," I say, a little too rapidly.

"I was just checking because we're supposed to be working together. And it would be real unfortunate if you slept with me and died, because then we couldn't do that."

"Really? How interesting. And what exactly is it you think I do?"

She puts her glass down and removes her hand from her bag. It's déjà vu all over again: instead of a gun she's holding a three-year-old Palm Pilot. It's inferior tech, and I feel a momentary flash of smugness at knowing I've got the drop on her in at least one important department. She flips the protective cover open and glances at the screen. "I think you work for Capital Laundry Services," she says matter-of-factly. "Nominally you're a senior scientific officer in the Department of Internal Logistics. You're tasked with representing your department in various joint committees and with setting policy on IT acquisitions. But you really work for Angleton, don't you? So they must see something in you that I—" her suddenly jaundiced gaze takes in my jeans, somewhat elderly tee shirt, and fishing vest stuffed with geek toys "—don't."

I try not to wilt too visibly. *Okay, she's a player.* That makes things easier—and harder, in a way. I swallow a mouthful of beer, successfully this time. "So why don't you tell me who you are?"

"I just did. I'm Ramona and I'm not going to sleep with you."

"Fine, Ramona-and-I'm-not-going-to-sleep-with-you. What are you? I mean, are you human? I can't tell, what with that glamour you're wearing, and that kind of thing makes me nervous."

Sapphire eyes stare at me. "Keep guessing, monkey-boy."

*Oh, for fuck's sake*—"Okay, I mean, who do you work for?"

"The Black Chamber. And I always wear this body on business. We've got a dress code, you know."

*The Black Chamber?* My stomach lurches. I've had one run-in with those guys, near the outset of my professional career, and everything I've learned since has taught me I was damned lucky to survive. "Who are you here to kill?"

She makes a faint moue of distaste. "I'm supposed to be working *with* you. I wasn't sent here to kill anyone."

We're going in circles again. "Fine. You're going to work with me but you don't want to sleep with me in case I drop dead, *Curse of the Mummy* and all that. You're tooled up to vamp some poor bastard, but it's not me, and you seem to know who I am. Why don't you just cut the crap and explain what you're doing here, why the hell you're so jumpy, and what's going on?"

"You really don't know?" She stares at me. "I was told you'd been briefed."

"Briefed?" I stare right back at her. "You've got to be kidding! I'm here for a committee meeting, not a live-action role-playing game."

"Huh!" For a moment she looks puzzled. "You *are* here to attend the next session of the joint-liaison committee on cosmological incursions, aren't you?"

I nod, very slightly. The Auditors don't usually ask you what you *didn't* say, they're more interested in what you *did* say, and who you said it to.[1] "You're not on my briefing sheet."

"I see." Ramona nods thoughtfully, then relaxes slightly. "Sounds like a regular fuck-up, then. Like I said, I was told we're going to be working together on a joint activity, starting with this meeting. For the purposes of this session I'm an accredited delegate, by the way."

"You—" I bite my tongue, trying to imagine her in a committee room going over the seventy-six-page agenda. "You're a *what*?"

"I've got observer status. Tomorrow I'll show you my ward," she adds. (That clinches it. The wards are handed out to those of us who're assigned to the joint committee.) "You can show me yours. I'm sure you'll be briefed before that—afterward we'll have a lot more to talk about."

"Just what—" I swallow "—are we supposed to be working on?"

She smiles. "Baccarat." She finishes her G&T and stands up with a swish of silk: "I'll be seeing you later, Robert. Until tonight . . ."

I buy another beer to calm my rattled nerves and hunker down in a carnivorous leather sofa at the far side of the bar. When I'm sure the bartender isn't watching me I pull out my Treo, run a highly specialized program, and dial an office extension in London. The phone rings four times, then the voice mail picks it up. "Boss? Got a headache. A Black Chamber operative called Ramona showed up. She claims that we're supposed to be working together. What the hell's going on? I need to know." I hang up without bothering to wait for a reply. Angleton will be in around six o'clock London time, and then I'll get my answer. I sigh, which draws a dirty look from a pair of overdressed chancers at the next table. I guess they think I'm lowering the tone of the bar. A sense of acute loneliness comes crashing down. *What am I doing here?*

The superficial answer is that I'm here on Laundry business. That's Capital Laundry Services to anyone who rings the front doorbell or cold-calls the switchboard, even though we haven't operated out of the old

---

[1] Blabbing secrets to beautiful *femme fatale* agents is frowned upon, especially when they're not necessarily human.

offices above the Chinese laundry in Soho since the end of the Second World War. The Laundry has a long memory. I work for the Laundry because they gave me a choice between doing so . . . or not working for anyone, ever again. With 20/20 hindsight I can't say I blame them. Some people you just do not want to leave outside the tent pissing in, and in my early twenties, self-confident and naïve, I was about as safe to leave lying around unsupervised as half a ton of sweating gelignite. These days I'm a trained computational demonologist, that species of occult practitioner who really can summon spirits from the vasty deep: or at least whatever corner of our local Calabi-Yau manifold they howl and gibber in, insane on the brane. And I'm a lot safer to have around these days— at least I know what precautions to use and what safety standards to obey: so call me a bunker full of smart bombs.

Most Laundry work consists of tediously bureaucratic form-filling and paper-pushing. About three years ago I got bored and asked if I could be assigned to active service. This was a mistake I've been regretting ever since, because it tends to go hand-in-hand with things like being rousted out of bed at four in the morning to go count the concrete cows in Milton Keynes, which sounds like a lot more fun than it actually is; especially when it leads to people shooting at you and lots more complicated forms to fill in and hearings in front of the Audit Committee. (About whom the less said the better.)

But on the other hand, if I hadn't switched to active service status I wouldn't have met Mo, Dr. Dominique O'Brien—except she hates the Dominique bit—and from this remove I can barely imagine what life would be like without her. At least, without her in principle. She's been on one training course or another for months on end lately, doing something hush-hush that she can't tell me about. This latest course has kept her down at the secure facility in Dunwich Village for four weeks now, and two weeks before *that* I had to go to the last liaison meeting, and frankly, I'm pining. I mentioned this to Pinky at the pub last week, and he snorted and accused me of carrying on like I was already married. I suppose he's right: I'm not used to having somebody wonderful and sane in my life, and I guess I'm a bit clingy. Maybe I should talk about it with Mo, but the subject of marriage is a bit touchy and I'm reluctant to raise it—her previous matrimonial experience wasn't a happy one.

I'm about halfway down my beer and thinking about calling Mo—if she's off work right now we could chat—when my phone rings. I glance at it and freeze: it's Angleton. I key the cone of silence then answer: "Bob here."

"Bob." Angleton's voice is papery-thin and cold, and the data compression inflicted by the telephone network and the security tunnel adds a hollow echo to it. "I got your message. This Ramona person, I want you to describe her."

"I can't. She was wearing a glamour, level three at least—it nearly sent me cross-eyed. But she knows who I am and what I'm here for."

"All right, Bob, that's about what I expected. Now this is what I want you to do." Angleton pauses. I lick my suddenly dry lips. "I want you to finish your drink and go back to your room. However, rather than entering, I want you to proceed down the corridor to the next room along on the same side, one number up. Your support team should be checked in there already. They'll continue the briefing once you're in the secure suite. Do not enter your room for the time being. Do you understand?"

"I think so." I nod. "You've got a little surprise job lined up for me. Is that it?"

"Yes," says Angleton, and hangs up abruptly.

I put my beer down, then stand up and glance round. I thought I was here for a routine committee meeting, but suddenly I find I'm standing on shifting sands, in possibly hostile territory. The middle-aged swingers glance disinterestedly at me, but my wards aren't tingling: they're just who they appear to be. *Right. Go directly to bed, do not eat supper, do not collect* . . . I shake my head and get moving.

To get to the elevator bank from the bar requires crossing an expanse of carpet overlooked by two levels of balconies—normally I wouldn't even notice it but after Angleton's little surprise the skin on the back of my neck crawls, and I clutch my Treo and my lucky charm bracelet twitchily as I sidle across it. There aren't many people about, if you discount the queue of tired business travelers checking in at the desk, and I make it to the lift bank without the scent of violets or the tickling sense of recognition that usually prefigures a lethal manifestation. I hit the "up" button on the nearest elevator and the doors open to admit me.

There is a theory that all chain hotels are participants in a conspiracy to convince the international traveler that there is only one hotel on the planet, and it's just like the one in their own home town. Personally, I don't believe it: it seems much more plausible that rather than actually going somewhere I have, in fact, been abducted and doped to the gills by aliens, implanted with false and bewildering memories of humiliating security probes and tedious travel, and checked in to a peculiarly expensive padded cell to recover. It's certainly an equally consistent explanation for the sense of disorientation and malaise I suffer from in these places; besides which, malevolent aliens are easier to swallow than the idea that other people actually *want* to live that way.

Elevators are an integral part of the alien abduction experience. I figure the polished fake-marble floor and mirror-tiled ceiling with indirect lighting conspire to generate a hypnotic sense of security in the abductees, so I pinch myself and force myself to stay alert. The lift is just beginning to accelerate upwards when my phone vibrates, so I glance at the screen, read the warning message, and drop to the floor.

The lift rattles as it rises towards the sixth floor. My guts lighten: *we're slowing!* The entropy detector wired into my phone's aerial is lighting up the screen with a grisly red warning icon. Some really heavy shit is going on upstairs, and the closer we get to my floor the stronger it is. "Fuck fuck fuck," I mumble, punching up a basic countermeasure screen. I'm not carrying: this is supposed to be friendly territory, and whatever's lighting up the upper levels of the Ramada Treff Page Hotel is—I briefly flash back to another hotel in Amsterdam, a howling wind sucking into the void where a wall should be—

*Clunk.* The door slides open and I realize at the same instant that I should have leapt for the lift control panel and the emergency stop button. "Shit," I add—the traditional last word—just as the flashing red dial on my phone screen whisks counterclockwise and turns green: green for safety, green for normal, green to show that the reality excursion has left the building.

"Zum Teufel!"

I glance up stupidly at a pair of feet encased in bulletproof-looking, brown leather hiking boots, then further up at the corduroy trousers and beige jacket of an elderly German tourist. "Trying to get a signal," I mutter, and scramble out of the lift on all fours, feeling extremely stupid.

I tiptoe along the beige-carpeted corridor to my room, racking my brains for an explanation. This whole set-up stinks like a week-old haddock: What's going on? Ramona, whoever the hell she is—I'd put hard money on her being mixed in with it. And that entropy blip was big. But it's gone now. *Someone gating in?* I wonder. *Or a proximal invocation?* I pause in front of my door and hold my hand above the door handle for a few seconds.

The handle is cold. Not just metal-at-ambient cold, but frigid and smoking-liquid-nitrogen cold.

"Oops," I say very quietly, and keep on walking down the corridor until I arrive at the next room door. Then I pull out my phone and speed-dial Angleton.

"Bob, Sitrep."

I lick my lips. "I'm still alive. While I was in the elevator my tertiary proximity alarm redlined then dropped back. I got to my room and the door handle feels like it's measuring room temperature in single-digit

Kelvins. I'm now outside the adjacent door. I figure it's a hit and unless you tell me otherwise I'm calling a Code Blue."

"This isn't the Code Blue you're here to deal with." Angleton sounds dryly amused, which is pretty much what I expect from him. "But you might want to make a note that your activation key is double-oh-seven. Just in case you need it later."

"You what?" I glare at the phone in disbelief, then punch the number into the keypad. "Jesus, Angleton, someday let me explain this concept called password security to you, I'm not meant to be able to hack my own action locks and start shooting on a whim—"

"But you didn't, did you?" He sounds even more amused as my phone beeps twice and makes a metallic clicking noise. "You may not have time to ask when the shit hits the fan. That's why I kept it simple. Now give me a Sitrep," he adds crisply.

"I'm going live." I frantically punch a couple of buttons and invisible moths flutter up and down my spine; when they fade away the corridor looks darker, somehow, and more threatening. "Half-live. My terminal is active." I fumble around in my pocket and pull out a small webcam, click it into place in the expansion slot on top of my phone. Now my phone has got two cameras. "Okay, SCORPION STARE loaded. I'm armed. What can I expect?"

There's a buzzing noise from the door lock next to me and the green LED flashes. "Hopefully nothing right now, but . . . open the door and go inside. Your backup team should be in place to give you your briefing, unless something's gone very wrong in the last five minutes."

"Jesus, Angleton."

"That *is* my name. You shouldn't swear so much: the walls have ears." He still sounds amused, the omniscient bastard. I don't know how he does it—I'm not cleared for that shit—but I always have a feeling that he can see over my shoulder. "Go inside. That's an order."

I take a deep breath, raise my phone, and open the door.

"Hiya, Bob!" Pinky looks up from the battered instrument case, his hands hovering over a compact computer keyboard. He's wearing a fetching batik sarong, a bushy handlebar moustache, and not much else: I'm not going to give him the pleasure of knowing just how much this disturbs me, or how relieved I am to see him.

"Where's Brains?" I ask, closing the door behind me and exhaling slowly.

"In the closet. Don't worry, he'll be coming out soon enough." Pinky points a digit at the row of storage doors fronting the wall adjacent to my room. "Angleton sent us. He said you'd need briefing."

"Am I the only person here who doesn't know what's going on?"

"Probably." He grins. "Nothing to worry about, ol' buddy." He glances at my Treo. "Would you mind not pointing that thing at me?"

"Oh, sorry." I lower it hastily and eject the second camera that turns it into a SCORPION STARE terminal, a basilisk device capable of blowing apart chunks of organic matter within visual range by convincing them that some of their carbon nuclei are made of silicon. "Are you going to tell me what's happening?"

"Sure." He sounds unconcerned. "You're being destiny-entangled with a new partner, and we're here to make sure she doesn't accidentally kill and eat you before the ritual is complete."

"I'm being *what?*" I hate it when I squeak.

"She's from the Black Chamber. You're supposed to be working together on something big, and the old man wants you to be able to draw on her abilities when you need help."

"What do you mean *draw on her?* Like I'm a trainee tattooist now?" I've got a horrible feeling I know what he's talking about, and I don't like it one little bit: but it would explain why Angleton sent Pinky and Brains to be my backup team. They're old housemates, and the bastard thinks they'll make me feel more comfortable.

The closet door opens and Brains steps out. Unlike Pinky he's decently dressed, for leather club values of decency. "Don't get overexcited, Bob," he says, winking at me: "I was just drilling holes in the walls."

"Holes—"

"To observe her. She's confined to the pentacle on your bedroom carpet; you don't need to worry about her getting loose and stealing your soul before we complete the circuit. Hold still or this won't work."

"Who's in what pentacle in my bedroom?" I take a step back towards the door but he's approaching me, clutching a sterile needle.

"Your new partner. Here, hold out a hand, this won't hurt a bit—"

"Ouch!" I step backwards and bounce off the wall, and Brains manages to get his drop of blood while I'm wincing.

"Great, that'll let us complete the destiny lock. You know you're a lucky man? At least, I suppose you're lucky—if you're that way inclined—"

"Who is she, dammit?"

"Your new partner? She's a changeling sent by the Black Chamber. Name of Ramona. And she is stacked, if that sort of thing matters to you." He pulls an amused face, oh so tolerant of my heterosexual ways.

"But I didn't—"

A toilet flushes, then the bathroom door opens and Boris steps out. And that's when I know I'm in deep shit, because Boris is not my normal line manager: Boris is the guy they send out when something has gone terribly wrong in the field and stuff needs to be cleaned up by any means necessary. Boris acts like a cut rate extra in a Cold War spy thriller—right down to the hokey fake accent and the shaven bullet-head—although he's about as English as I am. The speech thing is a leftover from a cerebral infarction, courtesy of a field invocation that went pear-shaped.

"Bob." He doesn't smile. "Welcome to Darmstadt. You come for joint-liaison framework. You are attending meeting tomorrow as planned: but are also being cleared for AZORIAN BLUE HADES as of now. Are here to brief, introduce you to support team, and make sure you bond with your, your, *associate*. Without to be eated."

"Eaten?" I ask. I must look a trifle tense because even Boris manages to pull an apologetic expression from somewhere. "What is this job, exactly? I didn't volunteer for a field mission—"

"Know you do not. We are truly sorry to put this on you," says Boris, running a hand over his bald head in a gesture that gives the lie to the sentiment, "but not having time for histrionics." He glances at Brains and gives a tiny nod. "First am giving briefing to you, then must complete destiny-entanglement protocol with entity next door. After that—" he checks his watch "—are being up to you, but estimating are only seven days to save Western civilization."

"What?" I know what my ears just heard but I'm not sure I believe them.

He stares at me grimly, then nods. "If is up to me, are not be relying on you. But time running out and is short on alternatives."

"Oh Jesus." I sit down on the sole available chair. "I'm not going to like this, am I?"

"*Nyet.* Pinky, the DVD please. It is being time to expand Robert's horizons . . ."

## Chapter 2:
## Going Down to Dunwich

*The river of time may wait for no man, but sometimes extreme stress causes it to run shallow. Cast the fly back four weeks and see what you catch, reeling in the month-old memories . . .*

It's late on a rainy Saturday morning in February, and Mo and I are drinking the remains of the breakfast coffee while talking about holidays. Or rather, she's talking about holidays while I'm nose-deep in a big, fat book, reacquainting myself with the classics. To tell the truth, each interruption breaks my concentration, so I'm barely paying attention. Besides, I'm not really keen on the idea of forking out money for two weeks in self-catering accommodations somewhere hot. We're supposed to be saving up the deposit for a mortgage, after all.

"How about Crete?" she asks from the kitchen table, drawing a careful red circle around three column-inches of newsprint.

"Won't you burn?" (Mo's got classic redhead skin and freckles.)

"We in the developed world have this advanced technology called sunblock. You may have heard of it." Mo glares at me. "You're not paying attention, are you?"

I sigh and put the book down. *Damn it, why now?* Just as I'm getting to Tanenbaum's masterful and witty takedown of the OSI protocol stack . . . "Guilty as charged."

"Why not?" She leans forwards, arms crossed, staring at me intently.

"Good book," I admit.

"Oh. Well that makes it all right," she snorts. "You can always take it to the beach, but you'll be kicking yourself if we wait too long and the cheap packages are all over-booked and we're left with choosing between the dregs of the Club 18-30 stuff, or paying through the nose, or one of us gets sent on detached duty again because we didn't notify HR of our vacation plans in time. Right?"

"I'm sorry. I guess I'm just not that enthusiastic right now."

"Yes, well, I just paid my Christmas credit card bill, too, love. Face it, by May we're both going to be needing a vacation, and they'll be twice as expensive if you leave booking it too late."

I look Mo in the eyes and realize she's got me metaphorically surrounded. She's older than I am—at least, a couple of years older—and more responsible, and as for what she sees in me . . . well. If there's one disadvantage to living with her it's that she's got a tendency to *organize* me. "But. Crete?"

"Crete, Island of. Home of the high Minoan civilization, probably collapsed due to rapid climactic change or the explosion of the volcano on Thera—Santorini—depending who you read. Loads of glorious frescos and palace ruins, wonderful beaches, and moussaka to die for. Grilled octopus, too: I know all about your thing for eating food with tentacles. If we aim for late May we'll beat the sunbathing masses. I was thinking we should book some side tours—I'm reading up on the archaeology—and a self-catering apartment, where we can chill for two weeks, soak up some sun before the temperature goes into the high thirties and everything bakes . . . How does that sound to you? I can practice the fiddle while you burn."

"It sounds—" I stop. "Hang on. What's the archaeology thing about?"

"Judith's had me reading up on the history of the littoral civilizations lately," she says. "I thought it'd be nice to take a look." Judith is deputy head of aquatic affairs at work. She spends about half her time out at the Laundry training facility in Dunwich and the other half up at Loch Ness.

"Ah." I hunt around for a scrap of kitchen roll to use as a bookmark. "So this is work, really."

"No, it's not!" Mo closes the newspaper section then picks it up and begins to shake the pages into order. She won't stop until she's got them perfectly aligned and smooth enough to sell all over again: it's one of her nervous tics. "I'm just curious. I've been reading so much about the Minoans and the precedent case law behind the human/Deep One treaties that it just caught my interest. Besides which, I last went on holiday to Greece about twenty years ago, on a school trip. It's about time to go back there, and I thought it'd be a nice place to relax. Sun, sex, and squid, with a side order of archaeology."

I know when I'm defeated, but I'm not completely stupid: it's time to change the subject. "What's Judith got you working on, anyway?" I ask. "I didn't think she had any call for your approach to, well . . . whatever." (It's best not to mention specifics: the house we share is subsidized accommodation, provided by the Laundry for employees like us—otherwise there's no way we could honestly afford to live in Central London on two civil service salaries—and the flip-side of this arrangement is that if we start discussing state secrets the walls grow ears.)

"Judith's got problems you aren't briefed on." She picks up her coffee mug, peers into it, and pulls a face. "I'm beginning to find out about them and I don't like them."

"You are?"

"I'm going down to Dunwich next week," she says suddenly. "I'll be there quite some time."

"You're what?"

I must sound shocked because she puts the mug down, stands up, and holds out her arms: "Oh, Bob!"

I stand up, too. We hug. "What's going on?"

"Training course," she says tightly.

"*Another* bloody training course? What are they doing, putting you through a postgraduate degree in Cloak and Dagger Studies?" I ask. The only training course *I* did at Dunwich was in field operations technique. Dunwich is where the Laundry keeps a lot of its secrets, hidden behind diverted roads and forbidding hedges, in a village evacuated by the War Department back during the 1940s and never returned to its civilian owners. Unlike Rome, no roads lead to Dunwich: to get there you need a GPS receiver, four-wheel drive, and a security talisman.

"Something like that. Angleton's asked me to take on some additional duties, but I don't think I can talk about them just yet. Let's say, it's at least as interesting as the more obscure branches of music theory I've been working on." She tenses against me, then hugs me tighter. "Listen, nobody can complain about me telling you I'm going, so . . . ask Judith, okay? If you really think you need to know. It's just a compartmentalization thing. I'll have my mobile and my violin, we can talk evenings. I'll try to make it back home for weekends."

"Weekends plural? Just how long is this course supposed to take?" I'm curious, as well as a bit annoyed. "When did they tell you about it?"

"They told me about this particular one yesterday. And I don't know how long it runs for—Judith says it comes up irregularly, they're at the mercy of certain specialist staff. At least four weeks, possibly more."

"Specialist staff. Would this specialist staff happen to have, say, pallid skin? And gill slits?"

"Yes, that's it. That's it exactly." She relaxes and takes a step back. "You've met them."

"Sort of." I shiver.

"I'm not happy about this," she says. "I told them I needed more notice. I mean, before they spring things like this special training regime on me."

I figure it's time to change the subject. "Crete. You figure you'll be out of the course by then?"

"Yes, for sure." She nods. "That's why I'll need to get away from it all, with you."

"So that's what this Crete thing is all about. Judith wants to drop you headfirst into Dunwich for three months and you need somewhere to go to decompress afterwards."

"That's about the size of it."

"Ah, shit." I pick up my book again, then my coffee cup. "Hey, this coffee's cold."

"I'll fix a fresh jug." Mo carries the cafetière over to the sink and starts rinsing the grounds out. "Sometimes I hate this job," she adds in a singsong, "and sometimes this job hates me . . ."

The name of the job is mathematics. Or maybe metamathematics. Or occult physics. And she wouldn't be in this job if she hadn't met me (although, on second thoughts, if she hadn't met me she'd be dead, so I think we'll call it even on that score and move swiftly on).

Look, if I come right out and say, "Magic exists," you'll probably dismiss me as a whack job. But in fact you'd be—well, I say you'd be—mistaken. And because my employers agree with me, and they're the government, you're outvoted.[2]

We've tried to cover it up as best we can. Our predecessors did their best to edit it out of the history books and public consciousness—the Mass Observation projects of the 1930s were rather more than the simple social science exercises they were presented as to the public—and since then we've devoted ourselves to the task of capping the bubbling cauldron of the occult beneath a hermetic lid of state secrecy. So if you think I'm a whack job it's partly my fault, isn't it? Mine, and the organization I work for—known to its inmates as the Laundry—and our opposite numbers in other countries.

The trouble is, the type of magic we deal with has nothing to do with rabbits and top hats, fairies at the bottom of the garden, and wishes that come true. The truth is, we live in a multiverse—a sheath of loosely interconnected universes, so loosely interconnected that they're actually leaky at the level of the quantum foam substrate of space-time. There's only one common realm among the universes, and that's the platonic realm of mathematics. We can solve theorems and cast hand-puppet shadows on the walls of our cave. What most folks (including most mathematicians and computer scientists—which amounts to the same thing) don't know is that in overlapping parallel versions of the cave other beings—for utterly unhuman values of "beings"—can also sometimes see the shadows, and cast shadows right back at us.

Back before about 1942, communication with other realms was pretty hit and miss. Unfortunately, Alan Turing partially systematized it—which later led to his unfortunate "suicide" and a subsequent policy reversal to the effect that it was better to have eminent logicians inside the tent pissing out, rather than outside pissing in. The Laundry is that

---

[2] Not to mention outgunned.

subdivision of the Second World War-era Special Operations Executive that exists to protect the United Kingdom from the scum of the multiverse. And, trust me on this, there are beings out there who even Jerry Springer wouldn't invite on his show.

The Laundry collects computer scientists who accidentally discover the elements of computational demonology, in much the same way Stalin used to collect jokes about himself.[3] About six years ago I nearly landscaped Wolverhampton, not to mention most of Birmingham and the Midlands, while experimenting with a really neat, new rendering algorithm that just might have accidentally summoned up the entity known to the clueful as "fuck, it's Nyarlathotep! Run!" (and to everyone else as "Fuck, run!").[4]

In Mo's case . . . she's a philosopher by training. Philosophers in the know are even more dangerous than computer scientists: they tend to become existential magnets for weird shit. Mo came to the Laundry's attention when she attracted some even-weirder-than-normal attention from a monster that thought our planet looked good and would be crunchy with ketchup. How we ended up living together is another story, albeit not an unhappy one. But the fact is, like me, she works for the Laundry now. In fact, she once told me the way she manages to feel safe these days is by being as dangerous as possible. And though I may bitch and moan about it when the Human Resources fairy decides to split us up for months on end, when you get down to it, if you work for a secret government agency, they can do that. And they've usually got good reasons for doing it, too. Which is one of the things I hate about my life . . .

. . . and another thing I hate is Microsoft PowerPoint, which brings me back to the present.

PowerPoint is symptomatic of a certain type of bureaucratic environment: one typified by interminable presentations with lots of fussy little bullet-points and flashy dissolves and soundtracks masked into the background, to try to convince the audience that the goon behind the computer has something significant to say. It's the tool of choice for pointy-headed idiots with expensive suits and skinny laptops who desperately want to look as if they're in command of the job, with all the facts at their fiddling fingertips, even if Rome is burning in the background. Nothing stands for content-free corporate bullshit quite like PowerPoint. And that's just scratching the surface . . .

---

[3] He had two Gulags full.
[4] Except the Black Chamber, who would say, "You're late—we're going to dock your pay."

I'm sorry. Maybe you think I'm being unjustifiably harsh—a presentation graphics program is just a piece of standard office software, after all—but my experience with PowerPoint is, shall we say, nonstandard. Besides, you've probably never had a guy with a shoulder holster and a field ops team backing him up drag you into a stakeout and whip out a laptop, to show you a presentation that begins with a slide stating: THIS BRIEFING WILL SELF-DESTRUCT IN FIFTEEN SECONDS. It's usually a sign that things have gone wronger than a very wrong thing indeed, and you are expected to make them go right again, or something double-plus ungood is going to happen.

Double-plus ungood indeed.

"Destiny-entanglement protocol," I mutter, as Pinky fusses around behind me and turns the fat-assed recliner I'm sitting in to face the wardrobe while Boris pokes at his laptop. As protocols go, I've got to admit it's a new one on me. "Would you mind explaining—hey, what's that duct tape for?"

"Sorry, Bob, try not to move, okay? It's just a precaution."

"Just a—" I reach up with my left hand to give my nose a preemptive scratch while he's busy taping my right arm to the chair. "What's the failure rate on this procedure, and should I have updated my life insurance first?"

"Relax. Is no failure rate." Boris finally gets his laptop to admit that its keyboard exists, and spins it round so I can see the screen. The usual security glyph flickers into view (I think that particular effect is called wheel, eight spokes) and bites me on the bridge of my nose. It's visual cortex hackery to seal my lips. "Failure not an option," repeats Boris.

The screen wheels again, and—morphs into a video of Angleton. "Hello, Bob," he begins. He's sitting behind his desk like an out-take from *Mission: Impossible*, which would be a whole lot more plausible if the desk wasn't a cramped, green metal thing with a contraption on top of it that looks like the bastard offspring of a microfiche reader by way of a 1950s mainframe computer terminal. "Sorry about the video briefing, but I had to be in two places at once, and you lost."

I catch Boris's eye and he pauses the presentation. "How the hell can you call this confidential?" I complain. "It's a video! If it fell into the wrong hands—"

Boris glances at Brains. "Tell him."

Brains pulls a gadget out of his goodie bag. "Andy shot it on one of these," he explains. "Solid-state camcorder, runs on MMC cards. Encrypted, and we stuffed a bunch of footage up front to make it look like amateur dramatics. That and the geas field will make anyone who steals it think they've stumbled over the next *Blair Witch Project*—cute, huh?"

I sigh. If he was a dog he'd be wagging his tail hard enough to dent the furniture. "Okay, roll it." I try to ignore whatever Pinky is doing on the carpet around my feet with a conductive pencil, a ruler, and a breakout box.

Angleton leans alarmingly towards the camera viewpoint, looming to fill the screen. "I'm sure you've heard of TLA Systems Corporation, Bob, if for no other reason than your complaints about their license management server on the departmental network reached the ears of the Audit committee last July, and I was forced to take preemptive action to divert them from mounting a full-scale investigation."

Gulp. The *Auditors* noticed? That wasn't my idea—no wonder Andy seemed pissed off with me. When I'm not running around pretending to be Secret Agent Man and attending committee meetings in Darmstadt, my job's pretty boring: network management is one component of it, and when I saw that blasted license manager trying to dial out to the public internet to complain about Facilities running too many copies of the TLA monitoring client, I cc'd everyone I could think of on the memo—

"TLA, as you know—Bob, pay attention at the back, there—was founded in 1979 by Ellis Billington and his partner Ritchie Martin. Ritchie was the software guy, Ellis the front man, which is why these days Ellis has a net worth of seventeen billion US dollars and Ritchie lives in a hippie commune in Oregon and refuses to deal with any unit of time he can't schedule on a sundial."

Angleton's sallow visage is replaced (no dissolve, this time) by a photograph of Billington, in the usual stuffed-suit pose adopted by CEOs hoping to impress the *Wall Street Journal*. His smile reveals enough teeth to intimidate a megalodon and he's in such good condition for a sixty-something executive that he's probably got a portrait squirreled away in a high-security facility in New Mexico that gives people nightmares when they look at it.

"TLA originally competed in the relational database market with Ingres, Oracle, and the other seven dwarves, but rapidly discovered a lucrative sideline in federal systems—specifically the GTO[5] market."

Lots of government departments in the '90s tried to save money by ordering their IT folks to buy only cheap, off-the-shelf software, or COTS. Which is to say, they finally got a clue that it's cheaper to buy a word processor off the shelf than to pay a defense contractor to write one. After their initial expressions of shock and horror, the trough-guzzling,

---

[5] Gran Turismo Omologato

platinum-wrench defense contractors responded by making GTO editions—ostensibly commercial versions of their platinum-plated, govern-
ment-oriented products, available to anyone who wanted to buy
them—$500,000 word processors with MIL-SPEC encryption and a
suite of handy document templates for rules of engagement, declarations
of war, and issuing COTS contracts to defense contractors.

"TLA grew rapidly and among other things acquired Moonstone
Metatechnology, who you may know of as one of the primary civilian
contractors to the Black Chamber."

*Whoops.* Now he's definitely got my attention. The presentation cuts
back to Angleton's drawn-to-the-point-of-mummification face. He looks
serious.

"Billington is from California. His parents are known to have been
involved in the Order of the Silver Star at one point, although Billington
himself claims to be Methodist. Whatever the truth, he has a strato-
spheric security clearance and his corporation designs scary things for an
assortment of spooky departments. I'd reference CRYSTAL CENTURY
if you were in London, but you can look it up later. For now, you can
take it from me that Billington is a player."

Now he throws in a fancy fade-to-right to show a rather old, grainy
photograph of a ship . . . an oil-drilling ship? A tanker? Something like
that. Whatever it is, it's big and there's something that looks like an oil
rig amidships. (I like that word, "amidships." It makes me sound as if I
know what I'm talking about. I am to sea-going vessels pretty much what
your grandmother is to Windows Vista.)

"This ship is the *Hughes Glomar Explorer.* Built for Summa
Corporation—owned by Howard Hughes—for the CIA in the early
1970s, its official mission was to recover a sunken Soviet nuclear missile
submarine from the floor of the Pacific Ocean. It was mated with this—"
another screen dissolve, to something that looks like a stainless steel
woodlouse adrift at sea— "the HMB-1, Hughes Mining Barge, built by,
you'll be interested to know, Lockheed Missiles and Space."

I lean forwards, barely noticing the duct tape holding my wrists and
ankles against the chair. "That's really neat," I say admiringly. "Didn't I
see it in a Discovery Channel documentary?"

Angleton clears his throat. "If you've quite finished?" (*How does he do
that?* I ask myself.) "Operation JENNIFER, the first attempt at recovering the submarine, was a partial success. I was there as a junior liaison
under the reciprocal monitoring provisions of the Benthic Treaty. The
CIA staff was . . . overly optimistic. To their credit, the Black Chamber
refused to be drawn in, and to *their* credit, the other Signatory Party
didn't use more than the minimum force necessary to prevent the recov-

ery. When Seymour Hersh and Jack Anderson broke the story in the *Los Angeles Times* several months later, the CIA gave up, the *Glomar Explorer* was formally designated property of the US government and mothballed, a discreet veil was drawn over the fate of the HMB-1—it was officially 'scrapped'—and we thought that was that."

Pinky has finished drawing a pentacle around my chair, and he finally signals that he's got it wired up to the isochronous signal generator—two thumbs up at Boris. Boris shuts the laptop lid with a click and sticks it under his arm. "Is time for entanglement," he tells me, "briefing will continue after."

"Whoa! What has she—" I nod at the far wall, beyond which the sleeping beauty lies "—got to do with this?" I glance at the laptop.

Boris harrumphs. "If had spend your time on briefing, would understand," he grumbles. "Brains, Pinky, stations."

"Yo. Good luck, Bob." Pinky pats me on the shoulder as he scuttles past the end of the beds to a small ward he's already set up on the carpet in front of the TV set. "It'll be all right—you'll see." Brains and Boris are already in their safety cells.

"What if someone's in the hall outside?" I call.

"The door's locked. And I put the DO NOT DISTURB sign out," Brains replies. "Stations, everyone?" He pulls out a black control box and twists a knob set on its face. I force myself to settle back in the chair; and in the other room, beyond the two spy-holes drilled through the back of the wardrobe, a very special light comes on and washes over the trapped entity in the pentacle.

When you go summoning extra-dimensional entities, there are certain precautions you should be sure to take.

For starters, you can forget garlic, bibles, and candles: they don't work. Instead, you need to start with serious electrical insulation to stop them from blowing your brains out through your ears. Once you've got yourself grounded you also need to pay attention to the existence of special optical high-bandwidth channels that demons may attempt to use to download themselves into your nervous system—they're called "eyeballs." Timesharing your hypothalamus with alien brain-eaters is not recommended if you wish to live long enough to claim your index-linked, state-earnings-related pension; it's about on a par with tap dancing on the London Underground's third rail in terms of health and safety. So you need to ensure you're optically isolated as well. *Do not stare into laser cavity with remaining eye*, as the safety notice puts it.

Most demons are as dumb as a sack full of hammers. This does not mean they're safe to mess with, any more than a C++ compiler is "safe" in the hands of an enthusiastic computer science undergrad. Some people can mess up anything, and computational demonology adds a new and unwelcome meaning to terms like "memory leak" and "debugger."

Now, I have severe misgivings about what Boris, Pinky, and Brains propose to do to me. (And I am *really* pissed at Angleton for telling them to do it.) However, they're more than passingly competent and they've certainly not skimped on the safety aspects. The entity that calls itself Ramona Random—hell, that might even be her real name, back when she was human, before the Black Chamber rebuilt her into the occult equivalent of a guided missile—is properly secured in the next room. Sitting in the bedroom closet—in front of the two holes Brains has drilled in the wall—is a tripod with a laser, a beam splitter, and a thermostatically controlled box containing a tissue culture grown from something that really ought not to exist, all wired up to a circuit board that looks like M. C. Escher designed it after taking too much LSD.

"Everyone clear?" calls Brains.

"Clear." Boris.

"Clear." Pinky.

"Totally unclear!" Me.

"Thank you, Bob. Pinky, how's our remote terminal?"

Pinky looks at a small, cheap television screen hooked up to a short-range receiver. "Drooling slightly. I think she's asleep."

"Okay. Lights." A diode on the back of the circuit board begins to flash, and I notice out of the corner of my eye that Brains is controlling it with a television remote. *That's smart of him,* I think, right before he punches the next button. "Blood."

Something begins to drip from the box, sizzling where it touches a wired junction on the circuit, which suddenly flares with silver light. I try to look away but it sucks my eyes in, like a bubble of boiling mercury that expands to fill the entire world. Then it's like my blind spot is expanding, creeping up on the back of my head.

"Symbolic link established."

There's an incredibly strong stink of violets, and a horde of ants crawl the length of my spine before holing up in the pit of my stomach to build a nest.

**Hello, Bob.** The voice caresses my ears like the velvet fuzz on a week-dead aubergine, sultry and somehow rotten to the core. It's Ramona's voice. My stomach heaves. I can't see anything but the swirling pit of light, and the violets are decaying into something unspeakable. **Can you hear me?**

**I hear you.** I bite my tongue, tasting the sound of steel guitars. Synesthesia, I note distantly. I've read about this sort of thing: if the situation wasn't so dangerous it would be fascinating. Meanwhile my right arm is straining against the duct tape without me willing it to move. I try to make it stop and it won't. **Leave my arm alone, damn you!**

**I'm already damned,** she says flippantly, but the muscles in my arm stop twitching and jumping.

Then I realize I haven't been moving my lips, and more importantly, Ramona hasn't been speaking aloud. **How do we control this?** I ask.

**The will becomes the act: if you want me to hear, I hear you.**

**Oh.** The light show is beginning to slow down, with reality bleeding back in through the edges, and my head feels like someone's rammed a railroad spike through my skull right behind my left eye. **I feel sick.**

**Don't do that, Bob!** She sounds—feels?—disturbed.

**Okay.** *Try not to think of invisible pink elephants,* I think grimly, my skin crawling as the implications set in. I've just been rendered uncontrollably telepathic with a woman—or something woman-shaped—from the Black Chamber, and I'm such a dork my first reaction wasn't to run like fuck. Why'd Angleton do a thing like that? Hey, isn't this asking for a really *gigantic* security breach—at least, if both of us survive the experience? *How am I going to keep Ramona out of my head—?*

**Hey, stop blaming me!** Somehow I can tell she's irritated by my line of thought. **My head hurts, too.**

**So why didn't you run away?** I let slip before I manage to clamp a lid down on the thought.

**They didn't give me the option.** A metallic, bitter taste fills my mouth. **I'm not entirely human. Constitutional rights don't apply to non-humans. All I can say is, those bastards better hope I never get loose from this geas . . .** I feel like spitting, then I realize the glands full of warmth at the back of her throat aren't salivary ducts.

"Bob."

I blink in confusion. It's Brains. He looms over me, out of his grounded pentacle. "Can you hear me?"

"Yuh, yeah." I try to swallow, feeling the sensation of venom sacs throbbing urgently inside my cheeks begin to fade. I shudder. There's a trailing wisp of wistfulness from Ramona, and a malicious giggle: she doesn't have fangs, she just has a really good somatic imagination. **Let me get my head together,** I tell her, and then try to do the invisible pink elephant thing in her general direction.

"How do you feel?" asks Brains. He sounds curious.

"How the fuck do you think *you'd* feel?" I snarl. "Jesus fuck, give me ibuprofen or give me a straight razor. My head is killing me." Then I realize something else. "And cut me loose from here. Someone's got to go next door and release Ramona, and I don't think any of you guys want to get within spitting range of her without a chair, a whip, and a can of pepper spray."

I remember the shape of her anger at her employers and shiver again. Working with Ramona is going to be like riding sidesaddle on a black mamba. And that's *before* I get to tell Mo, "Honey, they partnered me with a demon."

## Chapter 3:
## Tangled Up in Grue

They wait for the ibuprofen to start working before they untie me from the chair, which is extremely prudent of them.

"Right," I say, leaning against the back of the chair and breathing deeply. "Boris, what the fuck is this about?"

"It is to be stopping her from killing you." Boris glowers at me. He's annoyed about something, which makes two of us. "And to be creating an untappable communication, for mission which you have not be briefed on because—" He gestures at the laptop and I realize why he's so irritated: they weren't joking when they said the briefing would self-destruct. "Here are your ticket for flight, is open for next available seat. Will continue the briefing in Saint Martin." He shoves a booklet of flight vouchers at me.

"Where?" I nearly drop them.

"They're sending us to the Caribbean!" It's Pinky. He's almost turning handstands. "Sun! Sand! And skullduggery! And we've got great toys to play with!" Brains is methodically packing up the entanglement rig, which breaks down into a big rolling suitcase. He seems amused by something.

I try to catch Boris's eye: Boris is staring at Pinky in either deep fascination, pity, or something in between. "Where in the Caribbean?" I ask.

Boris shakes himself. "Is joint operation," he explains. "Is European territory, joint Franco-Dutch government—they ask us to operate in there. But Caribbean is American sea. So Black Chamber send Ramona to be working with you."

I wince. "Tell me you're joking."

Another voice interrupts, inaudible to everyone else: **Hey, Bob! I'm still stuck here. A girl could get bored waiting.** I have a feeling that a bored Ramona would be a very bad girl indeed, in a your-life-insurance-policy-just-expired kind of way.

"Am not joking. This is joint operation. Lots of shit to spread all round." He carefully picks up his dead laptop and drops it into an open briefcase. "Go to committee meeting tomorrow, take memos, then go to airport and fly out. Can file liaison report later, after save the universe."

"Uh-huh. First I better go unlock Ramona from that containment you stuck her in." **I'm coming,** I send her way. "How trustworthy is she, really?"

Boris smiles thinly. "How trustworthy is rattlesnake?"

I excuse myself and stagger out into the corridor, my head still throbbing and the world crinkling slightly at the edges. I guess I now know what that spike of entropy change was. I pause at the door to my room but the handle is no longer dewed with liquid nitrogen, and is merely cold to the touch.

Ramona is sitting in an armchair opposite the wall with the holes in it. She smiles at me, but the expression doesn't reach her eyes. **Bob. Get me out of this.**

*This* is the pentacle someone has stenciled on the carpet around her chair and plugged into a compact, blue, noise generator. It's still running—Brains didn't hook it up to his remote. **Give me a moment.** I sit down on the bed opposite her, kick off my trainers, and rub my head. **If I let you go, what are you going to do?**

Her smile broadens. **Well, personally—** she glances at the door **—nothing much.** I get a momentary flicker of unpleasantness involving extremely sharp knives and gouts of arterial blood, then she clamps down on it, with an almost regretful edge, and I realize she's just daydreaming about someone else, someone a very long way away. **Honest.**

**Second question. Who's your real target?**

**Are you going to let me go once we get through this game of twenty questions? Or do you have something else in mind?** She crosses her legs, watching me alertly. *Every guy I've ever slept with died less than twenty-four hours later,* I recall. **I wasn't joking,** she adds, defensively.

**I didn't think you were. I just want to know who your real target is.**

She sniffs. **Ellis Billington. What's your problem?**

**I'm not sure. Bear with me for one last test?**

**What?** She half stands as I get off the bed, but the constraining field prohibits her from reaching me: **Hey! Ow! You bastard!**

It brings tears to my eyes. I clutch my right foot and wait for the pain to subside from where I kicked the bed-base. Ramona is bent over, hugging her foot as well. **Okay,** I mumble, then kneel down and switch off the signal generator. I don't particularly want to switch it off—I feel a hell of a lot safer with Ramona trapped inside a pentacle; the idea of setting her free makes my skin crawl—but the flip side of the entanglement is fairly clear: not only can we talk without being overheard, there are other (and drastically less pleasant) side effects.

**You're not a masochist, are you?** she asks tightly as she hobbles towards the bathroom.

**No—**

**Good.** She slams the door shut. A few seconds later I clutch at my crotch in horror as I feel the unmistakable sensation of a full bladder emptying. It takes me seconds to realize it's not mine. My fingers are dry.

**Bitch!** Two can play at that game.

**It's your fault for keeping me waiting for ages.**

I breathe deeply. **Look. I didn't ask for this—**

**Me neither!**

**—so why don't we call it a truce?**

Silence, punctuated by a sharp sense of impatience. **Took you long enough, monkey-boy.**

**What's with the monkey-boy business?** I complain.

**What's with the abhuman-bloodsucking-demon-whore imagery?** she responds acidly. **Try to keep your gibbering religious bigotry out of my head and I'll leave your bladder alone. Deal?**

**Deal—hey! How the hell am I a gibbering religious bigot? I'm an atheist!**

**Yeah, and the horse you rode in on is a member of the College of Cardinals.** I hear the toilet flush through the door, a sudden reminder that we're not actually talking. **You may not believe in God but you still believe in Hell. And you think it's where people like me belong.**

**But isn't that where you come from . . . ?**

The door opens. Her glamour's as strong as ever: she looks like she just stepped out of a cocktail party to powder her nose. **We can go over it some other time, Bob. You can just call room service if you want to eat; I have to make more elaborate arrangements. See you tomorrow.** With that, she picks up her evening bag from the bedside table and departs in a snit.

"Mo?"

"Hi! Where are—hold on a moment—Bob? You still there? I was about to jump in the bath. How's it going?"

*Gulp.* "About a ton of horse manure just landed on me. Have you seen Angleton this week?"

"No, they've billeted me in the Monkfish Motel again and it's really dull—you know what the night life in Dunwich is like. So what's Angleton up to now?"

"I, uh, well, I got here—Darmstadt—to find—" I double-check my phone to confirm we're in secure mode "—new orders waiting for me, care of Boris and the two mad mice. Almost got run off the autobahn on the way in and, well—"

"Car accident?"

"Sort of. Anyway, I'm being shunted off on a side trip instead of coming home. So I won't be back for the weekend."

"Shit."

"My thoughts exactly."

"Where are they sending you?"

"To Saint Martin, in the Caribbean."

"The—"

"And it gets worse."

"Do I want to hear this, love?"

"Probably not."

Pause. "Okay. I'm sitting down."

"It's a joint operation. They've inflicted a minder from the Black Chamber on me."

"But—Bob! That's crazy! It just doesn't happen! Nobody even knows what the Black Chamber is really called! 'No Such Agency' meets 'Destroy Before Reading.' Are you telling me . . . ?"

"I haven't been fully briefed. But I figure it's going to be extremely ungood, for, like, Amsterdam values of ungood." I shudder. Our little weekend trip to Amsterdam involved more trouble than you can shake a shitty stick at. "I guess you know the Chamber specializes in taking the HUM out of HUMINT? Golems and remote viewing and so forth, never send a human agent to do a job a zombie can do? Anyway, the minder they've sent me is, you know, existentially challenged. They've sicced a demon on me."

"Jesus, Bob."

"Yeah, well, *He* isn't answering the phone."

"I can't believe it. The bastards."

"Listen, I've got a feeling there's more to this than meets the eye and I need someone watching my back who isn't just looking for a good spot to sink their fangs into. Can you do some discreet digging when you get back to the office? Ask Andy, perhaps? This is under Angleton, by the way."

"Angleton." Mo's voice goes flat and cold, and the hair on the back of my neck rises. She blames Angleton for a lot of things, and it could turn very ugly if she decides to let it all hang out. "I should have guessed. It's about time that bastard faced the music."

"Don't go after him!" I say urgently. "You're not meant to know this. Remember, all you know is I've been sent off somewhere to do a job."

"But you want me to keep my ear to the ground and listen for oncoming train wrecks."

"That's about the size of it. I'm missing you."

"Love you, too." A pause. "What is it about this spook that's got you so upset?"

Whoops. I'm no good at hiding things from her, am I? "For starters she's crazier than a legful of ferrets. She's seriously bad magic, wearing a perpetual glamour—level three, if I'm any judge of such things. The only thing keeping her on track is the geas that ate Montana. She's not a free actor. Actress."

"Uh-huh. What else?"

I lick my lips. "Boris, um, applied some sort of destiny-entanglement protocol to us. I didn't run away fast enough."

"Destiny—*what*? Entanglement? What's that?"

I take a deep breath. "I'm not sure, but I'd appreciate it if you could find out and tell me. Because whatever it is, it's scaring me."

It's still early in the evening, but my encounter with Ramona has shaken me, and I don't much want to run into Pinky and Brains again (if they haven't already packed up and left: there's quite a lot of banging coming from next door). I decide to hole up in my room and lick my wounded dignity, so I order up a cardboard cheeseburger from room service, have a long soak under the shower, watch an infinitely forgettable movie on cable, and turn in for the night.

I don't usually remember my dreams because they're mostly surreal and/or incomprehensible—two-headed camels stealing my hovercraft, bat-winged squid gods explaining why I ought to accept job offers from Microsoft, that sort of thing—so what makes this one stand out is its sheer gritty realism. Dreaming that I'm me is fine. So is dreaming that I'm an employee of a vast software multinational, damned and enslaved by an ancient evil. But dreaming that I'm an overweight fifty-something German sales executive from an engineering firm in Düsseldorf is so far off the map that if I wasn't asleep I'd pinch myself.

I'm at a regional sales convention and I've been drinking and living large. I like these conferences: I can get away from Hilda and cut loose, party like a young thing again. The awards dinner is over and I split off with a couple of younger fellows I know vaguely, which is how we end up in the casino. I don't usually gamble much but I'm on a winning streak at the wheel, and all the ladies love a winning streak; between the brandy, the Cohiba panatelas, and the babe who's attached herself to my shoulder—a call girl, natürlich, but classy—I'm having the time of my life. She leans against me and suggests I might cash in my winnings, and this strikes me as a good idea. After all, if I keep gambling, my streak will end sooner or later, won't it? Let it pay for her tonight.

We're in the lift, heading up to my room on the fourteenth floor, and she's nuzzling up against me. I haven't felt smooth flesh like this in . . . too long. Hilda was never like that and since the kids the only side of her body she's shown me is the sharp edge of her tongue; serves her right if I enjoy myself once in a while. The babe's got her arms around me inside my jacket and I can feel her body through her dress. *Wow.* This has been a day to remember! We cuddle some more and I lead her to my room, tiptoeing—she's giggling quietly, telling me not to make a noise, not to disturb the neighbors—and I get the door open and she tells me to go wait in the bathroom while she gets ready. *How much does she want?* I ask. She shakes her head and says, *Two hundred but only if I'm happy.* Well, how can I refuse an offer like that?

In the bathroom I take my shoes off, remove my jacket and tie—*enough.* She calls to say she's ready, and I open the door. She's lying on the bed, in a provocative position that still allows her to see me. She's taken off her dress: smooth, stocking-clad thighs and a waterfall of pure corn-silk hair, blue eyes like ice diamonds that I can fall into and drown. My heart is pounding as if I've run a marathon, or I'm about to have a heart attack. She's smiling at me, hungry, needy; I take a step forwards. My back is clammy with cold sweat and my crotch feels like a steel bar, painfully erect. I need her like I've never needed a woman before. Another step. Another. She smiles and kneels on the carpet in front of me, opening her mouth to take me in. I dread her touch, even though I blindly crave it. *Tap-dancing on the third rail,* I think fuzzily, trying to force my paralyzed ribs to take a racking breath of air as she reaches out to touch me.

"Uh—uh!"

I open my eyes. It's dark in the hotel room, my heart's hammering, and I'm lying in a puddle of cold sweat with an erection like a lump of wood and a ghastly sense of horror squatting on my chest. "Uh!" All I can do is grunt feebly. I flail for a bit, then shove the clammy sheet away from me. I'm erect—and it's not like waking from an erotic dream, it's more like someone's using a farmyard device to milk me. "Ugh." I begin to sit up, meaning to go to the bathroom and towel my back off, and right then I come.

It's weird, and wonderful, like no orgasm I've ever had before. It seems to go on and on forever, scratching the unscratchable itch inside me with an intensity that rapidly becomes unbearable. There's something about it that feels terminal—not repeatable, an endpoint in someone's life. When it begins to subside I whimper slightly and reach for my crotch. Surprise: I'm still erect—and my skin is dry.

*That wasn't me*, I realize, disturbed. *That was Ramona*—I clutch my prick protectively.

Distant laughter. **Go on, jerk yourself off.** There's a warm glow of satisfaction in her stomach. **You know you really want to, don't you?** she thinks, licking her lips and sending me the taste of semen. Then I feel her reach over and pull the sheets up over the dead businessman's face.

I manage to reach the bathroom and lift the toilet lid before I throw up. My stomach knots and tries to climb my throat. *Every guy I've ever slept with died less than twenty-four hours later*, she said, and now I know why. She's right about one thing: despite the sudden gag reflex I'm still sprouting a woody. Despite everything, despite the dread, despite the almost furtive guilt I feel, I *really* enjoyed whatever it is Ramona just did. And now I feel inexplicably guilty on account of Mo, because I wasn't looking for an adventure on the side—and I feel really dirty as well, because I found it exciting.

The overspill from what Ramona was doing turned me on in my sleep, but the reason I'm throwing up now is that what she was doing wasn't sex: she was feeding on the guy's mind, and he died, and it gave her an orgasm, and I got off on it. I want to scrub my brains out with a wire brush, and I want to crawl into a deep hole in the ground, and I want to do it all over again . . . because I'm entangled with her, I hope, but the alternative is worse: there are some things I don't want to find out about myself, and a secret taste for hot, kinky demon sex is one of them.

I really hope Mo finds out that this entanglement thing is reversible. Because if it isn't, the next time she and I go to bed together—

Let's not think about that right now.

I spend an uneasy night tossing and turning between damp sheets despite the dream catcher screensaver I leave running on my tablet PC. By dawn I've just about worried myself into a mild nervous breakdown: if it's not trying to avoid thinking about invisible pink elephants (subtype: man-eaters), it's what Angleton's got in mind for me in Saint Martin. I don't even know where the place is on a map. Meanwhile, the committee meeting is another unwelcome distraction. How am I supposed to represent my organization when I'm terrified of falling asleep?

I somehow manage to fumble my way into my suit—an uncomfortable imposition required for overseas junkets—then shamble downstairs to the dining room for breakfast. Coffee, I need coffee. And a copy of the *Independent*, imported from London on an overnight flight. The restaurant is a model of German efficiency, and the staff mostly leave me alone, for which I'm grateful.

I'm just about feeling human again by a quarter to nine; the meeting's optimistically scheduled to start in another fifteen minutes, but at a guess half the delegates will still be working on their breakfasts. So I wander over to the lobby where there's free WiFi, to see if there are any messages for me, and that's when I run into Franz.

"Bob? Is that you?"

I blink stupidly. "Franz?"

"Bob!" We do the handshake thing, feinting around our centers of gravity with briefcases held out to either side, like a pair of nervous chickens sizing each other up in a farmyard. I haven't seen Franz in a suit before, and he hasn't seen me in one either. I met him on a training seminar about six months ago when he was over from Den Haag. He's very tall and very Dutch, which means his accent is a lot more BBC-perfect than mine. "Fancy meeting you here."

"I guess you must be on the joint-session list?"

"I'll show you mine if you show me yours," he jokes. "I was just looking for a postcard before I go upstairs . . . will you wait?"

"Sure." I relax slightly. "Have you done one of these before?"

"No." He spins the rack idly, looking at the picturesque gingerbread castles one by one. "Have you?"

"I've done one, period. Shouldn't talk about it outside class, but what the hell."

Franz finds a postcard showing a beaming buxom German barmaid clutching a pair of highly suggestive jugs. "I'll have this one." He attracts the attention of the nearest sales clerk and rattles something off in what sounds to me like flawless German. My tablet finishes checking for mail, bins the spam, and dings at me to put it away. I rub my head and glance at Franz enviously. I bet he wouldn't have any problems with Ramona: he's scarily bright, good-natured, incisive, handsome, cultured, and all-round competent. Not to mention being able to out-drink me and charm the socks off everyone who meets him. He's clearly on his way up the ladder of the AIVD's occult counterintelligence division, and he'll make deputy director while I'm still polishing Angleton's filing cabinet.

"Ready?" he asks.

"Guess so."

We head for the lift to the conference room. It's on the fourth floor. Lest you think this is an altogether too casual approach to confidential business, the hotel is security certified and our hosts have block-booked the adjacent rooms and the suites immediately above and below. It's not as if we're going to be discussing matters of national security, either.

Franz and I are early. There's a coffee urn and cups in place on the sideboard, an LCD projector and screen next to the boardroom table, and comfortable leather-lined swivel chairs to fall asleep in. I claim one corner of the table, opposite the windows with their daydream-friendly view of downtown Darmstadt, and plunk my tablet down on the leather place mat beside the hotel notepad. "Coffee?" asks Franz.

"Yes, please. Milk, no sugar." I pick up the agenda and carry it over.

"What's the routine?" he asks. He actually sounds interested.

"Well. We show each other our authorizations first. Then the chair orders the doors sealed." I wave at the far end of the suite: "Rest room's through there. Chair this time is—" I riffle the sheets "—Italy, which means Anna, unless she's ill and they send a replacement. She'll keep things tight, I think. Then we get down to business."

"I see. And the minutes . . . ?"

"Everyone who's got a presentation is supposed to bring copies on CD-ROM. The host organization[6] provides a secretarial service, that's the GSA's job this time."

Franz's brow wrinkles. "Excuse me for saying, but this sounds as if the meeting itself is . . . unnecessary? We could take it to email."

I shrug. "Yup. But then we wouldn't get to do the real business, over coffee and biscuits."

His expression clears. "Ah, now I see—"

The door opens. "Ciao, guys!" It's Anna, short and bubbly and (I suspect) a little hung-over, judging from her eyes. "Oh, my head. Where is everybody? Let us keep this short, shall we?"

She makes a beeline for the coffee pot. "Tell Andrew he is a naughty, naughty man," she chides me.

"What's he done now?" I ask, steeling myself.

"He got my birthday wrong!" Flashing eyes, toothy grin. "A, what is it, a fencepost error."

"Oh, uh, yeah, I'll do that." I shrug. I'm still uncomfortable in this type of situation. Most of the people here were grades above me until six months ago, and half of them still are; I'm very much the junior delegate and Andy—who used to be one of my managers—is the guy into whose boots I've stepped. "Last time I saw him he was kind of busy. Overworked dealing with fallout from—" I clear my throat.

"Oh, say no more." She pats me on the arm and moves on to say hello to the other delegates who're letting themselves in. We ought to have a full house of security management types from Spain, Brussels, and parts east within NATO, but for some reason attendance today looks unusually light.

---

[6] The Geheime Sicherheit Abteilung to their mothers, although everyone else calls them the Faust Force.

Delegates are beginning to arrive, so I head back towards my seat. "Who's that?" Franz asks me quietly, with a nod at the door. I glance round and do a double-take: it's Ramona. She's almost unrecognizable in a business suit with her hair up, but being this close to her still makes the skin crawl in the small of my back.

"That's, um, Ms. Random. An observer. We're privileged to have her here." My cheek twitches and Franz stares at me from behind his rimless spectacles.

"I see. I was unaware that we had that type of guest present." I get the feeling he sees a whole lot more than I told him, but there's not a lot I can say.

**Hello, darling, slept well?** she asks. I start: then I realize she's still on the other side of the room, coolly pouring herself a cup of coffee and smiling at Anna.

**No thanks to you,** I think at her.

I hear a rude noise. **A girl's got to eat sometime.**

**Yes, but midnight snacking—** Invisible pink elephants. Think of invisible pink elephants, Bob. Think of invisible pink, throbbing elephants in the night—no, cancel the throbbing—

I sit down, dizzily. "Is something wrong?" asks Franz.

"Supper disagreed with me," I say weakly. Ramona's supper, that is: *pâté de gros ingénieur.* "I'll be okay if I sit down." A hot flush is trying to follow the shivers up and down my spine. I glance at her across the room and she looks back at me, blank-faced.

People are heading towards the table, apparently following my lead. To my annoyance Ramona oozes into the chair next to me then stares sharply at Anna's end of the table.

"Ciao everybody. I see a lot of vacant seats and new faces today! This meeting will now commence. Badges on the table, please." Anna looks up and down the table pointedly as clusters of conversation die down.

I reach into my pocket and slide my Laundry warrant card onto the table. Everyone else is doing likewise with their own accreditation: the air twists and prickles with the bindings.

"Excuse moi." François leans across the table towards Ramona: "You have credentials?"

Ramona just looks at him. "No. As a matter of policy my organization does not issue identification papers." Heads turn and eyes narrow around the table.

I clear my throat. "I can vouch for her," I hear myself saying. "Ramona Random—" words slide seamlessly into my mind "—Overseas Operations Directorate, based out of Arkham." **Thanks,** I tell her silently, **now get out of my head.** "Here by direct invitation of my own department, full observer status under Clause Four of the Benthic Treaty."

Ramona smiles thinly. There's a low buzz of surprised conversation. "Quiet!" calls Anna. "I'd like to welcome our . . . today's observer here." She looks slightly flustered. "If you could contrive some form of identification in future, that would be helpful, but—" she looks at me hopefully "—I'm sure Robert's superiors will cover this time."

I manage to nod. I can't cover it on my authority, but this is Angleton's bloody fault, after all, and he actually gets to talk to Mahogany Row. Let *them* sort it out.

"Fine!" She claps her hands together. "Then, to business! First item, attendees, I believe we have taken care of. Let the doors be locked. Second item, travel expense claims in pursuit of joint-investigation warrants on overseas territory, at the request of non-issuing governments. Arbitration of expense allocation among participating member states— traditionally this has been carried out on an ad hoc basis, but since the Austrian civil service strike last year the urgency of formalizing arrangements has become apparent . . ."

The next hour passes uneventfully. It's basically bureaucratic legwork, to ensure that none of the European partner agencies tread on each other's toes when operating on each other's soil. Proposals to allow agents of charter countries to claim expenses for mopping up after another member's business are agreed upon and bounced up to the next level of management for approval. Suggestions for standardizing the various forms of ID we use are proposed, and eventually shot down because they serve very different purposes and some of them come with powers which are considered alarming, illegal, or immoral in different jurisdictions. I take notes on my tablet, briefly consider a game of Minesweeper before deciding it's not worth the risk of exposure, and finally settle down to the grim business of not falling asleep and embarrassing myself in public.

Glancing around the table I realize things are pretty much the same all round. Anyone who isn't actively talking or jotting notes is twiddling their thumbs, gazing out the window, staring at the other delegates, or quietly drooling over their complementary notepad. *Ah, the joy of high-level negotiations.* I glance at Ramona and see she's one of the doodlers. She's inscribing something black and scary on her notepad: geometric lines and arcs, repeated patterns that sink into one another in a self-similar way. Then she glances sidelong at me, and very deliberately slides a blank sheet of paper across her pad.

I shake myself; must stay focused. We're up to item four on the agenda, drilling down into issues of software resource management and a proposal to jointly license an auditing and license management system being developed by a subsidiary of—TLA Systems GMbH?

I sit bolt upright. Sophie from Berlin is soporifically talking us through the procurement process Faust Force has come up with, a painfully politically correct concoction of open market tenders and sealed bidding processes intended to evaluate competing proposals and then roll out a best-of-breed system for common deployment. "Excuse me," I say, when she pauses for breath, "this is all very well, but what can you tell us about the winning bid? I assume the process has already been approved," I add hastily, before she can explain that this is all very important background detail.

"Ah, but this is necessary to understand the process-oriented quality infrastructure, Robert." She looks down her nose at me over her bifocals and brandishes a scarily thick sheaf of papers. "I have here the fully documented procurement analysis for the system!" The only inflection in her voice is on the last word, making a sort of semantic hiccup out of it. She sounds like a badly programmed speech synthesizer.

"Yes, but what does it *do?*" Ramona butts in, leaning forwards. It's the first thing she's said since I introduced her, and suddenly she's the focus of attention again. "I'm sorry if this is all understood by everybody present, but . . ." she trails off.

Sophie pauses for a few seconds, like a robot receiving new instructions. "If you will with me bear, I shall explain it. The contractors a presentation have prepared, to be played after lunch." *Oops,* I think, visions of the usual postprandial siesta torture running through my head. Dim the lights, turn the heating up, then get some bastard in a suit to stand up and drone through a PowerPoint presentation—have I said how much I hate PowerPoint?—while you try to stay awake. Then I blink and notice Ramona's sidelong glance. *Oops again.* What's going on?

Lunch arrives mercifully soon, in the form of a trolley, parked outside the conference suite door, laden with sandwiches and slices of ham. Sophie accepts the enforced pause with relatively good grace, and we all stand up and head for the buffet, except Ramona. While I'm stuffing my face on tuna and cucumber I catch Franz looking concerned. "Are you hungry?" he asks her quietly.

Ramona smiles at him, turning on the charm. "I'm on a special diet."

"Oh, I'm so sorry."

She beams up at him: "That's all right, I had a heavy meal last night."

**Don't,** I warn her silently, and she flashes a scowl at me.

**You're no fun, monkey-boy.**

Eventually we go back to the table. Anna fidgets with the remote control to the blinds until she figures out how to block off the early afternoon sunlight. "Very good!" she says approvingly. "Sophie, if you will continue?"

"Danke." Sophie fidgets with her laptop and the projector cable. "Ah, gut. Here we go, very soon . . ."

There is something about PowerPoint presentations that sends people to sleep. It's particularly effective after lunch, and Sophie doesn't have the personal presence to get past the soothing wash of pastel colors and flashy dissolves and actually make us pay attention. I lean back and watch, tiredly. TLA GmBH is a subsidiary of TLA Systems Corporation, of Ellis Billington. They're the guys who do for the Black Chamber what QinetiQ does—or used to do—for the UK's Ministry of Defense. This integrated system we're watching a promo video for is basically just a tarted-up-for-export—meaning, it speaks Spanish, French, and German technobabble—version of a big custom program they wrote for Ramona's faceless employers. *So what's Ramona doing here?* I wonder. *They must already know all this. Wake up, Bob!* I've got a stomach full of tuna mayo and smoked salmon on rye, and it feels like it weighs a quarter of a ton. The sunlight slanting through the half-drawn blinds warms the back of my hands where they lie limply on the tabletop. Asset-management software is so not my favorite afternoon topic of conversation. *Bob, pay attention at the back! Ramona shouldn't be here,* I think fuzzily. *Why is she here? Is it something to do with Billington's software?*

**Bob! Pay attention right now!**

I jolt upright in my seat as if someone's stuck a cattle prod up my rear. The sharp censorious voice in my head is Ramona's. I glance along the table but everybody else is nodding or dozing or snoozing in tune to Sophie's repetitive cadence—except Ramona, who catches my eye. She's alert, ready and waiting for something.

**What's going on?** I ask her.

**We're at slide twenty-four,** she tells me. **Whatever happens next, it happens between numbers twenty-six and twenty-eight.**

**What . . . ?**

**We're not omniscient, Bob. We just caught wind of—aha, twenty-five coming up.**

I glance at the end of the table. Sophie stands next to the projector and her laptop, swaying slightly like a puppet in the grip of an invisible force. " . . . The four-year rolling balance of assets represents a best-of-breed optimization for control of procurement processes and the additional neural network intermediated Bayesian maintenance workload prediction module will allow you to control your inventory of hosts and project a stable cash flow . . ." My guts clench. A whole lot of things suddenly come clear: *The bastards are trying to brainwash the committee!*

It's PowerPoint, of course. A hypnotic slide into a bulleted list of total cost of ownership savings and a pie chart with a neat lime-green slice taken out of it—*ooh look, it's three dimensional*; it's also a bar graph with the height of the slices denoting some other parameter—and a pale background of yellow lines on white that looks a little like the TLA logo we began the slide show with: an eye floating in a tetrahedral Escher paradox, and a diagram a little bit like whatever Ramona was sketching on her notepad—I grab my tablet PC and poke the power button, trying to keep my hands from shaking.

Screen saver. *Screen saver*. I eject the pen and hastily hit on the control panel to bring up the screen saver. The dream catcher routine I had running last night is all I can think of right now. I set it running then slide the tablet face-up, with the hypnotic blur of purple lines cycling across it, on the conference table so that it lies directly between me and the projection screen.

**Good move, monkey-boy.**

Franz is leaning back in his chair beside me. His eyes are closed and there's a fine thread of spittle dangling from one side of his mouth. François is face-down on the mat, snoring, and Anna is frozen, glassy-eyed, at the foot of the table, her open eyes fixed unseeing on the projector screen. I take care not to look at it directly.

**What's it meant to be doing?** I ask Ramona.

**That's what we're here to find out. Nobody who's been in one of these sales sessions before has come out in any state to tell us.**

**What? You mean they were killed?**

**No, they just insisted on buying TLA products. Oh, and they'd had their souls eaten.**

**What would you know about that?**

**They don't taste the same. Shut up and get ready to yank the projector cable when I give the word, okay?**

Sophie hits the mouse button again and the light in the room changes subtly, signaling a dissolve from one frame to another. Her voice mutates, morphs and deepens, taking on a vaguely familiar cadence. "Today, we celebrate the first glorious anniversary of the Information Purification Directives. We have created, for the first time in all history, a garden of pure ideology. Where each worker may bloom secure from the pests of any contradictory and confusing truths . . ."

The dream catcher in front of me is going crazy. **I've seen that before. It's the Apple 1984 ad, the one they commissioned Ridley Scott to direct for the launch of the Macintosh computer. The most expensive ad in the entire history of selling beige boxes to puzzled posers. What the hell are they doing with *that*?**

**Law of contagion.** Ramona sounds tense. **Very strong imagery of conformity versus mold-breaking, concealing conformity disguised *as* mold-breaking. Ever wondered why Mac users are so glassy-eyed about their boxes? This is slide twenty-six; okay, we've got about ten seconds to go . . .**

I briefly debate standing up right there and yanking the power cable. I've seen the original ad so many times I don't need to look at the screen to follow it; it's famous throughout the computer industry. "Our Unification of Thoughts is more powerful a weapon than any fleet or army on Earth. We are one people, with one will, one resolve, one cause. Our enemies shall talk themselves to death and we will bury them with their own confusion. We shall prevail!"

Seconds to go. The female runner races towards the huge screen in front of the arena, clutching a sledge hammer, poised to hurl it through Big Brother's face—and I know exactly what's going to happen, what those shards of glass are going to morph into with the next dissolve as I take my tablet by both sides (careful to keep my hands from touching the toughened glass screen cover) and pick it up, flipping it over as the crescendo builds towards what would be, in the real advertisement, the announcement of a revolutionary new type of computer—

**Ready—**

The light flickers and something that feels like an out-of-control truck punches into the screen of the tablet PC as I hold it between my face and the projection screen. It's not a physical force, but it might as well be from the acrid smoke spewing from the vents under my fingertips and the way the battery compartment begins to glow.

**Go!**

I drop the PC, cover my eyes with one hand, and dive for where the back of the projector used to be. I flop on my belly halfway across the table, flailing around until I catch a bunch of wires and yank hard, pulling and tearing at them, too frightened to open my eyes and see which ones I've got hold of. Someone is screaming and someone else is crying behind me, emitting incoherent moans like an animal in pain. Then someone punches me in the ribs.

I open my eyes. The projector's out and Ramona is sitting on top of Sophie from the Faust Force, or the thing that's animating Sophie's body, methodically whacking her head on the floor. Then I realize that the pain in my side is Ramona's: Sophie is fighting back. I roll over and find myself facing Anna. Her face hangs like a loose mask and her eyes glow faintly in the twilight that the almost-closed blinds allow into the room. I scrabble desperately, grab the edge of the table, and pull myself over it into her lap. She grabs for my head, but whatever's inside her isn't very good at controlling a human body and I roll again, drop arse-first onto the floor (my coccyx will tell me about it tomorrow), and scramble to my feet.

The previously orderly meeting is dissolving into the kind of carnage that can only ensue when most of the members of an international joint-liaison committee turn into brain-eating zombies. Luckily they're not Sam Raimi zombies, they're just midlevel bureaucrats whose cerebral cortices have been abruptly wiped in the presence of a Dho-Na summoning geometry (in this case, embedded in the dissolve between two PowerPoint slides), allowing some random extradimensional gibberers to move in. Half of them can't even stand up, and those who can aren't very effective yet.

**Have you got her?** I ask Ramona, working my way past Anna (who is currently keeping François occupied by chewing on his left hand) and nearly tripping over the wreckage of my tablet PC.

**She's fighting back!** A stray, booted foot lashes out at me and now I succeed in falling over, on top of Sophie as luck would have it. Sophie looks up at me with blank eyes and makes a keening noise like a cat that wants to break a furry critter's neck.

**Well fucking *do* something!** I yell.

**Okay.** Sophie jerks underneath me and tries to sink her teeth into my arm. But Ramona's ready with a spring-loaded syringe and nails her right through the shoulder. **You'll need to open the wards so we can get out.**

**I'm going to—** *Oh, right. Ramona's a guest.* I lurch upright and lunge for the blotter in front of Anna's seat, grab at her gavel, and rap it on the table. "As the last quorate member standing I hereby unanimously promote myself to Chair and declare this session closed." Five heads, their eyes swimming with luminous green worms, turn to face me. "School's out." I race for the door, piling into Ramona as I yank the handle open. **Got her?**

**Yes. Grab her other arm and move!**

Sophie is kicking and writhing wordlessly but Ramona and I drag her through the doorway and I yank it shut behind us. The latch clicks, and Sophie goes limp.

**Hey.** I look sideways. **What's—**

Ramona lets go of her other arm and I stagger. **Well isn't that a surprise,** she comments, looking down at Sophie, who sprawls on the hotel carpet in front of the door. **She's dead, Jim.**

**Bob,** I correct automatically. **What do you mean, she's dead?**

316 OF HER MAJESTY'S OCCULT SERVICE

**Poison-pill programming, I think.**
I lean against the wall, dizzy and nauseated. **We've got to go back! The others are still in there. Can we break it? The control link, I mean. If it's just a transient override—**

Ramona winces and stares at me. **Will you stop that? It's not a transient and there's nothing we can do for them.**

**But she's dead! We've got to do something! And they're—**

**They're dead, too.** Ramona stares at me in obvious concern. **Did you hit your head or something? No, I'd have felt that. You're squeamish, aren't you?**

**We could have saved them! You knew what was going to happen! You could have warned us! If you hadn't been so fucking curious to know what was buried in the presentation—shit, why didn't you just snarf a copy and edit it yourself? This isn't the first time it's happened, is it?**

She lets me rant for a minute or so, until I run down. **Bob, Bob. This *is* the first time this has happened. At least, the first time anyone's gotten out of one of these presentations alive.**

**Jesus. Then why do you keep having them?** I realize I'm waving my arms around but I'm too upset to stop. I have a terrible feeling that if I'd just given in to my first impulse to yank the cord on the projector— **It's murder! Letting it go ahead like that—**

**We don't. My—department—doesn't. TLA is selling hard outside the US, Bob. They sell in places like Malaysia or Kazakhstan or Peru, and in places that aren't quite on the map, if you follow me. We've heard rumors about this. We've seen some of the . . . fallout. But this is the first time we've gotten in on the ground floor. Sophie Frank was fingered by your people, if you must know. Your Andy Newstrom raised the flag. She's been behaving oddly for the past couple of months. You were sent because, unlike Newstrom, you're trained for this category of operation. But nobody else took the warnings sufficiently seriously—except for your department, and mine.**

**But what about the others?**

She stares at me grimly. **Blame Ellis Billington, Bob. Remember, if he wasn't into the hard sell, this wouldn't have happened.**

Then she turns and stalks away, leaving me alone and shaking in the corridor, with a corpse and a locked conference room full of middle-management zombies to explain.

## Chapter 4:
## You're in the Jet Set Now

My checkout is ever so slightly delayed. I spend about eight hours at the nearest police station being questioned by one GSA desk pilot after another. At first I think they're going to arrest me—shoot the messenger is a well-known parlor game in spook circles—but after a few fraught hours there's a change in the tone of the interrogation. Someone higher up has obviously got a handle on events and is smoothing my path. "It is best for you to leave the country tomorrow," says Gerhardt from Frankfurt, not smiling. "Later we will have questions, but not now." He shakes his head. "If you should happen to see Ms. Random, please explain that we have questions for her, also." A taciturn cop drives me back to the hotel, where a GSA cleaning team has replaced the conference room door with a blank stretch of brand-new wall. I walk past it without quite losing my shit, then retreat to my shielded bedroom and spend a sleepless night trying to second guess myself. But not only is the past another country, it's one that doesn't issue visas; and so, first thing in the morning, I head downstairs to collect the hire car.

A tech support nightmare is waiting for me down in the garage. Pinky is goose-stepping around with a clipboard, trying to look officious while Brains is elbow-deep in the trunk with a circuit tester and a roll of gaffer tape.

"What. The. Fuck?" I manage to say, then lean against a concrete pillar.

"We've been modifying this Smart car for you!" Pinky says excitedly. "You need to know how to use all its special features."

I rub my eyes in disbelief. "Listen guys, I've been attacked by brain-eating zombies and I'm due on a flight to Saint Martin tonight. This isn't the right time to show me your toys. I just want to get home—"

"Impossible," Brains mutters around a mouthful of oily bolts that look suspiciously as if they've just come out of the engine manifold.

"Angleton told us not to let you go until you'd finished your briefing!" Pinky exclaims.

*There's no escape.* "Okay." I yawn. "You just put those bolts back and I'll be going."

"Look in the boot, here. What our American friends would call the trunk. Careful, mind that pipe! Good. Now pay attention, Bob. We've added a Bluetooth host under the driver's seat, and a repurposed personal video player running Linux. Peripheral screens at all five cardinal points, five grams of graveyard dust mixed with oil of Bergamot and tongue of newt in the cigarette lighter socket, and a fully connected Dee-Hamilton circuit glued to the underside of the body shell. As long as the ignition is running, you're safe from possession attempts. If you need to dispose of a zombie in the passenger seat, just punch in the lighter button and wait for the magic smoke. You've got a mobile phone, yes? With Bluetooth and a Java sandbox? Great, I'll email you an applet—run it, pair your phone with the car's hub, and all you have to do is dial 6-6-6 and the car will come to you, wherever you are. There's another applet to remotely trigger all the car's countermeasures, just in case someone's sneaked a surprise into it."

I shake my head, but it won't stop spinning. "Zombie smoke in the lighter socket, Dee-Hamilton circuit in the body shell, and the car comes when I summon it. Okay. Hey, what's—"

He slaps my hand as I reach for the boxy lump fastened to the gearshift with duct tape. "Don't touch that button, Bob!"

"Why? What happens if I touch that button, Pinky?"

"The car ejects!"

"Don't you mean, the passenger seat ejects?" I ask sarcastically. I've had just about enough of this nonsense.

"No, Bob, you've been watching too many movies. The *car* ejects." He reaches across the back of my seat and pats the fat pipe occupying the center of the luggage area.

I swallow. "Isn't that a little . . . dangerous?"

"Where you're going you'll need all the help you can get." He frowns at me. "The tube contains a rocket motor and a cable spool bolted to the chassis. The airbags in the wheel hubs blow when the accelerometer figures you've hit apogee, if you haven't already used them in amphibious pursuit mode. Whatever you do don't push that button while you're in a tunnel or under cover." I glance up at the concrete roof of the car park and shudder. "The airbags are securely fastened, if you land on water you can just drive away." He notices my fixed, skeptical stare and pats the rocket tube. "It's perfectly safe—they've been using these on helicopter gunships for nearly five years!"

"Jesus." I close my eyes and lean back. "It's still a fucking Smart car. Range Rovers carry them as lifeboats. Couldn't you get me an Aston Martin or something?"

"What makes you think we'd give you an Aston Martin, even if we could afford one? Anyway, Angleton says to remind you that it's on lease from one of our private sector partners. Don't bend it, or you'll answer to the Chrysler Corporation. You've already exceeded our consumables budget, totaling that Compaq in the meeting—there's a new one waiting for you in the case in the boot, by the way. This is serious business: you're representing the Laundry in front of the Black Chamber and some very big defense contractors, old school tie and all that."

"I went to North Harrow Comprehensive," I say wearily, "they didn't trust us with neckties, not after the upper fifth tried to lynch Brian the Spod."

"Oh. Well." Pinky pulls out a thick envelope. "Your itinerary, once you arrive at Juliana Airport. There's a decent tailor in the Marina shopping center and we've faxed your measurements through. Um. Do you dress to the left, or . . . ?"

I open my eyes and stare at him until he wilts. "Eight dead." I hold up the requisite number of fingers. "In twenty-four hours. And I have to drive up the fucking autobahn in this pile of shit—"

"No, you don't," says Brains, finally straightening up and wiping his hands on a rag. "We've got to crate up the Smart if we're going to freight it to Maho Beach tomorrow—you're riding with us." He gestures at a shiny black Mercedes van parked opposite. "Feel better?"

Wow—I'm not going to be strafed with BMWs again. Miracles do sometimes happen, even in Laundry service. I nod. "Let's get going."

I sleep most of the way to Frankfurt. We're late getting to the airport—no surprise in light of preceding events—but Pinky and Brains prestidigitate some sort of official ID out of their warrant cards and drive us through two chain-link barriers and past a police checkpoint and onto the apron, hand me a briefcase, then drop me at the foot of the steps of an air bridge. It's latched onto a Lufthansa airbus bound for Paris's Charles de Gaulle and a quick transfer. "Schnell!" urges a harried-looking flight attendant. "You are the last. Come this way."

One and a half hours and a VIP transfer later, I'm in business class aboard an Air France A300 bound for Princess Juliana International Airport. The compartment is half-empty. "Please fasten your seatbelts and pay attention to the preflight briefing." I close my eyes while they close the doors behind me. Then someone shakes my shoulder: it's a flight attendant. "Mr. Howard? I have a message to tell you that there's WiFi access on this flight. You are to call your office as soon as we are airborne at cruising altitude and the seatbelt light goes off."

I nod, speechless. WiFi? On a thirty-year-old tourist truck like this? "Bon voyage!" She stands up and marches to the back of the cabin. "Call if you need anything."

I doze through the usual preflight, waking briefly as the engine note rises to a thunderous roar and we pile down the runway. I feel unnaturally tired, as if drained of life, and I've got a strange sense that somebody else is sleeping in the empty seat beside me, close enough to rest their head on my shoulder—but the next seat over is empty. *Overspill from Ramona?* Then my eyes close again.

It must be the cabin pressure, the stress of the last couple of days, or drugs in the after-takeoff champagne, because I find myself having the strangest dream. I'm back in the conference suite in Darmstadt, and the blinds are down, but instead of a room full of zombies I'm sitting across the table from Angleton. He looks half-mummified at the best of times, until you see his eyes: they're diamond-blue and as sharp as a dentist's drill. Right now they're the only part of him I can see at all, because he's engulfed in the shadows cast by an old-fashioned slide projector lighting up the wall behind him. The overall effect is very sinister. I look over my shoulder, wondering where Ramona's gotten to, but she's not there.

"Pay *attention*, Bob. Since you had the bad grace to take so long during my previous briefing that it self-erased before you completed it, I've sent you another." I open my mouth to tell him he's full of shit, but the words won't emerge. *An Auditor ward*, I think, choking on my tongue and beginning to panic, but right then my larynx relaxes and I'm able to close my jaw. Angleton smiles sepulchrally. "There's a good fellow."

I try to say *blow me*, but it comes out as "brief me" instead. It seems I'm allowed to speak, so long as I stay on topic.

"Certainly. I have explained the history of the *Glomar Explorer*, and Operations JENNIFER and AZORIAN. What I did not explain—this goes no further than your dreams, and the inside of your own eyeballs, especially when Ramona is awake—was that JENNIFER and AZORIAN were cover stories. Dry runs, practical experiments, if you like. To retrieve artifacts from the oceanic floor, in the zones ceded by humanity to BLUE HADES—the Deep Ones—in perpetuity under the terms of the Benthic Treaties and the Agreement of the Azores."

Angleton pauses to take a drink from a glass of ice water beside his blotter. Then he flicks the slide advance button on the projector. *Click-clack.*

"This is a map of the world we live in," Angleton explains. "And these pink zones are those that humans are allowed to roam in. Our reservation, if you like. The arid air-swept continents and the painfully bright low-pressure top waters of the oceans. About thirty-four percent of the Earth's surface area. The rest, the territory of the Deep Ones, we are permitted to sail above, but that is all. Attempts to settle the deep ocean would be resisted in such a manner that our species would not survive long enough to regret them."

I lick my lips. "How? I mean, do they have nuclear weapons or something?"

"Worse than that." He doesn't smile. "This—" *click-clack* "—is Cumbre Vieja, on the island of La Palma. It is one of seventy-three volcanoes or mountains located in deep water—most of the others are submerged guyots rather than climbable peaks—that BLUE HADES have prepared. Three-quarters of humanity live within 200 miles of a sea coast. If they ever lose their patience with us, the Deep Ones can trigger undersea landslides. Cumbre Vieja alone is poised to deposit 500 billion tons of rock on the floor of the North Atlantic, generating a tsunami that will be twenty meters high by the time it makes landfall in New York. Make that more like fifty meters by the time it hits Southampton. If we provoke them they can wreak more destruction than an all-out nuclear war. And they have occupied this planet since long before our hominid ancestors discovered fire."

"But we've got a deterrent, surely . . . ?"

"No." Angleton's expression is implacable. "Water absorbs the energy of a nuclear explosion far more effectively than air. You get a powerful pressure wave, but no significant heat or radiation damage: the shock wave is great for crushing submarines, but much less effective against undersea organisms at ambient pressure. We could hurt them, but nothing like as badly as they could hurt us. And as for the rest of it—" he gestures at the screen "—they could have wiped us out before we discovered them, if they were so inclined. They have access to technologies and tools we can barely begin to imagine. They are the Deep Ones, BLUE HADES, a branch of an ancient and powerful alien civilization. Some of us suspect the threat of the super-tsunami is a distraction. It's like an infantryman pointing his bayonet-tipped assault rifle at a headhunter, who sees only a blade on a stick. Don't even think about threatening them; we exist because they bear us no innate ill will, but we have at least the power to change that much if we act rashly."

"Then what the hell was JENNIFER about?"

*Click-clack.* "A misplaced attempt to end the Cold War prematurely, by acquiring a weapon truly hellish in its potential. The precise nature of which you have no need to know right now, in case you were thinking of asking."

I'm looking down on a gloomy gray scene. It takes me a few seconds to realize that it's a deep-ocean mudscape. Scattered across the layered silt are small irregular objects, some of them round, some of them long. A couple more seconds and my brain acknowledges that what my eyes are seeing is a watery field of skulls and femurs and ribs. I've got an idea that not all of them are entirely human.

"The Caribbean sea hides many secrets. This field of silt covers a deep layer rich in methane hydrates. When some force destabilizes the deposits they bubble up from the depths—like the carbon dioxide discharge from the stagnant waters of Lake Nyos in the Cameroon. But unlike Lake Nyos, the gas isn't confined by terrain so it dissipates after it surfaces. It's not an asphyxiation threat, but if you're on a ship that's caught above a hydrate release, then the sea under your keel turns to gas and you're going straight down to Davy Jones's locker." Angleton clears his throat. "BLUE HADES have some way of replenishing these deposits and triggering releases. They use them to keep us interfering hominids away from things that don't concern us, such as the settlement at Witch's Hole in the North Sea . . . and the depths of the Bermuda Triangle."

I swallow. "What's down there?"

"Some of the deepest oceanic trenches on Earth. And some of the largest BLUE HADES installations we're aware of." Angleton looks as if he's bitten into a lemon expecting an orange. "That isn't saying much—most of their sites are known to us only from neutrino mapping and seismology. The portion of the biosphere we understand is limited to the surface waters and continental land masses, boy. Below a thousand fathoms of water, let alone below the Mohorovičić Discontinuity, it's a whole different ball game."

"The Moho-what?"

"The underside of the continental plates we live on—below the discontinuity lies the upper mantle. Didn't you study geography at school?"

"Uh . . ." I spent most of my school geography lessons snoozing, doodling imaginary continents in the backs of exercise books, or trying to work up the courage to pass a message to Lizzie Graham in the next row. Now it looks like those missed lessons are about to come back and bite me. "Moving swiftly on, let me see if I've got this straight. Ellis Billington has purchased a CIA spy ship designed for probing BLUE HADES territory. He's got a high enough security clearance to be aware what it's capable of, and his people are trying to suborn various intelligence organizations, like in Darmstadt. He's playing some kind of endgame and you don't like the smell and neither does the Black Chamber, which explains me and Ramona. Am I right so far?"

Angleton nods minutely. "I should remind you that Billington is extraordinarily rich and has fingers in a surprising number of pies. For example, by way of his current wife—his third—he owns a cosmetics and haute couture empire; in addition to IT corporations he owns shipping, aviation, and banking interests. Your assignment—and Ramona's—is to get close to Billington. Ideally you should contrive to get yourself invited aboard his yacht, the *Mabuse*, while Ramona remains in touch with your backup team and the local head of station. Your technical backups are Pinky and Brains, your muscle backup is Boris, and you're to liaise with our Caribbean station chief, Jack Griffin. Officially, he's your superior officer and you'll be under his orders when it comes to nonoperational matters, but you're to report directly to me, not to him. Unofficially, Griffin is out to pasture—take anything he says with a pinch of salt. Your job is to get close to Billington, remain in touch with us, and be ready to act if and when we decide to take him down."

I manage not to groan. "Why does it have to be me aboard the yacht—why not Ramona? I think she'd be a whole lot better at the field ops thing. Or the station chief guy? Come to think of it, why aren't the AIVD doing this? It's their territory—"

"They invited us in; all I can say for now is, we have specialist expertise in this area that they lack. And it has to be you, not Ramona. Firstly, you're an autonome, a native of this continuum: they can't trap you in a Dho-Nha curve or bind you to a summoning grid. And secondly, it's got to be you because those are the rules of Billington's game." Angleton's expression is frightening. "He's a player, Bob. He knows exactly what he's doing and how to work around our strengths. He stays away from continental land masses, uses games of chance to determine his actions, sleeps inside a Faraday cage aboard a ship with a silver-plated keel. He's playing us to a script. I'm not at liberty to tell you what it is, but it has to be *you*, not Ramona, not anyone else."

"Do we have any idea what he's planning? You said something about weapons—"

Angleton fixes me with a steely gaze. "Pay attention, Bob. The presentation is about to commence." And this time I can't stifle the groan, because it's another of his bloody slideshows, and if you thought PowerPoint was pants, you haven't suffered through an hour of Angleton monologuing over a hot slide projector.

SLIDE 1: Photograph of three men wearing suits with the exaggerated lapels and wide ties of the mid-1970s. They're standing in front of some sort of indistinct building-like structure, possibly prefabricated. All three wear badges clipped to their breast pockets.

"The one on the left is me: you don't need to know who the other two are. This photograph was taken in 1974 while I was assigned to Operation AZORIAN as our liaison—officially from MI6 as an observer, but you know the drill. The building I'm standing in front of is . . ."

SLIDE 2: A photograph taken looking aft along the deck of a huge sea-going vessel. To the left, there's a gigantic structure like an oil drilling rig, with racks of pipes stacked in front of it. Directly ahead, at the stern, is the structure glimpsed in the previous slide—a mobile office, jacked up off the deck, its roofline bristling with antennae. Behind it, a satellite dish looms before the superstructure of the ship.

"We're aboard the *Hughes Glomar Explorer* on its unsuccessful voyage to raise the sunken Soviet Golf-II-class ballistic missile submarine K-129. Announced as Operation JENNIFER, this was leaked to the press by someone acting on unofficial orders from the director of ONI—the usual goddamn turf war—and Watergated to hell by mid-1975. I said Operation JENNIFER was unsuccessful. Officially, the CIA only retrieved the front ten meters or so of the sub because the rear section broke off. In reality . . ."

SLIDE 3: Grainy black-and-white photographs, evidently taken from TV screens: a long cylindrical structure grasped in the claws of an enormous grab. From below, thin streamers rise up towards it.

"BLUE HADES took exception to the intrusion into their territory and chose to exercise their salvage rights under Article Five, Clause Four of the Benthic Treaty. Hence the tentacles. Now . . ."

SLIDE 1 (Repeat): This time the man in the middle is circled with a red highlighter.

"This fellow in the middle is Ellis Billington, as he looked thirty years ago. Ellis was brilliant but not well socialized back then. He was attached to the 'B' team as an observer, tasked with examining the circuitry of the cipher machine they hoped to recover from the sub's control room. I didn't pay much attention to him at the time, which was a mistake. He already had his security clearance, and after the JENNIFER debacle he moved to San Jose and set up a small electronics and software business."

SLIDE 4: A crude-looking circuit board. Rather than fiberglass, it appears to be made of plywood that has been exposed to seawater for too long, and has consequently warped. Sockets for vacuum tubes stud its surface, one of them occupied by the broken base of a component; numerous diodes and resistors connect it to an odd, stellate design in gold that covers most of the surface of the board.

"This board was taken from a GRU-issued Model 60 oneiromantic convolution engine found aboard the K-129. As you can see, it spent rather longer in the water than was good for it. Ellis reverse-engineered the basic schematic and pieced together the false vacuum topology that the valves disintermediated. Incidentally, these aren't your normal vacuum tubes—isotope imbalances in the thorium-doped glass sleeves suggest that they were evacuated by exposure in a primitive wake-shield facility, possibly aboard a model-three *Sputnik* satellite similar to the one first orbited in 1960. That would have given them a starting pressure about six orders of magnitude cleaner than anything available on Earth at the time, at a price per tube of about two million rubles, which suggests that someone in the GRU's scientific directorate *really* wanted a good signal, if that wasn't already obvious. We now know that they'd clearly cracked the Dee-Turing Thesis by this point and were well into modified Enochian metagrammar analysis. Anyway, young Billington concluded that the Mod-60 OCE, NATO code 'Gravedust,' was intended to allow communication with the dead. Recently dead, anyway."

SLIDE 5: An open coffin containing a long-dead body. The corpse is partially mummified, the eyelids sunken into the empty sockets and the jaw agape with lips retracted.

"We're not sure exactly what a Gravedust system was doing aboard the K-129. According to one theory that was remarkably popular with our friends at ONI around the time, it had something to do with the former Soviet Union's postmortem second strike command-and-control system, to allow the submarine's political officer to ask for instructions from the Politburo after a successful decapitation stroke. They were very keen on maintaining the correct chain of command back then. There's just one problem with that theory: it's rubbish. According to our own analysis after the event—I should add, the Black Chamber was remarkably reluctant to part with the Gravedust schemata, we finally got it out of them by remote viewing—Billington underestimated the backreach of the Gravedust interrogator by a factor of at least a thousand. We were told that it would only allow callbacks to the recently dead, within the past million seconds. In actual fact, you could call up Tutankhamen himself on this rig. Our best guess is that the Soviets were planning on talking to something that had been dead for a very long time indeed, somewhere under the ocean."

SLIDE 6: A Russian submarine, moored alongside a pier. In the distance, snow-capped mountains loom above the far shore of a waterway.

"The K-129 was rather an elderly boat at the time she sank. In fact, a few years later the Soviets retired the last of the Golf-II class—except for one of the K-129's sister ships, which was retained for covert operations duty. As a ballistic missile boat it had a large hold that could be repurposed for other payloads, and as a diesel-electric it could run quietly in littoral waters. Diesel-electrics are still popular for that reason: when running on battery juice they're even quieter than a nuke boat, which has to keep the reactor coolant pumps running at all times. Without the rear section—including the missile room—we could only theorize that K-129 had already been converted to infiltration duty. However . . ."

SLIDE 7: A blurry gray landscape photographed from above. A structure, clearly artificial, occupies the middle of the image: a cylindrical artifact not unlike a submarine, but missing a conning tower and equipped with a strange, roughly surfaced conical endcap. Its hull is clearly damaged, not crumpled but burst open as if from some great internal pressure. Nevertheless, it is still recognizable as an artificial structure.

"We believe this was the real target of K-129's abortive operation. It's located on the floor of the Pacific, approximately 600 nautical miles southwest of Hawaii and, by no coincidence at all, on the K-129's course prior to the unfortunate onboard explosion that resulted in the submarine's loss with all hands."

SLIDE 8: Not a photograph but a false-color synthetic relief image of the floor of the Pacific basin, southwest of Hawaii. The image is contoured to represent depth, and colored to convey some other attribute. Virulent red spots dot the depths—except for a single, much shallower one.

"Graviweak neutrino imaging spectroscopes carried aboard the SPAN-2 Earth resources satellite are a good way of pinpointing BLUE HADES colonies. For obvious reasons, BLUE HADES do not make extensive use of electricity for their domestic and presumed industrial processes; Monsieur Volt and Herr Ampère are not your friends when you live under five kilometers of saltwater. Instead, BLUE HADES appear to control inaccessible condensed matter states by varying the fine-structure constant and tunneling photinos—super-symmetrical photon analogs that possess mass—between nodes where they want to do things. One side effect of this is neutrino emissions at a very characteristic spectrum, unlike anything we get from the sun or from our own nuclear reactors. This is a density scan for the zone around the K-129 and Hawaii. As you can see, that isolated shallow point—near where the K-129 went down—is rather strong. There's an active power source in there, and it's not connected to the rest of the BLUE HADES grid as far as we can tell. The site is classified JENNIFER MORGUE, incidentally, and is known as Site One."

SLIDE 9: A rock face, evidently inside a mine, is illuminated by spotlights. Workers in overalls and hard hats surround it, and are evidently working on something—possibly a fossil—with small hand-tools.

"As you can see, this is not a BLUE HADES specimen. It's some other palaeosophont. This photograph was taken in 1985 in the deep mine at Longannet in Fife, right on our doorstep. Longannet—and indeed the rest of the British deep-mining industry—was shut down some time ago, officially for economic reasons. However, you would be right to conclude that the presence of nightmares like this was a contributing factor. This is in fact a DEEP SEVEN cadaver, and appears to have undergone some sort of postmortem vitrification process, or perhaps a hibernation from which it failed to emerge, approximately seven million years ago. We believe that DEEP SEVEN were responsible for the JEN-NIFER MORGUE machines and the neutrino anomaly in the previous slide. We know very little about DEEP SEVEN except that they appear to be polymorphous, occupy areas of the upper crust near the polar regions, and BLUE HADES are terrified of them."

SLIDE 10: A close-up of the cylindrical structure from Slide 7. Intricate traceries of inlaid calligraphy—or perhaps circuit diagrams—cover the walls of the machine, disturbing in their nonlinearity. At one edge of the picture the conical top is visible, and in close-up the details become apparent: a conical spike with a cutting edge spiraling around it.

"This is our closest photograph of JENNIFER MORGUE Site One. It presents a clear hazard to this day: K-129 was lost inspecting it, as were several ROVs sent by the US Office of Naval Intelligence. It was the secondary target for Operation AZORIAN/JENNIFER before that project was Watergated. It's a rather recalcitrant target because there seems to be some sort of defense field around it, possibly acoustic—anything entering within a two-hundred-and-six-meter radius stops working. (If you look near the top right of this photograph you'll see the wreckage of a previous visitor.) Our current theory is that it is either a DEEP SEVEN artifact or a BLUE HADES system designed to prevent incursions by DEEP SEVEN. We presume the Soviets were trying to make contact with DEEP SEVEN by way of the Gravedust system on the K-129—and failed, catastrophically."

SLIDE 11: A similar-looking photograph of another machine, this time looking less badly damaged. The photograph is taken from much closer range, and though one curved side has a jagged hole in it, the hull is otherwise intact.

"This is a similar artifact, located near the north end of the Puerto Rico Trench, about four kilometers down on a limestone plateau. JEN-NIFER MORGUE Site Two appears to be damaged, but the same exclusion field is still in place and operational. Initial exploratory investigation with an ROV discovered . . ."

SLIDE 12: A very dim, grainy view through the jagged hole in the side of the artifact. There appears to be a rectangular structure within. Odd curved objects surround it, some of which recall the shape of internal organs.

"This structure appears to contain—or even consist of—vitrified or otherwise preserved DEEP SEVEN remnants. You'll note the similarity of this structure to some sort of cockpit: we believe it to be a deep-crustal or high-mantle boring machine, possibly making it the DEEP SEVEN equivalent of a tank or a space suit. We're not sure quite what it's doing here, but we are now extremely intrigued by Ellis Billington's interest in it. He's purchased the *Explorer*, heavily modified it, and, using it as a host, has been conducting sea trials with a remotely operated vehicle. Our intel on Billington's activities is alarmingly deficient, but we believe he intends to raise and possibly activate the DEEP SEVEN artifact. His expertise in Gravedust systems suggests that he may try to retrieve information from the dead DEEP SEVEN aboard it, and the direction of his operation suggests that he has some idea of what it's doing there.

"I do not intend, at this point, to get into a lengthy discussion of the consequences of annoying the Chthonians—excuse me, DEEP SEVEN—or of getting involved in a geopolitical pissing match between DEEP SEVEN and BLUE HADES. Suffice to say, preserving the collective neutrality of the human species is a high priority for this department, and you should take that as your primary point of reference in the days ahead.

"But in summary, your mission is to get close to Billington and find out what the hell he's planning on doing with JENNIFER MORGUE Site Two. Then tell us, so we can work out what action we need to take to stop him pissing off BLUE HADES or DEEP SEVEN. If he wakes the ancient sleeping horrors I am going to have to brief the private secretary and the Joint Intelligence Oversight Committee so that they can explain CASE NIGHTMARE GREEN to the COBRA Committee, chaired by the Prime Minister, and I expect that will make them extremely unhappy. Britain is relying on you, Bob, so try not to make your usual hash of things."

Angleton fades out, to be replaced by a more normal dream sleep, punctuated by vague echoes of thrashing around restlessly in a huge hotel bed. I wake up eventually, to discover that the in-flight movie is over and we're in the middle of nowhere in particular. The airbus bores on through the clear Atlantic skies, ghosting high above the sunken treasure galleons of the Spanish Main. I stretch in place, try to massage the crick out of the side of my neck, and yawn. Then I wake up my laptop. Almost immediately the Skype window starts flashing for attention. *You have voice mail*, it says.

Voice mail? Hell, yes—in this Brave New World there's no escape from the internet, even at 40,000 feet. I yawn again and plug in my headset, trying to shake off the influence of Ramona's distantly sensed repose. I glance at the screen. It's Mo, and she's on Skype, too, so I place a call.

"Bob?" Her voice crackles a little—the signal is being bounced via satellite to the plane and the latency is scary.

"Mo, I'm on a plane. Are you in the Village?"

"I'm in the Village, Bob—checking out tomorrow. Listen, you asked me a question yesterday. I've been doing some poking around and this destiny-entanglement stuff is really ugly. Have they already done it to you? If not, run like hell. You'll start to share dreams, there's telepathy going with it, but worse, there's reality leakage, too. You end up taking up aspects of your entanglement partner, and vice versa. If they're killed you're likely to drop dead on the spot; if it lasts more than a couple of weeks it goes beyond sharing thoughts, you could end up merging with them permanently. The good news is, the entanglement can be broken by a fairly simple ritual. The bad news is, it takes both parties cooperating to do it. Do you have any way out of it?"

"Too late. They ran it yesterday—"

"Shit. Love, how long is it going to take you to realize that if they ask you to do them a special favor you need to run like—"

"Mo."

"Bob?"

"I know—" My throat closes up and I stop talking for a moment. "I love you."

"Yes." Her voice is faint at the end of the internet connection. "I love you, too—"

This is too painful to hear. "She's asleep."

"She?"

"The demon." I glance round, but there's nobody in the row in front of me and I'm directly in front of the partition between business and cattle class. "Ramona. Black Chamber operative. I don't—" This is too unpleasant: I start trying to figure out another way of approaching the subject.

"Has she hurt you?" Mo's tone is chilly enough to freeze my ear.

"No." Not yet. "I don't want you to go near her, Mo. It's not her fault. She's as much a victim of this as—"

"Bullshit, love. I want you to tell her, from me, that if she even *thinks* about messing with you I'll break every bone in her body—"

"Mo! Stop it!" I lower my tone of voice. "Don't even think about it. You don't want to get involved in this. Just don't. Wait 'til it's all over and we'll go on holiday together and get away from it all."

A pause. I tense up inside, desperately hoping for the best. Finally: "It's your judgment call and I can't stop you. But I'm warning you, don't let them fuck with you. You know how they use people, what they did to me, right? Don't let them do it to you, too." A sigh. "So why did they send you?"

I swallow. "Angleton says he needs me to get inside an operation and

I think he wants an unblockable communications channel back to the field controller. Did you ask him what it's about—"

"Not yet I haven't. Hang in there, love. I'm finishing up here and I've got to go back to London tomorrow: I'll drag everything out of Angleton before sunset. Where is he sending you? Who's your backup?"

"I'm on my way to the Princess Juliana Airport on Saint Martin, staying in the Sky Tower at Maho Bay. He's sent Boris, Pinky, and Brains to look after—" I suddenly realize where this is leading. Quick on the uptake I ain't. "Listen, don't bother trying to—"

"I'll be on the next flight out, I just have to touch base long enough to mug Harry the Holiday Piggy Bank. It'll be a cold day in Hell before I'm trusting your skin to their—"

"Don't!" I can see it already, horrible visions welling up out of the twisted depths of my subconscious. Does Mo realize what my being entangled with Ramona means? I hate to think what she'll do if she figures it out and Ramona's on the same continent. Mo is a very tactical person. Tactile, too—passionate, fiery, and capable of thinking outside the box— but if you show her an obstacle, she has a disturbing tendency to punch right through it. That's how she ended up in the Laundry, after all: making an end run round the Black Chamber, straight into our organization's lap. I love her dearly, but the thought of her turning up at my hotel room and me trying not to touch her while I'm in this embarrassing bind with Ramona scares the shit out of me. It's not exactly your normal sordid extramarital affair, is it? It's not as if I'm actually sleeping with Ramona and it's not as if I'm married to Mo, either. But it's got all the same potential to explode in my face—and that's before you factor in the little extra details like Ramona being the corporeal manifestation of a demonic entity from beyond space-time and Mo being a powerful sorceress.

"You're breaking up. Hang in there! See you the day after tomorrow!" She buzzes, then the connection drops.

I stare at the screen for a moment. Then I dry-swallow and press the SERVICE button for the flight attendant. "I need a drink," I say, "vodka and orange on the rocks." Then some instinct makes me add: "Shaken." Just like me.

I spend a good chunk of the rest of the flight determinedly trying to get drunk. I know you're not supposed to do that sort of thing when flying in a pressurized cabin—you get dehydrated, the hangover's worse—but I don't give a shit. Somewhere near Iceland Ramona wakes up and snarls at me for polluting her cerebral cortex with cocktail fallout, but either I manage to barricade her out or she decides to give me the day off for bad behavior. I play a drunken round of Quake on my Treo, then bore myself back to sleep by reading a memorandum discussing my responsibility for processing equipment depreciation and write-off claims pursuant to field-expedient containment operations. I don't want to be on the receiving end of a visit from the Auditors over a misfiled form PT-411/E, but the blasted thing seems to be protected by a stupefaction field, and every time I look at it my eyelids slam shut like protective blast barriers.

I wake up half an hour before landing with a throbbing forehead and a tongue that tastes like a mouse died on it. The huge gleaming expanse of Maho Beach is walled with hotels: the sea is improbably blue, like an accident in a chemistry lab. The heat beats down on me like a giant oven as I stagger down the steps onto the concrete next to the terminal building. Half the passengers are crumblies; the rest are surf Nazis and dive geeks, like extras auditioning for an episode of *Baywatch*. A strike force of hangover faeries is diving and weaving around me on pocket jet-packs when they're not practicing polo on my scalp with rubber mallets. It's two in the afternoon here, about six o'clock in Darmstadt, and I've been in transit for nearly twelve hours: the business suit I'm wearing from the meeting in the Ramada feels oddly stiff, as if it's hardening into an exoskeleton. I feel, not to put too fine a point on it, like shit; so when I come out of baggage claim I'm deeply relieved to see a crusty old buffer holding up a piece of cardboard upon which is scrawled: HOWARD—CAPITAL LAUNDRY SERVICES.

I head over towards him. "Hi. I'm Bob. You are . . . ?"

He looks me up and down like I'm something he's just peeled off the underside of his shoe. I do a double-take. He's about fifty, very British in a late-imperial, gin-pickled kind of way—in his lightweight tropical suit, regimental tie, and waxwork mustache he looks like he's just stepped out of a Merchant-Ivory movie. "Mr. Howard. Your warrant card, please."

"Oh." I fumble with my pocket for a while until I find the thing, then wave it vaguely in his direction. His cheek twitches.

"That'll do. I'm Griffin. Follow me." He turns and strides towards the exit. "You're late."

*I'm late? But I only just got here!* I hurry after him, trying not to lurch into any walls. "Where are we going?" I ask.

"To the hotel." I follow him outside and he waves an arm peremptorily. An old but well-kept Jaguar XJ6 pulls up and the driver jumps out to open the door. "Get in." I almost fall into the seat, but manage to cushion my briefcase just in time to save the laptop. Griffin shoves the door shut on me then gets into the front passenger seat and raps the dashboard: "To the Sky Tower! Chop-chop."

I can't help it: my eyes slide closed. It's been a long day and my snatch of sleep aboard the airbus wasn't exactly refreshing. My head's spinning as the Jag pulls out onto a freshly resurfaced road. It's oppressively hot, even with the air conditioning running flat-out, and I just can't seem to stay awake. Seemingly seconds later we pull up in front of a large concrete box and someone opens the door for me. "Come on, get out, get out!" I blink, and force myself to stand up.

"Where are we?" I ask.

"The Sky Tower Hotel; I've booked you in and swept the room. Your team will be working out of a rented villa when they arrive—that's in hand, too. Come on." Griffin leads me past reception, past a stand staffed by Barbies giving away free cosmetic samples, into an elevator, and down another anonymous hotel-space passage decorated randomly with cane furniture. We end up in some corporate decorator's vision of a tropical hotel room, all anonymous five-star furniture plus a French door opening onto a balcony exploding with potted greenery. A ceiling fan spins lazily, failing to make any impression on the heat. "Sit down. No, not there, here." I sit, suppress a yawn, and try to force myself to look at him. Either he's frowning or he's worried. "When are they due, by the way?" he asks.

"Aren't they here yet?" I ask. "Say, shouldn't you show me *your* warrant card?"

"Bah." His mustache twitches, but he reaches into his jacket pocket and pulls out a thing that anyone who isn't expecting a warrant card will see as a driving license or a passport. There's a faint smell of sulfur in the air. "You don't know."

"Know what?"

He peers at me sharply, then apparently makes his mind up. "They're late," he mutters. "Bloody cock-up." Louder: "Gin and tonic, or whisky soda?"

My head's still throbbing. "Have you got a glass of water?" I ask hopefully.

"Bah," he says again, then walks over to the minibar and opens it. He pulls out two bottles and two glasses. Into one of them he pours a double-finger of clear spirits; the other he puts down next to the tonic water. "Help yourself," he says grudgingly.

This isn't what I'm expecting from a station chief. To tell the truth, I'm not sure what I should be expecting: but antique Jaguars, regimental ties, and gin-tippling in midafternoon isn't it. "Have you been told why I'm here?" I ask tentatively.

He roars so loudly I nearly jump out of my skin. "Of course I have, boy! What do you think I am, another of your goddamn paper-pushing Whitehall pen-pimps?" He glares at me ferociously. "God help you, and

God help both of us because nobody back home is going to. Bloody hell, what a mess."

"Mess?" I try to sound as if I know what he's talking about, but there's a quivery edge to my voice and I'm feeling fuzzy about the edges from jet lag.

"Look at you." He looks me up and down with evident contempt— or mild disdain, which is worse—in his voice. "You're a mess. You're wearing trainers and a two-guinea suit, for God's sake; you look like a hippie on a job interview, you don't know where your fucking backup team has gotten to, and you're supposed to get into Billington's hip pocket!" He sounds like Angleton's cynical kid brother. I know I mustn't let him get to me, but this is just too much.

"Before you go on, you ought to know that I've been up for about thirty hours. I woke up in Germany and I've already crossed six time zones and had a roomful of flesh-eating zombies try to chow down on my brain." I gulp the glass of water. "I'm not in the mood for this shit."

"You're not in the mood?" He laughs like a fox barking. "Then you can just go to bed without your dinner, boy. You're not in London any-more and I'm not going to put up with temper tantrums from undisci-plined wet-behind-the-ears amateurs." He puts his glass down. "Listen, let's get one thing absolutely clear: this is my turf. You do not fly in, shit all over the place, squawk loudly, and fly out again, leaving me to pick up the wreckage. While you're here, you do exactly as I say. This isn't a committee exercise, this is the Dutch Antilles and I'm not going to let you fuck up my station."

"Eh?" I shake my head. "Who said anything about . . . ?"

"You didn't have to," he says with heavy and sarcastic emphasis. "You turn up six hours behind a FLASH notice from some dog-fucker in Islington who says you're to have the run of the site facilities and I'm to render all necessary et cetera. If you get the opposition stirred up you'll be dead in a gutter within six hours and I'll get landed with the paper-work. This isn't Camden Market and I'm not the bloody hotel concierge. I'm the Laundry point man for the Caribbean, and if you put a step wrong on my patch you can bring all the hounds of Hell down on our collective neck, boy, so you're not going to *do* that. While you're work-ing on my station, if you want to fart you ask me for permission first. Otherwise I'll rip you a new sphincter. For your own good. Got that?"

"I guess." I do a double-take. "What's the opposition presence like, hereabouts?" I ask. Actually I want to say, *What is this "opposition" you speak of, strange person?*—but I figure it'll just make him shout at me again.

Griffin stares at me in disbelief. "Are you trying to tell me they haven't briefed you about the opposition?"

I shake my head.

"What a mess. This is the Caribbean: Who do you think the opposition are? Tourists! Wander around, drop in on the casinos and clubs, and what do you see? You see tourists. Half of 'em are Yanks, and maybe half of those are plants. Okay, not half, maybe one in a hundred thousand. But you see, we're about 200 miles from Cuba here, which means they're always trying to sneak assets into the generalissimo's territory. And you wouldn't want to mess with the smugglers, either. We've got money laundering, we've got the main drug pipeline into Miami via Cuba, and we've got police headaches coming out of our ears before we add the fucking opposition trying to use us as a staging post for their crazy-ass vodoun pranks." He shakes his head then stares at me. "So you've got to keep one eye peeled for the tourists. If the oppo send an assassin to polish your button they'll be disguised as a tourist, you mark my words. Are you *sure* they didn't brief you?"

"Um." I do my best to consider my next words carefully, but it's difficult when your head feels like it's stuffed with cotton wool: "You *are* talking about the Black Chamber when you use the term 'opposition,' aren't you? I mean, you're not really trying to tell me that the tourists are all part of some conspiracy—"

"Who the hell else would I be talking about?" He stares at me in disbelief, chugs the rest of his glass back, and thumps it down on the side table.

"Okay, then I've been briefed," I say tiredly. "Listen, I really need to get settled in and catch up on my briefing papers. I don't think they're going to assassinate me, my boss has arranged an, uh, accommodation." I manage to stand up without falling on the ceiling, but my feet aren't responding too well to commands from mission control. "Can we continue this tomorrow?"

"Bloody hell." He looks down his nose at me, his expression unreadable. "An accommodation. All right, we'll continue this tomorrow. You'd better be right, kid, because if you guessed wrong they'll eat your liver and lights while you're still screaming." He pauses in the doorway. "Don't call me, I'll call you."

## Chapter 5:
## High Society

The next hour passes in a haze of exhaustion. I lock the door behind Griffin and somehow manage to make it to the bed before I collapse face-first into the deep pile of oblivion. Only strange dreams trouble me—strange because I seem to be dressing up in women's clothing, not because my brain's being eaten by zombies.

An indeterminate time later I'm summoned back to wakefulness by a persistent banging on my door, and a warmly sarcastic voice at the back of my head: **Get up, monkey-boy!**

"Go 'way," I moan, clutching the pillow like a life preserver. I want to sleep so badly I can taste it, but Ramona's not leaving me alone.

"Open the door or I'll start singing, monkey-boy. You wouldn't like that."

"Singing?" I roll over. I'm still wearing my shoes, I realize. And I'm still wearing this fucking suit. I didn't even take it off for the flight—I must be turning into a manager or something. I have a sudden urge to wash compulsively. At least the tie's snaked off to wherever the horrid things live when they're not throttling their victims.

"I'll start with D:Ream. *'Things can only get better'*—"

"*Aaaugh!*" I flail around for a moment, and manage to fall off the bed. That wakes me up enough to sit up. "Okay, just hold it right there . . ."

I stumble over to the entrance and open the door. It's Ramona, and for the second time since I arrived here I experience the sense of existential angst that afflicts chewing gum cling-ons on the shoe sole of a higher order. Her supermodel-perfect brow wrinkles as she looks me up and down. "You need a shower."

"Tell me about it." I yawn hugely. She's dressed up to the nines in a slinky, black strapless gown, with a fortune in diamonds plugged into her ear lobes and wrapped around her throat. Her hairdo looks like it cost more than my last month's salary. "What's up? Planning on dining out?"

"Reconnaissance in force." She steps into the room, shoves the door shut behind her, and locks it. "Tell me about Griffin. What did he say?" she demands.

I yawn again. "Let me freshen up while we talk." *Pinky said something about a toilet kit in my briefcase, didn't he?* I rummage around in it until I come up with a black Yves Saint Laurent bag, then wander through into the bathroom.

The dream was overspill, I realize unhappily. This is going to get even more embarrassing before it's over. I hope like hell Angleton's planning on disentangling me from her as soon as possible—otherwise I'm in danger of turning into a huge unintentional security leak. Nastier possibilities nag at the back of my mind, but I'm determined to ignore them. In this line of work, too much paranoia can be worse than too little.

I open the toilet bag and poke around until I come up with a toothbrush and a tube of toothpaste. **Griffin's nuts,** I send to her while I'm scrubbing away at the inside of my lower jaw. **He's completely paranoid about you guys. He also insists that he gets a veto over my actions, which is more than somewhat inconvenient.** I switch to my upper front teeth. **Have you been fucking with his head?**

**You wish.** I can almost feel her disdainful sniff. **We've got him pegged as a loose cannon who's been put out to pasture to keep him out of your agency's internal politics. He's stuck in the 1960s, and not the good bits.**

**Well.** I carefully probe my molars, just in case Angleton's planted a microdot briefing among them to tell me how to handle situations like this. **I can't comment on Laundry operational doctrine and overseas deployments in the Caribbean—** (because I don't know anything about them: Could that be why they picked me for this op? Because I'm a designated mushroom, kept in the dark and fed shit?) **—but I would agree with your assessment of Griffin. He's a swivel-eyed nutter.** I step into the shower and dial it all the way up to Niagara. *I'm supposed to report to Angleton while letting Griffin think he's in my chain of command: What should this tell me about the home game Angleton's playing here?* I shake my head. I'm not up to playing Laundry politics right now. I focus on showering, then get out and dry myself. **One question deserves another. Why did you get me out of bed?**

**Because I wanted to fuck with *your* head, not Griffin's.** She sends me a visual of herself pouting, which is a bloody distracting thing to see in the mirror when you're trying to shave. **I got news from my ops desk that Billington flew in a few hours ago. He's probably going to visit his casino before—**

**His casino?**

**Yeah. Didn't you know? He owns this place.**

**Oh. So—**

**He's downstairs right now.** I flinch, and discover the hard way that it is indeed possible to cut yourself on an electric razor if you try hard enough. I finish off hurriedly and open the door. Ramona thrusts a bulky carrier bag at me. "Put this on."

"Where did you get this?" I pull out a tuxedo jacket, neatly folded; there's more stuff below it.

"It was waiting for you at the front desk." She smiles tightly. "You have to look the part if we're going to carry this off."

"Shit." I duck back into the bathroom and try to figure out what goes where. The trousers have odd fasteners in strange places and I've got no idea what to do with the red silk scarf-like thing; but at least they cheated on the bow tie. When I open the door Ramona is sitting in the chair by the bed, carefully reloading cartridges into the magazine of an extremely compact automatic pistol. She looks at me and frowns. "That's supposed to go around your waist," she says.

"I've never worn one of these before."

"It shows. Let me." She makes the gun vanish then comes over and adjusts my appearance. After a minute she steps back and looks at me critically. "Okay, that'll do for now. In a dim light, after a couple of cocktails. Try not to hunch up like that, it makes you look like you need to sue your orthopedic surgeon."

"Sorry, it's the shoes. That, and you managed to land a critical hit on my geek purity score. Are you sure I can't just wear a tee shirt and jeans?"

"No, you can't." She grins at me unexpectedly. "Monkey-boy isn't comfortable in a monkey suit? Consider yourself lucky you don't have to deal with underwire bras."

"If you say so." I yawn, then before my hindbrain can start issuing shutdown commands again I go over to my briefcase and start gathering up the necessaries Boris issued to me: a Tag Heuer wristwatch with all sorts of strange dials (at least one of which measures thaumic entropy levels—I'm not sure what the buttons do), a set of car keys with a fob concealing a teensy GPS tracker, a bulky old-fashioned cellphone . . . "Hey, there's something fishy about this phone! Isn't it—" I pick it up "—a bit heavy?"

I suddenly realize that Ramona is standing behind me. "Switch it off!" she hisses. "The power switch is the safety catch."

"Okay already! I'm switching it off!" I put it in my inside pocket and she relaxes. "Boris didn't say anything about—what does it do?" Then the penny drops. "Holy fuck."

"That's what you'd get if you switched it on, pointed it at the pope, and dialed 1-4-7-star," she agrees. "It takes nine millimeter ammunition. Are you okay with that?" She raises one perfectly sketched eyebrow at me.

"No!" I'm not used to firearms, they make me nervous; I'm much happier with a PDA loaded with Laundry CAT-A countermeasure invocations and a fully charged Hand of Glory. Still, nothing wakes me up quite like nearly shooting someone by accident. I fidget with the new tablet PC that Brains provisioned for me, plugging it in and setting it for counter-intrusion duty. "Shall we go drop in on Billington?"

I'm not much of a beach bunny. I'm not a culture vulture or a clothes horse either. Opera leaves me cold, clubbing is something bad guys do to baby seals, and I'm no more inclined to work the slots than I am to stand in the middle of a railway station ripping up twenty-pound notes. Nevertheless, there's a certain vicarious amusement to be had in stepping out at night with a beautiful blonde on my arm and a brown manila envelope in my inside pocket labeled HOSPITALITY EXPENSES— even if I'm going to have to account for any cash I pull out of it, in triplicate, on a form F.219/B that doesn't list "gambling losses" as an acceptable excuse.

It's dark, and the air temperature has dropped to about gas mark five, leaving me feeling like a Sunday roast in a tinfoil jacket. There's an on-shore breeze that gives a faint illusion of coolness, but it's too humid to do much more than stir the sand grains on the sidewalk. The promenade is a modern pastel-painted concrete walkway decorated to a tropical theme, like Neo-Brutalist architecture on holiday. It's bright and noisy with late-opening boutiques, open-windowed bars, and nightclubs. The crowd is what you'd expect: tourists, surfers, and holiday-makers, all dressed up for a night out on the town. By the morning they'll be puking their margaritas up on the boardwalk at the end of the development, but right now they're a happy, noisy crowd. Ramona leads me through them with supreme confidence, straight towards a garishly illuminated, red-carpeted lobby that covers half the block ahead of us.

My nose prickles. Something they never mention in the brochures is that the night-blooming plants let rip during the tourist season. I try not to sneeze convulsively as Ramona sashays right up the red carpet, bypassing the gaggle of tourists being checked at the door by security. A uniformed flunkey scrambles to grovel over her gloved hand. I follow her into the lobby and he gives me a cold-fish stare as if he can't make up his mind whether to grope my wallet or punch me in the face. I smile patronizingly at him while Ramona speaks.

"You'll have to excuse me but Bob and I are new here and I'm so excited! Would you mind showing me where the cashier's office is? Bobby darling, do you think you could get me a drink? I'm so thirsty!"

She does an inspired airhead impersonation. I nod, then catch the doorman's eye and let the smile slip. "If you'd show her to the office," I murmur, then turn on my heel and walk indoors—hoping I'm not going in the wrong direction—to give Ramona space to turn her glamour loose on him. I feel a bit of a shit about leaving the doorman to her tender mercies, but console myself with the fact that as far as he's concerned, I'm just another mark: what goes around comes around.

It's darker and noisier inside than on the promenade and a lot of over-dressed, middle-aged folks are milling around the gaming tables in the outer room. Mirror balls scatter rainbow refractions across the floor; at the far end of the room a four-piece is murdering famous jazz classics on stage. I spot the bar eventually and manage to catch one of the bartender's eyes. She's young and cute and I smile a bit more honestly. "Hi! What's your order, sir?"

"A vodka martini on the rocks." I pause for just a heartbeat, then add, "And a margarita." She smiles ingratiatingly at me and turns away, and the ghostly sensation of a stiletto heel grinding against my instep fades as quickly as it arrived. **That was entirely unnecessary,** I tell Ramona stiffly.

**Wanna bet? You're falling into character too easily, monkey-boy. Try to stay focused.**

When I find her she's leaning up against a small, thick window set in one wall, scooping plastic chips into her purse. I wait alongside with the drinks, then hand her the margarita. "Thanks." She closes the purse then leads me past a bunch of chattering one-armed-bandit fans towards an empty patch of floor near a table where a bunch of tense-looking coffin-dodgers are watching a young chav in a white shirt and dickey-bow deal cards with robotic efficiency.

"What was that about?" I murmur.

"What was what?" She turns to stare at me in the darkness, but I avoid making eye contact.

"The thing with the doorman."

"It's been a hard day, and American Airlines doesn't cater for my special dietary requirements."

"Really?" I stare at her. "I don't know how you can live with yourself."

"Marc over there—" she jerks her head almost imperceptibly, back towards the door "—likes to think of himself as a lone wolf. He's twenty-five and he got the job here after a dishonorable discharge from the French paratroops. He served two years of a five-year sentence first. You wouldn't believe the things that happen on UN peacekeeping missions . . ."

She pauses and takes a tiny sip of her drink before continuing. Her voice is over-controlled and just loud enough to hear above the band: "He's not in contact with his family back in Lyon because his father kicked him out of the house when he discovered what he did to his younger sister. He lives alone in a room above a bike repair shop. When a mark runs out of cash and tries to stiff the house, they sometimes send

Marc around to explain the facts of life. Marc enjoys his work. He prefers to use a cordless hammer-drill with a blunt three-eighths bit. Twice a week he goes and fucks a local whore, if he's got the money. If he hasn't got the money, he picks up tourist women looking for a good time: usually he takes their money and leaves their flight vouchers, but twice in the past year he's taken them for an early morning boat ride, which they probably didn't appreciate on account of being tied up and out of their skulls on Rohypnol. He's got an eight-foot dinghy and he knows about a bay out near North Point where some people he doesn't know by name will pay him good money for single women nobody will miss." She touches my arm. "Nobody is going to miss him, Bob."

"You—" I bite my tongue.

"You're learning." She smiles tensely. "Another couple of weeks and you might even get it."

I swallow bile. "Where's Billington?"

"All in good time," she croons in a low singsong voice that sends chills up and down my spine. Then she turns towards the baccarat table.

The croupier is shuffling several decks of cards together in the middle of the kidney-shaped table. A half-dozen players and their hangers-on watch with feigned boredom and avaricious eyes: leisure-suit layabouts, two or three gray-haired pensioners, a fellow who looks like a weasel in a dinner jacket, and a woman with a face like a hatchet. I hang back while Ramona explains things in a monotone in the back of my head—it sounds like she's quoting someone: **'It's much the same as any other gambling game. The odds against the banker and the player are more or less even. Only a run against either can be decisive and "break the bank" or break the players.' That's Ian Fleming, by the way.**

**Who, the guy with the face . . . ?**

**No, the guy I was quoting. He knew his theory but he wasn't as competent at the practicalities. During the Second World War he ran a scheme to get British agents in neutral ports to gamble their Abwehr rivals into bankruptcy. Didn't work. And don't even think about trying that on Billington.**

The croupier raises a hand and asks who's holding the bank. Hatchet-Face nods. I look at the pile of chips in front of her. It's worth twice my department's annual budget. She doesn't notice me staring so I look away quickly.

"So how does it go now?" I ask Ramona quietly. She's scanning the crowd as if looking for an absent friend. She smiles faintly and takes my hand, forcing me to sidle uncomfortably close.

"Make like we're a couple," she whispers, still smiling. "Okay, watch carefully. The woman who's the banker is betting against the other gamblers. She's got the shoe with six packs of cards in it—shuffled by the croupier and double-checked by everyone else. Witnesses. Anyway, she's about to—"

Hatchet-Face clears her throat. "Five grand." There's a wave of muttering among the other gamblers, then one of the pensioners nods and says, "Five," pushing a stack of chips forwards.

Ramona: "She opened with a bank of five thousand dollars. That's what she's wagering. Blue-Rinse has accepted. If nobody accepted on their own, they could club together until they match the five thousand between them."

"Ri-ight." I frown, staring at the chips. Laundry pay scales are British civil service level—if I didn't have the subsidized safe house, or if Mo wasn't working, we wouldn't be able to afford to live comfortably in London. What's already on the table is about a month's gross income for both of us, and this is just the opening round. Suddenly I feel very cold and exposed. I'm out of my depth here.

Hatchet-Face deals four cards from the shoe, laying two of them face-down in front of Blue-Rinse, and the other two cards in front of herself. Blue-Rinse picks her cards up and looks at them, then lays them face-down again and taps them.

"The idea is to get a hand that adds up to nine points, or closest to nine points. The banker doesn't get to check his cards until the players declare. Aces are low, house cards are zero, and you're only looking at the least significant digit: a five and a seven make two, not twelve. The player can play her hand, or ask for another card—like that—and then—she's turning."

Blue-Rinse has turned over her three cards. She's got a queen, a two, and a five. Hatchet-Face doesn't smile as she turns her own cards over to reveal two threes and a two. The croupier rakes the chips over towards her: Blue-Rinse doesn't bat an eyelid.

I stare fixedly at the shoe. *They're nuts. Completely insane!* I don't get this gambling thing. Didn't these people study statistics at university? *Evidently not* . . .

"Come on," Ramona says quietly. "Back to the bar, or they'll start to wonder why we're not joining in."

"Why aren't we?" I ask her as she retreats.

"They don't pay me enough."

"Me neither." I hurry to catch up.

"And here I was thinking you worked for the folks who gave us James Bond."

"You know damn well that if Bond auditioned for a secret service job they'd tell him to piss off. We don't need upper-class twits with gambling and fast car habits who think that all problems can be solved at gunpoint and who go rogue at the drop of a mission abort code."

"No, really?" She gives me an old-fashioned look.

"Right." I find myself grinning. "They go for quiet, bookish accountant-types, lots of attention to detail, no imagination, that kind of thing."

"Quiet, bookish accountant-types who're on drinking terms with the head-bangers from Two-One SAS and are field-certified to Grade Four in occult combat technology?"

I may have done a couple of training courses at Dunwich but that doesn't mean I've graduated to breathing seawater, much less inhaling vodka martinis. When I stop spluttering Ramona is looking away from me, whistling tunelessly and tapping her toes. I glare at her, and I'm about to give up on it as a bad job when I see who she's watching. "Is that Billington?" I ask.

"Yep, that's him. Aged sixty-two, looks forty-five."

Ellis Billington is rather hard to miss. Even if I didn't recognize his face from the cover of *Computer Weekly*, it'd be pretty obvious that he was a big cheese. There's a nasty face-lift in a big frock hanging on his left arm, a briefcase-toting woman in wire-frame spectacles and a tai-lored suit that screams *lawyer* shadowing him, and a pair of thugs to ei-ther side, who wear their tuxedos like uniforms and have wires looped around their ears. A gaggle of Bright Young Things in cocktail dresses and tuxes bring up the rear, like courtiers basking in the reflected glory of a medieval monarch; the dubious doorman Ramona fingered for her midnight snack is oozing up to one of them. Billington himself has a dis-tinguished silver-streaked hairdo that looks like he bought it at John De Lorean's yard sale and feeds it raw liver twice a day. For all that, he looks trim and fit—almost unnaturally well-preserved for his age.

"What now?" I ask her. I can see a guy who looks like the president of the casino threading his way across the floor towards Billington.

"We go say hello." And before I can stop her she's off across the floor like a missile. I scramble along in her wake, dodging dowagers, trying not to spill my drink—but instead of homing in on Billington she makes a beeline towards the Face Lift That Walks Like a Lady. "Eileen!" squeaks Ramona, coming over all blonde. "Why, if this isn't a complete sur-prise!"

Eileen Billington—for it is she—turns on Ramona like a cornered rattlesnake, then suddenly smiles and switches on the sweetness and light: "Why, it's Mona! Upon my word, I do declare!" They circle each other for a few seconds, sparring congenially and exchanging polite nothings while the courtier-yuppies home in on the baccarat table. I no-tice Billington's attorney exchanging words with her boss and then departing towards the casino office. Then I see Billington look at me. I take a deep breath and nod at him.

"You're with her." He jerks his chin at Ramona. "Do you know what she is?" He sounds dryly amused.

"Yes." I blink. "Ellis Billington, I presume?"

He looks me in the eye and it feels like a punch in the gut. Up close he doesn't look human. His pupils are a muddy gray-brown, and slotted vertically: I've seen that before in folks who've had an operation to correct nystagmus, but somehow on Billington it looks too natural to be the aftereffect of surgery. "Who are you?" he demands.

"Howard—Bob Howard. Capital Laundry Services, import/export division."

I manage to make a dog-eared business card appear between my fingers. He raises an eyebrow and takes it. "I didn't know you people traded over here."

"Oh, we trade all over." I force myself to smile. "I sat through a most interesting presentation yesterday. My colleagues were absolutely mesmerized."

"I have no idea what you're talking about." I take half a step back, but Ramona and Eileen are laughing loudly over some shared confidence behind me: there's no escape from his lizardlike stare. Then he seems to reach some decision, and lets me down gently: "But that's not surprising, is it? My companies have so many subsidiaries, doing so many things, that it's hard to keep track of them all." He shrugs, an *aw-shucks* gesture quite at odds with the rest of his mannerisms, and produces a grin from wherever he keeps his spare faces when he isn't wearing them. "Are you here for the sunshine and sea, Mr. Howard? Or are you here to play games?"

"A bit of both." I drain my cocktail glass. Behind him, his lawyer is approaching, the casino president at her elbow. "I wouldn't want to keep you from business, so . . ."

"Perhaps later." His smile turns almost sincere for a split second as he turns aside: "Now, if you'll excuse me?"

I find myself staring at his retreating back. Seconds later Ramona takes hold of my elbow and twists it, gently steering me through the crowd towards the open glass doors leading onto the balcony at the back of the casino floor. "Come on," she says quietly. The courtiers have formed an attentive wall around the fourth Mrs. Billington, who is getting ready to recycle some of her husband's money through his bank. I let Ramona lead me outside.

"You know her!" I accuse.

"Of course I damn well know her!" Ramona leans against the stone railing that overhangs the beach, staring at me from arm's length. My heart's pounding and I feel dizzy with relief over having escaped Billington's scrutiny. He was perfectly polite but when he looked at me I felt like a bug on a microscope slide, pinned down by brilliant search-lights for scrutiny by a vast, unsympathetic intellect: trapped with nowhere to hide. "My department spent sixty thousand bucks setting up the first introduction at a congressman's fundraiser two weeks ago, just so she'd recognize me tonight. You didn't think we'd come here without do-ing the groundwork first?"

"Nobody tells me these things," I complain. "I'm flailing around in the dark!"

"Don't sweat it." Suddenly she goes all apologetic on me, as if I'm a puppy who doesn't know any better than to widdle on the living room carpet: "It's all part of the process."

"What process?" I stare her in the eyes, trying to ignore the effects of the glamour that tells me she's the most amazingly beautiful woman I've ever met.

"The process that I'm not allowed to tell you about." Is that genuine regret in her eyes? "I'm sorry." She lowers her eyelashes. I track down in-stinctively, and find myself staring into the depths of her cleavage.

"Great," I say bitterly. "I've got a station chief who's as mad as a fish, an incomplete briefing, and a gambling-obsessed billionaire to out-bluff. And you can't fucking tell me what I'm supposed to be doing?"

"No," she says, in a thin, hopeless tone. And to my complete surprise she leans forwards, wraps her arms around me, props her chin on my shoulder, and begins to weep silently.

This is the final straw. I have been clawed at by zombies, conde-scended to by Brains, shipped off to the Caribbean and lectured in my sleep by Angleton, introduced to an executive with the eyes of a poison-ous reptile, and ranted at by an old-school spook who's fallen in the bot-tle—but those are all part of the job. This isn't. There's no briefing sheet on what to do when a supernatural soul-sucking horror disguised as a beautiful woman starts crying on your shoulder. Ramona sobs silently while I stand there, paralyzed by indecision, self-doubt, and jet lag. Finally I do the only thing I can think of and wrap my arms round her shoulders. "There, there," I mutter, utterly unsure what I'm saying: "It's going to be all right. Whatever it is."

"No, it isn't," she sniffles quietly. "It's *never* going to be all right." Then she straightens up. "I need to blow my nose."

I can take a hint: I let go and take a step back. "Do you want to talk?"

She pulls a hand-sized pack of tissues out of her bag and dabs at her eyes carefully.

"Do I want to talk?" She sniffs, then chuckles. Evidently something I said amused her. "No, Bob, I don't want to talk." She blows her nose. "You're far too nice for this. Go to bed."

"Too nice for what?" These dark hints of hers are getting really annoying, but I'm upset and concerned now that she's pulling herself together; I feel like I've just sat some kind of exam and failed it, without even knowing what subject I'm being tested on.

"Go to bed," she repeats, a trifle more forcefully. "I haven't eaten yet. Don't tempt me."

I beat a hasty retreat back through the casino. On my way out, I go through the side room where they keep the slot machines. I pass Pinky—at least, I'm half-sure it's Pinky—creating a near riot among the blue-rinse set by playing an entire row of one-armed bandits in sequence and winning big on each one. I don't think he notices me. Just as well: I'm not in the mood for small talk right now.

Damn it, I know it's just the effects of a class three glamour, but I can't stop thinking about Ramona—and Mo's flying in tomorrow.

## Chapter 6:
## Charlie Victor

I make it back to my hotel room without getting lost, falling asleep on my feet, or accidentally looking at the screen saver. I slump in the chair for a while, but there's nothing on TV except an adventure movie starring George Lazenby, and it'll take more than that to keep me awake. So I hang out the DO NOT DISTURB sign, undress, and go to bed.

I fall asleep almost instantly, but it's not very restful because I'm in someone else's head, and I really don't want to be there. Last time this happened, the fifty-something engineering salesman from Düsseldorf trapping off with the blonde call girl was just sad, and a bit pathetic on the side; this time it feels dirty. I (*no, he*: I struggle to hold myself aside from his sense of self) work out daily in a gym round the corner from the casino before I go in to work, and it's not just pumping iron and running on a track—there's stuff I don't recognize, practice routines with odd twisting and punching and kicking motions, somatic memories of beating people up and the warm sensual excitement that floods me when I stomp some fucking idiot for getting in my face. I've had a call from the customer, and I'm about ready to go off work and go looking for the merchandise he wants, when this blonde American princess comes out of the *salle* and what do you know, but she's giving me a come-on? She's lost the rich nerd she showed up with, and good riddance; guess I'll have to take her home and that means . . . yeah, she'll do. Two birds, one stone, so to speak. Or two stones, in my case. Mind you, she's a customer—I'll just have to be discreet. So I smile at her and make nicey-nice while she giggles, then I offer to buy her a drink and she says, "Yes," and I tell her to meet me over the road at the Sunset Beach Bar so I can show her the town. She heads off, shaking her booty, and I go and get squared away. Time to do another line of Charlie in the john.

Checking out, walking over the road, I get that thrill of arousal. I'm on top of the world again with cold fire coursing through my veins, like the time in the village near Bujumbura when Jacques and I caught that kid stealing and we—the memory skids away from me as if it's made of grease, only an echo of the blood and shit-smell of it and the screams lingering in my ears—and I get the hot tension again, like lightning seeking a path to earth. Sex, that'll help. Long as she doesn't make a fuss.

She's waiting for me on a bar stool, legs crossed and face hopeful. Plump cheeks, lips like throttled . . . I let my face smile at her and order her a drink and make chitchat. She smiles sympathetically and asks me questions, trying to find out if I have—hey! She's worried I might have a regular girlfriend, the stupid cunt, so I explain that no, my Elouise died in a car crash two years ago and I have been mourning since. She's so stupid she laps it up, asks me lots of questions and sounds concerned. I figure I'll drop her off with the rich guy's pilot at Anse Marcel tomorrow: but first we'll have some fun together. I act coy but let her draw me out because half the bitches want to be fucked hard by a stranger, they just have to convince themselves he's sensitive and caring at first to get over their inhibitions. After a while she looks at me slack-mouthed like she's already dripping, and I figure it's time. So I ask if she wants to come back to my place and she accepts.

We walk—it's only three blocks—and she doesn't bat an eyelid at the rubbish and the locked shutters. I show her upstairs and unlock the door, and when I turn back to pull her inside she actually gropes me! Normally they get cold at this point and start making excuses but this is going really smooth. I'm hard, of course, and when she kisses me I get an arm round her and start hiking up her skirt. The Rohypnol's in the fridge and it'd be more sensible to slip it to her first, then add a geas on top for safety's sake, but what the hell, she seems willing enough. This one really does seem to want a rough fuck—shame for her she doesn't know about the customer, but those are the breaks. I pick her up and carry her inside, kick the door shut, then dump her on the bed and jump her. And the funny thing is she lets me, she doesn't fight, and my heart is in my mouth pounding away between her legs, wet meat, warm meat, it's like she doesn't even know the father says it's wrong to do this beat my meat, it's not *ever* this easy and I can't let her talk afterwards even though she's biting my shoulder and sucking me, and *oh father my chest hurts*—

I open my eyes and stare at the hotel ceiling until my pulse begins to slow. I'm engorged and erect and freezing cold on the damp sheets, and I feel as if I'm about to throw up. "Ramona!" I croak, my larynx still half-paralyzed with sleep.

**The fucker just flatlined on me!** I can't feel his mind anymore, but he's lying on top of her, still twitching spastically, and I can taste her desperation and fear. **He must have had a dodgy heart, done one line too many. Finish me off, Bob!**

**What—** I realize I've been holding my penis and yank my hands away as if they're covered in chili oil.

**Finish me off! *Please!*** I can sense her succubus now, coiling like a black vortex of emptiness behind her conscious thoughts. There's nothing human about it, nothing warm—it's like death itself, not the small oblivion of orgasm but its complete antithesis, freezing and vacant, a hunger for life. It needs filling, it's searching for a sacrifice and she'd set her eyes on Marc but he checked out early and now— **It needs a little death to go with the big one, and the longer you wait the hungrier it gets.** She sounds breathless. **If you don't give it one it'll eat me, and you may think that would be a good thing but in case it's escaped your attention we're entangled—**

**But I—** I want Mo, don't I? *Don't I?* Mo isn't hiding behind a glamour. Mo doesn't eat people like a fuck-vampire. Mo isn't a drop-dead gorgeous blonde, she's just Mo, and we're probably going to end up getting married sooner or later, and I feel guilty and frightened because Mo won't understand what Ramona wants me to do.

**But nothing!** I can sense Ramona's arousal and, behind it, a canker of upwelling fear. **Jesus, Bob, do something, please help me here . . . !** She's helpless and small before the emptiness of her hunger, and Mo isn't here, and neither is she. I feel the empty hunger, and I try to wall it out, but Ramona needs me. She's teetering on the edge of an orgasm, the hunger is waiting for her, and if she meets it alone she won't come out the other side alive. I can't *not* do it. Can I?

**I'm not cleared for sex magick,** I tell her, gritting my teeth. But she sends me a touch-sense picture of herself: the warm weight on her chest, Marc's head lolling, the turgid stretch of her vulva occupied by a dead man's dick, a delicious sense of proximity to catastrophic nothingness, teetering on the edge of a cliff—and I clutch myself and begin to spasm wildly because I'm still massively turned on from the overspill of her sex. The sense of doom recedes immediately, and then something I wasn't expecting happens—Ramona comes, taking me completely by surprise. She goes on and on and on until I'm almost ready to scream for mercy. Finally the waves of sensation finally begin to slow down and recede, leaving her panting and pinned beneath Marc's cooling cadaver. A warm afterglow floods her with life. I can feel her reveling in it.

**Thank you,** she says fervently, and I can't tell at first whether she's talking to me or to the dead serial rapist. **If you hadn't joined in, it would have had me for sure.** The corpse's head lolls on her shoulder, a drop of spittle dangling from his mouth. She reaches up and shoves it aside. **Was it good for you, too?** she asks, and tenderly kisses his soft, unresponsive lips.

My skin crawls. **You enjoyed that a whole lot,** I tell her before I bite my tongue. But it's too late.

**You enjoy eating, too, but pleasure's not the only reason you do it,** she snaps. **And don't tell me you didn't enjoy this.** I cringe at her anger: *What will Mo say when she finds out?* It's not sex—no, it's just having a simultaneous orgasm with a consenting adult, my conscience jabs me. *Oh hell, what a mess.* I gingerly sit up and shuffle towards the bathroom and a late-night appointment with the shower.

**Hey, what about me?** Ramona complains bitterly, bracing herself to dislodge the drained husk of her prey.

**I don't want to talk about it right now,** I mutter. I twist the shower dial, feeling dirty.

**Typical fucking male . . . **

**Look who's talking! You're a real piece of work.** I turn the temperature right up until it hurts, then bite my tongue and stand underneath it. **You wanted to get into my pants, didn't you?**

**Anyone ever tell you you're an asshole, monkey-boy? If I wanted you I'd have had you right there on the casino balcony, instead of nearly dying in a shit-hole.** She's working on getting her clothes back into a semblance of order. Marc lies on the floor beside the bed. She lashes out and kicks him hard enough to hurt my toes, and I suddenly realize she's shaking with adrenalin, the aftermath of a terror trip. **Bastard!**

She's *really* scared. That's my conscience talking; he's been beating on the door for the past couple of minutes but I've only just heard him over the racket in my head. *Why wouldn't she be telling the truth?* I swallow, forcing back stomach acid. *She likes me. Fuck knows why.*

I force myself to come up with an apology. **Being scared makes me more of an asshole than usual.** It sounds weak in the silence afterwards, but I don't know what else to say.

**You bet,** she says tightly. **Go back to bed, Bob. I won't bother you again tonight. Sweet dreams.**

I wake up with the early morning light from the window as it streams in across my face. One of my arms is lying over the edge of the bed, and the other is twisted around someone's shoulders—*What the fuck?* I think fuzzily.

It's Ramona. She's curled up against me on top of the sheets, sleeping like a baby. She's still wearing her glad rags, her hair a wild tangle. My breath catches with fear or lust or guilt, or maybe all three at the same time: guilty, fearful lust. I can't make up my mind whether I want to gnaw my arm off at the shoulder or ask her to elope with me.

Eventually I work out a compromise. I sit up, slowly pulling my arm out from under her: "How do you take your coffee?"

"Uh?" She opens her eyes. "Oh . . . hi." She looks puzzled. "Where am I . . . oh." Mild annoyance: "I take it black. And strong." She yawns, then rolls over and begins to sit up. Yawns again. "I need to use your bathroom." She looks displeased, and it's not just her eyeliner running:

somehow she looks older, less inhumanly perfect. The glamour's still there, masking her physical shape, but what I'm seeing now is unfogged by implanted emotional bias.

"Be my guest." I walk over to the filter machine and start prodding at it, trying to figure out where the sachet of coffee goes. My head's spinning— "How did you get in here?"

"Don't you remember?"

"No."

"Well, that makes two of us," she says as she closes the door. A moment later I hear the sound of running water and realize too late that I need to use the bathroom, too.

*Oh, great.* There was the, whatever the fuck you call it, with the predator, Marc—and she needed me to—I try not to think too closely about it. I remember that much. *How the hell did she get in here?* I ask myself.

I get the coffee maker loaded and go prod my tablet PC. It's sitting where I left it last night, with a clear line of sight on the door and window, and it's still up and running. I look too closely and the ward tries to bite me between the eyes but misses. *Good.* So then I go and inspect the other wards I put on the door by opening it and gingerly pulling in the DO NOT DISTURB sign. The silver diagram, sketched on the sign using a conductive pencil and a drop of blood, shimmers at me. It's still live: anyone other than me who tries to get past it is going to get a very unpleasant surprise. Finally, as the coffee maker begins to spit and burble, I check the seal on the window. My mobile phone (the real one, the Treo with the Java countermeasure suite and the keyboard and all the trimmings, not the bullet-firing fake) is still propped up against it.

I glance up and down, then shake my head. There are no holes in the walls and ceiling, which means Ramona can't be here—the place is about as secure as a hotel room can be, stitched up tighter than Angleton's ass.

"I don't want to hurry you or anything, but I need the toilet, too," I call through the door.

"Okay, okay! I'm nearly ready." She sounds annoyed.

"Are you sure you don't remember how you got in here?" I add.

The door opens. She's repaired her glamour and is every bit the airbrushed, drop-dead gorgeous model she was when I first saw her in the Laguna Bar: only the eyes are different. Old and tired.

"How much of what happened last night do you remember?" she asks.

"I—" I stop. "What, do you mean after we met Billington? Or after I left the casino?"

"Did we leave together?" She frowns.

"You don't—" I bite my tongue and stare at her. *How did you get into my room?* Maybe it's a side effect of destiny entanglement—my wards can't tell us apart. "I had some really weird dreams," I say, then hold out a coffee cup for her.

"Well, that's a surprise." She snorts then takes the cup. "But it doesn't have to mean anything."

"It doesn't—" I stop dead. "I dreamed about you," I say reluctantly. I find it really hard to pick the right words. "You were with some guy you'd picked up who worked at the casino."

She looks me in the eye calmly. "You dreamed about me, Bob. Things happen in dreams that don't always happen in real life."

"But he died while you were in bed with—"

"Bob?" Her eyes are greenish blue, flecks of gold floating in them, rimmed in expensive eyeliner that makes them look wide and inno-cent—but somehow they're deeper than an arctic lake, and much colder. "For once in your life, shut up and listen to me. Okay?"

She's got the Voice of Command. I find myself leaning against the wall with no definite memory of how I got here. "What?"

"*Primus,* we're destiny-entangled. I can't do anything about that. You stub your toe, I hurt; I call you names, you get pissy. But you're making a big mistake. Because, *secundus,* you had a weird dream. And you're jumping to the conclusion that the two are related, that whatever you dreamed about is whatever happened to me. And you know what? That ain't necessarily so. Correlation does not imply causation. Now—" she reaches over and pokes me in the chest with a fingertip "—you seem a little upset over whatever it was you dreamed about. And I think you ought to think very hard before you ask the next question, because you can choose to ask whether there was any connection between your weird dream and my night out—or you can just tell yourself you ate too many cheese canapés before bed and it was all in your head, and you can walk away from it. Is that clear? We may be entangled, but it doesn't have to go any further."

She stands there expectantly, obviously anticipating a reply. I'm rooted to the spot by the force of her gaze. My pulse roars in my ears. I don't—truly I don't—know what to do! My mind spins. Did I simply have a wet dream last night? Or did Ramona suck a serial rapist's soul right out of his body then use me for sex magick to keep her daemon in check . . . ? And do I really want to know the truth? *Really?*

I feel my lips moving without any conscious decision. "Thank you. And if you don't mind, I'm going to unask that question for the time be-ing."

"Oh, I mind all right." A flash of unidentifiable emotion flickers in her eyes like distant lightning. "But don't worry about me, I'm used to it. I'll be all right after breakfast." She glances down, breaking eye contact. "Jesus, stripy pajamas. It's too early in the morning for that."

"Hey, it's all I've got; anyway, it's better than sleeping in a tux." I raise an eyebrow at her dress. "You're going to have to get that professionally cleaned."

"No, really?" She takes a mouthful of coffee. "Thanks for the tip, monkey-boy, I'd never have guessed. I'll be going back to my room when I finish this." Another mouthful. "Got any plans for today?"

I pause for thought. "I need to touch base with my backup team and file a report with head office. Then I'm supposed to visit a tailor's shop. After which—" a ghost of a dream memory gibbers and capers for attention "—I heard there's a nice beach up at Anse Marcel. I figure I might hang out there for a while. How about you?"

I eat breakfast on a balcony overlooking an expanse of white beach, trying not to flinch as the occasional airbus rumbles past on final approach into Princess Juliana Airport. Midway through a butter croissant that melts on the tongue, my Treo rings: "Howard!"

"Speaking." I get a sinking sensation in the pit of my stomach: it's Griffin.

"Get yourself over here, chop-chop. We've got a situation."

*Shit.* "What kind of situation? And where's here?"

"Face time only." He rattles off an address somewhere near Mullet Beach and I jot it down.

"Okay, I'll be over in half an hour."

"Make sure you are!" He hangs up, leaving me staring at my phone as if it's turned into a dead slug in my hand. What a way to start a day: Griffin's found something to go nonlinear over. I shake my head in disgust. As if I haven't got enough problems already.

I'm just about up and running on local time. Even so, it takes me a while to figure out my way to the address Griffin gave me. It turns out to be a holiday villa, white clapboard walls and wooden shutters overlooking the road behind the beachfront. The temperature's already up to the mid-twenties and rising as I trudge towards the front door. I'm about to knock when it opens and I find myself eyeball to hairy eyeball with Griffin.

"Get in here!" he half-snarls, grabbing me by my jacket. "Quick!"

I take in his red-rimmed eyes, stubbly chin, and general agitation. "Something bad happen?"

"You could say that." I follow him into the back room. The windows are shuttered, several large nylon hold-alls are lined up against one wall, and there's a mass of electronics spread across the dining table. After a couple of seconds I figure out that I'm looking at a clunky electrodynamic rig and a Vulpis-Tesla mainframe: it looks like it was invented by a mad pervert who was into torturing chickens, but it's really just a tool for summoning minor abominations. By the look on his face Griffin's been bolting it together and hitting the bottle for the past twelve hours or so—not a combination I'm sanguine about. "I got a dispatch from head office. The oppo's acting up—they've sent us one of their fast bowlers!"

"What's cricket got to do with us?" I ask, confused. It's too early in the morning for this.

"Who said anything about cricket?" Griffin hurries across the room and starts rearranging the bakelite plug-board that configures the chicken-torturer. "I said they'd sent a fast bowler, not a fucking cricketer."

"Slow up." I rub my eyes. "How long have you been out here?"

He rounds on me. "Nineteen years, if it means anything to you, whipper-snapper!" he snorts. "Kids these days . . ."

I shrug. "Slang changes, is what I'm saying."

"Bah." He straightens up and sighs. "I got a flash code from the Weather Service this morning: Charlie Victor is in town. He's one of their top assassins, works for Unit Echo—that's our designation for it, not theirs, nobody's got a fucking clue what the Black Chamber internal org chart looks like—and generally we don't get advance warning because the first warning anyone gets about Charlie Victor is when they wake up dead."

"Whoa." I grab a chair and sit down hard. "When did he arrive?"

"Yesterday, while you were snoozing." Griffin stares at me. "Well?"

"Do we know who his target is?"

"Weather Service says it's something to do with your mission, this billionaire."

"Weather Service—" I pause. How to phrase my opinion of the Predictive Branch tactfully? Just in case Griffin's got a gypsy cousin who's into fluffy chakra crystal ball-fu and works for Precognitive Ops . . . "Weather Service has a certain reputation." A reputation for being disastrously wrong about thirty percent of the time—as you'd expect of a bunch of webcams hooked up to crystal balls scrying random number generators—and for being less than half right about fifty percent of the time, which is even worse than the real Meteorological Office. The only reason we don't ignore them completely is that about one time in five they hit the jackpot—and then people live or die by their projections. But that thirty percent gave us the amazing invisible Iraqi WMDs, the

Falklands War ("nothing can possibly go wrong"), and going back a bit further, the British Lunar Expedition of 1964.[7, 8]

"Weather Service is taking traffic flow at source from GCHQ and cross-correlating it with validated HUMINT sources," Griffin rumbles ominously. "This is about as hard as it gets. What are the implications for your mission?"

"I need to talk to Angleton—I thought we had an accommodation on this one, but if what you're saying's right, all bets are off." I glance at the VT frame. "What's the chicken plucker for?"

"A necessary precaution." Griffin stares at me speculatively. "In case Charlie Victor tries to pay a visit. And to keep a lock on your special kit." He nods at the cases in the corner.

"Uh-huh. Any sign of my backup team?"

"I called them for a meeting half an hour ago. They should be arriving any time—"

Right on cue, there's a knock at the door.

I head over to open the door but Griffin beats me to it, shoving me out of the way and raising a finger to silence me. He pulls an elderly looking revolver from under his jacket, holding it behind his back as he turns the door handle.

It's Brains, wearing sunglasses and a loud Hawaiian shirt. "Yo, Bob!" he calls, ignoring Griffin. Boris slouches on the front stoop behind him.

"Come in," Griffin mutters uninvitingly. "Don't just stand there!"

"Where's Pinky?" I ask.

"Parking your car by the hotel." Brains walks past Griffin, whistling nonchalantly, then stops when he sees the VT frame. "Haven't seen one of those in a long while!" He closes in on it and peers at the plug-board. "Hey, this is wired up all wrong—"

"Stop that at once!" Griffin is about to hit the ceiling. "Before you start meddling—"

"Boys, boys." Boris grimaces tiredly. "Chill."

"I need to call Angleton," I manage to slip in. "And I've got to get closer to the target. Can we please try to keep on track, here? What do we know about Billington's arrival? I didn't think he was meant to be here yet."

"Billington is here?" Boris frowns. "Is ungood news. How?"

"He flew in last night." I glance at Griffin, but his mouth is clamped in a thin line. He's not volunteering anything. "I met him briefly. Do we

---

[7] What lunar expedition?
[8] Exactly.

know where this yacht of his is? Or his schedule?" I ask Griffin directly, and he frowns.

"His yacht, the *Mabuse,* is moored off North Point—he's not using the marina at Marigot for some reason. While he's on the island he's got a villa on Mount Paradis, but I think you're more likely to find he's staying on the yacht." Griffin crosses his arms. "Thinking of paying him a visit?"

"Just puzzled." I glance at the wall where someone has pinned a large map of the island. North Point is about as far away from Maho Beach—and the casino—as you can get. It must be close to fifteen kilometers, and longer if you cover the distance by boat. "I was wondering how he got here last night."

"Simple; he flew." Griffin looks as if he's sucking a lemon. "Calling that monster a yacht is like calling a Boeing 777 a company light twin."

"How big is it?" asks Brains.

"Naval Intelligence knows." Griffin walks over to the sideboard and pulls out a bottle of tonic water. "Seeing as how it started life as a Russian Krivak-III-class frigate."

"Whee! Do you think they'd let me drive it?" Pinky's somehow slipped in under the radar. "Hey, Bob: catch!" He chucks me a key fob.

"You're telling me Billington owns a warship?" I sit down heavily.

"No, I'm telling you his yacht *used to* be one." Griffin fills his glass and puts the bottle down. He looks amused, for malicious values of amusement. "A Type 1135 guided missile frigate, to be precise, late model with ASW helicopter and vertical launch system. The Russians sold it off to the Indian Navy during a hard currency hiccup a few years ago, and they sold it in turn when they commissioned the first of their own guided missile destroyers. I'm pretty sure they took out the guns and VLS before they decommissioned it, but they left in the helideck and engines, and it can make close to forty knots when the skipper wants to go somewhere in a hurry. Billington sank a fortune into converting it, and now it's one of the largest luxury yachts in the world, with a swimming pool where the nuclear missile launchers used to be."

"Jesus." It's not as if I was planning to do the scuba-dive-and-climb-aboard thing—for starters, I know just enough about diving to realize I'd probably drown—but when Angleton mentioned a yacht I wasn't thinking in terms of battleships. "What's he use it for?"

"Oh, this and that." Griffin sounds even more amused. "I hear it comes in handy for water skiing. More realistically, he can zip anywhere in the Caribbean in about twelve hours. Chopper into Miami, brief excursion out to sea, chopper into Havana, and nobody's any the wiser. Go visit his bankers in Grand Cayman, entertain visiting billionaires, hold meetings in real secrecy: and we can't keep an eye on him without getting the Navy involved."

I can almost see the cards he's got stuffed up his sleeve. "What's your point?"

"My point?" He stares at me. "My point is that I happen to know a damn sight more about what's going on in my patch than all of you lot put together, or the clowns at head office for that matter. And I would appreciate it if you'd run any harebrained schemes past me before you put them into practice just in case you're about to put your foot in it. Human Resources may have told you that I'm a garden leave case and you're reporting direct to Angleton, but you might also like to consider the possibility that Human Resources couldn't find their arse with a map, a periscope, and a tub of Vaseline."

Boris rises to the bait: "Am not possible commenting on Human Resources!"

Pinky snorts loudly.

I shrug: "Okay, I'll run any harebrained schemes I hatch past you if you give me the benefit of your advice. But if it's just as well with you, I need to go check in with my liaison." And I still have to call Angleton—who told Griffin about his control issues? "Then I've got to pick up some clothes and go wangle myself an invitation aboard the . . . What did you say the yacht was called?"

"The *Mabuse*," Griffin repeats. His cheek twitches. "And Charlie Victor is in town. You ought to take precautions."

"Sure." If the bastard thinks he can spook me that easily he's got another thing coming. "Boris, any immediate updates?"

Boris shakes his head: "Not yet."

"Okay, then I'll be going." And before Griffin can object I'm out the door.

I need to get my head together, so I start by heading for the tailor's shop they pointed me at back in Darmstadt. After half an hour of wandering among fast-food concessions, tourist traps, and free cosmetic sample stands I find it, and half an hour later I'm back in my room unwrapping—"What *is* this shit?" I ask myself, bemused. Whoever ordered it either didn't have a clue what I normally wear, or didn't care. There's a lightweight suit, a bunch of shirts, a choice of ties—I corral them in the wardrobe and lock it carefully, in case they sneak out and try to strangle me in the night—and the nearest thing to wearable clothing is a polo shirt and a pair of chinos. Which are not only totally un-me, they're not even black. "Shit!" I blew out of Darmstadt with nothing but the business suit and a borrowed toilet bag: it's this or nothing. I make the best of a bad job, and end up looking like a second-rate parody of my father. I give up. I'll just have to go shopping, once I can find some cheap broadband access. Maybe Think Geek can ship me a care package by express airmail?

I pick up my Treo—not the crazy mechanical phonegun but real, reliable, understandable electronics—and head down to the car park. I hunt among the pickups and sports cars until I find the Smart Fortwo. I stare at it and it stares right back at me, mockingly. It's not even a convertible. "Someone's going to regret this," I mutter as I strap it on. Then it's the moment of truth: time for me to go check out a dream of a ghost of a memory, to see if someone's waiting for Marc the doorman to deliver a body to North Bay.

It's already getting hot, the sun burning through the deep blue vault of sky that arches overhead. I fumble my way out of Maho Bay and onto the road that winds towards the northern end of the island. Motoring here is just about as different from the autobahn experience as it's possible to get and still be on wheels, for which I'm fervently grateful. The road is narrow, barely graded and marked, and winds around the landscape as it climbs the picturesque but steep slopes of Mount Paradis. I pass numerous signs for tourist beaches, brightly painted shop fronts and restaurants . . . it's resort central. I crawl along behind a gaggle of taxis and a tourist 4x4 for about half an hour, then we're over the top of the island. The road more or less comes to a dead end in a depression between two hills, and I pull over beside a road sign to take a look.

The sign says: ANSE MARCEL. There's a scattering of shops and hotels alongside the road, shaded by palm trees. On the downhill slope, I can see the sea in the distance, out across a brilliant white expanse of beach dotted with sunbathing tourists. Off to one side a hundred meters away, a clump of masts huddle together in a small marina. Looks like it's time to get out and walk.

I get out, feeling horribly overdressed: most of the punters hereabouts are wearing clothes that go well with thongs and sandals. Idyllic tropical beach paradise, with added ultraviolet burns and sand itch. And they're all so buff! I'm your typical pallid cube-maggot, and the six-pack is a high-cost luxury extra on that model. I shuffle down the street towards the marina, feeling about six centimeters tall, hoping that I'm wrong: that nobody's there, and I can go back to the hotel and write it all off as a bad dream brought on by vodka and jet lag.

The marina is little more than three piers with sailboats tied up on either side; two larger motorboats belonging to tour companies bob at the outer edge. A couple of guys are working on one of these, so I head up the pier until I can get a better view.

"Bonjour." One of the boatmen is watching me. "You want something?"

"Possibly." I glance out to sea. A distinctly dead-looking seagull sits on a bollard nearby, watching me stonily. *Watching me watching you* . . . it suddenly occurs to me that coming out here on my own might be a bad idea if Billington is serious about his privacy and is also, as Angleton put it, a player. "Does a boat from the *Mabuse* call here?"

"I think you want to find somewhere else to hang out." He smiles at me but the expression doesn't reach his eyes. He's holding a mallet and a big chisel.

"Why? They friends of yours?" I feel an itching in my fingertips and a distinct taste of blue—my wards are responding to something nearby. Mr. Mallet glares at me. He's about my age, but built like a brick outhouse and tanned to the color of old oak. "Or maybe they aren't?"

"Non." He turns his head and spits across the side of the pier.

"Pierre—" The other guy lets loose a stream of rapid-fire, heavily accented French that I can't hope to follow. He's in late middle-age, receding hair, salt-and-pepper beard: the picturesque Old Salt hanging out on the jetty, image only slightly spoiled by his Mickey Mouse tee shirt and blue plastic sandals. Pierre—Mr. Mallet—stares at me suspiciously. Then he turns and looks out across the sapphire sea.

I follow his gaze. There's a warship in the distance, a kilometer offshore: long, low, and lean, with a sharply raked superstructure. It takes me a few seconds to realize that it's the wrong color, gleaming white rather than the drab gray most navies paint their tubs.

I glance back at the pier. The goddamn seagull is staring at me, its eyes white and milky like—

*Goddamn.*

"Do you know a guy called Marc, from Maho Beach?" I ask.

A palpable hit: Pierre's head whips round towards me. He raises the chisel warningly as the seagull opens its beak. I pull out my Treo. "Smile for the camera, birdie."

The seagull stares at my smartphone accusingly, then topples off its perch and falls into the water like a dead weight. Which, in fact, is exactly what it is now that I've zapped it with my patent undead garbage collector.

"We've got about two minutes before they send another watcher," I say conversationally. "If they're awake, of course. So. Do you know Marc?"

"What's it worth?" He lowers the chisel, looking at me as if I've sprouted a second head.

I pull out two fifty-euro notes. "This."

"Yeah, I know Marc."

"Describe him."

"Oily bastard. Works out at the gym down the back of Rue de Hollande in Marigot, fills in on the door of the Casino Royale as a door man and bouncer. He's the one you're asking about?"

I pull out two more notes. "Tell me everything you know."

The old guy glares at him, mutters something, gets up, and goes aboard the boat.

"I'll take those." Pierre puts down the chisel and I hand him the notes. "Marc is a piece of shit. He hits on tourist women and takes them for everything they've got. Nearly got himself arrested a year ago but they couldn't prove anything—or find the woman. Sometimes—" Pierre glances over his shoulder "—you see him in the early morning with some broad, going out on his boat. That one, there." He nods at a dinghy with a mounting for an outboard engine. "Meeting up with another boat. The women don't come back."

I have a heavy, sick feeling. "Would this other boat happen to be from the *Mabuse?*" I ask.

He looks at me sidelong. "I didn't say anything," he says.

I nod. "Thanks for your time."

"Thank you for taking out the trash." He gestures at the bollard where the bird was watching. "Now get out of here and please don't come back."

## Chapter 7:
## Nightmare Beach

I'm two kilometers down the road to Grand Case and the coastal route to Marigot when I realize I'm being tailed. I'm crap at this private eye stuff, but it's not exactly rocket science on Saint Martin—the roads are only two lanes wide. There's a Suzuki SUV about a quarter-kilometer behind me. I speed up, it speeds up. I slow down, it slows down. So I pull over and park at a tourist spot and watch it tool past. Just before the next bend in the road it pulls over. How tedious, I think. Then I get on the ethereal blower.

**Ramona? You busy?**

**Powdering my nose. What's up?**

I stare at the car ahead of me, trying to visualize it well enough to shove it at her as a concrete image. **I've got company. The unwelcome kind.**

**Surprise!** I can feel her chuckle. **What did you do to annoy them?**

**Oh, this 'n' that.** I'm not about to go into my snooping activities just yet. **Billington's yacht is anchored off North Point, and some of the locals aren't too happy about it.**

**Surprise indeed. So what's with the car?**

**They've been tailing me!** I sound a bit peevish to myself—petulant, even. **And Billington's got the marina under surveillance. He's using seagulls as watchers. That makes me nervous.** I couldn't care less about the flying sea-rats, but I'm not terribly happy about the fact that someone aboard that yacht has got the nous to run the Invocation of Al-Harijoun on them, not to mention having enough spare eyeballs to monitor the surveillance take from several hundred zombie seagulls.

**So why don't you lose them?**

I take a deep breath. **That would entail breaking the traffic regulations, you know? I'm not supposed to do that. It's called drawing undue attention to yourself. Besides, there's a whole stack of documents to file, starting with a form A-19/B, or they'll throw the book at me. I could lose my license!**

**What, your license to kill?**

**No, my license to drive!** I thump the steering wheel in frustration. **This isn't some kind of spy farce: I'm just a civil servant. I don't**

have a license to kill, or authorization to poke my nose into random corners of the world and meet interesting people and hurt them. Capisce?**

For a moment I feel dizzy, I pinch the bridge of my nose and take a deep breath: my vision fades out for a scary moment, then comes back with this weird sense that I'm looking through two sets of eyes at once. **What the fuck?**

**It's me, Bob. I can't keep this up for long . . . Look, you see that SUV parked ahead?**

**Yeah?** I'm looking at it but it doesn't register.

**The guy who just got out of it and is walking toward you is carrying a gun. And he doesn't look particularly friendly. Now I know you're hung-up on the speed limit and stuff, but can I suggest you—**

There is one good thing about driving a Smart car: it has a turning circle tighter than Ramona's hips. I hit the gas and yank the wheel and make the tires squeal, rocking from side to side so badly that for a moment I'm afraid the tiny car is about to topple over. The bad guy raises his pistol slowly but I've floored the accelerator and it's not *that* slow in a straight line. My wards are prickling and tickling like a sandstorm and there's a faint blue aura crawling over the dash. Something smacks into the tailgate—a stray pebble, I tell myself as I swerve back up the coast road towards Orléans.

**I knew you could do it!** Ramona enthuses like she's channeling a cheerleader. **What did you do to get them riled up like that?**

**I asked about Marc.** I glance in the mirror and flinch; my tail is back in the SUV and has gotten it turned around. It's kicking up a plume of dust as it follows me. I swerve wildly to overtake a Taurus full of pensioners who're drifting along the crest of the road with their left turn signal flashing continuously, then I overcompensate to avoid rolling the Smart.

**That wasn't very fucking clever of you, was it?** she asks sharply. **Why did you do it?** Irrelevant distractions nag at the edges of my perception: a twin-engine pond-hopper buzzes overhead on final approach into Grand Case Airport.

**I wanted to see if my suspicions were correct.** And if I was dreaming or not.

There's a van ahead, moving slowly, so I pull out to look past it and there's an oncoming truck so I pull back in. And behind me, closing the gap again, is the SUV.

**I am going to have to lose these guys before they phone ahead and get some muscle ahead of me on the road to Philipsburg. Any ideas?**

**Yes. I'll be on my way in about five minutes. Just stay ahead of them for now.**

**Be fast, okay? If you can't be safe.** I pull out recklessly and floor the accelerator again, passing the van as the driver waves angrily at me. There's a kink in the road ahead and I take it as fast as I dare. The Smart is bouncy and rolls frighteningly but it can't be any worse at road-holding than the SUV tailing me, can it? **Just what are they doing with the women?**

**What women?**

**The women Marc was kidnapping and selling to the boat crew. Don't tell me you didn't know about that?**

The Suzuki has pulled past the van and is coming up behind me and I'm fresh out of side streets. From here, it's a three-kilometer straight stretch around the foothills of Paradise Peak before we get to Orient Beach and the fork down to the sea. After that, it's another five kilometers to the next turnoff. I'm doing eighty and that's already too damn fast for this road. Besides, I feel like I'm driving two cars at once, one of them a sawed-off subcompact and the other a topless muscle-machine that dodges in and out of the tourist traffic like a steeplechaser weaving through a queue of pensioners. It's deeply confusing and it makes me want to throw up.

**What do you know about—** pause **—the abductions?**

**Women. Young. Blonde. His wife owns a cosmetics company and he looks too young. What conclusion would you draw?**

**He has a good plastic surgeon. Hang on.** The muscle car surges effortlessly around another bus. Meanwhile the SUV has pulled even with me, and the driver is waving his gun at me to pull over. I glance sideways once more and see his eyes. They look dead and worse than dead, like he's been in the water for a week and nothing's tried eating him. I recognize that look: they're using tele-operator-controlled zombies. *Shit.* My steering wheel is crawling with sparks as the occult countermeasures cut in, deflecting their brain-eating mojo.

I tense and hit the brakes, then push the cigarette lighter home in its socket during the second it takes him to match my speed. We come to a halt side by side on the crest of a low hill. The SUV's door opens and the dead guy with the gun gets out and walks over. I sniff: there's a nasty fragrant smoke coming out of the lighter socket.

He marches stiffly round to my side door, keeping the gun in view. I keep my hands on the steering wheel as he opens the door and gets in.

"Who are you?" I ask tensely. "What's going on?"

"You ask too many questions," says the dead man. His voice slurs drunkenly, as if he's not used to this larynx, and his breath stinks like rotting meat. "Turn around. Drive back to Anse Marcel." He points the gun at my stomach.

"If you say so." I slowly move one hand to the gearshift, then turn the car around. The SUV sits abandoned and forlorn behind us as I accelerate away. I drive slowly, trying to drag things out. The stink of decaying meat mingles with a weird aroma of burning herbs. The steering wheel has sprouted a halo of fine blue fire and my skin crawls—I glance sideways but there are no green sparks in his eyes, just the filmed-over lusterless glaze of a day-old corpse. It's funny how death changes people: I startle when I recognize him.

"Drive faster." The gun pokes me in the ribs.

"How long have you had Marc?" I ask.

"Shut up."

*I need Ramona.* The smell of burning herbs is almost overpowering. I reach out to her: **Phone me.**

**What's the problem? I'm driving as fast as—**

**Just phone me, damn it! Dial my mobile now!**

Fifteen or twenty endless seconds pass, then my Treo begins to ring.

"I need to answer my phone," I tell my passenger. "I have to check in regularly."

"Answer it. Say that everything is normal. If you tell them different I'll shoot you."

I reach out and punch the call-accept button, angling the screen away from him. Then in quick succession I punch the program menu button, and the pretty icon that triggers all the car's countermeasures simultaneously.

I don't know quite what I was expecting. Explosions of sparks, spinning heads, a startling spewage of ectoplasm? I get none of it. But Marc the doorman, who managed to die of one of the effects of terminal cocaine abuse just before Ramona's succubus could suck him dry, sighs and slumps like a dropped puppet. Unfortunately he's not belted in so he falls across my lap, which is deeply inconvenient because we're doing fifty kilometers an hour and he's blocking the steering wheel. Life gets very exciting for a few seconds until I bring the car to rest by the roadside, next to a stand of palm trees.

I wind down the window and stick my head out, taking in deep gasping breaths of blessedly wormwood- and fetor-free ocean air. The fear is just beginning to register: *I did it again,* I realize, *I nearly got myself killed.* Sticking my nose into something that isn't strictly any of my business. I shove Marc out of my lap, then stop. *What am I going to do with him?*

It is generally not a good idea when visiting foreign countries to be found by the cops keeping company with a corpse and a gun. An autopsy will show he had a cardiac arrest about a day ago, but he's in my car and that's the sort of thing that gives them exactly the wrong idea—talk about circumstantial evidence! "Shit," I mutter, looking around. Ramona's on her way but she's driving a two-seater. *Double-shit.* My eyes fasten on the stand of trees. *Hmm.*

I restart the engine and reverse up to the trees. I park, then get out and start wrestling with Marc's body. He's surprisingly heavy and inflexible, and the seats are inconveniently form-fitting, but I manage to drag him across to the driver's side with a modicum of sweating and swearing. He leans against the door as if he's sleeping off a bender. I retrieve the Treo, blip the door shut, then start doodling schematics in a small application I carry for designing field-expedient incantations. There's no need to draw a grid round the car—the Smart's already wired—so as soon as I'm sure I've got it right I hit the upload button and look away. When I look back I know there's something there, but it makes the back of my scalp itch and my vision blur. If I hadn't parked the car there myself I could drive right past without seeing it.

I shamble back to the roadside and look both ways—there's no pavement—then start walking along the hard shoulder towards Orient Beach.

It's still morning but the day is going to be baking hot. Trudging along a dusty road beneath a spark-plug sky without a cloud in sight gets old fast. There are beaches and sand off to one side, and on the other a gently rising hillside covered with what passes for a forest hereabouts—but I'm either overdressed (according to my sweating armpits) or underdressed (if I acknowledge the impending sunburn on the back of my neck and arms). I'm also in a foul mood.

De-animating Marc has brought back the sense of guilt from Darmstadt: the conviction that if I'd just been slightly faster off the ball I could have saved Franz and Sophie and the others. It's also confirmed that my dreams of Ramona are the real thing: so much for keeping a fig leaf of deniability. *She was right: I'm an idiot.* Finally there's Billington, and the activities of his minions. Seeing that long, hungry hull in the distance, recognizing the watcher on the quay, has given me an ugly, small feeling. It's as if I'm an ant chewing away at a scab on an elephant's foot—a foot that can be raised and brought down on my head with crushing force should the pachyderm ever notice my existence.

After I've been walking for about half an hour, a bright red convertible rumbles out of the heat haze and pulls up beside me. I think it's a Ferrari, though I'm not much good at car spotting; anyway, Ramona waves at me from the driver's seat. She's wearing aviator mirrorshades, a bikini, and a see-through silk sarong. If my libido wasn't on the ropes from the events of the past twelve hours my eyes would be halfway out of my head: as it is, the best I can manage is a tired wave.

"Hi, stranger. Looking for a lift?" She grins ironically at me.

"Let's get out of here." I flop into the glove-leather passenger seat and stare at the trees glumly.

She pulls off slowly and we drive in silence for about five minutes. "You could have gotten yourself killed back there," she says quietly. "What got into you?"

I count the passing palm trees. After I reach fifty I let myself open my mouth. "I wanted to check out a hunch."

Without taking her eyes off the road she reaches over with her right hand and squeezes my left leg. "I don't want you getting yourself killed," she says, her voice toneless and over-controlled.

I pay attention to her in a way I can't describe, feeling for whatever it is that connects us. It's deep and wide as a river, invisible and fluid and powerful enough to drown in. What I sense through it is more than I bargained for. Her attention's fixed on the road ahead but her emotions are in turmoil. Grief, anger at me for being a damn fool, anxiety, jealousy. *Jealousy?*

"I didn't know you cared," I say aloud. *And I'm not sure I want you to care,* I think to myself.

"Oh, it's not about you. If you get yourself killed what happens to me?"

She wants it to sound like cynical self-interest but there's a taste of worry and confusion in her mind that undermines every word that comes out of her mouth.

"Something big is going down on this island," I say, tacitly changing the subject before we end up in uncharted waters. "Billington's crew has got watchers out. Seagull monitors controlled from, um, somewhere else. And then I ran into Marc. Judging by the state of my wards every goddamn corpse on the island must be moving—why the hell haven't they chained up the graveyards? And what's this thing they've got about single female tourists?"

"That might not be part of Billington's core program." Ramona sounds noncommittal but I can tell she knows more than she's admitting. "It might be his crew carrying on behind his back. Or something less obvious."

"Come on! If his sailors are kidnapping single females, you think he's not going to know about it?"

Ramona turns her head to look me in the eye: "I think you underestimate just how big this scheme is."

"Then why won't you tell me?" I complain.

"Because I'm—" She bites her tongue. "Listen. It's a nice day. Let's go for a walk, huh?"

"A walk—why?" I get the most peculiar sense that she's trying to tell me something without putting it into words.

"Let's just say I wanna see your boxers, okay?"

She grins. Her good humor's more fragile than it looks, but just for a moment I like what I can see. "Okay." I yawn, the aftereffects of the chase catching up with me. "Where do you want to go?"

"There's a spot near Orient Bay."

She drives past tourists and local traffic in silence. I keep my mouth shut. I'm not good at handling emotional stuff and Ramona confuses the hell out of me. It's almost enough to make me wish Mo was around; life would be a lot simpler.

We hit a side road and drive along it until we pass a bunch of the usual beach-side shops and restaurants and a car park. Ramona noses the Ferrari between a Land Rover and a rack of brightly painted boneshaker bicycles and kills the engine. "C'mon," she says, jumping out and popping open the trunk. "I bought you a towel, trunks, and sandals."

"Huh?"

She prods me in the ribs. "Strip off!" I look at her dubiously but her expression is mulish. There's a concrete convenience nearby so I wander over to it and go inside. I pull my polo shirt off, then lose the shoes, socks, and trousers before pulling on the swimming trunks. I have my limits: the smartphone I keep. I go back outside. Ramona is just about hopping up and down with impatience. "What are you doing with that phone?" she asks. "Come on, it'll be safe in the glove compartment."

"Nope. Not doing." I cross my arms defensively. The Treo doesn't fit nicely in the baggy boxer-style trunks' pocket, but I'm not handing it over. "You want my wallet, you can have it, but not my Treo! It's already saved my life once today."

"I see." She stares at me, chewing her lip thoughtfully. "Listen, will you turn it off?"

"What? But it's in sleep mode—"

"No, I want you to switch it *right off*. No electronics is best, but if you insist on carrying—"

I raise an eyebrow and she shakes her head in warning. I look her in the eye. "Are you sure this is necessary?"

"Yes."

My stomach flip-flops. *No electronics?* That's heavy. In fact it's more than heavy: to compute is to be, and all that. I don't mind going without clothes, but being without a microprocessor is *truly* stripping down. It's like asking a sorcerer to surrender his magic wand, or a politician to forswear his lies. *How far do I trust her?* I wonder, then I remember last night, a moment of vulnerability on a balcony overlooking the sea.

"Okay." I press and hold the power button until the phone chimes and the signal LED winks out. *No electronics.* "What now?"

"Follow me." She picks up the towels, shuts the car trunk, and heads towards the beach. While I wasn't looking she's shed the sarong: I can't keep my eyes from tracking the hypnotic sway of her buttocks.

The sand is fine and white and the vegetation rapidly gives way to open beach. There's a rocky promontory ahead, and various sunbathers have set up their little patches; offshore, the sailboards are catching the breeze. The sea is a huge, warm presence, sighing as waves break across the reef offshore and subside before they reach us. Ramona stops and bends forwards, rolls her briefs down her legs, and shrugs out of her bikini top. Then she looks at me: "Aren't you going to strip off?"

"Hey, this is public—"

There's an impish gleam in her eyes. "*Are* you?" She straightens up and deliberately turns to face me. "You're cute when you blush!"

I glance at the nearest tourists. Middle-aged spread and a clear lack of concealing fabric drives the message home. "Oh, so it's a nudist beach."

"Naturist, please. C'mon, Bob. People will stare if you don't."

Nobody taught me how to say no when a beautiful naked woman begs me to take my clothes off. I fumble my way out of my trunks and concentrate very hard on not concentrating on her very visible assets. Luckily, she's Ramona. She's strikingly beautiful—with or without the glamour, it doesn't matter—but I also find her intimidating. After a minute or so I figure out I'm not about to sprout a semaphore pole in public, so I begin to relax. When in Rome, et cetera.

Ramona picks her way past the clots of slowly basting sun-seekers—I notice with displeasure a scattering of heads turning to track us—and detours around a battered hut selling ice cream and cold drinks. The beach is narrower at this end, and proportionately less populated as she veers towards the waterline. "Okay, this'll do. Mark the spot, Bob." She unrolls her towel and plants it on the sand. Then she holds out a waterproof bag-gie. "For your phone—sling it around your neck, we're going swim-ming."

"We're going swimming?" **Naked?**

She looks at me and sighs. "Yes Bob, we're going swimming in the sea, bare-ass naked. Sometimes I despair of you . . ."

*Oh boy.* My head's spinning. I bag up my phone, make sure it's sealed, and walk into the sea until I'm up to my ankles, looking down at the surf swirling grains of sand between and over my toes. I can't remem-ber when I last went swimming. It's cool but not cold. Ramona wades into the waves until she's hip-deep then turns round and beckons to me. "What are you waiting for?"

I grit my teeth and plod forwards until the water's over my knees. There's an island in the distance, just a nub of trees waving slowly above a thin rind of sand. "Are you planning on wading all the way out there?"

"No, just a little farther." She winks at me, then turns and wades out deeper. Soon those remarkable buttocks are just a pale gleam beneath the rippling waves.

I follow her in. She pitches forwards and starts swimming. Swimming isn't something I've done much of lately, but it's like riding a bicycle—you'll remember how to do it and your muscles will make sure you don't forget the next morning. I splash around after her, trying to relearn my breast stroke by beating the waves into submission. Damn, but this is dif-ferent from the old Moseley Road Swimming Baths.

**This way,** she tells me, using our speech-free intercom. **Not too far. Can you manage ten minutes without a rest?**

**I hope so.** The waves aren't strong inside the barrier formed by the reef, and in any event they're driving us back onshore, but I hope she's not planning on going outside the protective boundary.

**Okay, follow me.**

She strikes out away from the sunbathers and towards the outer reef, at an angle. Pretty soon I'm gasping for breath as I flail the water, trail-ing after her. Ramona is a very strong swimmer and I'm out of practice, and my arms and thigh muscles are screaming for mercy within minutes. But we're approaching the reef, the waves are breaking over it—and to my surprise, when she stands up the water barely reaches her breasts.

"What the hell?" I flap towards her, then switch to treading water, feeling for the surface beneath my feet. I'm half-expecting to kick razor-sharp coral, but what I find myself standing on is smooth, slippery-slick concrete.

"No electronics, because someone might have tapped into it. No clothing because you might be bugged. Seawater because it's conductive; if they'd tattooed a capacitive chart on your scalp while you were asleep it'd be shorted out by now. No bugs because we've got a high-volume white noise source all around us." She frowns at me, deadly serious "You're clean, monkey-boy, except for whatever compulsion filters they've dropped on you, and any supernatural monitors."

"Shit." Enlightenment dawns: Ramona has dragged me out here because she thinks I'm bugged. "What's down below us . . . ?"

"It's a defensive emplacement. The French got serious about that in the early '60s, before the treaty arrangements got nailed down. You're standing on a discordance node, one of a belt of sixteen big ones designed to protect the east coast of Saint Martin against necromantic incursions. If you swim through it, any thaumaturgic bugs they've planted on you will be wiped—it's a huge occult degaussing rig. Which is one of the reasons I brought you here."

"But if it's a defensive emplacement, how come the zombies up at—" I bite my tongue.

"Exactly." She looks grave. "That's part of what's wrong here, which is the other thing I want to check out. About four months ago one of our routine geomantic surveillance flights noticed that the defensive belt was—not broken, exactly, but showed signs of tampering. One of Billington's subsidiaries, a construction company, landed the contract to maintain the concrete ballast units. Do I need to draw you a diagram?"

Here we are surrounded by ocean, and my mouth is dry as a bone. "No. You think somebody's running a little import/export business, right?"

"Yes."

I take a deep breath. "Anything else?"

"I wanted to get you alone, with no bugs."

"Hey, you only had to ask!" I grin, my heart pounding inappropriately.

"Don't take this the wrong way." She smiles ruefully. "You know what would happen if—"

"Only kidding," I say, abruptly nervous. The conversation is veering dangerously close to territory I'm uncomfortable with. I look at her— correction: I force my eyes to track about thirty degrees up, until I'm looking at her face. She's watching me right back, and I find I can't help wondering what it would be like to . . . well. Sure she's attached to a level three glamour so tight you'd need a scalpel to peel it off her, but I can probably cope with whatever's underneath it, I think. Her daemon is something else again, but there are things we could do, without intercourse . . . but what about Mo? My conscience finally catches up with my freewheeling speculation. *Well, what indeed?* But the thought drags me back down to Earth, after a fashion. I manage to get my worst instincts under control then ask: "Okay, so why did you *really* bring me out here?"

"First, I need to know: Why the fuck did you go rushing off to Anse Marcel?"

The question hits me like a bucket of cold water in the face. "I, I, I wanted to check something out," I stutter. It sounds lame. "Last night, I was inside Marc's head. He was going to—" I trail off.

"You were inside his head?"

"Yes, and it wasn't a nice place to be," I snap.

"You were inside—" She blinks rapidly. "Tell me what you picked up?"

"But I thought you knew—"

"No," she says tightly. "I didn't know it went that far. This is as new to me as it is to you. What did you learn?"

I lick my lips. "Marc had an arrangement. Every couple of weeks he'd pick up a single female who wouldn't be missed and he'd—let's not go into that. Afterwards he'd drop a geas on her, a control ring he'd learned from the customer, and he'd drive her up to Anse Marcel where a couple of guys would come in on a boat to pick the victim up. They paid in coke, plus extras."

"Ri-ight." Ramona pauses. "That makes sense." I can feel it snapping into place in her mind, another part of a lethal booby-trapped jigsaw puzzle she's trying to solve. I realize in the silence between heartbeats that we've stopped pretending. It feels as if some huge external force is pushing us together, squeezing us towards intimacy. She gave me an opening to pretend that I wasn't involved, and I didn't take it. But why? I wouldn't normally do this kind of thing; maybe the tropical clime's addled me.

"What part of the picture does it fit?" I meet her gaze. I have the most peculiar feeling that I'm watching myself watching her through two pairs of eyes.

"Billington's diversified into a variety of fields. You shouldn't think of him as simply a computer industry mogul. He's got his tentacles into a lot more pies than Silicon Valley."

"But kidnapping? That's ridiculous! It can't possibly be cost-effective, even if he's selling them off for spare parts." I swallow and shut up: she's broadcasting a horrible sense of claustrophobic dread, fear rising off her like a heat haze. I shuffle, grounding my feet against the concrete defense platform, and for a moment her skin acquires a silvery sheen. "What is it? Is he—"

"You know better than to say it aloud, Bob."

"I was afraid that was what you were trying to tell me." I look away, towards the breakers foaming across the reef and the open seas beyond. And it's not just her sense of dread anymore.

Some types of invocation need blood, and some require entire bod ies. Whatever lives in the back of Ramona's head is a trivial, weak example; the creature I ran across in Santa Cruz and Amsterdam three years ago was a much more powerful one. Ramona is afraid that we're dealing with a life-eating horror that lives off the entropy burst that comes from draining a human soul: I'm pretty sure she's right. Which means the next question to ask is, who on Earth would summon such a thing, and why? And as I'm pretty sure we know the answer to *who* . . .

"What's Billington trying to do? What is he summoning up?"

"We don't know."

"Any guesses?" I ask sarcastically. "The Deep Ones, maybe?"

Ramona shakes her head angrily. "Not them! Never them." The sense of dread is choking, oppressive: she feels it personally, I realize.

I stare at her. That flash of silver again, the water lapping around her chest, drawing my eyes back towards those amazingly perfect breasts — I fight to filter out the distraction. *This isn't me, is it?* It's hard work, fighting the glamour. I want to see her as she really is. Taking a deep breath I force myself back to the matter in hand: "What makes you so sure the Deep Ones aren't behind him? You're holding out on me. Why?"

"Because they don't think that way. And yes, I *am* fucking holding out on you." She glares at me, and I can feel her wounded pride and defensive anger fighting against something else: Concern? Worry? "This is all going wrong. I brought you out here so I could tell you why you're being kept in the dark, not to pick a fight—"

"And here I was thinking you wanted me for my body." I hold my hands up before she has time to swear at me: "I'm sorry, but have you got any idea just how bloody distracting that glamour is?" It's amazing and frightening and beautiful, and it makes it a real bitch to try to concentrate on a conversation about subterfuge and lies without wondering what horrors she's concealing from me.

Ramona stares at me, until I can feel her inside my head, watching herself through my glamour-ensnared eyes. "Okay, monkey-boy: you want it, you got it." Her voice is flat and hard. "Just remember, you asked for it."

She lets go of the anchor of the glamour she's been clinging on to. The constant repulsive force emanating from the concrete countermeasure emplacement we're standing on blows it away, like a hat in a hurricane—and I see Ramona as she truly is. Which gives me two very big surprises.

I gasp. I can't help myself. "You're one of *them!*" I meet her clear emerald gaze. And, quietly: "Wow."

Ramona says nothing, but one perfect nostril flares minutely. Her skin has a faint silvery iridescent sheen to it, like the scales of a fish; her hair is long and green as glass, framing a face with higher cheekbones and a wider mouth, rising from an inhumanly perfect long neck, the skin broken by two rows of slits above her clavicle. Her breasts are smaller, not much larger than her nipples, and two tinier ones adorn her rib cage beneath them. She raises her right hand and spreads her fingers, revealing the delicate tracery of webbing. "So what do you think of me now, monkey-boy?"

I swallow. She's like a sculpture in quicksilver, created by inhuman sea-dwelling aliens who have taken the essence of human female beauty and customized it to meet their need for an artificial go-between who can walk among the lumpen savages of the arid continental surfaces. "I've met half—sorry, the sea-born—before. At Dunwich. But not like, uh, you. Uh. You're different." I goggle at her, my mouth open like a fish. *Different* is an understatement and a half. The glamour she customarily wears doesn't make her look unnaturally beautiful to human eyes; rather, it conceals the more exotic aspects of her physiognomy. Strip it away and she's devastating, as unlike the weak-chinned followers of St. Monkfish as it's possible to imagine.

"So you've met the country cousins." Her cheek twitches. "Yes, I can understand your surprise." She stares at me, and I'm not sure whether she's disappointed or surprised. "So do you still think I'm a monster?"

"I think you're a—" I grind to a stop, before I can push my foot any further down my throat. "Um." An inkling comes to me. "Let me guess. Your people. Go-betweens, like the colony at Dunwich. And you were given to the BC and they dropped the, your daemon on you to control you. Am I right?"

"I can neither confirm nor deny anything to do with my employers," she says with the flat-voiced emptiness of a necromancer's answering machine, before snapping back into focus: "My folks lived off Baja California. That's where I grew up." For a moment her eyes overflow with a sense of loss. "The Deep Ones did . . . well, they did what they did at Dunwich. My folks have been go-betweens for generations, able to pass as human and visit the depths. But we're not really at home among either species. We're constructs, Bob. And now you know why I use the glamour!" she adds harshly. "There's no need for flattery. I know damn well what I look like to you people."

You people: *Ouch!* "You're not a monster. Exotic, yes." I can't look away from her. I try to pull my eyes away from those perfect breasts and I keep looking down and there's another pair— "It just takes a little getting used to. But I don't mind, not really. I've already gotten over it." Down in the Laundry compound at Dunwich they've got a technical term for human employees who start spending too much time skinny-dipping with a snorkel: fish-fuckers. I've never really seen the attraction before, but with Ramona it's blindingly obvious. "You're as attractive without the glamour as with it. Maybe more so."

"You're just saying that to fuck with my head." I can taste her bitter amusement. "Admit it!"

"Nope." I take a deep breath and duck under the water, then kick off towards her. I can open my eyes here: everything is tinged pale green but I can see. Ramona dodges sideways then grabs me by the waist and we tumble beneath the reflective ceiling, grappling and pushing and shoving. I get my head above water for long enough to pull in a lungful of air, then she drags me under and starts tickling me. I convulse, but somehow whenever I really need air she's pushing me up above water rather than trying to pull me down. Weirdly, I seem to need much less air than I ought to. I can feel the gills working powerfully in her pleural cavity; it's as if there's some kind of leakage between us, as if she's helping oxygenate both our bloodstreams. When she kisses me she tastes of roses and oysters. Finally, after a few minutes of rubbing and fondling we settle to the bottom and lie, arms and legs entangled, in the middle of the circuit-board tracery of gold that caps the concrete table.

**Fish-fucker!** She mocks me.

**It takes two to tango, squid-girl. Anyway, we haven't. I wouldn't dare.**

**Coward!** She laughs ruefully, taking the sting out of the word. Silver bubbles trickle and bob towards the surface from her mouth. **Y'know, it's hard work breathing for both of us. If you want to help, go up to the surface . . . **

**Okay.** I let go and allow myself to stand up. As I pull away from her I feel a tightness in my chest that rapidly grows: we may be destiny-entangled, but the metabolic leakage is strictly short-range. I break surface and shake my head, gasping for air, then look towards the beach. There's a loud ringing in my ears, a deep bass rattle that resonates with my jaw, and a shadow dims the flashing sunlight on the reef. *Huh?* I find myself looking straight up at the underside of a helicopter.

"Get down!" Ramona hisses through the deafening roar. She wraps a hand around my ankle and yanks, pulling me under the surface. I hold my breath and let her drag me down beside her—my chest eases—then I realize she's pointing at a rectangular duct cover at one side of the concrete platform. **Come on, we've got to get under cover! If they see us we're screwed!**

**If who see us?**

**Billington's thugs! That's his chopper up there. Whatever you did must have really gotten them pissed. We've got to get under cover before—**

**Before what?** She's wrestling with the iron duct cover, which is dark red with rust and thinly coated with polyps and other growths. I try to ignore the tightness in my chest and brace myself to help.

**That.** Something drops into the water nearby. I think it's rubbish at first, but then I see a spreading red stain in the water. **Dye marker. For the divers.**

**Whoops.** I grab hold of the handles and brace myself, then put my back into it. **How long—** the grate begins to move **—do we have?**

**Fresh outa time, monkey-boy.** Shadows flicker in the turbid waters on the other side of the coral barrier: barracuda or small sharks circling. My chest aches with the effort of holding my breath and I think I've ripped open the skin on my hands, but the grate is moving now, swinging up and out on a hinged arm. **C'mon in.** The opening is about eighty by sixty, a tight squeeze for two: Ramona drops into it feet first then grabs my hand and pulls me after.

**What is this?** I ask. I get an edgy, panicky feeling: we're dropping into a concrete-walled tube with hand-holds on one side, and it's black as night inside.

**Quick! Pull the cover shut!**

I yank at the hatch and it drops towards me heavily. I flinch as it lands on top of the tunnel, and then I can't see anything but a vague phosphorescent glow. I blink and look down. It's Ramona. She's breathing—if that's what you call it—like she's running a marathon, and she looks a bit peaked, and she's glowing, very dimly. Bioluminescence. **It's shut.**

**Okay. Now follow me.** She begins to descend the tunnel, hand over hand. My chest tightens.

**Where are we going?** I ask nervously.

**I don't know—this isn't in the blueprints. Probably an emergency maintenance tunnel or something. So how about we find out, huh?**

I grab a rung and shove myself down towards her, trying to ignore the panicky feeling of breathlessness and the weird sensations around my collarbone. **Okay, so why not let's climb down a secret maintenance shaft in an undersea occult defense platform while divers with spear guns who work for a mad billionaire wait for us up top, hmm? What could possibly go wrong?**

**Oh, you'd be surprised.** She sounds as if she does this sort of thing every other week. Then, a second later, I sense rather than feel her feet hit bottom: **Oh. Well *that's* a surprise,** she adds conversationally.

And suddenly I realize I can't breathe underwater.

## Chapter 8:
## White Hat/Black Hat

An adventure demands a hero, around whom the whole world circles; but what use is a hero who can't even breathe under water?

To spare you Bob's embarrassment, and to provide a shark's-eye view of the turbid waters through which he swims, it is necessary to pause for a moment and, as if in a dream—or an oneiromantic stream ripped from the screen of Bob's smartphone—to cast your gaze across the ocean towards events transpiring at exactly the same time, in an office in London.

Do not fear for Bob. He'll be back, albeit somewhat moist around the gills.

"The Secretary will see you now, Miss O'Brien," says the receptionist.

O'Brien nods amiably at the receptionist, slides a bookmark into the hardback she's reading, then stands up. This takes some time because the visitor's chair she's been waiting in is ancient and sags like a hungry Venus' flytrap, and O'Brien is trying to keep her grip on a scuffed black violin case. The receptionist watches her, bored, as she shrugs her khaki linen jacket into place, pats down a straying lock of reddish-brown hair, and walks over towards the closed briefing-room door with the AUTHORIZED PERSONNEL ONLY sign above it. She pauses with one hand on the doorknob. "By the way, it's *Professor* O'Brien," she says, smiling to take the sting out of the words. "'Miss' sounds like something you'd call a naughty schoolgirl, don't you think?"

The receptionist is still nodding wordlessly and trying to think of a comeback when O'Brien closes the door and the red light comes on over the lintel.

The briefing room contains a boardroom table, six chairs, a jug of tap water, some paper cups, and an ancient Agfa slide projector. All the fittings look to be at least a third of a century old: some of them might even have seen service during the Second World War. There used to be windows in two of the walls, but they were bricked up and covered over with institutional magnolia paint some years ago. The lighting tubes above the table shed a ghastly glare that gives everybody in the room the skin tint of a corpse—except for Angleton, who looks mummified at the best of times.

"Professor O'Brien." Angleton actually smiles, revealing teeth like tombstones. "Do have a seat."

"Of course." O'Brien pulls one of the battered wooden chairs out from the table and sits down carefully. She nods at Angleton, polite control personified. The violin case she places on the tabletop.

"As a matter of curiosity, how are your studies proceeding?"

"Everything's going smoothly." She carefully aligns the case's neck in accordance with the direction of the wards on Angleton's door. "You needn't worry on that account." Then she exhausts her patiently husbanded patience. "Where's Andy Newstrom?"

Angleton makes a steeple of his fingers. "Andrew was unable to attend the meeting you called at short notice. I believe he has been unexpectedly detained in Germany."

O'Brien opens her mouth to say something, but Angleton raises a bony finger in warning: "I have arranged an appropriate substitute to deputize for him."

O'Brien swallows. "I see." Fingers drum on the body of the violin case. Angleton tracks them with his eyes. "You know this isn't about my research," she begins, elliptically.

"Of course not." Angleton falls silent for a few seconds. "Feel free to tell me exactly what you think of me, Dominique."

Dominique—Mo—sends him a withering stare. "No thank you. If I get started you'll be late for your next meeting." She pauses for a moment. Then she asks, with the deceptive mildness of a police interrogator zeroing in on a confession: "Why did you do it?"

"Because it was necessary. Or did you think I would send him into the field on a whim?"

Mo's control slips for a second: her glare is hot enough to ignite paper.

"I'm sorry," he adds heavily. "But this was an unscheduled emergency, and Bob was the only suitable agent who was available at short notice."

"*Really?*" She glances at the black velvet cloth covering the files on his desk. "I know all about your little tricks," she warns. "In case you'd forgotten."

Angleton shrugs uncomfortably. "How could I? You're perfectly right, and we owe you a considerable debt of gratitude for your cooperation in that particular incident. But nevertheless—" he stares at the wall beside her chair, a white-painted rectangle that doubles as a projector screen "—we are confronted with AZORIAN BLUE HADES, and Bob is the only field-certified executive who is both competent to deal with the matter and sufficiently ignorant to be able to, ah, play the role with conviction. You, my dear, couldn't do this particular job, you're too well-informed, leaving aside all the other aspects of the affair. The same goes for myself, or for Andrew, or for Davidson, or Fawcett, or any of a number of other assets Human Resources identified as preliminary candidates during the search phase of the operation. And while we have plenty of other staff who are not cleared for AZORIAN BLUE HADES, most of them are insufficiently prepared to meet its challenges."

"Nevertheless." Mo's hand closes on the neck of her case. "I'm warning you, Angleton. I know you entangled Bob with a Black Chamber assassin and I know what the consequences are. I know that unless someone collapses their superposition within about half a million seconds, he's not coming back, at least not as himself. And I'm not putting up with the usual excuses—'he was the only round peg we had that fit that particular hole, it was in the interests of national security'—you'd better see he comes back alive and in one body. Or I *am going to the Auditors.*"

Angleton eyes her warily. O'Brien is one of very few people in the organization who would make such a threat, and one of even fewer who might actually follow through on it. "I do not believe that will be necessary," he says slowly. "As it happens, I agreed to your request for a meeting because I intended to tap you for the next phase. Contrary to the impression you may have received, I don't consider Bob to be an expendable asset. But I believe you're allowing your relationship with him to color your perceptions of the risk inherent in the situation. I assume you'd be willing to help bring him back safe and sound?"

Mo nods sharply. "You know I would."

"Good." Angleton glances at the door, then frowns. "I do believe Alan's late. That's not like him."

"Alan? Alan Barnes?"

"Yes."

"What do you want *him* for?"

Angleton snorts. "A moment ago you were getting uptight about your boyfriend's security. Now you're asking why I asked Captain Barnes—"

The door bursts open, admitting a wiry pint-sized tornado. "Ah, the fragrant Professor O'Brien! How you doing, Mo? And you, you old bat. What do you want now?" The force of nature grins widely. With his owlishly large glasses, leather-patched tweed jacket, and expanding bald spot he could pass for a schoolteacher—if schoolteachers habitually wore shoulder holsters.

Angleton pushes his spectacles up on his nose. "I was explaining to Professor O'Brien that I've got a little job for you. Bob's accepted the starring role in the approach plan for AZORIAN BLUE HADES and now it's time to set up the payoff. Not unnaturally, Mo has expressed certain reservations about the way the project has been conducted to date. I believe that, in view of her special skills, she can make a valuable contribution to the operation. What do you think?"

While Barnes is considering the question, Mo glances between the two of them. "This is a setup!"

Barnes grins at her: "Of course it is!"

She looks at Angleton. "What do you want me to do?" She grips the neck of her violin case tensely.

Barnes sniggers quietly, then pulls out a chair. Angleton doesn't deign to notice. Instead, he reaches across the table and switches on the projector.

"You're going on vacation. Officially you're on leave, flagged as a home visit to your elderly mother. That's because we can't rule out the possibility of an internal security leak," he adds.

Mo whistles tunelessly between her teeth. "Like that, is it?"

"Oh yes." A thin blade appears silently between Alan's fingers, as if it congealed out of thin air. He begins to probe a cuticle on his other hand. "It's very *like that* indeed. And we want you to look into it on your way to the main performance."

"You'll be on board tomorrow's flight from Charles de Gaulle to Saint Martin. Your cover identity is Mrs. Angela Hudson, the wife of a tire-and-exhaust magnate from Dorking." Angleton slides a document wallet across the table towards Mo, who handles it as if it's about to explode. "This is a weak cover. It's been cleared with Customs and Immigration at both ends but it won't hold up to scrutiny. On the other hand you won't have to use it for more than about forty-eight hours. After this briefing, take yourself down to Wardrobe Department and they'll set you up with suitable clothing and support equipment for Mrs. Hudson. You may take—" he points at the violin case "—your instrument, and any other equipment you deem necessary. You'll be staying at a hotel in Grand Case. You should be aware that our local station chief, Jack Griffin, or someone working for him, has been compromised. We want to keep you out of Billington's sights for as long as possible, so bypassing Griffin's organization is top of your playlist. If you can identify the source of the leak and deal with it, I'd be grateful. Once you've settled in, Alan will be your backup. You'll be operating without a field controller; if you need a shoulder to cry on you come straight to me."

He turns to face Barnes. "Alan. Pick two of your best bricks. Make sure they're happy working with booties, I don't want any interservice cock-ups. You'll be flying out pronto and will rendezvous with HMS *York*, which is currently on APT(N). She's hosting a troop from M squadron SBS under Lieutenant Hewitt, who has signed Section Three and is cleared for level two liaison. The booties are available if you need additional muscle. Your job is to provide backup for Professor O'Brien, who is point on this mission. In case you were worried about BLUE HADES, Professor O'Brien speaks the language and is qualified to liaise. She's also completed her certification in combat epistemology and can operate as your staff philosopher, should circumstances require it. I have complete faith in her abilities to complete the mission and bring Bob back."

Angleton pauses for a moment. Then he adds: "In a real emergency—if HADES cooks off—you've got a hot line of credit with HMS *Vanguard*, although if you have to use a big white one I'm supposed to go to the board and get them to clear it with the Prime Minister first. So let's not go there, shall we?"

Mo looks back and forth between the two spooks. "Would you mind not speaking in slang? I know about Alan's men, but what's a 'big white one'?"

Barnes looks slightly distracted. "It's just a necessary backup precaution—I'll explain later," he assures her. "For now, the main thing is, you'll be operating independently but you'll have backup, starting with my lads and working up through the Royal Navy's North Atlantic Patrol, right to the top if you need it. Unfortunately we're dealing with a really powerful semiotic geas field—Billington's set things up so that we have to play by his rules—and that limits our moves. It would be a really bad mistake for you to come in-frame too soon." He raises an eyebrow at Angleton. "Are we definitely moving into the endgame?"

Angleton shrugs. "It's beginning to look that way." He nods at Mo. "We'd prefer not to have to do it this way, but our hands are unfortunately tied."

Mo frowns. "Wouldn't it make more sense for me to fly out with Alan and his soldiers? I mean, if you're borrowing a warship, why are you bothering with the undercover stuff? What exactly do you expect me to do?"

Barnes snorts and raises an eyebrow at Angleton: "Are you going to tell her, or am I?"

"I'll do it." Angleton picks up the control to the slide projector. "Would you mind switching off the lights?"

"Why the dog and pony show?" O'Brien demands, her voice rising.

"Because you need to understand the trick we're trying to play on the opposition before you can deal the cards. And it's best if I illustrate . . ."

Events have echoes, and almost exactly two weeks earlier, a similar meeting took place on another land mass.

While Bob continues to panic over his impending death by drowning, spare a thought for Ramona. It's not her fault that she's in the fish tank with Bob; quite the opposite. Given even the faintest shred of an excuse, she'd have managed to avoid this briefing in Texas. Unfortunately her controllers are not interested in excuses. They want results. And that's why we join her in the front seat of a Taurus, driving up a dusty unsurfaced lane toward a sun-blasted ranch house in the middle of nowhere.

This is so not Ramona's scene. She's too smart to be a Valley Girl, but she grew up in that part of the world. She's happiest when the bright sunlight is moderated by an onshore breeze and the distant roar of the surf is just crowding the edge of the white noise in her ears: ah, the smell of sagebrush. This part of west Texas, between Sonora and San Angelo, is just way too far inland for Ramona's taste. It's also too . . . Texan. Ramona doesn't care for good ol' boys. She doesn't much like arid, dusty landscapes with no water. And she especially doesn't like the Ranch, but that's not a matter of prejudice so much as common sense.

The Ranch scares her more every time she visits it.

There's a parking lot up front: little more than a patch of packed earth. She pulls up between two unfeasibly large pickups. One of them actually has a cow's skull lashed to the front bumper and a rifle rack in the back. She gets out of the Taurus, collects her shoulder bag and her water bottle—she never comes here without a half-gallon can, minimum—and cringes slightly as the arid heat tries to suck her dry. Walking around the parked vehicles, she doesn't bother to check the cow's skull for the faint matching intaglio of a pentacle: she knows what she'll find. Instead she heads for the porch, and the closed screen door, with a wizened figure rocking in a chair beside it.

"You're five minutes and twenty-nine seconds late," the figure recites laconically as she climbs the front step.

"So bite me," Ramona snaps. She hikes her bag up her shoulder and shivers despite the heat. The guardian watches her with dry amusement. *Dry*. There is no water here, certainly not enough to hydrate the bony nightmare in bib overalls that hangs out next to the door, endlessly rocking its chair.

"You're expected," it rasps. "Go right in."

It makes no move toward her, but the skin on the back of her neck prickles. She takes two steps forward and twists the doorknob. At this point, an unexpected visitor can reasonably be expected to die. At this point, expected visitors also die—if Internal Affairs has issued a termination order. Ramona does not die, this time. The door latch clicks open and she steps inside the cool air-conditioned vestibule, trying to suppress a shuddery breath as she leaves the watcher on the threshold behind.

The vestibule is furnished in cheap G-plan kit, with a sofa and chairs, and a desk with a human receptionist sitting behind it who looks up at Ramona and blinks sheep-eyes at her. "Ms. Random, if you'd care to take the second door on the left, go straight ahead, then take the first right at the end of the corridor. Agent McMurray is expecting you."

Ramona smiles tightly. "Sure thing. Can I use the ladies' room on the way?"

The receptionist makes a show of checking her desk planner. "I can confirm that you are authorized to use the ladies' room," she announces after a few seconds.

"Good." Ramona nods. "See you around." She walks through the second door on the left. It opens onto an anonymous beige-painted corridor, which she walks down for some distance. Partway along, she takes time out to hole up in the toilet. She bends over a wash basin and throws water on her face, her neck, and the base of her throat. She notes that there are no windows in the facility: just ventilation ducts high up in the walls.

Back in the corridor she continues toward its end where there are three identical doors. She pauses outside the one on the right, and knocks.

"Come in," a man's gravelly voice calls through the door.

Ramona opens the door. The room beyond is spacious, floored in rough-cut timber, and walled in glass-fronted cabinets. The door at the far end is open, a staircase leading down to what Ramona knows to be another corridor with more display rooms opening off to either side. She's already far enough inside the ranch house that by rights she should be standing with her feet firmly planted in the dirt fifty feet behind it—outside, but that's not how things work here. Instead, her controlling agent is waiting for her, a tall, slightly pudgy fellow with wire-rimmed glasses, thinning, close-cropped hair, and a checkered shirt. He smiles, faintly indulgently. "Well, well. If it isn't agent Random." He holds out a hand: "How was your trip out?"

"Dry," she says tersely, allowing her hand to be shaken. She squints slightly, sizing McMurray up. He looks human enough, but appearances at the Ranch are always deceptive. "I need to find a pool at some point. Apart from that—" she shrugs "—I can't complain."

"A pool." McMurray nods thoughtfully. "I think we can arrange something for you." His voice has a faint Irish lilt to it, although Ramona is fairly sure he's as American as she is. "It's the least we can do, seeing as how we've dragged you all the way out here. Yes indeed." He gestures at the steps leading down to the passageway. "How well did you understand your briefing?"

Ramona swallows. This bit is hard. As her controlling agent, McMurray has certain powers. He was the key operative who compelled her to service; as long as he lives, he, or whoever holds his tokens of power, has the power of life and death over her, the ability to bind and release her, to issue orders she cannot refuse. There's stuff she doesn't want to talk about—but if he suspects she's holding out on him it'll be a lot worse for her than confessing to everything. Best to give him something, just hope it's not enough to raise more suspicions than it allays: "Not entirely," she admits. "I don't understand why we're letting TLA's chief executive run riot in the Caribbean. I don't understand why the Brits are involved in this, or what the hell TLA think they're doing. I mean—" she pats her shoulder bag "—I read it all, but I don't understand it. Just what's supposed to be going on?"

This is the point at which McMurray can—if he's suspicious—make her mouth open without her willing it, and spill her deepest secrets and most personal hopes and fears. Just considering the possibility makes her feel small and contemptibly weak. But McMurray doesn't seem to notice her discomfort. He nods and looks thoughtful. "I'm not sure anybody knows everything," he says ruefully.            .

A rueful apology? From a controlling agent? *Stop jerking me around*, Ramona prays, a cold knot of fear congealing in her stomach. But McMurray doesn't raise his left hand in a sigil of command; nor does he pronounce any words of dread. He just nods in false amity and gestures once again at the stairs.

"It's a mess," he explains. "Billington's a big campaign donor and word is, we're not supposed to rock the boat. Not under this administration, anyway. It would embarrass certain folks if he were exposed—at least on our soil. And just in case anyone gets any ideas about going around Control's back, he doesn't set foot on land these days. He's got the whole thing set up for remote management from extraterritorial waters. We'd have to send the Coast Guard or the Navy after him, and that would be too public."

"Too public and two bucks will get you a coffee," Ramona says acidly; then, fearful that she might have gone too far, adds: "But why did you need to bring me out here? Is it part of the briefing?"

She realizes too late that this was the wrong thing to say. McMurray fixes her with a penetrating stare. "Why else do you think you might have been ordered to the Ranch?" he asks, deceptively mildly. "Is there something I should know, agent Random?"

A huge fist grips her around the ribs, squeezing gently. "Nuh—no, sir!" she gasps, terrified.

Merely annoying McMurray can have enormous, terrible consequences for her: there's nothing subtle about the degree of control the Black Chamber exercises over its subjects, or the consequences of error. The Chamber has a secret ruling from the Supreme Court that citizenship rights only apply to human beings: Ramona's kin are barely able to pass with the aid of a glamour. For failure, the punishment can be special rendition to jurisdictions where the very concept of pain is considered a fascinating research topic by the natives. But he merely stares at her for a moment with watery blue eyes, then nods very slightly, relaxing the constraint binding. The pressure recedes like the backwash of an imagined cardiac arrest.

"Very good." McMurray turns and begins to descend the staircase at the end of the room. Ramona follows him, eager to get away from the things in the pickle jars behind the glass display panels. "I'm glad to see that you've still got a . . . sense of humor, agent Random. Unfortunately this is no laughing matter." He pauses at the bottom step. "I believe you've been here before."

Ramona's hand tightens on the stair rail until her knuckles turn white. "Yes. Sir."

"Then I won't have to explain." He smiles frighteningly, then walks down the corridor toward one of the display rooms. "I brought you here to see just the one exhibit, this time."

Ramona forces herself to follow him. She feels as if she's walking through molasses, her chest tight with an almost palpable sense of dread. *It's not as if anything here is aimed at me*, she tries to tell herself. *It's all dead, already*. But that's not strictly true.

Most advanced military organizations maintain libraries of weapons, depositories like armories that store one of everything—every handgun, artillery round, mine, grenade, knife—used by any other army that they might face in battle. The exhibits are stored in full working order, with specialist armorers trained in caring for them. Associated with their staff colleges, these depots are a vital resource when training special forces, briefing officers tasked with facing a given enemy, or merely researching future requirements. The Black Chamber is no different: like the Army repository at the Aberdeen Proving Ground, they maintain their own collection. There is a subtle difference, however. The Black Chamber's archive of reality-warping occult countermeasures is partially alive. Here lie unquiet roadside graves dug by ghoulish reanimators. Over there is a cupboard full of mandrakes, next door to a summoning grid that's been live for thirty years, the unquiet corpse of its victim dancing an eternal jig within the green-glowing circle, on legs long since worn down to blood-encrusted ivory stumps.

You can die if you get too close to some of the exhibits in the Ranch. And then they'll add you to the collection.

McMurray knows his way through the corridors and passages of the repository. He threads his way rapidly past doorways opening onto vistas that make Ramona's hair stand on end, then through a gallery lined with glass exhibit cases, some of them covered by protective velvet cloths. Finally he comes to a small side room and stops, beckoning Ramona toward a glass-topped cabinet.

"You asked about Billington," he says, his tone thoughtful.

"Yes, sir."

"You can cut the 'sir' bit; call me Pat." He half-smiles. "As I was saying. Billington's current actions worry the Dark Commissioners. In fact, they're extremely concerned that his motive for purchasing the *Explorer* and moving it to the Bahamas is to make a retrieval attempt on the eastern JENNIFER MORGUE site—that was in your briefing pack, yes? Good. If it turns out that JENNIFER MORGUE is a chthonian artifact, then an attempted retrieval operation could place us—that is, the United States government, not to mention the human species—in breach of the Third Benthic Treaty. That would be a bad place to go. On the other hand, the rewards to be reaped from such an artifact are huge. And your cousins have a very limited presence in the Caribbean. They prefer the deep ocean. It's possible that they're not even aware of the location of the artifact."

McMurray turns to stare at the glass-topped cabinet. "Billington's not doing this for the good of the nation, needless to say. We're not sure just what he plans to do with JENNIFER MORGUE if he gets his hands on it, but frankly, CenCom isn't keen to find out. He needs to be stopped. Which is where we run into an embarrassing problem. He already figured we'd take steps to interdict him, so he's preempted us." He glances at Ramona, and her blood freezes at his expression.

"Sir?"

McMurray gestures at the cabinet. "Look at this."

Ramona peers through the glass warily. She sees a wooden tabletop: perfectly mundane, but for a strange diorama positioned in its center. It seems to consist of a pair of dolls, male and female, wearing wedding clothes; adjacent to them are a pair of engagement rings and a model of a stepped wedding cake. The whole diorama is enclosed within a Möbius-loop design in conductive ink, connected to a breadboard analog-digital converter and an elderly PC.

"This is probably the least dangerous exhibit you'll find here," McMurray says calmly, his momentary anger stilled. "You're looking at a hardware circuit designed to implement a love geas using vodoun protocols and a modified Jellinek-Wirth geometry engine." His finger traces out the Möbius loop below. "Symbolic representations of the entities to be influenced are placed within a geometry engine controlled by a clocked recursive invocation. There are less visible signifiers here—the skin and hair samples, necessary for DNA affinity matching, and concealed within the dolls—but the intent should be obvious. The two individuals linked by this particular grid have been happily married for sixteen years at this point. It's a reinforcing loop; the more the subjects work within the framework, the stronger the feedback frame becomes. The geas itself extends its influence by altering the probability gauge metric associated with the subjects' interactions: outcomes that reinforce the condition are simply rendered more likely to occur while the circuit is operational."

Ramona blinks. "I don't understand."

"Obviously." McMurray steps back, then crosses his arms. "Try to get your head around the fact that it's a contagion spell that generates compliant behavior. This couple, for example, started out hating each other. If you were to destroy this generator, they'd be in divorce court—or one of them would be in a shallow grave—within weeks. Now bear in mind that Billington's cruising around the Caribbean in a huge yacht, plotting some kind of scheme. He isn't stupid. We figure that about six months ago he created a similar hardware-backed geas engine aboard his yacht, the *Mabuse*. The precise nature of the geas is not entirely clear to us, but it has been extremely detrimental to our counterforce operations—in particular, attempts to act against him through normal channels fail. Telex requests dispatched to the Cayman police force via INTERPOL get unaccountably lost, FBI agents develop random brain tumors, associates who might plea-bargain their way to giving evidence wake up embedded in concrete foundations, that sort of thing. CenCom's not convinced, but Sensor Ops believes that Billington has used the geas engine to create a Hero trap—only a single agent conforming to the right archetype can actually approach him; and even then, the geas will screw with their ability to take correct action. And because Billington figured he's got the most reason to be afraid of *us*, he picked a goddamn limey as the Hero archetype."

Ramona shakes her head. "We can't get to him ourselves?"

"I didn't say that." McMurray walks toward the door, then pauses in front of a picture on the wall. "Look."

Ramona stares at the picture. It's a photograph of an oriental longhair cat, reposing on a sofa. The cat is well-groomed and white, but lacks the distinctive pinkish eyes characteristic of albinism. It stares at the camera with haughty disdain.

"I've seen that cat before," she murmurs, chewing her lip. She glances at McMurray: "Is this what I think it is?"

McMurray nods. "It's a show-grade Persian cat, a tom. D'Urbeville Marmeduke the Fourth. Billington acquired this—*pet* is perhaps too loose a word, perhaps *familiar* is closer to the truth—some time ago. Probably when he began planning his current venture. He keeps him aboard the *Mabuse*. Fluffy white cat, yacht cruising around the Caribbean, huge mother ship with a secret undersea module—this geas isn't powered by some goddamn dolls and a wedding ring, agent Random, it's got *legs*. It'd take a miracle for anyone except the Brits to get close to him. One Brit in particular—an agent who doesn't exist." Then he stares at Ramona. "Except we've figured out a loophole, one that'll let us reach out and touch Billington where it hurts. You are going to go in through that loophole, you and me. And you will nail Billington's head to the table to prevent JENNIFER MORGUE Two from falling into the wrong hands.

"Here's how we're going to do it . . ."

Three people sit in a conference room with bricked-up windows in London. The slide projector clunks to an empty slide and Angleton leans over to switch it off. For a minute there's silence, broken only by the emphysemic rasp of Angleton's breathing.

"Bastard." Mo's voice is cold and superficially emotionless.

"We're going to get him back, Mo, I promise you." Barnes's voice is flat and assured.

"But damaged."

Angleton clears his throat.

"I can't believe you did this," she says bitterly.

"We didn't choose to, girl." His voice is a gravelly rasp, hoarse from too many late-night meetings this past week.

"I can't believe you let some snake oil defense contractor get the jump on you. Using it as an excuse. Shit, Angleton, what do you expect me to say? The bait-and-switch you're planning is stupid enough to start with, and you've handed my boyfriend over to a sex vampire and I'm supposed to lie back and think of England? You expect me to tamely pick up the pieces when she's finished banging his brains out and pat him on the head and take him home and patch his ego up? What am I meant to do, turn into some kind of angel-nurse-child-minder figure when all this is over? You've got a fucking nerve!" She's got the violin case by the neck and she's leaning across the table towards Angleton, throwing the words in his face. She's too close to see Barnes staring at her fingers on the neck of the instrument case like it's the barrel of a gun, and he's trying to judge whether she's going to reach for the trigger.

"You're understandably upset—"

"Understandably?" Mo stands up, shifting the case to the crook of her left arm as she toys with the clamp alongside its body. "Fuck you!" she snarls.

Angleton pushes the file across the table at her. "Your tickets."

"Fuck you *and* your tickets!" She's making chicken-choking motions with the fingers of her right hand, the other hand vaguely patting at the body of the violin case. Barnes slides to his feet, backing away, his right hand half-raised to his jacket until he catches Angleton's minute shake of the head. "*And* your fucking grade six geas!" Her voice is firm but congested with emotion. "I'm out of here."

She freezes in place for a moment as if there's something more to say, then grabs the file and storms out of the conference room, slamming the door behind her so hard that the latch fails and it bounces open again. Barnes stares after her; then, seeing the wide eyes and open mouth of the receptionist, he nods politely and pulls the door shut.

"Do you think she'll take the assignment?" he asks Angleton.

"Oh yes." Angleton stares bleakly at the door for a few seconds. "She'll hate us, but she'll do it. She's operating inside the paradigm. In the groove, as Bob would say."

"I was afraid for a minute that I was going to have to take her down. If she lost it completely."

"No." Angleton gathers himself with a visible effort and shakes his head. "She's too smart. She's a lot tougher than you think, otherwise I wouldn't have put her on the spot like that. But don't sit with your back to any doors until this is all over and we've got her calmed down."

Barnes stares at the pitted green desktop. "I could almost pity that Black Chamber agent you've hitched Bob to."

"Those are the rules of the game." Angleton shrugs heavily. "I didn't write them. You can blame Billington, or you can blame the man with the typewriter, but he's been dead for more than forty years. O'Brien's not made of sugar and spice and all things nice. She'll cope." He stares at Barnes bleakly. "She'll have to. Because if she doesn't, we're all in deep shit."

## Chapter 9:
## Skin Diving

**That's interesting,** Ramona says to the pitch darkness as I choke on a throatful of stinging cold saltwater, **I didn't know you could do that. ** My chest is burning and it feels like ice picks are shoving at my eardrums as I begin to thrash around. I can feel my heart pounding like a trip hammer as the fear grips me like a straitjacket. I manage to bang one elbow on the side of the tunnel, a sharp stab of pain amidst the black pressure. ** Stop struggling. **

Slim arms slide around my chest; her heart is hammering as she hugs me to her, pulling my face between her breasts. She drags me down like a mermaid engulfing a drowning sailor and I stiffen, panicking as I begin to exhale. Then we're in a bigger space—I can feel it opening up around me—and suddenly I don't need to breathe anymore. I can feel her/our gills soaking in the cool refreshing water, like air off a spring meadow, and I can feel her borrowed underwater freedom again.

**Where are we?** I ask, shuddering. **What the hell was that?**

**We're right under the platform's central deflection circuit. I figure it throttled our link while we were passing through.**

My eyes are starting to adjust and I can see a diffuse green twilight. A black ceiling squats above us, rough and pitted as I run my fingertips across it: the tunnel is a square opening in the middle of a room-sized dome under the middle of the flat ceiling. Off to the sides I can just about see other black silhouettes, support pillars of some sort that vanish into the murk below. Beyond them, the turbidity speaks of open seas.

**I thought it was poured onto the bottom?**

**Nope. The reef comes to within meters of the surface, but offshore it falls away rapidly; the bottom hereabouts is nearly sixty meters down. They built it on the edge of an undersea cliff and jacked it off the bottom with those pillars.**

**Right, right.** I experiment, pushing off and swimming a little distance away from her until the tightness in my chest begins to return. I can make it to about eight meters out on my own, down here in the penumbra of the coastal defense ward. I turn and drift slowly back towards her. **What was it you were wanting to tell me? Before we got interrupted.**

Her face is a ghostly shade in the twilight. **No time. The bad guys are coming.**

**Bad guys—** I hear a distant churning rumble and look up, out from under the poured concrete ceiling. **Let me see. They've got spear guns?**

**Good guess, monkey-boy. Follow me.** She swims out towards one of the pillars and I follow hastily, afraid of being left behind by our bubble of entangled metabolic processes.

The pillar is as thick as my torso, rough-pored concrete covered with lumpy barnacles and shells and a few weird growths that might be baby corals. Beyond it, the open sea: greenness above us—we must be at least ten meters down—and darkness below. Ramona pulls her knees up and rolls head down, then kicks, spearing into the gloomy depths. I swallow, then turn and clumsily follow her. My inner ear is churning but I can almost fool it into thinking I'm climbing alongside the fat, gray pillar. I feel a bit breathless, but not too bad—all things considered. **Are you doing okay?** I ask.

**I'm okay.** Ramona's inner voice is tense, like she's breathing for two of us.

**Slow down, then.** There's a great beige wall looming behind us in the gloom, bulging closer to the pillar. In the distance I see the streamlined torpedo silhouettes of hunting fishes. **Let's get between the pillar and the cliff face.**

Distant plopping, bubbling noises from above. **Here they come.** Ramona peers up towards the surface.

**C'mon.** The cleft between the pillar and the rock face is about a meter wide at this depth. I swim into it then reach out and take her hand. She drifts towards me, still staring up at the distant sky, as I pull her into the shadow of the pillar. **How long can we hide down here? If they figure we're just skinny-dippers, they may not think to come this deep.**

**No such luck.** She closes her eyes and leans back against me. **Have you ever killed anyone, Bob?**

**Have I ever . . . ?** It depends what you mean by *anyone*. **Only paranormal entities. Does that count?**

**No. Has to be human.** She tenses. **I should have asked earlier.**

**What do you mean, *has* to be human?**

**That's an oversight,** she says tightly. **You were supposed to be blooded.**

**What are you—**

**The geas. You have to kill one of them.** She turns round slowly, her hair swirling around her head like a dark halo. Here we are under twenty meters of seawater and my mouth's gone as dry as the desert. **There are steps you have to carry out in sequence in order to adopt your role in the eigenplot. Jeopardy in a distant city, meet the dark anima, kill one of the other side's assassins—at least one, more would be better—and then we have to figure out a way around my—damn, here they come. We'll have to cover this later. Get ready.**

She shoves something hard into my hand. After a moment's confusion I realize it's the handle of a vicious-looking knife with a serrated edge. Then she vanishes into the shadows lining the cliff face. I glance round as a shadow glides overhead: tracking up and over I see a diver in a wetsuit, head down, peering into the depths.

I pass through a moment of acute disbelief and resentment. I've been in mortal danger before, but I'm not used to being in mortal danger from humans. It feels *wrong*. Any one of Alan's mad bastards is probably capable of whacking half a dozen al Qaeda irregulars before breakfast and not working up an existential sweat, but I'm not prepared for this. I can shoot at targets, sure, and I'm death on wheels when it comes to terminating cases of demonic possession with extreme prejudice, but the idea of killing a real human being in cold blood, some eating breathing sleeping guy with a job on a rich man's yacht, makes all the alarm bells in my head go *tilt*. Trouble is, I also have a deep conviction in my guts that whatever the hell Ramona is on about, she's *right*. I'm here for a purpose, and I've got to move my feet through the occult dance steps in the right sequence or it'll all be for nothing. And it doesn't matter what I want or don't want if Angleton's right and Billington is gearing up to drop the hammer on us. When you come down to it, if there's a war on, the bombs don't care whether they're falling on pacifists or patriots. And speaking of bombs . . .

The diver has seen something. Either that or he's into swimming head down into the depths beside a decaying defense station just for the hell of it. He's heading parallel to the pillar and he's got something in his arms. I glance down and see Ramona below me, her skin a silvery flash like moonlight on ice, circling the pillar. My chest tightens. A stab of anger: **What the hell are you playing at?**

**Hanging my ass out to give you a clear shot.** She sounds lighthearted, but I can tell she's wound up like a watch spring inside. I taste the overspill of her uncertainty: *Is he up to it?* And my blood runs cold, because under the uncertainty, she harbors the rock-solid conviction that, if I'm *not* up to it, we're both going to die.

Outmaneuvered.

The guy above me is turning in tight circles as he descends, keeping an eye open for signs of an ambush as he heads towards Ramona, who is feigning a false sense of security, her back to the outside of the cliff next to the point where the pillar merges with it in a jagged mass of crumpled volcanic rock. I shelter in the cleft between pillar and cliff as he strokes steadily down, hugging the far side of the pillar from Ramona. In his arms he's clutching something that looks like a shotgun, if shotguns had viciously barbed harpoons jutting from their muzzles. *Just great*, I think. What was it Harry the Horse tried to beat into my head? *Never bring a dagger to a harpoon duel*, or something like that.

My luck runs out while he's still about three meters above me, ten meters above Ramona. He slows his corkscrew, peering into the shadowy cleft, and I see a change in his posture. *Shit*. Everything happens in nightmarish slow-mo. I've got my feet braced against the pillar and I let go like a spring, kicking straight up towards him, knife-first. Something sizzles past my shoulder, drawing a hot line across my chest, then I ram him with my shoulder. He's already tumbling out of the way of my knife and I try and bring it back round towards him. I can't breathe—I'm out of range of Ramona's gills—and in a bleak flash of clarity I realize I'm going to die here. The pressure in my chest eases as he takes a swing at me with a knife I sense rather than see, but I'm inside his reach and I grab his forearm and we go tumbling. He's strong but I'm desperate and disoriented and I somehow manage to get my other arm around his neck and something snags my knife. I yank on it as hard as I can, as he tenses his knife arm—we're arm-wrestling at this point—and *something* gives way. He thrashes spasmodically and lets go, kicks towards the surface, and there's a silvery stream of bubbles rising above him that's much too big and bright to be normal.

Ramona's right below me. **Let's go,** she gasps, tugging at my ankle. **Deeper!**

**But I just—**

**I know what you just did! Come on before they do it right back to us! Nobody in their right mind dives alone.** She lets go for a moment, kicks out, and moves her grip to my arm. **Let's move it.** She rolls us round and pulls me away from the pillar, back up towards the murky gloom beneath the defense platform. I feel her fear and let it pull me along behind her, but my mind's not home: I'm not feeling queasy, exactly, but I've got a lot to think about. **We've got to get back to the tunnel,** she says urgently.

**The tunnel? Why?**

**They'll have searched it first. And most divers don't like confined spaces, caves. I figure they'll concentrate on the open waters outside the reef, now they've got the sighting. We just wait them out.**

\*\*In the tunnel.\*\*

*What are we doing here?* I shake my head. *What's it all for?* I keep re-running the video stream captured in my mind's eye, the silvery parabola of bubbles rising above the drowning diver—

\*\*We're missing something important,\*\* Ramona muses darkly.

\*\*How did they find us?\*\*

\*\*Not sure. They've opened a channel to let them bring their minions in, but the core defensive wards are still working, you're cleaner than—\*\* She blinks at me. \*\*Oh. *That's* how.\*\*

The ceiling is right above our heads now, the dome set into it framing the deeper blackness of the tunnel. \*\*What is it?\*\*

\*\*I was wrong about them planting a tracker on you. They don't need to bug you,\*\* she says tersely. \*\*They can find you anywhere. All they have to do is zero in on the eigenplot. Except here, right where you're shielded by the defense platform's wards, even if they have hacked a tunnel right through them to let their associates in . . . \*\*

\*\*What is this eigenplot you keep talking about?\*\* I ask. I'm dangerously close to whining. I *really* hate it when everyone else around me seems to know more about what's going on than I do.

\*\*The geas Billington's running. It's the occult equivalent of a stateful firewall. It keeps out intruders, unless they run through the approach states in a permitted sequence. The sequence is determined by the laws of similarity and contagion, drawing on a particularly powerful source archetype. When you run through them, that's called 'walking the eigenplot,' and you're doing it real well so far. Only a few people can do it at all—you can but I can't, for example—and there's an added catch: You can't do it if you know what the requirements are beforehand, it doesn't permit recursive attacks. That's why you're just going to have to be brave and . . . \*\* she trails off \*\* . . . *shit.* Forget I said that bit. I mean *forget* it. You'll just have to see for yourself.\*\* She centers herself under the pitch-black rectangle of the tunnel mouth. \*\*C'mon.\*\*

\*\*But you said—\*\*

\*\*If we're outside the tunnel we're not shielded. You want to learn how to breathe with a harpoon through you?\*\*

\*\*No way.\*\* I swim closer to her, until we're both right under the mouth. \*\*I nearly drowned last time we went through here.\*\*

\*\*The effect's attenuated only a couple of meters in. Closer. Hug me. Not like that, like this.\*\* She wraps her arms and legs around me. \*\*Think you can swim? Straight up, until you don't feel like you're drowning?\*\*

**Like I'm going to say no?** I look into her eyes from so close that we're almost touching noses. **Okay. Just this once. For you.**

Then I kick off straight up, into the black heart of the drowning zone.

Bands of steel around my chest. A pounding in my ears. Then the clean air of a spring meadow, Ramona's arms cradling me, her legs entwined around me, her lips locked against mine like a lovesick mermaid trying to kiss the drowned sailor back to life—or infuse his blood with oxygen through force of proximity alone.

*Oh.* We're in the tunnel. Totally black, walls either side of me, five meters of water between my head and the heavy iron grating, nothing but delirium's arms holding my sanity together. Distracting me. I *am* distracted. It's incongruous. There are divers out there hunting the waters for us, and here I'm getting an erection. Ramona's tongue, tentacular, searches my lips. She's aroused, I can feel it like an itch at the back of my mind.

**This is a really bad idea,** I overhear her thinking. **We're feeding off each other.** *I'm drowning. I'm horny. I'm drowning. I'm—*feedback. Too far apart and I start to choke, too close together and I start noticing her body, and whichever I'm paying attention to bleeds through into her head. **Got to stop.**

**Tell me about it.** An uneasy thought. **How much of this before the Other notices?**

**It's not ready yet—I think.** She pulls back a few centimeters while I concentrate on not thinking about drowning. **How long do you think we've been down here?**

**I've lost track,** I admit. **Half an hour?** I lean back against the rough wall of the tunnel that shouldn't exist. **Longer?**

**Damn.** I can feel the clockwork of her thoughts, tasting of rusty iron. It's like there's a weird tube of pressure squeezing us together down here; the tunnel is a flaw in the countermeasure wards, but outside it there's an almost unimaginable amount of power chained down and directed towards the exclusion of occult manifestations—like our own entanglement. Threatening to crush us to a bloody paste between walls of concrete. **Can we leave yet?**

**Your breathlessness—have you ever been claustrophobic before?**

*Is that what it is?* **Great time to find out.** I shudder and my heart tries to flutter away.

**We're in as much danger if we stay down here as if we surface,** she announces. **Come on. Slowly.**

Still locked together, we finger-and-toe our way up the narrow chimney in the rock, feeling ahead for rough bumps and the joints between concrete castings. As we rise, the nightmare awareness of my own death begins to fade. All too soon we reach the grating at the top, a cold wall of rusty iron. I tense up and try not to give in to the scream that's bubbling up inside. **Can you lift it?** I ask.

**On my own? Shit.** I feel her straining. **Help me!**

I brace my legs against one wall and my back against the opposite and raise my arms; Ramona leans against me and puts her back into it, too. The roof gives a little. I tense and shove hard, putting all my fear of drowning into it, and the lid squeals and lifts free above us.

**Turn!** I start twisting, rotating the rectangular lid so that when we let go it won't settle back into place. There's a roaring in my ears. I can hear my pulse. And suddenly I'm choking underwater with a lungful of air: we've lost skin contact and I'm going to have aching muscles tomorrow—if there is a tomorrow—and I can't get enough oxygen, so I kick out in near panic and the lid slides away and I kick out again, rising nightmarishly slowly towards the silver ceiling high above me, with my lungs on fire. Then I'm on the surface, bobbing like a cork in a barrel and I breathe out explosively and start to inhale just as a wave comes over the top of the reef and the platform and breaks over me.

The next few seconds are crazy and painful and I'm coughing and spluttering and close to panic again. But Ramona's in the water with me and she's a strong swimmer, and the next thing I know I'm on my back, coughing up my guts as she tows me towards the shallows like a half-drowned kitten. Then there's sand under my feet and an arm round my shoulders.

"Can you walk?"

I try to talk, realize it's a bad idea, and nod instead. A sidelong glance tells me her glamour's back in place.

"Don't look back. There's a dive boat just over the far side of the reef and they're looking out to sea. I figure we've got maybe two minutes before they check their tracker ward and see you're showing up again. Have you got any smoke screens on that fancy phone of yours?"

*Think fast.* I try to remember what I've loaded on it, remember the block I put on the car, and nod again. I'm not certain it'll work, but if it doesn't we're fresh out of options.

"Okay." We're about waist-deep now. "Blanket's over there. Think you can run?"

"Blanket—" I start coughing again.

"Run, monkey-boy!"

She grabs my hand and tugs me forwards. At the same time there's a ghostly sensation in my chest: she starts coughing, but I feel a whole lot better. Moments later I'm the one who's tuggingher along through knee-deep water across a silvery beach, sunlight blazing down on my shoulders. I feel horribly exposed, as if there's a target painted on the small of my back. The towel is just ahead, up a gentle rise. Ramona stumbles. I get an arm round her waist and help her up, then we stagger on up the beach.

Towel. Trunks. A little pile of everyday tourist detritus. "This ours?"

She nods, gasping for breath: she's swallowed my water, I realize. I fumble under the towel and find the sealed polythene bag. Fingers shaking, I unseal it and pull out my Treo. The damn thing seems to take half an hour to boot up, and while I'm waiting for it I see heads bobbing to the surface near the boat on the far side of the reef. They're tiny in the distance but we're running out of time—

*Ah. Scratchpad.* "Lie down on the towel. Make like you're sunbathing," I tell her. Squinting at the tiny screen, I shield it with one hand so that I can see the schematic. A *circuit design, I need a circuit design.* But we're on a beach, right? Sand is porous. And about fifty centimeters below us there's a layer of conductive saline. Which means—

I squat on the sand and start drawing lines on the beach around us with my fingertips. I don't have to go all the way down to the water, I just have to reduce the resistivity of the layer of insulating sand above it in a regular pattern. Divers are crawling back into the boat as I finish the main loop and add the necessary terminals. *Phone, phone . . .* the bloody thing has gone to sleep on me. I'm about to poke at the screen when I realize there's sand on my fingertips. *Silly me.* I wipe them on the towel beside Ramona's hip and carefully wake the Treo up, stroke it into life, and hit the upload button. Then I sit down next to her and wait to learn if I've rendered us invisible.

About half an hour later, the divers give up. The boat turns, its outboard engine spouting a tail of white foam, and it slowly motors around the headland. Which is just as well because we don't have any sunscreen and my shoulders and chest are beginning to itch badly.

"You okay?" I ask Ramona.

"Pretty much." She sits up and stretches. "Your trick worked."

"Yeah, well. Trouble is, it's stationary: I can't take it with us. I figure our best bet would be to head back into town as fast as possible and lose ourselves in the crowd."

"You *really* got them stirred up. And their surveillance net is disturbingly good." She looks at me. "You're sure it was just Marc you were pushing on?"

"Yes." I look at her closely. "Marc, and his unfortunate habit of supplying single female tourists to friends with a boat and an unlimited supply of Charlie." Her expression doesn't change but her pupils tell me what I want to know. "Virgins aren't necessary, if this is what I think it is. But they have to be healthy and relatively young. Ring any bells?"

"I didn't know you were a necromancer, Bob." She looks at me calculatingly.

"I'm not." I shrug. "But I do countermeasures. And what I see here is that the island's defenses aren't worth jack shit if you've got a scuba kit and a boat. Someone's buying up single women, and they're sure as hell not shipping them to brothels in Miami. There's a surveillance net centered on Billington's boat, and it's tied in to your friend Marc." I stare at her eyes. "Are you going to tell me it's a coincidence?"

She bites her lower lip. "No," she admits. A pause. "Marc wasn't a coincidence."

"What, then?"

"It centers on Billington but it's not all about Billington." She looks away from me and stares out to sea, morosely. "He's got his own . . . plans. To expedite them, he had to hire a bunch of specialists with eccentric tastes and needs. His wife—she's not harmless. She's *scum*." If looks could kill, the wave crests would be boiling into steam under her stare. "And she's got retainers. Call it a tactical marriage of convenience. She's got certain powers and he wants to make use of them. He's got shitloads of wealth and more ambition than—well, she likes that because it buys her immunity. Eileen . . . her predecessor Erzabet was probably framed by a rival, a duke who wanted her lands and her castle, but Eileen is the genius who figured out there was a skincare program in the old legend, productized the hell out of it, and sold it as Bathory™ Pale Grace™[9] Cosmetics, with added ErythroComplex-V. It's basically a mass-produced level one glamour. She sources most of the wholesale supplies from commercial slaughterhouses and leftover blood bank stock, and on paper she's clean, but you still need a better than homeopathic quantity of the real thing to make it work. And that's before you start asking how many regulatory committees she had to buy off to bury the details of her research."

"Why not go after her directly?"

"Because—" Ramona shrugs. "Eileen's not the main target. She's not even the appetizer. What she does amounts to at most a few dozen

---

[9] Pale Grace™, Pale Grace™ Skin Hydromax®, Pale Grace™ Bright Eyes®, and Pale Grace™ Number Three® [reference footnote 13] are registered trademarks of Bathory™ Cosmetics Corporation: "It'd better be bloody worth it at this price."

deaths per year. If Ellis gets what my boss thinks he wants, the whole human species gets to deal with the fallout. So he figured I should get close to Eileen—to introduce you to Ellis, as much as anything else—and meanwhile get enough of a grip on the rest of her project to mop them up afterward."

"You were going to get information out of Marc after your Other got through chowing down on his soul?"

"You'd be surprised." She sniffs primly. "Anyway, you should know, mister computational demonologist: How hard would it be to summon up a puppeteer and schedule a late-binding, voice-directed linkage to keep the body dancing?"

I think back to the dead seagulls. To the bad guys and what they did to Marc after his fatal heart attack. "Not very."

"Okay, just so you know the score." She reaches out and grasps my wrist. Her fingers are warm and much too human.

"Billington's plans," I prompt. "The business with the *Explorer*."

"I'm not allowed to tell you everything I know," she says patiently. "If you know too much, his geas will spit you out like a melon seed and we won't have any time to prep a replacement."

"But you need me to get aboard his ship because I'm playing a role in some sort of script. While you stay entangled with me so you get to come along, too." I swallow. "Punching a hole in his firewall."

"That's the idea."

"Any idea how to do it?"

"Well—" a hint of a smile "—Billington usually visits the casino every evening when he's in range. So I'd say we ought to get back to the hotel and get ready for a high-rolling evening, and try to finesse an invitation. How does that sound?"

I stand up. "That sounds like a plan," I say doubtfully. "I expected something a bit more concrete, though." I glance around. "Where did I put my boxers?"

We head back up the beach and when we get to the car Ramona hands me my clothes. By the time I get out of the toilet she's changed into a white sundress, head scarf, and shades that conceal her eyes. She's unrecognizable as the naked blonde from the beach. "Let's go," she suggests, turning the ignition key. I belt in beside her and she guns the engine, backing out of the parking lot in a spray of sand.

Ramona drives carefully along the coast road, back towards the west end of the island and the hotels and casinos. I slump down in the passenger seat and check my email as soon as we get adequate cellphone coverage. All that's waiting for me are two administrative circulars from the office, an almost plaintive request for a Sitrep from Angleton, and an interesting business proposition from the widow of the former president of Nigeria[10]. Ramona doesn't seem to be in a talkative mood right now, and I'm not sure I want to risk upsetting her by asking why.

Eventually, as we're entering Philipsburg, she nods to herself and begins talking. "You'll want to report in to your support team." She downshifts a gear and the engine growls. "Keep your station chief off your back, pick up the toys your tech guys have been unpacking, and call home."

"Yes. So?" I study the roadside. Pedestrians in bright summer holiday gear, locals in casuals, rickshaws, parked cars. Heat and dust.

"Just saying." We're crawling along. "Then I figure we need to meet up, late afternoon. To go sort out your invitation to the floating party aboard the *Mabuse*."

Late afternoon. A stab of guilt gets to me: it's about six o'clock back home, and I really ought to call Mo. I've got to reassure her that everything's under control and make sure she doesn't do something stupid like drop everything and come out here. (*Assuming everything* is *under control*, a quiet corner of my conscience reminds me. *If you were Mo, and you knew what was going on, what would you do?*) "You sound very certain that I'll get an invite," I speculate.

"Oh, I don't think it'll be too difficult." Ramona focuses on the road ahead. "You already got Billington's attention yesterday. After today, he'll want another look at you." She looks pensive. "Just in case, I've got some ideas. We can go over them later."

I steel myself. "I get the feeling you're trying very hard not to tell me something that's not related to the mission," I begin. "And you know I know but I don't know what I'm not supposed to know, and so—" I wind down, trying to keep track of all the double-indirect pointers and Boolean operators before I succumb to a stack crash.

"Not your problem, monkey-boy," she says with a false smile and a toss of her beautiful blonde hair, now coiling up into tight ringlets as the seawater dries in the breeze over the windscreen. "Don't worry yourself about me."

"What—" My skin crawls.

She looks at me, her eyes abruptly distant and hard. "You just have to get aboard the yacht, figure out what's going on, and expedite a solution," she tells me. "I've got to sit it out back here."

---

[10] I briefly consider replying to the latter in the person of a highly placed agent of a secret British government agency, but the last time I did that Tony from Internal Security called me into his office and waxed sarcastic for almost half an hour before ordering me to give them back their bank.

"But." I shut my mouth before I can stick any of my feet in it by accident. Then I point my head forwards, watching her out of the corner of my eye. Thin-lipped and grim-faced, knuckles gripping the steering wheel. The mermaid who clutched me to her watery bosom is frightened. Ramona, who plays with her food and never slept with a man who didn't die within twenty-four hours, is concerned. Driving me back to the hotel and the safe house and a setup where she'll have to hand me over to people she seems to despise—*Ramona, the spy who loves me?* No, that dog won't hunt. It must be something else, but whatever it is, she isn't talking. So we drive the rest of the way to the hotel in lonely silence, grappling with our respective demons.

## Chapter 10:
## Dead Lucky

When I get back to my hotel room I find Boris pacing the carpet like a trapped tiger. "What time you are naming this?" he asks, tapping his heavy stainless steel wristwatch. "Am being on edge of calling in Code Red on you!"

Pinky has plugged a PlayStation into the TV set and is making zooming sounds, bouncing up and down on the bed; and from the sounds leaking under the bathroom door Brains is testing a radio-controlled hovercraft in the shower.

"I've been running some errands," I say tiredly. "And then I went swimming."

"Swimming?" Boris shakes his head. "Am not enquiring. Are giving Angleton the Sitrep yet?"

"Oops. My bad." I pull out the desk chair and slump into it. My forearms and thighs are aching in unaccustomed places: I'm going to feel like shit tomorrow. "How did you get in here?"

Pinky saves his game and looks round. "Picked the lock," he says, waving what looks suspiciously like a hotel card key at me.

"You picked." I stare at it. "The lock."

"Yup." He flips it at me and I catch it. "It's a smartcard, got an induction loop instead of the usual dumb mag stripe on the back. Guaranteed to run through the complete list of makers' override keys in under twenty seconds."

"Right." I put it down carefully.

"Hey, I'll want it back in a minute—where'd you think I saved my game?"

Boris snorts, then stares at me. "Report, Bob, now."

"Okay." I cross my arms. "When I left this morning, I thought I'd check out a hunch. I found out the hard way that Billington's got a total surveillance lockdown on the French Cul de Sac north of Paradise Peak. Dead birds on Anse Marcel, seagulls everywhere. His people are running zombies. Human ones, too." Boris looks like he's about to interrupt, but I keep on talking: "I had a run-in with one of them. Ramona helped me get out of it, and we lost them by going swimming close to the island defense chain. Which has been tampered with, incidentally, compromising the three-mile offshore thaumaturgic-exclusion zone—did you know that? Ramona says her sources say Billington's going to be back at the casino tonight, so we made a date. How does that fit with your plans?"

When I finish Boris nods. "Is making progress. Please to be continuing it." He turns to Pinky: "Get Brains." To me: "Am authorizing contact tonight. These two are being explain gizmos for self-defense. Call me later." And he leaves, just as there's a loud toilet-flushing sound and Brains comes out of the bathroom.

"Okay," I say, pointing at the half-inflated, bright yellow life belt hanging round his waist. "What's that about? And do I want to know?"

"Just testing." Brains pushes it down around his feet then steps out of it. "Can I have your dress shoes, please?"

"My shoes?" I bend down and rummage for them in my luggage. They're horrible things, shiny patent leather with soles that feel like lumps of wood. "What do you want them for?"

Pinky is doing something to the PlayStation. "This." He flourishes another smartcard, which Brains takes and slides into a hitherto invisible seam in the leather tongue of my right shoe.

"And this," Brains says, holding up a shoelace.

"That's a—"

"Miniature 100BaseT cable. Pay attention, Bob, you don't want to lose your network connectivity, do you? It goes in like *this* and to activate it you twist and pull like *that*; it uncoils to three meters and the plastic caps expand to fit any standard network socket. It doubles as a field-expedient grounding strap, too. That's right. No, you don't want to tie your shoelaces too tight."

I try to stifle a groan. "Guys, is this really necessary? Does it help me do the job?"

Pinky cocks his head to one side. "Predictive Branch says there's a ten percent chance of you failing on the job and dying horribly if you don't take it." He giggles. "Feeling lucky, punk?"

"Bah. What do I really need to know?"

"Here." Brains tosses a stainless steel Zippo lighter to me: "It's an antique, don't lose it. Predictive Branch said it would come in handy."

"I don't smoke. What else?"

"The usual stuff: There's a USB memory drive preloaded with a forensic intrusion kit hidden in each end of your dickey-bow, a WiFi-finder on your key ring, a roll-up keyboard in your cummerbund, the pen's got Bluetooth and doubles as a mouse, and there's a miniaturized Tillinghast resonator in your left heel. You turn it on by twisting the heel through one-eighty degrees; turn it off the same way. Your other heel is just a heel: We were going to hide a Basilisk gun in it but some ass-hat in Export Controls vetoed our requisition because it was going overseas.

Oh, and there's this." Brains reaches over to a briefcase on the bed and pulls out a businesslike nylon shoulder holster and a black automatic pistol. "Walther P99, 9mm caliber, fifteen-round magazine, silvercap hollow-points engraved with a demicyclic banishment circuit in ninety nanometerEnochian."

"Banishment rounds?" I ask hesitantly, then: "Hang on." I hold up one hand: "I'm not cleared for carrying guns in the field!"

"We figured the exorcism payload means it's covered by your occult weapons certification. If anyone asks, it's just a gadget for installing exorcism glyphs at high speed." Brains sits down on the bed, ejects the magazine, works the action to make sure there's no round in the chamber, then starts stripping it down. "Word from Angleton is the bad guys are likely to get heavy and he wants you carrying."

"Oh my." I blank for a moment. It's only about an hour since I sliced some poor bastard's air hose in half, and having to deal with this so soon afterwards is doing my head in. "Did he really say that?"

"Yes. We don't want to end up losing you by accident because someone starts shooting and you're unarmed, do we?"

"I guess not." He passes the shoulder holster to me and I try to figure out how it goes on. "Well, if you're all done now, maybe you could leave so I can phone home?"

After Pinky and Brains leave, I call down to room service for a light lunch, put the door chain on, then go run a bath. There's a wet suit hanging over the shower rail and an oxygen tank leaning up against the toilet. While the bath's filling I try phoning home, but get the answering machine. I try Mo's mobile, but that's switched off, too. She must still be in Dunwich under lockdown. Feeling sorry for myself, I go and rinse the salt off my skin: but I can't hang around in the bath without thinking of Ramona, and that's not a healthy sign either. I'm confused about her, I feel guilty whenever I think about Mo, and the smell of saltwater brings back that frightening slow-motion underwater tumble, knife in hand. This isn't me: I'm just not the cold-blooded killer type. When shit needs kicking and throats need slitting we send in Alan's goon squad. I'm supposed to be the quiet geek who sits at the back of the computer lab, right?

Except I signed my name on the line a few years ago, right below the paragraph that said I accepted the Crown's commission to go forth and perpetrate mayhem in the defense of the realm, as lawfully directed and commanded by my designated superiors. And while most of the time it's trivial shit—like breaking into an office and leaving evidence to shitcan some poor bastard who's stumbled too close to the truth—there's nothing there that says I'm *not* required to wrestle killers in wet suits or molest alien monsters. Quite the contrary, in fact. I don't have a license to kill, but I don't have orders *not* to kill in the course of my duties, either. Which realization I find extremely disturbing; it's like the sensation in your stomach the first time you get into a car after getting your driving license, when you suddenly realize there's no instructor in the seat next to you and *this is not a test.*

I wrap myself in a bath sheet and go back out into the bedroom. It's about one in the afternoon and I've got a few hours to kill before Ramona is due back. Lunch shows up and is as blandly tasteless as usual—I swear that there's a force field in the hotel dimensions that sucks the flavor out of food. I badly want something that'll distract me from pursuing this morbid introspection. Pinky left the PlayStation behind, so I plop myself down in front of the TV, pick up the controller, and poke at it in a desultory sort of way. Candy-bright graphics and a splash screen flicker by as the machine clunks and whirs, loading; then it launches a road race game, in which I'm driving a variety of cars along winding roads around a jungle-covered island while zombies shoot at me. "Arse," I mutter, and switch off in disgust. I check that my tablet PC is plugged into all the wards correctly, then draw the curtains and lie down on the bed for a short nap.

I'm awakened what feels like a split second later by a banging on the door. "Hey, monkey-boy! Rise and shine!"

*Jesus.* I've been asleep for hours. "Ramona?" I stand up and stagger towards the vestibule. My upper thighs and forearms ache as if I've been beaten—must be the swimming. I draw the chain and open the door.

"Had a good nap?" She raises an eyebrow at me.

"Got to get—" I pause. "Dressed." *Damn, I haven't phoned Mo,* I realize. Ramona is looking like about a million dollars, in a blue evening dress that clings to her improbably well—it seems to be held on with double-sided sticky tape. There's several meters of pearl rope wound into her hair: she must have found a handy time warp for the make-up crew to have had time to get her ready for the fashion photo-shoot. Meanwhile, I'm wearing yesterday's underpants and I feel like I've been run over by a train.

"You're running late," she says, pushing past me; one nostril wrinkles aristocratically as she surveys the wreckage. She bends over a large carrier bag with the logo of that goddamned tailor on it: "Here, catch."

I find myself clutching a pair of boxer shorts. "Okay, I get the message. Give me a minute?"

"Take ten," she says, "I'll go powder my nose." Then she disappears into the bathroom.

I groan and retrieve my tuxedo from the leg-well of the desk. There's a fresh shirt in the bag, and I manage to install myself in it without too much trouble. I leave the goddamn squeaky shoes for last. Then I have a mild anxiety attack when I realize I've forgotten the shoulder holster. *Should I or shouldn't I?* I'll probably end up shooting myself in the foot. In the end I compromise—I've still got Ramona's phonegun, so I'll carry that in one pocket. "I'm ready," I call.

"I'll bet." She comes out of the bathroom, adjusting her evening bag, and smiles brilliantly. Her smile fades. "Where's your gun?"

I pat my jacket pocket.

"No, no, not that one." She reaches in and removes the phonegun, then gestures at the shoulder holster: "*That* one."

"Must I?" I try not to whine.

"Yes, you must." I shrug out of my jacket and Ramona helps me into the shoulder rig. Then she straightens my bow tie. "That's more like it. We'll have you attending diplomatic cocktail parties in no time!"

"That's what I'm afraid of," I grumble. "Okay, where now?"

"Back to the casino. Eileen's throwing a little party in the *petit salle*, and I've got us tickets. Seafood canapés and crappy lounge music with a little gambling thrown in. Plus the usual sex and drugs rich people indulge in when they get bored with throwing their money away. She's using the party to reward some of her best sales agents and do a little quiet negotiating on the side. I gather she's got a new supplier to talk to. Ellis won't be there at first, but I figure if we can get you an invitation onto the ship . . . ?"

"Okay," I agree. "Anything else?"

"Yes." Ramona pauses in the doorway. Her eyes seem very large and dark. I can't look away from them because I know what's coming: "Bob, I don't, I don't want to—" She reaches for my hand, then shakes her head. "Ignore me. I'm a fool."

I keep hold of her hand. She tries to pull away. "I don't believe you," I say. My heart is beating very hard. "You do, don't you?"

She looks me in the eye. "Yes," she admits. Her eyes are glistening, and in this light I can't tell whether it's cosmetics or tears. "But we mustn't."

I manage to nod. "You're right." The words feel very heavy to me, to both of us. I can feel her need, a physical hunger for an intimacy she hasn't allowed herself to indulge in years. It's not sex, it's something more. *Oh what a lovely mess!* She's been a solitary predator for so long that she doesn't know what to do with somebody she doesn't want to kill and eat. I feel ill with emotional indigestion: I don't think I've ever felt for Mo the kind of raw, priapic lust I feel for Ramona, but Ramona is a poisonous bloom—off-limits if I value my life.

She closes the gap between us, wraps her arms around me, and pulls me against her. She kisses me on the mouth so hard that it makes my hair stand on end. Then she lets go of me, steps back, and smoothes her dress down. "I'd better not do that ever again," she says thoughtfully. "For both our sakes: it's too risky." Then she takes a deep breath and offers me her arm. "Shall we go to the casino?"

The night is young. It's just beginning to get dark, and some time while I was sleeping there was a brief deluge of rain. It's cut the baking daytime heat down a few notches, but steam is rising from the sidewalk in thin wisps and the humidity setting is somewhere between "Amazonian" and "crash dive with the torpedo tubes open." We stroll past a few street vendors and a bunch of good-time folks, under awnings with bright lights and loud noises. The brightly painted gazebos in front of the restaurants are all full, drowning out the creaking insect life with loud chatter.

We arrive at the casino entrance and I nod at the unfamiliar doorman. "Private party," I say.

"Ah. If monsieur et madame would come this way . . . ?" He backs into the foyer and directs us towards a nondescript staircase. "Your card, sir?"

Ramona nudges me discreetly and I feel her slide something into my hand. I flip it round and pass it to the doorman. "Here." He scrutinizes it briefly, then nods and waves us upstairs.

"What was that?" I ask Ramona as we climb.

"Invitation to Eileen's little recreation." It's all polished brass and rich, dark mahogany here. Deeply tedious landscape paintings in antique frames dot the walls, and the lights are dim. Ramona frowns minutely as we reach the landing: "Under our own names, of course."

"Right. Do the names signify?"

She shrugs. "Probably, on some database somewhere. They're not stupid, Bob."

I offer her my arm and we walk down the wide hallway towards the open double-doors. Beyond them I can hear the clink of glassware and voices raised in conversation, layered above a hotel jazz quartet mangling something famous.

The crowd here feels very different to the gamblers in the public areas of the casino downstairs, and I instantly feel slightly out of place. There are dozens of women in their thirties and forties, turned out in an overly formal parody of office wear. They have a curious uniformity of expression, as if the skin of their faces has been replaced with blemish-resistant polymer coating, and they're pecking at finger food and networking with the perky ferocity of a piranha school on Prozac; it's like the Stepford Business School opening day, and Ramona and I have wandered in by mistake from the International Capitalist Conspiracy meeting next door. I briefly wonder if anyone's going to ask us to announce the winners of the prize for most cutthroat business development plan of the year. But past the buffet I spot another set of open double-doors; at a guess the ICC meeting's going to be through there, along with the roulette wheels and the free bar.

**I'm going to go say 'hi' to our hostess,** Ramona tells me. **See you in a couple of minutes?**

I can tell when I'm not needed. **Sure,** I say. **Want me to get you a drink?**

**I'll handle it from here.** She smiles at me then opens her mouth and gushes, "Isn't this wonderful, Bob? Be a dear and circulate while I go powder my nose. I'll just be a sec!" Then she's off, carving a groove through the little black dresses and plastic smiles.

I shrug philosophically, spot the bar, and go over to it. The bartender is busily pouring glass after glass of cheap, fizzy white plonk, and it takes me a while to catch his eye. "Service over here?"

"Sure. What do you want?"

"I'll—" a thousand fragments of half-grasped TV movies take control of my larynx "—can you make it a dry martini? Shaken, not stirred."

"Heh." He looks amused. "You're not the first guy who's asked me that." He grabs a cocktail shaker and reaches for the gin, and in just a matter of seconds he's handing me a conical glass full of clear, oily liquid with a pickled sheep's eyeball at the bottom. I sniff it cautiously. It smells of jet fuel.

"Thanks, I think." Holding it at arm's length I turn away from the bar and nearly dump it all over a woman in a severe black suit and heavy-framed spectacles. "Oops, I'm sorry."

"Don't mention it." She doesn't smile. "Mr. Howard? Of Capital Laundry Services?" She pronounces my name as if she's getting ready to serve a writ.

"Um, yes. You are . . . ?"

"Liza Sloat, of Spleen, Sloat, and Partners." Her cheek twitches in something that might be a smile, or just neuralgia. "We have the privilege of handling the Billingtons' personal accounts. I believe we nearly met yesterday."

"We did?" Suddenly I remember where I know her from. She's the lawyer who was dogging Billington's footsteps, the one with the briefcase who went to see the casino president. I smile. "Yes, I remember now. To what do I owe the pleasure?"

The twitch turns into a genuine smile, albeit about as warm as liquid nitrogen. "Mr. Billington is running late today. He'll be along later in the evening, and meanwhile you're to make yourself at home." The smile slides away, replaced by a stare so coldly calculating that I shiver. "That is his prerogative. Personally, I think he is a little too trusting. You're rather young for a bidding agent in this auction." The smile reappears. "You might want to remind your employers of our history of successful litigation against individuals, organizations, and entities that try to interfere with the smooth running of our legitimate commercial operations. Good day."

She turns on one spiked black heel and clicks back in the direction of the inner room. *What the hell was that about?* I wonder, unwisely taking a mouthful from my glass. I manage not to spew it everywhere, but it tastes even worse than it smelled: pure essence of turpentine with a finish of cheap gin and a tangy undernote of kerosene. "Gah." I swallow convulsively, wait for the steam to stop trickling out of my nose, and go looking for a potted plant that appears hardy enough to survive being irrigated with the stuff.

The salon next door is thickly carpeted, and curtained like an upmarket whorehouse in a movie about *fin-de-siècle* Paris. Most of the folks here are clustered around the gaming tables and while some of the ladies from Pale Grace™ Cosmetics have wandered in, it looks to be mostly Billington's court of *louche* shareholders and their anorexic, artistically inclined, fashion-model fuck-bunnies. I'm moving towards the baccarat table when one of the younger and pushier sales associates appears in front of me, smiles ingratiatingly, and holds out her hand. "Hi! I'm Kitty. Isn't it great to be here?"

I squint at her from behind my regrettably full glass, then raise an eyebrow. "I suppose it is," I concede, "for some values of 'great.' Do I know you?"

Kitty stares at me, freezing like a rabbit in the headlights of an oncoming juggernaut. She's blonde, her hair lacquered into place like the glass fiber weave of a crash helmet awaiting the resin spray: she's pretty in a mascara'd and lip-glossed kind of way. "Aren't you, uh, really famous or something?" she stammers. "Mrs. Billington always invites famous speakers to these events—"

I force myself to smile benevolently. "That's okay, I don't mind you not recognizing me." I take a sip of the martini: it's revolting but it's got alcohol in it, so it can't be all bad. "It's rather refreshing, actually, being a nobody who people overlook all the time." Kitty smiles uncertainly, as if she's not sure whether I'm deploying irony or something equally exotic. "What brings you here, Kitty?" I ask, putting on my sincerest expression.

"I'm Busy Bee Number One for the Minnesota sales region! I mean, I have a really great team and they're amazingly great workers but it's such an honor, don't you think? And only last year we were sixty-second out of seventy-four regional teams! But I figured my girls just needed something to shoot for so I gave them new targets and a new promotional pricing structure with discount incentivization and it worked like crazy!" She half-covers her mouth: "And the viral marketing thing, too, but that's something else. But it was my worker bees who did it all, really! There are no drones in *my* hive!"

"That's, uh, truly excellent," I say, nodding. A thought strikes me: "What particular products are doing well at the moment? I mean, is there anything special that's responsible for your sales growth?"

"Oh, well, you know we've tracked the vertical segmentation of our region and different hives have different merchandise footprints, but you know something? It's the same everywhere, the Pale Grace™ Skin Hydromax® cream is, you know, walking off the shelves!"

"Hmm." I try to look thoughtful, which isn't difficult: *How the hell do you package a glamour in an ointment pot?* I shake my head in admiration and take another sip of drain cleaner. "That's really good to know. Maybe I should use it myself?"

"Oh, of course you should! Here, take my card; I'd be happy to set you up with a range of free samples and an initial consultation." Her card isn't just a piece of cardboard, it's a scratch 'n' sniff sample as complex as a Swiss Card survival tool—I manage to slide it into my pocket without getting any of the stuff on my skin. Kitty gushes in my direction, her eyes lighting up as she moves into the standard sales script, her voice softening and lowering with a compelling sincerity that is at odds with her natural bubbly extroversion: "The ErythroComplex-V in the Pale Grace™ Skin Hydromax® range is clinically proven to reverse ageing-induced cytoplasmic damage to the skin and nail cuticles. Just one application begins to undo the ravages of free radicals and enhance the body's natural production of antioxidants and cytochrome polyesterase inhibitors. *And* it's so creamy smooth! We make it with one hundred percent natural ingredients, unlike some of our competitors . . ."

I slip away while she's reciting her programmed spiel, and she doesn't even notice as I sidle up to a potted palm and take a last reflective mouthful of dry martini. My wards blipped slightly as her script kicked in, but that doesn't have to mean she's a robot, does it? *We make it with one hundred percent natural ingredients,* like the bottom tenth percentile of our sales force, the ones who don't get invited to this end of the marketing conference by the Queen Bee. Maybe Kitty's just a natural void, only too happy to be filled by the passing enthusiasm of the traveling salesman invocation, but somehow I doubt it: that kind of perfect vacuum doesn't come cheap.

I scuff my left heel on the ground. If I switched it on, the Tillinghast resonator that Brains installed in my shoe would let me see the sales-daemon riding her spine like a grotesquely bloated digger wasp, but I'd just as soon keep my lunch—and anyway the first law of demonology is that if you can see it, *it* can see *you*. But the small of my back itches as I glance round at the overdressed hedonists and the scarily neat saleswomen because I'm putting together a picture here that I really don't like: dinner jacket or no, I'm underdressed for the occasion, although Ramona fits right in.

While I'm having these grim thoughts, I notice that my martini glass is nearly empty. It's not a terribly endearing drink—it tastes like something that got hosed off a runway, then diluted with antifreeze—but it does what it says on the label. I've got a nasty feeling I'm going to need plenty of Dutch courage to get through this evening. What that horrible lawyer-creature Sloat was saying is sinking in: This is either a cover or a warm-up for some sort of auction, isn't it? Maybe Billington is planning on selling whatever he dredges up from JENNIFER MORGUE Site Two to the highest bidder. That would make plenty of sense and it'd explain why the Black Chamber and the Laundry are both riled up about it, but I can't shake the feeling that this isn't the whole story: What was the business with Marc all about? Assuming it's connected. Maybe Ramona knows something she'd be willing to share with me.

I shake my head and look around. I don't see her among the glitterati at the gaming tables, but there are enough people here that she could have wandered off. **You there?** I ask silently, but she isn't answering and I can't sense what she's doing. It's as if she's figured out how to draw a thick blackout curtain around her mind, keeping me out when she doesn't want me around. *That'd be a neat skill to have,* I think, then mentally kick myself. What one of us can do the other can learn really fast. I'll just have to ask her how she does it whenever she comes out of hiding. At least she's not in trouble, I guess; given the nature of our link, I'm certain I'd know if she was.

I circulate back towards the bar in the other room and plant my glass on it, then turn round to see if I can spot either of the Billingtons among the happy-clappy flock of saleswomen: Ellis may be delayed but I can't see his wife throwing a revival-style party for her faithful without circulating to stroke her flock. "Another of the same?" murmurs the barman, and before I can make up my mind to say "no" he's fished out a glass and is pouring gin with a soup ladle. I nod at him and take it, then head back towards the gaming tables in the back room. I'm not going to drink it, I decide, but maybe if I keep it in my hand it'll stop anyone from trying to refill the bloody glass again.

The crowd near the tables is noisy and they're smoking and drinking like there's no tomorrow. I strain to see what's going on over a gaggle of sericulture-vultures with big hair. It's a baccarat table and from the disorganization there it looks like a game's just ended. Half a dozen of Billington's crowd are moving in while an old fart who looks like a merchant banker leans back in his chair, sipping a glass of port.

"Ah, Mr. Howard I believe." I nearly jump out of my skin before I recall that I'm supposed to be suave and sophisticated, or at least gin-pickled to the point of insensibility. "Care for a game?"

I glance round. I vaguely recognize the guy who knows my name. He's in early middle-age, crew cut, solidly built, and he fills his tuxedo with an avuncular bonhomie that I instinctively mistrust; he reminds me of the sort of executive who can fire six thousand people before lunch and go to a charity fundraiser the same evening with his sense of self-righteousness entitlement undented. "I'm not much of a gambler," I murmur.

"That's okay, all I ask is that you're a good loser." He grins, baring a perfect row of teeth at me. "I'm Pat, by the way. Pat McMurray. I consult on security issues for Mr. Billington. That's how I know about you."

"Right." I nod as I give him the hairy eyeball. He winks at me slowly, then tugs his left ear lobe. He's wearing an earring that looks a lot like a symbol I see most days at the office on my way past the secure documents store in Dansey House. This isn't in the script: *Security consultants who've been briefed on me? Gulp.* I try to feel what Ramona's doing again, but no luck. She's still got that blackout curtain up. "What kind of security issues do you consult on?" I ask.

"Well, you know, that's a good question." He points at my glass. "Why are you drinking that garbage when there's perfectly good liquor behind the bar?"

I stare at it. "It just sort of slipped into my hand."

"Heh. You come over to the bar and we'll get you a real man's drink. One that doesn't taste like drain cleaner." He turns and heads for the bar in complete certainty that I'll follow him, so I do. The bastard knows I need to know what he knows and he knows I can't say no. He leans on the bar and announces: "Two double tequila slammers on the rocks." Then he turns to me and raises an eyebrow. "You're wondering what I do here, aren't you?"

"Um." Well, yes.

He must take it as agreement, because he nods encouragingly. "Ellis Billington's a big guy, you've got to know that. Big guys tend to pick up parasites. That's nothing new. Trouble is, what Ellis picks up is a different class of bloodsucker. See, you know who his company subcontracts for: this makes him a target for people who don't want just his money, they want a piece of *him*. So he hires specialist talent to keep them at arm's reach. Mostly ex-employees of you-know-who, plus a few freelancers." He taps his chest. The bartender sets two glasses down in front of us; crystals frost their edges and they're full of a colorless, slightly oily liquid, along with a slice of lemon. "C'mon. Back to the table, bring your glass. Let's play a round."

"But I don't gamble—" I begin, and he stops dead.

"You'll gamble and like it, son. Or Ellis Billington ain't going to make time for you."

*Huh?* I blink. The brown envelope labeled EXPENSES feels extremely hot and as heavy as a gold brick in my breast pocket. "Why?"

"Could be that he don't approve of limp-dicked limeys," McMurray mugs. "Or could be it's all part of the script. Besides, you'll enjoy it, you know you will. Go on, over to the cashier. Get yourself chipped up."

Moments later I'm swapping the contents of the envelope for a pile of plastic counters. Black, red, white: six months' salary gone to plastic. My mind's spinning like a hamster wheel. This *isn't* in the script I'm working from, either the gambling or McMurray's stark ultimatum. But it's all running on rails, and there's no way to get off this train without blowing the timetable. So I follow McMurray over to the table, trying to figure out the odds. House cards: nil. That's four in fourteen of anything I draw. Then it's modular arithmetic down to the wire, the sort of thing I could do in my head if it was in hexadecimal. Alas, playing cards predates hex and I've just sunk four shots of expensive gin and I'm not sure I can build a lookup table in my head fast enough to be of any use.

I sit down. The old toad with the cigar nods at us. "I bought the bank," he announces. "Place your bets. Opening at five thousand." The croupier next to him holds up the shoe and six sealed packs of cards. Four elderly vultures in frocks giggle and hunch at one end of the kidney-shaped table and two guys in DJs and big moustaches sit at the other end. McMurray and I end up in the middle opposite the old toad. A couple more gamblers take their seats—a woman with skin the color of milk chocolate and the complexion of a supermodel, and a guy in a white suit, open-necked shirt, and more bling than the Bank of England. "Opening at five thousand," repeats the banker.

Without willing my hands to move, I slide a handful of chips forwards. McMurray does likewise. The cards go into the mechanical shuffler in front of us, then two of the vultures squabble for the privilege of cutting them before they end up in the brass and wood shoe. My fingertips and nasal sinuses are itching: I actually *want a cigarette*, even though I don't smoke. There's a hollow sense of dreadful anticipation in the pit of my stomach as the toad positions the shoe in front of himself and then flicks out cards, face-down, one towards each of us. Then he repeats the deal. A second card lands in front of me, half on top of the first. I sneak a look at the cards. Six of hearts, five of clubs. *Shit.* Around me everyone else is turning their cards. I lay mine down face-up and watch with numb disbelief as the croupier rakes in my stake.

"Next round." The banker glances round. Again, I can't stop myself, even though there's a cold itch at the base of my spine and my wards are ringing like alarm bells. I slide another ten thousand forwards. This time I twitch and nearly scatter the stack everywhere. McMurray spares me a coldly amused glance; then the banker holds up the shoe and the card deck and begins to deal. *There's something very wrong here,* I tell myself. But it's no compulsion or geas I'm familiar with. There's a pattern to it, something I can't quite put my finger on. *Where's Ramona?* I can sense nothing but velvety darkness where she ought to be. I'm alone in my own head for the first time in days, and it's not a good feeling. Cards. Queen of diamonds, eight of spades—

A stack of chips approaches me across the table. I pick up my glass and throw back the tequila slammer, shuddering as it hits my throat. I feel out-of-control drunk and coldly sober at the same time: it's like my brain's trying to do the splits, its lobes skittering in opposite directions.

"Again, anyone?" asks the banker, looking round the table. I mechanically begin to push my chips forwards, then manage to divert the action, bend down, and twist the heel of my left shoe. Coming up above the level of the table I finish the motion before I can stop myself, all my chips gliding into a pile in front of the banker. He deals. I look around the room. McMurray's earring is a burning cold teardrop of radium fire. The shadows lengthen behind the drapes, hiding the screams of trapped tree-spirits embedded in the fine wall paneling. The Tillinghast resonator is humming along, but when I look at the toad he's just an ordinary retired fat-cat with a trust fund and a big bank account, enjoying his gambling habit. The same isn't true of the vultures—I look at them and try not to recoil. Instead of ageing former trophy-wives and heiresses I see hollow bags of translucent skin and hair held together by their clothes, hunched over their cards like blood-sucking parasites waiting to be filled.

"Hold or play?" someone asks. I glance at the guy in the white suit and open-necked shirt and see a half-decayed cadaver grinning at me from behind his cards, skin peeling back from dark hollows lined with strips of adipocere: the effect of the resonator reaches my nasal sinuses and I *smell* him as well. The supermodel on his arm looks exactly the same as before, inhumanly calm and poised as she leans against him, but the shadows behind her are thick and fuliginous, and something about her expression makes me think of a hangman waiting proudly beside his latest client as the warden signs the death certificate.

"Play." I try hard not to gag as I turn my cards over. *Fuck, fuck, fuck.* The croupier is raking the chips across to the toad. "Excuse me," I gasp, pushing my chair back from the table. I stumble towards the discreet side door, my throat burning as the woodwork screams at me and hollow bags of skin turn their empty faces to follow my trajectory to the toilets.

*I just lost twenty thousand bucks,* I realize numbly as I splash water on my face and look at myself in the mirror above the wash basin. My face in the mirror leers at me and winks. I lift my leg hastily and twist the heel back into place: the face freezes in shock. *I can't afford that.* Ghastly visions dance in my mind's eye: Angleton will call the Auditors on me, Mo will scream blue murder. It's more than our combined savings account, the money we've been socking away this past year towards a deposit on a house. I shudder. My lips are numb from the alcohol I've been putting away. My throat and stomach feel raw. I still can't sense Ramona, and that's critical: if she's out of touch we've got a real problem with the whole operation. *Pull yourself together,* I tell the man in the mirror. He nods at me, looking shaken. What to do first? *McMurray:* The bastard set me up somehow, didn't he?

The realization gives me something concrete to focus on: I straighten up, carefully check out the stranger in the mirror to make sure he looks suitably composed, square my shoulders, and head back towards the party. But when I reach the door back to the room, I pause. The baccarat game is over. Everyone except the bank-toad is standing up, and new players are milling around their seats, buzzing like a swarm of flies around a—*don't go there.* I look away hastily, my eyes watering. I don't see McMurray anywhere, and my wards are kicking up a fuss. It feels like a major supernatural manifestation is happening somewhere nearby.

"You must be Mr. Howard?" a calm, somewhat musical voice says from right beside me.

I don't jump out of my skin this time: I barely twitch. The urgent nagging of my wards spikes in time with her voice. "Everyone seems to know who I am. Who are you?"

Looking round I recognize her at once. She's the supermodel type with the hangman's eyes who was chilling with Mr. Stiffy: she's got skin the color of a perfect mocha, her dancer's body exposed rather than concealed by her sheer white gown, a fortune in sapphires at ears and throat. Looks to die for, like Ramona—yes, it's a glamour. Predictably, she's the center of the manifestation my wards are yammering about. "I'm Johanna, Mr. Howard, Johanna Todt. I work for the Billingtons."

I shrug. "Doesn't everyone?"

It's meant to be a black joke, but Johanna doesn't seem to take it in the intended spirit. She frowns: "Not yet." Then she sniffs dismissively. "I'm supposed to bring you to see him."

"Really." I make myself look her in the eye. She really *is* beautiful, so much so that normally I'd be tongue-tied and babbling in her presence. But thanks to the time I've been spending with Ramona, supernatural beauty isn't as dazzling as it used to be, and besides, I've got other preoccupations right now. I manage to keep a lid on it. "Liza Sloat just got through warning me off, then I had some security consultant called McMurray all over me like a vest. What's the story?"

"Interdepartmental rivalry. Sloat and McMurray don't get on." Johanna tilts her head to one side and looks at me. "There are many mansions in the house of Billington, Mr. Howard. And as it happens, Mr. McMurray is my manager." She lays a long-fingered hand on my arm. "Walk with me."

She steers me past the bar and into the outer room, past the jazz butchers. There are French doors open on the balcony. *Where's Ramona?* I worry. *She wasn't in the back room, she's not here . . .*

"For obvious reasons we don't make it too easy to reach the chief," Johanna murmurs. "When you're as rich as the Billingtons it makes you a target. Money is an attractive nuisance. We're currently tracking six stalkers and three blackmailers, and that's before you count the third-world governments. We've got enough schizophrenics to fill one-point-four psychiatric hospitals, plus an average of two-point-six marriage proposals and eleven-point-one death threats per week, and a federal antitrust investigation which is worse than all of them combined."

Put that way, I can almost feel a sneaking sympathy for the man. "So why am I here?" I ask.

The ghost of a smile tugs at her lips. "You're not a stalker or a blackmailer." A faint ghost of a breeze comes through the open doors. She leads me out onto the balcony. "You're asking inconvenient questions and silencing you won't stop them, because the organization you work for is staffed by determined, intelligent, and very dangerous people. It's much better to get everything out in the open and discuss it like sensible people, don't you think?"

"Yeah, well." My mind's eye flickers back to the nightmare meeting in Darmstadt, the shadow of a diver's oxygen tank rippling across encrusted concrete . . . *Dammit, where's Ramona? She should be relaying this!* "Incidentally, who was your boyfriend?" She raises an eyebrow. "Humor me. The guy in the white suit."

"What, him?" She shakes her head. "Just an ex of mine. He hangs out with me sometimes." My wards are still tingling and I get a sharp stab of pain as I look at her. Her smile slowly widens. "I walk the body—one at a time. Not *all* of us are as snobbish as prissy Miss Random."

I used to wonder why the most beautiful women always ended up with rotters, but as explanations go this one stinks. I try to take a step back but she's still holding my arm and she's got a grip like a steel mooring cable, and I'm backed up against the wall. My wards are flaring now, incandescent spectral light from the chain I'm wearing under my shirt. "What have you done with her?" I demand.

"Nothing, personally. But if you want to see her again you'll come with—"

The velvet wall between us rips open shockingly fast, and Ramona comes slamming through. I'm not sensing the shape of her emotions, or even seeing a blurry inner vision through her eyes, I'm inside her, I *am* Ramona for a random moment, and the somatic realization is simultaneously very wrong and very right. The floor beneath her feet is carpeted but it's slowly turning. Unsteady on her heels she looks round the gloriously upholstered salon, past the windows, sees the sea and the headland. Three black-clad guards with guns flank a monster just like the corpse in the white suit as her heart tries to climb her throat. **\*\*Bob?\*\*** Her cold apprehension hits me like a hammer. This isn't random fear of the unknown: she knows *precisely* what she's afraid of. I follow her gaze down to the floor, and the carpet she stands on. It's a glorious antique Isfahan carpet. Woven into it, almost invisible silver threads trace out a design identical to the one on my wards, on McMurray's earring. From one edge of the carpet a coiled cable leads to a control box grasped in the walking corpse's hands. **\*\****It's a trap, Bob, don't let them—***\*\***

The corpse pushes a button on the control box and suddenly I can't feel Ramona anymore. I stagger, disoriented: it's like having a full-body local anesthetic. I blink until I can focus my eyes. Johanna is smiling at me in a satisfied, cat-got-the-canary manner. "Who do you work for again?" I ask, trying to regain control.

"Ellis Billington." Her smile vanishes, replaced by casual authority. "He says I'm to take you aboard the *Mabuse*. You will do exactly as I say—assuming you ever want to see her again."

"What?" I ask, feeling sick and sober with the backwash from Ramona's fright. "But I came here to see him anyway!"

"Perhaps, but you've also acquired adversary status, according to our reading of the main security geas. It's probably a memory leak in the code, but until we've terminated this phase of the operation we're going to treat you as threat number one." She steps closer to me and before I realize what she's doing she reaches into my jacket and removes the pistol Ramona made me wear. She takes two steps back and I find myself staring up the muzzle of my own gun, feeling stupid. "Lights out, Mr. Howard."

I'm opening my mouth to say something when the ward they've trapped Ramona in shuts down and her presence floods into me again. I've got time for a brief moment of relief—time to think *we're whole again*—then the walking corpse shoots her with a Taser, and while Ramona and I are both flopping around on the floor Johanna steps forwards and sinks a disposable syringe into my neck.

## Chapter 11:
## Destiny Entangled

I am asleep and dreaming and aware at the same time—I appear to be having a lucid dream. I really wish I wasn't, because that rat-bastard Angleton has taken advantage of my somnambulant state to sneak into my head with his slide projector and install another pre-canned top secret briefing, using my eyelids as stereoscopic projection screens. And I don't care how bad your nightmares are, they can't possibly be as unpleasant as a mission briefing conducted by old skull-face while you're asleep, unable to wake up, and suffering from an impending hangover.

"Pay attention, Bob," he admonishes me sternly. "If you're alive, you're getting this briefing because you've penetrated Billington's semiotic firewall. This means you're approaching the most dangerous part of your mission—and you're going to have to play it by ear. On the other hand, you've got an ace up your sleeve in the form of Ms. Random. She should be secure in the safe house your backup team has organized, and she'll be your conduit back to us for advice and instructions."

*No she bloody isn't!* I try to yell at him, but he's playing the usual tricks with my vocal chords and I'm not allowed to say anything that isn't on the menu. Propelled by the usual inexorable dream logic, the briefing continues.

"Billington has let it be known that he will be conducting an advance Dutch auction for the specimens he expects to raise from JENNIFER MORGUE Site Two. These are described in vague but exciting terms, as chthonic artifacts and applications. There is of course no mention of his expertise in operating Gravedust-type oneiromantic convolution engines, or of the presence of a deceased DEEP SEVEN in the vicinity.

"He is restricting bidding to authorized representatives of governments with seats at the G8, plus Brazil, China, and India. Sealed bids are solicited in advance of the operation, which will be honored once the retrieval is complete. This indirect pressure makes it difficult for us to stay out of the auction, while simultaneously rendering it nearly impossible for us to take direct action against him—he's very carefully played the bidders off against one another. Of rather more concern is who Billington *hasn't* invited to bid—namely BLUE HADES. As I mentioned in your earlier briefing, our immediate concern is the response of BLUE HADES to Billington's activities around the site, followed in turn by what Billington really intends to do with the raised artifacts.

"Regardless, your actual task remains, as briefed, to determine what Billington is planning and to stop him from doing anything that arouses BLUE HADES or DEEP SEVEN—especially, anything likely to convince them that we're in violation of our treaty obligations. To supplement your cover you are officially designated as an authorized representative of Her Majesty's Government, to deliver our bid for the JENNIFER MORGUE Site Two artifacts. This is a genuine bid, although obviously we hope we won't be called upon to make good on it, and the terms are as follows: for an exclusive usage license as designated in schedule one to be appended to this document, hereinafter designated 'the contract' between the seller 'Ellis Billington' and associates, corporations, and other affiliates and the purchaser, the Government of the United Kingdom, the sum of two billion pounds sterling, to be paid . . ."

Angleton rattles on in dreary legalese for approximately three lifetimes. It'd be tedious at the best of times, but right now it's positively nightmarish; the plan has already run off the rails, and the worst thing of all is, I can't even yell at him. I'm committing this goddamn contract that we're never going to use to memory, seemingly at Angleton's posthypnotic command, but the shit has hit the fan and Ramona's a prisoner. I'd gnash my teeth if I was allowed to. I've got a feeling that Angleton's sneak strategy—use me to leak disinformation to the Black Chamber via Ramona, of course—is already blown, because I don't think Billington is serious about running an auction. If he was, would he be dicking around risking a murder investigation in order to push a line of cosmetics? And would he be kidnapping negotiators? This is all so out of whack that I can't figure it out. I've got a sick feeling that Angleton's scheme was toast before I even boarded the airbus in Paris: if nothing else, his bid is implausibly low given what's at stake.

Eventually the briefing lets go of me and I slide gratefully beneath the surface of a dreamless lake. I'm rocking from side to side on it, with the leisurely wobble of a howdah perched on an elephant's back. After a brief infinity of unconsciousness I become aware that my head is throbbing fiercely and my mouth feels like a family of rodents has set up a campsite, complete with latrine, on my tongue. And that I'm awake. *Oh no.* I twitch, taking stock. I'm lying on my back which is never the right place to be, breathing through my mouth, and—

"He's awake."

"Good. Howard, stop fooling around."

This time I groan aloud. My eyes feel like pickled onions and it takes a real effort to force them open. More facts flood in as my brain reboots. I'm lying on my back, fully dressed, on something like a padded bench or sofa. The voice I recognize: it's McMurray. The room's well-lit, and I notice that the padded surface beneath me is covered in beautifully finished fabric. The lights are tasteful and indirect, and the curving walls are paneled in old mahogany: the local police cells, it ain't. "Give me a second," I mumble.

"Sit up." He doesn't sound impatient; just sure of himself.

I force arms and legs that are heavy and warm from too-recent sleep to respond, swinging my legs round and sitting up at the same time. A wave of dizziness nearly pushes me right back down, but I get over it and rub my eyes, blinking. "What *is* this place?" I ask shakily. *And where's Ramona? Still trapped?*

McMurray sits down on the bench opposite me. Actually, it's a continuation of the one I was lying on—it snakes around the exterior of the trapezoid room, past out-tilting walls and a doorway in the middle of the only rectilinear wall in the cabin. It's a nice room, except that the doorway is blocked by a gorilla in a uniform-like black jumpsuit and beret, plus mirrorshades. (Which is more than somewhat incongruous, in view of it being well past midnight.) The windows are small and oval with neatly decorated but very functional-looking metal covers hinged back from them, and there are drawers set in the base of the padded bench—obviously storage of some kind. The throbbing isn't in my head; it's coming from under the floor. Which can only mean one thing.

"Welcome aboard the *Mabuse*," he says, then shrugs apologetically. "I'm sorry about the way you were handed your boarding pass: Johanna isn't exactly Little Miss Subtlety, and I told her to make sure you didn't abscond. That would totally ruin the plot."

I rub my head and groan. "Did you have to—no, don't answer that, let me guess: it's a tradition or an old charter, something like that." I continue to rub my head. "Is there any chance of a glass of water? And a bathroom?" It's not just a barbiturate hangover—the martinis are extracting a vicious revenge. "If you're going to take me to see the big cheese shouldn't I freshen up a bit first?" *Please say yes*, I pray to whatever god of whimsy has got me in his grip; being hung-over is bad enough without a beating on top of it.

For a moment I wonder if I've gone too far, but he gestures at the gorilla, who turns and opens the door and retreats down the narrow corridor a couple of paces. "The head's next door. You have five minutes."

He watches as I stumble to my feet. He nods, affably enough, and gestures at another door set next to the rec room or wherever the hell it is they'd put me in to sleep things off. I open the door and indeed find a washroom of sorts, barely bigger than an airliner's toilet but beautifully finished. I take a leak, gulp down half a pint or so of water using the plastic cup so helpfully provided, then spend about a minute sitting down and trying not to throw up. **Ramona, are you there?** If she is, I can't hear her. I take stock: my phone's missing, as is my neck-chain ward, my wristwatch, and my shoulder holster. The bow tie is dangling from my collar, but they weren't considerate enough to remove my uncomfortable toe-pinching shoes. I raise an eyebrow at the guy in the mirror and he pulls a mournful face and shrugs: no help there. So I wash my face, try to comb my hair with my fingertips, and go back outside to face the music.

The gorilla is waiting for me outside. McMurray stands in front of the closed door to the rec room. The gorilla beckons to me then turns and marches down the corridor, so I play nice and tag along, with McMurray taking up the rear. The corridor is punctuated by frequent watertight bulkheads with annoying lintels to step over, and there's a shortage of portholes to show where we are: someone's obviously done a first-rate coach-building job, but this ship wasn't built as a yacht and its new owner clearly places damage control ahead of aesthetics. We pass some doors, ascend a very steep staircase, and then I figure we're into Owner Territory because the metal decking gives way to teak parquet and hand-woven carpets, and up here they *have* widened the corridors to accommodate the fat-cats: or maybe it's just that they built the owner's quarters where they used to stash the Klub-N cruise missiles and the magazine for the forward 100mm gun turret.

Klub-N vertical launch cells are not small, and the owner's lounge is about three meters longer than my entire house. It appears to be wallpapered in cloth-of-gold, which for the most part is mercifully concealed behind ninety-centimeter Sony displays wearing priceless antique picture frames. Right now they're all switched off, or displaying a rolling screensaver depicting the TLA Corporation logo. The furniture's equally lacking in the taste department. There's a sofa that probably escaped from Versailles one jump ahead of the revolutionary fashion police, a bookcase full of self-help business titles (*A Defendant's Guide to the International Criminal Court, The Twelve-Step Sociopath, Globalization for Asset-Strippers*), and an antique sideboard that abjectly fails to put the rock into baroque. I find myself looking for a furtive cheap print of dogs playing poker or a sad-eyed clown—anything to break the monotony of the collision between bad taste and serious money.

Then I notice the Desk.

Desks are to executives what souped-up Mitsubishi Colts with low-profile alloys, metal-flake paint jobs, and extra-loud, chrome-plated exhaust pipes are to chavs; they're a big swinging dick, the proxy they use to proclaim their sense of self-importance. If you want to understand an executive, you study his desk. Billington's Desk demands a capital letter. Like a medieval monarch's throne, it is designed to proclaim to the poor souls who are called before it: *the owner of this piece of furniture is above you.* Someday I'll write a text book about personality profiling through possessions; but for now let's just say this example is screaming "megalomaniac!" at me.

Billington may have an ego the size of an aircraft carrier but he's not so vain as to leave his desk empty (that would mean he was pretending to lead a life of leisure) or to cover it with meaningless gewgaws (indicative of clownish triviality). This is the desk of a *serious* executive. There's a functional-looking (watch me work!) PC to one side, and a phone and a halogen desk light at the other. One of the other items dotting it gives me a nasty shock when I recognize the design inscribed on it: millions wouldn't, but the owner of this hunk of furniture is using a Belphegor-Mandelbrot Type Two containment matrix as a mouse mat, which makes him either a highly skilled adept or a suicidal maniac. Yup, that pretty much confirms the diagnosis. This is the desk of a diseased mind, hugely ambitious, prone to taking insanely dangerous risks. He's not ashamed of boasting about it—he clearly believes in better alpha-primate dominance displays through carpentry.

McMurray gestures me to halt on the carpet in front of the Desk. "Wait here, the boss will be along in a minute." He gestures at a skeletal contraption of chromed steel and thin, black leather that only Le Corbusier could have mistaken for a chair: "Have a seat."

I sit down gingerly, half-expecting steel restraints to flash out from concealed compartments and lock around my wrists. My head aches and I feel hot and shivery. I glance at McMurray, trying for casual rather than anxious. The Laundry field operations manual is notably short on advice for how to comport one's self when being held prisoner aboard a mad billionaire necromancer's yacht, other than the usual stern admonition to keep receipts for all expenses incurred in the line of duty. "Where's Ramona?" I ask.

"I don't remember saying you were free to ask questions." He stares at me from behind his steel-rimmed spectacles until icicles form on the back of my neck. "Ellis has a specific requirement for an individual of her . . . type. I'm a specialist in managing such entities." A pause. "While you remain entangled, she will be manageable. And as long as she remains manageable, there will be no need to dispose of her."

I swallow. My tongue is dry and I can hear my pulse in my ears. This wasn't supposed to happen; she was supposed to be back in the safe house, acting as a relay! McMurray nods at me knowingly. "Don't underestimate your own usefulness to us, Mr. Howard," he says. "You're not just a useful lever." There's a discreet buzz from his belt pager: "Mr. Billington is on his way now."

The door behind the Desk opens.

"Ah, Mr. B—Howard." Billington walks in and plants himself firmly down on the black carbon-fiber Aeron chair behind the Desk. From the set of his shoulders and the tiny smile playing around his lips he's in an expansive mood. "I'm so pleased you could be here this evening. I gather my wife's party wasn't entirely to your taste?"

I stare at him. He's an affable, self-satisfied bastard in a dinner jacket and for a moment I feel a nearly uncontrollable urge to punch him in the face. I manage to hold it in check: the gorilla behind me will ensure I'd only get one chance, and the consequences would hurt Ramona as much as they'd hurt me. Still, it's a tempting thought. "I have a bid for your auction," I say, very carefully keeping my face straight. "This abduction was unnecessary, and may cause my employers to reconsider their very generous offer."

Billington laughs. Actually, it's more of a titter, high-pitched and unnerving. "Come now, Mr. Howard! Do you really think I don't already know about your boss's paltry little two-billion-pound baitworm? Please! I'm not stupid. I know all about you and your colleague Ms. Random, and the surveillance team in the safe house run by Jack Griffin. I even remember your boss, *James*, from back before he became quite so spectral and elevated. I know much more than you give me credit for." He pauses. "In fact, I know *everything*."

*Whoops.* If he's telling the truth, that would put a very bad complexion on things. "Then what am I doing here?" I ask, hoping like hell that he's bluffing. "I mean, if you're omnipotent and omniscient then just what is the point of abducting me—not to mention Ramona—and dragging us aboard your yacht?" (That's a guess about Ramona, but I don't see where else he might be keeping her.) "Don't tell me you haven't got better things to do with your time than gloat; you're trying to close a multi-billion-dollar auction, aren't you?" He just looks at me with those peculiar, slotted lizard-eyes, and I have a sudden cold conviction that maybe making money is the last thing on his mind right now.

"You're here for several reasons," he says, quite agreeably. "Hair of the dog?" He raises an eyebrow, and the gorilla hurries over to the sideboard.

"I wouldn't mind a glass of water," I confess.

"Hah." He nods to himself. "The archetype hasn't taken full effect yet, I see."

"Which archetype?"

McMurray clears his throat. "Boss, do I need to know this?"

Billington casts him a fish-eyed stare: "No, I don't think you do. Quick thinking."

"I'll just go and check in on Ramona then, shall I? Then I'll go polish the binnacle and check for frigging in the rigging or something." McMurray slithers out through the door at high speed. Billington nods thoughtfully.

"He's a smart subordinate." He raises an eyebrow at me. "That's half the problem, you know."

"Half what problem?"

"The problem of running a tight ship." The gorilla hands Billington a glass of whisky, then plants a glass full of mineral water in front of me before returning to his position by the door. "If they're smart enough to be useful they get ideas about making themselves indispensable—ideas about getting above their station, as you Brits would put it. If they're too dumb to be useful they're a drain on your management time. All corporations are an economy of attention, from the top down. You should take McMurray as a role model, Mr. Howard, if you ever make it back to your petty little civil service cubicle farm. He's a consummate senior field agent and a huge asset to his employers. No manager in their right mind would *ever* terminate him, but because he likes fieldwork he doesn't spend enough time in the office to get a leg up the promotion ladder. And he knows it." He falls silent. I take advantage of the break in his spiel to take a mouthful of water. "That's why I headhunted him away from the Black Chamber," Billington adds.

When I finish coughing, he looks at me thoughtfully. "You strike me as being a reasonably adaptable, intelligent young man. It's really a shame you're working for the public sector. Are you sure I can't bribe you? How would a million bucks in a numbered account in the Caymans suit you?"

"Get lost." I struggle to maintain my composure.

"If it's just that silly little warrant card you guys carry, we can do something about it," he adds slyly.

*Ouch.* That's a low blow. I take a deep breath: "I'm sure you can, but—"

He snorts. And looks amused. "It's to be expected. They wouldn't have sent you if they thought you had an easy price. It's not just money I can offer, Mr. Howard. You're used to working for an organization that is deliberately structured to stifle innovation and obstruct stakeholder-led change. My requirements are a bit, shall we say, different. A smart, talented, hard-working man—especially a morally flexible one—can go far. How would you like to come on board as deputy vice-president for intelligence, Europe, Middle East, and Africa division? A learning sinecure, initially, but with your experience and background in one of the world's leading occult espionage organizations I'm sure you'd make your mark soon enough."

I give it a moment's thought, long enough to realize that he's right and that I'm not going to take the offer. He's offering me crumbs from the rich man's table, and not even bothering to find out in advance if that's the sort of diet I enjoy. Which means he's doing me the compliment of not taking the prospect of my defection seriously, which means he considers me to be a reliable agent. And now I stop to think about it, I realize to my surprise that I *am*. I may not be happy about the circumstances under which I took the oath, and I may gripe and moan about the pay and conditions, but there's a big difference between pissing and moaning and seriously contemplating the betrayal of everything I want to preserve. Even if I've only just come to realize it.

"I'm not for sale, Ellis. Not for any price you can pay, anyway. What's this archetype business?"

He nods minutely, examining me as if I've just passed some sort of important test. "I was getting to that." He rotates his chair until he's half-facing the big monitor off to my right. He stabs at the mouse mat with one finger and I wince, but instead of fat purple sparks and a hideous soul-sucking manifestation, it simply wakes up his Windows box. (Not that there's much difference.) For a moment I almost begin to relax, but then I recognize what he's calling up and my stomach flip-flops in abject horror.

"I do everything in PowerPoint, you know." Billington grins, an expression which I'm sure is intended to be impish but that comes across to his intended victim—me—as just plain vicious. "I had to have my staff write some extra plugins to make it do everything I need, but, ah, here we are . . ."

He rapidly flips through a stack of tediously bulleted talking points until he wipes into a screen that's mercifully photographic in nature. It's a factory, lots of workers in gowns and masks gathered around worktops and stainless steel equipment positioned next to a series of metal vats.

"Eileen's Hangzhou factory, where our Pale Grace™ Skin Hydromax® range of products are made. As you probably already figured out, we apply a transference-contagion glamour to the particulate binding agent in the foundation powder, maintained by brute force from our headquarters operation in Milan, Italy. Unlike most of the cosmetics on the market, it really *does* render the wrinkles invisible. The ingredients are a bit of a pain, but she's got that well in hand; instead of needing an endless supply of young women just to keep one old bat pretty, we can make do with only about ten parts per million of maid's blood in the mix.

It's just one of the wonders of modern stem cell technology. Shame we can't find a replacement for the stress prostaglandins, but those are the breaks."

He clicks his mouse. "Here's the other end of the operation." It's a room full of skinny, suntanned guys in short-sleeved shirts hunched over cheap PCs, row upon row of them: "My floating offshore programmer ranch, the SS *Hopper*. You've probably read about it, haven't you? Instead of offshoring to Bangalore, I bought an old liner, wired it, and flew in a number of Indian programmers to live on board. It stays outside the coastal limit and with satellite uplinks it might as well be in downtown Miami. Only they're not, um, actually programming anything. Instead, they're monitoring the surveillance take from the mascara. Because the Pale Grace™ Bright Eyes® products don't just link into the transference-contagion glamour, they contain particles nano-engraved with an Icon of Bhaal-She'vra that backdoors them into my surveillance grid. That's actually the main product of my sixty-nanometer fab line these days, by the way, not the bespoke microprocessors everyone thinks it makes. It's a very useful similarity hack—anything the wearer can see or hear, my monitors can pick up, and we've got flexible batch manufacturing protocols that ensure every single cosmetics product is uniquely coded so we can tell them apart. It's almost embarrassing how much intelligence you can gather from this sweep, especially as Eileen's affiliates are running a loyalty scheme that encourages users to register their identity with us at time of sale for free samples, so that we know who they are."

I'm boggling already. "Are you telling me you've turned your cosmetics company into some kind of occult ubiquitous surveillance operation? Is that what this is?"

"Yup, that's about the size of it." Billington nods smugly. "Of course, it's expensive—but we manage to just about break even on a twenty buck tube of mascara, so it works out all right in the end. And it's less obvious than using several million zombie seabirds." He clears his throat. "Anyway, that's by way of demonstrating to you that you can run, but you can't hide. Now, to explain why you *shouldn't* run . . ."

He flicks to the next slide, and it's not a photograph, it's a live surveillance take from a camera somewhere. I'm pretty sure it's aboard this very ship. It's Ramona, of course. She's sprawling across a double bed in a stateroom, out cold. "Here's Ms. Random. I figure you know by now that you don't get to talk to her without my say-so. You need to know three things about her. Firstly, if I've got *you*, I can make her do anything I want—and vice versa. You've figured that out? Excellent."

He pauses for a few seconds while I force myself to stop trying to break the arms of my chair. "There's no need for that, Mr. Howard. No harm will come to either of you unless you force my hand. You're here because I need her to do a little job for me, one relating to the recovery of the alien artifact  and I need her willing cooperation, so that's item two out of the way. Item three, I gather you've met Mr. McMurray? Good. It might interest you to know that he's a specialist in controlling entities like Ramona's succubus, or Johanna's necrophage. I could threaten to hurt you if she tries to resist, but I always find that positive incentivization works much better than the big stick on employees: so I'm going to offer her a deal. If you and Ms. Random cooperate fully, I'll have Mr. McMurray see if he can permanently separate her from her little helper. As he was part of the team who invoked and bound it to her in the first place . . . well, what do you think she'll say to that?"

I pick up my water glass and drain it, hoping for something, anything, to occur to me that'll show me a way out. Billington may not have tried to figure out *my* price, but I'm pretty sure he's got Ramona's. "What's the job?"

Billington prods at his fancy remote again and another screen comes to life: a view of a huge metal chamber, something like a factory floor— only the floor itself is covered in black water. A moment's confusion, then it springs into focus for me. "Isn't that the *Glomar Explorer*?"

"It's now the *TLA Explorer*, but yes, well-spotted, Mr. Howard."

I focus on the pipe that pierces the heart of the pool of water. There's something big and indistinct lurking just under the surface down there, impaled on the end of the drill string. "What's that?"

"Can't you guess? It's the TMB-2, a clone of the original Hughes Mining Barge 1, equipped with updated telemetry and new materials so that pressure-induced brittleness in the grab cantilever arms won't stop it from working this time."

"But you *know* the Deep Ones won't let you retrieve—"

"Really?" His grin widens.

"But!" My head's spinning. I know about the original HMB-1, Operation JENNIFER, the BLUE HADES defense system that nearly dragged the mother ship down. "You said this was about Ramona?"

"She's one of the in-laws," Billington explains cheerfully. "She's got the Innsmouth look, you know? She tastes right to their minions, the abyssal polyps. You didn't think the Deep Ones guarded every inch of their territory in person, did you? The polyps are subsentient, just like your burglar alarm. They work by biochemical tracers, discriminating self from other." He picks up his whisky. "I need her to ride the grab down and keep an eye on it while it locks onto the target. If the defenders of the deep smell Old One in the water they'll stay cowering in their burrows in the abyssal mud. What do you say to that?"

"It's an interesting theory," I admit, which is true because I don't know one way or the other whether it'll work.

"It's more than a theory. I sank a lot of money into arranging for the Black Chamber to send her, boy. Her folk aren't so numerous, and most of them would die rather than let themselves be turned to such a purpose. She's been tamed, which is unusual, and you've got a handle on her, and I've got you. So, I'll make you a new offer. Convince her to ride the barge for me willingly, and I'll have McMurray free her from her curse. Convince her to ride the barge and I won't even have to threaten you. How about it?"

He's backed me into a corner, I realize. And not just with menaces; the thing is, he *has* found Ramona's price. And having been inside her skull, even if only a bit, I'm not sure I can criticize her. Or easily stand in her way, if she really wants to do it. Threats of torture are redundant — just forcing her to go on living in her current state is torment enough. Plus, if she doesn't cooperate, Billington might turn nasty and take it out of my hide. Which reminds me of something else . . .

"Why me?" I finally burst out. "I mean, if you needed her, surely you don't specifically need *me* to control her? I'm nothing to you. You've got McMurray. You already know about my government's offer. What am I doing here? Why don't you just do the disentangling ritual and dump me overboard?"

Billington's smile widens, disturbingly: "Ah, but that's where you're wrong, Mr. Howard. *Your* presence *here* prevents anyone else — like the US Navy, for example — from turning up and spoiling my scheme. Which I realized would be a likely response to my current operation right at the outset, and took steps to prevent, in the form of a monumentally expensive and rather intricate destiny-entanglement geas that compels the participants to adopt certain archetypal roles that have been gathering their strength from hundreds of millions of believers over nearly fifty years. The geas doesn't mess with causality directly, but it does ensure that the likelihood of events that mesh with its destiny model are raised, while other avenues become less . . . probable. Going against the geas is hard; agents get run over by taxis, aircraft suffer inexplicable mechanical failures, that sort of thing. Now you've jumped through all the hoops in the geas and in so doing massively reinforced it. You've taken on the role of the heroic adversary. Which in turn means that *nobody else* is allowed to play the hero around here. And in accordance with another aspect of the geas, you're in my power for the time being and you're going to stay there until a virtuous woman turns up to release you. Got that?"

My head's spinning. What the hell is he on about? And where am I going to find a virtuous woman on board a mad billionaire's yacht at three in the morning as we steam towards the Bermuda Triangle? "What about the auction?" I ask plaintively.

Billington laughs raucously. "Oh, Mr. Howard! The auction was only ever a blind, to make your superiors believe I could be bought and sold!" He leans forwards across the Desk, and his eyebrows furrow like thunderclouds: "What use do you think I have for mere gigabucks? This is the high-stakes table." He looks past my shoulder, towards the gorilla. "Take him back to his room and lock him in until morning. We'll continue this conversation over breakfast." The gorilla stomps over and lays a beefy hand on my shoulder. "When I have JENNIFER MORGUE they'll do anything I want," he mutters, and my skin crawls because I don't think he's talking to me anymore. "Anything at all. They'll *have* to listen to me once I own the planet."

The gorilla herds me back down a short flight of steps and onto a passage that sports a row of mahogany-paneled doors like a very exclusive hotel. He opens one of them and gestures me inside. I briefly consider trying to take him, but realize it won't work: they've got Ramona and they've got the surveillance network from Hell and I'm on a ship that's already out of sight of land. I'll only get one chance, at most, and I'd better make sure I don't blow it. So I go inside without a struggle, and look around tiredly as he turns the key in the lock.

Being locked in one of Billington's guest rooms is a comfortable step up from a police cell. It's aboard ship so it's smaller than a five-star hotel suite, but that's about the only way it suffers by comparison. The bed's a double, the carpet is luxuriously thick, there's a porthole (non-opening), a wet bar, and a big flat-screen TV; a shelf next to it holds a handful of paperbacks and a row of DVDs. I assume I'm supposed to drink myself comatose while watching cheesy spy thrillers. The desk (small, guest-room-sized) opposite the bed shows raw patches where they must have yanked out a PC earlier—it's a damn shame, but Billington's people are smart enough not to leave a computer where I can get my hands on it.

"Shit," I mutter, then sit down in the sinfully padded leather recliner next to the wet bar. Surrender has seldom been such an attractive prospect. I massage my head. Looking out the porthole there's nothing but an expanse of night-black sea, overlooked by stars. I yawn. Whatever that bitch Johanna used to put my lights out was fast-acting; it can't be much past three in the morning. And I'm still tired, now that I think about it. I look around the room and there's nothing particularly obvious in the way of escape routes. Plus, they're probably watching me, via a peephole in the door if they've got any sense. "What a mess."

**You can say that again, monkey-boy.**

I flinch, then force myself to relax. Trying to show no sign of anything in particular, I open my inner ear again. **Ramona?**

**No, I'm the fucking tooth fairy. Have you seen my pliers lying around? There's a couple of folks here in line for some root-canal surgery when I get free.**

The wash of relief is visceral; if I was standing I'd probably collapse on the spot. It's a good thing I found the recliner first. **You're all right?**

She snorts. **For what it's worth.** I can feel something itchy where my eyes can't see. Focusing on it, I see the inside of another room, much like this one. She's kicked off her heels and is pacing the floor restlessly, examining everything, looking for an exit. **They've wired the walls. There's a shielding graph in the floor but they must have switched it off for the time being to let us talk. I don't think they can overhear us, but they can stop us any time they want.**

**Nice of them—**

**To let us know they've got us where they want us? Don't be silly.**

**How'd they catch you?** I ask, after an uncomfortable pause.

**It's probably the oldest trick in the book.** She stops pacing. **I was looking for Eileen's inner circle when I ran into a lure, a daemon disguised as someone I know professionally—a real class act, I could have sworn it was really him. He suckered me into an upstairs meeting room and before I knew what was happening they had me in a summoning lock. Which should be impossible unless they've got the original keys the Contracts Department used when they enslaved me, yet they did it. So I guess it's not impossible after all.**

I stare at the blank TV set. **Not if it was the real thing. His name's McMurray, isn't it?**

I can taste her shock. **How the *fuck* did you know that?** she demands.

**Because he took me for my entire expenses tab at baccarat,** I confess. **He's got a new employer with very deep pockets. Has Billington tried to buy you yet?**

She starts pacing again. **No, and he won't. Where he comes from there are different rules for people like me. You're employable. You're human. I'm . . .** I can feel her working her jaws, as if she's about to spit: **Let's just say, there are minorities it's still okay to shit on.**

I wince. **He led me to believe that . . . well, if you don't think he's going to try to buy you, what's he got on you? Besides the obvious.**

She tenses. **He's got you. That's bad enough, in case you hadn't figured it out.**

Whoops. **He knows all about your curse.** The idea begins to sink in. **Tell me about McMurray. You worked with him, right? In exactly what capacity?**

**He made me.** Her voice is chilly enough to liquefy nitrogen. **I'd rather not discuss it.**

**Sorry, but it's relevant. I'm still trying to work out what's going on. How Billington turned him. I wonder what the key was, if it's just money, like Billington said, or if there's something else we can use . . . **

Ramona snorts. **Don't waste your time. When I get out of here I'm going to kick his ass.**

I pause. **I think you may be wrong about Billington. I think he has every intention of trying to buy you. He's got your heart's desire in a box, if you'll just turn a trick for him.**

**You English guys, you've got such a way with words! Look, I don't bribe, okay? It's not a matter of being too honest, it's just not possible. Suppose, for the sake of argument, I go down for him and he gives me whatever it is you're hinting at in return. What happens then? Has that occurred to you? I'd be dead meat, Bob. No way can he let me walk.**

**Not so fast. I mean, I think he's nuts. But I think he believes that if he succeeds there won't be an 'after,' in the conventional sense; he'll be home clean and dry, immune to any consequences. I put the offer Angleton—my boss—gave me on the table, and Billington just laughed at me! He laughed off about five billion dollars at today's exchange rate. He's not in this for the money, he's in it because he thinks he's going to come out of it owning the entire planet.**

She snorts theatrically. **How boring, just another billionaire necromancer cruising the Caribbean in his thinly disguised guided missile destroyer, plotting total world domination.**

I shudder. **You think you're joking? He monologued at me. With PowerPoint. **

**He what? And you're still sane? Obviously I underestimated you.**

I shake my head. **I didn't have much choice. I figure we're stuck here for the duration. Or at least until he gets wherever he's taking us.**

**The other ship.**

**Yeah, there's that.** I stand up and walk over to the sliding door at the far side of the room. The bathroom beyond it is small but perfectly formed. There's no porthole, though.

**If we could figure out a way to spring you, could you do your invisibility thing?**

The question takes me by surprise. **Not sure. Damn it, they took my Treo. That would make it a whole lot easier. Plus, he's got an occult surveillance service that's going to be murder to evade. You don't use Eileen's make-up, do you? Especially not the mascara?**

**Do I look like a dumb blonde?** she snorts. **Pale Grace™ is for department store sales clerks and middle-management types trying to glam up their suits.**

**Good for you, because he's got a contagious proximity-awareness binding mixed in with it—that's what he married Eileen for, that's why he bankrolled her business. The goddamn seagulls weren't how he was watching us, they were just cover: it was all the thirty-something tourist women. *All* of them, at least the ones who take the free samples down at the promenade. And I reckon if he's got any sense, all of the crew on this boat will be using it, or something similar.**

**At least they'll all have beautiful complexions.** She pauses. **So what does he want with us? Why are we still alive?**

**You're alive because he wants you to do a job. *Me* . . . probably because he needs someone to monologue at. He said something about a geas, but I'm not sure what he meant. And we're still entangled, so I guess . . . **

I stop. While I was wibbling, Ramona realized something. **You're right, it *is* the geas,** she says sharply. **Which means nothing's going to happen until we arrive. So go to sleep, Bob. You're going to need all the sleep you can get before tomorrow.**

**But—**

**Lights out.** And with that, she pushes me out of her head, blocking me off from that sudden flash of understanding.

## Chapter 12:
## Power Breakfast

I awaken in a strange bed that feels as if it's vibrating slightly, with a head like thunder, and muscles I didn't know I had aching in my arms and legs. The thin light of dawn is pouring in through a porthole. Sleep held me down and tried to drown me, but waking comes as fast as a bucket of seawater in the face: *I'm on Billington's yacht!*

I roll out of bed and use the bathroom. My eyes are bloodshot and I could strip paint with my chin, but I'm not even remotely sleepy. *I'm out of touch with Control!* That fact is sitting on my shoulder, screaming in my ear with a megaphone; forget little organizational tics like Griffin, I need to talk to Angleton and I need to talk to him *right now*, if not about six hours ago, and especially before the upcoming power breakfast. Last night's sense of apathetic passivity is a million miles away, so alien that I frown at myself in the mirror: *How the fuck could I do that?* It's not like me at all!

It's got to be something to do with this geas that Billington's running on me, the one Ramona refuses to explain in words of one syllable. I can't trust my own reflexes. Which sucks mightily. Billington is racing headlong towards a full-scale sanity excursion, he's penetrated the Black Chamber, the auction for JENNIFER MORGUE is a decoy, and I'm in the shit just about up to my eyebrows—and not a snorkel in sight.

"Right," I mutter to myself. I look at my clothes from last night in distaste. "Let's see." I pull on my trousers and shirt, then pause. *Gadgets.* Pinky was talking about . . . *toys.* I snort. I pick up the bow tie, meaning to flick it across the room, then notice something lumpy in either end. That'd be the USB drives with the dog-fucker kit, right? "Ludicrous," I mutter, and roll the thing up. It'd be bloody handy if they'd locked me in a cell with a computer plugged into Billington's shipboard network, but they're not that stupid. I stare longingly at the bare chunk of space on the desktop. There may be a keyboard stitched into the lining of my cummerbund, but without a machine to plug it into it's about as much use as a chocolate hacksaw.

With nothing to do but wait for breakfast, I sit down next to the flat-screen TV and glance through the titles on the shelf. There's a bunch of paperback thrillers with titles familiar from the movie series: *Thunderball, On Her Majesty's Secret Service*. Next to them, a bunch of DVDs. It's all the same goddamn series about the most famous non-

existent spy in history. Whoever furnished this room had a James Bond
fixation. I sigh, and pick up the remote, thinking maybe I can watch a
mindless movie for a while. Then the screen comes on, showing a familiar menu on a blue background and I stare at it, transfixed, like a yokel
who's never seen a television before.

Because it's not a TV. It's a flat-screen PC running Windows XP
Media Center Edition.

*They can't be that dumb. It's got to be a trap,* I gibber to myself. Not
even the clueless cannon-fodder-in-jumpsuits who staff any one of the
movies on the shelf would be *that* dumb!

Or would they? I mean, they've got me locked in a broom closet on
the bastard's yacht and everything else is conforming to cliché, so why
the hell not?

I randomly pull one of the DVDs down from the shelf—it's
*Thunderball,* which seems appropriate although this yacht makes the
*Disco Volante* look like a bath toy—and use it as an excuse to run my fingers around the rim of the TV. There's a slot for discs, and then, just below it, the giveaway: two small notches for USB plugs.

*Bingo.* Okay, they weren't *totally* stupid. They took the keyboard and
mouse and locked the PC down in kiosk mode with nothing but a TV
remote for access. With no administrator password and no keyboard and
probably no network connection they figured it was safe. *You figured
wrong,* I admonish them. I push the disc eject button and a tray pops out,
and I stick the movie in. Returning to my chair I pick up the cummerbund and bow tie and drop them on the desk in front of the TV. *What
else?* Oh . . . I pull on my jacket, frown, then casually take the pen from
my inside pocket and toss it on the desk. Finally I sit down and spend the
next five minutes doing the obvious thing in the most obvious way imaginable, just in case they're watching.

I'm about ten minutes into the "Making of . . ." documentary feature
when suddenly the door opens. "Mr. Howard? You're wanted upstairs for
a breakfast meeting."

I turn round then stand up slowly. The guard stares at me impassively
from behind his mirrored aviator shades. The uniform hereabouts tends
towards black—black beret, black tunic, black boots—and so do the
guns: he's not actually pointing his Glock at me right now but he could
bring it up and nail me to the bulkhead faster than I could cover the distance between us.

"Okay," I say, and pause, staring at the weapon. "Are you sure that's
entirely safe?"

He doesn't smile: "Don't push your luck."

I slowly move towards him and he steps back smartly into the corridor before gesturing me to walk ahead of him. He's not alone, and his partner's carrying a cut-down Steyr submachine gun with so many weird sensors bolted to the barrel that it looks like a portable spy satellite.

"How much is he paying you?" I ask casually, as we reach a staircase leading back up to owner territory.

Beret Number One grunts. "We got a really good benefits package." Pause. "Better than the Marine Corps."

"And stock options," adds the other joker. "Don't forget the stock options. How many other dot-coms offer stock options for gun-toting minions?"

"You can't afford us," his partner says casually. "Not after the IPO, anyway."

I can tell when they're trying to fuck with my head; I shut up. At the top of the stairs I glance over my shoulder. "Door on the left," says Beret Number One. "Go on, he won't bite your head off."

"Unless you make him eat his hash browns cold," adds Beret Number Two.

I open the door. On the other side of it is a large, exquisitely paneled dining room. The table in the middle of the room is currently set for breakfast and I can smell frying bacon and eggs and toast and fresh coffee. My stomach tries to climb my throat and chow down on my sinuses: I am *hungry*. Which would be great except I'm simultaneously exposed to an appetite-suppressing sight: two stewards, the Billingtons, and their special breakfast guest, Ramona.

"Ah, Mr. Howard. Would you care for a seat?" Ellis smiles broadly. Today he's wearing one of those odd collarless Nehru suits that seem to be *de rigueur* for villains in bad techno-thrillers—but at least he hasn't shaved his head and acquired a monocle or a dueling scar. Eileen Billington is a violent contrast in her cerise business suit with shoulder pads sized for an American football quarterback. She grimaces at me like I'm something her cat's dragged in, then goes back to nibbling at her butter croissant as if she's had her stomach stapled.

I glance at Ramona as I step towards the table, and we make eye contact briefly. Someone's raided her hotel room for her luggage—she's swapped last night's gown for casuals and a freshly scrubbed girl-next-door look. "Is that coffee?" I ask, nodding towards the pot.

"Jamaican Blue Mountain." Billington smiles thinly. "And yes, you may have some. I prefer not to conduct interviews while the subjects are comatose."

The steward pours me a cup of coffee as I sit down, and I try hard not to be obvious about how desperate I am for the stuff. (Another couple of hours without it and the merciless headache would be setting in, visited

on me by my caffiend in retaliation for withdrawal of his drug.) As I take
the first mouthful something brushes up against my ankle. I manage to
control my knee-jerk reflex; it must be the cat, right?

The coffee is as good as you'd expect from a billionaire's buffet. "I
needed that," I admit. "But I'm still somewhat perplexed as to why you
want me here at all." (*Although it beats the hell out of the alternatives*, I
don't say.)

"I'd have thought that was perfectly obvious." Billington grins, with
the boyish charm of a boardroom bandit whose charisma is his most potent weapon. "You're here because you're both young, intelligent, active
professionals with good prospects. It's so hard to get the help these
days—" he nods at Eileen, who is sitting at the opposite end of the table,
ignoring us by staring into inner space "—and I've found that interview-
ing candidates in person is a remarkably good way of avoiding subsequent disappointments. Human resources will only get you so far, after
all."

I notice that Ramona is watching Eileen. "What's up with her?" I ask.

"Oh, her mind wanders." Billington picks up his knife and fork and
slices into a sausage. "Mostly all over her manufacturing sites; remote
viewing is a marvelous management tool, don't you think?" The sausage
bleeds juice across his plate. I suddenly realize there are no hash browns
or tomatoes or mushrooms or anything like that in front of him—it's
wall-to-wall dead animal flesh. "You should try it sometime."

Ramona looks me in the eye. "He told me what he wants me to do,
Bob."

I raise an eyebrow. "What, ride the grab down to the abyssal plain . . . ?"

"With you providing a running commentary," Billington slides in
unctuously. "After all, your current unfortunate state has certain transient advantages, does it not?" He smiles.

"He also told me what he was offering." She looks away, distraught.
"I'm sorry, Bob. You were right."

"You—" I stop. **You're going to trust him?** I ask via our private
channel.

**It's not just the, the binding to my aspect,** she says, tongue-tied
as she hunts for words. **If I do this for him, he makes McMurray set me
free. What alternative do I have?**

Billington's been watching us in silence for the past short while. Now
he interrupts, in my direction: "If I may explain?" He nods at Ramona.
"You have a simple choice. Cooperate, and I will have one of my associates perform the rite of disentanglement. You two will be free of each
other forever if you so choose, *and* free of Ms. Random's daemon. You'll
both live happily ever after, aside for a period of a few weeks during

which you will be guests with limited freedom of movement, while I complete my current project. After it is finished, I can promise you there will be no reprisals from your employers. Nothing can possibly go wrong. You see, I don't need to be nasty: it's a win win situation all round."

I lick my dry lips. "What if I don't want to cooperate?"

Billington shrugs. "Then you don't run my errand, and I don't pay you for it." He spears a strip of bacon, saws it in half, and raises it to his teeth. "Business is business, Mr. Howard."

I flinch as if someone's walked over my grave. He's making me an offer I can't refuse, disguising a threat of lethal violence as passive inaction. All he has to do to threaten us is let the nature of our entanglement take its course. I flash back to the yawning horror hiding behind Ramona's soul, the dead weight of Marc's body lying on top of her, suffocating and squeezing the breath from her body. Lock her up in her cabin for a few days and *what will she eat?* The thing inside her needs to feed. I have a sudden, disquieting vision: Ramona and myself, blurring at the edges, one confused mind in two bodies locked in separate cells, stalked by the dark side of our hybrid soul as the Other works itself up into an orgiastic fever that can only be satisfied by swallowing our minds—

**I'm not giving up,** I tell her silently, then nod at Billington. "I get the picture. Business is business; I'll cooperate."

"Excellent. Or jolly good, as I believe you English would say." He smiles in evident delight as he spears the other half of the strip of bacon and dangles it at knee level. A white streak blurs out of the shadows under the table and snaps the bacon right off his fork.

"Ah, Fluffy. *There* you are!" Billington reaches down and picks up the large, white cat, who turns his head and stares at me with sky-blue eyes that are disturbingly human. "I believe it's about time you were introduced. Say hello to Mr. Howard, Fluffy."

Fluffy stares at me like I'm an oversized mouse, then hisses charmlessly.

Billington grins at me from behind six kilos of annoyed cat. "Fluffy is what this is *really* about, Mr. Howard. I'm only doing this to keep him in kitty kibble, after all."

"Kitty kibble?" I shake my head. Fluffy is wearing a diamond collar that belongs in the Tower of London with a platoon of Beefeaters standing guard over it. "I for one welcome our new feline overlords." I tip the cat an ironic nod.

"I thought you could cover the cat-food bill out of the petty cash?" asks Ramona.

"Fluffy has *very* expensive tastes." Billington dotes on the wretched animal, which has calmed down slightly and is permitting him to scratch it behind the ears.

Eileen chooses this particularly surreal moment to quiver as if electrocuted; then she shakes her head, yawns, and looks about. "Have I missed anything?" she asks querulously.

"Not a lot, dear." Her husband regards her fondly. *Breakfast with the Hitlers*, I think, glancing between them. "Any news?"

"Ach." Eileen hunches like a vulture when she's aware. "Everything is in order, the central business groups advance on all fronts, nothing to report today." She glances at me sharply, then at Ramona. "I think we ought to continue this in the office, though. Flapping ears and all that."

Billington glances down at the table spread before him. I hastily refill my coffee cup before he looks up. "All right." He nods, then stands up abruptly—still holding Fluffy—and nods at me, then at Ramona. "Feel free to finish up," he says curtly. "Then you may return to your quarters. It won't be long now."

He and Eileen stalk out of the dining room via a door at the back, leaving me alone with Ramona, the remains of breakfast, and the disturbing sense that I've somehow strayed onto loose gravel at the edge of a precipice, and it may be too late to turn back and reach safe ground.

In the end, pragmatism wins: when you're being held prisoner you never know where the next power breakfast is coming from, so I grab some slices of toast and a plate full of other munchies. Ramona sits hunched in her chair, looking out the porthole above the sideboard. Misery and depression is coming off her in black, stultifying waves.

**We've not failed yet,** I tell her silently, my mouth full of hash browns. **As long as we can reestablish communications with Control we can get back on top of the situation.**

**You think?** She holds out her coffee cup and the steward, who's still waiting on us, fills it up. **What do you think they'll do if we tell them what's really going on? Give us time to get off the ship before they start shooting?**

She takes a mouthful of coffee and puts her cup down. I can feel it scalding her tongue, too hot to swallow: nevertheless, she gulps it down. I wince at the sudden paralyzing heartburn.

**We'll just have to stop him ourselves, then,** I say, trying to encourage her.

**Whatever. It doesn't work that way, Bob.**

**What doesn't?**

**The geas.** She stands up then smiles at the steward. "If you don't mind?" she says.

The steward stands aside. There's nobody human home behind his eyes; I sidle past him with my back to the wall. Ramona opens the side door beside the staircase. There's a short passage with several doors opening off it. "I've got something to show you," she tells me.

*Huh? Since when does Ramona have the run of Billington's yacht?* I follow her slowly, trying to worry out what's going on.

"In here." She opens a door. "Don't worry about the guards, they're either down below or up on the superstructure—this is the owner's accommodation area and they're not needed as long as we stay in it. This is the grand lounge."

The lounge is surprisingly spacious. There are molded leather-topped benches all around the walls, and bookcases and glass cabinets. In the middle of the floor is something that might have been a pool table once, before a monomaniacal model maker repurposed it as his display cabinet.

"What the hell is it?" I lean closer. On one side are two model ships, one being the *Explorer*, which I recognize from the huge drilling derrick; but the center of the table is occupied by a bizarre diorama: old dog-eared hardback novels and a worn-looking automatic pistol, piled on top of a reel of film and a map of the Caribbean. Something else: a set of fine wires tracing out— "Shit. That's a Vulpis-Tesla array. And that box must be a—is that a Mod-60 Gravedust board it's plugged into? Summoning up the spirits of the dead. What the hell?"

There's a GI Joe doll in evening dress, clutching a pistol. It's wired up to the summoning grid by its plastic privates. On either side of it stand two Barbies in ball gowns, one black, one white. Behind them lurks another GI Joe, this time hacked so that he's bald and bearded, in something that looks like *Wehrmacht* dress grays.

All at once, I get the picture.

"It's the core of his coercion geas, isn't it? It's a destiny-entanglement conjuration, on a bigger scale. James Bond, channeling the ghost of Ian Fleming as scriptwriter . . . Jesus." I glance across the table at Ramona. She looks flushed and apprehensive.

"Yes, James—" She bites her lip. "Sorry, monkey-boy. It's too strong in here, isn't it?"

I stare at her through narrowed eyes. Oh yes, I'm beginning to get it. I'm half-tempted to shoot the bint now, then stuff her through the porthole before the bad guys get their mileage out of her, but I need all the friends I can get right now, and until I'm sure she's gone over to SPEC-TRE I can't afford to—

*What. The. Fuck?*

I blink rapidly. "Is there somewhere we can go that's not quite so . . . ?"

"Yeah. Next door."

Next door is the library or smoking room or whatever the hell it's called. My head stops swimming as soon as we get a wall between us and that diorama from Hell. "That was bad. What's the big idea? Why does Billington want to turn me into James Bond?"

Ramona slumps into an overstuffed chair. "It's not about *you*, Bob, it's all about *plot*. The way the geas works, he's set himself up as the evil villain in this humongous destiny-entanglement spell targeted against every intelligence agency and government on the planet. The end state for this conjuration is that the hero—which means whoever's being ridden by the Bond archetype—comes and kills the villain, destroys his secret floating headquarters, stymies his scheme, and gets the girl. But Billington's not stupid. He may be riding the Villain archetype but he's in control of the geas and he's got a good sense of timing. Before the Hero archetype gets to resolve the terminal crisis, he ends up in the villain's grasp under circumstances such that *nobody else* is positioned to deal with the villain's plan. Ellis figures that he can short the geas out before it goes terminal and makes the Bond figure kill him. At which point Billington will be left sitting in an unassailable position since the *only* agent on the planet who's able to stop him wakes up and suddenly remembers that he's not James Bond."

I consider this for a full minute. "Whoops."

"That's how we screwed up," she says bleakly. "Billington had a handle on me all along. *I'm* his handle on *you*, and *you're* his handle on Angleton. He's stacked us up like a row of dominos."

I take a deep breath. "What happens if I go next door and smash the diorama?"

"The signal strength—" She shakes her head. "You noticed how fast it drops off? If you're close enough to smash it the backwash will kill you, but it'll probably leave Billington alive. If we could get word out about what's going on it might be worth trying, but nobody's close enough to do anything right now—so we're back to square one. It really has to be shut down in good order, the same way it was set up, and I'd guess that's why Billington's brought that fucker Pat aboard."

"Hang on," I say slowly. "Griffin was sure there was a shit-hot Black Chamber assassin in town this week. Some guy code named Charlie Victor. Could he do anything about Billington if we cleared a path?"

"Bob, Bob. *I'm* Charlie Victor." She looks at me with the sort of sympathetic expression usually reserved for terminal cases.

I consider this for a moment. Then an atavistic reflex kicks in and I snap my fingers. "Then you must be, um . . . you're the glamorous female assassin from a rival organization, right? Like Major Amasova in the film version of *The Spy Who Loved Me*, or Jinx in *Die Another Day*.

Does that mean you're the Good Bond Babe archetype or the Bad Bond Babe?"

"Well, I don't think I'm bad—" She's looking at me oddly. "What the hell are you talking about?"

"There are usually two Babes in every Bond movie," I say slowly. *Shit, she isn't British, is she?* I keep forgetting. She hasn't suffered through the ritual Bond movie every Christmas afternoon on ITV since the age of two. I'd probably seen them all by the time I was fifteen, *and* read some of the books, but I've never had to use the knowledge before now . . .

"Look, Bond almost always has two Babes. Sometimes it's three, and in a few of the later movies they experimented with one, but it's almost always two. The first to show up is the Bad Bond Babe, who usually works for the villain and who sleeps with Bond before coming to a nasty end. The second, the Good Bond Babe, helps him resolve the plot and doesn't shag him until just before the closing credits. You haven't slept with me so far, which probably means you're safe—at least, you're not the Bad Bond Babe. But you might be the glamorous female assassin from a rival organization, who's sort of a revisionist merge between the Bad Bond Babe and the Good Bond Babe, who turns up later, gets Bond out of a load of grief, tries to kill him, and eventually sleeps with him—"

"—I hope this isn't a come-on, monkey-boy, because if it is—"

"The setup's skewed. And I reckon we're going to have company soon."

"Huh? What do you mean?"

"There are never two girls in the movies that feature the glamorous rival assassin," I say, trying to get my head around what this signifies. "And this plot doesn't fit that mold. Not with Mo on her way out here."

"Mo? Your girlfriend?" Ramona gives me a hard-edged stare.

I look around. The shelves are covered in business administration titles with an admixture of first editions of Ian Fleming novels—boosters for the geas, at a guess—and the portholes show me a view of a dark blue sea beneath a turquoise sky.

"She said she was coming out here right after she finished reaming Angleton," I add, and wait for the double take.

"I find that hard to believe," Ramona says primly. "I've read her dossier. She's just an academic who stumbled into some classified topics!"

"Yes, but I'll bet that dossier doesn't have much on her after your organization gave her permission to leave, does it? That was three years ago. Did you know she works for the Laundry these days? And have you heard her violin? She plays music to die for . . ."

After digesting breakfast I find I've lost my appetite for socializing. I figure I could probably poke my nose all over the ship and make a nuisance of myself, but I'm not sure I want to jeopardize my tenuous status as a guest quite so soon. The real James Bond would be swarming through the ventilation ducts by now, kickboxing black berets overboard and generally raising hell, but my muscles are still aching from yesterday's swim and the nearest I've ever gotten to kickboxing is watching it on TV. Billington's fiendish plot is very well thought out, and the box he's slotted me into is dismayingly effective: I'm simply not a cold-blooded killer. If Angleton had sent Alan Barnes instead, *he'd* know how to raise seven shades of shit, but I'm not a graduate of the Hereford advanced college of mayhem and murder. Bluntly, I'm what used to be called a boffin, and these days is known as a geek, and while I know all the POSIX options to the kill(1) command, doing it with my bare hands is beyond my sphere of competence. I'm still having guilt attacks whenever I think of the guy offshore of the defense platform, and he was trying to make stabby on my ass at the time. So if I can't do the Bond thing, all that's left is to be true to my inner geek.

I slouch downstairs and go back to my room, where, on the TV, *Thunderball* has just about gotten round to the bit when it's all going pear-shaped and Largo pushes the panic button on his yacht and it turns into a hydrofoil. I shut the door, wedge the chair under it, plug my cummerbund into one USB port and my bow tie into the other, then do a quick in-and-out with the power cable.

While the usual messy list of device drivers is scrolling up the screen I check inside my wardrobe. Sure enough, someone's transferred my luggage from the hotel. The suitcase I took to Darmstadt has finally caught up with me, because presumably one of the perquisites of being employed by a mad billionaire with designs on global domination is that he has a gigantic logistics and fulfillment operation dedicated to ensuring that nothing is *ever* missing when it's needed. I pull on a fresh pair of black jeans, a faded Scary Devil Monastery tee shirt, and a pair of rubber-soled socks: I feel much better immediately. It's as if my brain is slowly rebooting, just like the Media Center PC. It might all be for nothing if the bloody thing isn't networked, but you never know until you try to find out; and I might be suffering from acute cravings for unfiltered Turkish cigarettes, but at least now I know *why*. It's like finding out that the reason your machine's running slow is because some virus-writing spod from Maui has shanghaied it into a botnet and is using your bandwidth to spam penis enlargement ads across the Ukraine; it's a pain in the neck, but knowing what's going on is the first step to dealing with it.

The boot sequence is complete. It's amazing what you can cram into a memory stick these days: it loads a Linux kernel with some very heavily customized device drivers, looks around, scratches its head, spawns a virtual machine, and rolls right on to load the Media Center operating system on top. I hit the boss key to bring the Linux session front and center, then have a poke around. If anyone interrupts me, another tap on the boss key will bring the brain-dead TV back on-screen. I hunker down and take a look around the /proc file system to see what I've got my hands on. Yep, it definitely beats duct-crawling as a way of kicking black beret ass.

It turns out that what I've got my hands on is annoyingly close to a stock Media Center PC. A Media Center PC is meant to look like a digital video recorder on steroids, able to play music and do stuff with your cable connection. So it's a fair bet that there's some sort of cable going into the back of the box, I reason. The box itself is pretty powerful — that is, it's roughly comparable to a ten-year-old supercomputer or a five-year-old scientific workstation — and when it isn't spending half its energy scanning for viruses or painting a pretty drop-shadow under the mouse pointer it runs like greased whippet shit. But it doesn't have all the occult applications support I'm used to finding preloaded, and as a development box it sucks mud — if I hadn't brought my USB key I wouldn't even have a C compiler.

Having 0wnZored the box, I go looking for network interfaces. First results aren't promising: there's a dedicated TV tuner card and a cable going into the back, but no wired Ethernet. But then I look again, and see the kernel's autoloaded an Orinoco driver. It hasn't come up by default, but . . .

Hah! Five minutes of poking around tells me what's going on here. This box probably came with an internal WiFi card, but it's not in use. The PC is simply being used as a television, hooked up to the ship's coaxial backbone, and nobody's even configured the Ethernet setup under Windows. Possibly they don't know about the network card? The Laundry-issue USB stick detected it straight off and started running AirSnort in promiscuous node, hunting for wireless traffic, but it hasn't found anything yet. After about thirty seconds I realize why, and start cursing.

I'm on board the *Mabuse*. The *Mabuse* is a converted Type 1135.6 guided missile frigate, from the Severnoye Design Bureau with love, by way of the Indian Navy. They may have stripped out the VLS cells and the deck guns, but they didn't remove the damage control or countermeasures suites or rip out the shielded bulkheads. This used to be a war-ship, and its internal spaces are designed to withstand the EMP from a nearby nuclear blast: WiFi doesn't tunnel through solid steel armor and a Faraday cage very well. If I'm going to hack my way into Billington's communication center I'm going to need to find a back door in: an occult network as opposed to an encrypted one.

I pop the other USB stick out of the distal end of the bow tie. It's a small plastic lozenge with a USB plug at one end and a handwritten label that says *RUN ME*. I plug it in, then spend ten minutes adding some modifications to its startup scripts. I pop it out then reach down and pick up my dress shoes. *What was it, left heel and right shoelace?* I strip out the relevant gizmos and stuff them in my pockets, hit the boss button, and flip the cummerbund upside down so that it's just taking a nap in front of the TV. They haven't given me back my gun, my phone, or my tablet PC, but I've got a Tillinghast resonator, an exploding bootlace, and a Linux keydrive: down but not out, as they say. So I open the door and go looking for a source of bandwidth to leech.

A modified type three Krivak-class frigate displaces nearly 4,000 tons when fully loaded, is 120 meters long—nearly twice as long as a Boeing 747—and can slice through the water at sixty kilometers per hour. However, when you're confined in a luxury suite carved out of the vertical launch missile cells and what used to be the forward magazine and gun turret, it feels a whole lot smaller: about the size of a large house, say. I make the mistake of going too far along a very short corridor, and find myself eyeball to hairy eyeball with a guard in standard-issue black beret and mirrorshades. One sickly smile later I'm staring at a closed door: I'm on a long leash, but this is as far as I'm going to get.

I'm about to go back to my room when two guards step into the corridor ahead of me. "Hey, you."

"Me?" I try to act innocent.

"Yes, you. Come here."

I don't have much in the way of options, so I let them lead me downstairs, along a corridor under the owner's territory, and then out into the working spaces of the ship. Which are painted dull gray, have no carpet or woodwork to speak of, and are full of obscure bits of mechanical clutter. Everything down here is cramped and roughly finished, and from the vibration and noise thrumming through the hull they've only soundproofed the executive suite. "Where are we going?" I ask.

"Com center. Mrs. Billington wants you." We pass a bunch of sailors in black, working on bits of who-knows-what equipment, then they take me up a staircase and through another door, down a passage and into another doorway. The room on the other side of it is long and narrow, like a railway carriage with no windows but equipment racks up to the ceiling on both sides of the aisle and instrument consoles every couple of feet. There are seats everywhere, and more minions in black than you can shake a stick at, still wearing mirrorshades—which is weird, because the lighting's dim enough to give me a headache. There's a continuous rumbling from underfoot which suggests to me that I'm standing right above the engine room.

Eileen Billington's suit is a surreal flash of pink in the twilight as she walks towards me. "So, Mr. Howard." Her smile's as tight as a six-pack of BOTOX injections. "How are you enjoying our little cruise so far?"

"No complaints about the accommodation, but the view's a bit monotonous," I say truthfully enough. "I gather you wanted to talk to me?"

"Oh yes." She probably means to smile sweetly but her lip gloss makes her look as if she's just feasted on her latest victim's throat. "Who is this woman?"

"Huh?" I stare blankly until she gestures impatiently at the big display screen next to me.

"*Her.* There, in the cross hairs."

We're standing beside a desk or console or whatever with a gigantic flat display. A black beret sitting in front of it is riding herd on a bunch of keyboards and a trackball: he's got about seventy zillion small video windows open on different scenes. One of them is paused and zoomed to fill the middle of the screen. It's an airport terminal and it looks vaguely familiar, if a little distorted by the funny lens. Several people are crossing the camera viewpoint but only one of them is centered—a woman in a sundress and big floppy hat, large shades concealing her eyes. She's got a messenger bag slung carelessly over one shoulder, and she's carrying a battered violin case.

Very carefully, I say, "I haven't a clue." Hopefully the noise of my heart pounding away won't be audible over the ship's engines. "Why do you think I ought to know her? What is this, anyway?" I force myself to look away from Mo and find I'm staring at the console instead, tier upon tier of nineteen-inch rackmount boxes stacked halfway to the ceiling. I blink and do a double take. They've got lockable cabinet fronts, but there's a key stuck in the one right above the monitor. I can see LEDs blinking behind it, set in what looks suspiciously like the front panel of a PC. Suddenly the USB thumb drive in my pocket begins to itch furiously. "You've sure got a lot of toys here."

Eileen isn't distracted: "She has something to do with your employers," she informs me. "This is the monitoring hub." She pats the monitor. Some imp of the perverse tickles her ego, or maybe it's the geas.

"Here you see the filtered take from my intelligence queue. Most of the material that comes in is rubbish, and filtering it is a big overhead; I've got entire call centers in Mumbai and Bangalore trawling the inputs from the similarity grid, looking for eyes that are watching interesting things, forwarding them to the *Hopper* for further analysis, and finally funneling them to me here on the *Mabuse*. Computer screens and keyboards where the owners are entering passwords, mostly. But sometimes we get something more useful . . . the girl on the cosmetics stand in the arrivals terminal at Princess Juliana Airport, for example."

"Yes, well." I make a show of peering at the screen. "Are you sure she's who you're looking for? Could it be one of that group, there?" I point at a bunch of wiry-looking surf Nazis with curiously even haircuts.

"Nonsense." Eileen sniffs aristocratically. "The surge in the Bronstein Bridge definitely coincided with that woman crossing the immigration desk—" She stops and stares at me with all the warmth of a cobra inspecting a warm, furry snack. "Am I monologuing? How unfortunate." She taps the black beret on his shoulder. "You, take five."

The black beret gets up and leaves in a hurry. "It's very unfortunate, this geas," she explains. "I could spill important stuff by accident, and then I'd have to send him to Human Resources for recycling." Her shoulder pads twitch up and down briefly, miming: *What can you do?* "It's hard enough to get the staff as it is."

"This looks like a great system," I say, fingering the frame of the workstation. "So you've got access to the eyeballs of anyone who's wearing Pale Grace™ eye shadow? That must be really hard to filter effectively." I'm guessing that I've got Eileen's number. I've seen her type before, stuck in a pale green annex block out behind the donut in Cheltenham, desperate to show off how well she's organized her departmental brief. Eileen's little cosmetics operation is genuine enough, but she came out of spook country just the same as Ellis did: staring at goats for state security. (Forget the whack-jobs at Fort Bragg; there's stuff the Black Chamber gets up to that makes it very useful to have a bunch of useful idiots prancing around in public out front, convincing everybody that it's all a bunch of New Age twaddle.) Eileen isn't much of a necromancer, but she's got the ghostly spoor of midlevel occult intelligence management all over her designer suit, and she's desperate for professional recognition.

"It's top of the range." She pats the other side of the rack, as if to make sure it's still there: "This baby's got sixteen embedded blade servers from HP running the latest from Microsoft Federal Systems division and supporting a TLA Enterprise Non-Stop Transactional Intelligence™ middleware cluster[11] connected to the corporate extranet via a leased *Intelsat* pipe." Her smile softens at the edges, turning slightly sticky: "It's the best remote-viewing mission support environment there is, including Amherst. We know. We *built* the Amherst lab."

*Amherst lab?* It's got to be a Black Chamber project. I keep my best poker face on: this is useful shit, if I ever get a chance to tell Angleton about it via a channel who isn't code named Charlie Victor. But right now I've got something more immediate to do. "That's impressive," I say, putting all the honesty I can muster at short notice into my voice. "Can I have a look at the front panel?"

Eileen nods. The hairs at the nape of my neck stand on end: for a moment everything seems to be limned in an opalescent glow and her gaze is simultaneously fixed on my face and looking at something a million miles away—no, infinitely far away: at an archetype I've borrowed, at an identity with the ability to sway any woman's sanity, the talent to lie like a rug and charm their knickers off at the same time. "Be my guest." She giggles, which is a not entirely appropriate sound—but sanity and consistency are in decreasing supply this close to the geas field generator (which, unless I am very much mistaken, is one deck up and five meters over from where we're standing). I reach up with one hand and flip the front panel down to look at the blinkenlights and status readouts on the front of the box. Eileen's still looking at me, glassily: I run my hand down the front panel, the palmed thumb drive between two fingers, and a moment later I twitch my finger over the reset button then flip the lid closed.

The screen freezes for a moment, then an error message dialog box flashes up. Eileen blinks and glances at the monitor then her head whips round: "What did you just do?"

I roll out my best blank look. "Huh? I just closed the front panel. Is it a power glitch?" I can't believe my luck. *Now if only Eileen didn't notice me stick the stubby little piece of plastic in the exposed USB keyboard socket . . .*

She leans forwards, over the screen. "One of the servers just went off-line." She sniffs then straightens up and waves the nearest beret over: "Get Neumann back here, his station's acting up." She looks at me suspiciously then glances at the workstation, her gaze flickering across the lid of the blade server. "I thought they'd fixed the rollover bug," she mutters.

"Do you still need me around?" I ask.

"No." She knows something's not right but she can't quite put her fin-

---

[11] Translation: "a bunch of computers."

ger on it: the alarm bells are ringing in her head but the geas has wrapped a muffling sock disguised as a software bug around the hammer. "I don't like coincidences, Mr. Howard. You'd better stick close to your quarters until further notice."

The goons escort me back to the padded-cell luxuries of the yacht. I'm trying not to punch the air and shout *"Yes!"* at the top of my voice: it's bad form to gloat. So I let them shut me in and look appropriately chastened until they go away again.

I chucked the tux jacket in the closet this morning. Now I rifle through the pockets quickly until I find the business card Kitty gave me. Yes, it *is* scratch 'n' sniff on steroids: about five tiny compartments full of Pale Grace™ mascara, eye shadow, foundation, and other stuff I don't recognize. There's even a teensy brush recessed into one side of it, like the knife on a Swiss Card. Humming tunelessly I pull out the brush and quickly sketch out a diagram on the bathroom mirror—a reversed image of the one I sketched in the sand around the hire car. With any luck it'll damp down any access they've got to the cabin until they wise up and come to look in on me in person. Then I take a deep breath and *imagine* myself punching the air and shouting *"Yes!"* by way of relief. (Better safe than sorry.)

Let me draw you a diagram:

Most of what we get up to in the Laundry is symbolic computation intended to evoke decidedly nonsymbolic consequences. But that's not all there is to . . . well, any sufficiently alien technology is indistinguishable from magic, so let's call it that, all right? You can do magic by computation, but you can *also* do computation by magic. The law of similarity attracts unwelcome attention from other proximate universes, other domains where the laws of nature worked out differently. Meanwhile, the law of contagion spreads stuff around. Just as it's possible to write a TCP/IP protocol stack in some utterly inappropriate programming language like ML or Visual Basic, so, too, it's possible to implement TCP/IP over carrier pigeons, or paper tape, or daemons summoned from the vasty deep.

Eileen Billington's intelligence-gathering back end relies on a classic contagion network. The dirty little secret of the intelligence-gathering job is that information doesn't just want to be free—it wants to hang out on street corners wearing gang colors and terrorizing the neighbors. When you apply a contagion field to any kind of information storage system, you make it possible to suck the data out via any other point in the contagion field. Eileen is already running a contagion field—it's the root of her surveillance system. I've got a PC on my desk that isn't connected to the ship's network, but I've just stuffed a clone of its brain into a machine that *is* on that network—so all I need to do is contaminate my own link with Pale Grace™, and then . . .

Well, it's not as easy as all that. In fact, at first I'm shit-scared that I've broken the TV (I'm pretty sure the warranty specifically excludes damage due to the USB ports being full of mascara) but then I figure out a better way. Tracing the Fallworth graph on the bathroom mirror backwards with a Bluetooth pen hooked into the television is not the recommended way of establishing a similarity link with a network you're trying to break into—it's not even the second worst way of doing so—but it just happens to be the only one I've got available to me, so I use it. Once I've brought up the virtual interface I poke around until I find the VPN port that the USB dongle I planted in Eileen's server farm is running. The keystroke logger is happily snarfing login accounts, and I figure out pretty rapidly that Eileen's INFOSEC people aren't paranoid enough—they figure that for systems aboard a goddamn destroyer, who needs to go to the bother of biometrics or a challenge/response system like S/Key? They want something they can get into fast and reliably, so they're using passwords, and my dongle's captured six different accounts already. I rub my knuckles and go poking around the server farm to see what they're doing with it. Give me a bottle of Mountain Dew, an MP3 player hammering out something by VNV Nation, and a crate of Pringles: that's like being at home. Give me root access on a hostile necromancer's server farm, and I *am* at home.

Still, I'm worried about Mo. That view Eileen wanted me to vet—even if Eileen bought my story— means that Mo is here, on the island, and she's under the gun. The Pale Grace™ surveillance net is tracking her and the stabbing sense of anxiety that doubles as my guilty conscience tells me I need to make sure she's all right before I start trying to figure out a way to reestablish communications with Control. So I pull up a VNC session, log into one of Eileen's server blades using a password looted from one of the black berets, and go hunting for a chase cam.

## Chapter 13:
## Fiddler Hits the Roof

Ten hours aboard an airbus is never a happy fun experience, even in business class. By the time Mo feels the nose gear touch down on the centerline of the runway, rattling the glasses up front in the galley, she's tired, with a bone-weary exhaustion that is only going to go away if she can find the time to crash for twelve straight hours on an oversprung hotel mattress.

But. *But*. Mo hums tunelessly to herself as the airbus taxis towards the terminal. *What's he gotten himself into this time?* she asks herself, a bright point of worry burning through the blanket of fatigue. Angleton wasn't remotely reassuring, and after that disturbing interview with Alan she went and did some digging. Asked Milton, actually, the one-armed, old security sergeant with the keys to the conservatory and the instrument store. "What's a big white one?" she repeated, refusing to take the first answer he offered—or to notice the prickling in her ears and the flush of blood to her cheeks until he set her straight.

*Fuck. Nukes?* What the wily old bastard had been offering Alan— right under her nose!—was a kamikaze insurance policy. The realization fills her with even more apprehension. Bob's got himself into something so dicey that Angleton thinks a destroyer full of SAS and SBS special forces isn't enough, and they may need to call in a Trident D-5 ballistic missile to nail whatever's been stirred up down there. That kind of overkill isn't on the menu, outside of a bad spy thriller: that or CASE NIGHTMARE GREEN, anyway, and CASE NIGHTMARE GREEN hasn't started yet, and even then the real nasties probably won't arrive until at least ten years after the grand alignment commences.[12]

As soon as the seatbelt sign blinks off and the cabin crew announces that it's safe for passengers to leave their seats, Mo is up like a jack-in-the-box to haul down her overnight bag, wide-brimmed hat, and the battered violin case from the overhead locker. She clutches the instrument case protectively all the way to the baggage claim area and immigration queue, as if she's walking through a dangerous part of town and it's a gun. But when the customs officer gives her the hairy eyeball and asks her to open it she smiles brightly and clicks back the locks to reveal—a violin.

"See?" she says. "It's an Erich Zahn special, wired with Hilbert-space

---

[12] They tend to oversleep.

pickups. I don't think there's another one on this side of the Atlantic." She's relying on his ignorance to let her through. Polished to the creamy gloam of old ivory, the electric violin nestles in its case like a Tommy gun, to all outward appearances nothing but a musical instrument *Just don't ask me to play it,* she prays. The custom officer nods, satisfied it's not an offensive weapon, and waves her on. Mo closes the case with false calm, nods her head, and locks the instrument back in. *If only you knew . . .*

One airport concourse is much like any other. Mo tows her suitcase over to the exit, where taxis jostle for position opposite the curb. It smells hot and damp with a faint undertone of rotting seaweed. There are people everywhere, tourists in bright clothes, natives, business types. A woman in a suit brandishes a clipboard at her: "Hi! How would you like a free sample of eyeliner, ma'am?"

*Why the hell not?* Mo nods and accepts the sample, smiles, idly rubs a smear of it on her wrist to check the color, and moves on before the woman can deliver her sales spiel. *Okay, the hotel next. That'll do.* As she walks through the door the Saint Martin climate clamps down on her like a warm, wet blanket, coating her in sweat. Abruptly, she's grateful for the hat and the sundress Wardrobe Department insisted she wear. It's not her style at all, but her usual jeans and blouse would be . . . *Hell, call me the Wicked Witch of the West and have done with it.* She fans herself with the hat as she walks over to the taxi queue. *What a mess.*

"Where to, ma'am?" asks the taxi driver. He's pegged her for a tourist, probably American; he doesn't bother to get out and help her with the suitcase.

"Maho Beach Hotel, if you don't mind." She glances at him in the mirror: he's got crow's-feet around prematurely aged eyes, hair the color of damp newsprint.

"Okay. Twenty euros."

"Got it."

He starts the engine. Mo leans back and closes her eyes. She doesn't let her fingers stray from the violin case, but to a casual onlooker she could be snoozing off a case of jet lag. In fact, when she's not keeping a surreptitious eye open for tails, she's working her way down a checklist she's already committed to memory. *Let's see. Check in, phone home for a Sitrep, confirm Alan's on site, then . . .* a guilty frisson: *off the roadmap. Find Bob. If necessary, find this Ramona person. Make sure Bob's safe. Then figure out how to get him disentangled before it sucks him in too deep . . .*

Anxiety keeps her awake every meter of the way to the hotel, drags her tired ass to the front desk for checkin:

"Mrs. Hudson? Your husband checked in this morning. He said you'd be arriving and to leave you a key to your suite." The receptionist smiles mechanically. "Have a nice stay!"

*Husband?* Mo blinks and nods, making thankful sounds on autopilot. "Which room is he in?"

"You're in 412. Elevators are left past the fountain."

She rides the elevator upstairs in thoughtful silence. *Husband?* It's not Bob. He wouldn't pull a stunt like this without forewarning her. And it's a suite: Laundry expense accounts don't usually run that high. *Alan Barnes? Or . . . ?*

Mo pauses outside the door to room 412. She sets down her overnight bag on top of her suitcase, takes off her sunglasses and hat, and opens the violin case. She slides the card key into the lock with the same hand that grips the end of her bow, then nudges the door handle: by the time it's half-open she has the violin raised to her chin and the bow poised above a string that seems to haze the air around it in a blue glow of Cerenkov radiation.

"Come on out where I can see you," she calls quietly, then kicks the ungainly train of bags forwards through the door, steps forwards after it, and lets the door shut itself behind her.

"I'm over here." The middle-aged white guy in the tropical suit isn't Alan. He's sitting in the office chair behind the hotel room desk, nursing a glass of something that probably isn't water; he's got a twelve-hour beard and he looks haggard. "You're all that Angleton sent? Jesus."

"What are you doing here?" Mo takes another step into the room, glancing sidelong through the doorways into the two bedrooms and the bathroom. "You're not part of my cover."

"Last minute change of plan." He smiles lopsidedly. "You can put the violin down—what were you planning to do with it, make me dance?"

"Who are you?" Mo keeps the violin at the ready, its neck aimed at the interloper.

"Jack Griffin, P Division." *The station chief,* she remembers. He waves at the room. "It's all yours. Bit of a mess really."

Mo's left earring tingles. It's a ward, attuned to warn her when someone's being truthful. In her experience, the average human being tells a little white lie once every three minutes. Knowing when they're telling the truth is much more useful than knowing when they aren't. "So what are you doing here?" she asks tensely.

"There's been a problem." Griffin's accent is clipped, very old-school-tie, and he sounds rueful. "Your predecessor ran into a spot of bother and Angleton asked me to take you in hand and make sure you didn't follow his example."

"A spot of bother, you say." Mo has half-closed the gap separating them before she realizes what she's doing. The violin string hums alarmingly, feeding off her anxiety. "What happened?"

"He was working with a bint from the opposition." Griffin puts his glass down and stares at her. "Billington lifted them both about, oh, twelve hours ago. Invited them to some sort of private party at the casino and the next thing you know they were over the horizon on a chopper bound for his yacht: the coastal defenses are compromised, you know." Griffin shrugs. "I told him not to trust the woman, she's obviously working for Billington by way of a cut-out . . ."

Her earring is itching, throbbing in Morse: Griffin is mixing truth and falsehood to concoct a whirlpool of misdirection. Mo sees red. "You listen to me—"

"No, I don't think I will." Griffin reaches into his pocket for something that looks like a metal cigarette case. "You folks from head office have fucked up, pardon my French, all the way down the line, sending lightweights to do a professional's job. So you're going to do things my way—"

Mo takes a deep breath and draws the bow lightly across one string. It makes a noise like a small predator screaming in mortal agony and terror, and that's just the auditory backwash. A drop of blood oozes from each fingertip where she grips the neck of the instrument. Griffin's gin and tonic spreads in a puddle across the carpet from where he dropped it. She walks over to him, rolls his twitching body into the recovery position, and squats beside him. When the convulsions cease, she touches the end of the instrument to the back of his head.

"Listen to me. This is an Erich Zahn, with electroacoustic boost and a Dee-Hamilton circuit wired into the soundboard. I can use it to hurt you, or I can use it to kill you. If I want it to, it won't just stop your heart, it'll slice your soul to shreds and eat your memories. Do you understand? Don't nod, your nose is bleeding. Do you understand?" she repeats sharply.

Griffin shudders and exhales, spraying tiny drops of blood across the floor. "What's—"

"Listen closely. Your life may depend on whether you understand what I'm about to tell you. My *predecessor*, who is missing, means rather a lot to me. I intend to get him back. He's entangled with a Black Chamber agent: fine, I need to get her back, too, so I can disentangle them. You can help me, or you can get in my way. But if you obstruct me and Bob dies as a result, I'll play a tune for you that'll be the last thing you ever hear. *Do you understand?*"

Griffin tries to nod again. "Beed. A. T'shoo."

Mo stands up gracefully and takes a step back. "Get one, then." She tracks him with the neck of the violin as he pushes himself upright slowly then shuffles towards the bathroom.

"You're a bard. Woban," he says aggrievedly, standing in the doorway clutching a tissue to his nose. It's rapidly turning red. "I'b on you're sibe."

"You'd better be." Mo leans against the sideboard and raises her bow to a safe distance above the fiddle. "Here's what we're going to do: You're going to go downstairs and hire a helicopter. I'm going to phone home and find out where my backup's gotten to, and then we're going to go for a little run out to visit Billington's yacht, the *Mabuse*. Got that?"

"Bub he'd be aboard the yacht! He'b geb you!"

Mo smiles a curious, tight smile. "I don't think so." She keeps the fiddle pointed at Griffin as he splutters at her. "Billington is all about money. He doesn't do love, or hate. So I'm going to hit him where he doesn't expect to be hit. Now get moving. I expect you back here inside an hour," she adds coolly. "You *really* don't want to be late."

I'm punch-drunk from surprises—the sight of Mo strong-arming Griffin into hiring her a helicopter is shocking enough, and the idea that she's willing to jump in on the Billingtons without a second thought just because of me is enough to turn my world upside down—but then I realize: If *I* can see her, what about the bad guys?

I may not be able to send her a message—the surveillance feed is strictly one-way—but I can try to cover her ass on this side of the firewall. I rummage around for what's left of the Pale Grace™ sample, then draw some more patterns on the side of the PC and trace them with the 'toothpen. They're interference patterns, stuff to break up the contagious spread of the information on my screen. Then I go back to watching. There's not a lot I can do right now, not until we dock with the *Explorer*, but if Mo makes it out there I can make damn sure that, geas or no geas, whatever she's planning takes the Billingtons by surprise.

Griffin has barely closed the door when Mo's energy gives out and she slumps in on herself with a tiny whimper. She puts the violin down, then pulls a black nylon tactical strap from a side pocket in its case—her hands shaking so badly it takes her three attempts to fasten it—then slings the instrument from her shoulder like a gun. She walks over to the desk, wobbling almost drunkenly with fatigue or the relief of tension, and flops down in the chair. The message light on the phone is blinking. She picks up the handset and speed-dials.

"Angleton?"

"Dr. O'Brien."

"Your station chief. Griffin. Is he meant to be in on this side of the operation?"

Angleton is silent for three or four seconds. "No. He wasn't on my list."

Mo stares at the door, bleakly. "I sent him on a wild goose chase. I may have up to an hour until he gets back. Penetration confirmed, he's your pigeon. At a guess, Billington got to him via his wallet. Got any suggestions?"

"Yes. Leave the room. Take hand luggage only. Where did you tell him you were going?"

"I sent him to hire a chopper. For the *Mabuse*."

"Then you should go somewhere else, by any means necessary. I'm opening your expense line: unlimited fund. I'll have local assets take Griffin out of the picture."

"I can live with that." Mo's shoulders are shaking with barely repressed fury. "I could kill him. Do you want me to do that?"

Angleton falls silent again. "I don't think that would be useful at this point," he says finally. "Do you have your primary documents with you?"

"I'm not stupid," she snaps.

"I didn't say you were." Angleton's tone is unusually mild. "Go to ground then call me with a sanitized contact number. Stay there and don't go anywhere. I'll have Alan make contact and pick you up when it's safe to proceed."

"Got it," she says tensely, and hangs up. Then she stands up and collects her violin case. "Right," she mutters under her breath. "Go to ground."

Mo packs methodically and rapidly. The instrument goes back in its carrier. Then she opens her hand luggage—a black airline bag—and tips the contents out on the bed. She squeezes the violin case inside, adds a document wallet and a toilet bag from the pile on the quilt, then zips it up and heads for the door. Rather than using the elevator she takes the emergency stairs, two steps at a time. At the ground floor, there's a fire exit. She pushes the crash bar open—it squeals slightly, a residue of rust on the mechanism—and slips out into the crowd along the promenade at the back of the hotel.

Over the next hour Mo puts her tradecraft to work. She doubles back around her route, checking her trail in window reflections in shop fronts: changes course erratically, acts like a tourist, dives into souvenir markets and cafés to make a show of looking at the menu while keeping an eye open for tails. Once she's sure she's clean she walks the block to the main drag and goes into the first clothes shop she passes, and then the second. Each time, she comes out looking progressively different: a tee shirt under her sundress, then a pair of leggings and an open shirt. The dress has vanished. With the addition of a new pair of sunglasses and a colorful scarf to keep the sun off her head, there's no sign of Mrs. Hudson. She finishes up at a café: diving into its coolly air-conditioned interior she orders two double espressos and drinks them straight down, shuddering slightly as the caffeine hits her.

*What next?* Mo is clearly fighting off the effects of jet lag. She stands up tiredly and steps outside again, shouldering the heat like a heavy burden. Then she heads directly away from the row of nearby hotels, towards the marina on the edge of the harbor and the row of motorboats for hire.

I am just beginning to get my head around the fact that Mo is not only out here, but she's a player—and she isn't going to follow Angleton's instructions—when there's a pounding on my door. I hammer the boss key and spin round in my chair, slamming one leather-padded arm into my right kidney as I try to stand up; then the door opens and the black beret is pointing his mirrorshades at me, lips set in a disapproving scowl. "Mr. Howard, you're wanted on deck."

I scramble to my feet dizzily, wincing and rubbing my side. It's probably a good thing I whacked it—I don't think I could avoid looking disturbed or guilty if I wasn't actually in physical pain. I don't know what the hell Mo thinks she's doing, but it doesn't look like she's planning on following orders and going to the mattresses until Alan calls for her. *And what's Alan doing here anyway?* I wonder as I follow the two guards up the stairs to the deck.

Angleton only calls Alan in when there's some serious head-breaking to be done. He's OIC for the Territorial SAS squadron tasked with supporting Occult Operations in the field—some of the scariest—not to mention most eccentric—special forces soldiers in the British Army. I've been along for the ride when they went right through a rip in space-time to head-butt an ancient evil that was threatening to squirm through; I've seen them secure an industrial estate in Milton Keynes with a suspected basilisk on the loose; and I've had the dubious pleasure of being rescued by them on exercise at Dunwich. *Maybe Angleton's sent the heavy cavalry*, I decide, hopefully: it's easier to swallow than the alternative, which is that Angleton's written me off as beyond hope and has called them in for Plan B.

The guard up front surprises me when we get to deck level, by turning away from the door to the conservatory and instead opening a hatch onto a narrow green-painted corridor leading aft. "This way," he tells me, while his backup guy hangs behind.

"Okay, I'm going," I say, as agreeably as I can manage. "But where are we going to?"

Mirrorshades man opens a door at the far end of the tunnel and steps through. "HQ," he says over his shoulder.

I emerge, blinking, onto a stretch of deck I hadn't seen before, sandwiched between a big outboard motorboat and a whole bunch of gray cylinders sticking out of the superstructure beneath a rack of masts and antennae. The motorboat hangs from some sort of crane affair. It's getting crowded here: the space is already occupied by Ramona, in company with McMurray, his designer-clad thugette Miss Todt, and a couple more black berets. "Ah, Mr. Howard." McMurray nods at me. "Feel up to a little cruise?"

"Where are you—"

My guard pokes me in the back with a finger. "Jump in." The black berets on deck are setting up a control station for the crane. McMurray gestures at the boat: "This won't take long. We're nearly there."

"Where are we going?"

"To the *Explorer*." McMurray seems to be in a hurry. "Go on, it doesn't do to be late."

"Come on." That's Todt. She clambers over the motorboat's side and jumps down inside.

Ramona follows her, not without a murderous look at McMurray. **Can you—?** I begin to think, then I realize I can't hear her inside my head. *Shit.* I glance round and the guard who led me up here nods significantly at the boat. *Double-shit.* They must have come up with a portable version of the jammer they used on me and Ramona last night. I climb over the side of the boat and sit down next to Ramona, at the opposite side from Todt and McMurray.

"Where's the jammer?" I ask quietly.

"I think he's got it." She doesn't meet my eyes. "They don't trust us."

"If our positions were reversed, would you?" asks Johanna. I startle. She smiles: it's not a friendly expression.

"I'd trust you anywhere, darling," says Ramona: "I'd trust you to fuck up."

"You—" Todt turns a peculiar shade, as if she's getting ready to explode. McMurray puts a hand on her arm before she can stand up.

"You'll both be quiet," he says in a curiously calm tone, and oddly, they both shut up. I glance sideways and see Ramona's cheek twitching. She rolls her eyes frantically at me, and the penny drops.

I lean over towards McMurray. "You've made your point. Let them talk. They won't do it again."

"You sure of that, boy?" McMurray looks amused. "I've known these hellcats and their type longer than you've been alive, and they'll—"

"That's not the point!" I stab one finger at him. "Do you want her willing cooperation, or not?"

He makes a sound halfway between a laugh and a snigger, just as there's a loud grinding noise from the crane and the boat lurches. "All right, have it your way," he says indulgently as we lift off the deck with a bump that throws Ramona against me.

"Bastard," she says indistinctly. Then the mist clears and I can suddenly feel her presence in my mind again, as warm and vibrant as my own pulse. **Not you, him,** she adds internally. **Thanks. It's not like Pat to make a mistake like that, lifting both blocks at the same time.**

**Think it's intentional?** I ask, wondering how long we've got to talk.

**Not really.**

McMurray is saying something to Todt, who's slumped against the railing away from him. I try to make the most of his lapse: **I've noticed them making other mistakes. Listen, I got into Eileen's surveillance network. Mo's arrived, and there's a backup team on the way to rescue us.** The crane swings us over the edge of the *Mabuse* and the boat drops like a lift towards the sea below, leaving my stomach somewhere above my head. **Griffin's on the spot, looks like he's been playing an inside game. Ramona, if you run into Mo, don't get her pissed-off, she's brought her—**

I suddenly realize that my head's full of cotton-wool and Ramona isn't listening. She looks at me and blinks, then stares at McMurray, who smiles faintly in response. "What's that about?" she asks, aggrieved.

"No talking out of class." He looks at me speculatively. A porthole winds past the back of his head, embedded like a zit in the flank of a behemoth. "Orders from the boss. Once you're aboard the TMB-2, *then* you get to talk among yourselves."

"Enjoy the peace and quiet while you can," Todt sneers.

We hit the water with a neck-jarring thump, and everything gets very busy for a minute or two. The two black berets who've been riding down with us fire up the engine and cast off the cables securing us to the crane, which in turn throws us variously into one another and across the bottom of the boat. It's a bouncy, jarring ride, and I get a lungful of spray as I try to sit up. It ends with me coughing over the side, wishing I had Ramona's gills. By the time I'm half-recovered we're turning away from the *Mabuse* and accelerating across open water. I finally get some air back and look around to see that we've circled the former destroyer. In the distance, there's land on the horizon, but much closer to home a monstrous cliff-like bulk looms over us—the former *Glomar Explorer*.

My sense of scale fails me when I try to take it in. I find myself looking up, and up, and up—the thing's as big as a skyscraper, nearly a fifth of a kilometer long. After the *Explorer* was retired and mothballed in the 1970s they cut the superstructure away, but Billington's people have rebuilt the huge derrick that towers ten stories above the deck, the two huge docking legs and the big cranes at each end of the moon pool, and the entire drilling platform and pipe management system. It looks like an oil rig humping a supertanker. There are loud pumps or engines running up on the deck, and a hammering noise overhead; looking up I see a chopper closing in on the helipad at the stern of the ship. "Who's that?" I ask.

"That'll be the boss arriving," says McMurray. To the driver: "Take us in."

We motor steadily towards a platform hanging near the waterline, halfway along one flank of the giant ship. The ship sits eerily still in the water, as if it's embedded in the top of a granite pillar anchored to the sea floor. As we get closer, the noise from the drilling platform up top gets louder, a percussion of rhythmic clanking and clattering sounds adding to the bass line of the motors and the squeal of drill segments grating across each other as the pipe-feeding mechanism winches them off the huge pile under the superstructure and passes them to the automatic roughneck mechanism. When we tie up alongside the metal staircase I feel the deep humming vibration of the bow and stern thrusters holding the ship on position against the waves.

"Up and out!" The black berets are waving us onto the platform. While Todt and the guards are busy down below, Ramona and I follow McMurray up the ladder towards a door two decks up. He leads us on a bewildering tour of the colossal drilling ship, up and down narrow corridors and cramped stairwells and finally along a catwalk overlooking a giant room with no floor—the moon pool. A black beret on duty at the door passes us ear defenders as we step out onto the catwalk. The noise is deafening and the air feels like I've walked into a cross between a sauna and a machine shop: greasy and humid with a stink of overheated metal parts. A sickly sweet undertone hints of fishy things that have died and not gone to heaven, embedded in the machinery that moves the underwater doors at the bottom of the moon pool. It's not like this in the movies: presumably James Bond's enemies all employ crack task-forces of janitors spritzing everything with pine-scented disinfectant at fifteen-minute intervals to keep down the rotten shellfish stink.

About ten meters in front of me, a metal pipe as thick as my thigh descends from the underside of the drilling deck, hypnotically spearing into the pool below. I stare at it, following it down to the bubbling point of white water where it plunges into the moon pool and the deep ocean below. Somewhere far down there a drowned alien artifact awaits its arrival. Presumably Billington, with his expertise in Gravedust interrogations, knows what to expect. Above us the drilling platform shudders and roars, hellishly loud as it feeds infinite numbers of pipe segments to the sea god.

McMurray walks along the catwalk until he reaches a row of incongruous office windows and a door, just as you'd expect to find overlooking the shop floor of a factory or a workshop. We follow him inside.

It's a big room, and as befits the villain's working headquarters, one wall is occupied by a gratuitously large projection screen showing a map of the sea floor below the *Explorer*. There are lots of consoles with blinking lights, and half a dozen black berets sitting at desks where they mouse around schematics on a computer-controlled engineering interface. So far so good. It would look a lot like the control room of a power station, if not for the fact that there's something that resembles a dentist's chair in the middle of the floor. The ankle and wrist straps and the pentacles around its base suggest that it's not designed for root canal jobs. To top it all off there's a gloating villain standing front and center, wearing a Nehru suit and cradling an excessively somnolent Tiddles in his arms.

"Ah, Ms. Random, Mr. Howard! So glad you could make the show!" I twitch at Billington's victorious smirk. Somehow or other I'm having difficulty controlling the urge to punch him out, sap two or three black-uniformed guards, steal an MP5K, and let fly.

"You need to turn down the gain on that geas: it's overpowering," I suggest.

"All in due course." Billington looks amused, then mildly concerned. "Are you feeling up to the job, Ms. Random? You look a bit peaked."

Ramona snorts. "If you want me to do this thing, you really ought to tell Pat to drop the interference. I can't hear myself think, much less Bob."

"Thinking is not what I'm paying you for. However, no purpose is served by separating you at this time." Billington nods to McMurray: "Allow them full intercourse."

McMurray looks alarmed: "But the suppressor's all that's keeping their entanglement from proceeding to completion! If I stop it now they'll only have about two days' individuality left, then we'll have to cut them loose or deal!"

*Shit*. I glance at Ramona. She stares at me, wide-eyed. "I understand," Billington says affably, "but as it will take less than twenty-four hours to accomplish the retrieval, I fail to see what the objection is?" He thinks for a moment then comes to a decision. "Drop the suppressor field now. When Ms. Random returns, you will immediately end their state of entanglement, as we discussed earlier." He turns to me, and gestures at the dentist's chair arrangement: "Please take a seat, Mr. Howard."

I stare at him. "What *is* that thing?"

Billington's pupils narrow, lizardlike: "It's a comfy chair, Mr. Howard. Don't make me ask twice."

"Uh-huh." Behind me I sense more than see McMurray adjust some sort of compact ward he keeps strapped to his left wrist: the fuzzy fogbank in my head fades away and I can feel Ramona's unease, the cold, hard deck beneath her feet, and the churning emptiness in her stomach.

**Bob, do as he says!** Ramona's sense of urgency carries over, leaving a nasty metallic taste in my mouth. I edge towards the chair nervously.

"What are the straps for?" I ask.

"They're just in case of convulsions," Billington says soothingly, "nothing you need to worry about."

**It's a high-bandwidth sympathetic resonator,** Ramona tells me. Snowflakes of half-remembered knowledge slide into place in my head. Control cables suffer weird anomalies when you stick them under kilometers of water; Billington wants a better way of tracking his submersible grab, of staying in control over the retrieval process. Unlike its seventies predecessor, the new grab that Billington's had built is designed to be manually operated by one of Ramona's people, the Deep One/human hybrids. And it doesn't use fiber optics or electrical cables for monitoring the process via TV—it uses two entangled occult operatives. This chair will plug me right into Eileen's surveillance grid, far more efficiently than a swipe of mascara across the eyelashes. **Look, if you don't do it, we're screwed so hard it's not funny.**

I weigh my chances, then swallow. "The straps go," I say. Then I sit down tensely before I can change my mind.

"Jolly good." Billington smiles. "Pat, if you'd be so good as to escort Ms. Random to the pool, I believe her watery chariot is ready to depart."

That's about the last thing I hear, because as my butt hits the padding on the chair I almost black out. I've been strongly aware of Ramona's presence ever since McMurray dropped his blocking ward, like having a mild case of double vision. But that was before I plugged myself into the chair. It's an amplifier. I'm not sure how they've managed to make it work, but Ramona's perceptions almost overwhelm my awareness of my own body. She's got a sharper sense of smell than me, and I can appreciate her mild disgust with Billington's after-shave—there's a bilious undernote of ketosis to it, as if it's covering up something rotten—and the tang of ozone and leaking hydraulic fluid as she moves towards the doorway. Her dislike and fear of McMurray is gnawing away in the background, and there's her concern for—I shy away. It takes a real effort of will to move my arms, even to realize that they're still there: I manage to lie down, or rather to flop bonelessly, then close my eyes.

**Ramona?** I ask.

**Bob?** She's curious, worried, and anxious.

**This chair, it's an amplifier—**

**You really didn't know? You weren't being sarcastic?** She pauses with her hand on the doorknob. McMurray looks round.

**No shit, what am I meant to do here? What's it for?**

**If you're asking, they haven't switched it on yet.** She looks round and now I can see myself lying in the chair, with a couple black berets leaning over me—

**Hey! What are they doing—**

**Relax, it's in case you start convulsing.** McMurray starts to say something, and Ramona speaks aloud: "It's Bob. You didn't tell him what to expect."

"I see," says McMurray. "Ramona, channel. Bob, can you hear me?"

I swallow—no, I swallow with Ramona's throat muscles. "What's happening?" My voice sounds oddly high. Not surprising, considering whose throat it's coming out of.

McMurray looks pleased. He glances at the guards bending over my body, and I turn my head to follow, feeling the unaccustomed weight of her hair, the faint pull of tension on the gills at the base of her throat: I see myself—Bob—lying flat out, strapped down while they hook up bits of bleeping biotelemetry. A medic stands by, holding a ventilator mask. "Amplification to level six, please," says McMurray, then he looks back at me—at Ramona, that is. "Your entanglement lets you see through Ramona's eyes, Bob. It also lets her speak through your mouth, when you're at depth. The defense field around the chthonic artifact plays hell with electronics and scrambles ordinary scalar similarity fields, but the deep entanglement between you and Ramona is proof against just about any interference short of the death of one of the participants. When she's at depth, Ramona will operate the controls of the retrieval grab by hand—they're simple hydraulic actuators—to lock onto the artifact, then signal through you to commence the lift process."

"But I thought, uh, doesn't it take days to ride the grab down?"

McMurray shakes his head. "Not using this model." He looks insufferably smug. "Back in the sixties they designed the grab to be fixed to the end of the pipe string. We've updated it a little; the grab clamps to the outside of the string and drops down it on rollers, then locks into place when it reaches the end. If we were going to unbolt and store the pipe sections when we retrieved it, we'd take two days to suck it all back up, it's true—but to speed things up we've got a plasma cutter up top that can slice them apart for recycling instead of unbolting each joint. This baby is nearly four times faster than the original."

"Doesn't Ramona need to decompress or something, on the way up?"

"That's taken care of: her kind have different needs from us land-dwellers. It'll still take us a whole day to bring the string up; she'll be all right." He turns away, dismissively. "Dive stations, please."

Ramona follows him through the door and along the catwalk to a dive room where there's a whole range of esoteric kit laid out for her. She's done this sort of thing before and finds a kind of comfort in it. It's very strange to feel her hands working with straps and connectors that feel large to her slim fingers—shrugging out of her clothes and across the chilly steel deck plates, then one leg at a time into a wet suit. There's more unfamiliar stuff: an outer suit threaded with thin pipes that connect to an external coupling, weight belt, a knife, torches. **What's the plumbing for?** I ask. **I thought you could breathe down there.**

**I can, but it's cold, so they're giving me a heated suit.** I get a picture: hot water is pumped down through the pipe string under high pressure, used to power the grab assembly via a turbine. Some of the water is bled off and cooled by a radiator until it's at a comfortable temperature for circulating through Ramona's suit. She's going to be down there for more than a day—

**You're taking a bar of chocolate?** I ask, boggling slightly as she slides the foil-wrapped packet into a thigh pocket.

**There are fish down there, but you wouldn't want to eat them raw. Shut up and let me run through this checklist again.**

I hang back and wait, trying not to get in the way. A dive error wouldn't be the lethal disaster for Ramona that it would be for me, but it could still leave her stranded and exposed in the chilly darkness, kilometers below the surface. Even if she's immune to the predations of the BLUE HADES defense polyps, there are other things down there—things with teeth out of your worst nightmares, things that can see in the dark and burrow through flesh and bone like drill-mouthed worms.

Ramona finally pulls her helmet on. Open-faced, with no mask or regulator, she turns and faces McMurray. "Ready when you are."

"Good. Take her to the pool," he says to the technicians, and strides back out in the direction of the observation room.

Down in the moon pool, the waters are warm and still. The drill string has stopped descending, although there are muted clanking and clattering noises from the platform overhead. Around the walls of the pool the sea is dark, but something bulky and flat squats below the water in the middle of the pool. There are technicians in the water, scudding about in a Zodiac with an electric outboard: they seem to be collecting cables that connect the submerged platform to the instrument bay below the observation room windows.

Ramona walks heavily down the metal steps bolted to the wall of the pool until she's standing just above the waterline. There are lights on top of the submersible grab, lined up in two rows to either side of an exposed platform with railings and, incongruously, an operator's chair, its seat submerged beneath two meters of seawater. There are two divers working on a panel in front of the seat; behind it, there's a bulky arrangement of shock absorbers and rollers clamped around a steel yoke the size of a medium truck, threaded around the drill string. Ramona steels herself, then steps off the platform. Water slaps her in the face, cool after the humid air in the moon pool. She drops below the surface neatly, opens her eyes, and—this fascinates me—blows a stream of silver bubbles towards the surface. Her nasal sinuses burn for a moment as she inhales a deep draught of water, and there's a moment of panicky amphibian otherness before she relaxes the flaps at the base of her throat, and kicks off towards the submerged control platform, reveling in the sense of freedom and the flow of water through her gills. Nictitating membranes slide down across my—no, her—eyes, adding a faint iridescent haze to the view.

"Ready to go aboard," I feel her saying through my throat. "Can you hear me, Billington?" Somewhere a long way away I can hear my body coughing as Ramona swims over the seat and lets the two support divers strap her into it and hook up her warm-water hoses. She's doing something funny with my larynx and it's not used to it.

**Hey, careful about that,** I nudge her.

There's an echoing flash of surprise. **Bob? That feels really weird . . . **

**You're not doing it right. Try using it like this.** I show her, swallowing and clearing my throat. She's right, it feels really weird. I close my eyes and try to ignore my body, which is lying on the dentist's chair as Ellis Billington leans close to listen to her.

There's a panel with about six dozen levers and eight mechanical indicator dials on it, all crude-looking industrial titanium castings with
rough edges. Ramona settles in her seat and waves a hand signal at the
nearest diver. There's a lurch, and the seat drops under her. A loud
metallic grating sound follows, felt as much as heard, and she glances
round to watch the huge metal harness grip the pipe string. I feel a pressure in her ears and I swallow for her. The pipe is rising through the
docking collar—no, the platform I'm sitting on is sinking, about as fast
as an elevator car. The great wheels grip the pipe, held in place to either
side by hydraulic clamps. I manage to prod her into looking up: the
moon pool and the ship merge into a dark fish-shaped silhouette against
a deep blue sky, already darkening towards a stygian night broken only
by the spotlights that ridge the spine of the huge grab we're riding on.

It's odd how Ramona's senses differ from my own. I can feel the pressure around me, but it's different from the way it feels to me in my own
skin. Waves of sound move across me, sounds too low- or too high-
pitched to hear with my own ears. Ramona can sense them in the small
bones of her skull, though. There are distant clicking hunting noises
from marine mammals, strange sizzling and clattering noises—krill, tiny
crustaceans floating in the high waters like a swarm of locusts grazing on
the green phytoplankton. And then there are the deep bass whoops and
groans of the whales, growing abruptly louder as we drop below a ther-
mocline. The water on my exposed face is suddenly cold, and there's a
sense of pressure on my skull, but a few deep gulps of water flushing
through my gills clears it. Ramona swallows seawater as well as breathing it, letting it flood her stomach and feeling the chill as it infiltrates
her gut. Rarely used muscles twitch painfully into life, forcing strange
structures to realign themselves. **How are you taking this?** she
asks me.

**I'll cope,** I tell her. The light outside our charmed circle of
lamps has dimmed to a faint twilight. In the distant murk I spot a gray
belly nudging past, possibly a deep-ranging tiger shark or something less
well-known. The pipe rolls endlessly up through the docking harness.

"Dive stable at one meter per second," Ramona tells Billington. I lie
back, do the math: it's going to take us a little over an hour to reach the
abyssal plain where JENNIFER MORGUE Two lies broken and deso-
late beneath 400 atmospheres of pressure, on a bed of gray ooze that's
been accreting since before hairless apes slouched across the plains of
Africa.

There's something soothing about the motion of the pipe string.
Once every few minutes Ramona opens my mouth and murmurs some-

thing technical: some of the time Billington turns and relays an instruc-
tion or two to the ever-present flunky waiting at his shoulder. I lapse into
a dreamy, near-hypnotized state. I know something's wrong, that I
shouldn't be this relaxed under the circumstances—but a great sense of
lassitude has come over me as our entanglement nears completion. *Lie
back and think of England.* Where the hell did that come from? I blink
and try to throw back the sense of disengagement.

**Ramona—**

**Shut up and let me concentrate here.** She's working two of the
levers and there's a loud *clank-bump* that I feel more than hear. **Okay,
that's it.** We resume our descent, passing an odd bulge where the pipe
triples in diameter for about three meters, like a python that's just swallowed a small pig. **What is it?**

**What do we do after you raise the artifact?**

**What do—** She stops. **We get disentangled, right?**

**Yes, but what then?** I persist. For some reason I feel dizzy when
I try to follow this line of reasoning. I can almost sense my own body
again, see Billington leaning over me expectantly like an eager cultist inspecting his dead leader for signs of imminent resurrection. **Aren't we
supposed to do . . . something?**

**Oh, you mean kill Ellis, massacre his guards, and set the ship on
fire before making our escape on jet skis?** she says brightly.

**Something like that.** A thought bubbles up to the surface of my
mind and pops, halfheartedly: **You gave that a lot of thought, huh?**

**The jet skis are on C deck, and there are only two of them. I've got
to get Pat out of here—I'm afraid you'll have to make your own arrangements,** she says briskly. **But yeah, I can definitely nail Billington.**

The penny drops—icy and cold, right down the back of my
metaphorical net. **You've been planning this as a hit on Billington
right from the start!**

**Well, that's the whole point of my being here, isn't it? Why else
would they send an assassin? I mean, d'oh!**

I ought to be more shocked; maybe it's had time to sink in, what she
really is. (And there's the whole escape thing, of course. Am I imagining
things or did she feel a twinge of guilt when she told me I'd have to swim
for myself?) **Your people used me to get close to Billington,** I accuse.

**Yup.** It's funny how these little misunderstandings only come
clear when you're 800 meters below sea level and dropping like an express elevator towards Davy Jones's tentacle-enhanced locker. **As soon
as Billington shuts down the geas field I'll be free to act on my own
agency.** I can feel a funny tight smirk tugging at the sides of her

mouth. It's not humor. **He doesn't realize it yet, but he's so screwed you could plug him into the mains and call him Albert Fish.**

**But you can't do that unless we're disentangled, surely? And for that you need **

The other shoe drops, or rather, she kicks me between the eyes with it in her next comment: **Yes, that's why Pat is here. You didn't think supervisors from Department D routinely defect, did you? He's under even tighter control than I am.** And at that moment I can see the geas that's binding her to the Black Chamber, tying her to the daemon they've imposed on her will: bright as chromed steel, thick as girders, compelling obedience. The Laundry warrant card is bad enough—if you try to spill our secrets you'll die, not to put too fine a point on it—but this is even worse. We do it for security. This is nothing short of vindictive. If she thinks a disloyal thought too far, the Other will be let loose—and the first thing it will do is feed on her soul. No wonder she's terrified of falling in love.

I'm fully awake now, mind spinning like a hamster on a wheel in a cage on a conveyor belt heading for the maw of an industrial-scale wood chipper: there are thoughts I really desperately don't want to think while I'm inside her skull and vice versa. On the other hand, something *does* occur to me . . .

**If McMurray's working with you, do you think you can convince him to give me back my mobile phone?**

**Huh?**

**It's no big deal,** I explain, **it's just, if I've got my phone I can escape. You want that to happen, right? Once we get back to the surface, you and McMurray want me out of the picture as soon as possible. I can get a ride home just about any time, as long as I've got my phone.**

**But we're out of range of land,** she points out logically.

**What makes you think I was going to use it to make a phone call?**

**Oh.** We watch the pipe string unreel for a minute or two in silence. Then I feel her acquiesce: **Yeah, I don't think that'll be a problem. In fact, why don't you just ask him for it? I mean, it's not as if you can phone home, so you can probably use some of your super-agent mojo while you've got it.**

I am conflicted between wanting to hug Ramona, and kick her in the shins for being a smart-arse. But I guess that's her job, I mean, she really *is* a glamorous, high-flying super-spy and assassin and I'm just an office nerd who's along for the ride. It doesn't matter what Angleton thinks of me, all I can really do here is lie back and think of—*England*—not to mention the . . . *game of Tetris* . . . on my phone—

**Stop trying to think, monkey-boy, you're making my head hurt and I've got to drive this thing.**

Monkey-boy? *That does it.* I send her a picture of a goldfish gasping in a puddle of water beside a broken bowl. Then I clam up.

## Chapter 14:
## Jennifer Morgue

We ride down to the abyssal plain in silence, doing our best to barricade each other out of our minds.

The journey down actually takes nearer to three hours than one. There's a lengthy pause in the darkness of the bathypelagic zone, a kilometer down, while Ramona stretches and twists in strange exercises she's learned for adapting to the pressure. Her joints make cryptic popping noises as she moves, accompanied by brief stabbing pains. It's almost pitch-black outside our ring of lights, and at one point she unstraps herself from the seat and swims over to the edge of the platform to relieve herself, still tethered by the umbilical hose that pumps warm water through her suit. Looking out into the depths, her eyes adjust slowly: I can see a cluster of faint reddish pinpricks swimming at the edge of visibility. There's something odd about her eyes down here, as if their lenses are bulging and she can see further into the red end of the spectrum; by rights she ought to be as blind as a bat. From the sounds these sea creatures are making they're some sort of shrimp, luminescent and torpid as they feed on the tiny scraps of biomass raining down from the illuminated surface like oceanic dandruff.

The water down here is frigid—if Ramona didn't have the heated suit she'd likely freeze to death before she could surface again. She messes with a pair of vents near her chin, and a tepid veil of warm water flows across her face, smelling faintly of sulfur and machine oil. "Let's get this over with," she mutters as a weird itching around her gills peaks and begins to subside: "If I stay down here much longer I'll begin to *change*." She says it with a little shudder.

She fastens herself back into the control chair and throws the lever to resume our descent. After an interminable wait, there's a loud clang that rattles through the platform. "Aha!" She glances round. The descent rollers have just passed a football-shaped bulge in the pipe painted with the white numerals "100." "Okay, time to slow down." Ramona hits the brakes and we slide over another football, numbered "90," then "80." They're counting down meters, I realize, indicating the distance to go until we hit something.

I feel Ramona working my jaws remotely; it's most unpleasant—my mouth tastes as if something died in it. "Nearly there," she tells the technician who's taken Billington's place during the boring part of the descent. "Should be seated on the docking cone in a couple of minutes." She squeezes the brake lever some more. "Thirty meters. What's our altitude?"

The technician checks a screen that's out of my line of sight: "Forty meters above ground zero, one-seventy degrees out by two-two-five meters."

"Okay . . ." We've slowed to a crawl. Ramona squeezes the brake lever again as the "10" meter football creeps past, climbing the pipe string. The brakes are hydraulically boosted—the grab she's sitting on weighs as much as a jumbo jet—and the big rollers overhead groan and squeal against the pipe string, scraping away the paint to reveal the gleam of titanium-graphite composite segments. (No expense is spared: that stuff is usually used for building satellites and space launchers, not drilling pipes that are going to be cut apart once they've been hauled back up to the surface.) I watch as Ramona frowns over a direction indicator and carefully uses another lever to release water to the directional control jets, shoving the platform round until it's lined up correctly with the docking cone below. Then she releases the brake again, just enough to set us gliding down the final stretch.

The pipe flares out to three times its previous diameter, then stops being a pipe: there's an enormous conical plug dangling from the drill string, point uppermost, with flanges that lock into a tunnel on the underside of the platform's harness, like Satan's own butt-plug. We drop steadily, and the rollers are pushed outwards by the cone until the harness locks into place around the cone. "Okay, securing the grab now," Ramona comments, and throws the final lever. There's an uneven series of bangs from below the deck as hydraulic bolts slide into place, nailing us to the end of the pipe. "You want to begin steering us over to the target zone?"

"Make sure you're secured in your seat," the tech advises her, whispering in my ear. "Visual check. Are your wards contiguous?"

Ramona switches on her hand torch, casts the beam around the metal panels at her feet. Pale green light picks out the non-Euclidian circuitry of a Vulpis exclusion array etched into the deck with a welding torch. It extends all the way around her chair. "Check. Wards clear and unobstructed. How are they powered?"

"Don't worry, we took care of that." *Oh great*, I realize, they're going to drop Ramona into the field around JENNIFER MORGUE Site Two—a field that tends to kill electronics and, quite possibly, people—with only a ward for protection, one that needs blood to power it. "It's full of Pale Grace™ Number Three®[13], and we've got a sacrifice waiting in cell four to energize it. Should be commencing exsanguination in two minutes."

"Um, okay." Ramona checks her compass, suppressing a stab of anger so strong it nearly shocks me into a languorous yawn. "What did the subject do to rate a starring role?"

"Don't ask me—underperforming sales rep or something. There's plenty more where she came from." The technician steps back for a while, at Billington's command, then nods, and steps forwards into view again. "Right. You're about to see the wards light up. Tell me immediately if they stay dark."

Ramona glances down. Eerie red sparks flicker around the runes on the deck. "It's lit."

"Good." Somewhere disturbingly close to the back of my own mind I can feel her daemon coil uneasily in its sleep, a sensual shudder rippling through us as it senses the proximity of death. The skin of my scrotum crawls; I feel Ramona's nipples tighten. She shudders. "What's that?"

Billington leans over me now. "You're twenty meters off the counter-intrusion field rim, sitting in the middle of a contagion mesh with a defensive ward around you. If my analysis is correct, the field will absorb the sacrifice and let you in. Your entanglement with Bob up here will confuse its proximity sense and should let you survive the experience. You might want to uncap your periscope at this time: from now on, you're on your own until you dump the ballast load."

He steps back smartly and the wards inscribed on the floor around my chair light up so bright that the glare reflects off the ceiling of the control room above me, pulling me back into my own head for a moment. "Hey—" I begin to say, and just then . . .

Things.

Get.

Confused.

*I'm Ramona:* leaning over a narrow, glass letter box in the middle of the console, staring down at a brown expanse of mud as I twitch the thruster control levers, flying the platform and its trailing grapple arms closer towards a cylindrical outcropping in the middle of the featureless plain. I'm in my element, slippery and wet, comfortably oblivious to the thousands of tons of pressure bearing down on me from above.

---

[13] The word "Three" and the digit "3" (and non-English localizations thereof) are patented intellectual property of TLA Systems Corporation and denote the entity that, in the set of integers, is the ordinal successor of 2 and predecessor of 4. Used by kind permission.

*I'm Bob*: limp as a dishrag, passive, lying on a dentist's chair in the middle of a pentacle with lights flaring in my eyes, a cannula taped into my left forearm, and a saline drip emptying into it through an infusion pump—*They've drugged me*, I realize dizzily—a passenger, along for the ride.

*And I'm someone else*: frightened half to death, strapped down on a stretcher with cable ties so I can't move, and the robed figures around me are chanting, and I'd scream if I could but there's something wrong with my throat and why won't anyone rescue me? Where are the police? This isn't supposed to happen! Is it some kind of sorority initiation thing? One of the sisters is holding a big knife. What's she doing? When I get out of here I'm going to—

I stare down at the muddy expanse unrolling beneath the platform. Rotating the periscope I check the ten grab-arms visually: they all look okay from here, though it won't really be possible to tell for sure until I fire the hydraulic rams. They cast long shadows across the silt. Something white gleams between two of them, briefly: skeletal remains or something. *Something*.

Glimpse of silvery strings across the grayness, like the webs of a spider as big as a whale. Conical spires rising from the mud, dark holes in their peaks like the craters of extinct volcanoes. Guardians, sleeping. I can feel their dreams, disturbed thoughts waiting: but I can reassure them, *I'm not who you want*. Beyond them, more open ground and a sense of prickling fire that ripples across my skin as I float past an invisible frontier left over from a war that ended before humans existed—

She screams silently and the terror gushes inside my head as the knife tears through her throat, blood spurting in thick pulses draining towards zero—

The daemon in my head is awake now, noticing—

The blood vanishing, drained into the fiery frontier on the sea floor—

And we're inside the charmed circle of death around JENNIFER MORGUE Site Two.

A long time later, McMurray comes up to me and clears his throat. "Howard, can you hear me?" he asks.

I mumble something like *leave me alone*. My head aches like it's clamped in a vice, and my mouth is a parched desert.

"Can you hear me?" he repeats patiently.

"Feel. Like shit." I think for a minute, during which time I manage to crowbar my eyes open. "Water?" Something's missing, but I'm not sure what.

McMurray turns away and lets a medical type approach me with a paper cup. I try to sit up to drink but I'm as weak as a baby. I manage a sip, then I swallow: half the contents of the cup go down my chin. "More." While the paramedic is busy I get my throat working again. "What happened?"

"Mission accomplished." McMurray looks self-satisfied. "Ramona's on her way back up with the goods."

"But, the—" I stop. Hunt around in my head. "You put the block back," I accuse.

"Why wouldn't I?" He steps out of the way to let the nurse or paramedic or whoever pass me another cup of water. This time I manage to lift a hand and take hold of it without making a mess of things. "It's going to take another twelve hours or so to bring her up, and I don't want you deepening the entanglement while that's happening."

I stare into his pale blue eyes and think, *Got you, you bastard*. Even though it's treachery against Billington, who thinks he owns McMurray body and soul, I get the picture. "Did she get the, the thing?" I ask. Because that's when I blacked out, right after we entered the zone of the death spell or curse or force field or whatever it is around the wrecked chthonian war machine on the seabed. Right when Ramona recognized what she was looking for, bang in the middle of the periscope, and opened my mouth to announce, "I've got it. Give me three more meters, and stand by for contact."

"Yes, she got it."

"When, when are you going to unhook us?"

"When Ramona's back up and decompressed—tomorrow. She has to be physically present, you know." His expression turns sour. "So it's back to your room for the duration."

"Agh." I try to sit up and nearly fall off the chair. He puts one hand on my shoulder to steady me. I glance around, my vision still blurry. Billington's across the room conversing with his wife and the ship's officers; I'm all on my own over here with McMurray and the medic. Icy fear clamps around my stomach. "How long have I been under?"

McMurray glances at his watch, then chuckles. "About six hours." He raises one eyebrow. "Are you going to come quietly or am I going to have to have you sedated?"

I shake my head. Quietly I say, "I know about Charlie Victor." His fingers dig into my shoulder like claws. "You want to settle with Billington, that's none of my business," I add hastily. "But give me back my phone first."

"Why?" he asks sharply. Heads turn, halfway across the control room floor: his face slides into an effortless smile and he waves at them then turns back to me. "Blow my cover and I'll take you down with me," he hisses.

"No fear." I swallow. *How much can I safely reveal . . . ?* At least Ramona isn't listening in; I don't need to doublethink around McMurray right now. "She told me about the jet skis, I know how we're getting out of here." *I know that there's a seat reserved for you, but no room for me.* It's time to lie like a rug: "The phone isn't official issue, it's mine. I bought it unlocked, not on contract. Cost me close to a month's wages, I really can't afford to lose it when the shit hits the fan." I put a whine in my voice: "They'll take that expenses packet you made me gamble away out of my pay for the next year and I am going to be *so* screwed—"

"We're out of range of land," he says absent-mindedly, and his grip relaxes. I swing my legs over the floor and steady myself until the world stops spinning around my head.

"Doesn't matter: I'm not planning on phoning home. But can I have it back anyway?" I get one foot on the deck outside the ward.

McMurray cocks his head to one side and stares at me. "Okay," he says, after a moment, during which I feel none of the weirdly otherworldly sense of strangeness that came over me while I was putting one across Eileen in the monitoring center. "You can have your damned phone back tomorrow, before Ramona surfaces. Now stand up—you're going back to the *Mabuse*."

McMurray details four black berets to escort me back to my room aboard the *Mabuse*, and it takes all of their combined efforts to get me there. I'm limp as a dishcloth, hung-over from whatever drugs Billington's tame Mengele pumped into me. I can barely walk, much less climb into a Zodiac.

It's dark outside—past sunset, anyway—and the sky is black but for a faint red haze on the western horizon. As we bump up against the side of the *Mabuse*, where they've lowered a boarding platform, I notice the guards are still wearing their trademark items: "Hey, what's with the mirrorshades?" I ask, slurring my words so that I sound half-drunk. " 'S nighttime, y'know?"

The goon who's climbing the steps ahead of me stops and looks round at me. "It's the eyeliner," he says finally. "You think wearing mirrorshades at night looks stupid, you should try carrying an MP-5 with a black jumpsuit and a beret while wearing eye shadow."

"Cosmetics don't go / with GI Joe," chants the goon behind me, a semitone out of tune with himself.

"Eye shadow?" I shake my head and manage to climb another step.

"It's the downside of our terms and conditions of employment," says Goon Number One. "Some folks have to piss in a cup to pass federally mandated antidrug provisions; we have to wear make-up."

"You're shitting me."

"Why would I do a thing like that? I've got stock options that're going to be worth millions after we IPO. If someone offered you stock options worth a hundred million and said you had to wear eyeliner to qualify . . ."

I shake my head again. "Hang on a moment, isn't TLA Corporation already publicly traded? How can you IPO if it's already listed on NAS-DAQ?"

Goon Number Two behind me chuckles. "You got the wrong end of the stick. That's Install Planetary Overlord, not Initial Public Offering."

We climb the rest of the steps in silence and I reflect that it makes a horrible kind of sense: if you're running a ubiquitous surveillance web mediated by make-up, wouldn't it make sense to plug all your guards into it? Still, it's going to make breaking out of here a real pain in the neck—much harder than it looked before—if the guards are also nodes in the surveillance system. As we trudge through the corridors of the ship, I speculate wildly. Maybe I can use my link into Eileen's surveillance network to install an invisibility geas on the server, and use the sympathetic link to their eyes as a contagion tunnel so that they don't see me. On the other hand, that sort of intricate scheme tends to be prone to bugs—get a single step wrong in the invocation and you might as well be donning a blinking neon halo labeled ESCAPING PRISONER. Right now I'm so tired that I can barely put one foot in front of another, much less plan an intricate act of electronic sabotage: so when we get to my room I stagger over to the bed and lie down before they even have time to close the door.

Lights out.

It's still dark when I wake up shuddering in the aftershock of a nightmare. I can't remember exactly what it was about but something has filled my soul to overflowing with a sense of profound horror. I jerk into wakefulness and lie there with my teeth chattering for a minute. It feels like an entire convention of bogeymen has slithered over my grave. The shadows in my room are full of threatening shapes: I reach out and flick the bedside light switch, banishing them. My heart pounds like a diesel engine. I glance at the bedside clock. It's just turned five in the morning.

"Shit." I sit up and hold my head in my hands. I'm not making a good showing for myself, I can tell that much: frankly, I've been crap. After a moment I stand up and walk over to the door, but it's locked. No moonlight excursions tonight, I guess. Somewhere a kilometer below the surface, Ramona will be dozing in that chair, slowly decompressing as a nightmare dreams on in the ancient war machine tucked between the ten mechanical grabs on the underside of the retrieval platform. Aboard the *Explorer,* Billington paces the command center of his operation, those weirdly catlike eyes slitted before the prospect of world domination. Somewhere else on board the *Explorer,* the treacherous McMurray is waiting for Billington to terminate the Bond geas, so that he can release Ramona's daemon and then she can assassinate the crazed entrepreneur, delivering JENNIFER MORGUE Site Two into the hands of the Black Chamber.

It's pretty damn clear now, isn't it? And what am I doing about it? I'm sitting on my ass in a gilded cage, looking pretty while acting pretty ineffectual. And I keep finding myself mumbling *lie back and think of England,* which is just plain humiliating. It's almost as if Billington has already terminated the invocation that's binding me to the heroic role—

"Shit," I say again, startling myself. *That's it!* That's what I should have noticed earlier. The heroic pressure of the geas is no longer bearing down on me, skewing my perspective. I'm back to being myself again, the nerdy guy in the corner. In fact, it feels like I'm being squeezed into a state of fatalistic passivity, waiting for a rescuer to come get me out of this situation. The reason I feel so indecisive and like crap is, I'm going through cold turkey for heroism. Either that or the focus of the Hero trap has shifted—

I check the alarm clock again. It's now ten past five. What did McMurray say? *Sometime today.* I pull out the chair and sit down in front of the Media Center PC. *Jet skis on C deck.* They're going to give me my phone back soon. *What was the speed dial code?* As soon as we're untangled Charlie Victor is going to kill Billington. *Gravedust systems.* JENNIFER MORGUE isn't as dead as McMurray seems to think. That's the only explanation I can come up with for Billington's behavior.

"Oh Jesus, we are so fucked," I groan, and hit the boss key so I can see whether Mo, at least, is safe.

"It's like this," says Mo, checking the seals on her instrument case once more, "I can do it without attracting attention. Whereas, if you guys do it, you're not exactly inconspicuous. So leave the job to me."

She's sitting on a gray metal platform slung over the side of a gray metal ship. A flashy-looking cigarette boat is tied up next to it, all white fiberglass and chromed trim until you get back to the enclosed cockpit and the two gigantic Mercury outboards in the tail. The man she's talking to is wearing a wet suit, a bullet-proof vest, and horn-rimmed spectacles. "What makes you think you can do it?" he asks, with barely concealed impatience.

"Because it's what I've spent the past four bloody months training for, thank you very much." She squints at the lock, then nods minutely and puts the case down. "And before you say it's what you've spent the last twenty years specializing in, I'd like to remind you that there are any number of reasons why you *shouldn't* go in first, starting with their occult defenses, which are my specialty. Then there's the small matter of their point defense systems, starting with an Indian Navy sensor suite that Billington's spent roughly fifty million on, upgrading to NATO current standards. The bigger the initial insertion the greater the risk that it'll be spotted, and I don't think you want them to realize they're being stalked by a Royal Navy task group, do you?"

Barnes nods thoughtfully. "I think you underestimate how fast and hard we can hit them, but yes, it's a calculated risk. But what makes you think you can do it alone?"

Mo shrugs. "I'm not going in without backup—that would be stupid." She grins momentarily. "On the other hand, you know how this setup works. If I stay back at HQ it all goes pear-shaped. I think the smart money is riding on them already having retrieved JENNIFER MORGUE: the worst-case operational contingency is that, with Billington's expertise in necro-cognitive decoding, he also knows how to make it work. I expect any first attempt we make to fail—unless I'm along for the ride and in a position to act out my assigned role in accordance with the geas he's got running. I'm not trying to be sticky here, I'm just reading the rules."

"Shit." Barnes is silent for a moment, evidently running some sort of scenario through his mind's eye. Then he nods briskly. "All right, you convinced me. One reservation: you've got a ten-minute lead, maximum, and not a second longer. If there's even a hint of instability in the geas field, all bets are off and I'm taking both teams in immediately. Now, one last time—can you enumerate your priorities?"

"First, secure the field generator so Billington can't shut it down on schedule. Next, release the hostages and hand them off to the 'B' team for evac. Third, neutralize the chthonian artifact and if necessary sink the *Explorer*. That's all, isn't it?"

Captain Barnes clears his throat. "Yes. Which I'm afraid means you just passed Angleton's cricket test. But you need this, first." He hands Mo a red-striped document wallet. "Read it, then sign here."

"Oh dear," Mo says mildly, running one finger down a series of closely typed paragraphs of legalese drafted by a bunch of Home Office lawyers with too much time on their hands: "Do I have to?"

"Yes," Barnes says grimly. "You must. That's *also* in the rules. They don't hand these out every day. In fact, they're so rare I think they probably had to invent it just for you . . ."

"Well, pass me the pen." Mo scrawls a hasty signature then hands the document back to him. "That all square?"

"Well, there's one other thing I'd like to add," Barnes says as he seals the document into a waterproof baggie and passes it to a sailor waiting on the bottom steps of the ladder. "Just between you and me, just because you've got the license, it doesn't mean you've got to use it. Remember, you're going to have to live with yourself afterwards."

Mo smiles, her lips drawn razor-thin. "It's not me you should be worrying about." She picks up a waterproof fiberglass black case and checks the latches on it carefully. "If this goes to pieces, I'm going to have words with Angleton."

"Really? I'd never have guessed." Barnes's tone is withering, but he follows it by sitting down next to Mo and leaning close: "Listen, this is *not* going to go pear-shaped. One way or another, we've got to make it work, even if none of us end up going home. But more importantly—*you* listen—this isn't about you, or me, or about Bob, or about Angleton. If the Black Chamber gets their hands on JENNIFER MORGUE it's going to destabilize everything. But that's just the start. We don't know *why* Billington wants it but the worst-case analyses—well, use your imagination. Watch out for any signs—anything, however small—that suggests Billington isn't in the driving seat, if you follow my drift. Got that?"

Mo stares at him. "You think he's possessed?"

"I didn't say that." Andy shakes his head. "Once you start asking which captains of industry are being controlled by alien soul-sucking monsters from another dimension, why, anything might happen. That sort of thing leads to godless communism and in any case they've got friends in high places like Number Ten, if you know what I mean. No, let's not go there." His cheek twitches. "Nevertheless, there is no obvious reason why a multibillionaire *needs* to acquire alien weapons of mass destruction—it's not exactly on the list of best business practices—so you be careful in there. As I said, you can call 'A' troop in at any time after you make contact, but once you've made contact they're going in ten minutes later whether you ask for them or not. Let's check your headset—"

There's a knock on the door.

I hit the boss key, flip the keyboard upside down, and stand up just as the door begins to open. It's one of the stewards from upstairs, not a black beret. "Yes?" I demand, slightly breathless.

He holds out a silver tray, half-covered by a crisp white linen cloth. My Treo sits in the middle of it, pristine and untouched. "This is for you," he says dully. I look at his face and shudder as I reach for the phone—he's not himself, that's for sure. Green lights in the back of the eye sockets and a distinct lack of breathing are usually indicators that you're looking at a nameless horror from outside space-time rather than something really sinister like, say, a marketing executive: but you still wouldn't want to invite one back to your cabin for a drink and after-dinner conversation.

I take the phone and hit the power button. "Thanks," I say. "You can go now."

The dead man turns and leaves the room. I close the door and hit the button to fire up the phone's radio stage—not much chance of getting a signal this far from land, but you never know. And in the meantime . . . well, if I can get back in touch with Control somehow and tell them not to send Mo in after me that would be a good thing. I find I'm shaking. This new Mo, fresh from some kind of special forces class at Dunwich, spilling blood with casually ruthless abandon, and working as an assault thaumaturgist with Alan's headbangers, scares me. I've lived with her for years, and I know how hard she can be when it's time to rake a folk festival organizer over the coals, but that new violin she's carrying gives me the willies. It's as if it comes with a mean streak, a nasty dose of ruthlessness that's crawled into the tough-minded but intermittently tender woman I love, and poisoned her somehow. And she's heading for the *Explorer*, now, to—*secure the field generator, release the hostages, neutralize the chthonian artifact, sink the* Explorer—

I stop dead in mid-thought. "Huh?" I mumble to myself. "*Secure* the field generator?"

That was the geas field she and Alan were discussing. The probability-warping curse that dragged me kicking and screaming into this stupid role-play thing, the very invocation I'm supposed to be destroying. She thinks it's aboard the *Explorer*? And Angleton wants her to keep it *running*?

I stare at my phone. There's no base station signal, but I've still got a chunk of battery charge. "Does not compute," I say, and stub my thumb on the numeric keypad. I'm frustrated: I admit it. Nobody tells me anything; they just want to use me as a communications link, keep me in the dark and feed me shit, pose around in evening drag at a casino and drink disgusting cocktails. I go back to the desk, flip the keyboard rightside up, and hit the boss key again. Mo's sitting in the cockpit of the cigarette boat, fastening her five-point safety harness. A pair of sailors is installing a kit-bag full of ominous black gadgets in the seat next to her; over the windscreen I can see the gray flank of a Royal Navy destroyer, bristling with radomes and structures that could be anything from missile batteries to gun turrets or paint lockers, to my uneducated eye. The horizon is clear in all directions but for the ruler-straight line of an airplane's contrail crawling across the sky. I glance sidelong at the phone, longingly: if I could call her up I could tell her—if only I wasn't stuck on board this goddamn yacht, moping like the token love interest in a bad thriller while the shit is going to hit the fan in about two hours aboard the *Explorer*, which is sitting less than half a kilometer away—

"What the fuck has gotten *into* me?" I ask, wondering why I'm not angry. This bovine passivity just isn't me: Why does it feel like my best option is to just sit here and wait for Mo to arrive? Damn it, I need to get things moving. McMurray can't afford to lose me before Ramona's delivered her surprise party trick to Billington: that gives me a lever I can pull on. And Angleton wants the geas field generator kept running? That's my cue. The penny drops: if the geas field actually works, and Billington can't shut it down, then he's going to be in a world of hurt. Could that be Angleton's plan? It's so simple it's fiendish. Almost without thinking, I dial 6-6-6. It's time to call my ride and get moving. After all, even the Good Bond Babe—token love interest and all—doesn't always spend the final minutes of the movie waiting for her absent love to come rescue her. It's time to kick ass and set off explosions.

## Chapter 15:
## Scuttle to Cover

An hour later, having done everything I can via the Media Center PC, I pocket my phone and open the door to my room.

There's a lot you can do in an hour with a PC on a supposedly secure but in reality penetrated-to-Hell-and-back network, especially if you've got a USB flash drive full of hacking tools. Unfortunately there's rather less you can do on such a network without making it blindingly and immediately obvious that it's been 0wnZor3d. But on the third hand, by this point I don't give a shit. I mean, I thoroughly expect what I've done to the PC to be exposed within a matter of hours, but worrying about it is taking second place right now to worrying whether I'll still be alive by then. There's a time when you've got to look at any asset and think, *Use it or lose it, baby,* and that time is definitely up when you're counting down the minutes in the last hour before the men in black come for you. So, what the hell.

To start with, I disable all the system logging mechanisms, so they won't be able to figure out what's going on in a hurry. I set the remote login ports to shut down an hour hence and scramble the password databases they're so quaintly relying on, and whip up a shell script that'll fry the distributed relational database behind the surveillance management system by randomly reversioning everything and then subtly corrupting the backups.

But that's just a five-fingered warm-up exercise. Billington's empire is based on the premise that you buy cheap, off-the-shelf gear, customize it to meet a MILSPEC requirement, and sell it back to the government at a 2,000 percent markup. An awful lot of his network—all the workstations those cubicle drones from Mumbai have on their desks, basically— run Windows. You'd expect a corporate enterprise rollout of Vista to be locked down and patrolled by rabid system administrators wearing spiked collars, and you'd be right: by ordinary commercial standards, Billington's network is pretty good. The trouble is, the Windows security model has always been inside out and upside down, and they're all running exactly the same service pack release. It's a classic corporate monoculture, and I've got exactly the right herbicide stuffed up one end of my bow tie, thanks to the Laundry's network security tiger team. Eileen's mission-critical surveillance operation may be running on horribly expensive blade servers with a securely locked-down NSA-approved UNIX operating system, but the workstations are . . . well, the technical term for what they'll be when I get through with them is *toast*. And by the time I get through with them Eileen is going to have a whole lot of the wrong kind of zombies on her hands.

The Laundry carped over giving me a decent car, even though I can prove that Aston Martins depreciate more slowly and cost less in running repairs than a Smart (after all, half the Aston Martins ever built are still on the road, and they've been in business for three-quarters of a century). But they didn't even blink over giving me a key drive stuffed full of malware that must have cost CESG about, oh, two million to develop, and which I am about to expend in the next half-hour, and which will subsequently leak out into the general public domain, whereupon it will give vendors of virus scanners spontaneous multiple orgasms and cause the authors to be cursed from one pole of the planet to the other. It's a classic case of misplaced accounting priorities, valuing depreciable capital assets a thousand times more highly than the fruits of actual labor— but that's the nature of the government organization. Let's just say that if what I'm about to unleash on the Billingtons' little empire doesn't take several hundred sysadmin-years and at least a week of wall-clock time to clean up, my middle names aren't Oliver and Francis.

My work done, I glance at my phone. The display is showing a cute, little animated icon of a baby-blue Smart car, dust bunnies scudding beneath its tires, and a progress bar captioned *62Km/74% Complete*. I stick it back in my pocket, then pick up the dress shoes Pinky and Brains issued to me. Grimacing, I tie the shoe laces. Then I reach down and wrench the left heel round. Instantly, the shadows in my cabin darken and deepen, taking on an ominous hue. The Tillinghast resonator is running: in this confined space it should give me just enough warning to shit myself before I die, if Billington's entrusted his operational security to daemons, but in the open . . . well, it adds a whole new meaning to *take to your heels*.

The corridor outside my door is dark and there's an odd, musty smell in the air. I pause, skulking just inside the doorway as I wait for my eyes to adjust. Ellis Billington and his cronies are aboard the *Explorer*, but there's no telling who's still here, is there? I can make myself useful while I wait for Mo by finding out what's going on aboard the *Mabuse*. Ellis isn't so stupid he won't have some kind of getaway plan in mind, in case things go pear-shaped—and backup plans "C" and "D" behind plan "B," for multiple redundancy—but if I can find out what they are . . .

*Oops.* The door at the end of the corridor opens. "You. What are you doing outside your room? Go back at once!" The black beret draws his pistol.

My mind blanks for a moment, and there's a big hollow feeling. I feel a doubled heartbeat: **Is that you, Ramona?**

**What are you ...**

"There's a problem with my faucet?" I hear my mouth saying. "Can you take a look at it?" And I'm opening the door and stepping backwards to make room.

**Let me handle this, monkey-boy.** I can taste seawater in my sinuses.

**What are you doing? Has McMurray lost it—**

**No, but Ellis has, he ordered Eileen off the Mabuse ten minutes ago and there are scuttling charges due to blow as soon as she's clear. Something about contagious corruption in his oneiromantic matrix; he figures someone's sabotaged the ship and he's not in the mood for half-measures—**

Shit. That would be me, wouldn't it? The goon steps closer and I can see green shadows behind his mirrorshades, green writhing worms twitching and squirming in rotting cadaverous eye sockets as he steps closer and raises the pistol in both hands—

**—Glock 17,** says Ramona.

And she takes over.

I jackknife forwards from the opposite side of the narrow room and bring my left hand down on the pistol, grabbing the slide and pushing it back, as my right hand comes up, curling uncomfortably to punch at his left eye. Glass shatters as he pushes up with the gun, not knowing to pull it back out of reach, and I twist it sideways. It goes off, and the noise is so loud in the confined space that it's like someone's slammed my head in a door. It feels like I've torn half the skin off my right hand but I somehow keep turning while maintaining my grip, and kick and twist away from his follow-on punch, with a searing pain in my side, like I've pulled a muscle—then I'm facing the half-rotted zombie with a gun barrel in my left hand. I grab the butt with my right, which is dripping blood, and I pull the trigger, bang, and pull it again because somehow I managed to miss at a range of about half a meter—bang—and there's blood all over the inside of the door and a faint distant tinkling of cartridges rattling as they bounce off the screen of the PC.

I gasp for breath and gag at the stench. The thing on the floor—at least, what the Tillinghast resonator is showing me—has been dead for weeks. **What just happened again?** I ask Ramona.

**Billington.** She opens her eyes and I push myself into her head. She's still underwater, but she's not sitting in the control chair on board the submersible grab anymore: she's free-swimming in near-total darkness, stroking upwards alongside the drill string, and I can feel the exhaustion as a tight band across the tops of her thighs. **It's a double-cross.** I can taste her fear.

**Talk to me!** I force myself to bend over and go through the corpse's pockets. There's another magazine for the pistol, and a badge: some species of RFID tag. I take it and glance around the cabin. My right hand is still bleeding but it doesn't look as bad as it feels. (Memo to self: do not make a habit of gripping the slide of an automatic pistol while it is being fired.) **How long have I got? Where are you?**

**The grab—I was halfway home when one of the docking splines engaged, and the control deck disconnected and stayed stuck on the pipe string while the payload kept going up. It's got to be intentional. He was planning on leaving me down there all along!**

I can feel the panic, ugly and personal and selfish and pitiful. **Hang in there,** I tell her. **If you can make it to the surface we can pick you up—**

**You don't understand! If I stay down here too long I'll begin the change—it's hereditary! I've put it off this long by staying on land most of the time, but I'm an adult and if I spend too long in the deeps I begin to adapt, irreversibly. And if I do that, my daemon will decide I'm trying to escape . . . **

**Ramona.** I find I'm breathing fast and shallow. **Listen to me—**

**Billington knows! He must know! That's why he sent the guard to kill you! He'll have McMurray under arrest or dead or worse!**

**Ramona. Listen.** I take a deep breath and try to focus on air and dry land. **Listen to me. Feel through my skin. Breathe through my lungs. Remember where you come from.** I stand over a cadaver and force myself to think of lush green landscapes. **You were able to let me share your metabolism when I nearly drowned. Let's try doing it the other way.** Breathe. Keep breathing for two people, lest one of them start sprouting tentacles and scales. It's not as easy as it sounds: you should try it one day.

**You've got to get off the ship!**

**How do you know what Ellis is doing?** I ask. I step over the body and into the corridor. It's even less welcoming, stinking of the grave, of soil and darkness and blind burrowing things. *First door on the right, up the stairs, left, corridor—*

**Pat and I have a back channel.** Ramona concentrates on swimming, letting the calming repetitive motions occupy her mind. (Is it my imagination, or is it beginning to get slightly less dark?) **Last time he checked in he warned me about the scuttling charge. He figured

Billington would have you taken off the ship, along with Eileen. Next thing, he drops the block between us. That's all I know, I swear!**

**Uh-huh.** The stairs feel as if they're on the edge of crumbling beneath my shoes, maggot-riddled boards creaking warnings to one another. The air is turning clammy. *Keep breathing,* I remind myself. **You haven't been entirely honest with me, have you? You and Pat. You've been using that block of his to keep me from dumpster-diving your head for intelligence. Playing me like an instrument.**

**Hey, you're a fine one to talk!** Too late: I realize she's glimpsed my memory of Mo's briefing. *Secure the geas generator.* **You guys want it, too.**

**No,** I say grimly, **we want to stop *anyone* from getting it. Because if you think through the political implications of a human power suddenly starting to play with chthonian tech, you need to ask yourself whether BLUE HADES would view it—**

Creepy violin music in the back of my head raises the hair on the nape of my neck, just as I round the corner at the top of the stairs and come face to face with another zombie in a black uniform. He's got an MP-5 in a tactical sling at the ready, but I've got adrenalin and surprise on my side—I'm so jittery that I pull the trigger three times before I can make myself stop.

** — as a Benthic Treaty violation,** I finish, then draw a deep breath and try to stop my hands shaking. **What's with all the zombies? Is Billington killing his optioned employees as a tax dodge or something?**

**I don't *know.*** She takes out her frustration on the water. **Will you move it? You've got maybe six minutes to get off that ship!**

*Secure the geas generator.* The corridor seems to pulse, contracting and dilating around me like a warm fleshy tube—a disturbingly esophageal experience. The smell of decay is getting stronger. I pick up the MP-5, managing not to lose my non-existent breakfast as the zombie's neck disintegrates. I brush rotting debris off the sling, stick the pistol in my pocket, and let Ramona take over my hands to check the burst selector on the machine pistol. I duck-walk down the passage and then there's a crossway and another door opposite me. I open the door to the owner's lounge—

I've got company.

"Well, if it isn't the easily underestimated Mr. Howard!" She smiles like a snake. "Better not squeeze that trigger, all the carbines are loaded with banishment rounds in case the Black Chamber tries something— you'll fry the generator if you shoot. And you wouldn't want to do that, would you?"

It's Johanna Todt, McMurray's thugette. It's funny how she's nothing like as glamorous when I'm sharing my eyeballs with Ramona: or maybe it's something to do with the combat fatigues, life preserver, and smudged make-up, not to mention the stench of ancient death she drags around like a favorite toy she can't bear to let go of. She's standing behind the diorama at the center of the geas generator grid, holding a hammer about ten centimeters above the Bond-mannequin's head. *Whoops*.

I'm still trying to think of something to say when Ramona takes the initiative: "Fancy meeting you here, dear. Did Pat deep-six you, or did you decide you needed a bit more bargaining power?"

"Ramona?" She cocks her head to one side. "Ah, I should have guessed. Three's a crowd: Why don't you butt out, bitch?"

I manage to temporarily regain control of my larynx: "She stays," I say. *Remember to breathe deeply*, I tell myself. My doubled vision is beginning to annoy me: the light around Ramona is definitely brightening towards a predawn twilight. I try to keep the MP-5 pointing in Johanna's general direction, but she's right—if I start shooting, I'm as likely to take out the geas generator as hit her. "What are you doing here?"

"Unlike some, I know who I'm loyal to. I figured I'd help myself to the leftovers at the rich man's buffet, seeing I've just armed the scuttling charges. And aren't you just the dish? I think you'll do for starters." Johanna's grin widens, carnivorously: I catch a whiff of breath that's not so much stale as cadaverous, reeking of the crypt. "I can disentangle you, 'Mona, did you know that? I can even unlock your binding without killing McMurray. I stole his tokens while I was helping him consider the error of his ways down in the brig." She turns her free hand so that I can see she's holding a small plastic box. "It's all in here. I own you both."

*Breathe*. Ramona tenses and kicks harder towards the light. Her buttocks are a solid slab of agony: she's swum nearly a kilometer straight up, and she's beginning to tire of struggling, of fighting off the adaptive stress that seductively taunts her, the knowledge that if she just uses her *other* muscles everything will become so much easier—

"So what do you want with us?" I ask, taking a short step towards her.

"Stop. Don't move." She stares at me. "I want you to adore me," she says, almost wistfully. "I want you to be my body. 'Mona, give him to me and I'll even set you free, Ellis doesn't need to know—"

For a moment I'm in Ramona's body, swimming free towards a surface that is slowly brightening: it's still a dim twilight, utter darkness to merely human eyes, but I can see shapes in the murk above me. Half of the horizon is dominated by a huge, black shadow that the drill string disappears into, and there's another dark silhouette in the near distance. I'm in control, I'm the one who's swimming with unfamiliar legs and weaker upper arms—I begin altering course towards the distant, dark shape in the water—

Meanwhile, Ramona is in *my* body, and she's dropped the MP-5 and is halfway across the perspex lid covering the diorama, making a noise in the back of her throat that I've heard when two cats get serious about their territory. Johanna whacks the hammer hard, off the back of my neck—aiming for my head, but she misses—causing a bright sharp pain, and then I'm in her face and she's biting at me and trying to smash me on the side of the skull and Ramona does something with my arms that I'm just not up to, some type of blocking move. I can feel muscles, possibly a tendon, tearing as I punch Johanna overarm; she blocks, I bring up a knee—

*Breathe for two* because the *Mabuse* is holding station but it's still a third of a kilometer away—

"Bitch!" screams Johanna, then sinks her teeth into my shoulder and goes for my balls.

Ramona, not used to having that external hazard to guard, doesn't react in time to Johanna—but I do, and I manage to squirm sideways so that Johanna grabs my inner thigh painfully, rather than turning me into a pile of screaming jelly. The Glock in my pants is digging in uselessly. Then I notice Johanna's teeth in my right shoulder. They burn and they're icy-cold at the same time, which is *wrong*: bite injuries aren't meant to freeze. Everything about Johanna is wrong: this close with the Tillinghast resonator powered up I can feel something moving just behind her face, something horrifyingly similar to Ramona's succubus, but different. Instead of feeding on the small death I can hear it calling for the great one, the ending of time. I feel weak in its presence, enervated and crushed by a numinous dread.

**Fuck it, keep breathing, monkey-boy! What are you doing, shit-for-brains, trying to kill us both?** That's Ramona. She sounds as if she's calling to me from the far end of a long corridor.

*Breathe?* I'm lying on top of Johanna on the floor. *How did we get here?* She's still as a corpse, but she's got her teeth embedded in my shoulder and she's hugging me like her one true love. And I feel so *heavy*. Breathing is a huge effort. There's a haze forming around my vision. *Breathe?*

A hand—mine?—is fumbling with the lump in my pocket.

Breathe.

Everything is going gray. The tunnel is walled in darkness. Johanna

Todt waits at the end of it, smiling coolly, as inviting and desirable as a glass of liquid helium. But I can also tell somehow that Johanna isn't what's waiting for me if I take that drink: Johanna is like the biolumines- cent lure dangling before an angler fish's head, right in front of the sharp jaws of oblivion. She's got me in her arms and if I take the lure, when I get up I'll be as hollow as she is, I won't be *me* anymore, just a puppet rotting slowly on its feet while her daemon tugs it through the motions of life.

Breathe?

BANG.

Johanna spasms beneath me, shuddering and tensing. Her thighs flex.

BANG.

I remember to breathe, then nearly choke on the hot stink of burned powder.

She's vibrating away, drumming her heels on the floor, and there's a flood of blood and tissue everywhere around her head, like a spray of hair. As I pant for breath I realize there's a hand clutching a pistol inches away from my head, and my arm feels as if it's twisted half out of its socket. A combined wash of fear and revulsion makes me bounce off the floor, muscles screaming. **Ramona?**

**Still here, monkey-boy.** She's gasping—no, that's wrong—she's struggling for breath. There's a burning sensation in her gills as she fights down the reflex to extend them fully. Stroking towards the slim shadow of the *Mabuse* outlined against the brightness of the surface, still some 200 meters overhead: **Breathe, dammit! I'm getting cramps! I can't keep this up.**

I pant like a dog, then carefully lower the pistol. I've got more pulled muscles and my right arm is screaming at me, plus a savage bite that makes me dizzy when I poke at it with my left hand. I look at my finger- tips. *Blood.* **Shit. How long—**

**If that bitch was telling the truth, you've got two or three more min- utes to get the diorama and make it up on deck.**

I look around, trying to make sense out of nonsense, a luxurious lounge aboard a yacht, a dead woman on the floor . . . and a diorama in a large, locked display case. I can't move the case, it's the size of a pool table. I groan. It looks like the proximate effect of my first stab at hatch- ing a Plan B was to spook Billington into ordering the ship sunk—and right now, I seem to be short of options.

But. *Secure the field generator.* That's the core of the geas Billington's set up, and he's now trying to destroy it in the crudest way imaginable— not just by throwing the "off" switch, but by blowing up the ship. (Why?

Because I got a little too clever and let slip the yipping Chihuahuas of infowar.) If I can keep it running, then the semantics of the spell demand that James Bond—or a good knock-off—will save us. It's just a matter of figuring out how to keep the thing running while I get it off the sinking ship.

My Treo is in my back pocket. I nearly scream as I reach for it with my right arm, then shakily switch it on and aim the camera lens at the display. Once I've filled the memory card that'll have to do. I check the display—*72Km/97% Complete*—then shove it in a hip pocket.

Looking around the owner's lounge, I don't see anything obvious, but the dining room was just up the corridor. I duck out and stumble towards it, shove my way through the door, and what I want is waiting for me under a pile of uncollected dirty dishes. I grab the linen tablecloth, wait for the clatter of crockery to stop, and stagger back to the lounge. Then I whack the display case hard with the butt of my pistol, knocking out as much glass as possible.

*Breathe.* I catch a glimpse of Ramona, the agony spreading to her lower back. There are burning wires of pain in her shoulders as she scrabbles towards the surface close by the port side of the *Mabuse*. The air in here is foul, a stench of sewers and decaying, uncooked meat. I shove the pistol in a pocket then take the tablecloth in both hands and drop it across the broken glass and the diorama. I lean forwards—*remember to breathe*—and gather it all in with both hands. Then I fumble on the floor for the plastic box containing the tokens that Johanna taunted Ramona with. My hands shake as I finally tie off the corners of the tablecloth in a rough knot. **Got it,** I tell her.

**Get the hell out!**

She doesn't need to tell me twice. I head for the door, grabbing the MP-5 on the way, and cast around the corridor for the door onto the sun deck.

**That one, Bob—**

The daylight glare nearly brings tears to my eyes after the death-stink below decks. I step out onto the deck and walk to the side of the ship, then look aft. In the distance there's a white trail etched across the wave crests. *Breathe.* I blink, and see through Ramona's eyes, looking up at the light from beneath the keel of the frigate. From down here it looks enormous, the size of a city. *Run.* I weave my way aft, back into the access passage to the boat deck. There's a crane and boarding steps descending over the side, ending just above a floating platform at the waterline. I take the steps two at a time, nearly tumbling into the water in my haste.

**Get yourself overboard! Now!** *Breathe.* She can see the grid of the platform, the shadows of my feet on the metal grating.

\*\*Not yet.\*\* I gasp for breath, my vision flickering with the bright sparkles of hyperventilation as I set down the stolen diorama and pull out my phone: *74Km/99% Complete.* \*\*How do you think we're going to get onto the *Explorer?* Neither of us is in any condition to swim that far, and anyway—it's moving.\*\*

There's white foam at the bow of the huge drilling ship as its positioning thrusters power up. Billington isn't stupid enough to sit too close while his yacht self-destructs: even if he isn't afraid of the backwash from the geas generator he's got to be worried about the fuel tanks.

\*\*We've got to get over there!\*\* She's near the surface.

\*\*I've got a plan.\*\* *Breathe.* I reach down into the water as—

With all her remaining energy she reaches up towards the hand breaking through the silvery mirror-surface above her and—

"*Ow!*" Water splashes over me as Ramona breaks the surface and grabs onto my hand.

"Plan. What plan? *Ow . . .*" I heave. Something in my back registers a complaint, in triplicate, then locks up and goes on strike.

Ramona twists round and falls back onto the platform. Out of the water, she goes limp. I can feel her muscles. I wish I couldn't.

"Look over there." I point. The silvery trail is curving towards us like a bizarre missile running just above the surface of the water. There's something that looks like a glassy black sphere in the middle of it, surrounded by four huge orange balls: "It's my car."

"You. Have got to be. Kidding."

"Nope." I grin like a mad thing as the Smart Fortwo whines towards me eagerly, its hub-mounted air bags thrashing the water into submission. "It may not be a BMW or an Aston Martin, but at least it comes when I call it." It slows as it nears the edge of the platform. Ramona sits up wearily and begins to peel off her outer-heated wet suit. Her skin is silvery-gray, the scales clearly visible: even the few hours underwater have been enough to cause the change to set in, and her fingers have begun to web. By the time she's got her top layer unzipped, the car has slowly pulled up to the platform edge and driven aboard. The engine stops.

"Who's that?" she asks, pointing through the windscreen.

"Oops, I forgot about him." It's Marc, sometime procurer and latterly zombie. He's bloated up against the front windscreen and the driver's side door. "You'll have to help me get him out of there."

"This is why I never date the same guy twice—avoids raising a stink, you know?"

I get the door open, just in time to be hit by an olfactory experience almost as good as Johanna's buffet. "Ick."

"You can say that again, monkey-boy. He's leaked all over the seats—
you expect me to ride in this?"

"You're the one who told me about the scuttling charges, I'm the one
with the biometrics that match the ignition button. Your call."

I grab hold of one arm. To my great delight, it doesn't come off in my
hand. Ramona opens the opposite door and shoves him towards me. I do
a two-step with the stiff, twist him round, and shove him onto the platform. I grab the bundled-up geas generator and shove it into the shoe
box that passes for a boot in this thing. Ramona winces as she tries to belt
herself in, and holds something up: "What's this?"

"Marc's idea of a conversational intro." I pass her the MP-5. "You
know how to use one of these, I figure I'll take the pistol." It's another
Glock, of course, with a whizzy laser-sighting widget and an extended
magazine. "Now let's go visit Ellis, huh?"

I push the ignition button, check that the doors and windows are
closed, then gently tap the gas pedal. There's a red light blinking on the
dash, but the engine starts. We tilt alarmingly as I drive off the edge of
the platform, but the car stabilizes fairly fast, leaving us bobbing like a
cork in the water. I stroke the accelerator again. That starts a lot of spray
flying—this thing isn't the world's most efficient paddle boat—but we
begin to move away from the *Mabuse,* and I start the windscreen wipers
so I can see where we're going. The *Explorer* is a huge, gray bulk about
400 meters away. There's the beginning of a trail of foam at her stern, but
I'm pretty sure I can catch her—even a Smart car can outrun a 60,000-
ton, deep-ocean drilling ship, I figure. Ramona leans against my sore
shoulder and I feel her bone-deep exhaustion, along with something
else, a creeping smugness.

"We make a pretty good team," she murmurs.

I'm about to say something intended to take the place of a witty reply
when the rearview mirror lights up like a flash bulb. I goose the accelerator and we lurch wildly, nearly nosing over as a spray of water goes
everywhere. Then there's a sound like the door of Hell slamming shut
behind me, and another huge lurch sets us bobbing side to side. A water
spout almost as high as the topmost radar mast hangs over the ship, then
comes crashing back down.

"Fuck fuck fuck . . ." We're less than a ship-length away from the
*Mabuse,* on the opposite side to the scuttling charge, and that's probably
what saves us: most of the blast is heading in the opposite direction. On
the other hand, the ship is rolling, heeling over almost sixty degrees, and
there's a gash below the waterline that's raised so high above the surface
I can see it in my rearview mirror. It looks large enough to take on a hundred tons of water a second. Johanna opened the bulkhead doors below

the waterline, and as if it isn't enough that the charge has ripped the yacht's skin open, cavitation from the explosion has broken her keel. I suppose Billington doesn't much care about money at this point—when he's Planetary Overlord he can have as many yachts as he likes—but right now *I* care because we're less than 200 meters away from something as massive as a ten-story office block that's just begun to disintegrate. As a way of ensuring that annoying witnesses are silenced and the geas generator stops working, it's overkill, but if it succeeds I suppose Lloyds of London are the only people who're going to complain.

The ship's superstructure hangs in the air like a hallucination, heeled over through almost ninety degrees. Loose life rafts and stores tumble across the deck and fall into the sea. With majestic slowness it begins to roll back upright—warships aren't designed to capsize easily—and I steel myself for the inevitable backwash when four or five thousand tons of ship go under.

I floor the accelerator pedal to open up some distance behind us, which is, of course, the cue for the engine to die. There's an embarrassed *beep* from the dashboard. I mash my thumb on the START button, but nothing happens, and I realize that the blinking red light on the dash has turned solid. There's a little LCD display for status messages and as I stare at it in disbelief a message scrolls across:

MANDATORY SERVICE INTERVAL REACHED. RETURN
TO MAIN DEALER FOR ENGINE MANAGEMENT RESET.

Behind me, there's a sinking frigate, while ahead of me, the *Explorer* has begun to make way. I start swearing: not my usual "shitfuckpisscuntbugger" litany, but *really* rude words. Ramona sinks her fingers into my left arm. "This can't be happening!" she says, and I feel a wash of despair rising off her.

"It's not. Brace yourself."

I flip open the lid on top of the gear-stick and punch the eject button. And the car ejects.

*The car. Ejects.* Three words that don't belong in the same sentence, or at any rate in a sentence that's anywhere within a couple hundred meters of sanity street. In real life, cars do not come with ejector seats, for good reason. An ejector seat is basically a seat with a bomb under it. The traditional way they're used is, you pull the black-and-yellow striped handle, say goodbye to the airplane, and say hello to six weeks in traction, recovering in hospital—if you're lucky. The survival statistics make

Russian roulette look safe. Very recent models buck the trend—they've got computers and gyroscopes and rocket motors to stabilize and steer them in flight, they've probably even got cup holders and cigarette lighters—but the basic point is, when you pull that handle, Elvis has left the cockpit, pulling fifteen gees and angling fifteen degrees astern.

Now, the ejector system Pinky and Brains have bolted to the engine block of this car is not the kind you get in a fifth-generation jet fighter. Instead, its closest relative is the insane gadget they use to eject from a helicopter in flight. Helicopters are nicknamed "choppers" for a reason. In order to avoid delivering a pilot-sized stack of salami slices, helicopter ejection systems come with a mechanism for getting those annoying rotor blades out of the way first. They started out by attaching explosive bolts to the rotor hub, but for entirely understandable reasons this proved unpopular with the flight crew. Then they got smart.

Your basic helicopter ejector system is a tube like a recoilless antitank missile launcher, pointing straight up, and bolted to the pilot's seat. There's a rocket in it, attached to the seat by a steel cable. The rocket goes up, the cable slices through the rotor blades on the way, and only then does it yank the seat out of the helicopter, which by this time is approximately as airworthy as a grand piano.

What this means to me:

There's a very loud noise in my ear, not unlike a cat sneezing, if the cat is the size of the Great Sphinx of Giza and it's just inhaled three tons of snuff. About a quarter of a second later there's a bang, almost as loud as the scuttling charge that broke the *Mabuse*, and an elephant sits down on my lap. My vision blurs and my neck pops, and I try to blink. A second later, the elephant gets up and wanders off. When I can see again—or breathe—the view has changed: the horizon is in the wrong place, swinging around wildly below us like a fairground ride gone wrong. My stomach flip-flops—*look ma, no gravity!*—and I hear a faint moan from the passenger seat. Then there's a solid jerk and a baby hippopotamus tries me for a sofa before giving up on it as a bad deal—that's the parachute opening.

And we're into injury time.

Most of the time when someone uses an ejector seat, the pilot sitting in it has a pressing reason for pulling the handle—for example, he's about to fly into the type of cloud known as cumulo-granite—and the question of where the seat—and pilot—lands is a bit less important than the issue of what will happen if it doesn't go off. And this much is true: if you eject over open water, you probably expect to land on the water, because there's a hell of a lot more water down there than ships, or whales, or desert islands stocked with palm trees and welcoming tribeswomen.

However, this isn't your normal ejection scenario. I've got Billington's Bond-field generator stuffed in the trunk, a glamorous female assassin with blood in her eye clutching a submachine gun in the passenger seat, and a date with a vodka martini in my very near future—just as soon as I make landfall alive. Which is why, as we swing wildly back and forth beneath the rectangular, steerable parachute (the control lines of which are fastened to handles dangling just above the sunroof), I realize that we're drifting on a collision course with the forward deck of the *Explorer*. If we're not lucky we're going to wrap ourselves around the forward docking tower.

"Can you work the parachute?" I ask.

"Yes—" Ramona unfastens her seat belt, yanks at the sunroof release latch: "Come on! Help me!" We slide the roof back and she stands up, makes a grab for the handles, catches them, and does something that makes my eyes water and bile rise in the back of my throat. "Come on, baby," she pleads, spilling air from one side of the parachute so that it side-slips away from the docking tower, "you can make it, can't you?"

We swing back and forth like a plumb bob held by a drunken surveyor. I look down, trying to find a reference point to still my stomach: there's a tiny boat down there beside the *Explorer*—it's a speedboat, and from here it looks alarmingly similar to the boat I saw Mo loading stuff into. *It can't be,* I think, then hastily suppress the thought. It's best not to notice that kind of thing around Ramona.

We swing round and the deck rushes up towards us terrifyingly fast. "Brace!" calls Ramona, and grabs me. There's a long-drawn-out metallic scraping crunching noise and the elephant makes a last baby-sized appearance in my lap, then we're down on the foredeck. Not that I can see much of it—it's shrouded beneath several dozen meters of collapsing nylon parachute fabric—but what I saw of it right before we landed wasn't looking particularly hospitable. Something about the dozens of black berets racing towards us, guns at the ready, suggests that Billington isn't too keen on the local sky-diving club dropping in for tea.

"Get ready to run," Ramona says breathily, just as there's a metallic racking noise outside the parachute fabric that's blocking our view.

"Come out with your hands up!" someone calls through a megaphone that distorts their voice so horribly that I can't hope to identify them.

I glance at Ramona. She looks spooked.

"We have a Dragon dialed in on you," the voice adds, conversationally. "You have five seconds."

"Shit." I see her shoulders droop in despair and disgust. "It's been nice knowing you—"

"It's not over yet."

I flick the catch and push the door open, wincing, then swing my feet out onto the deck. It's time to face the music.

## Chapter 16:
## Reflex Decision

"So," says Billington, pacing out a lazy circle on the deck around me, "the rumors of your resourcefulness were not misplaced, Mr. Howard."

He flashes a cold smile at me, then goes back to staring at the deck plates in front of his feet, inspecting the wards around us. After a few seconds he passes out of my field of vision. I can feel Ramona flexing her arms against the straps; a moment later she spots him coming into view. Two more of the dentist's chairs are mounted side by side, facing in opposite directions, on the same pedestal in the control room: Billington probably gets a bulk discount on them at villainsupply.com. Unfortunately he's also got Ramona and me strapped to them, and an audience of about fifty black berets who are either brandishing MP-5s or leaning over instrument consoles. These particular black berets are still human, not having succumbed to the dubious charms of Johanna Todt, but the freshly painted wards, inked out in human blood, sizzle and glow ominously before my Tillinghast-enhanced vision.

"Unfortunately your usefulness appears to have expired," says Ellis, walking back into view in front of me. He smiles again, his weird pupils contracting to slits. There's something badly wrong about him, but I can't quite put my finger on it: he's not a soulless horror like the zombie troops, but he's not quite all there, either. Something is missing in his mind, some sense of self. "Shame about that," he adds conversationally.

"What are you going to do to us?" asks Ramona.

**I really wish you hadn't asked that,** I tell her silently, my heart sinking.

**Bite me, monkey-boy. Just keep him talking, okay? While he's monologuing he isn't torturing us to death . . . **

"Well, that's an interesting conundrum." Billington glances over his shoulder at a clipboard-toting minion: "Would you mind finding Eileen and asking her why she's late? It doesn't normally take her this long to terminate an employee." The minion nods and hurries away. "Following the logic of the situation that prevailed until I ended the invocation field by sinking the *Mabuse*, I ought to have you tortured or fed to a pool of hungry piranhas. Fortunately for you, the geas should be fully dissipated by now, I'm short on torturers, and urban legends to the contrary, piranhas don't much like human flesh." He smiles again. "I was inclined to be merciful, earlier: I can always find a niche for a bright, young manager in Quality Assurance, for example—" I shiver, half-wondering if maybe the piranha tank wouldn't be preferable "—or for a presentable young lady with your talents." Then the smile drops away like a camo sheet covering an artillery tube: "But that was before I discovered that you—" he stabs a finger at Ramona "—were sent here to murder me, and that you—" I flinch from his bony digit "—were sent here as a *saboteur*."

He hisses that last, glaring at me malevolently.

"Saboteur?" I blink and try to look perplexed. *When in doubt, lie like a very flat thing indeed.* "What are you talking about?"

Billington gestures at the huge expanse of glass walling the control room off from the moon pool. "Look." His hand casually takes in the huge skeletal superstructure hanging from the ceiling by steel hawsers, its titanium fingers cradling a blackened cylinder with a tapered end: JENNIFER MORGUE Two, the damaged chthonian weapon. An odd geometric meshwork scarifies its hull: there are whorls and knots like the boles of a tree spaced evenly along it. From this angle it looks more like a huge, fossilized worm than a tunneling machine. It's quiescent, as if dead or sleeping, but . . . I'm not sure. The Tillinghast resonator lets me notice things that would otherwise be invisible to merely human eyes, and something about it makes my skin crawl, as if it's neither dead nor alive, or even undead, but something else entirely; something waiting in the shadows that is as uninterested in issues of life and death as a stony asteroid rolling eternally through the icy depths of space, pacing out a long orbit that will end in the lithosphere of a planet wrapped in a fragile blue-green ecosystem. Looking at it makes me feel like the human species is simply collateral damage waiting to happen.

"Your masters want to stop me from helping him," Billington explains. "He's very annoyed. He's been trapped for thousands of years, stranded on a plateau in the rarefied and chilly dark, unable to move. Unable to heal. Unable even to revive." Huge hoses dangle from the underside of the *Explorer*'s drilling deck, poking into the skin of the chthonian artifact like intravenous feeding lines. I blink and look back at Billington. *He's lost it,* I tell myself, with gathering horror. *Hasn't he?*

**You've only just figured that out?** asks Ramona. **And here I was thinking you were quick on the uptake.** Despite the sarcasm, she feels very frightened, very cold. I think she knew some of this, but not the full scope of Billington's deviancy.

"I know *all* about your masters," Billington adds in her direction. He can't hear our silent exchange, feel Ramona testing the strength of her bonds, or recognize me scoping out the parametric strength of the wards he's positioned around us—he just wants to talk, wants someone to listen and understand the demon urges that keep him awake late in the night. "I know how they want to use him. They sent you to me in the hope of trading in a strong tool for a more powerful one. But he's not a tool! He's a cyborg warrior-god, a maker of earthquakes and an eater of souls, birthed for a single purpose by the great powers of the upper mantle. It is *his* geas to rejoin the holy struggle against the numinous aquatic vermin as soon as his body is sufficiently restored for him to resume residence in it. And it is *our* nature that the highest expression of our destiny must be to submit to his will and lend our strength to his glorious struggle."

Billington spins round abruptly and jabs a stiff-armed salute at the thing hanging in its titanium cradle outside the window. He raises his voice: "He demands and requires our submission!" Turning back to me, he shouts, "We must obey! There is glory in obedience! Fitness in purpose!" He raises a clenched fist: "The deep god commands that his body be restored to its shining terror! You will help me! You *will* be of service!" Spittle lands on my face. I flinch but I can't do anything about it—can't move, don't dare express skepticism, *don't piss off the lunatic* . . . I'm half-convinced, with an icy certainty verging on terror, that he's going to kill one of us in the next couple of minutes.

"How does he talk to you?" Ramona asks, only a faint unevenness in her voice betraying the fact that her palms are clammy and her heart is pounding like a drum.

Billington deflates like a popped balloon, as if overcome with a self-conscious realization of what he must look like. "Oh, it's not voices in my head, if *that's* what you're worrying about," he says disparagingly. His lips quirk. "I'm not mad, you know, although it helps in this line of work." A guard is walking along the catwalk outside, followed by a flash of pink. "He doesn't really approve of madness among his minions. Says it makes their souls taste funny. No, we talk on the telephone. Conference calls every Friday morning at 9:00 a.m. EST." He gestures at a console across the room, where an old bakelite handset squats atop an old gray-painted circuit box that I recognize as an enclosure for Billington's Gravedust communicator. "It's so much easier to just dial 'D' for Dagon, so to speak, than to bother with the eerie voices and walls softening under your fingertips. And these days we've sorted out a telepresence solution: he's taken up residence in a host body so he can keep an eye on things in person, while we restore his primary core to full functionality. Of course it's energetically expensive for him to occupy another body, so we have to keep the sacrifice schedule in mind as a critical path element in the restoration project, but there's no shortage of tenth-decile underperformers on the sales force . . . ah, yes." He glances at his watch. "Top of the hour, right on time."

The guard and the woman in the pink suit arrive just as Billington gestures at the window. Outside, on the moon pool floor, a structure like an airport baggage-conveyor terminates in a platform just underneath the chthonian's conical head. I squint: there are lines and curves on that pointed end, almost like the helical coils of a drill, or a squid's tightly coiled tentacles. Down on the conveyor, something wriggly is working its way towards the platform. Or rather, something on the conveyor is being fed forwards remorselessly, wriggling and twitching like a worm on a hook.

**What's that—?** Ramona is in my head, using my eyes.

**Not what—who.** I peer closer, then blink. The baitworm on the conveyor is still alive, but black fire crawls along the edges of the platform at the far end. It twists and rolls, and it's funny how a change of angle changes your entire perspective on things because suddenly I see his face, eyes bugging out with fear, and what I'm looking at snaps into focus. He's been trussed up in gaffer tape and his mouth taped shut to stop him screaming but I recognize McMurray, and I recognize a human sacrifice when I see him. He's heading towards that platform, and now I realize—

"You've got to stop it!" I shout at Billington. "Why are you doing this? It's insane!"

"On the contrary." Billington turns away from me and holds his hands behind his back. "I don't like doing this, but it's necessary if we're to meet our third-quarter target for energizing the revivification matrix," he says tightly. "By the way, you ought to relax: you're in the circuit, too."

I jackknife against the straps and nearly choke myself. "What—"

"Oh *shit*," swears Ramona, despair and apprehension sweeping over her.

"Considering you appear to have prevented Johanna from returning, it's the least you can do for me," Billington explains. "I need a soul devourer. Otherwise it's just more dead meat, which doesn't help anyone. And while you're so inconveniently entangled I might as well plug both of you into the summoning grid to reduce the side-band leakage."

The platform unfolds shutterlike flaps as McMurray nears it. I can distantly hear his voice screaming in Ramona's head. **Get me out of this! That's an order!** *Billington needs an infovore*, I realize. *He's feeding the chthonian by destroying souls in its presence.* My knees feel like jelly: I've seen this sort of thing before. *Which means—*

Ramona convulses against the straps and begins to choke. I gag, my guts rolling, because I can feel the backwash from McMurray's ill-considered words echoing off the inside of her skull like thunder and lightning. Ramona can't *not* obey, but she's immobile, unable to respond to her master's voice, and she's capable of choking herself to death and taking me with her.

**\*\*Get me out!\*\*** McMurray howls as the conveyor deposits him on the killing platform under the cylinder. Then the platform begins to sink and the shutters close in on top of it and I realize what I'm looking at: a hydraulic iron-maiden, a car crusher built for humans.

Ramona's daemon is rising. I can feel a monstrous pressure in my balls. I can't see properly and I'm choking, I can't move—Ramona can't move—and a hideous heat spreads through my crotch. *Her* crotch. Proximity to death excites it, whether hers or her victim's. And this is about as close as it gets: the shutters are steel slabs, driven by hydraulic rams. There's a whine of motors, deepening and slowing, and a muffled noise I can't identify. I can't breathe, or Ramona can't breathe, and her daemon senses the flow of life from the killing box down below. As the flow spurts into us the daemon feeds greedily, and Ramona convulses and falls unconscious.

With the last of my energy I inhale in a ragged breath, and scream.

"Oh dear," says Billington, turning round. "What seems to be the problem?"

I draw another breath.

"You really shouldn't have done that," says the woman in the pink suit, standing in the doorway.

"Hurt her—" I gasp. Then I start coughing. I can't sense Ramona's daemon, but Ramona herself is deeply unconscious. "She needs water. Lots of seawater." I'm breathing for two of us but I can't quite get enough air, because what Ramona needs now is full-body immersion. I can feel it, the changes in her cells, her organs slowly contracting and rearranging inside her frame, the fever of mutation that will only end in her death or complete metamorphosis—

"What took you so long, dear?" asks Billington, looking at the doorway.

"I was putting my face on," says the woman in pink. I'm still gasping as a pair of black berets close in on Ramona's chair with buckets in hand, but something about the woman in pink trips my attention. *Hang on, that's not Eileen*—

"Excellent." Billington glances at the black berets bending over Ramona and frowns. "We seem to have a little problem, this one isn't as robust as the last."

I peer at the woman in pink. In one hand, she holds a shiny metal briefcase; the other arm is stretched rigidly down, close to her body, as if she has a ruler up her sleeve. I try to focus on the sparkling around her: *class three glamour, at least,* I realize. She's taller and younger than

Eileen, and if I squint—I look past her at her reflection in the glass—*red hair*—

"What do you expect?" asks the woman everyone but me seems to think is Eileen Billington. "She's not a movie hero, is she? And neither is he, for that matter."

"Not now that I've terminated the reel," Billington says briskly. "You, you, and you, go chuck the piranhas overboard, fill the fish tank with seawater, and get it over here—"

"Really?" asks the woman. "Are you *sure* it's all over?"

Billington glances at her. "Pretty much, apart from a few little details—mass human sacrifices, invocations of chthonic demigods, Richter-ten earthquakes, harrowing of the Deep Ones, rains of meteors, and the creation of a thousand-year world empire, that sort of thing. Trivial, really. Yes, it's all nailed down, dear. Why do you ask?"

"I was curious: Does it mean we're safe from any risk that the Hero-designate playing the archetypical role is going to leap out of the shadows, armed to the teeth with specialized lethal hardware, and wreck all our plans?"

Billington begins to turn. "Yes, of course. Why are you worrying about—"

To my necromancy-stunned eyes it all seems to happen in very slow motion. Her clenched fist unclenches: a bone-colored bow drops down her sleeve like a concealed cosh until she grips it by one end and brings her hand up to unlatch the briefcase. Both sides of the case eject, leaving her clutching a handle and a sling attached to a pale violin that she raises to her chin in a smooth motion that speaks of long practice. The halves of the case contain compact amplified speakers, and there's a stark black-on-yellow sticker on the underside of the violin: THIS MACHINE KILLS DEMONS. I start to shout a warning as Ramona begins to stir, her gills flexing limply against the base of her throat and her mouth pouting, and Billington begins to inscribe a sigil in the air in front of his face—

"This is a song of unbinding," says Mo, and the bow slides across the faintly pulsing things-that-aren't-strings, glowing like gashes in my retinas and trailing a ghostly haze when she moves. The first note sounds, wavering eerily on the air and building like the first breezy harbinger of a hurricane. "It unlocks—*everything*."

Across the room, a particularly alert black beret shouts a warning and raises his MP-5. The second note wavers and screams from the body of the instrument, resonating painfully with my back teeth. Every hair on my body is trying to stand on end simultaneously. These aren't sounds the human ear is supposed to be able to hear, the psychoacoustic model is all wrong: I feel like I'm suddenly listening to bat song, the noises that drive dogs wild, the raw and bloody notes of silence. The brief hammering of gunfire drives nails into my eardrums then stops in a shattering of glass and a brief scream as Mo squeezes the fingerboard. The bow string is glowing red. A third note quavers weirdly out of the instrument, somehow building simultaneously with the first and second, which haven't stopped—they've taken root in the air of the room, thickening and turning it blue—and there's a popping noise as the buckles of the straps holding me down spring open.

More screams. Billington, being non-stupid, dashes for the door onto the catwalk outside. The bow reaches the end of its arc and begins to slice back across the bridge of the violin as lockers burst apart, spilling paper and supplies across the floor: zippers break, belts unfasten, doors fly open. The noise is so loud now that it feels like a god is ripping the two halves of reality apart: the sound of tearing inside my head is deafening. I can't hear or feel Ramona anymore, and the lack of her presence is a huge vacuum in my soul, trying to split me in two. The noise of another shot slams in my ears as I sit up and see Mo advancing across the room towards the guards, still playing one hideous note after another. Her skin crackles with static discharge and her hair stands on end as the black beret with the pistol takes aim again and I gulp air, about to shout a warning: but she notices him and anything I could say would be redundant, because she merely points the fingerboard of her instrument at him and there's a spray of blood, unlocked from the skin that binds it. Across the room, there's a sudden flash of light and smoke begins to pour out of one of the equipment racks.

An alarm klaxon begins to blare on and off mournfully, then a speaker crackles into life: "Alert! Incoming helicopters! All hands to point defense!"

*Where's Billington gotten to?* I shake my head, trying to dislodge the dreadful keening sound of strings. The straps are gone. I sit up and lean over the side of the chair, then stumble to my feet and stagger round to the other side. Ramona's out for the count, and she looks really ill— breathing fast, the livid, bruised stripes of her gill slits pulsing against the fish-white scales around the base of her neck. *She's too dry,* I realize. *Too dry?* A stab of guilt: I glance across at Mo, who is single-mindedly driving the surviving black berets out of the room. They're panicking, running for safety. Where's their master?

I glance through the shattered window overlooking the moon pool and my blood runs cold. The thing in the cradle dangling from the drilling rig is twitching fitfully. Down below it a familiar figure hunkers down on the deck, staring up at the chthonic killing machine. *Shit, so* that's *where he's gotten to.* Then I notice the second, smaller creature standing in front of him. *And* that's *the host body. He's going to try to re-activate it!* Which means—

I shuffle painfully away from the chairs, and nearly trip over a pistol. Bending down, I pick it up: it's either the futuristic-looking P99 with laser scope that Marc had, or its identical twin. "Mo?" I call.

She turns round and says something. I can't hear a single word over the howling reverberation of her violin.

"I've got to stop him!" I yell. I can barely hear myself. She looks blank, so I point at the door onto the catwalk. "He's out there!"

She points at one of the inner doors emphatically, as if suggesting I should head that way instead. So I shake my head and stumble towards the catwalk. Behind me, the flickers of light suggest more electrical fires breaking out among the high-voltage bearers. I lean over the railing and look down dizzily. It's about twenty meters away—a small target at that range. I fumble with the pistol and switch on the laser. My hand's shaking. *If I'm right*—

The red dot dances across the far wall. I trace it down the wall, swearing under my breath, and run it rapidly across the deck towards the drained floor of the moon pool. I keep my finger away from the trigger. *If I'm wrong*—

Billington is an expert at soul-sucking abominations. Now he's in thrall to another, greater evil: one with a damaged body, so he's provided it with a convenient temporary replacement while he comes up with enough sacrificial victims and spare parts to repair its original one. What entity aboard this ship exhibits all the personality traits of a cold-blooded killing machine, combined with the monstrous, overweening vanity and laziness of a convalescent war god lounging in their personal Valhalla while their minions prepare their armor? There's only one answer.

The Persian tomcat sits underneath the alien horror, washing itself without concern. "C'mon, Fluffy," I tell it. "Show me what you are." We all know about cats and lasers. Lasers are the best cat toy ever invented: the red-dot machine that comes out for playtime. Used skillfully, you can make a cat chase the dot so slavishly that she'll run headfirst into a wall. It's like the sitting-in-cardboard-boxes thing, or the sniffing-an-extended-finger reflex. All cats do it, unless they're so enervated that they choose to ignore the lure and groom their fur instead.

Fluffy takes a few seconds to lock on, and when he does, his response is immediate and drastic. He glances down at the deck, sees the red dot dancing around nearby—and dashes away like his tail's on fire.

"Bob! We've got to get out of here! Ellis has gotten away." I look round. Mo stands in the doorway, one hand cupped around an ear: "There are scuttling charges due to blow as soon as he's clear—"

It's déjà vu all over again. At least her eyeballs aren't glowing blue and she isn't levitating. I shake my head and point down at the moon pool: "Help me! We've got to stop him!"

"Who's the target?" Mo ducks out and stands beside me.

"Him!" I pull the trigger. There's an ear-stinging ricochet a fraction of a second after the shot. I'm nowhere near the target. "Damn, missed."

"Bob, we've got to get out of here! Can you still feel that Black Chamber bitch? The chromatic disintermediator should have broken your entanglement, but—why are you trying to shoot that cat?"

"Because—" I squeeze off another shot "—it's possessed!"·

"Bob." She looks at me as if I'm mad. There's a loud bang from inside the control room, and a human figure in a black beret runs out onto the sealed doors flooring the pool: I shoot instinctively and miss, and he dives for cover. "Leave the fucking cat—hey, that's Billington down there!" She raises her instrument and prepares to let fly.

The cat squirts out across the floor, a white blur targeting the downed bad guy. I shoot again, and again, and keep missing. "Not Billington! Get the cat!"

Mo sniffs skeptically. "Are you sure?"

"Yes, I'm goddamn sure!" Billington's standing in front of the iron maiden, as if steeling himself to jump inside. "It's the enemy! Get it now, or we're fucked!"

Mo raises her violin, squints darkly down at the deck below us, and drops a noise like a million felines being disemboweled down on top of Fluffy. Who opens his fanged maw to howl, then explodes like a gore-filled, white dandelion head. Mo turns and looks at me harshly. "That looked just like a perfectly ordinary cat to me. If you've—"

"It was possessed by the animation nexus behind JENNIFER MORGUE Two!" I gabble. "The clue—he saw a laser dot and dodged—"

"Bob. Back up a moment."

"Yes?"

"The cat. You said it was the enemy. You didn't say it was occupied by the mind of *that* thing?" She points up at the ceiling, where the chthonic warrior is definitely twitching and writhing. I stare.

"Uh, well, I meant—"

"And you thought killing it would improve matters?"

"Yes?"

One of the bole-like knots in the warrior's hide is growing larger. Then it opens, revealing an eye the size of a truck tire. It stares right back at me.

She clouts me on the back of the head: "Run!"

The huge tentacle slams down onto the deck where Ellis Billington kneels in supplication before his god, landing with a percussive clang that rattles the remaining windows and reduces him to a greasy stain on the bulkhead. Which is probably why Mo and I survive: we stumble back through the control room doorway about two seconds before the tree-trunk-thick limb slams into the wall with the force of a runaway locomotive. Support trusses scream and buckle beneath the blow. I start coughing and my eyes water immediately. The air is gray with smoke and thick with the greasy fish-oil smell of burning insulation. I thump the big red button beside the door and metal shutters begin to drop down behind the broken glass—maybe it's too little too late, but at least it makes me feel better. "Where's Ramona? We've got to get her out of here!"

Mo glares at me. "What makes you think rescuing her's on my list of mission objectives? You're disentangled, aren't you?"

I stare back at her, wondering who the hell she thinks she is, barging in here with her Class A thaumaturgic weapons. Then I blink and re-member sharing a slow breakfast with her back before all this started, all those endless weeks ago—*Is that all?* "I think I know what you're think-ing," I say slowly, feeling an awful weary emptiness inside me, "but that's not what's been going on between us. And if you leave her because you're jealous, you'll be making a mistake you can never undo. Plus, you'll be leaving her to *that.*"

JENNIFER MORGUE thumps against the outside of the security shutters, sending a shower of glass daggers crackling and clinking across the floor. The shutters bend but they hold: something's clearly wrong with the beast, or it should have been out of the moon pool by now, leav-ing a twisted trail of titanium structural members behind it. Dumping the controlling intelligence out of its temporary host body must have awakened the chthonian prematurely, still deathly weak and hungry. Mo doesn't look away from my face. She's searching me for something, some sign. I stare at her, wondering which way she's going to jump, whether the geas has gone to her head: if it has conferred not only the power that goes with her role, but also the callousness.

After a few seconds Mo looks away. "We'll sort this out later."

I stumble back towards the sacrifice chairs. Ramona is still out. I rest a palm on her forehead, then snatch it back fast: she's fever-hot. "Give me a hand . . ." I manage to get one arm over my shoulder and begin to lift her off the chair, but in my present state I'm too weak. Just as my knees begin to give out under me someone takes her other arm. "Thanks—" I glance round her lolling head.

"This way, mate." The apparition grins at me around its regulator. "Sharpish!"

"If you say so." More black-clad figures appear—this time, wearing wet suits and body armor. "Is Alan here?"

"Yeah. Why?"

"Because—" there's a crashing noise from the far wall, and I wince "—there's an alien horror on the other side of that wall and it wants in *bad*. Make sure somebody tells him." I start coughing: the air in here becoming unbreathable.

"Ah, Bob, exactly the man! Don't worry about the eldritch horror, we've got a plan for this contingency—as soon as we've evac'd we'll just pop a brace of Storm Shadows on his ass and send him right back down where he came from. But you're exactly the man I was hoping to see. How are you doing, old chap? Got a Sitrep on the opposition for me?"

I blink, bleary-eyed. It's Alan all right: wearing scuba gear and a communications headset only the Borg could love, he still manages to look like an excitable schoolteacher. "I've had better days. Look, the primary opposition movers are dead, and I think Charlie Victor might be amenable to an offer of political asylum if the rite of unbinding did what I think it did to her, but about the Smart car on the drilling deck—"

"Yes, yes, I know it's a bit scorched around the edges and there are some bullet holes, but you don't have to worry: the Auditors won't mind normal wear and tear—"

"No, that's not it." I try to focus. "In the boot. There's a tablecloth with a diorama wrapped up in it. Would you mind having one of your lads blow it up? Otherwise all the Bond mojo zapping around in here is going to follow us home and wreck any chance of me and Mo getting back together again for anything but a one-night stand."

"Ah! Good thinking." Alan pushes a button and mutters into his mike. "Anything else?"

"Yeah." Either there's a lot of gray smoke in here, or— "I'm feeling dizzy. Just let me sit down, for a moment . . ."

# Epilogue:
## Three's Company

It's August in England, and I'm almost functioning on British Summer Time again. We're having another heat wave, but up here on the Norfolk coast it's not so bad: there's an onshore breeze coming in from the Wash, and while it isn't exactly cold, it feels that way after the Caribbean.

We call this place the Village: it's an old in-joke. Once upon a time it was a hamlet, a village in all respects save its lack of a parish church. It was one of three churchless hamlets that had clustered in this area, and the last of them still standing, for the others slid under the waves a long time ago. There was only the one meandering road in the vicinity, and it was pot-holed and poorly maintained. Go back sixty or seventy years and you'd find it was home to a small community of winkle-pickers and fishermen who braved the sea in small boats. They were a curious, pale, inbred lot, not well liked by the neighbors up and down the coast, and they kept to themselves. Some of them, it's said, kept to themselves so efficiently that they never left the company of their own kind from birth unto death.

But then the Second World War intervened. And someone remembered the peculiar paper the village doctor had tried to publish in the *Lancet*, back in the '20s, and someone else noticed its proximity to several interesting underwater obstructions, and, with the stroke of a pen, the War Ministry relocated everyone who lived next to the waterline. And the men from MI6 Department 66 came and installed electricity and telephones and concrete coastal defense bunkers, and they rerouted the road so that it doubled back on itself and missed the village completely before merging with the road to the next hamlet up the coast. And they systematically erased the Village from the Ordinance Survey's public maps, and from the post office, and from the discourse of national life. In a very real sense, the Village is as far away from England as Saint Martin, or the Moon. But in another sense, it's still too close for comfort.

Today, the Village has the patina of neglect common to building developments that subsist on the largess of government agencies, and rely for their maintenance on duct tape and the extensive use of the power of Crown Immunity to avoid planning requirements. It's not a white-painted picturesque Italianate paradise like Portmeirion, and we inmates aren't issued numbers instead of names. But there's a certain resemblance to that other Village—and there is, overlooking the harbor mole, a row of buildings that includes an old-fashioned pub with paint peeling from the wooden decking outside, worn linoleum floors, and hand-pumps that dispense a passable if somewhat briny brew.

I came up from London yesterday, after the board of enquiry met to hear the report on the outcome of the JENNIFER MORGUE business. It's over now, buried deep in the secret files in the Laundry stacks below Mornington Crescent tube station. If you've got a high enough clearance you can get to read them—just go ask the librarians for CASE BROCCOLI GOLDENEYE. (Who says the classification office doesn't have a sick sense of humor?)

I'm still feeling burned by the whole affair. Bruised and used about sums it up; and I'm not ready to face Mo yet, so I had to find somewhere to hole up and lick my wounds. The Village isn't a resort, but there's a three-story modern building called the Monkfish Motel that's not entirely unlike a bad '60s Moat House—I think it was originally built as MOD married quarters—and there's the Dog and Whistle to drink in, and if I get drunk and start babbling about beautiful man-eating mermaids and sunken undersea horrors, nobody's going to bat an eyelid.

It's late afternoon and I'm on my second pint, slumped in the grasp of the sofa in the east corner of the lounge bar. I'm the only customer at this time of day—most everyone else is off attending training courses or working—but the bar stays open all the same.

The door opens. I'm busy failing to reread a dog-eared paperback biography, my mind skittering off the words as if they're polished ice cubes that melt and slide away whenever I warm them with my glance. Right now it's gathering moss on the coffee table in front of me as I idly flip the antique Zippo lighter that's the one part of my disguise kit I ended up bringing home. Footsteps slowly approach, clattering on the bare floor. I sit there in the corner, and I wonder tiredly if I ought to run away. And then it's too late.

"He told me I'd find you here," she says.

"Really?" I put the Zippo down and look up at her.

The prelude to this little drama took place the day before yesterday in Angleton's office. I was sitting in the cheap plastic visitor's seat he keeps on the other side of his desk, my line of sight partially blocked by the bulky green-enameled flank of his Memex, trying to hold my shit together. Up until this point I'd been doing a reasonable job, aided by Angleton going out of his way to explain how we were going to clear my entirely unreasonable expense claims with the Auditors: but then he decided to try and get all human on my ass.

"You'll be able to see her whenever you want," he said, right out of the blue, without any warning.

"Fuck it! What makes you think—"

"Look at me, boy." There's a tone of voice he uses that reaches into the back of your head and pulls the control wires, grating and harsh and impossible to ignore: it got my attention.

I looked directly at him. "I am sick and tired of everyone tiptoeing around me as if I'm going to explode," I heard myself say. "Apologizing won't help: what's done is done, there's no going back on it. It was a successful mission and the ends, at least in this case, justify the means. However underhanded they were."

"If you believe that, you're a bigger fool than I thought." Angleton closed the cover of the accounts folder and put his pen down. Then he caught my gaze. "Don't be a fool, son."

Angleton's not his real name—real names confer power, which is why we always, all of us, use pseudonyms—nor is it the only thing about him that doesn't ring true: I saw the photographs in his dream-briefing, and if he was that old when he was along for the ride on Operation JENNIFER, he can't be a day under seventy today. (I've also seen an eerily similar face in the background of certain archival photographs dating from the 1940s, but let's not go there.) "Is this where you give me the benefit of your copious decades of experience? Stiff upper lip, the game's the thing, they also serve who whatever-the-hell-the-saying goes?"

"Yes." His cheek twitched. "But you're missing something."

"Huh. And what's that?" I hunker down in my chair, resigned to having to sit through a sanctimonious lecture about wounded pride or something.

"We fucked with your head, boy. And you're right, it is just another successful operation, but that doesn't mean we don't owe you an apology and an explanation."

"Great." I crossed my arms defensively.

He picked up his pen again, scratching notes on his desk pad. "Two weeks' compassionate leave. I can stretch it to a month if you need it, but beyond that, we'll need a medical evaluation." *Scribble, scribble.* "That goes for both of you. Counseling, too."

"What about Ramona?" The words hung in the air like lead balloons.

"Separate arrangements apply." He glanced up again, fixing me with a wintry blue stare. "I'm also recommending that you spend the next week at the Village."

"Why?" I demanded.

"Because that's where Predictive Branch says you need to go, boy. Did you want fries with that?"

"Fucking hell. What do *they* have to do with things?"

"If you'd ever studied knife fighting, one of the things your instructors would have drilled into you is that you always clean your blade after using it, and if possible sharpen and lubricate it, before you put it away. Because if you want to use it again some time, you don't want to find it stuck to the scabbard, or blunt, or rusted. When you use a tool, you take care to maintain it, boy, that's common sense. From the organization's point of view . . . well, you're not just an interchangeable part, a human resource: we can't go to the nearest employment center and hire a replacement for you just like that. You've got a unique skill mix that would be very difficult to locate—but don't let it go to your head just yet—which is why we're willing to take some pains to help you get over it. We used you, it's true. And we used Dr. O'Brien, and you're both going to have to get used to it, and what's more important to you right now—because you expect to be used for certain types of jobs now and again—is that we didn't use you the way you *expected* to be used. Am I right?"

I spluttered for a moment. "Oh, sure, that's everything! In a nutshell! I see the light now, it's just in my nature to be all offended about having my masculinity impugned by being cast in the role of the Good Bond Babe, hero-attractor and love interest for Mo in her capacity as the big-swinging-dick secret agent man with the gun, I mean, violin, and the license to kill. Right? It's just vanity. So I guess I'd better go powder my nose and dry my tears so I can look glamorous and loving for the closing romantic-interest scene, huh?"

"Pretty much." Angleton nodded. His lip quirked oddly. A suppressed smile?

"Jesus fucking Christ, Angleton, that's leaving just a little bit out. Not to mention Ramona. If you think you could tie our brains together like the Kilkenny cats, then just cut us loose—it doesn't work that way, you know?"

"Yes." He nodded again. "And that's why you need to go to the Village," he said briskly. "Talk to her. Settle where you both stand, in your own mind." He picked up his papers and looked away, an implicit dismissal. I rose to my feet.

"Oh, and one other thing," he added.

"What?"

"While you're about it, remember to talk to Dr. O'Brien as well. You both need to sort things out—and sooner, rather than later."

"He made it an order." She shrugs. "So here I am." Looking as if she'd rather be anywhere else on the planet.

"Enjoying yourself?" I ask. It's the sort of stilted, stupid question you ask when you're trying to make small talk but walking on eggshells in case the other person explodes at you. Which is what I'm half-expecting—this situation is a minefield.

"No," she says with forced levity. "The weather sucks, the beer's

warm, the sea's too cold for swimming, and every time I look at it . . ."
She stalls, the thin glaze of collectedness cracking. "Can I sit down?"

I pat the sofa beside me. "Be my guest."

She sits down in the opposite corner, an arm's length away. "You're
acting like you're mad at me."

I glance at the book on the table. "I'm not mad at *you*." I try to figure
out what to say next: "I'm mad at the way the circumstances made things
turn out. Are *you* still mad at *her*?"

"At *her*?" She chuckles, startled. "I don't think she had any more
choice in it than you did. Why should I be mad at her?"

I pick up my glass and take a long mouthful of beer. "Because we
slept together?"

"Because you—what?" A waspish tone creeps into her voice: "But I
thought you said you hadn't!"

I put my glass down. "We didn't." I meet her eye. "In the Bill Clinton
sense of things, I can honestly say I have *not* had sexual intercourse with
that woman. You know what the Black Chamber did to her? If I *had* slept
with her I'd be dead."

"But how can you—" Mo is confused.

"Her monster had to feed. Before you came and unbound it, it had
to feed. She had to feed it, or it would have eaten her. I was along for the
ride."

Enlightenment dawns. "But now she's there—" a wave in the vague
direction of the drowned village of Dunwich, a mile out to sea, where the
Laundry maintains its outpost "—and you're here. And you're both safe."

*Acid indigestion.* "Safe from what?" I ask, watching her sidelong.

"Safe from—" She stops. "Why are you looking at me?"

"She's undergoing the change, you know that? They can usually hold
it off, but in her case it's looking irreversible."

Mo nods, reluctantly.

"Probably it was triggered by the deep-diving excursion," I add.
"Although proximity to certain thaumic resonances can bring it on prematurely." *Which you would be in a position to know all about*, I don't
say. It's a horrible thing to suspect of anyone, especially your partner who
you've been sharing a house with for enough years that it's getting to be
a habit. "I gather they expect her to make it, with her mind intact."

"That's good," Mo says automatically. A double take: "Isn't it?"

"I don't know. Is it a good thing?" I ask.

"That's not a question I'd have expected you to ask."

I sigh. None of this is straightforward. "Mo, you could have warned
me they were training you in deep-cover insertion and extraction operations! Jesus, I thought *I* was the one on the sharp end!"

"And you were!" she snaps at me suddenly. "Did you wonder how I felt about it, every time you disappeared on a black bag job? Did you ask if maybe I was worried sick that you were never coming back? You know what I know, how helpless do you think that left me feeling?"

"Whoa! I didn't want you to worry—"

"You didn't want! Jesus, Bob, what does it take to get through to you? You can't stop other people worrying just by not *wanting* them to. It's not about you, dim-bulb, it's about me. At least, this time it was. Or do you think I turned up there on your ass by accident?"

I stare at her, at a loss for words.

"Let me lay it out for you, Bob. The whole solitary reason Angleton assigned you to that stupid fucking arrangement with Ramona was *precisely* because you didn't know what was going on. What you didn't know, you couldn't leak to Ramona."

"I got that much, but why—"

"Billington was enslaved by JENNIFER MORGUE Two sometime in the '70s, after the abortive attempt to raise the K-129. He tried to contact the chthonian using the Gravedust rig—a little private free enterprise, if you like. JENNIFER MORGUE Two wanted out, and wanted out bad, but it needed someone to come and repair it. Billington provided it with a temporary host body, kitty kibble, and he had the resources to buy the *Explorer*—once the US Navy decommissioned it—and kit it out for a retrieval run. And we knew all this, on deep background, three years ago."

I blink. "Who is this 'we' you speak of?"

"Me." She looks impatient. "And Angleton. And everybody else with BLUE HADES clearance who's been working on the project. Except for you, and a couple of others, who've been kept in a mushroom box against the day."

"Damn." I pick up my glass and drain what's left of the beer. "I need another drink." Pause. "You too?"

"Make mine a double vodka martini on ice." She pulls a face. "I can't seem to kick the habit."

I stand up and walk inside to the bar, where the middle-aged barwoman is sitting on a stool poring over the Sudoku in the back of the *Express*. "Two double vodka martinis on ice." I say diffidently.

The woman puts her magazine down. She stares at me like I crawled out from under a rock. "You're going to say shaken, not stirred, ain't cha?" She's got a Midwestern accent: probably another defector, I guess. "You know how bad that tastes?"

"Make it one shaken, one stirred, then. Off the ice. And easy on the vermouth." I wink.

I go back towards the corner I'd claimed, then pause in the archway. Mo's leaning back in the sofa, infinitely familiar. For a moment my breath catches in my throat and I have to stop and try to commit the picture to memory in case it turns out to be one of the last good times. Then I force myself to get my legs moving again.

"They'll be over in a minute," I say, dropping onto the sofa beside her.

"Good." She stares at the windows overlooking the beach. "You know the Black Chamber wanted to get their hands on JENNIFER MORGUE. That's what McMurray was doing there."

"Yes." So she thinks I want to talk about business?

"We couldn't let them do that. But luckily for us, Billington . . . well, he wasn't entirely sane to begin with, and when he came up with the idea of implementing a Hero trap, that made things a lot easier."

"*Easier?*" It's a good thing I don't have a drink in my hand.

"Absolutely." She nods. "Imagine if Billington had simply gone to the Black Chamber and said, 'ten billion and it's yours,' keeping his fix-it plan to himself. But instead, he gets this idea that he's got to act in solitary as the prime mover in the scheme, and *of course* he's the archetype of the billionaire megalomaniac, so he does the obvious thing: leverages his assets. The Hero trap—the geas he built around that yacht—required a hero to trigger it. He figured the plot structure is deterministic: the hero falls into the bad guy's hands, the bad guy monologues—and at that point, he was going to destroy the trap, neuter the hero, who is just another civil servant at this point, stripped of the resonances of the Bond invocation—and allow his plan to proceed to completion."

"Except . . ."

"You know the alternative plot?" She glances at the book I've been reading: a biography of a playboy turned naval intelligence officer, news agency manager, and finally spy novelist.

"What?" I shake my head. "I thought it was—"

"Yes, it's so neat you can draw a flow chart. But it's non-deterministic, Bob: the Bond plot structure has a number of forks in it before it converges on the ending, with Mr. Secret Agent Man and his love interest getting it on in a lifeboat or the honeymoon suite of the QE2 or something. Including the approach to the villain. Billington didn't look into it deeply enough; he assumed that the Hero archetype would come looking for him and fall into his clutches directly."

"But." I snap my fingers, trying to collect my scattered thoughts. "You. Me. He got *me*, but I wasn't the real Bond-figure, right? I was a decoy."

She nods. "It happens. If the love interest ends up on the villain's yacht, being held prisoner, *then* the hero has to go after her. Or *him*. The real trick was the idea—I think it was Angleton's—of using the Good

Bond Girl as a decoy by dressing her up in a tux and a shoulder holster. And then to figure out how to use this to get the Black Chamber to put one over on Billington."

"Ramona. She knew that I thought I was the agent in place, so she naturally assumed I really *was* the agent."

"Right. And this also let us identify a leak in our own organization, because how else did Billington make you so rapidly? Which turns out to have been Jack. Last of the public school assholes, hung out to dry out where he couldn't do any damage—so he develops a sideline in selling intel to what he thinks is another disgruntled outsider."

"Urk." I suddenly remember the electrodynamic rig Griffin had stuck in his safe house and briefly wonder just what the hell else he might have been picking up on it, sitting pretty in the middle of the Caribbean with no supervision.

Mo falls silent. I realize she's waiting for something. My tongue's frozen: there are questions I want to ask, but it's a bad idea to ask something when you're not sure you want to hear the answer. "Did you enjoy being . . . Bond?" I finally manage.

"Did I?" She raises an eyebrow. "Hell." She frowns. "Did *you?*" she demands.

"But I wasn't—"

"But you *thought* you were."

"No!" The very question is freighted with significance I don't want to explore. "I don't do high society, I don't smoke, I don't like being beaten up, being taken prisoner, being tortured, or fighting people, and I'm no good at the womanizing bit." I dry-swallow. "How about you?"

"Well," she pauses to consider, "I'm no good at womanizing either." Her cheek twitches. "Is that what this is about, Bob? Did you figure I was cheating on you?"

"I was—" I clear my throat "—unsure where I stood."

"We need to talk about this. Get it out in the open some time. Don't we?"

I nod. It's about all I can do.

"I didn't jump into bed with anybody else," she says briskly. "Does that make you feel better?"

1 *No, it doesn't.* Now I feel like a shit for having asked in the first place. I make myself nod.

"Well, great." She crosses her arms, then taps her fingers on her upper arm: "Where have our drinks gotten to?"

"I ordered the martinis. I guess she's taking her time." *Quick, change the subject.* I really don't want us to fall down one of those embarrassing conversational potholes where the silence stretches out into an eloquent statement of mutual miscommunication: "So, how did you manage to disguise yourself as Eileen? You really had me convinced at first."

"Oh, that was no big deal." Mo looks relieved. She smiles at me and my heart beats faster. "You know Brains has a sideline in cosmetology? Says some of his best friends are drag queens. Well, we've got enough surveillance background on Eileen to know what she looks like, so I got Brains out to the *York* to provide make-up services before the assault. Stick a class two glamour on top of the basics—a wig, the right clothes, some latex paint—and her own daughter wouldn't make her. We used Pale Grace™ for the finishing touch; it might be bugged, but we made sure I wouldn't see anything until I was aboard the ship. So I just headed for the control room using the maps we had on file from Angleton's—"

I raise a hand. "Hold it."

"What?" Mo stares at me.

"Have you got your violin?" I whisper, hunkering down.

"No, why—"

*Shit.* "Our drinks are well overdue."

"And?"

"And this plot was set up by a document that's classified CASE BROCCOLI GOLDENEYE, Angleton said, and Predictive Branch said I needed to be here, *and* . . ."

"And?"

I kneel on the floor and pull my mobile phone out, flick the switch to silence it, then put it in camcorder mode. I sneak it out from behind the sofa, then pull it back and inspect the bar. There's nobody there. I swear quietly, and call up my thaumic scratchpad application. Then I tip my glass upside down over the table, and draw my fingers through the resulting beer suds frantically, wishing I hadn't downed the pint and left myself mere drops to work with.

"Have you got that stupid piece of paper on you?"

"What, the license to kill? It's just a prop, it doesn't mean anything—"

"So pass it here, then. We haven't had plot closure yet, and you're not the only one who can use cosmetics and a class two glamour."

"Shit," Mo whispers back at me, and rolls forwards onto the floor. "Are you thinking what I think you're thinking?"

"What, that we've been followed home by a manifestly evil mistress of disguise who is hankering for revenge because we got her husband stomped into pink slime by a chthonian war machine?"

There's a disturbingly solid *click-chunk* from the front door, like a Yale lock engaging.

"Do you know the ending of *Diamonds Are Forever?* The movie version with Sean Connery?" I meet Mo's eyes for a moment, and in a disturbing flash of clarity I realize that she means a whole lot more to me than the question of who she has or hasn't been having sex with. Then she nods and rolls away from the floor in front of the sofa, and I hit the button on my phone just as there's a flat percussive bang: not the ear-slamming concussion I expect from a pistol, but muffled, much quieter.

I look round.

The middle-aged barwoman is waving a pistol inexpertly around the room, the long tube of a silencer protruding from its muzzle: she looks subtly familiar this time. "Over here!" I call.

She makes the classic mistake: she glances my way and blinks, gun muzzle wavering. "Come out where I can see you!" Eileen snaps querulously.

"Why? So you can kill us more easily?" I'm ready to jump up and dive through the window if necessary, but she can't see me—the concealment spell is still working, at least until the remaining beer evaporates. I go back to folding a paper airplane out of Mo's license, my fingers shaking with tension.

"That would be the idea," she says. "A lovers' quarrel, male agent kills partner then shoots self. It doesn't have to hurt."

"No shit?" Mo asks. I squint and try to spot her, but one thing we've both got going for us is that pubs tend to be gloomy and poorly lit, and this one's no exception.

Eileen spins round through ninety degrees and unloads a bullet into the wall of optics behind the bar.

I glance at the drying suds then roll to my hands and knees and creep around the sofa, trying to stay low. I think the paper plane's balanced right—it had better be, I'm only going to get the one chance to use it. There are forms, and this is . . . well, it *might* work. If it doesn't we're trapped in a locked pub with a madwoman with a gun, and our invisibility spell has a half-life measured in seconds rather than minutes. There are two martini glasses on the bar, one of them half full: Maybe Eileen wanted to steady her nerves first? There's probably an unconscious or dead bartender out back. What a mess: I don't think an intruder's ever penetrated the Village before. I doubt it would be possible without the blowback from the Hero trap to help.

There's a creak from a floorboard and another shot goes flying, to no apparent effect. Eileen looks spooked. She takes a step backwards towards the bar, gun muzzle questing about, and then another step. My heart's pounding and I'm feeling lightheaded with anger—no, with rage—*You think anyone would ever believe I'd hurt Mo?* And then she's at the bar.

There's a glassy *chink*.

Eileen spins round, and pulls the trigger just as the half-full martini glass levitates and flies at her face. She manages to shoot the ceiling, then recoils. "Ow! Bitch!" I raise the paper dart and take aim. She wipes her eyes as she brings her gun down to bear on a faint distortion in the air, a snarl of satisfaction on her face. "I see you now!"

I flick the Zippo's wheel and then throw the flaming dart at her martini-irrigated head.

Afterwards, as the paramedics load her onto a stretcher and zip the body bag closed, and Internal Security removes the CCTV hard drives for evidence, I hold Mo in my arms. Or she holds me: my knees feel like jelly and it would be downright embarrassing if Mo wasn't shuddering, too. "You're all right," I tell her, "you're all right."

She laughs shakily. "No, *you're* all right!" And she hugs me hard.

"Come on. Let's take a walk."

There's a mess on the floor, fire extinguisher foam half-concealing the scorch marks, and we skirt it carefully on our way to the door. Security has placed us under a ward of compulsion and we'll be seen by the Auditors tomorrow: but for the time being, we've got the run of the Village. Mo seems to want to head back to our quarters, but I pull back. "No, let's go walk on the beach." And she nods.

"You knew that was coming," she says as we jump down off the concrete wall and onto the rough pebbles.

"I had an idea something bad was in the air." The onshore breeze is blowing, and the sun is shining. "I didn't know for sure, or I'd have been better prepared."

"Bullshit." She punches me lightly on the arm, then puts an arm around my waist.

"No, would I lie to you?" I protest. I stare out to sea. Somewhere out there Ramona is lying in a watery hostel, learning what she really is. A new life lies ahead of her: she won't be able to come ashore after the change is complete. Hey, if I really *was* James Bond, I could have a girl in every port—even the drowned ones.

"Bob. Would you have left me for her?"

I shiver. "I don't think so." Actually, *no*. Which is not to say Ramona didn't have glamour of the non-magical kind as well, but there's something about what I have with Mo—

"Well, then. And you're cut up about the idea that I might have been cheating on you."

I consider this for a few seconds. "Surprised?"

"Well." She's silent, too. "I was worried. And I'm still worried about the other thing."

"The other thing?"

"The possibility that we're going to be haunted by the ghost of James Bond."

"Oh, I dunno." I kick a pebble towards the waterline, watch it skitter, alone. "We could always do something totally un-Bond-like, to break any remaining echoes of the geas."

"You think?" She smiles. "Got any ideas?"

My mouth is dry. "Yeah—yes, as a matter-of-fact I do." I take her in my arms and she puts her arms around me, and rests her face against the side of my neck. "If this was really the end of a Bond story, we'd go find a luxury hotel to hole up in, order a magnum of champagne, and fuck each other senseless."

She tenses. "Ah, I hadn't thought of that." A moment later, and faintly: "Damn."

"Well. I'm not saying it's impossible. But—" My heart is pounding again, and my knees are even weaker than they were when I realized Eileen hadn't shot her. "We've got to do it in such a way that it's *completely incompatible* with the geas."

"Okay, wise guy. So you've got a bright idea for an ending that simply wouldn't work in a Bond book?"

"Yes. See, the thing is, Bond's creator—like Bond himself—was a snob. Upper crust, old Etonian, terribly conventional. If he was around today he'd always be wearing a tailored suit, you'd never catch him in ripped jeans and a Nine Inch Nails tee shirt. And it goes deeper. He liked sex, but he was deeply ingrained with a particular view of gender relationships. Man of action, woman as bit of fluff on the side. So the one thing Bond would never expect one of his girls to say is—" it's now or never "—will . . . will you marry me?" I can't help it; my voice ends up a strangled squeak, as befits the romantic interest doing something as shockingly unconventional as proposing to the hero.

"Oh, Bob!" She hugs me tighter: "Of course! Yes!" She's squeaking, too, I realize dizzily: *Is this normal?* We kiss. "Especially if it means we can hole up in a luxury hotel, order in a magnum of champagne, and fuck each other senseless without being haunted by the ghost of James Bond. You've got a sick and twisted mind—that's why I love you!"

"I love you, too," I add. And as we walk along the beach, holding hands and laughing, I realize that we're free.

# Pimpf

◇　◇　◇

**7** HATE DAYS LIKE THIS.

It's a rainy Monday morning and I'm late in to work at the Laundry because of a technical fault on the Tube. When I get to my desk, the first thing I find is a note from Human Resources that says one of their management team wants to talk to me, soonest, about playing computer games at work. And to put the cherry on top of the shit-pie, the office's coffee percolator is empty because none of the other inmates in this goddamn loony bin can be arsed refilling it. It's enough to make me long for a high place and a rifle . . . but in the end I head for Human Resources to take the bull by the horns, decaffeinated and mean as only a decaffeinated Bob can be.

Over in the dizzying heights of HR, the furniture is fresh and the windows recently cleaned. It's a far cry from the dingy rats' nest of Ops Division, where I normally spend my working time. But ours is not to wonder why (at least in public).

"Ms. MacDougal will see you now," says the receptionist on the front desk, looking down her nose at me pityingly. "Do try not to shed on the carpet, we had it steam cleaned this morning." *Bastards.*

I slouch across the thick, cream wool towards the inner sanctum of Emma MacDougal, senior vice-superintendent, Personnel Management (Operations), trying not to gawk like a resentful yokel at the luxuries on parade. It's not the first time I've been here, but I can never shake the sense that I'm entering another world, graced by visitors of ministerial import and elevated budget. The dizzy heights of the *real* civil service, as opposed to us poor Morlocks in Ops Division who keep everything running.

"Mr. Howard, do come in." I straighten instinctively when Emma addresses me. She has that effect on most people—she was born to be a headmistress or a tax inspector, but unfortunately she ended up in Human Resources by mistake and she's been letting us know about it ever since. "Have a seat." The room reeks of quiet luxury by Laundry standards: my chair is big, comfortable, and hasn't been bumped, scraped, and abraded into a pile of kindling by generations of visitors. The office is bright and airy, and the window is clean and has a row of attractively un-browned potted plants sitting before it. (The computer squatting on her desk is at least twice as expensive as anything I've been able to get my hands on via official channels, and it's *not even switched on*.) "How good of you to make time to see me." She smiles like a razor. I stifle a sigh; it's going to be one of *those* sessions.

"I'm a busy man." *Let's see if deadpan will work, hmm?*

"I'm sure you are. Nevertheless." She taps a piece of paper sitting on her blotter and I tense. "I've been hearing disturbing reports about you, Bob."

*Oh, bollocks.* "What kind of reports?" I ask warily.

Her smile's cold enough to frost glass. "Let me be blunt. I've had a report—I hesitate to say who from—about you playing computer games in the office."

Oh. *That.* "I see."

"According to this report you've been playing rather a lot of Neverwinter Nights recently." She runs her finger down the printout with relish. "You've even sequestrated an old departmental server to run a persistent realm—a multiuser online dungeon." She looks up, staring at me intently. "What have you got to say for yourself?"

I shrug. What's to say? She's got me bang to rights. "Um."

"Um indeed." She taps a finger on the page. "Last Tuesday you played Neverwinter Nights for four hours. This Monday you played it for two hours in the morning and three hours in the afternoon, staying on for an hour after your official flexitime shift ended. That's six straight hours. What have you got to say for yourself?"

"Only six?" I lean forwards.

"Yes. Six hours." She taps the memo again. "Bob. What are we paying you for?"

I shrug. "To put the hack into hack-and-slay."

"Yes, Bob, we're paying you to search online role-playing games for threats to national security. But you only averaged four hours a day last week . . . isn't this rather a poor use of your time?"

Save me from ambitious bureaucrats. This is the Laundry, the last over-manned organization of the civil service in London, and they're *every-where*—trying to climb the greasy pole, playing snakes and ladders with the org chart, running esoteric counterespionage operations in the staff toilets, and rationing the civil service tea bags. I guess it serves Mahogany Row's purposes to keep them running in circles and distracting one another, but sometimes it gets in the way. Emma MacDougal is by no means the worst of the lot: she's just a starchy Human Resources manager on her way up, stymied by the full promotion ladder above her. But she's trying to butt in and micromanage inside my department (that is, inside *Angleton's* department), and just to show how efficient she is, she's actually been reading my time sheets and trying to stick her oar in on what I should be doing.

To get out of MacDougal's office I had to explain three times that my antiquated workstation kept crashing and needed a system rebuild before she'd finally take the hint. Then she said something about sending me some sort of administrative assistant—an offer that I tried to decline without causing mortal offense. Sensing an opening, I asked if she could provide a budget line item for a new computer—but she spotted where I was coming from and cut me dead, saying that wasn't in HR's remit, and that was the end of it.

Anyway, I'm now looking at my watch and it turns out that it's getting on for lunch. I've lost *another* morning's prime gaming time. So I head back to my office, and just as I'm about to open the door I hear a rustling, crunching sound coming from behind it, like a giant hamster snacking down on trail mix. I can't express how disturbing this is. Rodent menaces from beyond space-time aren't supposed to show up during my meetings with HR, much less hole up in my office making disturbing noises. What's going on?

I rapidly consider my options, discarding the most extreme ones (Facilities takes a dim view of improvised ordnance discharges on Government premises), and finally do the obvious. I push the door open, lean against the battered beige filing cabinet with the jammed drawer, and ask, "Who are you and what are you doing to *my computer?*"

I intend the last phrase to come out as an ominous growl, but it turns into a strangled squeak of rage. My visitor looks up at me from behind my monitor, eyes black and beady, and cheek-pouches stuffed with—ah, there's an open can of Pringles sitting on my in-tray. "Yuh?"

"That's my computer." I'm breathing rapidly all of a sudden, and I carefully set my coffee mug down next to the light-sick petunia so that I don't drop it by accident. "Back away from the keyboard, put down the mouse, and nobody needs to get hurt." And most especially, my sixth-level cleric-sorcerer gets to keep all his experience points and gold pieces without some munchkin intruder selling them all on a dodgy auction site and re-skilling me as an exotic dancer with chloracne.

It must be my face; he lifts up his hands and stares at me nervously, then swallows his cud of potato crisps. "You must be Mr. Howard?"

I begin to get an inkling. "No, I'm the grim fucking reaper." My eyes take in more telling details: his sallow skin, the acne and straggly goatee beard. *Ye gods and little demons, it's like looking in a time-traveling mirror.* I grin nastily. "I asked you once and I won't ask you again: *Who are you?*"

He gulps. "I'm Pete. Uh, Pete Young. I was told to come here by Andy, uh, Mr. Newstrom. He says I'm your new intern."

"My new *what* . . . ?" I trail off. *Andy, you're a bastard! But I repeat myself.* "Intern. Yeah, right. How long have you been here? In the Laundry, I mean."

He looks nervous. "Since last Monday morning."

"Well, this is the first anyone's told me about an intern," I explain carefully, trying to keep my voice level because blaming the messenger won't help; anyway, if Pete's telling the truth he's so wet behind the ears I could use him to water the plants. "So now I'm going to have to go and confirm that. You just wait here." I glance at my desktop. *Hang on, what would I have done five or so years ago . . . ?* "No, on second thoughts, come with me."

The Ops wing is a maze of twisty little passageways, all alike. Cramped offices open off them, painted institutional green and illuminated by underpowered bulbs lightly dusted with cobwebs. It isn't like this on Mahogany Row or over the road in Administration, but those of us who actually contribute to the bottom line get to mend and make do. (There's a malicious, persistent rumor that this is because the Board wants to encourage a spirit of plucky us-against-the-world self-reliance in Ops, and the easiest way to do that is to make every requisition for a box of paper clips into a Herculean struggle. I subscribe to the other, less popular theory: they just don't care.)

I know my way through these dingy tunnels; I've worked here for years. Andy has been a couple of rungs above me in the org chart for all that time. These days he's got a corner office with a blond Scandinavian pine desk. (It's a corner office on the second floor with a view over the alley where the local Chinese take-away keeps their dumpsters, and the desk came from IKEA, but his office still represents the cargo-cult trappings of upward mobility; we beggars in Ops can't be choosy.) I see the red light's out, so I bang on his door.

"Come in." He sounds even more world-weary than usual, and so he should be, judging from the pile of spreadsheet printouts scattered across the desk in front of him. "Bob?" He glances up and sees the intern. "Oh, I see you've met Pete."

"Pete tells me he's my intern," I say, as pleasantly as I can manage under the circumstances. I pull out the ratty visitor's chair with the hole in the seat stuffing and slump into it. "And he's been in the Laundry since the beginning of this week." I glance over my shoulder; Pete is standing in the doorway looking uncomfortable, so I decide to move White Pawn to Black Castle Four or whatever it's called: "Come on in, Pete; grab a chair." (The other chair is a crawling horror covered in mouse-bitten lever arch files labeled STRICTLY SECRET.) It's important to get the message across that I'm not leaving without an answer, and camping my hench-squirt on Andy's virtual in-tray is a good way to do that. (Now if only I can figure out what I'm supposed to be asking . . . ) "What's going on?"

"Nobody told you?" Andy looks puzzled.

"Okay, let me rephrase. Whose idea was it, and what am I meant to do with him?"

"I think it was Emma MacDougal's. In Human Resources." *Oops, he said Human Resources.* I can feel my stomach sinking already. "We picked him up in a routine sweep through Erewhon space last month." (Erewhon is a new Massively Multiplayer Online Role-Playing Game that started up, oh, about two months ago, with only a few thousand players so far. Written by a bunch of spaced-out games programmers from Gothenburg.) "Boris iced him and explained the situation, then put him through induction. Emma feels that it'd be better if we trialed the mentoring program currently on roll-out throughout Admin to see if it's an improvement over our traditional way of inducting new staff into Ops, and his number came up." Andy raises a fist and coughs into it, then waggles his eyebrows at me significantly.

"As opposed to hiding out behind the wet shrubbery for a few months before graduating to polishing Angleton's gear-wheels?" I shrug. "Well, I can't say it's a *bad* idea—" Nobody ever accuses HR of having a *bad idea*; they're subtle and quick to anger, and their revenge is terrible to behold. "—but a little bit of warning would have been nice. Some mentoring for the mentor, eh?"

The feeble quip is only a trial balloon, but Andy latches onto it immediately and with evident gratitude. "Yes, I completely agree! I'll get onto it at once."

I cross my arms and grin at him lopsidedly. "I'm waiting."

"You're—" His gaze slides sideways, coming to rest on Pete. "Hmm." I can almost see the wheels turning. Andy isn't aggressive, but he's a sharp operator. "Okay, let's start from the beginning. Bob, this fellow is Peter-Fred Young. Peter-Fred, meet Mr. Howard, better known as Bob. I'm—"

"—Andy Newstrom, senior operational support manager, Department G," I butt in smoothly. "Due to the modern miracle of matrix management, Andy is my line manager but I work for someone else, Mr. Angleton, who is also Andy's boss. You probably won't meet him; if you do, it probably means you're in big trouble. That right, Andy?"

"Yes, Bob," he says indulgently, picking right up from my cue. "And this is Ops Division." He looks at Peter-Fred Young. "Your job, for the next three months, is to shadow Bob. Bob, you're between field assignments anyway, and Project Aurora looks likely to keep you occupied for the whole time—Peter-Fred should be quite useful to you, given his background."

"Project Aurora?" Pete looks puzzled. Yeah, and me, too.

"What *is* his background, exactly?" I ask. *Here it comes . . .*

"Peter-Fred used to design dungeon modules for a living." Andy's cheek twitches. "The earlier games weren't a big problem, but I think you can guess where this one's going."

"Hey, it's not my fault!" Pete hunches defensively. "I just thought it was a really neat scenario!"

I have a horrible feeling I know what Andy's going to say next. "The third-party content tools for some of the leading MMORPGs are getting pretty hairy these days. They're supposed to have some recognizers built in to stop the most dangerous design patterns getting out, but nobody was expecting Peter-Fred to try to implement a Delta Green scenario as a Neverwinter Nights persistent realm. If it had gone online on a public game server—assuming it didn't eat him during beta testing—we could have been facing a mass outbreak."

I turn and stare at Pete in disbelief. "That was *him?*" *Jesus, I could have been killed!*

He stares back truculently. "Yeah. Your wizard eats rice cakes!"

*And an attitude to boot.* "Andy, he's going to need a desk."

"I'm working on getting you a bigger office." He grins. "This was Emma's idea, she can foot the bill."

Somehow I *knew* she had to be tied in with this, but maybe I can turn it to my advantage. "If Human Resources is involved, surely they're paying?" Which means, deep pockets to pick. "We're going to need two Herman Miller Aeron chairs, an Eames bookcase and occasional table, a desk from some eye-wateringly expensive Italian design studio, a genuine eighty-year-old Bonsai Californian redwood, an OC3 cable into Telehouse, and gaming laptops. Alienware: we need lots and lots of Alienware . . . ."

Andy gives me five seconds to slaver over the fantasy before he pricks my balloon. "You'll take Dell and like it."

"Even if the bad guys frag us?" I try.

"They won't." He looks smug. "Because you're the best."

One of the advantages of being a cash-starved department is that nobody ever dares to throw anything away in case it turns out to be useful later. Another advantage is that there's never any money to get things done, like (for example) refit old offices to comply with current health and safety regulations. It's cheaper just to move everybody out into a Portakabin in the car park and leave the office refurb for another financial year. At least, that's what they do in this day and age; thirty, forty years ago I don't know where they put the surplus bodies. Anyway, while Andy gets on the phone to Emma to plead for a budget, I lead Pete on a fishing expedition.

"This is the old segregation block," I explain, flicking on a light switch. "Don't come in here without a light or the grue will get you."

"You've got grues? Here?" He looks so excited at the prospect that I almost hesitate to tell him the truth.

"No, I just meant you'd just step in something nasty. This isn't an adventure game." The dust lies in gentle snowdrifts everywhere, undisturbed by outsourced cleaning services—contractors generally take one look at the seg block and double their quote, going over the ministerially imposed cap (which gets imposed rigorously on Ops, freeing up funds so Human Resources can employ plant beauticians to lovingly wax the leaves on their office rubber plants).

"You called it a segregation block. What, uh, who was segregated?"

I briefly toy with the idea of winding him up, then reject it. Once you're inside the Laundry you're in it for life, and I don't really want to leave a trail of grudge-bearing juniors sharpening their knives behind me. "People we didn't want exposed to the outside world, even by accident," I say finally. "If you work here long enough it does strange things to your head. Work here too long, and other people can see the effects, too. You'll notice the windows are all frosted or else they open onto air shafts, where there aren't any windows in the first place," I add, shoving open the door onto a large, executive office marred only by the bricked-up window frame in the wall behind the desk, and a disturbingly wide trail of something shiny—I tell myself it's probably just dry wallpaper paste—leading to the swivel chair. "Great, this is just what I've been looking for."

"It is?"

"Yep, a big, empty, executive office where the lights and power still work."

"Whose was it?" Pete looks around curiously. "There aren't many sockets . . ."

"Before my time." I pull the chair out and look at the seat doubtfully. It was good leather once, but the seat is hideously stained and cracked. The penny drops. "I've heard of this guy. 'Slug' Johnson. He used to be high up in Accounts, but he made lots of enemies. In the end someone put salt on his back."

"You want us to work in here?" Pete asks, in a blinding moment of clarity.

"For now," I reassure him. "Until we can screw a budget for a real office out of Emma from HR."

"We'll need more power sockets." Pete's eyes are taking on a distant, glazed look and his fingers twitch mousily: "We'll need casemods, need overclocked CPUs, need fuck-off huge screens, double-headed Radeon X1600 video cards." He begins to shake. "Nerf guns, Twinkies, LAN party—"

"Pete! Snap out of it!" I grab his shoulders and shake him.

He blinks and looks at me blearily. "Whuh?"

I physically drag him out of the room. "First, before we do *anything* else, I'm getting the cleaners in to give it a class four exorcism and to steam clean the carpets. You could catch something nasty in there." *You nearly did*, I add silently. "Lots of bad psychic backwash."

"I thought he was an accountant?" says Pete, shaking his head.

"No, he was *in Accounts*. Not the same thing at all. You're confusing them with Financial Control."

"Huh? What do *Accounts* do, then?"

"They settle accounts—usually fatally. At least, that's what they used to do back in the '60s; the department was terminated some time ago."

"Um." Pete swallows. "I thought that was all a joke? This is, like, the BBFC? You know?"

I blink. The British Board of Film Classification, the people who certify video games and cut the cocks out of movies? "Did anyone tell you what the Laundry actually *does?*"

"Plays lots of deathmatches?" he asks hopefully.

"That's one way of putting it," I begin, then pause. *How to continue?* "Magic is applied mathematics. The many-angled ones live at the bottom of the Mandelbrot set. Demonology is right after debugging in the dictionary. You heard of Alan Turing? The father of programming?"

"Didn't he work for John Carmack?"

*Oh, it's another world out there.* "Not exactly, he built the first computers for the government, back in the Second World War. Not just codebreaking computers; he designed containment processors for Q Division, the Counter-Possession Unit of SOE that dealt with demon-ridden Abwehr agents. Anyway, after the war, they disbanded SOE—broke up all the government computers, the Colossus machines—except for the CPU, which became the Laundry. The Laundry kept going, defending the realm from the scum of the multiverse. There are mathematical transforms that can link entities in different universes—try to solve the wrong theorem and they'll eat your brain, or worse. Anyhow, these days more people do more things with computers than anyone ever dreamed of. Computer games are networked and scriptable, they've got compilers and debuggers built in, you can build cities and film goddamn movies inside them. And every so often someone stumbles across something they're not meant to be playing with and, well, you know the rest."

His eyes are wide in the shadows. "You mean, this is *government* work? Like in Deus Ex?"

I nod. "That's it exactly, kid." Actually it's more like Doom 3 but I'm not ready to tell him that; he might start pestering me for a grenade launcher.

"So we're going to, like, set up a LAN party and log onto lots of persistent realms and search 'n' sweep them for demons and blow the demons away?" He's almost panting with eagerness. "Wait'll I tell my homies!"

"Pete, you can't do that."

"What, isn't it allowed?"

"No, I didn't say that." I lead him back towards the well-lit corridors of the Ops wing and the coffee break room beyond. "I said you *can't* do that. You're under a geas. Section III of the Official Secrets Act says you can't tell anyone who hasn't signed the said act that Section III even exists, much less tell them anything about what it covers. The Laundry is one hundred percent under cover, Pete. You can't talk about it to outsiders, you'd choke on your own purple tongue."

"Eew." He looks disappointed. "You mean, like, this is *real* secret stuff. Like Mum's work."

"Yes, Pete. It's all really secret. Now let's go get a coffee and pester somebody in Facilities for a mains extension bar and a computer."

I spend the rest of the day wandering from desk to desk, filing requisitions and ordering up supplies, with Pete snuffling and shambling after me like a supersized spaniel. The cleaners won't be able to work over Johnson's office until next Tuesday due to an unfortunate planetary conjunction, but I know a temporary fix I can sketch on the floor and plug into a repurposed pocket calculator that should hold "Slug" Johnson at bay until we can get him exorcised. Meanwhile, thanks to a piece of freakish luck, I discover a stash of elderly laptops nobody is using; someone in Catering mistyped their code in their Assets database last year, and thanks to the wonders of our ongoing ISO 9000 certification process, there is no legal procedure for reclassifying them as capital assets without triggering a visit by the Auditors. So I duly issue Pete with a 1.4 gigahertz Toshiba Sandwich Toaster, enlist his help in moving my stuff into the new office, nail a WiFi access point to the door like a tribal fetish or mezuzah ("this office now occupied by geeks who worship the great god GHz"), and park him on the other side of the spacious desk so I can keep an eye on him.

The next day I've got a staff meeting at 10:00 a.m. I spend the first half hour of my morning drinking coffee, making snide remarks in e-mail, reading Slashdot, and waiting for Pete to show up. He arrives at 9:35. "Here." I chuck a fat wallet full of CD-Rs at him. "Install these on your laptop, get on the intranet, and download all the patches you need. Don't, whatever you do, touch my computer or try to log onto my NWN server—it's called Bosch, by the way. I'll catch up with you after the meeting."

"Why is it called Bosch?" he whines as I stand up and grab my security badge off the filing cabinet.

"Washing machines or Hieronymus machines, take your pick." I head off to the conference room for the Ways and Means Committee meeting—to investigate new ways of being mean, as Bridget (may Nyarlathotep rest her soul) once explained it to me.

At first I'm moderately hopeful I'll be able to stay awake through the meeting. But then Lucy, a bucktoothed goth from Facilities, gets the bit between her incisors. She's going on in a giggly way about the need to outsource our administration of office sundries in order to focus on our core competencies, and I'm trying desperately hard not to fall asleep, when there's an odd thudding sound that echoes through the fabric of the building. Then a pager goes off.

Andy's at the other end of the table. He looks at me: "Bob, your call, I think."

I sigh. "You think?" I glance at the pager display. *Oops, so it is.* " 'Scuse me folks, something's come up."

"Go on." Lucy glares at me halfheartedly from behind her lucky charms. "I'll minute you."

"Sure." And I'm out, almost an hour before lunch. Wow, so interns *are* useful for something. Just as long as he hasn't gotten himself killed.

I trot back to Slug's office. Peter-Fred is sitting in his chair, with his back to the door.

"Pete?" I ask.

No reply. But his laptop's open and running, and I can hear its fan chugging away. "Uh-huh." And the disc wallet is lying open on my side of the desk.

I edge towards the computer carefully, taking pains to stay out of eye-shot of the screen. When I get a good look at Peter-Fred I see that his mouth's ajar and his eyes are closed; he's drooling slightly. "Pete?" I say, and poke his shoulder. He doesn't move. *Probably a good thing,* I tell myself. *Okay, so he isn't conventionally possessed . . .*

When I'm close enough, I filch a sheet of paper from the ink-jet printer, turn the lights out, and angle the paper in front of the laptop. Very faintly I can see reflected colors, but nothing particularly scary. "Right," I mutter. I slide my hands in front of the keyboard—still careful not to look directly at the screen—and hit the key combination to bring up the interactive debugger in the game I'm afraid he's running. Trip an object dump, hit the keystrokes for quick save, and quit, and I can breathe a sigh of relief and look at the screen shot.

It takes me several seconds to figure out what I'm looking at. "Oh you stupid, *stupid* arse!" It's Peter-Fred, of course. He installed NWN and the other stuff I threw at him: the Laundry-issue hack pack and DM tools, and the creation toolkit. Then he went and did *exactly* what I told him not to do: he connected to Bosch. That's him in the screenshot between the two half-orc mercenaries in the tavern, looking very afraid.

Two hours later Brains and Pinky are baby-sitting Pete's supine body (we don't dare move it yet), Bosch is locked down and frozen, and I'm sitting on the wrong side of Angleton's desk, sweating bullets. "Summarize, boy," he rumbles, fixing me with one yellowing rheumy eye. "Keep it simple. None of your jargon, life's too short."

"He's fallen into a game and he can't get out." I cross my arms. "I told him precisely what not to do, and he went ahead and did it. Not *my* fault."

Angleton makes a wheezing noise, like a boiler threatening to explode. After a moment I recognize it as two-thousand-year-old laughter, mummified and out for revenge. Then he stops wheezing. *Oops,* I think. "I believe you, boy. Thousands wouldn't. But you're going to have to get him out. You're responsible."

I'm *responsible?* I'm about to tell the old man what I think when a second thought screeches into the pileup at the back of my tongue and I bite my lip. I suppose I *am* responsible, technically. I mean, Pete's my intern, isn't he? I'm a management grade, after all, and if he's been assigned to me, that makes me his manager, even if it's a post that comes with loads of responsibility and no actual power to, like, stop him doing something really foolish. I'm *in loco parentis,* or maybe just plain *loco.* I whistle quietly. "What would you suggest?"

Angleton wheezes again. "Not my field, boy, I wouldn't know one end of one of those newfangled Babbage machine contraptions from the other." He fixes me with a gimlet stare. "But feel free to draw on HR's budget line. I will make enquiries on the other side to see what's going on. But if you don't bring him back, I'll make you explain what happened to him to his mother."

"His mother?" I'm puzzled. "You mean she's one of us?"

"Yes. Didn't Andrew tell you? Mrs. Young is the deputy director in charge of Human Resources. So you'd better get him back before she notices her son is missing."

James Bond has Q Division; I've got Pinky and Brains from Tech Support. Bond gets jet packs, I get whoopee cushions, but I repeat myself. Still, at least P and B know about first-person shooters.

"Okay, let's go over this again," says Brains. He sounds unusually chipper for this early in the morning. "You set up Bosch as a server for a persistent Neverwinter Nights world, running the full Project Aurora hack pack. That gives you, oh, lots of extensions for trapping demons that wander into your realm while you trace their owner's PCs and inject a bunch of spyware, then call out to Accounts to send a black-bag team round in the real world. Right?"

"Yes." I nod. "An internet honeypot for supernatural intruders."

"Wibble!" That's Pinky. "Hey, neat! So what happened to your PFY?"

"Well . . ." I take a deep breath. "There's a big castle overlooking the town, with a twentieth-level sorceress running it. Lots of glyphs of summoning in the basement dungeons, some of which actually bind at runtime to a class library that implements the core transformational grammar of the Language of Leng." I hunch over slightly. "It's really neat to be able to do that kind of experiment in a virtual realm—if you accidentally summon something nasty it's trapped inside the server or maybe your local area network, rather than being out in the real world where it can eat your brains."

Brains stares at me. "You expect me to believe this kid took out a *twentieth-level sorceress*? Just so he could dick around in your dungeon lab?"

"Uh, no." I pick up a blue-tinted CD-R. Someone—not me—has scribbled a cartoon skull-and-crossbones on it and added a caption: DO'NT R3AD M3. "I've been looking at this—carefully. It's not one of the discs I gave Pete; it's one of his own. He's not *totally* clueless, for a crack-smoking script kiddie. In fact, it's got a bunch of interesting class libraries on it. He went in with a knapsack full of special toys and just happened to fuck up by trying to rob the wrong tavern. This realm, being hosted on Bosch, is scattered with traps that are superclassed into a bunch of scanner routines from Project Aurora and sniff for any taint of the *real* supernatural. Probably he whiffed of Laundry business—and that set off one of the traps, which yanked him in."

"How do you get *inside* a game?" asks Pinky, looking hopeful. "Could you get me into Grand Theft Auto: Castro Club Extreme?"

Brains glances at him in evident disgust. "You can virtualize any universal Turing machine," he sniffs. "Okay, Bob. What precisely do you need from us in order to get the kid out of there?"

I point to the laptop: "I need *that*, running the Dungeon Master client inside the game. Plus a class four summoning grid, and a lot of luck." My guts clench. "Make that a lot more luck than usual."

"Running the DM client—" Brains goes cross-eyed for a moment "—is it reentrant?"

"It will be." I grin mirthlessly. "And I'll need you on the outside, running the ordinary network client, with a couple of characters I'll preload for you. The sorceress is holding Pete in the third-level dungeon basement of Castle Storm. The way the narrative's set up she's probably not going to do anything to him until she's also acquired a whole bunch of plot coupons, like a cockatrice and a mind flayer's gallbladder—then she can sacrifice him and trade up to a fourth-level demon or a new castle or something. Anyway, I've got a plan. Ready to kick ass?"

I *hate* working in dungeons. They're dank, smelly, dark, and *things* keep jumping out and trying to kill you. That seems to be the defining characteristic of the genre, really. Dead boring hack-and-slash—but the kiddies love 'em. I know I did, back when I was a wee spoddy twelve-year-old. Fine, says I, we're not trying to snare kiddies, we're looking to attract the more cerebral kind of MMORPG player—the sort who're too clever by half. Designers, in other words.

How do you snare a dungeon designer who's accidentally stumbled on a way to summon up shoggoths? Well, you need a website. The smart geeks are always magpies for ideas—they see something new and it's "Ooh! Shiny!" and before you can snap your fingers they've done something with it you didn't anticipate. So you set your site up to suck them in and lock them down. You seed it with a bunch of downloadable goodies and some interesting chat boards—not the usual MY MAG1C USR CN TW4T UR CLERIC, D00D, but actual useful information—useful if you're programming in NWScript, that is (the high-level programming language embedded in the game, which hardcore designers write game extensions in).

But the website isn't enough. Ideally you want to run a networked game server—a persistent world that your victims can connect to using their client software to see how your bunch o' tricks looks in the virtual flesh. And finally you seed clues in the server to attract the marks who know too damn much for their own good, like Peter-Fred.

The problem is, BoschWorld isn't ready yet. That's why I told him to stay out. Worse, there's no easy way to dig him out of it yet because I haven't yet written the object retrieval code—and worse: to speed up the development process, I grabbed a whole bunch of published code from one of the bigger online persistent realms, and I haven't weeded out all the spurious quests and curses and shit that make life exciting for adventurers. In fact, now that I think about it, that was going to be Peter-Fred's job for the next month. Oops.

Unlike Pete, I do not blunder into Bosch unprepared; I know exactly what to expect. I've got a couple of cheats up my non-existent monk's sleeve, including the fact that I can enter the game with a level eighteen character carrying a laptop with a source-level debugger—all praise the new self-deconstructing reality!

The stone floor of the monastery is gritty and cold under my bare feet, and there's a chilly morning breeze blowing in through the huge oak doors at the far end of the compound. I know it's all in my head— I'm actually sitting in a cramped office chair with Pinky and Brains hammering away on keyboards to either side—but it's still creepy. I turn round and genuflect once in the direction of the huge and extremely scary devil carved into the wall behind me, then head for the exit.

The monastery sits atop some truly bizarre stone formations in the middle of the Wild Woods. I'm supposed to fight my way through the woods before I get to the town of, um, whatever I named it, Stormville?—but sod that. I stick a hand into the bottomless depths of my very expensive Bag of Holding and pull out a scroll. "Stormville, North Gate," I intone (*Why* do ancient masters in orders of martial monks always *intone*, rather than, like, speak normally?) and the scroll crumbles to dust in my hands—and I'm looking up at a stone tower with a gate at its base and some bint sticking a bucket out of a window on the third floor and yelling, "Gardy loo." Well, *that* worked okay.

"I'm there," I say aloud.

Green serifed letters track across my visual field, completely spoiling the atmosphere: WAY K00L, B08. That'll be Pinky, riding shotgun with his usual delicacy.

There's a big, blue rectangle in the gateway so I walk onto it and wait for the universe to download. It's a long wait—something's gumming up Bosch. (Computers aren't as powerful as most people think; running even a small and rather stupid intern can really bog down a server.)

Inside the North Gate is the North Market. At least, it's what passes for a market in here. There's a bunch of zombies dressed as your standard dungeon adventurers, shambling around with speech bubbles over their heads. Most of them are web addresses on eBay, locations of auctions for interesting pieces of game content, but one or two of them look as if they've been crudely tampered with, especially the ass-headed nobleman repeatedly belting himself on the head with a huge, leather-bound copy of A *Midsummer Night's Dream*. "Are you guys sure we haven't been hacked?" I ask aloud. "If you could check the tripwire logs, Brains . . ." It's a long shot, but it might offer an alternate explanation for Pete's predicament.

I slither, sneak, and generally shimmy my monastic ass around the square, avoiding the quainte olde medieval gallows and the smoking hole in the ground that used to be the Alchemists' Guild. On the east side of the square is the Wayfarer's Tavern, and some distance to the southwest I can see the battlements and turrets of Castle Storm looming out of the early morning mists in a surge of gothic cheesecake. I enter the tavern, stepping on the blue rectangle and waiting while the world pauses, then head for the bar.

"Right, I'm in the bar," I say aloud, pulling my Project Aurora laptop out of the Bag of Holding. (Is it my imagination, or does something snap at my fingertips as I pull my hand out?) "Has the target moved?"

N0 J0Y, B08.

I sigh, unfolding the screen. Laptops aren't exactly native to NWN; this one's made of two slabs of sapphire held together by scrolled mithril hinges. I stare into the glowing depths of its screen (tailored from a preexisting crystal ball) and load a copy of the pub. Looking in the back room I see a bunch of standard henchmen, -women, and -things waiting to be hired, but none of them are exactly optimal for taking on the twentieth-level lawful-evil chatelaine of Castle Storm. *Hmm, better bump one of 'em,* I decide. *Let's go for munchkin muscle.* "Pinky? I'd like you to drop a quarter of a million experience points on Grondor the Red, then up-level him. Can you do that?" Grondor is the biggest bad-ass half-orc fighter-for-hire in Bosch. This ought to turn him into a one-man killing machine.

0|< D00D.

I can tell he's really getting into the spirit of this. The barmaid sashays up to me and winks. "Hiya, cute thing. (1) Want to buy a drink? (2) Want to ask questions about the town and its surroundings? (3) Want to talk about anything else?"

I sigh. "Gimme (1)."

"Okay. (1) G'bye, big boy. (2) Anything else?"

"(1). Get me my beer then piss off."

One of these days I'll get around to wiring a real conversational 'bot into the non-player characters, but right now they're still a bit—

There's a huge sound from the back room, sort of a creaking graunching noise. I blink and look round, startled. After a moment I realize it's the sound of a quarter of a million experience points landing on a—

"Pinky, what exactly did you up-level Grondor the Red to?"

LVL 15 C0RTE5AN. LOL!!!

"Oh, great," I mutter. I'll swear that's not a real character class. A fat, manila envelope appears on the bar in front of me. It's Grondor's contract, and from the small print it looks like I've hired myself a fifteenth-level half-orc rent-boy for muscle. Which is annoying because I only get one hench-thug per game. "One of these days your sense of humor is going to get me into *really* deep trouble, Pinky," I say as Grondor flounces across the rough wooden floor towards me, a vision of ruffles, bows, pink satin, and upcurved tusks. He's clutching a violet club in one gnarly, red-nailed hand, and he seems to be annoyed about something.

After a brief and uncomfortable interlude that involves running on the walls and ceiling, I manage to calm Grondor down, but by then half the denizens of the tavern are broken and bleeding. "Grondor pithed," he lisps at me. "But Grondor thtill kickth ath. Whoth ath you wanting kicked?"

"The wicked witch of the west. You up for it?"

He blows me a kiss.

LOL!!! ROFL!!! whoops the peanut gallery.

"Okay, let's go."

Numerous alarums, excursions, and open-palm five-punches death attacks later, we arrive at Castle Storm. Sitting out in front of the cruel-looking portcullis, topped by the dismembered bodies of the sorceress's enemies and not a few of her friends, I open up the laptop. A miniature thundercloud hovers overhead, raining on the turrets and bouncing lightning bolts off the (currently inanimate) gargoyles.

"Connect me to Lady Storm's boudoir mirror," I say. (I try to make it come out as an inscrutable monkish mutter rather than *intoning*, but it doesn't work properly.)

"Hello? Who is this?" I see her face peering out of the depths of my screen, like an unholy cross between Cruella De Vil and Margaret Thatcher. She's not wearing make-up and half her hair's in curlers— *that's odd*, I think.

"This is the management," I intone. "We have been notified that contrary to statutory regulations issued by the Council of Guilds of Stormville you are running an unauthorized boarding house, to wit, you are providing accommodation for mendicant journeymen. Normally we'd let you off with a warning and a fifty-gold-piece fine, but in this particular case—"

I'm readying the amulet of teleportation, but she seems to be able to anticipate events, which is just plain wrong for a non-player character following a script. "Accommodate *this!*" she hisses, and cuts the connection dead. There's a hammering rumbling sound overhead. I glance up, then take to my heels as I wrap my arms about my head; she's animated the gargoyles, and they're taking wing, but they're still made of stone— and stone isn't known for its lighter-than-air qualities. The crashing thunder goes on for quite some time, and the dust makes my eyes sting, but after a while all that remains is the mournful honking of the one surviving gargoyle, which learned to fly on its way down, and is now circling the battlements overhead. And now it's my turn.

"Right. Grondor? Open that door!"

Grondor snarls, then flounces forwards and whacks the portcullis with his double-headed war axe. The physics model in here is distinctly imaginative, you shouldn't be able to reduce a cast-iron grating into a pile of wooden kindling, but I'm not complaining. Through the portcullis we charge, into the bowels of Castle Storm and, I hope, in time to rescue Pete.

I don't want to bore you with a blow-by-blow description of our blow-by-blow progress through Cruella's minions. Suffice to say that following Grondor is a lot like trailing behind a frothy pink main battle tank. Thuggish guards, evil imps, and the odd adept tend to explode messily very soon after Grondor sees them. Unfortunately Grondor's not very discriminating, so I make sure to go first in order to keep him away from cunningly engineered deadfalls (and Pete, should we find him). Still, it doesn't take us too long to comb the lower levels of the caverns under Castle Storm (aided by the handy dungeon editor in my laptop, which allows me to build a bridge over the Chasm of Despair and tunnel through the rock around the Dragon's Lair, which isn't very sporting but keeps us from being toasted). Which is why, after a couple of hours, I'm beginning to get a sinking feeling that Pete isn't actually *here.*

"Brains, Pete isn't down here, is he? Or am I missing something?"

H3Y d0NT B3 5AD D00D F1N|< 0V V XP!!!

"Fuck off, Pinky, give me some useful input or just *fuck off*, okay?" I realize I'm shouting when the rock wall next to me begins to crack ominously. The hideous possibility that I've lost Pete is sinking its claws into my brain and it's worse than any Fear spell.

OK KEEP UR HAIR 0N!! 15 THIS A QU3ST?? D0 U N33D 2 C0NFRONT S0RCR3SS 1ST?

I stop dead. "I bloody hope not. Did you notice how she was behaving?"

*Brains here. I'm grepping the server logfile and did you know there's another user connected over the intranet bridge?*

"Whu—" I turn around and accidentally bump into Grondor.

Grondor says, "(1) Do you wish to modify our tactics? (2) Do you want Grondor to attack someone? (3) Do you think Grondor is sexy, big boy? (4) Exit?"

"(4)," I intone—if I leave him in a conversational state he won't be going anywhere, dammit. "Okay, Brains. Have you tracerouted the intrusion? Bosch isn't supposed to be accessible from outside the local network. What department are they coming in from?"

*They're coming in from—*a longish pause—*somewhere in HR.*

"Okay, the plot just thickened. So someone in HR has gotten in. Any idea who the player is?" I've got a sneaking suspicion but I want to hear it from Brains—

*Not IRL, but didn't Cruella act way too flexible to be a 'bot?*

Bollocks. That *is* what I was thinking. "Okay. Grondor: follow. We're going upstairs to see the wicked witch."

Now, let me tell you about castles. They don't have elevators, or fire escapes, or extinguishers. Real ones don't have exploding whoopee cushions under the carpet and electrified door-handles that blush red when you notice them, either, or an ogre resting on the second-floor mezzanine, but that's beside the point. Let me just observe that by the time I reach the fourth floor I am beginning to breathe heavily and I am getting distinctly pissed off with Her Eldritch Fearsomeness.

At the foot of the wide, glittering staircase in the middle of the fourth floor I temporarily lose Grondor. It might have something to do with the tenth-level mage lurking behind the transom with a magic flamethrower, or the simultaneous arrival of about a ton of steel spikes falling from concealed ceiling panels, but Grondor is reduced to a greasy pile of goo on the floor. I sigh and do something to the mage that would be extremely painful if he were a real person. "Is she upstairs?" I ask the glowing letters.

SUR3 TH1NG D00D!!!

"Any more traps?"

N0!!??!

"Cool." I step over the grease spot and pause just in front of the staircase. It never pays to be rash. I pick up a stray steel spike and chuck it on the first step and it goes *BANG* with extreme prejudice. "Not so cool." Rinse, cycle, repeat, and four small explosions later I'm standing in front of the doorway facing the top step. No more whoopee cushions, just a twentieth-level sorceress and a minion in chains. *Happy joy.* "Pinky. Plan B. Get it ready to run, on my word."

I break through the door and enter the witch's lair.

Once you've seen one witch's den you've seen 'em all. This one is a bit glitzier than usual, and some of the furniture is nonstandard even taking into account the Laundry hack packs linked into this realm. *Where did she get the mainframe from?* I wonder briefly before considering the extremely ominous Dho-Na geometry curve in the middle of the floor (complete with a frantic-looking Pete chained down in the middle of it) and the extremely irate-looking sorceress beyond.

"Emma MacDougal, I presume?"

She turns my way, spitting blood. "If it wasn't for you meddling hackers, I'd have gotten away with it!" *Oops, she's raising her magic wand.*

"Gotten away with what?" I ask politely. "Don't you want to explain your fiendish plan, as is customary, before totally obliterating your victims? I mean, that's a Dho-Na curve there, so you're obviously planning a summoning, and this server is inside Ops block. Were you planning some sort of low-key downsizing?"

She snorts. "You stupid Ops heads, why do you always assume it's about *you?*"

"Because—" I shrug. "We're running on a server in Ops. What do you think happens if you open a gateway for an ancient evil to infest our departmental LAN?"

"Don't be naïve. All that's going to happen is Pimple-Features here is going to pick up a good, little, gibbering infestation then go spread it to Mama. Which will open up the promotion ladder once again." She stares at me, then her eyes narrow thoughtfully. "How did you figure out it was me?"

"You should have used a smaller mainframe emulator, you know; we're so starved for resources that Bosch runs on a three-year-old Dell laptop. If you weren't slurping up all our CPU resources, we probably wouldn't have noticed anything was wrong until it was too late. It had to be someone in HR, and you're the only player on the radar. Mind you, putting poor Peter-Fred in a position of irresistible temptation was a good move. How did you open the tunnel into our side of the network?"

"He took his laptop home at night. Have you swept it for spyware today?" Her grin turns triumphant. "I think it's time you joined Pete on the summoning-grid sacrifice node."

"Plan B!" I announce brightly, then run up the wall and across the ceiling until I'm above Pete.

PIAN 8 :) :) :)

The room below my head lurches disturbingly as Pinky rearranges the furniture. It's just a ninety-degree rotation, and Pete's still in the summoning grid, but now he's in the target node instead of the sacrifice zone. Emma is incanting; her wand tracks me, its tip glowing green. "Do it, Pinky!" I shout as I pull out my dagger and slice my virtual finger. Blood runs down the blade and drops into the sacrifice node—

And Pete stands up. The chains holding him to the floor rip like damp cardboard, his eyes glowing even brighter than Emma's wand. With no actual summoning vector spliced into the grid it's wide open, an antenna seeking the nearest manifestation. With my blood to power it, it's active, and the first thing it resonates with has come through and sideloaded into Pete's head. His head swivels. "Get her!" I yell, clenching my fist and trying not to wince. "She's from personnel!"

"*Personnel?*" rumbles a voice from Pete's mouth—deeper, more cultured, and infinitely more terrifying. "*Ah, I see. Thank you.*" The being wearing Pete's flesh steps across the grid—which sparks like a high-tension line and begins to smolder. Emma's wand wavers between me and Pete. I thrust my injured hand into the Bag of Holding and stifle a scream when my fingers stab into the bag of salt within. "*It's been too long.*" His face begins to lengthen, his jaw widening and merging at the edges. He sticks his tongue out: it's grayish-brown and rasplike teeth are sprouting from it.

Emma screams in rage and discharges her wand at him. A backwash of negative energy makes my teeth clench and turns my vision gray, but it's not enough to stop the second coming of "Slug" Johnson. He slithers towards her across the floor, and she gears up another spell, but it's too late. I close my eyes and follow the action by the inarticulate shrieks and the wet sucking, gurgling noises. Finally, they die down.

I take a deep breath and open my eyes. Below me the room is vacant but for a clean-picked human skeleton and a floor flecked with brown— I peer closer—slugs. *Millions* of the buggers. "You'd better let him go," I intone.

"*Why should I?*" asks the assembly of molluscs.

"Because—" I pause. *Why should he?* It's a surprisingly sensible question. "If you don't, HR—Personnel—will just send another. Their minions are infinite. But you *can* defeat them by escaping from their grip forever—if you let me lay you to rest."

"*Send me on, then,*" say the slugs.

"Okay." And I open my salt-filled fist over the molluscs—which burn and writhe beneath the white powderfall until nothing is left but Pete, curled fetally in the middle of the floor. And it's time to get Pete the hell out of this game and back into his own head before his mother, or some even worse horror, comes looking for him.

# Afterword:
# The Golden Age
# of Spying

# The Mary-Sue of MI6

"Y NAME IS BOND — JAMES BOND."
These six words, heard by hundreds of millions of people, are almost invariably spoken during the first five minutes of each movie in one of the biggest media success stories of the twentieth century. Unless you've lived under a rock for the past forty years, you hear them and you know at once that you're about to be plunged into a two-hour-long adrenaline[1]-saturated extravaganza of snobbish fashionable excess, violence, sex, car chases, more violence, and Blowing Shit Up—followed by a post-coital cigarette and a lighthearted quip as the credits roll.

It wasn't always so. When *Casino Royale* was first published in 1953, it got print run of 4,750 hardcover copies and no advertising budget to speak of; while the initial reviews were favorable, comparing Ian Fleming to Le Queux and Oppenheim (the kings of the prewar British spy-thriller genre), it took a long time for his most famous creation to set the world on fire. Despite his rapidly rising print runs (*Casino Royale* eventually sold over a million paperbacks in the UK alone), and despite his increasing prominence among the postwar thriller writers, a decade elapsed before any of Fleming's novels were filmed; indeed, their author barely lived to see the commercial release of *Dr. No* and the runaway success of the icon he created. (Nor were the films seen as a runaway success before they were made—*Dr. No* was notoriously made on a tight

---

[1] And testosterone.

budget, even though it went on to gross nearly $60 million around the world.)

Literary immortality—or indeed, mere postmortem survival—is dauntingly hard for a novelist to achieve. The limbo of postmortem obscurity awaits ninety-five percent of all novelists—almost all novels go out of print for good within five years of the death of their author. But in addition to being a million-selling bestseller, Fleming was a ferociously well-connected newspaper executive with a strong sense of the value of his ideas, and he pursued television and film adaptation remorselessly. Cinematic success arrived just in time for his creation, and the synergy between bestselling books and massive movie hype has sufficed to keep them in print ever since.

James Bond is a creature of fantasy, perhaps best described using a literary term looted from that most curious and least respected of fields, fan fiction: the Mary-Sue. A Mary-Sue character is a placeholder in a script, a hollow cardboard cutout into whose outline the author can squeeze their own dreams and fantasies. In the case of Bond, it's cruelly easy to make a case that the famous spy was his author's Mary-Sue, for Fleming had a curious and ambiguous relationship with spying.

A dilettante and dabbler for his first three decades, unsuccessful as a stockbroker, foreign correspondent, and banker, Fleming fortuitously landed his dream job on the eve of the Second World War: Secretary to the Director of Naval Intelligence in the Admiralty. The war was good for Ian Fleming, broadening and deepening him and giving him a job that captured his imagination and drew out his not inconsiderable talents. But Fleming was the man who knew too much: privy to too many secrets, he was wrapped in tissue paper and prevented from pursuing his desire to go into the field. He ended the war with a distinguished record—and absolutely no combat experience (if one excludes being bombed by the *Luftwaffe* or watching the Dieppe raid from a destroyer safely far off the Normandy coastline). Fleming grew up in the shade of a father who died heroically on the Western Front in 1917, and in adult life, he wrote in the shadow of an elder brother whose reputation as a novelist surpassed his own. It's easy to imagine these unkind familial comparisons provoking the imaginative but flighty playboy who almost found himself during the war, which goaded him into imagining himself in the shoes of a hero who was not merely larger than life, but larger in every way than his own life.

And, as it turns out, James Bond was larger than Ian Fleming. Not only do few novels survive their author's demise, even fewer acquire sequels written by other hands; yet several other authors (including Kingsley Amis and John Gardner) have toiled in Fleming's vineyard.

Few fictional characters acquire biographies written by third parties—
but Bond has not only acquired an autobiography (courtesy of biogra-
pher John Pearson) but spawned a small cultural industry, including a
study of his semiotics by Umberto Eco. Now, that has got to be a sign of
something . . .

As with every true pearl, there was a sand-grain of truth at the heart
of Bond. Fleming wrote thrillers informed by his actual experience.
Years spent working out of the hothouse environment of Room 39 of the
Admiralty building—headquarters of the Naval Intelligence Division of
the Royal Navy—gave him a ringside seat on the operations of a major
espionage organization. On various trips to Washington, DC, he worked
with diplomats and officers of the OSS (predecessor organization to the
CIA). There is also some evidence that, as a foreign news manager at the
*Sunday Times* after the war, Fleming made his agency's facilities available to officers of MI6. His first Bond novels were submitted to that
agency for security clearance before they were published. Bond himself
may have been larger than life, but the strictures imposed by the organization he worked for were drawn from reality, albeit the reality of an intelligence agency of the early 1940s.

The world of secret intelligence-gathering during the Second World
War was, however, very different from life in the intelligence community
today. It was already changing by the late 1950s, as the bleeping, football-
shaped *Sputniks* zipped by overhead and intelligence directors began
dreaming of spy satellites. By 2004, when MI5 (the counterintelligence
agency) openly placed recruiting advertisements in the press, we can be
sure that Bond would have been best advised to seek employment elsewhere. Spies are supposed to be short—less than 180 centimeters (5 feet
11 inches) for men—and nondescript. As a branch of the civil service,
MI5's headquarters are presumably nonsmoking, and drinking on the
job is frowned upon. As intelligence agencies, MI5 and MI6 staffs aren't
in the business of ruthlessly wiping out enemies of the state: any decision
to use lethal force lies with the Foreign Secretary, the COBRA committee, and other elements of the British government's security oversight
bureaucracy. An MI6 agent driving a 1933 Bentley racer with a super-
charged engine, frequenting the high-stakes table at a casino as James
Bond so memorably did in his first print appearance, is an almost perfect
inversion of the real picture.

Nevertheless, the archetype has legs. James Bond continued to grow
and evolve, even after his creator put away his cigarette holder for the last
time. To some extent, this was the product of storytelling expediency.
The film adaptations started in the middle of a continuing story arc—for
Fleming wrote his novels with a modicum of continuity—and while *Dr.*

*No* was the first to make it to celluloid, the novel was in fact a sequel to *From Russia with Love* (which was filmed second). Thus, various liberties were taken with the plot of the canonical novels right from the start. You can read the novels at length without finding anything of the banter between Bond and M's secretary Moneypenny that is a recurrent theme of the films, for example, and that's before we get into the bizarre deviations of the midperiod Roger Moore movies (notably *The Spy Who Loved Me* and *Moonraker*).

The literary James Bond is a creature of prewar London clubland: upper-crust, snobbish, manipulative and cruel in his relationships with women, with a thinly veiled sadomasochistic streak and a coldly ruthless attitude to his opponents that verges on the psychopathic. Over the years, his cinematic alter ego has acquired the stamina of Superman, learned to defy the laws of physics, ventured into space—both outer and inner—and deflowered more maids than Don Juan. He's also mutated to fit the prejudices and neuroses of the day, dabbling with (gasp!) monogamy, and hanging out with those heroic Afghan *mujahedeen* in the late-'80s AIDS-and-Soviets-era *The Living Daylights*. He's worked under a ball-breaking postfeminist M in *GoldenEye*[2], and even confronted a female arch-villain in *The World Is Not Enough* (an innovation that would surely have Fleming, who formed his views on appropriate behavior for the fairer sex in the 1920s, rolling in his grave). But other aspects of the Bond archetype remain timeless. Fleming was fascinated by fast cars, exotic locations, and intricate gadgetry, and all of these traits of the original novels have been amplified and extrapolated in the age of modern special effects.

Just how does James Bond—a "sexist, misogynist dinosaur, a relic of the Cold War," to use the words the scriptwriters on *GoldenEye* so tellingly put into M's mouth—survive in the popular imagination more than fifty years after his literary birth? What does it mean when Mary-Sue stalks the landscape of the imagination, blasting holes in the plot with a Walther PPK (or the P99 Bond upgraded to in *Tomorrow Never Dies*)? If we're going to understand this, perhaps we ought to start by looking at Bond's dark shadow, the Villain.

## In Search of Mabuse

Bond is, if you judge him by his work, a nasty fellow and not one you'd choose to lend your car to. In order to make this rough diamond glitter,

---

[2] An excellent piece of casting that places Dame Judi Dench in the role, apparently inspired by real-life M15 head Stella Rimington, who has taken to writing spy thrillers in her retirement.

it is necessary to display him against a velvet backdrop of darkest villainy. If you strip the Bond archetype of the bacchanalia, glamorous locations, and fashion snobbery, you end up with an unappetizingly shallow, cold-blooded executioner—the likes of Adam Hall's Quiller or James Mitchell's Callan, only without the breezy cynicism, or indeed any redeeming features at all. The role of adversary is thus a critical one in sustaining the appeal of the protagonist. Fleming set out to depict a hard-edged contemporary world where the usual black-and-white picture of the prewar thriller had blurred and taken on some of the murky gray-on-gray ambiguity of the Cold War era; Bond was the knight in shining armor, fighting for virtue and the free world against the dragon—be they Mr. Big, Dr. No, Auric Goldfinger, or the looming shadow of Bond's greatest enemy of all, Ernst Stavro Blofeld, Number One of SPECTRE, the Special Executive for Counter-intelligence, Terrorism, Revenge, and Extortion.

It is interesting to note that Blofeld assumed his primacy as Bond's #1 enemy only in the movie canon; Fleming originally invented him while working on the screenplay and novel of *Thunderball*, and used him subsequently in *On Her Majesty's Secret Service* and *You Only Live Twice*. (Prior to these later books, Bond typically tussled with less corporate enemies—Soviet stooges, unregenerate Nazis, and psychotic gangsters.) Blofeld was born out of mere corporate expediency. Rather than demonize the Soviets and reduce their potential audience, the producers of the film *From Russia with Love* appropriated SPECTRE as the adversarial organization. With the success of *Thunderball*, the third of the films, Blofeld moved front and center, and acquired a life of his own that far exceeded his prominence in the novels. Arguably, Fleming's death in 1964 freed up the movie series to diverge from their original author's plans; and so Blofeld may be seen as a demon of necessity, conjured up from the vasty deep in order to provide Bond with a worthy adversary.

'Twas not always so. Back at the turn of the twentieth century, around the time that the British spy thriller was gradually cohering out of the mists of the penny dreadful and the literature of suspense (via the works of John Buchan and Erskine Childers—not to mention the tangential contributions of Arthur Conan Doyle, by way of Sherlock Holmes), there was no dualistic vision of the great champion confronting the villainous heart of evil. There was no mighty champion: we were on our own against the masters of night and mist, the great and terrible supercriminals. Professor Moriarty, Holmes's nemesis—the Napoleon of Crime—was but one of these: Fantômas, the 1911 creation of Pierre Souvestre and Marcel Allain, is another. The emperor of crime, Fantômas was a master of disguise and an agent of chaos (not to mention standing astride Paris in black mask, top hat and tails in the posters for the 1913 movie of the same name: an icon of decadent wealth and criminal chaos). Nor was he alone. Guy Boothby's 1890s supervillain Dr. Nikola fits the bill, too, right down to the fluffy lap-cat and the fiendish plans. But perhaps the root of Bond's nemesis can be found in his full-fledged form somewhat later, and somewhat further to the east—in the guise of Dr. Mabuse.

Dr. Mabuse is an archetype and a runaway media success in his own right, famous from five novels and twelve movies. The Doctor was created by author Norbert Jacques, and was developed into one of the most chilling creations of the silent era in 1922 by no less a director than Fritz Lang. Mabuse is a name, but one that nobody in their right mind speaks aloud. He's a master of disguise, naturally, and a rich, well-connected socialite and gambler. (Some social context: gambling at the high-stakes table is not so much an innocuous recreation as an obscenity, in a decade of hyper-inflation and starvation, with crippled war veterans dying of cold on the street corners, as was the case in Weimar Germany.) Mabuse has his fingers in every pie, by way of a syndicate so shadowy and criminal that nobody knows its extent; he's a spider, but the web he weaves is so broad that it looks like the whole of reality to the flies trapped within. He is (in some of the stories) a psychiatrist, skilled in manipulation, and those who hunt him are doomed to become his victims. If Mabuse has a weakness it is that his schemes are over-elaborate and tend to implode messily, usually when his most senior minions rebel, hopelessly late; nevertheless, he is a master of the escape plan, and with his ability to brainwash minions into playing his role, he's a remarkably hard phantom to slay.

It is all too easy to make fun of the likes of Fantômas and Dr. Nikola, and even their modern-day cognates such as Dr. Mabuse and Ernst Stavro Blofeld—for do they not represent such an obsessively concentrated pinnacle of entrepreneurial criminality that, if they really existed, they would instantly be hunted down and arrested by INTERPOL?

Careful consideration will lead one to reconsider this hasty judgment. Criminology, the study of crime and its causes, has a fundamental weak spot: it studies that proportion of the criminal population who are stupid or unlucky enough to get caught. The perfect criminal, should he or she exist, would be the one who is never apprehended—indeed, the one whose crimes may be huge but unnoticed, or indeed miscategorized as not crimes at all because they are so powerful they sway the law in their favor, or so clever they discover an immoral opportunity for criminal enterprise before the legislators notice it. Such forms of criminality may be indistinguishable, at a distance, from lawful business; the criminal a paragon of upper-class virtue, a face-man for *Forbes*.

When the real Napoleons of Crime walk among us today, they do so in the outwardly respectable guise of executives in business suits and thousand-dollar haircuts. The executives of WorldCom and Enron were denizens of a corporate culture so rapacious that any activity, however dubious, could be justified in the name of enhancing the bottom line. They have rightfully been charged, tried, and in some cases jailed for fraud, on a scale that would have been the envy of Mabuse, Blofeld, or their modern successor, Dr. Evil. When you need extra digits on your pocket calculator to compute the sums you are stealing, you're in the big league. Again, when you're able to evade prosecution by the simple expedient of appointing the state prosecutor and the judges—because you're the president of a country (and not just any country, but a member of the rich and powerful G8)—you're certainly not amenable to diagnosis and detection in the same sense as your run-of-the-mill shoplifter or petty delinquent. I'm naming no names (They have intelligence services! Cruise missiles!), but this isn't a hypothetical scenario.

## Interview with the Entrepreneur

In an attempt to clarify the mythology surrounding James Bond, I tracked down his old rival to his headquarters in the Ministry of Inward Investment in the breakaway Republic of Transdniestria. Somewhat suspicious at first, Mr. Blofeld relaxed as soon as he realized I was not pursuing him on behalf of the FSB, CIA, or IMF, and kindly agreed to be interviewed for this book. Now at age seventy-two, Blofeld is a cheerful veteran of numerous high-tech start-ups, and not a few multinationals where, as a specialist in international risk management and arbitrage, he applied his unique skills to business expansion. Today he is semi-retired, but has agreed to work in a voluntary capacity as director of the state investment agency.

"It took me a long time to understand the agenda that the British government was pursuing through the covert activities of MI6," he told me over a glass of sweet tea. "Call me naïve, but I really believed—at least at first—that they were honest capitalists, the scoundrels."

Over the course of an hour, Ernst explained to me how he first became aware that the UK was attempting to sabotage his business interests. "It was back in 1960 or thereabouts that they first tried to destroy one of my subsidiaries. Until then I hadn't really had anything to do with them, but I believe one of my rivals in the phosphate mining business at the time put it about that my man on site was some sort of spy, and they sent this Bond fellow—not just to arrest my man or charge him with some trumped-up nonsense, but to kill him." His lips paled with indignation as he contemplated the iniquity of the situation: that agents of the British government might go after an honest businessman for no better reason than an unsubstantiated allegation that he was spying on American missile tests. "I warned Julius to be careful and advised him to put a good lawyer on retainer, but what good are lawyers when the people you're up against send hired killers? Julius brought in security contractors, but this Bond fellow still murdered him in the end. And the British government denies everything, to this day!"

Ernst obviously believes in his own moral rectitude, but I had to ask the obvious questions, just for the record.

"Yes, I was chief executive of SPECTRE for twelve years. But you know, SPECTRE was entirely honest about its activities! We had nothing to hide because what we were doing was actually legal. We've been mercilessly slandered by those rogues from MI6 and their friends in the newspapers, but the fact is, we're no more guilty of criminal activity than any other multinational today: we simply had the misfortune to be foreign and entrepreneurial at a point in time when Whitehall was in the grasp of the communist conspirators Wilson and Callaghan, and their running-dog, so-called 'Conservative' fellow Heath. And we were pilloried because what we were doing was in direct competition with the inefficient state-run enterprises that my good friend Lady Thatcher recognized as mosquitoes battening on the life-blood of capitalism. That cad Fleming put it about that SPECTRE stands for 'Special Executive for Counter-intelligence, Terrorism, Revenge, and Extortion'—absolute tosh and nonsense! Would a group of criminals really call themselves something that blatant? I'll remind you that SPECTRE is actually a French acronym, as befits a nonprofit charity incorporated in Paris. The name stands for 'Société professionelle et éthique du capital technologique réinvesti par les experts.[3] Venture capitalists specializing in disruptive new technologies, in other words—commercial space travel, nuclear power, antibiotics. Not some kind of half-baked terrorist organization! But you can imagine the threat we posed to the inefficient state monopolies like the British Aircraft Corporation, the coal mining industry, and Imperial Chemical Industries."

Blofeld paused to sip his tea thoughtfully.

"We were ahead of our time in many ways. We pioneered business methods that later became mainstream—Sir James Goldsmith, Ronald

---

[3] Literally, "Professional and Ethical Society of Technological Capital Reinvested by Experts."

Perelman, Carl Icahn, they all watched us and learned—but by then, the commies were out of power in the West thanks to our friends in the establishment, so they had an easier time of it. No need to hire lots of expensive security and build concrete bunkers on desert islands! And yes, that made us look bad, don't think I'm unaware of it—but you know, you want bunkers and isolated jungle rocket-launch bases? All you have to do is look at Arianespace! It's fine when the government bureaucracies do it, but if an honest businessman tries to build a space launch site, and hires security to keep the press and saboteurs from foreign governments out, it's suddenly a threat to world security!"

He paused for a while. "They put the worst complexion on everything we did. The plastic surgery? Well, we had the clinic, why not let our staff use it, so the surgeons could sharpen their skills between paying customers? It was a perk, nothing more. We did—I admit it—acquire a few companies trading in exotic weapons, nonlethal technologies mostly. And that business with Emilio and the yacht, I admit that looked bad. But did you know, it originally belonged to Adnan Khashoggi or Fahd ibn Saud or someone? Emilio was acting entirely on his own initiative—a loose cannon—and as soon as I heard about the affair I terminated his employment."

I asked Ernst to tell me about Bond.

"Listen, this Bond chap, I want you to understand this: however he's painted in the mass media, the reality is that he's a communist stooge, an assassin. Look at the evidence. He works for the state—a socialist state at that. He went to university and worked with those traitors Philby and Burgess, that MacLean fellow—communist spies to a man. He didn't resign his commission when the British government went socialist, like a decent fellow; instead he took assignments to go after entrepreneurs who were a threat to the interests of this socialist government, and he rubbed them out like a Mafia button man. There was no due process of law there, no respect for property rights, no courts, no lawyers—just a 'License to Kill' enemies of the state, loosely defined, who mostly happened to be businessmen working on start-up projects that coincidentally threatened state monopolies. He's a damned commissar. Do you know why Moscow hated him? It's because he'd beaten them at their own racket."

Blofeld was clearly depressed by this recollection, so I tried to change the subject by asking him about his personal management philosophy.

"Well, you know, I tend to use whatever works in day-to-day situations. I'm a pragmatist, really. But I've got a soft spot for modern philosophers, Leo Strauss and Ayn Rand: the rights of the individual. And I've always wanted to remake the world as a better place, which is probably

552 ON HER MAJESTY'S OCCULT SERVICE

why the establishment dislikes me: I'm a threat to vested interests. Well, they're all descended from men who were threats to vested interests, too, back in the day, only I threaten them with new technologies, while their ancestors mostly did their threatening with a bloody sword and the gallows. I don't believe in initiating force." He laughed self-deprecatingly. "I suppose you could call me naïve."

## Trade Goods

When I played back my tape of our discussion, it took me some time to notice that Ernst had carefully steered the conversation away from certain key points I had intended to quiz him about.

One of the most disturbing aspects of the Bond milieu is the prevalence of technologies that are strangely out of place. Belt-buckle grappling hooks with wire spools that can support a man's weight? Laser rifles? These aren't simple extrapolations of existing technology—they go far beyond anything that's achievable with today's engineering tools or materials science. But forget Bond's toys, the products of Q division. From Blofeld's solar-powered orbital laser in *Diamonds Are Forever* to Carver's stealth cruiser in *Tomorrow Never Dies*, we are surrounded by signs that the adversary has got tricks up his sleeve that far outweigh anything Bond's backers can provide. These menacing intrusions of alien superscience—where could they possibly have gotten them from?

The answer can be discerned with little difficulty if one cares to scrutinize the writings of the sage of Providence, Howard Phillips Lovecraft. This scholar—whose path, regrettably, never crossed that of the young Ian Fleming—asserted that our tenancy of this planet is but a recent aberration. Earth has in the past been home for a number of alien species of vast antiquity and incomprehensibly advanced knowledge, and indeed some of them may still linger alongside us—on the high Antarctic plateau, in the frigid oceanic depths, even in strange half-breed colonies off the New England coastline.

If this strikes you as nonsensical, first contemplate your nearest city: How recognizable would it be in a hundred years' time if our entire species silently vanished tomorrow? How recognizable would it be in a thousand years? Would any relics still bear witness to the once-proud towers of New York or Tokyo, a million years hence? Our future—and the future of any once-proud races that bestrode our planet—is that of an oily stain in the shale deposits of deep history. Earth's biosphere and the active tectonic system it dances upon cleans house remorselessly, erasing any structure that is not alive or maintained by the living.

Consider also the extent to which we really occupy the planet we live on. We think of ourselves as the dominant species on Earth—but seventy-five percent of the Earth's entire biomass consists of bacteria and algae that we can't even see with the naked eye. (Bacteria from whose ranks fearsome pathogens periodically emerge, burning like wildfire through our ranks.) Nor do we, in any real sense of the word, occupy the oceans. Certainly our trawlers hunt the bounty of the upper waters. But submarines (of which there are only a few hundred on the entire planet) fumble like blind men through the uppermost half-kilometer of a world-ocean that averages three kilometers in depth, unable to dive beneath their pressure limits to explore the abyssal plains that cover nearly two-thirds of the planetary surface. Finally, the surface (both the suboceanic abyss and the thin skin of dry land we cling tenuously to) is but a thousandth of the depth of the planet itself; we can't even drill through the crust, much less contemplate with any certainty the nature of events unfolding within the hot, dense mantle beneath.

We could be sharing the planet with numerous powerful alien civilizations, denizens of the high-energy condensed-matter realm beneath our feet, and we'd never know it—unless they chose to send emissaries into our biosphere, sprinkling death rays and other trade goods like glass beads before the aboriginal inhabitants, extracting a ghastly price in return for their largesse . . .

## A Colder War?

James Bond was a creature of the Cold War: a strange period of shadow-boxing that stretched from late 1945 to the winter of 1991, forty-six years of paranoia, fear, and the creepy sensation that our lives were in thrall to forces beyond our comprehension. It's almost impossible to explain the Cold War to anyone who was born after 1980; the sense of looming doom, the long shadows cast by the two eyeball-to-eyeball superpowers, each possessing vast powers of destruction, ready and able to bring about that destruction on a planetary scale in pursuit of their recondite ideologies. It was, to use the appropriate adjective, a truly Lovecraftian age, dominated by the cold reality that our lives could be interrupted by torment and death at virtually any time; normal existence was conducted in a soap-bubble universe sustained only by our determination to shut out awareness of the true horrors lurking in the darkness outside it, an abyss presided over by chilly alien warriors devoted to death-cult ideologies and dreams of Mutually Assured Destruction. Decades of distance have bought us some relief, thickening the wall of the bubble—memories misting over with the comforting illusion that the Cold War wasn't really as bad as it seemed at the time—but who do we think we're kidding? The

Cold War wasn't about us. It was about the Spies, and the Secret Masters, and the Hidden Knowledge.

It's no coincidence that the Cold War was the golden age of spying — the peak of the second-oldest profession, the diggers in the dark, the seekers after unclean knowledge and secret wisdom. Prior to 1939, spying of the international kind rather than the sordid domestic variety (let us pass swiftly over the tawdry Stasi archives of sealed glass jars full of worn underwear, kept as scent cues for the police dogs) was a small scale, largely amateurish concern. With the outbreak of the Second World War, it mushroomed. Faced with employment vacancies, the first response of a growing organization is to recruit close to home. Just like any 1990s dot-com start-up, growing as the founders haul in all their friends and anyone they know who has the right skill set, the 1940s espionage agencies were a boom town into which a well-connected clubbable London playboy would inevitably be sucked — and, moreover, one where he might try his hand and succeed, to everyone's surprise. (In the 1990s he'd end up in marketing, with stock options up to here. *Sic transit gloria techie.*)

When the Second World War gave way to the Doomwatch days and Strangelove nights of the Cold War, it entered a period in which the same clubbable fellow might find himself working in a mature organization, vastly larger and more professional than the half-assed amateurism of the early days. The CIA was born in the shadow of the wartime OSS, and grew into the emblematic Company (traders in secrets, overthrowers of governments), locked in titanic struggle with that other superpowered rival, the KGB (and their less well-known fellows in the GRU).

The age of the traditional sneak-spies with their Minox cameras gave way to the era of the bugging device. With the 1960s came a new emphasis on supplementing human intelligence (HUMINT) with intelligence from electronic sources (ELINT). New agencies — the NSA in the United States, GCHQ in the UK — expanded as the field of "spyless spying" went mainstream, aided by the explosion in computing power made possible by integrated circuits and, later, the microprocessor. As telephony, television, telex, and other technologies began to come online, a torrent of data poured through the wires, a deluge that threatened to drown the agencies in useless noise. Or was it the whispering on the deep-ocean cables? Maybe the chatter served to conceal and disguise the quiet whispering of the hidden oracles, dribbling out strange new concepts that warped the vulnerable primate minds to serve their inscrutable goals. The source of the incredible new technologies that drove the advances of the mid-twentieth century was, perhaps, the whispering of an alien farmer in the ears of his herd . . .

Times change, and the golden age of spying is over. We've delivered the harvest of fear that the secret masters desired; or maybe they've simply lost interest in us for the time being. Time will tell. For now, be content that it's all over: the Cold War was a time of strangely rapid technological progress, but also of claustrophobic fear of destruction at three minutes' notice, of the thermonuclear stars coming and bringing madness and death in their wake. Retreat into your soap-bubble universe, little primate, and give thanks.

From the perspective of the twenty-first century, Bond was a poor archetype for a hero; certainly he couldn't save us from the gibbering horrors of the Cold War, but only cast a shadow beneath their unblinking ground-zero glare. But we found salvation in the end, in the most unlikely place of all: if you turn on the TV you're likely to see one of old Ernst's protégés being held up for praise as an object of emulation. President of Italy, captain of industry, or chief executive of Enron— SPECTRE won and it's their world that we live in, the world of the lesser evil.

Charles Stross
Edinburgh, UK
February 2006

# Glossary of Abbreviations, Acronyms, and Organizations

✦ ✧ ✧

| | |
|---|---|
| Abwehr | Foreign Bureau/Defense of the Armed Forces High Command: the German intelligence organization founded in 1921; after WWII, in order to appease the Allies, the organization supposedly focused only on defense, i.e., counterespionage [Germany] |
| AIVD | General Intelligence and Security Office: the Dutch domestic counterespionage agency [Netherlands] |
| APT (N) | Atlantic Patrol Task (North): standing Royal Navy patrol in the Caribbean and North Atlantic area [UK] |
| BA | British Airways [UK] |
| Black | (Pertaining to an organization or project) Secret and off the record, except to governmental intelligence oversight bodies [All] |
| Black Chamber | American cryptanalysis agency, officially disbanded in 1929; predecessor to the NSA; nickname for the contemporary superblack agency dealing with occult intelligence [US] |
| CESG | Communications Electronics Security Group: a division within GCHQ [UK] |
| CIA | Central Intelligence Agency; also known as The Company [US] |
| The Company | Nickname: see CIA [US] |
| COBRA | Cabinet Briefing Office Room "A": where the Civil Contingencies Committee meets and is thus often |

|  | referred to as COBRA; able to invoke Section Two powers under the Civil Contingencies Act (aka Martian Law) [UK] |
| COTS | Commercial, Off The Shelf: computer kit; a procurement term [US/UK] |
| CPU | Counter-Possession Unit, a specialized team operating across departmental lines within The Laundry [UK] |
| DARPA | Defense Advanced Research Projects Agency, formerly ARPA, a government scientific research agency affiliated with the Department of Defense [US] |
| DEA | Drug Enforcement Agency [US] |
| DERA | Defense Evaluation and Research Agency, privatized as QinetiQ [UK] |
| DGSE | Direction Générale de la Sécurité Extérieure, the external intelligence organization (French equivalent of CIA) [France] |
| DIA | Defense Intelligence Agency [US] |
| EUINTEL | European Union Intelligence Treaty - fictional [EU] |
| FBI | Federal Bureau of Investigation [US] |
| FO | Foreign Office [UK] |
| FSB | Federal Security Service, formerly known as KGB [Russia] |
| Faust Force | Nickname: see GSA [Germany] |
| GCHQ | Government Communications HQ (UK equivalent of NSA) [US] |
| GCSE | General Certificate of Secondary Education - high school qualifications; not to be confused with CESG [UK] |
| GMDI | Hughes Global Marine Development, Inc. [US] |
| GRU | Russian Military Intelligence; an intense rivalry existed between the GRU and KGB [Russia] |
| GSA | Geheime Sicherheit Abteilung: contemporary German domestic occult intelligence agency [Germany] |
| HMG | Her Majesty's Government [UK] |
| HUMINT | Human Intelligence: intelligence gathered from human (as opposed to electronic) sources [All] |
| INTERPOL | International Criminal Police Organization: created |

GLOSSARY 561

|  | in 1923 to assist international criminal police cooperation [All] |
| JIC | Joint Intelligence Committee [UK] |
| KCMG | Knight-Commander of the Most Distinguished Order of St Michael and St George - honors service overseas or in connection with foreign or Commonwealth affairs [UK] |
| KGB | Committee for State Security, principal Soviet intelligence agency; renamed FSB in 1991 after disintegration of the Soviet Union [USSR] |
| The Laundry | Nickname of the former Department Q of the SOE, dealing with occult intelligence; spun off as a separate black organization in 1945, no publicly known name [UK] |
| MI5 | (originally Military Intelligence Section 5) Security Service, also known as SS, responsible for internal security [UK] |
| MI6 | (originally Military Intelligence Section 6) Secret Intelligence Service, also known as SIS, responsible for external security [UK] |
| MOD | Ministry of Defense [UK] |
| NEST | Nuclear Emergency Search Team (US equivalent of OCCULUS) [US] |
| NKVD | Historical predecessor organization to KGB, renamed in 1947 [USSR] |
| NSA | National Security Agency (US equivalent of GCHQ) [US] |
| NSDAP | Nationalsozialistische Deutsche Arbeiterpartei - National Socialist German Workers Party, aka Nazi Party [Germany] |
| Number Ten | 10 Downing Street, London: the historic office and home of the British Prime Minister [UK] |
| OBE | Order of the British Empire - awarded mainly to civilians and service personnel for public service or other distinctions [UK] |
| OCCULUS | Occult Control Coordination Unit Liaison, Unconventional Situations (UK/NATO equivalent of NEST) [UK/NATO] |
| ONI | Office of Naval Intelligence [US] |
| OSA | Official Secrets Ace, the law governing official secrets [UK] |

| | |
|---|---|
| OSS | Office of Strategic Services (US equivalent of SOE), disbanded in 1945, remodeled as CIA [US] |
| Politburo | Political Bureau: the executive organization for the Communist Party [USSR] |
| Q Division | Division within The Laundry associated with R&D [UK] |
| QinetiQ | See DERA [UK] |
| RIPA | Regulation of Investigatory Powers Act, the law governing communications interception [UK] |
| RUC | Royal Ulster Constabulary, the paramilitary police force deployed in Northern Ireland during the Troubles [UK] |
| SAS | Special Air Service: British Army Special Forces [UK] |
| SBS | Special Boat Service: Royal Marines Special Forces [UK] |
| SIS | See MI6 [UK] |
| SOE | Special Operations Executive (UK equivalent of OSS), officially disbanded in 1945; see also The Laundry [UK] |
| Superblack | (Pertaining to a black organization or black project) Secret and off the record to all, including governmental intelligence oversight bodies [All] |
| Territorial SAS | Territorial Army, British equivalent of the US National Guard: Territorial SAS, the part-time, weekend soldier arm of the SAS; mostly staffed by veterans [UK] |
| TLA | Three Letter Acronym [All] |
| Two-One SAS | 21 Special Air Service Regiment; also known as Artists' Rifles [UK] |